looking forward to reading *The Trouble with Polly Brown* as soon as it is published.

Tears of joy and sadness alternately filled my eyes as I read the adventures of this lovable orphan named Polly Brown. This spellbinding novel contrasts good and evil in a most amazing way. Polly Brown will motivate any reader to live a better life, with more courage and kindness. And I just adored the chapters of *The Trouble with Polly Brown*, which you kindly let me preview.

Thank you for coming to our school to speak. You had a profound effect on our students sharing your insights on life, self-respect, and relationships, and thank you for personally reading excerpts of your book *Polly Brown*. You gave our students an experience they will treasure for a lifetime. It is my prayer and desire as a Reading Teacher that other students across this country will get the opportunity to hear you speak and to read your books. You are a great and noble author!

I've just finished reading the draft copy of *The Trouble with Polly Brown* and it is fantastic, just brilliant! As I was reading it, I was imagining it as a movie! You have a talent most people could only wish for. The book from start to finish was superb, and I was honestly unable to put down. I actually stayed up almost a whole night to finish it.

I am an avid reader with a Master's degree in English, so when I say that you are truly one of the best authors, I really mean it. I can hardly wait for the second in the trilogy. You deserve a blockbuster.

We've been to your Tearoom, Tricia, you are a wonderful person and author, and you truly deserve to have your own TV show. You are so warm and captivatingly funny, you truly come across to everyone you meet.

I am a pastor of a large church and when I came across your book I decided to place a few copies in our church library. I was amazed by the response to *Polly Brown*. I had mothers ringing me up saying that reading this book made them want to be better mothers.

The Trouble with Polly Brown tugs at the emotional heartstrings—you want to laugh, cry, and love Polly throughout, a desperate girl in a desperate world, dealing with many real life issues, bullying included. This book should be taken up by every school across the country. The ongoing painful world of Polly Brown is so beautifully written from the heart.

The Trouble with Polly Brown

Tricia Bennett

CREATION HOUSE

THE TROUBLE WITH POLLY BROWN by Tricia Bennett
Published by Creation House Books
A Charisma Media Company
600 Rinehart Road
Lake Mary, Florida 32746
www.charismamedia.com

Design Director: Bill Johnson
Cover design by Terry Clifton

Visit the author's Web site: http://www.hopeinyourheart.com

The characters portrayed in this book are fictitious unless they are historical figures explicitly named. Otherwise, any resemblance to actual people, whether living or dead, is coincidental.

Library of Congress Control Number: 2011928569
International Standard Book Number: 978-1-61638-600-9

First edition

11 12 13 14 15 — 987654321
Printed in Canada

I dedicate this book to my very dear brother
Anthony, who while on this earth suffered much at
the hands of others.

****

He will wipe away our tears.

ACKNOWLEDGMENTS

T IS A well-known fact that writing an acknowledgment section at the beginning of the book is a most splendid opportunity to make mention and acknowledge all those amazing people who have come into my life and in doing so have made me richer as a person.

There are too many wonderful people I should be thanking, and if your name does not appear, then please forgive me now.

First, I wish to thank my husband, John, for all his encouragement and support. Then I have need of thanking my very special daughter, Antonia, along with Isaac, my little grandson. Antonia has been one of my chief fans. Then I must make mention of my two sons Reuben and James, whom I miss terribly as they reside back in England. I wish to also send my love to two very special foster daughters, Emma and Anna.

My eldest son, Reuben, has just completed serving his second tour on the front lines in the British Army in Afghanistan. He lost a number of his mates on both tours. He is a paratrooper with the Second Battalion, and I could never be prouder than I am of him. I must use this occasion to honor all the special men from his regiment who up until this very minute have lost their lives or limbs fighting to maintain our freedom.

I also wish to thank every American soldier, especially those fighting in Afghanistan and Iraq, and I weep for every mother who has lost a son or daughter in this desperately sad and prolonged war.

Next I move on to my sister-in-law Stephanie, her husband, Gavin, and my four lovely and very special nephews and nieces—Jay, Dylan, Emily, and Eleanor. Stephanie has also spent many years fostering children as well as working with the local schools and their problem families. I love this woman with my whole heart.

I must use this occasion to make mention of my favorite organization—Guardian ad Litem. These volunteer workers are the best. If they had been around when my brothers and I went through the system, I am sure things would have been very different. They will never know how much good they are doing by getting involved in the lives of vulnerable children in foster care.

I want to thank the girls in the faith dorm at Lowell Correctional Institution in Ocala, Florida; these precious women have encouraged and inspired me to actively pursue my commission of being a mouthpiece for those who literally have no voice.

It therefore gives me great joy to make mention of a wonderful children's home that truly does love and care for orphaned children, many of whom would not have lived through their childhood let alone get to see their adult lives if it had not been for the dedication and devotion of Pat and Linda Manfredi. This couple is not daunted by challenges that many others would shun, and they run this home with absolutely no government assistance. These children are often in need urgent medical care when they arrive in America. I have therefore asked their permission to place their contact details just in case there may be some readers who would wish to help sponsor a child in their care. You may contact them through their website at www.TheCarpenters-HouseofLakeCounty.com.

I would also like to use this occasion to give a big thank you to Pastor Jim Brissey and his beautiful wife, Jean, who have the biggest, most generous hearts I've ever known. My husband and I have joined this couple a number of times on their regular visits to the local prisons where they give help and hope to despairing inmates. They also put on events for the homeless where they can be fed and clothed even while having their hair cut. You can contact them at their website www.highergroundministries.org should you wish to show any kind of support.

Next I would like to thank Jim and Darlene for all their enthusiasm and support. Jim is a first-class artist and illustrator, who, having read my book, has taken to drawing the most wonderful and inspirational illustrations of my self-published younger book *Princess Polly*, as well as drawing pictures of my English tearoom in Wildwood.

Next I move on to Pastor Steve Yates (a well-known pastor and motivational speaker) and his lovely wife, Chinita, and family for all the encouragement they have been to us in our ups and downs (especially the downs!).

Next is a very special lady named Therese Gaudette. I met Therese when she invited me to speak at her Writers Club. She loved *Polly Brown* so much that she offered her services to help me with *The Trouble With Polly Brown*. Therese, I cannot thank you enough for all your help, support, and overwhelming encouragement. You, my dear, are such a blessing!

I could not write these acknowledgments without making mention of a very extraordinary woman I have come to know and love called Jamie Clarke. This dedicated woman has for a number of years run a school for supposed no-hopers, and with her help and determination she has literally turned around the life of many an unfortunate child. I don't think this supercharged passionate woman has the remotest understanding of what the word *impossible* means! She also runs a center that supplies food, clothing, and counseling for the homeless and destitute. Amazingly there is always a big smile on her face and a light in her eyes as she recounts some latest amazing miracle that just took place. You, my dear, are a star.

I would like to make mention of Pastor Dan and Michele Binion. Michele works alongside me in our Polly's Pantry Tearoom in Wildwood, Florida.

I would also like to use this opportunity to say a special thank-you to Mike and Susie Collins, who took me in when, at seventeen years of age, I attempted to end everything. This amazing couple would see me through many storms in my life—and all this when they were trying to raise their own family, which turned out to be seven gorgeous girls and one boy. I have to add that this exceptional family has always reminded me of the Waltons!

Next I want to give a big thank-you to Len and Stacie Pedrick and their whole family. They are a ray of sunshine in our lives. Whenever we need a meal and a hug, it's to this couple we turn. Although I have to add that nearly all our visits require us to join them in lengthy karaoke sessions, as she and her young daughter Tori are mighty fine singers!

Then there are Tom and Maura, another outstanding couple who travel the country as a singing duo. Maura is Irish, need I say more! They never fail to bring tears to my eyes, for their singing is truly inspirational. This delightful couple has hearts of pure gold and a real sweetheart of a mother who makes the best cup of tea outside of England. We really love you.

Talking of Ireland, I want to say a big thank-you to two rather special ladies who originated from County Cork in Ireland. Yes, Kate O'Brien, you are the inspiration behind one of the main characters in my books. Your love and deep understanding of the downcast and downtrodden, as well as your incredible wit, have always brought a smile to my heart and face. You are a very special and gifted lady. Next I wish to say thank you to Olive Franklin for the hundreds of times she allowed me to share food at her table and the thousand or so hours she then freely counseled me until I finally learned to stand on my own two feet.

Next I move on to Billy and Shannon and family for all their help and encouragement.

Then I wish to personally thank a wonderful family who live in England and have done so much to help their community as well as support my son Reuben and my daughter Antonia. So Machelle, Jerome, Caleb, Teheillah, Micah, Koah, Sharmah, Beulah, Avodah, and Yehshaw, I cannot express how grateful I feel toward you and your family. You have shown yourself true by being there for my children when I was on the other side of the world. I hear nothing but praise when they talk about you and your family.

I also wish to thank Rosalyn and the Women of Wildwood Charity group. I have just become a member of this amazing group of feisty ladies, most of whom are educators who raise money that gives youngsters the opportunity to continue on in their education. They also raise money to give a second-chance grant to some older deserving person who wants to make it through college.

Next I would like to say a big thank-you to my special friends Dale and Carolyn, Derek and Darren. They befriended us when we knew hardly a soul over here.

I would also like to mention my lovely Spanish friend and interpreter Kenilia Perez as well as Danny and their very two very precious girls Stephanie and Grace.

Then there are Al and Vivienne Levine and their equally precious family. Vivienne is a dab hand at winning cookery competitions! We love you loads.

We must also make mention of our dear friend Watchman, who is also a regular visitor in the schools and prisons and has his own school of rap for poor but talented musicians. You're the best.

Which brings me to our closest friends that I left behind in England. As well as David and Tisha Knowles, I wish to say the biggest thank-you to Steve and Georgie Bailey and their terrific family. Polly's favorite teachers in book one are based on this exceptional couple! We had our children at the same time, and we've weathered many storms together.

Next I want to thank Doctor Vija Sodera, a talented physician, author, and musician, and his family for their support and friendship.

I also wish to say thank you to Jacinta here in Florida and her beautiful children. This single mother has most definitely been both an inspiration and help to me.

Finally I wish to make mention of my two surviving brothers Francis and Vincent. I wish to honor both of them as they were, to quote Dickens, "my companions in misery." I know we have grown apart, and I trust there will come a day when we will hold and hug each other once more; until such time, please know that I love you both.

And last but not least I wish to thank the mayor of Wildwood, Mr. Ed Wolf, for his continued support. This kind man came up trumps when on more than one occasion we urgently needed his help and support.

Lastly I would like to thank all my faithful customers who bring friend after friend to visit our Polly's Pantry Royal Tearoom situated just outside the Villages retirement community here in Wildwood, Florida. I want to thank so many of you for sending me personal gifts such as the hand-sewn apron with Polly's Pantry on the front, and the Harrods teddy bear, just to mention a few. There have been too many gifts and letters to make mention of them all, but I assure you now that these acts of human kindness never fail to touch me deeply.

We would also like to thank Allen Quain and all the staff at Creation House who have worked so hard to produce this book.

CONTENTS

Chapter One
BACK AT THE CASTLE

*A*RE WE ALL sitting comfortably?" the aged storyteller politely inquired, his steely blue eyes content to survey the continuously growing crowd as they weaved in and out of the aisles in search of a spare seat. As he continued to wait for his audience to settle down, he allowed a quizzical, if somewhat bemused, look to slowly spread across his craggy, deeply lined face, which bore testimony to many past and personal tragedies.

Needless to say there came a point when, with his patience wearing thin, he decided that this was indeed the perfect moment to bring the noisome crowd to order. He cleared his throat and began. "It has become most apparent that there are many newcomers amongst my audience, most of whom do not have youth on their side. So pray, would someone do me a great kindness in explaining this rather peculiar phenomenon?"

A number of hands hurriedly shot into the air before a young and bright pigtailed girl, who could wait no longer, rose to her feet. Then with the wide-eyed innocence of a dewy-eyed doe, she poignantly addressed the storyteller.

"Dear sir, I tell you no lie when I say that ever since you closed your book and ordered us to go home to our families, we all have found ourselves completely overwhelmed with the story of Polly, so much so that we were instinctively filled with the most extraordinary desire to tell everything we learned to not only friend and family but absolute strangers as well. Such was the compulsion within. So forgive us, sir, if we mistakenly passed on what was intended for our ears only. For if this is the case, well then, we all stand horribly guilty of letting you down."

1

The young, pigtailed girl stopped mid-sentence, for a nervous tickle had found its way into the back of her throat, causing her to cough somewhat. "Excuse me, sir," she mumbled, going the brightest shade of pink as she politely put her hand up to her mouth to stifle any further unseemly splutters.

"Young lady, pray take your time, and continue on only when you feel ready," encouraged the storyteller, giving her a warm and friendly wink.

The young girl responded with a sweet if not slightly nervous smile before continuing on with her story. "Well, of those grown ups who cared to listen, most then requested permission to accompany us back here, for they too wished to hear firsthand all that remained to be told of this unusual but wonderful tale. So please, I beg you, allow them to stay, for I assure you they will remain as quiet as church mice, and all present have given their personal assurance that they will be no trouble whatsoever!" she very adamantly stated before rather touchingly clasping hold of her father's strong hand for the purpose of gaining further moral support.

The storyteller's smile widened as he considered the earnest sincerity of the young girl's persistent pleas, and it was only a matter of seconds before the other children joined in and begged for their parents and grandparents to be allowed to stay and listen in on Polly's further adventures.

"We promise you they won't make any noise whatsoever," the children chanted over and over in perfect unison.

Eventually, albeit reluctantly, the storyteller found himself caving in to the children's rather unusual request. "Very well then, as long as they do as they're told and remain as silent as the night," he said slightly tongue in cheek as a somewhat bemused look settled across his face. He then leaned over to blow away the thin film of dust that had settled on the pages of the thick book, which held many a story yet to be told.

As he began to finger the well-read pages, he hesitated briefly before deciding that this must surely be the perfect moment to caution his extremely attentive audience. His tone was gentle, yet serious. "It is right that this story be told to grown-ups and children alike, but I would not be doing my job properly if I did not take the time to warn all present that you will at times feel deeply stirred within your soul as I turn page after page to reveal more of young Polly's sad and troubling young life as she continues on with her personal journey. It is true to say that such terrible things still take place in many a children's home all over the world and will surely never cease until those who truly care rise from their dormant slumber to take some form of expedient affirmative action. So, may Polly's story serve a much higher cause than just to tickle your ears. Yes, may it also stir in your bosom a fresh and fervent determination to show more love and understanding to your own offspring, but may it also arouse a deep compassion to reach out and touch the poor and defenseless in our midst, who battle on in this life with little or no hope to be found."

The room fell into a deathly hush. You could have heard a pin drop as all present seemed to mull over the storyteller's gentle but deeply convicting words. Never one to be in a hurry, he used the moment to take a deep breath and further study his audience, which rather alarmingly had not only quadrupled in size but appeared to come from every conceivable background.

And so it was on that otherwise ordinary day that the rich found themselves sitting alongside the poor, black touching elbows with white, and an honorable Indian chief who wished to take notes found himself borrowing the mighty pen of the determined politician seated right beside him as they all waited with bated breath and much anticipation for the storyteller to begin.

"Now purely for the sake of those who have only just cared to join us I feel it would be good to tell something of her journey so far," the storyteller suggested. "So those among you who are already familiar with the story, I would ask that you bear with me and be patient a moment longer so that I can quickly fill in the uninitiated amongst us.

"Polly and her two brothers had been sent to the orphanage at a very young age. Her elder brother, Thomas, became very sick and died, leaving Polly and her younger brother, James, at the mercy of their cruel guardians, known to all as the Scumberrys.

"Life for Polly was so unbearable that hardly a day went by without her praying or sending a letter to God asking for His personal help, for she felt she had nobody else to turn to. Her two favorite schoolteachers, who gave her hope, moved on, and the social services, for no apparent reason, seemed to have entirely abandoned her and her family. As she had no living relatives to visit and thus keep an eye on her and her younger brother, she was left to the mercy of her guardians, who compelled all the children to keep secret everything that took place within their walls, the family motto being 'What happens in the castle stays in the castle.' Failure to adhere to this command brought very severe consequences.

"One day help arrived in the form of two rather strange ragamuffins, one who went by the name of Ralph, the other, Hodgekiss. Polly was quickly befriended by these kind gentleman of the road, and there came a day when they gave her an invitation to come to tea at their house, which happened to be in a magical land called Piadora, a land where all her pain would cease and where all her dreams could and would come true.

"However, before she committed to leaving the home to go on this journey, she was warned that the journey would at times be perilously dangerous, and most who started the journey failed to ever make it to the end. If Polly was to run with this challenge, she would be allowed to take only one favorite item with her. Polly chose to take her tatty blue elephant, whose name is Langdon. The reason for her choice was simple: an elephant never forgets, and this elephant was very special, as he carried every tear she had ever cried.

"Despite many fears and misgivings, Polly soon found herself on a whirlwind adventure that was filled with tough tests and character-building challenges. On the journey she meets some very unusual characters who were there either to help or hinder her quest. There also came a time when she was informed that she must bury Langdon if she was to move on. This proved to be one of the hardest decisions of all.

"Polly finally met a young black boy named Aazi, who, just like herself, had suffered much. He was therefore equally determined to face every fresh crisis and fight every battle in his personal quest to also make it to Piadora. However, tragedy struck again, and Polly once more found herself alone as she continued to be forced to face her fears and doubts.

"Finally, against all odds, she made it to the kingdom of Piadora. Here, for the first time ever, Polly experienced the joy and happiness she had always been denied. She was no longer the good-for-nothing pauper she had always been led to believe she was, but she was transformed into a real and very caring princess. In Piadora, Polly is reunited with not only her brother Thomas but also Aazi. Langdon was also once more returned to her. The story should have ended there and would have done so, if only Hodgekiss hadn't called her to one side to show her other suffering people whom she alone could help. She was then given the hard choice of staying in Piadora and living happily ever after or returning to her difficult life in the orphanage, where she would be given countless opportunities to touch the lives of many others. Polly, being Polly, realized that there really was no choice, and so, against her better judgment, she agreed to return once more to the orphanage and to a life of deprivation and misery under the tyrannical rule of her cruel and heartless guardians Mr. and Mrs. Scumberry.

"So, if we are all comfortably settled, then allow me the privilege of starting the next chapter. Yes, I will begin where we left off, with Polly having arrived back at the castle after her eventful, if not immensely challenging, journey to the wondrously glorious and visually stunning, inexplicably breathtaking kingdom of Piadora."

<hr />

Having been dismissed from Uncle Boritz's abysmally untidy study, an aimless Polly then made her miserable way down the long corridor to continue on with the relentless cleaning chores that most would agree had unfairly been assigned to her. In this latest family meeting she had been warned by her uncle that she was never again to make tea and sandwiches for the assortment of undesirables who regularly rang the doorbell begging for a little something to eat and drink. In this most private of meetings she was also to be threatened with all sorts of terrible punishments if she even dared strike up a conversation with any future callers to the castle. All this left Polly despairing as to whether she would ever be fortunate enough to once more meet up Ralph or Hodgekiss, those two thoroughly loveable gentlemen of the road who had indeed become very dear to her. Polly sighed deeply as she wondered what to do next.

Moments later she espied her brother James in the distance in his usual trance he headed toward the stairs, carefully holding a model plane in his outstretched hand. She knew with much certainty that he was headed for the boys' dormitory to place this newly built model beside all his other prize exhibits.

She knew that these planes were so precious to him purely because he had to work very hard to save the large amount of pennies that were required to buy the kits. This he did by helping Mr. Johnston dig over his beloved vegetable patch on the weekends. James was also very clever when it came to bartering various things with other boys at the school they attended. He therefore counted these models as his most important and therefore prized possessions.

Polly smiled to herself as she thought how preoccupied he had been putting this last plane kit together. She could not help but admire his tenacity as he picked up one tiny piece after another to painstakingly glue together until the model plane or military tank finally emerged. She knew for certain she did not have the patience for such things. As Polly reflected on all this, a few of the other children raced past, carelessly knocking into her and causing her to stumble as they tried to get to kitchen door first.

"Hey, watch where you're going," she mumbled as she rubbed her upper arm, momentarily stopping to check for bruising.

Polly smiled and secretly rebuked herself for being so peevishly miserable, for as she looked down at the signet ring that still remained on the middle finger of her left hand, twisting it 'round and 'round, it once more reassured her that Piadora, with its Hoolie Koolie and Hubber Blubber trees, had not just been a figment of her seemingly wild and out-of-control imagination. She had to admit that she felt pretty upset, if not a tad angry, that her punishment had been extended for a further three months, especially as she believed she had done nothing to deserve the extra time. But as she continued to twist the ring on her finger, she reasoned that three more months on "Relinquishment of all privileges and enjoyments," better known as ROPE, was indeed a small price to pay when she had just come back from the most wonderfully harmonious place that could ever possibly exist. This in itself would surely have been enough!

But the icing on the cake was that she now believed, for the first time in her miserable existence, that she had finally found real, true friends she could cherish forever, friends like Aazi, as well as the thoroughly likable lads Justin Kase and Justin Thyme, whom she felt the deepest bond with as a direct result of all the trials they had survived. And then the cherry on top of the cake was surely to see her beloved brother Thomas not only safe from all harm but now so deliriously happy and content that it was almost impossible to imagine he had ever been otherwise. Just witnessing his newfound joy had provoked such a deep sense of gratitude in her.

When all was said and done, she knew there was no price tag she could even begin to put on having been given that rare, once-in-a-lifetime opportunity to partake in such an incredibly amazing journey, one that had taken her to a place that up until now had only ever existed in her wildest dreams and beyond, a land where all reference to pain and suffering was treated by all residents as nothing more than a contemptible byword that they no longer wished to be reminded of or indeed ever give another moment's thought to, for all inhabitants of Piadora lived in a place that could well be renamed "Land of Utter Bliss." Piadora had indeed proven itself to be the place where every elusive childhood dream was miraculously resurrected and brought to fruition. She therefore had little choice but to admit that even if she were to be sentenced to a whopping seventy-seven years on ROPE, only to emerge a wizened, toothless old lady, she would still have chosen to embark on the journey to Piadora.

"Well, I'd better just grit my teeth and try to make the best of it," she quietly resolved, at the same time reaching deep into her pocket until her fingers made contact with a small but thickly folded piece of paper. "If I keep my head down and do nothing further to upset my aunt and uncle, well, who knows, they may even cut my sentence in half," she murmured, at the same time unconsciously shaking her head as if to suggest that the likelihood of that happening was very remote, for compassion or mercy was indeed in very short supply when it came to both her guardians. Polly pulled the piece of paper from her pocket and caressed it between her fingers, and as she did so, she felt a warm, tingly sensation run the whole length of her body.

"Thank goodness I remembered to ask dear Aazi for a forwarding address. I bet he's struggling just as much as I am since leaving Piadora to go back to his homeland," she mumbled, her smile deepening as she instantly pictured his impish little dark face with its show-stopping smile.

"I must not leave it too long to write to him, although I have to confess to having absolutely no idea what it might cost to send a letter halfway around the globe. Oh, well. I will have to address that little problem when the time comes," she muttered as she slipped the precious piece of paper back into her pocket for safekeeping.

By the time Polly finally completed the ridiculously lengthy list of tasks Aunt Mildred had so considerately pinned on the kitchen wall for Polly's benefit, it was very late into the evening and so way past her bedtime. So it was that a very bleary-eyed Polly found herself holding on ever so tightly to the banister as she struggled to haul her aching body slowly and exhaustedly up each step of the winding oak staircase. With every step she took she could hear her joints creaking and cracking in unison with every piece of oak flooring that her feet bore down on. She willed herself to make it as far as the dormitory and then farther still until she reached her bed, which happened to lie at the farthest end of the room.

Her rickety iron bed with its thin sheet and blanket looked so inviting as it beckoned her toward it, and in that moment she desired deep sleep above all other creature comforts. "It's now much too late to write Aazi a letter," she muttered under her breath. "Never mind. Who knows? Maybe I'll have some time at school tomorrow. Yes, I will stay inside at break time and find an empty classroom. That way I can privately pour out all that is on my heart without any fear of Gailey Gobbstopper or one of the others getting their grubby little mitts on it, for I fear they would most likely destroy it or, worse, use it to make even more fun of me," she murmured.

Polly declined to use the bathroom that evening, even though she knew it was of the utmost importance to brush her teeth. The urgent need to collapse took preeminence, and so she slowly shuffled like a shackled prisoner across the bedroom floor as she headed toward her bed. That night Polly never even bothered to get out of her daytime clothes and into her thin, worn-out pajamas, so extreme was her exhaustion.

THE TROUBLE WITH POLLY BROWN

After peeling back the bedclothes, she dropped like a lifeless corpse onto the bed, her face instantaneously buried as she hit the thin pillow like a dead man. Finally she came up for breath and to grab hold of Langdon, her beloved blue elephant. Sniffing, she moved Cecil, her giraffe, over to one side. "Sorry old chap, but it looks as though you're still required to guard my pajamas for a little while yet," she whispered as her thoughts went back to her last will and testament, which she had written while kneeling in the freezing snow on the mountainside. Just thinking back to that episode had Polly instantly sitting bolt upright in the bed as though she had just been plugged into a million volts of electricity. She hastily attempted to switch on the bedside lamp, and in doing so a large number of books crashed to the floor.

"Oh no!" She gulped suddenly, feeling both anxious and afraid that the commotion would most certainly have woken up some of the girls, and that meant only one thing. Without further adieu, Polly threw herself back under the bedclothes, as if by doing this it would prevent the inevitable vitriolic barrage of abuse that would now rain down from actually hurting her. She plugged her ears with her fingers, for she knew for sure that the next few minutes would have all the girls hurling every imaginable insult in her direction. As she cowered under the bedclothes like a wounded animal, she could only pray that their rage and fury would miraculously subside and so not turn into a physical beating for her.

"Shut up and go to sleep, you stupid fat toad, or I'll give you a hard smack in the kisser," came the loud, irate voice of one of the older girls whose bed was farther down the room and near the door.

"Yeah, shut your gob and turn off that bloomin' light before I get out of bed to come over and punch your lights out, you stupid little toe rag," another angry voice threatened.

"She'll get more than a fat lip if I am forced to get involved," another voice boomed across the room in her direction.

Polly ignored the wild and unkind threats as she came up from under the bedclothes and began to frantically but quietly rummage through the locker drawer in search of her precious gold book.

"Phew! For one awful moment I thought it had been stolen," she whispered before gently closing the drawer and turning off the light to once again settle back down under her thin blanket.

"Sorry, everyone. Have a good night."

"You'll soon be sorry, yer little guttersnipe, if yer don't shut yer mouth and let us get some shut eye," snarled another voice in the dark that Polly instantly recognized as being that of Gailey Gobbstopper.

As Polly lay on her back with her hands tucked behind her head, staring into the darkness, she struggled to accept the horrid truth that she was, as usual, wide awake and therefore in for another grueling night of sleeplessness. "Oh no, I really can't do this any longer," she unhappily groaned.

Suddenly and therefore most unexpectedly, she felt the strange, tingly sensation return, only this time it was stronger than ever as wave after wave rolled over her tired body, systematically caressing each and every aching joint. Polly had no way of truly understanding what was happening to her, but nothing really needed any sort of reasonable explanation, for in all sincerity she was way beyond all that! After all, it was more than enough that she be consumed with such overpowering and wonderful feelings that in no time at all had her filled to capacity with the most wholesome, inexplicable gratitude.

Polly soon found herself struggling to remain awake, for her eyelids became heavier and heavier, as though they were supernaturally forced to surrender to sleep. No sooner had her top and lower lids met to momentarily fuse together than she felt the gentle touch of a hand tenderly run the whole length of her brow, taking with it all her anxious thoughts and feelings that haphazardly and insidiously raced around her mind day and night without fail. Then all tormenting thoughts were powerfully swept away, causing Polly to enter into the deepest state of relaxation.

"Hmm…I must be in heaven," she muttered under her breath. Then like the patient about to go under the knife who surrenders willingly or unwillingly to the power of the anesthesia, she likewise went into a seemingly comatose state of mind, and all too soon she found herself right back in Piadora.

Polly immediately let out a small giggle as she observed dear sweet Stanley Horlicks, the old school caretaker, who having hopped his way through the final chalk square, stood tall and proud as he was proclaimed to indeed be the winner of the hopscotch finale.

THE TROUBLE WITH POLLY BROWN

He really is having the time of his life! It is so wonderful to see him so spontaneously free and happy after years struggling with that awfully horrid back pain, she cheerfully thought. Moments later she then watched on as dear Stanley received his prize, which turned out to be a disgracefully enormous knickerbocker glory ice cream that was smothered in thick, gooey hopscotch sauce and generously topped with crumbly flakes of chocolate. "Ooh, he's so lucky," she whispered, licking her lips as she imagined dear Stanley handing her a spoon before telling her to dig in.

She had so little time to respond before she suddenly felt the warm, soft sand beneath her feet as she raced as hard as she could after her dear young friend Aazi. She could hear him burst into fits of laughter as he then playfully pulled her to the ground, taking the wind out of her sails as she fell backward onto the silky smooth sand, which very quickly had her struggling to regain her breath. Aazi then disappeared as quickly as he had appeared.

But it was not over, for as Polly let out a small gasp, she suddenly felt the sweet, warm breath of her beloved brother Thomas brush across her face as though he were playfully kissing her on the cheek. "Thomas, is that really you?" she joyfully whispered.

"Who else could it be?" he mischievously replied as he then excitedly produced another painting that he had been hiding behind his back. "You haven't been to this place yet," he animatedly informed her as he waved the freshly painted picture in front of her face. "It is so utterly breathtaking that I was left with no choice but to paint it for you, my dear sister," he beamed. Then another huge smile lit up his face further as, still pointing at his picture, he showed her a cool and sparkling brook meandering its way through a lush and fertile valley.

As Polly stared at his painting feeling awestruck by its beauty, she considered that the scene looked so strangely real that it might well jump right out from the canvas.

"But I must go now, for not a moment passes that does not have me feeling the urge to get out my brush and palette to start another painting. Oh, Polly, can you believe it? I have seen so much incredible beauty here in Piadora that I feel utterly compelled to continue painting forever and ever if necessary. And what's more, I have the distinct feeling that even if I were to be granted a further million years to paint all I have so far seen, it would be nothing but a mere drop in the ocean. Therefore it would in no way be long enough," he said with a lighthearted laugh as he planted another warm kiss on her cheek before giving her a spontaneous but much needed hug.

"My dear sister, please know that I love you so very, very much, and every time my paint brush touches the canvas, I paint for you," he said as he tenderly took hold of her hand to give it one final and very tight brotherly squeeze before vanishing into thin air.

As Polly continued to lie motionless in her bed while being utterly mesmerized by the moment, she became aware of a couple of cold, wet tears trickling unchecked down her face, but as she did not wish to move a muscle, she declined to brush them away, preferring to allow them to continue merrily strolling down her cheeks before disappearing beneath her chin to then disperse.

No sooner had Thomas disappeared than she found herself overwhelmed by the deliciously hazy aroma of jasmine and sweet honeysuckle, which had her immediately believing she was back in one of Piadora's many indescribably delightful gardens. Moments later she found herself sitting under the shade of a magnificently majestic Hoolie Koolie tree, momentarily lost in the sweetest, inescapable communion with her close friend Hodgekiss. More puzzling still was that every unspoken communication between them found Polly experiencing the keenest, deepest sense of unimaginable joy that pervaded every cell and corpuscle within her body and so had every hair follicle on the surface of her skin standing to attention.

Polly lay in the bed completely motionless, for she feared if she moved a muscle or had even the slightest nervous twitch, all these new and intensely profound feelings would instantly leave, never to return. She therefore prayed with all her heart and might that this utterly intoxicating, heavenly experience would continue to abide as long as possible, if not forever.

Eventually she took another deep gasp as she made her way up some wide steps and opened the huge but now very familiar door that led directly into the Princesses School of Training. An abundance of fresh tears rolled freely down her face as once again she found herself standing outside Mrs. O'Brien's classroom peering through the window. Polly watched on as her beloved and saintly teacher rolled out the pastry, at the same time keeping her girls amused with a number of humorous, if not slightly questionable, stories regarding her child-hood days back in County Cork, Ireland. Polly turned her attention to the large stove and could clearly see chopped-up apples bubbling away in a copper-based pan, and she knew without a shadow of doubt that appletude pie was once again on the menu.

"Dear, sweet Mrs. O'Brien, oh how I miss you so very much," she quietly moaned.

As Polly continued to watch, she could smell the delicious, sweet pastry wafting in front of her nose, and instantly her mouth began to water, causing her empty stomach to rumble like a waste disposal. Polly wanted more than anything to open the classroom door and enter, but something held her back. Perhaps it was the knowledge that if she were to place even one foot into the room, well then, she would never again want to leave. As Polly deep down knew that this could not be, she courageously chose to content herself by just watching, her nose glued to the window in the same manner as when she passed her favorite tea room in the High Street back home.

"Hmm…lovely jubbly," she whispered as her eyes began feasting on the number of freshly baked apple pies that, after leaving the hot oven, sat cooling on a table as they waited for the eager girls to dust them over with fine icing sugar.

"Girls, girls, remember that just as we sprinkle these pies generously with sugar, so we must endeavor to consistently sprinkle the lives of all around us with the sweetest and kindest acts of warmth and gener-osity," Mrs. O'Brien loudly commented as she purposely leaned over shoulder after shoulder in order to make sure the girls were following her instructions to the letter.

As Polly listened to her teacher's heartwarming and most compel-ling advice, she suddenly felt the same invisible hand that earlier on had wiped her brow now gently plunge into the core of her being, and like a specialist surgeon, those hands tenderly took hold of her heart.

Polly held in her breath and listened intently to the hypnotic beat of her heart as something unimaginably precious was delicately placed into its very center. She thought she could hear a faint whisper in her ear, and it seemed to repeat over and over, "Never be afraid, for I hold you always in the palm of my hand." Bizarre as all this might seem, even hearing those simple words helped her to lay all fear to rest.

Added to this was the harsh fact that every waking moment of her life had found her constantly struggling to fight off a subversive and hideously foul morass of pure evil that desired to drag her down into its thick and choking abyss, so surely what was taking place in this small space in time must come from the other end of the hemisphere, perhaps beyond infinity itself! One thing was certain, and this was that the whole unimaginably overwhelming experience seemed far beyond any words of description and therefore way beyond the scope of the human mind with its rational grasp of all things considered tangible and therefore real. Whatever it was, it clearly stood firmly on the side of good, as all fear was immediately vanquished, and she found herself revived with fresh hope that sought to exchange her ever-grieving heart for a deep and timeless abiding joy.

Eventually Polly slowly and most reluctantly opened her eyes, and in doing so, she was instantly brought back to Earth with a bump, for all too quickly she realized she was once again lying on the thin and lumpy horsehair mattress of her old, rickety iron bed. Polly pulled the thin blanket up to her chin, for despite being in the middle of summer and so presumably less cold, she still found herself shivering from head to toe. "Oh why, oh why, did I ever allow myself to be talked into leaving Piadora to come back to this draughty hate-filled castle?" she sighed. "I must be stupidly crazy after all."

Polly gave another shudder that went the full length of her spine. "Come on, Langdon, you're not doing your job properly. You, my young man, are meant to keep me warm as toast, for I am in most urgent need of some shut-eye, as I'll have you know I've got school tomorrow," she said as she nuzzled her face into her confidante's very floppy blue ear. She then miraculously fell into the best and deepest sleep she had ever known, a gentle slumber where all nightmarish dreams and torment are swiftly banished, replaced only by the sweetest, fanciful dreams filled to bursting with endless possibilities as well as the purest contentment, dreams that should rightfully fill the hearts and minds of each and every sweet-smelling, tender child as they lie tucked up tight in their beds, feeling deliciously safe and loved.

Chapter Two
THE CHOCOLATE-SEALED LETTER

*T*HE NEXT MORNING found Polly up and out of bed much earlier than usual, as rather miraculously she found herself feeling surprisingly good on the inside and so extremely optimistic about her day to come. With so much time on her hands, she thought this might well be as good a time as any to pen Aazi his very first letter from her. She had absolutely no idea what to say in the letter except that she was already missing him. So after tearing a sheet of paper from an old, unwanted exercise book, she began to put pen to paper with the full intention of writing down some of her deepest innermost thoughts.

Dear Aazi,

I trust this letter finds you safe and well. I hope you don't mind me asking, but what is it like for you living with your uncle? I hope for your sake he is much kinder than Uncle Boritz. Are you able to attend school? If so, can you give me some details so that I can compare it with mine?

This coming Friday our school will be showing us the first of many films about life in Africa, and I have to tell you that as a result of meeting you, I'm truly looking forward to learning more about your wonderful country and your people.

Although we are well into the month of June, sadly to date we have not seen much sun. In England when it rains and rains for days on end, it seems to

affect everybody I meet. The grown-ups in particular are noticeably far more miserable and moody. In
fact, if truth be told, they most definitely become
decidedly peevish!

Zimbabwe sounds such an awfully nice place to live,
especially as I'm told that the sun shines gloriously
all year round. How unfair this all seems! I mean,
our weather is so miserably cold and blustery, and
yours, well, it sounds so perfect that this surely
must go a long way in explaining why you, my little
friend, are constantly smiling.

I confess to missing you so very much; therefore,
one of my latest dreams that I've now added to my
ever growing wish list is to one day pay you a little
visit. Until then I have little choice but to content
myself with closing my eyes, and then I can clearly
see your beautiful, smiling face with those big, white
chompers, although I might add that even this has
its pitfalls, as I now spend a large percentage of my
days bumping into walls and doors in my ridiculously
desperate endeavor to keep your impish features
constantly fresh and alive in my memory. Yes, if the
truth be known, I am indeed covered from head to
toe in minor bluish bruises and bumps, but who
cares?

I am therefore waiting with bated breath and the
greatest anticipation to receive my first ever letter
from you.

Take care. Sincerely yours. Oodles and poodles of
love.

Polly, xxxx

PS: Stupid me. I forgot to ask, Do you miss Piadora as much as I do? What a ridiculous question. Of course you do! I know this might sound a bit peculiar, but I feel much more grown up as a result of all the trials that we both faced getting there. Yes, so much older and wiser, although to be honest I'm a little unsure as to whether the wiser bit is a good thing or not. What do you think, Aazi? Should we leave stuff like being wise well alone, as most grown-ups tend to suffer from far too much wisdom for their own good? Please write and tell me your truest thoughts on all such matters, as well as anything else you just might care to.

Polly then rummaged around in her locker drawer as she searched for an item she knew was there. Why? you might ask. Well, simply because she had hidden it there herself several weeks previously.

"Yes, thank goodness I've finally found it," she delightedly whispered to herself as out from the drawer came a small, round, and very dubious-looking lump of chocolate. She used force to squash the slightly stale and therefore hardened chocolate outer shell between her thumb and index finger until the gooey caramel inside the chocolate began to ooze its way out. Then when she was fully satisfied that it was now suitably mushy, she took her chocolate-covered thumb and pressed down hard on the paper in a manner that suggested she might well be sealing an important legal document. She had seen this done before on a number of legal documents Uncle Boritz carelessly left lying around his study. The only difference was that his splodge was done with melted red wax and not chocolate. She then blew on the paper in her bid to encourage the thick but deliciously melted splodge of gooey chocolate to dry thoroughly.

"Terrific. An excellent job done, if I say so myself," she pronounced, a little on the smug side. She then reached for her pen to add a further PS alongside the dried-out chocolate imprint that was now firmly attached and now weighing down the bottom of her letter.

THE CHOCOLATE-SEALED LETTER

Finally, with her letter now finished off to her complete satisfaction, Polly rustled around in her drawer until she came across an old, yellowing miscellaneous envelope. After slipping the letter into the envelope, she then sealed it down with a quick lick of her tongue.

Afterward she applied a quick squirt of very cheap cologne that had been given to her by someone who no longer cared for its smell. She placed the envelope under her nose to give it a quick sniff. "Mmm, it now smells fabulously gorgeous," she brightly declared. Turning it over, she proceeded to copy down the address he had written on a small scrap of paper, all the time wondering how on earth she would ever pay for the stamp that was now required if it was to have any hope of getting to its final destination.

Happily, that very necessary moment of inspiration was about to come forth. She had just written SWALK ("sealed with a loving kiss") on the back of the envelope, which she followed up by giving the envelope an impromptu kiss, when out of the blue she had that most essential moment of enlightenment. "I know. I'll pay a visit to dear, sweet lavender-and-lace Mrs. April Strudel and ask to be allowed to take her dogs for a walk. She always says yes, as the dogs need the regular exercise, and she never fails to give me a few pennies as a thank-you. Yes, I do believe those precious but yappy little pups are about to get more exercise than they ever dreamed of, as I intend to write many insightful letters to Aazi in the coming months."

Polly was now perfectly satisfied that she had hit on the best solution to her problem, so she tucked the precious envelope into her schoolbag for safety and then paid a quick visit to the bathroom to wash and brush her teeth. Polly spent double the time brushing them that morning, as she knew she had to make up for the previous evening when she had failed to give them the necessary brush that they deserved and required. As soon as she was dressed in her uniform, she sat on her bed and concentrated on filling her disgracefully tatty schoolbag with all necessary apparatus she would need for lessons that day.

She was in the process of doing a final meticulous check of her timetable when she drew in a deep breath, covering her mouth as she expressed great horror that she was missing some important and very essential items. She also knew without a shadow of a doubt that without these elusive items, there was not the teeniest chance of her day going even remotely well. She had completely forgotten that on the previous Friday her biology teacher, Mrs. Prunella McGillicuddy, had requested that every student bring to class a couple of sheep's eyes for the purpose of dissection.

Polly had at the time been horrified by what she considered to be a hideously gruesome request, and so she felt very relieved when other students wasted no time in voicing their objections. The girls in particular complained loudest. They were, after all, by far the fairer sex and therefore understandably squeamish when it came to complying with their teacher's latest and most unreasonable demand. The girls promptly gathered around to discuss ways of getting out of this extraordinarily unpleasant task, and Leander Robinson, a normally exemplary pupil, even had the temerity to stand up and blatantly challenge her teacher regarding the health implications associated with bringing such revolting items onto the school premises. Yes, if Polly remembered rightly, Leander had told Mrs. McGillicuddy in no uncertain terms that to be given such a sordid task was not only unhygienic but to her mind "very distasteful," so there would be serious ramifications if she was to be punished for her failure to comply. In view of all this, she would be calling the health department ASAP as well as taking the day off school, and that was that!

Angelica Clodsworthy seized the occasion to add her full support to the ever-growing and now highly contentious debate by belligerently stating that to be forced to carry such downright disgusting items in her schoolbag was downright vulgar, and so like her best school chum Leander, she too would be taking the day off school—oh, as well as calling the health department to add her name to the list of complainants. Besides, heaven forbid, but what if the revolting items were to somehow leak into her lunch box? It didn't bear thinking about, so there was no way she would be cooperating with her teacher's plainly ghoulish request, and that was that!

At the time of this rather unexpected and most hostile uprising, Polly had felt secretly pleased that for once it was other pupils and not just her showing a bit of what was likely be perceived as "rebellious and absurdly unacceptable behavior" by Mr. Edwood Batty, the school's omnipotent, hard-nosed headmaster.

Mrs. McGillicuddy had, of course, gone nuts! "How dare any of you question what I, your teacher, ask you to do," she shrieked, lengthy strands of her spittle flying through the air before landing on Polly's already badly stained blazer. A horrified Polly, who had been standing slightly to the left of her teacher as she prepared to hand in her overdue homework, hurriedly took a few steps backward, for she knew that once Mrs. McGillicuddy worked herself into a frenzy, well then, there was clearly plenty more spittle on its way, for this lady could produce more frothy foam than a large cup of Italian cappuccino!

Polly had always felt sorry for this teacher, and she could not help but wonder how the dear lady ever became a biology teacher. There was never any question that she loved all creatures great and small—and I might add, with an absolute passion—but was this the only essential criteria required that granted her the necessary permission to inflict her teaching skills on young, very innocent pupils? Polly was not on her own in her belief that Mrs. Prunella McGillicuddy was way out of her depth and therefore entirely unsuited to the post, although she remained at a loss as to what post, if any, would be suitable for their desperately high-strung teacher of biology.

Prunella, or rather, Mrs. McGillicuddy, was of an undeterminable age. She could have been thirty, or she could just as easily have been sixty. Polly had tried very hard to work out the poor darling's correct age but had finally conceded that to guess right was clearly an impossible task. The poor woman lived up to her name, for Polly sadly noted that her heavily lined face was indeed as shriveled as a dried-up prune, with lips as cracked as a tight walnut as they did their utmost to hide her distressingly prominent buck teeth. She always had her greasy, unkempt hair haphazardly stacked in the most untidy bun, which appeared as though it might well be home to families of mice, if not other unwelcome visitors, such as head lice. Many a time Polly had noticed odd and sometimes very large bits of twig and bark intertwined with her straggly, wispy hair, and so she naturally presumed that her teacher lived in a log cabin in the heart of a forest. For why else would she have small parts of a tree sprouting from her head daily?

Her gaunt face was framed by the thickest and most unfashionably square glasses ever created, which turned her eyes into hideously monstrous saucers. Add to this thick, sprouting nasal hair, as well as a dark, defining shadow over her lips that bore much resemblance to a mustache, and it was sorely evident that nature had not been the remotest bit provident or kind to this extraordinary woman.

It also had Polly wondering how on earth her teacher had ever managed to get hitched and go from Miss to Mrs. In the end she could only presume that Mr. McGillicuddy likewise must also be in receipt of some equally thick and very distasteful optic lenses that happily prevented either party from viewing the other clearly. But at the end of the day, Polly wondered, did any of this really matter? For as every old sock finds an old shoe, they had rather miraculously found each other.

There had in the past been a disturbing number of occasions when this wholly unpredictable woman had flown into such a scary rage that it had forced each and every member of the class to seriously question not only her age but also her actual origins. I mean, did she really have the same human characteristics as the rest of us? Or had some very thoughtful extraterrestrials concluded that for the higher good of man and science they would generously bequeath this good woman to Planet Earth? And more to the point, if this was found to be the case, how had she been assigned their biology teacher?

So Polly felt very sorry for Mrs. "Warts and Whiskers" McGillicuddy, because to be born looking quite this ugly wasn't nice at all, and Polly sincerely believed she understood this more than anybody else, what with her own personal connections to Quasimodo, better known as the Hunchback of Notre Dame.

As Polly made her way to the bus stop to catch the bus to school, she wondered what if anything she could do at this late hour to lay her hands on some eyeballs and thereby save the day. If you rightly remember, she had started the day feeling so very optimistic, but now all that was a thing of the past, for as soon as she stepped out of the door, those mischievous black clouds had, as usual, come out of hiding with only one cruel intention in mind, and this was to spend the day stalking her and making her life as miserable and downcast as they possibly could.

But this was not her only problem, for as she sat on the bus looking out of the window, she pretty soon became aware that none of girls from Snobbits Preparatory School for Young Ladies were on the bus. She found this very puzzling, as they always took the same bus for at least part of the journey. Had the school closed down? She sincerely hoped not. Polly decided to get off the bus early and head into the village in the forlorn hope that the village butcher might just happen to have a few spare eyeballs that maybe had been hidden from view and were therefore still lying around in his huge walk-in freezer.

As she stepped off the bus she prayed hard for a miracle, for she knew she had little or no excuse for not turning up at class without them. There could be no denying that her teacher had gone to great lengths, even advising all pupils to pay a visit to their family butchers over the weekend with the intention of ordering some, just in case they were not readily available. "Upon receipt of the goods, these items should immediately be refrigerated or at the very least stored in a cool pantry for the remainder of the weekend, as this will keep them both fresh and moist," she had dutifully informed the class.

"Failure to refrigerate these specific items will most certainly cause severe deterioration, and before too long they will indeed be transformed into highly pungent, rubberized Ping Pong balls. As you can

THE TROUBLE WITH POLLY BROWN

well imagine, in this event there is a high probability that they would begin bouncing off the table long before your surgical knife has even the privilege of making the smallest incision into the retina. I therefore strongly advise that you all follow my instructions to the letter, and this will go a long way toward making this latest assignment hugely successful. Do I make myself clear?"

"Yes, miss," the whole class answered back in depressingly rehearsed monosyllabic tones.

Polly was quick to notice that a number of the boys then quickly grouped, and despite their loud guffaws, drowning out much of their silly and very juvenile conversation, she distinctly heard them make up plans to put the eyeballs to the Ping Pong test if and when they got the opportunity. So Polly knew that if nothing else, Monday would more than likely turn out to be a very interesting day.

As the students had slowly filed out of the classroom that Friday afternoon, Mrs. McGillicuddy had most been most conscientious to repeat her warning. "Under no circumstances leave this assignment to the last minute; otherwise you may find to your peril that due to high demand, the eyeballs are completely out of stock."

"Yes, miss," they once more chanted in dreary unison.

"May I also use this occasion to remind all present that failure to bring eyeballs to Monday's lesson will, I assure you, result in a most severe reprimand," she had harshly warned. So although Polly did not relish this latest assignment at all, she still had the sense to acknowledge that she would need to show that she had exhausted every possible avenue in her attempt to get hold of some eyeballs, and so without further delay she headed into the shop of Brutus McClintock, the village butcher.

Her visit was sadly cut short due to the fact that the last set of eyeballs had only minutes earlier been purchased by Billy Blunkett, who had the good fortune of pipping her to the post, as his bus had rolled into the station five minutes earlier than hers. As Polly and Billy were for some unfathomable reason sworn enemies, Polly had little hope of coaxing or persuading Billy to part with even one of the gory little monsters. So as she stood most forlorn at the butcher's counter, she knew those miserably insufferable clouds that hung over her head were, as usual, up to no good as they sought to wreck this day in a manner similar to that of every other day of her doomed life.

"Sorry, luv, you're right out of luck today, for they've all goon, deary, for let me tell ya we've 'ad such a run on sheep's eyes this weekend. But tell yer wot, we still 'ave loads of pig trotters, as well as a fridge full of kidneys and lush livers, and more sheep's heads than I care to count, all minus their eyeballs of course! So, my sweetie pie, would any of these other items be of any use to yer?"

"I am altogether ruined!" she glumly grunted, shaking her head as she wondered what, if anything, to do next.

Polly made a further deep groan, and after thanking the young butcher's assistant for his help, she made haste to leave the shop, as she now needed to run as fast as her legs would carry her, for she knew with much certainty that she stood to be in further trouble if she turned up late for school assembly.

———

Ten minutes later witnessed a very hot and sweaty Polly racing full pelt down the long corridor as she ran with all her might toward the main hall for the usual Monday morning assembly. Polly screeched to a halt outside the hall entrance and quickly placed her ear up to the door in a desperate bid to determine just how late she was. "Phew! I just made it in the nick of time," she loudly gasped before prying open the door to creep in and find an empty seat on which to perch. Luckily nobody important noticed her sneak in so disgracefully late, as all eyes were closed for the start of morning prayers. Polly shut her eyes tight and joined in as though she had been there all the time.

After a few well-meaning prayers that were mainly concentrated on petitioning God to mercifully send as much help as He could possibly muster to each and every perilous corner of the globe where both strife and conflict abounded, they were all then instructed to once more stand to their feet to sing Hymn 102, "Onward Christian Soldiers," from the thick hymnal. As was customary and much to the annoyance of all those around her, Polly, as a matter of habit, immediately filled her lungs to capacity and then sang out heartily, mustering all her might behind each and every verse of the stirring hymn, which never failed to inspire her. But then most of the rousing hymns found her singing robustly louder than those around her, and so like most things, this too deeply aggravated and troubled many other concerned individuals when it came to the subject of Polly Brown.

When the hymn finally came to an end, the pupils were then ordered to remain standing for a continuance of morning prayers. Five minutes later—and thank goodness—Mr. Batty was almost finished.

"Dear God, we finally bring before You all the poor and less fortunate children around the globe who face terrible struggles such as poverty and hunger, as well as many other unimaginable trials every day of their young lives, and we ask that You may grant them supernatural comfort in their hour of need. Amen."

"Amen...amen," Polly excitedly roared, again much to the annoyance of all the other staff and pupils in morning assembly.

One of her forlorn teachers shot her a stern look, which Polly completely ignored as she happily slumped down onto her chair, for the headmaster now wished to address the whole school as a matter of urgency.

As Polly sat back in her seat, her eyes began surveying the long lines of pupils, and she made a loud distressing gasp. As she continued to look down the aisle, a look of pure disbelief etched across her face. She could not fail to notice that Billy Blunkett had not only unwrapped the brown paper bag but was now proudly handing around his personal set of gunk-filled eyeballs as though they were a pair of highly prized marbles. Polly watched on, feeling most indignant. Moments later all his mates were giving the eyeballs a good, long sniff before squeezing them between their fingers, quietly guffawing amongst themselves as they took it in turn to think of new and ingenious things to do with the eyeballs that might get them a cheap laugh. Needless to say, Polly was not the least bit amused. In fact, she remained thoroughly peeved as she continued to watch, for she rightly believed that had her bus arrived five minutes earlier, then those eyeballs would certainly have been in her rightful possession and not Billy's. How jolly unfair everything in her life was.

Chapter Three
THE EULOGY OF STANLEY HORLICKS

*D*R. EDWOOD BATTY, the school's most excellent and formidable headmaster, stood silent and solemn for a whole five minutes while he waited for each and every noisome pupil to settle down, along with all idle and mindless chatter to cease. While waiting, he chose to raise a hand to his face and began rubbing his chin with the tips of his fingers as though checking that his razor had done a thorough job in removing all unwanted stubble. This man knew with great assurance that cleanliness was indeed the prerequisite to true godliness, so for his face to show anything of a six o'clock shadow would have been most indelicate and embarrassing for the poor man.

Seemingly satisfied that he had shaved his chin to within an inch of pure perfection, he rewarded himself with a smug grin, affirmation that his face had not only survived the shave without mark or blemish but that also it now felt as soft as a newborn baby's bottom. With his chin inspection over, Polly watched as he then moved with a show of great decorum toward the middle of the stage to stand like a powerful politician behind the cedar wood podium. Removing his hands from his jacket pockets, he then clasped both sides of the stand for support as over his horn-rimmed spectacles he looked down into the sea of youthful, spotty faces that served to fill the large auditorium like tightly packed sardines in a can to well over its total capacity.

"Snodgrass, remove that foul and loathsome gum from your overworked orifice immediately! Then come and see me in my office at morning break," he sternly ordered.

All over the hall great volumes of chewing gum were instantaneously swallowed down as scarlet-faced pupils turned to focus their attention on their fellow chum who, having been caught illegally chomping, was now rather unfavorably in the limelight. A heavy-set Snodgrass immediately went a deep purple as he struggled to his feet. Removing the chewing gum from his mouth, he then clumsily headed off toward the nearest bin to dispense with a large lump of the offensive sticky substance.

The headmaster waited patiently until he returned to his seat before making a loud cough, his cue to let all know that he had something of great importance that they were all about to be notified of. Clearing a lump from his throat, he then began to address the whole school. "It is with the greatest sadness that I am compelled to reveal to all present that our dear caretaker, Stanley Horlicks, sadly passed away over the weekend." The sound of deep breaths being drawn could clearly be heard all around the auditorium as shocked staff and pupils attempted to take in this very unexpected, sad piece of news.

"Oh, dear Stanley, bless his little cotton socks," Polly deeply sighed.

"Cor, the old boy's finally popped his clogs," Molly Sutcliffe's unashamedly loud voice boomed down the line of seated pupils.

"Shh. All of you do as you're told and be quiet!" one of the many English teachers sternly ordered.

"As a school we wish to honor this gentle and meek man to whom we are deeply indebted for his many years of service to this wonderful school. Stanley Horlicks could accurately be termed an 'old-school' gentleman. From the simplest of acts, such as opening doors for young ladies and teachers to pass through, this magnanimous-hearted man showed consideration for others in everything he did and said. Although I have to say that as a rule of thumb he was not a man given to many words, he still managed to encourage teachers and pupils alike," said the headmaster, his voice faltering as he struggled to remain solemn and thereby unaffected.

Polly, who for once in her life was drinking in every word the headmaster uttered, began to furiously nod her head in agreement. She then turned to the girl on her left and whispered with a sigh, "Oh, if only everyone knew just how happy he is now, they would never be this sad."

"Shh, maggot face, or you'll get us both in trouble," the very irate fellow pupil with the ginger hair rather nastily snapped back.

　　　THE TROUBLE WITH POLLY BROWN

Polly sniffed as under her breath she muttered, "Eleanor Boodle-butt, you needn't be so jolly rude!" She then huffily folded her arms, at the same time moving farther back on her seat as she redirected her full attention to the headmaster's touching and very endearing speech regarding dear Stanley.

"I have to say that one of Stanley's many talents was that he could rather cleverly spot an illegally disposed-of lump of chewing gum stuck under a table from as far away as twenty or even thirty meters for that matter."

Embarrassed titters followed by smatterings of laughter quickly broke out around the hall as countless pupils privately conceded to being among those guilty of such a deplorable act of gross misconduct. Polly noticed that Mr. Batty paused to draw breath while shrewdly observing his pupils to make quick mental notes of those laughing the loudest, as these were obviously the worst offenders. For the first time in history he now knew each and every culprit by name!

Clearing his throat once again, he then continued to proceed. "As Stanley went about his daily cleaning tasks, this man was meticulous in all he did. He never looked upon his job as though it were some-thing beneath him. On the contrary, he did everything to the best of his ability, yes, with excellence and pride, and all this despite his poor health. Sadly, I never had the time to get to know Stanley prop-erly, as my job dictates that I must get forty-eight hours out of each twenty-four-hour day, but while sifting through the school archives I discovered a few very interesting facts concerning our now dearly departed school caretaker.

"Stanley served his country well by enlisting into the military when World War II broke out. This exemplary and very brave young man went on many harrowing missions but was eventually forced to leave the services after sustaining terrible leg injuries whilst in the trenches in France. Stanley was hospitalized in a military facility for almost a year as he struggled to learn to walk again.

"With his shining military career over, he was forced to take what might seem to man y as a very low and menial job, for it was at this stage of his life that he became this school's most cheerful cleaner. But Stanley's story does not end there, for the school records show that a number of years later saw our great and mighty country battling with some of the most severe and terrible storms she had ever witnessed. These ferocious storms destroyed whole villages and caused serious flooding and inestimable damage throughout our great land. Sadly, many great landmarks were lost forever, and countless families were not only uprooted but also lost everything, including beloved members of their families. Amidst all this confusion and crisis, dear Stanley, on discovering that the school's roof had been ripped off and other parts of the building had been severely damaged, willingly chose to set up home in one of the school outhouses and refused to leave the site until the school had been completely renovated and restored to its original glory. To this day his little stove, tin kettle, and tea-filled caddy remain in the outhouse as a visual reminder of this humble man's life.

"Yes, my friends, this is a story of a remarkable and very noble gentleman who never felt the need to blow his own trumpet but spent his entire life putting others first. I hasten to add that we could all do well to learn something from this quiet-spirited, unassuming man. And so I for one fully intend to be at his funeral, if only to let his family know what a special and outstanding person Stanley Albert Horlicks truly was. This earth will never quite be the same without him, so may he rest in pieces....er, I mean in peace."

The sound of sniffling and snuffling could clearly be heard all around the hall as teachers and pupils brought out a tissue or two to wipe away a tear or blow a troubled nose as it finally dawned on all present that dear, dependable Stanley really wasn't ever coming back.

"Stanley leaves behind a widow, Edith, five children, and I believe some twenty-six grandchildren in all. It was Stanley's express wish that instead of flowers, all donations should go to charities that help servicemen. Personally speaking, I cannot think of a more worthy cause than to honor those men and women here and abroad who risk their lives daily in order to protect us and in doing so keep our world both safe and prosperous. We will therefore be looking to give a handsome donation to such a truly worthy cause.

"Finally, I have been in touch with Father Constantinople, and he has yet to confirm the date and time of Stanley's funeral, details of which will be posted as soon as possible on the school notice board situated in the foyer. May I use this occasion to remind all pupils present that, as the funeral will be taking place during school hours, if any among you wish to attend, then I most certainly will require a written letter of permission from your respective parents. Do I make myself clear?"

"Yes, sir," was the quick response from all the pupils seated in the auditorium.

Mr. Batty took a deep breath and jangled a bunch of keys that were deep in his trouser pocket. To Polly it looked like he was privately congratulating himself on a speech well given. He was about to turn away from the podium when he suddenly turned back around as though he had absentmindedly left out something important that he needed to say. "However, before I dismiss you all from this assembly, I do have one final request. As Stanley's departure has been so sudden and unexpected, we have not had the time or the wherewithal to find a suitable replacement to take up the position of cleaner. So until such times as we do, I would like to humbly suggest that previously guilty parties should resist all further carnal and most inconsiderate acts of dispensing their lumps of chewing gum under the furniture. Instead, it would be much appreciated if you would be more thoughtful and opt to discard this undeniably revolting stuff in the bins provided. Thank you. You are all dismissed. Now please exit the hall in a quiet and orderly fashion."

Polly stood up to leave the hall and was very happy to suddenly catch sight of her younger brother James as he too stood in line waiting his turn to leave the hall and get to his classes. Once again she broke the school code of conduct, which was never to leave your class line, but Polly, being Polly, seemed always to be more moved by the emotion of the moment in preference to the cold, harsh rules of school officialdom.

She thought nothing of the consequences as she broke with school code to leave her class line and race over to speak to him.

"Psst, James. Let's meet up at lunch break," she gently whispered. James pulled a face as if to say he did not fully believe she would do as she said.

"Promise?" he mumbled loudly.

"Yes, I promise," she replied, giving him a meaningful look, as she was most eager to get his full consent.

"Well, that would be nice. I'll save you a seat," he said, still holding back as he forced a half-hearted smile.

Polly grabbed hold of his arm and responded by giving him a full smile. "See you at lunch break," she said, giving his arm a friendly tug.

"OK, Polly. See you at lunchtime, and try hard not to be late."

Chapter Four
ANOTHER BRICK IN THE WALL

*P*OLLY RACED BACK to join her line as her class slowly filed out of the hall and headed toward their first class of the day. She remained true to form as she wandered down the long corridors, deep in anxious thought and therefore totally oblivious to anything and everything going on around her.

However, today of all days was going to change that for good, for suddenly she was rather rudely interrupted by a complete stranger, who not only had the sheer audacity to sidle right up to her but then rather rudely began to interrupt her private and most important chain of thought. "Sorry to be such a nuisance, but please could you point me in the right direction? I am supposed to be joining a physics group, and you seem like a really friendly face."

Polly responded by raising a disturbed eyebrow before turning full circle to scrutinize his face in a manner that might suggest he were merely some out-of-focus photograph pinned on a wall.

"I am new to this school, and as of yet I have no timetable on which to rely, so I'm entirely at your mercy," he said with pleading eyes as he pulled a soppy face that would suggest he was as helpless and defenseless as a week-old puppy dog.

Well, if he thought the "I'm really helpless trick" would work on Polly, he was sadly very mistaken, for she still failed to communicate as much as a friendly vibe or utterance as rather rudely she continued to stare right through him.

"Hello, anyone there? I'd be extremely grateful and indebted to you if you would do all within your power to help me." The polite and friendly voice continued on, a keen sense of urgency now betraying more than a hint of exasperation.

Still Polly managed to have a blank expression written all over her face as she stood right in front of him to take a long, hard look at his features. He was tall, a bit of a beanpole really. His hair was jet black and slightly unruly, and Polly was convinced that if Mr. Batty saw that it went way past his shirt collar, well, he would be in serious trouble, and at the very least he would be ordered to cut off the ponytail or face the consequences! Otherwise, he was indeed a very presentable specimen, for she observed that his jacket was pristine clean, his trouser seams immaculately pressed, his shoes brushed to a shine, and as for his tie, well, that too was as perfectly straight as his beautiful ultrawhite teeth!

Polly was certain that he was at least a few years older, and so if she was heading for twelve, well then he must be fourteen coming on fifteen. His eyes were a pleasant muddy brown, and his nose was inoffensively chiseled. To add to the dramatic impact, his lips held a slight pout that had Polly musing he must surely play some form of wind instrument. Add to all this the ruddiest cheeks she had ever seen outside of the winter months, and it all went to make up an unusual but strangely handsome boy. *Yes, he must have aristocracy hidden somewhere in his ancestral line,* Polly bemusedly thought as pictures of famous composers such as Mozart and Brahms with their weird hairdos and long, hooked noses erratically flashed through her mind.

"Sorry, what were you asking?" she queried as she now appeared to directly, if not a little condescendingly, look him in the eye. His face changed, as if he instantly wished he'd stopped someone else—in fact anyone else—who was walking down the corridor, instead of her.

"Science block. Any idea?" he dared to once again ask, all the while pulling a playful long face.

Still Polly was slow to answer as she struggled to come out of her constant daydreaming, which over the years she had expertly honed to an art form.

"Umm, physics…Now, let me see. Is it down the left-hand corridor or the right?"

"Sorry, I should have introduced myself. My name is Will; full title, William Ogilvy Montgomery, at your service. And if you'd be so terribly kind as to help me out, well, then, I promise to return the favor," he said as he anxiously placed a hand on her arm in his very admirable attempt to keep her full attention. "I'm excellent at helping out with mathematics and/or French homework, and even though my history has in the past been described as both evasive and boorish, I will willingly offer any help that is required. So tell me, what's your name?"

"Oh, I'm Polly, Polly Brown to be precise."

"Well, nice to meet you Polly. I do hope we can be friends," he said in a voice much too cheerful for her liking. He then proceeded to further shock her by keenly holding out his hand in what was presumably intended to be a kind and friendly gesture. A shocked and confused Polly stared down at his outstretched hand as she battled to find the right words.

"Oh, um…Yes, well I guess we could be friends," was her sickeningly slow response, as it slowly began to dawn on her that someone was trying heroically hard to be nice to her and, better still, might actually want to become her friend. Polly finally jumped to attention and timidly placed her hand out to shake his. "Thank you, er…er…"

"Will, William Montgomery," he quickly interjected as he continued to help her out.

"Er, yes. Will. That would be really nice," she said, giving a gentle smile as she finally dared to limply shake his hand.

Will smiled back, but mainly, it appeared, from relief. "Well, Polly, as my mind-reading skills have yet to be honed to perfection, I do still need your expert help in pointing me in the right direction," he said, giving a light laugh.

"Oops, sorry," she spluttered, suddenly feeling shy and a bit of an idiot. Finally she became helpful enough to direct him toward the science block. "Go through the double doors, and then turn left. Don't stop until you reach the end of that corridor. At the end of the corridor you need to take a sharp right into a link corridor, and then halfway down that corridor you will see a rather battered-looking blue door that leads into the science block."

"Thanks again, Polly," he said, breaking into a very generous smile, a smile, I might add, she truly didn't deserve.

"Don't mention it. Glad to be of some service," she said, entirely breaking with tradition by feigning a half smile.

"Well, I hope to catch up with you later," he said as he hurried off in the direction Polly had shown him. Polly nodded, her smile becoming wider as she watched the crazy new boy unwittingly bump into a large group of pupils, as he wasn't properly looking where he was going.

"Maybe we could meet up at lunchtime?" Will shouted back in her direction as he stooped to pick up a pile of his books and papers that now littered the floor of the link corridor. Polly's face immediately went a significant scarlet in color as she considered his kind proposal to meet up. She therefore waved a quick good-bye and then with much relief turned on her heels to venture down a different corridor, as she had a class that she would be late to if she didn't hurry up.

"My goodness, he's drop dead gorgeous!" she giggled to herself. "This could turn out to be a good day after all," she declared as with a rarely seen smile on her face she hugged her books tightly to her chest and proceeded to march most determinedly toward the biology classroom.

<hr/>

Polly entered the noise-filled classroom long before her teacher and so quickly made her way toward an empty desk near the back of the room. Then, dropping her schoolbag down beside the chair, she slumped wearily down into her seat and found the time to ponder just how good a mood her unpredictable teacher would be in on this fine Monday morning. She did not have to wait too long to find out. Mrs. McGillicuddy entered the room in her usual frantic manner and shuffled toward her desk with the purpose of dispensing with her two heavy, stuffed-to-the gunnels carrier bags.

Polly observed the bags and immediately began to play the game that she always played, which was to attempt to guess quite what was in the overloaded bags and therefore absolutely necessary if her harebrained teacher was to safely make it through another day without any sudden, unexpected catastrophe. "Here we have a pair of matching candelabras recently valued by Sotheby's to be worth an astounding six thousand pounds. Do we have a buyer? Going...going...gone. Yes, sold to fellow classmate George Edgebaston for a modest forty-six hundred pounds. And what do we have next? Ah, yes, a metal cage. This cage comes complete with drinking receptacle and a seriously rusty hamster wheel that promises to keep the flab off your hamster's hips and so could easily be considered the ideal home for a mouse, hamster, or pet rat. This prized possession will cost you a mere two shillings and sixpence. So, do we have a taker? Next we have a rather splendid cracked cereal bowl, still encrusted with the remains of this morning's bran flakes. Oh, dear, what a mistake. For she clearly didn't mean to bring this in; rather, it was intended for the washing-up bowl!"

Polly could easily play this stupid game for the whole lesson and often did, as she automatically switched off as her teacher droned on and on about dreary things such as lymphatic systems and epithelial tissue. I mean, what was the purpose of learning all about the functions of the human body, and from such a hysterical woman, when everything else in Polly's life lay on the floor in tatters.

Did she need to know what her kidneys did or didn't do when all she wanted was to survive another day without a beating or further unjust punishments? No, it was settled. Just coping with all the anxiety and torment raging inside her daily was more than enough to keep her totally occupied without being forced to learn hundreds of challenging names of body parts as well as their bodily functions. These tongue-twister names were obviously made up thousands of years ago by a number of very bored professors who could have put their talents to much better use by making up a variety of new board games. Instead of which, all over the globe poor, desperate schoolchildren were gnashing and grinding their teeth as they struggled to get their tongues 'round words that would put most people into an instant coma and were absolutely ghastly, if not impossible, to spell correctly. There were words like *subcutaneous, mitochondria, cardiovascular,* and other terminology that might as well be Polish or Greek as far as Polly was concerned, for it was all gobbledygook to her. So with Polly's anxious mind already in overdrive, it was time as usual for it to go into total shutdown.

With her shabby, old-fashioned, fur-lined coat now hanging rather sloppily over her chair and the blackboard thoroughly wiped down, Mrs. McGillicuddy turned and ordered her pupils to stop all unnecessary conversation, for the morning lesson had now begun.

"Pay attention, everybody! Kindly unwrap your eyeballs and then proceed to place them carefully on the metal trays sitting in front of you," she commanded in her usual frenzied, high-pitched voice. She then marched around the room in her thick, calf-length tweed skirt and heavy Doc Martens boots, stopping at every desk en route to supply each student with a pair of tweezers as well as a small, silver-colored sharp knife that was required for dissecting small objects.

Of course, when she arrived at Polly's desk, there was not a measly eyeball in sight, just an empty tray with Polly sitting at her empty desk looking decidedly sheepish.

"Brown, I order you now to produce your eyeballs."

Polly remained silent.

"Brown, please do as you're told and get out your eyeballs," she fumed.

"Um, guess what? I don't have any."

"Unbelievable. Quite, quite…unbelievable," her teacher roared as she began to foam from the mouth. "Well, I guess we'll have to remove the ones in your head, if you really don't have any for this lesson."

"I'm so very sorry," Polly awkwardly muttered.

"Sorry means nothing when coming from your lips, girl," her angry teacher spat out.

For the next awkward twenty seconds her teacher stood frozen to the spot as she waited for one of Polly's usual most insightful explanations as to why there were no sheep's eyeballs staring up at her from the steel tray.

Polly could only shrug her shoulders as she spluttered an apology.

"Girl, get up from your seat and go stand facing the wall at the back of the classroom!" her teacher screamed, her eyes virtually exploding from their sockets. Polly watched as in just a matter of a few seconds her teacher's whole body began shaking violently, as she experienced her own very private volcanic tremor that, given time, would release seismic amounts of pent-up energy. If recorded, they would measure way beyond any Richter scale.

"I'm so sorry, miss, but, well, is there any way one of the other pupils could loan me one of their spare eyeballs to dissect? For if you look over toward Eleanor Boodlebutt you will see a number of eyeballs that before you entered the room were being used by some to bide away the time with a quick game of marbles," she said as she directed her teacher's gaze toward Eleanor's desk, which had, as she so rightly stated, a number of abandoned eyeballs stacked into a small, ghoulish pile. "So please, miss, say yes," she begged. Polly's voice then began to falter as she stared directly into the demonized eyes of her now severely strained teacher.

"Brown, how dare you be so insolent as to even think you can answer me back! Let me tell you now that even if there were enough leftover eyeballs to build an impressive monument to Winston Churchill, I would still refuse to permit any of the other students to help you out. And the simple reason is that I would consider such charity to be in your case a most futile exercise that would only serve to further develop your already sharpened skills in sheer laziness," she spat, her huge eyes rolling 'round and 'round in mind-boggling and perfectly synchronized hypnotic circles.

"Yes, miss," Polly whispered.

Her teacher then moved closer until she was almost cheek to cheek with poor Polly, her lips quivering like warmed, wobbly red jelly as she mercilessly continued on with her most severe reprimand. "Yes, Polly Fester Brown, I would have you made aware that your rudeness knows no bounds, for you are a continual sufferance to me. You, my girl, are not only slothful, but you are also the only student who regularly turns up at class without your homework completed or the necessary equipment required," she roared.

Polly began to feel very dismayed, but not, I might add, as a result of her teacher's voracious and very personal attack but rather because through the side of her eye she observed a large, fresh amount of frothy spittle merrily making its way down the lapel of her already badly stained school jacket.

A small and stifled, "Oh, yuck," was all she could manage to mutter under her breath. Polly, horrified, stood glued to the spot, fighting off the strongest urge to race to the washroom as her whole body yearned to hurriedly strip of her blazer in order to rinse it under running water until all visible evidence had been washed down the sink. She could only take a deep gulp, for wisdom told her that to even momentarily take her eyes off Mrs. McGillicuddy at this point in the proceedings would indeed have grave consequences.

Meanwhile, her fellow pupils broke out into spontaneous laughter as they rocked backward on their chairs mouthing the word *Fester* to each other. Mrs. McGillicuddy remained oblivious as to why she had provoked such raucous laughter, but to be perfectly honest, she was far too deep into her personal tirade to really care.

"Yes, young lady, I have yet to understand your sloppy approach to biology, as well as every other subject in the school curriculum, and so you will face the consequences of your shameful disobedience by going over to stand by the wall for the duration of this lesson. Do I make myself abundantly clear? Or shall we argue this one further?"

Billy Blunkett, who was sitting across from her desk, discreetly pried open the lid of his desk and take out his long ruler. With the aid of a thick rubber band securely placed around the head of the ruler, he took aim. "Hey, Fester. Gotcha!" he shouted loudly as the elastic band flew at lightning speed through the air and hit her smack on the cheek before falling to the ground. All the class began to titter, as their absent-minded teacher had inadvertently and incorrectly called her Fester instead of Esther, and this mishap had now given them a nice, new name to mischievously plague her with.

Polly hung her head in shame as she rubbed her marked and stinging cheek before standing up to abandon her desk and make her way toward the back of the classroom. She sadly knew with the deepest assurance that long before the dinner bell rang, her cruel, new name would have made its way down the lengthy, gossip-filled corridors of the school and would by dinnertime be on the tongue of every crass boy in the school, who, while stuffing humongous amounts of slimy green cabbage down their throats, would only stop chewing to have a good laugh at her expense. Worse still, by midafternoon her new name would have gone far beyond the school gates, as it continued to travel on overfilled school buses and trains. By teatime, heaven forbid, it would surely be on the lips of every child back at the castle. "Psst... Polly Esther...Polly Fester. Ha ha."

Polly's already deeply depressed heart sunk further still as she went on to picture Gailey Gobbstopper chanting it over and over in the late hours of the night as she lay in the next bed, only an arm's distance away from Polly. "I might as well face the firing squad now, for my life is well and truly over," she mumbled as in complete misery she took up her routine position of standing and staring at the blank wall in front of her.

As Polly stood mindlessly facing the wall, she broke into what was to be the first of many large yawns as she began doing the same thing as usual, to count every brick in the wall. She had done this same thing countless times, so it no longer held even the teeniest amount of fascination or excitement whatsoever. *Hello, wall. Here we are again, happy as can be. So what's new today? Shall we play "thick as a brick"? You make up the questions, and I'll try and guess the answers.*

So as Polly stood for what seemed an eternity making up endless silly and downright mindless games to pass away the time, the rest of the class quietly got down to the serious task of cutting into corneas and sticking pins through irises as they dissected the hideously slimy balls of flesh-covered matter. Polly could hear the neverendingly slow tick tock of the clock on the wall, something of an unusual occurrence in Mrs. McGillicuddy's normally chaotic lessons. Then, would you believe it? Just fifteen minutes before the end-of-lesson bell was due to ring, oversensitive Laura Jackson chose rather inconveniently to drop to the floor in a very alarming fainting fit. A shocked Mrs. McGillicuddy wasted no time as she raced over to where Laura lay flat as an ironing board on the classroom floor with Denise Bunter overdramatically slapping her exercise book in the poor girl's deathly white face in a desperate effort to bring her 'round.

All the class quickly left their desks and began to crowd 'round in the hope of getting the best view possible. "Cor, she really 'as gone pale! Like the blood's been sucked right out of 'er," Druzilla Bostock observed, as along with the other pupils she attempted to inch nearer Laura's limp body, which still lay stretched out like a corpse on the classroom floor.

"Ouch! You've just stamped on me little finger," Denise yelled up at the circle of concerned faces that were eagerly crowding in. "'Ere move back a bit. Give me a breather, for there's not enough room to swing a cat with you lot hovering over her like she's a goner," she continued to shout.

"'Ere, miss, I think seein' all that disgustin' fluid squirtin out the eyeballs was just too much for her to cope with, for she's always been terribly squeamish, I'll have you know." Amy Kershaw went on to helpfully inform Mrs. McGillicuddy, "Just five minutes ago she told both me and Denise that she was on the verge of throwing up everywhere. Go on, tell her, Denise. Isn't that what Laura told us?" She gave Denise an almighty nudge.

"Yes, it's true. That's exactly what she said," Denise rather huffily confirmed, looking very annoyed that Amy had gotten in first when she alone wanted to be the chosen one when it came to relaying the full extent of the gory facts

"So, miss, shall we call for an ambulance?" Denise excitedly asked.

"Ambulance? I sincerely hope that will not be necessary. After all, she's only fainted, so you can quickly dispel that thought from your mind, Denise dear," Mrs. McGillicuddy snorted as she finally managed to force her way through the crowd of overexcited pupils to take a closer look at the poor girl and hopefully take her pulse.

Denise, who was still wildly flapping her textbook in poor Laura's ashen face, was clearly in no mood to listen to her teacher. To Polly it seemed she had long made up her mind that this unexpected crisis was going to turn into a very exciting adventure for her. "Well, miss, I can't get as much as a faint pulse, and her breathing sounds mighty peculiar to me. So, don't you think she might need her heart shocked back to life with those paddles that doctors use? I've seen it done on *Emergency Ward 10*. Do you ever watch that program? It comes on straight after *Coronation Street*, and my mum and I think it's almost as good as *Coronation Street*, 'cos it's very gory, as well as incredibly exciting. So please, miss, please tell me that I can go with her in the ambulance."

"Enough, Denise! Here, now do as I say, and place these smelling salts directly under her nose. Hopefully this in itself will be enough to revive her," Mrs. McGillicuddy instructed as she then began taking some deep breaths in a bid to stop herself from shaking like a leaf. Denise reluctantly grabbed the smelling salts from her teacher and began to wave them under her friend's nose. Much to Denise's obvious utter disappointment, Laura instantly began to moan, and then this was followed up with a series of loud coughs and splutters.

Seconds later found her sitting up straight, sipping cold water from a Styrofoam cup, and happily, apart from her watery eyes, there was not a hint to suggest that moments earlier she had been out for the count on the classroom floor. All this left Denise looking forlorn that the drama was almost over—and without any hope whatsoever of a dramatic race to the hospital in the back of an ambulance!

Mrs. McGillicuddy, on the other hand, looked instantly relieved as she watched Laura's cheeks return to their healthy pink color, as this surely meant there was no further cause for concern. However, she declared her decision to err on the side of caution and so personally escort Laura down to the nurse's sick bay just in case. "Listen up, all of you! I have to leave the room for five minutes. Please do me the service of remaining calm and quiet as you clean up after yourselves. Pelligrim, thank you for taking the initiative to collect up all the surgical knives and tweezers. Please leave them soaking in a bowl of soapy detergent."

"Yes, miss," Anthony Pelligrim swiftly replied. Mrs. McGillicuddy was about to advance toward the door with Laura in tow when something else caught her attention.

"Druzilla Bostock, kindly stop using the tweezers to pluck your eyebrows, for need I constantly remind you that these implements are the sole property of the school and therefore are only meant to be used for the distinct purpose for which they were originally purchased, namely that of dissecting small animals as well as other small insects? Do I make myself clear?"

"Yes, perfectly, miss," replied a blushing Druzilla as she hurriedly popped her mirror back into her schoolbag before contemptuously dropping the tweezers into the large receptacle that goody-two-shoes Anthony Pelligrim was now aggressively holding up to her face as he wormed his way around the desks. Druzilla then turned to face her best friend Eleanor Boodlebutt and in a loud voice said, "Well, if anyone could really do with the help of some surgical tweezers, it's got to be Miss "Bombshell" McGillicuddy. Perhaps the school should do us all a favor and invest in some large, oversized tweezers, as well as a mammoth-sized scalpel for her benefit," she huffily stated through pouting lips as she tossed her long fringe to one side.

All those in the near vicinity who heard Druzilla's cheap remarks appeared to think them very funny. One brazen student even dared to stand behind Mrs. McGillicuddy as he mischievously held up a hastily drawn picture of their slightly off-the-wall teacher in a barber's chair ready and most willing to go under the knife. Luckily her teacher was partially deaf, so she carried on yelling her orders oblivious to the latest insults regarding her persona.

"Pelligrim, I am also giving you and Blunkett the responsibility of collecting all the soiled dissecting trays from the desks, for these also require cleaning. Please fill up a sink with hot water, and don't forget to add a squirt of sterilizing solution. I will get the next class to finish any leftover tasks. Do I make myself perfectly clear? I will be back in five minutes after I've assisted Laura here down to the sick bay."

No sooner than the door was closed behind their teacher than total chaos broke loose as the boys seized the opportunity they had in all earnest been praying for. Polly turned around to see Ben Hogwhistle, who had earlier elected himself the official collector of all leftover and abandoned eyeballs, begin to lop eyeball after eyeball in the direction of the girls. Eleanor Boodlebutt was the first to let out a shrill scream as a disgustingly smelly eyeball landed smack bang in the center of her lap. From then on it was a scene of pure chaos as distraught girls ducked and dived from the slimy offensive weapons that were being hurled through the air at great speed and mainly in their direction. And this mass hysteria continued for some time as they ran around the room screaming with eyeballs stuck to their flowing locks or, worse, down the front of their blouses.

One missed its target completely, only to land stuck to the ceiling light that hung high above their teacher's desk. Billy Blunkett spied it first, so he quickly jumped onto the desk, trying desperately to retrieve the eyeball, as he wanted to throw it at Linda Trotsky as retribution for unforgivable past offenses in and out of the classroom. As he stood on tiptoe in an attempt to reach the shade, another eyeball landed with a splat on the light shade, making Billy even more excited, as he now had two potential missiles within his grasp. Sadly, even on tiptoe he was unable to reach the light, so he was forced to abandon ship. Jumping down from the desk, he then raced over to join the other boys, who by now were itching to get their hands on some of the leftover balls that Ben was rather selfishly hogging all to himself.

Sure enough, Ben soon found himself fighting off all the other boys.

"Aw, come on, Ben. Do the decent thing and share 'em, for we all want some fun as well," they cried as they jumped him and then dragged him down onto the floor. With the weight of all the boys on top of him, the eyeballs began, one by one, to pop out of his trouser pockets, where they had been stuffed earlier for purposes of security.

As all hands went after the mischievous little blighters that were now slowly rolling across the floor, Anthony Pelligrim managed to pry one out of Ben's clenched fist. He then threw it as hard as he could toward Samantha Jackson, who, due to quick thinking, dove under the teacher's desk just in time to avoid all contact with eyeball.

But sadly, this was not to be the case where Mrs. McGillicuddy was concerned, for she had unwittingly chosen a most unfortunate moment in time to reenter the classroom. The gunk-filled eyeball soared through the air at great speed, almost shaving the very whiskers off her chin as it whizzed past, determined to reach its chosen target, which was the blackboard. It landed with an almighty splat. Their shocked teacher's jaw dropped farther still as she was forced to watch as the offensive material then slowly slithered down the full length of the blackboard before landing at her feet.

Then, as if things couldn't get worse, one of the eyeballs that previously had been stuck to the light shade finally released itself to drop down onto the arch of her glasses before plopping onto the floor to join the other squashed eyeball that already lay as stark evidence of the students' blatantly unforgivable mischief. What rotten luck this all was!

Mrs. McGillicuddy stood frozen to the spot, her eyeballs exploding from their sockets, her face utterly distorted with rage as she let out one of her infamously death-defying screeches, which unbelievably could set off a major landslide in the farthest regions of Nepal or Bangladesh. It never failed to send all pupils instantly rigid with fear.

"G–g–get out of here right now, you miserable bunch of misfits!" she screamed as she grabbed her waste paper basket to mindlessly throw it at the rebel pupils. All the rubbish emptied out as it flew through the air before crash landing just inches away from where Polly stood, though at Mrs. McGillicuddy's entrance she had smartly turned back to face the wall. Their teacher, still engulfed by pure rage, then grabbed a potted plant that stood innocently on her desk, and this too made its merry way through the air as she contemptuously took aim. Dirt and petals floated through the air long before the pot hit the floor, making a terrible noise as it was smashed to smithereens.

While all this further destruction took place, Polly turned again to face her teacher, if only to see what else might happen, and as she turned 'round, she noticed that the other eyeball that previously had been clinging for life to the lampshade had now finally released itself and was now jubilantly making a beeline for the bun on top of her teacher's head.

Polly swung back 'round to once again face the wall, her eyes shut tight and not daring to breathe as she feared what might happen next. Luckily for everyone concerned, Mrs. McGillicuddy remained entirely oblivious to the latest happening as she angrily raged on and ordered all pupils to leave the classroom—and pronto! "I cannot believe it! I just leave the room for five minutes due to a crisis, and this is what you do to pay me back, you miserable wretches," she screeched in such high-pitched tones that they threatened to shatter the large windows of the laboratory. "Now get out of my sight, the lot of you!"

None of the pupils wasted any time in obeying their emotionally erratic teacher's distressed request. They all raced over to their desks, and in record time gathered up their belongings before heading out of the classroom at top speed, feeling very relieved to have escaped without some form of serious punishment.

Polly, believing the word *all* to mean just that, said her quick good-byes to the wall and then made her way back to her desk to pick up her schoolbag to leave with the rest of the class and head to the next lesson. But as she began to make her way toward the exit, she heard the fear-invoking voice of her teacher from behind her. "And where, precisely, do you think you are going?" she boomed. "I'm talking to you. Yes, you, Polly Brown! So unless there are angelic beings in this room that cannot be seen with the naked eye, do me the courtesy of facing me when I'm talking to you."

Polly swung around on her heels to face her accuser. "I'm awfully sorry, Mrs. McGillicuddy, but I thought you said we should all leave and go to our next class," a very confused Polly blurted out.

"Yes, but this command in no way applies to you, girl. I'm sorry, Brown, but I am holding you entirely responsible for clearing up this disgraceful mess. So you can start right now by getting down on all fours to begin picking up all the broken pieces of the flower pot. When this is done, please go and fill up one of the buckets, grab a mop, and start cleaning. And when you're finally finished, allow me to tell you that the headmaster is expecting you to report to his office before lunchtime."

"Yes, miss," Polly miserably muttered.

"Goodness gracious me! I hadn't noticed the terrible state the walls are now in," she announced, reeling back in shock. "Brown, I order you to climb up on a chair and immediately begin the task of cleaning off all the ghastly muck that is now dripping down off the walls."

"Yes, miss," Polly once more responded as she despairingly dropped her bag to the floor by her teacher's desk before making her way toward the store cupboard in search of suitably abrasive cleaning materials. As her eyes scrutinized the mess on the walls, she was left with little doubt that this cleanup session would be a long and arduous task, for the biology room more resembled a violent crime scene than a classroom, with all the walls smothered with blood, ghoulish tissue, and membrane that still continued to drip down the walls. So, with oversized yellow rubber gloves on both hands and mop under one arm, she picked up the bucket of soapy water and headed toward the worst-affected area of the classroom.

After a long time cleaning and scrubbing, Polly poured the dirty water down the sink and then pealed off the sweaty oversized yellow gloves. She felt pleased with herself as she surveyed the cleaned-up room. "There. This room looks so much cleaner, even though it now smells high of bleach."

Satisfied with her work, Polly put both mop and bucket back into the store cupboard and then proceeded to make her way toward her teacher's desk. She stupidly hoped for a bit of praise—after all, she had done a very thorough job of cleaning down the walls—but she also thought that to be dismissed without any further recriminations, much less further exclusive servings of her teacher's frothy spittle, well, that would be considered a good thing for which she would be truly grateful.

As she stood on the other side of the desk from her teacher, believing herself to be well out of harms way, Polly began to seriously weigh whether it was right to leave for the next lesson without making mention of that little something that had earlier caught her eye. Was it kind or fair to leave without saying a measly word? It might after all mean further humiliation for her teacher if she were to enter the tutors' private recreation room still blissfully unaware of this unusual item that was still garnishing her hair.

"You are dismissed to leave, and may I remind you yet again that this lunchtime, you, Polly Brown, have an appointment with the headmaster. So be sure to turn up; otherwise, you will have me to answer to, and as surely as I live, I promise to make it my personal mission to make your school life a living hell."

"It already is," Polly quietly mumbled under her breath.

"So do I make myself clear? " her teacher said through gritted teeth as she rather condescendingly dismissed Polly with a mere flick of the wrist, her eyes never leaving the papers in front of her as she continued on with her marking.

"Thank you, Mrs. McGillicuddy," Polly muttered under her breath as she stooped down to pick up her schoolbag and exit the classroom.

That should have been the end of it, but then Polly—being Polly—rather stupidly and unwisely allowed her conscience to dictate that this was the opportune moment for open and honest dialogue to take over. And so, in her bid to be her usual helpful self, she opened her mouth and nervously began. "Oh, by the way, Mrs. McGillicuddy, I beg you not to take offense, but you still have some, um, leftover spittle on your mustache, I mean, upper lip, and well, umm—" she lowered her eyelids as she then pointed toward her teacher's head—"and umm, you also have a stray sheep's, um…. eyeball attached to the top of your haystack. I mean adorning your, um, hair."

Mrs. McGillicuddy shot up from her desk, her thinly framed torso rigid, as though it had just been plugged into an electric socket, causing a thousand live volts to shoot through each and every wiry vein. Polly took a nervous step backward as she beheld her teacher's quivering lips once more begin to foam. Polly believed she was well on the way to becoming something of an expert when it came to correctly evaluating as to whether an eruption was imminent. Frightened, she wondered who would take the next step. If it was up to Polly, she would have turned on her heels and raced out of the room without as much as a glance backward. But for now she was trapped, as her trembling teacher made the first move, raising both shaky hands up to her head as she attempted to remove the offensive, slippery item along with the usual bits of flora that were sticking to her haphazardly held together bun.

"Girl, get out of here now!" Mrs. McGillicuddy ordered in little more than a hoarse whisper, the blood draining from her taut face as her eyes then began their weird, pulsating movements that scared the life out of most people.

In that instant Polly recognized the familiar rumblings and so knew for sure that the much-promised volcanic eruption was now very imminent! Wisely, she turned on her heels, and after closing the door behind her, she ran down the long corridor as fast as her legs could carry her, all the time wondering why things had, as usual, taken such a terrible turn for the worse. Would she ever get things right and so begin to make any sort of promising progress? As things stood, she very much doubted it.

Chapter Five
NO JOLLY EYEBALLS

*A*s SHE MADE her way down the steep concrete staircase heading for the next lesson, she could not help but wonder why she alone was being sent for punishment, especially as she had not managed to get her hands on even one greasy, slimy ball, that is, until it came time to clean up the disgraceful mess. Not only did this feel grossly unfair to Polly, but it also served to confirm her strong conviction that because she was a child in care, she was a little miss nothing nobody from the castle, yes, a hideous, ugly blob that deserved to be cruelly laughed and sneered at. Would there ever be anyone who would willingly choose to stand up for her? Sadly, she thought not.

As she made her way toward the classroom, her mind went back in time to one of her earliest days at infant school, and it was sorely evident that her struggle with self-doubt and self-loathing had been there right from the start, only back then it had no name—just pain. She was only five at the time, and she distinctly remembered a play-time where a fight broke out with another girl the same age named Sally Smith. The fight was over a doll that they both wanted to play with, and so it was really a silly argument. It was only a stupid doll after all, but when Sally pulled Polly's hair and told her that everybody in the class called her "Smelly Welly," Polly instantly felt as though a knife had just been plunged into her stomach and then viciously twisted. She remembered her stomach felt knotted and mashed up as it immediately went into a spasm, causing her to feel physically sick and dizzy.

Polly had felt utterly incapable of retaliating or giving her accuser as good as she got. She just stood dazed and in a state of temporary paralysis as those ugly words churned around in her head while repetitiously stabbing at her heart. It had left her questioning, What exactly was wrong with her? Why couldn't she stand up for herself? Now that she was a lot older, she felt she knew the answer, for while all the other children had an abundance of relatives—mums, dads, aunts, uncles, and cousins—who repeatedly impressed on them just how special and how proud of them they were, she had nobody to give her such choice and affectionate accolades.

She had watched on as proud mums and dads came to watch their rising star perform in school plays or to parent evenings where their faces lit up as they helplessly gloried in their child's academic achievements while teachers heaped praise upon praise concerning their little Johnny or Sally. But she had never had anyone to turn up at a school concert and sing her praises or feel proud of her. She had no father to call her "little princess" or even just tell her she was good at something. She also had no sweet-smelling mother to gently kiss her forehead or put a plaster on her scraped knee or read her an uplifting bedtime story; therefore, she was left struggling her way through life with no inner stuffing or outer protective armor when it came to the cruel taunts of others. If they said she was smelly, then she was smelly. If they said she was a freak, then that was what she was, for sadly the words tore into her already mangled heart like a serrated knife, leaving her incapable of shrugging off or using any other alternative methods to fend off the cruel and ugly words and jibes of others.

Sadly, she had discovered at a very early age that children can be so terribly cruel. As an infant she had not been supplied with the ability to dismissively toss aside all insults to give way to reason. She never once considered being outraged enough to think, "Who on earth do they think they are? And why are they talking such rubbish, for my mum and dad think I'm great, and my Aunt Betsy thinks I'm the bees knees." Instead, like a sponge, she just absorbed every cruel and painful taunt that arose daily from childish playground skirmishes and grievances, and she could only think to run away and hide as, banging her head against a wall, she gave vent to pitiful cries of utter desperation and loneliness that would, if left unchecked, quickly turn to self-loathing as she learned to despise herself.

She was left feeling angry and frustrated, as well as believing that she might well have fared better if she had lived out her life in a wheelchair, for at least then she might be treated more fairly. However, her wheelchair was invisible to the naked eye, but all the same, it was a restrictive wheelchair. To her way of thinking, to be born into this world without the solace and protection of a proud and loving family was to come into this life seriously disabled. So, the question resounding through her thoughts that day was, Would things ever get any better or easier for her? Somehow she didn't think so.

Due to the cleaning up that she had been forced to stay behind and do, she was now seriously late for her geography lesson, and this sad fact got her into further trouble, as she was now the only student out of the whole class who was unable to fulfill the set tasks in the allotted time given by their teacher. She was therefore out of favor with this teacher, who at the end of the lesson was so disgusted he ordered her to do a detention in order to finish the work.

On arriving extremely late to the next class, Polly then dutifully proceeded to hand Mr. Warlord, her history teacher, a small, hand-written note from Mrs. McGillicuddy. The scrawled note merely asked for Polly to be excused fifteen minutes early from the lesson, as the headmaster had officially requested a private audience with her down in his office.

"All right, Brown. In trouble again? This letter had better be official, or else," he gently threatened.

"Yes, I promise you it is," Polly rather sullenly sniffed.

"Right, then. Don't just stand here gawking; go and sit at your desk, and I will tell you when it is time for you to leave, although I have to say that it is hardly worth you joining this lesson, as you are indeed fifteen minutes late, and you are required to leave fifteen minutes earlier than the rest."

"Sorry, sir," Polly lamely muttered.

"Well, do the board work, Brown, for you have only half an hour with which to do the task in hand," her unsympathetic history teacher muttered. "Oh, and if there is any catching up to do, well, then you will have to finish off the work in an after-school detention. Do I make myself clear?"

"Perfectly," she wearily groaned as, dragging her heels in the same fashion as her schoolbag, she turned and slunk the short distance to the only unclaimed desk in the room.

As Polly endeavored to fully immerse herself in her work, she completely forgot to look up at the clock, her teacher likewise.

Suddenly the loud, grating noise of the school bell rang indiscriminately down the long corridors, joyfully informing all grateful students that they could finally close their textbooks, for glorious lunchtime had finally arrived. None of her carefree classmates wasted any time grabbing up their personal belongings as all the cheerfully chatter-filled pupils exited the room, heading for the canteen.

On hearing the bell, a forlorn Polly looked up and loudly gasped. "Oh, help! I am now stupidly and hopelessly late for my appointment with the headmaster," she cried as she hastily gathered up her belongings and then made a desperate dash to try and exit the classroom ahead of the other pupils in order to make her way to the headmaster's office as quickly as she was able.

No one had cared to remind Polly to leave the classroom early, and no one cared that in being ordered to go to the headmaster's office it was highly probable that after being disciplined she would be ordered to leave the school premises immediately—and all because she had failed to obtain a couple of stupid, stinky eyeballs. If she was sent home, then sadly she would miss lunch altogether, and with it went her one and only opportunity to satisfactorily fill her otherwise empty belly. But who else cared if that happened? Only Polly, for only her belly would feel the terrible pangs that hunger brings. It would mean she would remain hungrier than ever, as back at the castle decent food was always in such short supply. She was in truth quite accustomed to the long wait until suppertime, but even when this frugal, unsatisfying meal was placed in front of her, it barely made any difference to her rumbling stomach, which loudly churned over, as it wished to constantly remind her that it would really like to feel more content.

All this was why she relied so heavily on school lunches, for it was the one decent and nutritious meal that gave her the necessary strength to make it through each and every school day. Without a satisfied stomach, she quickly became restless and weary and then found it impossible to stay awake and fully alert, especially in the afternoon lessons. Sadly, her tiredness had always been incorrectly interpreted by the teachers, for in their ignorance they preferred to believe that she suffered from consistent bouts of acute laziness; she was regularly punished for having such a slovenly attitude in the classroom. Understandably, it all made her really unpopular with her teachers, who without the full facts seemed so ready and willing to punish her further. It really was a vicious circle from which there appeared to be no answer or welcome release.

Of course, in all the turmoil Polly had clean forgotten she had made a fervent promise to meet up this lunchtime with her younger brother James, as they needed some personal, private time to talk over many issues that were badly troubling him. Polly slung her tatty-looking schoolbag over her heavily burdened shoulder, and with her heart and head stooped low, she raced as fast as she was able down the steep flight of stairs heading for the headmaster's office.

After standing for an indeterminate amount of time outside his office, Mr. Batty finally poked his head around the door. "Get into my office now, girl," he petulantly growled. Polly did as she was told, and once in his office she stood quietly in front of his oversized desk, her head remaining low while she watched as for the second time in less than a week her name was yet again written into his big black detention book. He then momentarily peered up from his desk to check the full facts that Mrs. McGillicuddy had so rather helpfully scribbled in her note to him, as all such things needed to be thoroughly and most accurately recorded before he could move on to suitably admonish her.

"Now then, Brown, according to the note I have in front of me, you, my girl, as per usual, failed to turn up at class with the necessary equipment, namely sheep's eyes. And all this is in spite of being reminded by your teacher last Friday before leaving the school to go home. Speak up, girl. Is this true?" he roared as he began to confront her over this latest gross misdemeanor.

"Yes, sir. It's all true," a now squirming Polly mumbled under her breath, lowering her eyelids at the same time so as not to give any further reasons for him to take offense.

"Hmm, I have to say that it's quite...quite...remarkable just how many times you are sent down to my office for failing to turn up at lessons without the correct equipment on your person. Isn't that true, Brown?"

Polly did the only thing she could do, and that was to nod her head in complete agreement and mumble a "yes, sir."

Mr. Batty drew a deep and very soul-destroying breath of despair before once more picking up his personalized pen. Without wasting any further time, he then proceeded to dip the brass nib into the ink pot, all the time muttering under his breath as he reached over for his black book.

With the book now open at a fresh page, he gave another deeply depressing sigh.

"Reason for Brown's latest detention: no jolly eyeballs," he said in a loud and very determined fashion as, rolling his eyes to the heavens to express his complete exasperation, he then accurately scribbled this latest very relevant piece of information into the correctly marked-out column of the incidents page. Having done this, he then went on to pen the day of the week, followed by the month and year. Satisfied that this latest diabolical offense was now safely logged for the whole of eternity, he exhaustedly pushed the book to one side, and after exhaling another of his loud and deeply depressing sighs, he reluctantly pulled himself up from his seat to stand with his eyes firmly shut for what seemed like an eternity.

"Hmm. All this does not sit well with me," he muttered as he walked toward the window and began staring into the distance.

As usual, Polly found the deafening silence very intimidating as she pondered what might happen next, so she began to make loud, nervous coughing noises, not because a mischievous tickle had found its way to the back of her throat but because she presumed that he had completely forgotten that she was in the same room.

Finally, like a man holding the burdens of the entire world on his shoulders alone, he moved away from the window and headed toward her. It was at this specific point in the meeting that Polly began to tremble from head to toe.

Closing his eyes, he then took yet another painfully deep breath as though preparing to invoke the power required to further discipline her. Picking up his thin cane, which had in its time been swiped over many a trouser pant of a rebellious insubordinate pupil, he then courageously edged forward toward her, tapping the stick gently across the palm of his hands as, inching nearer, he continued to intimidate her. Soon he stood just a matter of feet away from her. Bending over toward her, he began to stare directly into her face, their noses almost touching, and for the next few minutes he said not a word but continued to give young Polly his infamous evil eye that had most pupils quivering and shaking in their boots, they were so filled with fear.

Eventually he gave a loud snort and began. "Hmm. I fear for you, Brown, truly I do," he murmured, grinding his teeth as he approached her. "Yes, you are indeed one monster mistake, that's for sure," he stated in his usual abrasive manner as he rubbed his chin and continued to contemplate what punishment he should mete out. "Yes, what, if anything, are we to do with you? Personally speaking, I very much believe you to be thoroughly beyond all hope of redemption," he sighed.

"Now, I know that all of this means diddly-squat to you, my dear girl, for you are way beyond hope, but it all leaves me wondering as to what more, if anything, we can do to help you."

Polly remained with her head stooped and her eyes firmly shut as she tried to stop shaking.

"Right, Brown. Kindly remind me, which hand is it that you write with?"

"My right hand, sir," Polly mumbled.

"Good, then stretch out your left hand immediately. Come on, girl, show me your palm."

Mr. Batty raised the thin cane high into the air and brought it down swiftly.

Polly let out a tiny yelp as her open hand then automatically sprung to a close. She struggled to endure the intensely excruciating pain. Her eyes quickly filled up with tears as, embracing the painfully throbbing palm, she clenched her teeth as tightly as her closed fist, but still she was unable to prevent a strangled sob from escaping.

That bitterly anguished whimpering momentarily gave renewed hope and purpose to Mr. Batty.

"Good. I hope it hurts for days to come, for I believe corporal punishment is the only thing that gets your undivided attention," he sternly remonstrated.

Placing his cane to one side, the freshly energized headmaster stood up straight, and after inhaling deeply through his nose, he launched headfirst into his usual monotone rhetoric that, like an old and stuck gramophone record, could and probably would go on for hours. Polly was fully conversant with this excruciatingly painful scenario, for Uncle Boritz used the selfsame harrowing and mind-numbing method of torture, which was clearly designed to so wear the guilty party down they would eventually find themselves begging forgiveness for all crimes past and present—oh, as well as all those to come.

Luckily for Polly, she knew his time was nearly up when his long-winded, turgid speech got to the bit about her being one of the worst troublemakers who had ever crossed the doorway of this otherwise exemplary, high-achieving school. As usual, she remained compliant as she tried her best to look remorseful and listen intently to all he had to say. To answer back or even try to explain why she had come to school without the stupid eyeballs would only have served to make things far worse for her.

Finally and much to her relief, Polly, still clutching her stinging hand, found herself being dismissed from his presence.

"Girl, you are dismissed to go to lunch, and when you get back to class, you must try your hardest to do the right thing for once. However, from tomorrow onward you will attend lunchtime detention classes until I state otherwise. Do I make myself clear?"

"Yes, sir. Loud and clear," a very relieved Polly muttered as she tried hard to forget her stinging hand.

"Any further acts of defiance will be dealt with immediately, for you, my girl, need to know that you are only a hare's whisker away from being indefinitely suspended, if not altogether expelled from this school."

Polly would not hang around too long to become the recipient of any further menacing looks or remonstrations. She quickly swung around, and with her good hand she hurriedly reached for the door-knob, with the full intention of getting out of his office as fast as her legs would allow. But as she turned the door knob, she once again rather stupidly felt compelled to open her mouth, which in hindsight was her second very unwise move of the day and one that she would live to deeply regret.

"Mr. Batty, sir," she said as rather stupidly she turned to walk the few paces back toward his desk. "Please, may I be granted permission to speak, for I cannot leave your office without telling you that I really loved everything, yes everything, you had to say in assembly today regarding dear, sweet Stanley. He was, as you so rightly suggested, such a lovely man, and your touching words really went a long way in expressing and capturing this fact, making it such a wonderfully positive speech. Yes, it was lovely, really it was," she said dreamily, as she continued to pay absolutely no notice to the increasingly sour look on her headmaster's now very contorted face.

"But I also need to confess to feeling very troubled by all this profound sadness and grief surrounding his departure, so allow me to share with you that over the weekend—and as unbelievable as all this might seem—I briefly had the great privilege of bumping into dear Stanley in Piadora."

"Pia–what?" he stammered, lurching forward toward her face.

"Yes, Piadora, and I have to say that I've never seen him so terribly happy and pain free. I actually watched him play skittles as well as hopscotch with a group of friends," Polly casually informed him in her normal, very matter-of-fact manner while caressing her painful fingers. "And then would you believe it? He did a number of very impressive cartwheels as he made his way across a poppy field before the silly man decided it was time to climb a sky-high tree."

Sad as all this may seem, a very unversed Polly cheerfully and naively carried on with her appraisal, foolishly believing his silence meant that like a dried-up sponge he was not only drinking in but also thoroughly appreciating her. Polly—being Polly—brightly chirped on and on while remaining completely oblivious to the mounting tension that was fast growing in his study.

"I am telling you all this because I really don't think Stanley would want any of us to feel sad or unhappy now that he has gone. So Mr. Batty, don't hold back. Please tell me now. What do you think?"

A fuming Mr. Batty stood in a stupefied silence, his arms sanctimoniously folded and pressed hard into his chest as he struggled to remain fully composed and in full control, all the while searching his mind in the forlorn hope of finding suitably charitable words with which to respond. There were none to be found.

His heart began to pound erratically, and his tongue remained in perpetual spasm as it forcibly cleaved to the roof of his mouth. Try as he may, no words, kind or otherwise, would come forth. None whatsoever! For here, this day, in his office, he had been forced against his will to listen while this scruffy, illiterate, insufferable, and downright impertinent pupil thought it her God-given duty to tell him the most plainly fanciful and ridiculous stories he had ever heard regarding his school's dearly departed cleaner, stories that had this aged and severely pain-racked former school caretaker now playing childish school yard games in some hocus-pocus place called Piadora! How dare she!

Finally, and against all odds, he found his tongue.

"Brown, you recalcitrant misfit! You, girl, have successfully managed to rattle my cage, for how dare you presume to have the right to address me with such preposterously hideous and despicably outrageous ramblings? You foolish and most insolent girl!" he spluttered.

"Never in my life have I heard such utter balderdash! Get out of here immediately before I am forced to give you another hard stroke of the cane," he thundered as he continued to gnash his teeth. "And what's more, Brown, if you have even the teeniest modicum of decency hiding away in there"—he stretched out his hand to give her head a hard knock with his closed fist—"well then, you will not breathe one word of this hysterically offensive twaddle to any of his relatives. Answer me now, girl. Do you hear me?" he chokingly continued to splutter.

"Yes, Mr. Batty," Polly muttered, moving her head to one side just in time to escape one of his famous hard and malicious thumps.

Mr. Batty chose to completely ignore the bell as he continued on in his tedious, old-fashioned way to try and instill some sense into the grey matter that he could only presume lodged somewhere between both ears of this insanely stupid girl's head. Finally when he had completely run out of rhetoric, he looked down at his watch and sniffed.

"Oh, and one more thing, Brown. You can be very certain that I will be contacting your guardians concerning this latest piece of inexcusable, unwarranted, and unruly behavior. Do you hear me?" he raged.

"I'm truly sorry, sir, for I wasn't trying to be rude or to offend you. I know it sounds pretty daft, but I really did see Stanley, and he's so terribly happy, really he—"

"Silence! I order you to be silent, you ridiculously impudent child," he roared as, foaming from the mouth, his hand spontaneously hit the desk top. For the first time ever he failed most abysmally to curb his rage.

"Yes, sir," Polly replied, rather desperately placing a hand over her mouth.

"Brown, mark my words. If I hear even one more word spew forth from your runaway mouth, you will, I assure you, be in serious trouble. Do you hear me, you treacherous and uncouth little madam? Now get out of my office immediately!" he roared as he then marched most determinedly toward the door of his office. Then with the office door wide open, he then overdramatically and officiously gesticulated with a sweep of his right arm to suggest that she instantly leave his presence.

Polly didn't hesitate. She turned on her heels, and with her head hung low as usual and still rubbing her hand, she made haste to leave his office. "I'm not lying, I'm telling you the truth. Stanley is happier now than he's ever been," she mumbled loudly as she made haste to quickly exit his office.

The now very distraught headmaster thrust his head around the door and shouted down the corridor after her. "And Brown, don't even think of attending the funeral service. Do you hear me?" he ferociously barked.

Slamming the office door, he shakily headed over toward his desk, still feeling ridiculously overemotional. He was left with little choice but to admit that he felt stretched to his very limit. He was extremely angry to be feeling this way. He was, after all, the headmaster of a large school, and so to be consumed by such deep runaway feelings seemed unacceptably wrong. As he continued to experience the deepest sense of despair and agitation, he knew he had to do something, and quick, for he felt utterly spent. So, placing his outstretched hands on the desk in front of him, he took several deep breaths before audibly commanding his tattered nerves to calm down. It took a further three gulps of water from his glass before enough peace and tranquility entered his body and began restoring his deeply distressed mind, thus enabling him to pick up the telephone and begin dialing.

As he agitatedly stood by his desk listening to the ringing tone, he took further deep breaths, all the time pondering how this young, meddlesome upstart who went by the name Polly Brown could get so deeply under his skin and in doing so trouble him so very, very much. Finally, he heard a click, followed by a voice on the other end of the line.

"Good afternoon, do I have the castle?...I do. Well, that's wonderful.... Yes, I need to speak to my good friend....Yes, yes. Is dear Boritz available?...Yes....Yes....As per usual it is regarding Polly Brown's latest dreadful and downright insensitive behavior....Oh, he's unavailable at present?...Well, do please do me the consideration of asking him to contact me at his earliest convenience....Oh, you want me to hold on?...You say he's coming to the phone right now? Well, thank you so very much. I appreciate your help.

"Good morning, Boritz, old chap. It's Batty here....Thank you for asking....I am indeed in splendid health....Yes, I can confirm I am free for a round of golf this weekend....Just say a time, and I will be there....I do hope old Ebenezer Glumchops will be joining us....You say the old codger can make it? Well, splendid news, old chap. Now, while I'm on the line, don't forget to remind Mildred that Agnes has gone ahead and booked a table for four at the Toad in the Hole for eight o'clock next Wednesday evening. No, wait. What am I thinking? It's gone from the four of us to a table for six. I hope you don't mind, old boy, but I've taken the liberty of inviting dear Egor Treblinka and his wife, Ethel, to join us all. He's assured me that he will not discuss teeth, dentures, crowns, orthodontics, or any other related subject, and so I hope you don't mind, old sport. For as the saying goes, the more the merrier, eh? Oh, and please do try to remember that it's meant to be formal evening wear.

"Now then, as you specifically requested, I am also phoning to give you an update on the Brown girl....Yes, I have had an absolute belly full of her insolence. I do believe she's becoming more socially unacceptable by the minute, and therefore her ludicrous behavior almost certainly requires heavy monitoring, for she has me on the verge of doing things that the law most certainly prohibits me from carrying out....

"Yes, I know you too find her quite impossible. In fact, I have no idea how you and Mildred cope with her at all! As far as I am concerned both of you are indeed angels on assignment. It is true to say that we too have her at this school under some sufferance, Boritz, let me assure you now....Hmm...well, if something isn't done, and soon, then quite frankly I am of the growing opinion that in no time she will be beyond any form of suitable rehabilitation. Polly Brown is indeed a very disturbed and troubled mite....Hmm...hmm...

"Quite. I am therefore more than happy to write a report from an educational standpoint expressing my deepest concerns as to the poor girl's mental health. If I am to believe all you are saying with regard to her unruly behavior back at the castle, then I am of the opinion that some form of institutionalization appears to be the only alternative and safe solution for this highly problematic child. Trust me when I say I will give you all the support you require....Yes, absolutely, old chap, and it goes without saying, you scratch my back, and I'll definitely scratch yours....And you too....So I bid you good day and look forward most expectantly to a pleasant round of golf with Glumchops and your good self this coming Saturday. Agnes would also wish for me to send her kindest regards to Mildred."

Mr. Batty placed the phone back down on the receiver and then called out to his secretary, Miss Eva Beava, to come into his office, as he was in dire need of a strong cup of tea to restore his sense of well-being. He also needed to dictate a most urgent and important letter to his dear friend Mr. Scumberry showing his support and therefore adding his voice to the growing number of professionals who were known to be very concerned with Polly Brown's unruly behavior. His dear friend also required that a copy of this letter be sent to another friend and colleague, who went by the name of Dr. Nick Ninkumpoop, head of the Bureau for Mental Health Resources and Child Psychiatric Disorders.

<hr />

Meanwhile, back in Piadora Stanley Horlicks went on to win the latest round of the junior hopscotch championships. (I say junior, because in order to make it into the senior championships you had to be a lot older than our dear Stanley was.) Upon finding himself completely overwhelmed by the most unspeakable joy that he could hardly contain, Stanley then chose to whirl like a spinning top through a lush meadow, occasionally breaking out into cartwheels as he foolishly attempted to release some of this newly found and very excessive happiness. It didn't work, for he was to remain totally drunk and filled to overflowing with a most unprecedented amount of unspeakable joy.

He then went on to skip through a field of buttercups, his senses still completely overwhelmed by a ridiculous amount of irrepressible joy, all the while remaining blissfully unaware of all controversy he was now causing back at his old school. Had he known, he would quite rightly, as dear Polly dared to suggest, have been most perplexed, as well as deeply saddened. But as neither sadness nor ugly, petty disputes are welcome visitors in Piadora, it was best that he be left totally in the dark concerning such trivial earthly matters.

Chapter Six
LET'S GET TOGETHER

*B*Y BEING CALLED to the headmaster's office, Polly had avoided the usual stampede as crazily deranged, empty-bellied pupils hurtled like runaway steamrollers down the long corridors in a mad dash to be first in line for the canteen. Having spent quite a lengthy amount of time in the headmaster's office, she felt certain the line would be very short, and so she would be sitting down to eat in no time at all. She was once again wrong, for as she neared the hall she was dismayed to see how tiresomely long the line still was. Polly stopped in her tracks and took in a deep breath as she continued to follow after the unenticing smell of boiled cabbage and undercooked dumplings as their distinctive smell wafted down the long corridors of education. As she stood patiently at the very end of the hopelessly long dinner queue, she was forced to listen in on the moans and groans of the pupils around her as they attempted to guess what was on the menu for today.

"I wish this line was quicker, for I'll bloomin' starve to death before long," one boy loudly moaned.

"I bet by the time we get our dinner the only grub left will be braised liver casserole with slimy mildew cabbage," another tall, spotty lad churlishly moaned.

"Oh, boy. I hope not, for I do so hate liver," whined another.

"Well, you never know. We might be in luck and find there's still some hearty beef and vegetable stew left," another lad merrily piped up.

"Oh, yuck! I absolutely loathe their overcooked vegetables, especially the carrots, for they always look far more like dog turds," another plumpish boy added, giving a disgustingly loud belch that had all his school chums laughing out loud.

"Gross!" the other boys in the line cried out.

"Yeah, I'd rather have a couple of cheese and marmite sandwiches," he moaned.

Polly grimaced as standing in line she was forced to listen to their gruesome and horridly visual descriptions.

"Well, as long as there's still some nice pud for dessert, then I really don't mind if the first course turns out to be kidneys with mashed spuds or rattlesnake pie with beans," chipped in another chubby cheeked boy as he jostled his way into the queue.

"Don't get your high hopes up, for I'm fairly certain it's frog's spawn for pud," a sandy-haired boy piped up.

"Frog's spawn?" another lad questioned.

"Yeah, mate. Tapioca pudding."

"Oy, mate. We've been waiting here for ages, so don't push in," another lad sniffed before giving him a friendly shove.

As Polly continued to listening in, she wondered if the boys would remain so fussy if they had the misfortune to live up at the castle. For as decent food was such a rarity, she considered every school meal to be a sumptuous treat that found her savoring every tiny morsel that passed between her lips to settle oh so briefly on her tongue. As she stood listening to the lads' bitter winging, she considered herself very fortunate that so far Uncle Boritz had never considered adding sheep's eyes to the list of cheap and cheerful foods that would not only prove cost efficient but would be greatly misrepresented as he informed the starving little mites of their most impressive nutritional value. Heaven forbid that such a revolting dish as stewed sheep eyeballs would surreptitiously find their way onto the castle menu, even if they were served up with lumpy mash, brown gravy, and accompanied by stodgy, undercooked dumplings!

Minutes later found Polly standing up at the serving hatch still nursing her wounded hand as with the other hand she impatiently waited to be handed a hot plate of food. "Hmm, nice. Lancashire hotpot," she appreciatively murmured as she brought the plate right up to her nose before making a beeline for the cutlery station.

Out of the corner of her eye she suddenly noticed her younger brother, James, sitting alone, head down over an empty dinner plate and looking very rejected at the end of a long, rubbish strewn dinner table.

"Oh my goodness!" she cried as she suddenly remembered her commitment to him. This, of course, caused her to speed things up, as she desperately needed to catch up with him. With the necessary utensils clutched tightly in her hand, Polly wormed her way through the crowd of hungry students as she furiously attempted to reach his table.

Sadly, she was too late. Before she could get his attention he pushed his empty plate to one side and then stood up from where he was seated to head toward the nearest available exit. Polly, in her desperation, called out after him, but the noise in the room was far too loud for her brother to hear. She could only watch, helpless, as her younger brother departed the dining hall totally unaware that Polly had done all in her power to catch up with him and thereby fulfill her promise.

Polly let out a loud groan as rather despondently she dropped her plate onto the table nearest her before slumping miserably down on the first available seat. As she reached over toward the water jug, she heard a voice from behind that she recognized. "Hi, Polly. I hope you've reserved this seat for me." Polly turned and looked up and was pleasantly surprised to see it was the face of the new boy who earlier in the day had introduced himself as Will.

"I thought you were joking when you said we would meet up again at lunchtime," Polly openly admitted as he put his dinner plate down on the table next to hers before pulling up a chair in order to sit down beside her.

"Now, why would I do a thing like that?" he asked as he took hold of his fork and proceeded to tuck into a disgracefully large mountain of food piled high on his plate. "This grub may be lukewarm, but gosh isn't it good?" Will stated as he hungrily continued to devour everything in sight. "I'm ravenous. I swear I could easily eat a whole horse!"

I bet you could, followed closely by an overweight camel for desert, Polly thought privately as she observed him gulping down extraordinarily large mouthfuls from his plate.

"You'd better slow down, or you'll find yourself suffering severe stomach cramps before the day is up," she warned out of great concern.

Will dropped his fork onto his plate and laughed out loud. "All right then, Dr. Brown. I will slow down, but only if you agree to tell me more about yourself."

Polly immediately stopped eating and looked him straight in the eye. "Are you serious?" she asked.

"Yes, very," came the swift reply. "I want to know absolutely everything there is to know about you," he emphatically stated as he then gave her a slightly lopsided but impish grin.

"Everything?"

"Yes, everything. And I think everything means leaving nothing out," he said, giving a slow, wide grin that exposed his perfect white teeth. Polly remained fixated by his beautifully straight teeth, blissfully unaware that her mouth had dropped wide open.

"You'll pretty soon be catching flies if you sit with your mouth wide open much longer," Will kindly advised.

Polly snapped her mouth shut but continued to search his face, scrutinizing his every facial movement as she waited expectantly for the bubble to burst. *And this must happen soon*, she privately thought. *Yes, just like it always has before. Come on, Will, I'm waiting. Let me help you out here as you spring the good news on me by saying something really hurtful and unkind. Something like, "Gotcha! Sorry, but at the end of the day I was put up to this. You know what I mean, new boy and all that. Put to the test. Yep, you know how it goes. I was told that if I wanted to be part of the 'in' crowd then the super challenge of the day was for me to work out precisely who is the saddest, most pathetic loser in the school and then pretend to make friends with them. So I guess it's you, Polly Brown. So forgive my insincerity, but it really was nice meeting you."*

Polly anticipated he would then blush a bit, as if to imply he was really a decent sort of guy on a different day, oh and of course in a completely different setting. Please understand, for what else was he supposed to do? Anyone put in his position would do likewise, wouldn't they? He would then turn 'round to give the thumbs up to a large group of fellow pupils watching on from the other side of the hall, who, laughing uncontrollably, would fall off their seats as they signaled to him that he'd definitely made the grade and was therefore fully initiated, the grand prize being that he was now a fully paid-up member of the school's privileged and elite inner sanctum.

"Yes, Will. I'm waiting…"

Finally Will broke the uncomfortable silence. "Polly, help me out here. Is there something wrong? Otherwise something I should know about?

"No, no. Quite what do you mean?" she spluttered.

"Well, I feel that for some unfathomable reason my presence is making you terribly uncomfortable, so perhaps it would be better for both of us if I just move to another table to finish my lunch," he said. Without any further hesitation he began to get up from his chair to move to another table.

As he picked up his plate and turned to leave, Polly finally came to her senses and reached over to cautiously place her hand over his so as to prevent him from leaving. "Oh, no. Will, please don't go. Not just yet anyway," she begged.

Will stopped in his tracks and then sunk back down onto his chair. "Go on then. I'm all ears," he wearily stated.

"Forgive my apparent rudeness. It's just that—" Polly swallowed and then stuttered as she struggled to find the right words. Feeling like a real lemon and therefore at a complete loss for words, she reached out and picked up her fork to begin playing with her mainly untouched meal that was now stone cold.

"Is there something wrong with your hand, Polly, for you keep wincing like you're in some sort of pain?" he cautiously asked.

"Oh nothing, Will. Really, it's nothing. Honest," she replied as she then quickly removed her left hand from view by placing it on her lap.

She then bravely continued battling on in her quest to find the right words, words that would remain inoffensive but would suitably disclose why she was behaving so badly, yes so dispassionately cold and indifferent toward him, when actually she wanted his companionship more badly than she could ever dare admit.

Will, looking somewhat reluctant, sat back in the chair, his arms folded in front of him while he waited for her to fully explain herself, or at the very least, do all within her power to persuade him to stay.

"OK, Miss Misery Guts! Here's your one and only opportunity to explain to me why I am getting the cold shoulder treatment."

Polly was slow to speak, as she didn't wish to make herself too vulnerable, for this kind of situation was all too familiar to her. She would misguidedly open up from the heart, allowing her guard of self-protection to come down only to find out time and time again she really was a stupid fool. She had been kicked in the teeth more times than she cared to count, as she found herself further misunderstood, if not downright rejected. She wisely reasoned that she had only known Will for a short time, in fact, less than a day.

So let's face hard, cold facts, she thought to herself. Would he really still want her friendship once he discovered that she was just one of the many delinquent orphans who only due to the benevolence of a most philanthropic dowager were allowed to live in a castle? And as if all this was not enough, had he not taken the time to notice how severely stained her tatty, moth-eaten school blazer looked? I mean, as her jacket was only dry cleaned once a year, any idiot with half a functioning brain could easily work out the whole year's dinner menu from the many accidental spillages that now remained as disgraceful evidence down the front of her blazer. If he had, he would surely realize that she came from the poorer side of town.

He spoke so nicely, yes, slightly plum in mouth, and she could not help but notice how smartly dressed he was. His whiter-than-snow shirt was so crisp and clean, and his pressed trousers and jacket were immaculate. Worse still, he looked decidedly intelligent, so surely it would be more natural for him to choose to socialize with the other "highly intelligent" specimens, who donned thick glasses and armed themselves with even thicker books as with a distinct air of superiority and grandiose they strode with great purpose down the maze of long school corridors.

So, it made little or no sense whatsoever for him to spend any time or be seen corresponding with such a born loser. It was obvious to Polly that once Will had been at the school for a little more time, he would become more clear thinking. And when this inevitable realization took place, would he still think she was worth knowing? Polly's head was swimming with all these seriously troubling questions that had her feeling constantly exhausted as well as deeply confused. She decided it was surely in her best interest to discourage the friendship at this very early stage, for this way she could empower herself, yes, to protect herself from being seriously hurt.

Suffice it to say, she had little or no idea how to play this one, and needless to say it showed!

"Look, Polly, I have no idea as to what is going on in that pretty little head of yours—"

Pretty? Did he call me pretty? This unfamiliar and therefore unnatural and very painful word shot through her head like a commuter train hurtling at full speed through an underground station.

"Polly! Are you listening to a single word that I'm saying?" Will anxiously asked.

Polly took in a deep breath before answering. "Will, I have really enjoyed this lunchtime far more than you could ever realize, so please forgive my hesitancy. It's just that as well as being very touched, I'm equally curious as to why out of a whole school of almost eight hundred pupils you would wish to seek me out. Yes, me of all people, for I am not the best person for you to be seen hanging around. Put bluntly, it certainly won't get you the popularity vote with pupils or, sadly, any of the teachers."

Will smiled and then leaned back in his chair and began to laugh out loud.

Polly took immediate offense.

"Tell me, what's so funny, Will?" she cried as she now betrayed a keen sense of annoyance.

"Oh, now I see where the root of the real problem lies. I perceive that I'm looking at a real 'Billy No-Mates.' True or false?" he asked, his eyes remaining stubbornly fixed on hers as he waited patiently for an answer.

Polly remained curiously silent, her cheeks burning like the hot plates on a recently stoked-up stove as she casually continued to rearrange the cold food on her plate.

"Come on, Polly. Tell me that I'm right," he continued to urge.

Polly chose to remain vacant as she pushed the limp, unsavory-looking vegetables to the side of her plate, all the while remaining secretly puzzled as to how this interesting boy who was at least two years her senior could so easily have her whole innards feeling like a pile of rubble by one casual remark that totally took her off guard.

"Tell me something, Will. What does the word *insolent* mean?"

"I think it means 'disrespectful,' but don't just take my word on that."

"Oh, great, and have you any idea what *uncouth* means?"

"Hmm, I think that means 'ill mannered' or 'unrefined,' hmm— maybe even 'clumsy.'"

"Oh, good grief! Well, what about *recalcitrant*, or how about *treacherous*? What do those horrible-sounding words mean?"

"Hold on, Polly. You're going way too fast, for I'm not a walking dictionary. But tell me truthfully, why are you asking?"

"Oh, nothing, it's just that…Oh, never mind. It's all too much bother, really it is," she quietly sniffed as she experienced further distress at what those ill-fated words had finally revealed concerning her true disposition. Was she really that ill-mannered and unrefined? And as for disrespectful, never in a month of Sundays had she ever intended to be rude or discourteous to anyone, let alone a teacher. She instinctively knew that teachers worked harder than most, and she truly respected them for their dedication to their profession. So how did she alone manage to portray herself as having little to no respect for them? Oh, what a terrible problem to all she so sadly and much against her will had become.

Will watched on as though eagerly awaiting an answer as she continued halfheartedly to prod the food on her plate with her fork. The silence felt decidedly long and awkward.

Finally he decided to take matters into his own hands. "Look, Polly, I wasn't trying to be facetious, for I too have a history. And I know you're probably thinking, 'Goodness, he's a bit weird or abnormal,' or how about, 'He's just not normal!' Go on, admit it."

Polly looked up from her plate to wrinkle up her nose, but she still remained deathly quiet, leaving poor Will to carry on regardless.

"Well, at the end of the day I have to conclude that *normal* only applies to the knob on the washing machine, for as far as I'm concerned, we all go 'round at different spins, and so in my book, whoever we are, or whatever we are, well, that should be OK."

Polly couldn't believe her ears, for finally she'd met someone who saw things from the same perspective. Up until this moment she had believed herself to be alone in her thinking. After all, who has the right to decide what's OK and therefore acceptable, as opposed to what's not and therefore kooky? Who decided whether you were to be included as part of the in crowd or otherwise excluded to then be treated with pure contempt by others? Why should hideously unkind judgments be at the disposal of the beautiful-looking or the physically athletic pupils in the school? Were they within their rights to maliciously name-call or deem other pupils to be outcasts, nerds, or misfits?

Did these elite groups of students have the right to regularly send hideously spiteful letters about her and others around the classroom? To the girls concerned, this was seen as little more than light amusement to help them through another desperately boring day at school. However, for those at the receiving end, it felt very different. In fact, without wishing to appear too dramatic, it was life-threatening.

Sadly, this was indeed Polly's field of expertise, for she knew firsthand all there was to know about the subject of bullying. She had always lived in fear at home and at school, and there had never been any help from anyone. No, not one teacher or helper or social worker, for that matter, had ever come to her aid. Sometimes the threats came in the form of signals, like an index finger ominously swiped across a throat, or other messages, such as when upon opening her desk she would discover a frightening message that warned, "Watch your back, Brown, or you're dead."

Of course, all these notes were always absent of any signature whatsoever, for that would require her oppressors to be brave enough to own their words, but such cowardly creatures rarely come out in the open, preferring to opt for complete anonymity as they continue on with their cruel, sadistic, abusive oppression—and in most cases without fear of any repercussions.

Even using the school toilets created tension as she tried to fight off bullies determined to grab hold of her head, and after bashing it against one of the metal changing room lockers, they would then unceremoniously stuff her head as far down the toilet bowl as they were able and for as long as they could without actually drowning her. This inhumane practice was sadly considered very normal, and it was not just Polly but also overweight pupils, timid pupils, and pupils with thick, national health glasses who suffered. Come to think of it, any pupils who did not match up to some unwritten criteria were regularly subjected to this, and worse. On one occasion when she was using the toilets, a group of girls had thrown a bucket of water over the toilet door, drowning her in water. Polly missed the next lesson, as she stayed behind and attempted to dry her hair and clothes. Her failure to turn up at the lesson ended with a visit to the headmaster's office and a further lunchtime detention. To rat on her fellow pupils would certainly have meant further degradation the next time they caught up with her, so she had no choice but to quietly endure further punishment for bunking lessons.

Then there were the blatant, hideous lies that were fully intended to demean and degrade her in front of the boys. Yet again the girls making up the lies saw it all as merely having a bit of fun at the expense of others, of course! Polly knew with absolute clarity that they were nothing but filthy lies made up by the prettier and more popular girls in class so they could feel good and powerful. She also believed that if most students were stupid and susceptible enough to listen to and not question the lies, then those lies would stick and so might just as well be the truth. After all, why would anyone with even the teeniest amount of conscience spread wicked lies just for the sheer fun of it?

Whoever made up the ridiculously trite saying "Sticks and stones will break my bones, but words will never harm me" obviously needed to pay a visit Polly's world, if only for a day, for her life bore testimony to the fact that physical injuries, given time, will heal, but a destroyed reputation, well, that lives on forever! Sad to say, but she had known a small handful of decent, sensitive souls who, having constantly suffered and endured such malicious and injurious lies and wickedness, had come to the sad and unthinkable decision that the only way to permanently end this abuse was to bring their own young and tortured lives to a most terrible and permanent end.

Polly knew with great clarity that she had no power whatsoever to stop these weak, cowardly bullies in their tracks, for any form of retaliation only made things a whole heap worse, so just like her life back at the castle, she felt she had little choice other than to remain completely demoralized and powerless. Every day she was forced to gather up courage and brave the school corridor as she walked past these shallow, hedonistic students huddled together, immersed in conversation as all in the group shared their latest foul feast of spicy, character-destroying

THE TROUBLE WITH POLLY BROWN

tidbits. She knew these pernicious character assassinations were done purely for amusement purposes, and they cared nothing in terms of consequences, as they felt it was their right and virtue to systematically pull hers as well as other vulnerable students' reputations apart.

All this in mind, Polly nodded her head at Will, for she was in total agreement with her new friend, and she really did appreciate the analogy of the washing machine, for it truly made her smile.

Witnessing Polly's assent by a small nod of her head encouraged Will to take things further. "Polly, perhaps it would be helpful if, when it seems right, we could disclose to each other some of our best hidden secrets, and then you will know for sure that all my intentions are entirely honorable, hand on heart," he stated, giving yet another irresistible smile as he lay an arm across his chest, pointing directly to where he believed his heart presumably lay.

Polly groaned and gave another consenting nod before giving herself permission to half-smile.

"There, that's more like it. I was beginning to think you saw me as something of a freak or monster! Look, I had better be on my way, as my English class starts in less than five minutes, but how about coming back to my place for a while after school. I'm afraid my house may well shock you, for I warn you now that it's a bit of a tip. But if you can see past the mess, well then, I'd love you to come and pay an impromptu visit to my world."

"I'm awfully sorry, Will, but that really won't be possible. I have duties that I need to attend to after school that sadly prevent me from saying yes."

"Well then, what about after school tomorrow? I make a great cup of tea, really I do. And for such a lovely lady, well I might even consider handing out a scrumptious biscuit or two," he said optimistically in his gentle but very persuasive manner.

Polly smiled but still continued to shake her head.

"Wednesday? Thursday?"

Still Polly shook her head.

"OK then, Miss Popularity! What about sometime over the weekend? Can you see your way to somehow squeezing me into your overbooked social calendar?" he asked in a voice oozing great charm as he pulled out all the stops in his attempt to win her over and thereby get her full agreement.

"We'll see," was all Polly could come up with in response to her new friend's eager suggestion.

Completely undeterred, Will stood up to leave the table, and after gently pushing his chair to one side, he bent over to whisper in her ear. "I'm not about to give up on you, Polly Brown. You will be a good friend to me. Just you wait and see."

Meanwhile, back in Piadora Ralph turned to face Hodgekiss. "My! Wasn't it a reckless, if not most splendid idea of yours to move Will over to Polly's school? Thank goodness he has the tenacity and character to persevere with young Polly, for I do believe there are times when she rather unwittingly plays very hard to get.

Hodgekiss nodded his head in agreement. "Yes, but considering all she has been through, I am more than delighted to observe that she has over time made a tremendous amount of progress."

"Hmm. Needless to say, her trials are about to deepen, and then, Hodgekiss, you must surely agree that she will be in need of a strong shoulder for support," Ralph stated, a deep and perplexed look of concern written all over his face as he anxiously beheld his master's loving eyes.

"And to cry on?" Hodgekiss interjected.

"Yes, and sadly, to cry on."

Chapter Seven
MISS SCRIMP 'N' SAVE

*P*OLLY JUST ABOUT made it through the afternoon lessons without any further trouble or mishap, and soon she found herself sitting on a train with her eyes temporarily closed and her head back as she tried to rest. She felt unusually tired, and she just wished that she might get through the evening chores without physically collapsing.

Soon the train pulled into the station, and after exiting the station, she crossed the road to stand in line with all the other pupils by the bus stop. After finding a seat on the bus, Polly once more closed her eyes, and this time all she could do was think about her new friend, Will. "Dear God, please let Will turn out to be my first ever true and loyal school friend," she quietly whispered under her breath.

She then picked up her schoolbag and spent a few minutes rummaging through it until she finally pulled out an exercise book. Polly opened the thin book and ripped out a clean sheet of paper. Then, taking a pen from her pencil case, she began to write another letter to her dear, much-missed friend Aazi.

Dear Aazi,

I do hope this letter finds you in extraordinarily good health. Every day I hope and pray for some word of you, but sadly to date I have heard nothing. This in itself has me feeling both worried as well as anxiously concerned for you. I therefore beg you to write to me, as I long to hear how you are getting on. Currently nothing much has changed in my sad little life, for I am still little more than a horrible stench under my guardians' noses, and despite all my efforts to be good, I seem to always be in hot water (that means "trouble"). With all the chores I am expected to complete at home, it leaves me little time to do my homework, so then I am in even more trouble at school.

James, my younger brother, seems more distant than ever, as we rarely get the time to just be together as brother and sister. This makes it all the more difficult for me to bear. I love him so dearly, and I wish I could rescue us both from this awful place. Sometimes I despair that things could or will ever change.

Even our very precious time together now seems such a thing of the past that I do all I can to constantly recall those very special moments that I am most grateful we got to share.

On a much lighter note, a new boy has started at my school. His name is William, but we all call him Will for short. Anyway, he seems really nice and kind, and can you believe it? He appears to want to be friends with me. I must tell you privately that this really troubles me, because I have no idea as to the real reason behind why he is being so kind to a person such as me. I have to be honest and upfront when I tell you that my school is filled to overflowing with really pretty girls who are far more intelligent than I could ever hope to be and who come from the sort of nice families that I could only ever dream of being a part of, so it makes no sense at all that he should want to be seen hanging around with a useless urchin such as the likes of me.

THE TROUBLE WITH POLLY BROWN

I will try my very best to approach this friendship with extreme caution, and time alone will surely tell if he is the real deal, as opposed to just another artful imposter!

Anyway, Aazi, I am sorry this letter is short, so sadly lacking in any really interesting information, but the school bus is about to pull into the bus station, and from the moment I arrive back at the castle it's one chore after another until bedtime finally arrives. So I send you all my love and wait with bated breath as well as great anticipation to hear all your news, good and bad. Please, please, I beg you to answer my letters, for I am beginning to feel hopelessly sad that something is very wrong or that I have unwittingly offended you, something I seem very clever at doing, according to many of my teachers, as well as my guardians. Well, I must sign off now.

Affectionately yours.

Oh, and oodles and poodles of love!

Polly, xxxxxxxx *Polly*

PS: As per usual, please disregard all ridiculous rules regarding hygiene and just lick off yet another piece of rather yummy squashed and squidgy choco-late. Don't wait. Just do it.

PPS: Aazi, I do feel the need to get something off my chest that is causing me great concern. In an earlier letter I mentioned that for a season the school would be showing us a number of films about everyday life in Africa. Well, over the past three months or so we have seen probably five or six films showing different regions of your beautiful country. Aazi, I have to concede to feeling most alarmed and shocked to discover that nobody on the African continent appears to wear any clothes whatsoever! And of the few tribes that do, most are still unbelievably very scantily clad. So my question to you is simply this, Are clothes so disgracefully expensive that they are beyond one's purse, or is this more a case of personal preference?

I for one realize that the weather is extremely hot and humid, and I fully realize that this must also save on the washing bill, but I have to say that personally speaking I would feel most embarrassed to be out and about without a single stitch of clothing on my person. In England, people are expected to be a little more discreet, and so we do our utmost to cover up at all times, purely, I suppose, as a matter of decency. So if I were you, I would at least be on the look out for a loincloth or two! I would therefore be very grateful if you would explain this one to me. Oh, I hope my asking hasn't offended you. (Can't really believe I'm asking about this, but I wouldn't be me if I didn't!)

PPPS: Oh, I've completely forgotten my last point, so will most likely write it down in my next letter.

After producing an old, yellowing envelope from her bag, she then rummaged in her blazer pocket until she found a certain item she was looking for. After producing a small chocolate, she removed the foil wrapper and then proceeded to roll the chocolate between her fingers until it became melted. Satisfied that it was now sufficiently gooey, she then squashed the chocolate down hard on the bottom corner of the letter.

"There, finished," she whispered as she slipped the letter into the envelope, and then, using her tongue, she licked the envelope before firmly sealing it down.

As she remained seated on the bus, she once again noted that there was not one single girl from Snobbits Preparatory School on the bus, and come to think of it, she hadn't seen Mrs. O'Brien, their teacher, either for a long time—come to think of it, not since she returned from Piadora. All this was becoming very disconcerting for her, for Mrs. O'Brien had definitely told Polly that she too had to leave Piadora and make her way back to the school; otherwise, the girls would be without a cookery teacher. So what in the world was going on that could satisfactorily explain their continued absence from the bus stop?

In no time at all the bus came to a halt at the place where she normally got off. But today Polly still had one very urgent matter that needed to be taken care of, to once more visit dear, delightful Mrs. April Strudel and politely offer to take her yappy little dogs for a long walk to exercise them, so she stayed on the bus until it reached the village.

The sweet-smelling lavender-and-lace lady was, as always, overcome with delight at Polly's generous offer to walk her dogs, and so she paid Polly handsomely for her services. She then dropped an extra penny into Polly's hot little hand when she saw that both her usually over-excited pups had come back from their regular walk looking more exhausted and worn out than ever, so they were very ready for an afternoon nap.

"Same time next week," Polly shouted at the slightly deaf, sweet-smelling lady as she waved her good-bye and hurriedly headed for the post office to get her stamp before the office shut for the day.

"Phew! Thank goodness. As usual I've only just made it just in time," she said, beaming from ear to ear as she gladly passed the money over to a middle-aged woman who sat the other side of the glass counter.

"This is becoming quite a habit," the mean woman sourly sniffed as she grabbed hold of the money.

"What do you mean?" Polly innocently asked, giving another huge smile.

"Turning up here when I am just about to close the counter," the po-faced lady bitterly stated.

"Oh, I am so sorry, but I am so very happy to be here posting another letter to my friend."

"Has he ever replied to even one of your endless letters?" the miserable and moody lady sourly questioned Polly.

"Well, if I'm honest, to date, as you rightly suggest, I have not received a reply. But that does not mean I won't, for you see he lives in the jungle in darkest Africa, so I imagine that it is probably much more difficult for him to get to a post office."

"If you'll believe that, then you'll believe anything!" she snarled.

"Oh, I know he'll write eventually, for he's such a lovely person. Just you wait and see," Polly stated in a very matter-of-fact tone of voice as she continued to beam from ear to ear.

The frosty looking lady in the horn-rimmed spectacles failed to respond with any form of kind gesture, other than to slip a small, single postage stamp under the glass counter along with a halfpenny in change before abruptly pulling the blind down to show the office was now officially shut. Polly failed to take any offense at the lady's surly behavior because she was so caught up in the moment of posting yet another very important letter to her friend. She was also equally delighted to realize that she still had enough change leftover to buy four Black Jacks at the sweetshop, two for her and two for her younger brother, James.

She was in the process of sticking the stamp to the envelope when the distinctive red mail van on its last mission of the day pulled up at the curb. As the postman, with keys in hand, leapt out of the van and made his way toward the red pillar box that required emptying, Polly completely took him by surprise as she rushed over and stuffed her precious letter into his open hand.

"Please, Mr. Postman, take the greatest care with this important letter and faithfully promise me that it won't get lost at sea," she begged. "It is going many miles over land and ocean, and at all costs it must get into the hands of a most special friend of mine."

The postman smiled and promised that, as with all her other letters, this would be as safe as houses all the while her letter remained in his possession. He also suggested that Polly should try and have a little more faith in the British postal service, as he went on to remind her that it was considered the most efficient service in the world and had Her Majesty's personal seal of approval.

"Yes, young lady, that is why it is called the Royal Mail," he indignantly sniffed.

"Oh," gasped a sincerely repentant Polly as secretly she thought back to all the letters she had previously posted to God, letters that she concluded He couldn't possibly have received; otherwise, He would surely have been gentleman enough to reply to them!

Polly smiled at the postman and told him that as a result of his genuine and most sincere promise, she could now trust him with her whole life—oh, as well as with her precious letter, of course! "Oh, Mr. Postman, let me tell you, you're such a darling angel," she cried as she grabbed hold of the poor, unsuspecting postman's hand and then gave it an overwhelmingly long and seriously hearty shake.

With his full sack of letters and small parcels bundled into the back of the mail van, the now shaky and overemotional postman wiped away a tear and then waved good-bye to Polly before turning the key in the engine to set off down the lane. As the engine came to life, there was a loud, strange noise, followed by a series of very disconcerting rumbles. Polly stopped in her tracks and watched as hundreds of white feathers very mysteriously shot out from the undercarriage of the van as it then sped off like a rally car down the long and winding country lane.

As Polly stood transfixed by the feathers dancing around in front of her, a gust of wind unexpectedly forced the feathers higher up into the air until they came to circle above her head before floating down to land near her feet. *How perfectly strange,* Polly thought to herself, as in what might be considered a stupefied trance she turned on her heels to head back to the castle.

⚬•⊷•⚬

On Polly's arrival back at the castle, she was to be pleasantly surprised to hear firsthand that Uncle Boritz and Aunt Mildred were not at home, nor would they be coming back any time soon. "They had to go to London on a matter of the greatest urgency. That's all I or any of us know at the moment," Natalie Nitpick whispered in hushed but very officious tones. "So sadly for all of us, the recently arrived ex-prison warden has been authorized to take complete charge until they return," she continued to inform, as though she believed it to be her personal duty to relay all relevant and important information on to Polly, as well as any other passerby, whether they cared to ask or not.

"You mean Miss Scrimp?"

"Who else?"

"Does that mean I've finally got an evening free from horrid chores?" Polly wistfully asked.

"No such luck, Polly," Natalie promptly replied. "Aunt Mildred has seen to it that you are kept busy, for she has left you her latest very lengthy list of duties. You can't miss it, for it's pinned to the wall above the kitchen sink."

Polly wearily made her way up the creaky oak staircase heading for the dormitory to change out of her school uniform into clothes more appropriate for hard work. On her way back down the stairs, she bumped into James, her younger brother, who was sitting on the bottom stair holding one of his model air planes but looking very glum and miserable.

Polly felt overwhelmed with remorse. She had no way of explaining that it was not entirely her fault that she had failed to meet up with him at lunchtime, but sadly she knew no excuse would work. She had, as usual, let him down, and the realization that they were drawing further apart than ever was oh so painful. They had already lost their beloved brother, Thomas, so surely it was time for them to close ranks and become close, and yet sadly the opposite seemed to be happening. Words failed her, and it was true to say that since she had returned from Piadora, they had not spoken as much as one kind sentence to one another. In fact, it was farther back than then, for if she rightly remembered, she had not really spoken to him since before dear Thomas's funeral. She therefore felt terribly guilty, as being his older sister it was surely her responsibility to be there for him. She believed that his heart must surely be broken by the death of Thomas, so she knew his loneliness must match hers, but how could she communicate the love and compassion she felt inside when they rarely had the luxury of just being together to enjoy each other's company as brother and sister?

Polly slowly forced herself to sit down on the staircase and snuggle up beside him before tentatively placing an arm around his shoulder. "James, we need to talk, and I have no way of saying how sorry I am for letting you down at school today. I have no excuse whatsoever, but all I can say is I really love you, and I know of no way of making things right between us," she whispered, her cracking voice completely betraying the anguished pain behind her words as she willed herself not to start crying. James made no response to her appeal, so Polly could only think to hug him tighter, her eyes brimming with tears as she considered the sad fact that she had no words left to express her pain at letting him down.

She knew that no words would suffice. No apology could act as balm on a gaping, open wound, and she was left feeling that her only hope lay in the fact that maybe one day he might come to a full realization of the truth. If then he understood, then surely forgiveness would finally flow.

Polly hugged him tighter than ever. James shrugged off her expression of love by removing her arm from his shoulder before placing his model plane by his side. He then buried his face in his hands as if to express that all communication was over. They were now way past any hope of sorting things out.

Though hurt by his blatant rejection, Polly pretended that all was well, and so she continued on.

"Hey, is this the plane you've been working on?" she brightly asked as she picked up the model to further admire it. "Why, James, you've done a really wonderful job," she enthused. "So tell me, what's this one called?"

James lifted his head just enough to mumble. "It's a Spitfire, and I would tell you its complete history if you ever cared to take the time to listen."

Polly broke into a smile. "Now, you know time is one thing I don't have, James, but I wish I did," she said, giving a heavy sigh to express something of her deep regret. "I think it's remarkable just how much you know about planes, tanks, and ships. You're incredible, and I can say hand on heart that as usual you've done a really brilliant job."

Polly carefully placed it back on the staircase before throwing caution to the wind by replacing her arm back around his slumped shoulder to give it a firm squeeze. "You always do such a beautiful job on your models. I wish we had more pocket money than a meager penny a week, because I would buy you every model kit that exists," she said, giving him another hug. James remained cold and unmoved despite her generous display of affection, but Polly—being Polly—was not about to give up.

"Oh, dear brother of mine, can't we call a truce? I know there must be times when you think that I don't care, but let me assure you that nothing could ever be further from the truth," she said, giving another deep and troubling sigh as she reached out to tilt his chin upward and observe for herself his pale, withdrawn-looking face. Looking him directly in the eyes she softly continued on. "You know as well as I do that the boys' wing of the castle is completely out of bounds to us girls, so apart from school there seems to be very little time left for anything other than horrid chores. But it doesn't mean I don't care," she desperately cried.

"Truth is, I really love you, and sometimes I love you oh so much that it truly hurts. Yes, James, it's like a physical pain that will not go away, because everything inside of me yearns to free us both forever from this horrid, hate-filled castle," she earnestly cried out, all the while patiently hoping for some positive form of response from James. Anything!

Still he sat with his head between his hands as though he wasn't listening to a word she was saying.

"I know, like me, you must be feeling terribly sad and alone, especially now that Thomas is no longer with us," she sniffed, her eyes filling with fresh tears as she thought back to the funeral and also because she witnessed a sudden show of pain on her younger brother's wearied face. Polly seized the moment by grabbing hold of one of his small hands before gently squeezing it.

"James, we will never, ever forget Thomas—no, not even for one minute will he be out of our prayers. I promise you, hand on heart, that we will be reunited with him, and that wonderful day will be filled with great joy. This I promise," she stated with great authority, mingled with immense tenderness.

As she talked on, Polly suddenly witnessed the first signs of hope in James, for she saw a lone tear race unchecked down his left cheek before pausing to momentarily dangle beneath his chin. She quickly moved forward, and with her hand she gently wiped it away.

"Look, James, maybe we can talk again later this evening if by some unforeseen miracle I can get through my chores early," she tenderly whispered in his ear.

James once more buried his head in his hands, but eventually he reached out just enough to place a hand on hers as if to say that even though he was furious with her, he was still touched that she had made the effort to sit down with him and at least try to explain herself. True, it had not changed much, but even so, it had momentarily formed a bridge between them. Polly gave his hand another friendly squeeze and then stood up to leave.

"Look, as usual I'm very late starting my chores, James, and if I don't hurry up and start the tea soon, I will be in even deeper trouble." James looked up and nodded, and as he did Polly could have sworn she saw even more tears welling up in his eyes. "See you later," she said, giving him a long and lingering smile before heading off toward the kitchen to begin the evening duties.

As she walked, she thought about the tasks at hand. "Right, I've got to clean the bathrooms, wash the kitchen floor, cook tea, followed by a mountain of ironing, and then before I go to bed I must polish the shoes all by myself as surprise, surprise Cecilia is off sick again! Oh, great! Nothing new, but just as I suspected, there will be no time to catch up on my homework, which is now beginning to seriously mount up."

Polly was still deciding the best order in which to tackle the mountain of tasks when Miss Scrimp perkily marched through the open kitchen door and sidled right up her. She gave Polly a quick elbow in the ribs and then turned to face her, eyeball to eyeball.

"Polly, as you can see, I have once more been left in charge, and even though I have only been in this new post a number of months, I fully intend to stay and make my mark. So, understand me when

I categorically state that there will be no slacking whatsoever," she loudly and curtly muttered.

"Yes, Miss Scrimp," Polly wearily muttered.

Suddenly one of the boys entered the kitchen and informed Miss Scrimp that there was a tramp at the door asking for a cup of tea and something to eat. "He also asked to see Polly," the boy breathlessly stated.

"Sorry, Polly. You know the rules as well as I do. Uncle Boritz has clearly specified that you are no longer allowed any form of communication with the transients and vagrants who ring the doorbell, and this means you are forbidden from taking mugs of tea or any food out to them. With that said, you can make the tea and cheese sandwich, but then I will have to order one of the other children to take it out. Have I made myself clear?"

"Perfectly, Miss Scrimp."

"Good, because may I remind you that it will be my neck on the chopping block if they discover otherwise!"

"Yes, Miss Scrimp. I will not disobey your orders."

"Oh good, and please don't think that while the cat's away, the mice can be allowed to play, for I assure you I will be standing over you to make sure that every task is done to dear Mildred's highest standards. So chop, chop! There's no time left for loitering. After putting the kettle on, you will need to head over to the sink, for there are a large number of potatoes in the sink that require peeling," the old battle-ax snorted as once more she sunk one of her razor-sharp elbows directly into Polly's arm. "When you're on ROPE, don't expect life to be a bundle of fun. Oh, and before you start on the potatoes, this large tin of jam needs the furry green-and-gray mold scraped off the surface. Just get as much off the top as you can, and then stir in the rest," she brusquely ordered.

"Oh, please, Miss Scrimp. As my guardians are away, can't you just turn a blind eye and allow me to throw it away? It looks really disgusting."

"Girl, stop your insolence now, and just do as I say, for if I say scrape, then that's what you'll do. We're here to save money, not throw it away. Do you understand?"

"Yes, Miss Scrimp."

"Well, then repeat after me: 'It's my duty to be thrifty at all times; therefore, I will always seek to save whatever can be saved.'"

"Yes, Miss Scrimp."

"It's called being cost effective, I'll have you know."

Polly grimaced as she considered what she was being asked to do.

"Well, what are you waiting for, child? Or do you need reminding that mold is, in fact, very good for you. Rest assured it's considered by many to be good, wholesome bacteria that will serve nicely to protect you from all sorts of detestable illnesses. Joseph Lister was, after all..."

Polly gave a resigned smile as she glumly thought how odd it was that everybody she knew had such blind faith in Uncle Boritz and his profound words of wisdom that they all happily recited them verbatim at every opportune moment. Yes, if Uncle Boritz stated with much authority that eating serious amounts of gray fungi and festering mold was not only good for you but could actually save your life as it medicinally acted to ward off all horrid, ghastly germs, well then, it was the best thing for you, end of story. And so Polly grew to understand that his word on every imaginable subject was not only supreme but actually precedent and therefore not open to reason, unable to be changed, tampered with, or violated in any shape or form, unless, of course, you desired to challenge his supreme lordship and thereby land up on trial in one of his man-made court-martials.

Polly made tea and sandwiches, and then she went on to successfully scrape off what she deemed to be a reasonably decent amount of gray mold from the surface area of the jam. She then dutifully went to a drawer in search of a wooden spoon to do as she had been ordered, and this was to stir the residual spunky-looking mold into the rest of the jam. Miss Scrimp stood watching on, her severely wrinkled and withered arms folded as her never-blinking, cold, beady eyes bore into the nape of Polly's neck. Polly imagined her mind was in constant overdrive as she continued to scheme all sorts of extra mealy-minded ways to make Polly work harder and thus more efficiently.

Miss Scrimp was a waspish sort of woman with grayish, paper-thin skin and severely slit eyes, which truly resembled the narrow windows of some bygone fortress tower. And, I might add, when this fearsome woman was on the war path, it would be no lie to suggest that many a fiery arrow seemed to shoot from them. Her misshapen beak was long and narrow, as were her yellowing, razor-sharp teeth, which appeared as though with one bite they could easily crunch straight through to the bone of her unsuspecting victim like a hungry-bellied barracuda. The remainder of her slight torso appeared like a cardboard cut-out, for it was minus even an ounce of unwanted flesh, and the bones of her rib cage were so clearly visible that they could easily be counted, and often were by the children as she stood, hand on hip, officiously screaming out her orders.

She had thinning, wiry hair scraped into a very formidable-looking bun and equally thin and permanently pursed lips that no longer bore testimony to a mustache, as quite recently Aunt Mildred had seen it as her duty to introduce the woman to the art of clinical waxing. However, any further feminist acts were to be considered an absolute no-no. She wore sensible, flat shoes all the time and equally sensible long-hemmed skirts that did a painfully poor job in hiding her excessively saggy knees.

But this hauntingly fragile image was one of pure deceit, for not only did this woman have the masculine hands of a carpenter—large, rough, and extensively cracked—but her record for accurately hitting her target, mainly that of a child's ear as he or she passed by, was, to say the least, impeccable! Perhaps much of this precision had been honed when as a young adult she had been something of a champion log thrower. At least, this was among much of the salacious gossip that was now regularly being bandied around the castle.

In the weeks and months since this woman had taken up the appointment, she had more than delighted the Scumberrys with her absolute professionalism. "I have the ideals of Hitler and the barbaric determination of Mussolini," she would bark at the terrified children if they dared to sass her. Of course, most of the children had little to no idea as to quite whom she was referring to, as they were not the least familiar with Hitler or Mussolini. All the same, they could not fail to get a very clear picture of where she was coming from.

Her excuse for having such unsightly, blemished hands was the long length of time they were subjected to chemically based detergents as she scrubbed away from dawn to dusk in the washroom. Sadly, this sanctimonious woman's tongue was also believed to have been accidentally dipped in a large bowl of caustic soda, for every word that spewed forth from her lips carried with it the harshest and meanest criticism and judgments. They never failed to chill each and every child down to the very marrow of his or her bones.

As if all this wasn't enough, she had also been blessed with obscenely large feet, and many a child's trouser pant bore testimony to her specialist skills as they raced down the corridors trying very hard to stay well out of reach of her boot.

Polly noted that there was not a single item of jewelry adorning her heavily lined turkey neck, for such self-indulgence was deemed absolutely unnecessary. Neither was there the faintest whiff of anything womanly or sweet-smelling, as this might cause a certain amount of confusion to the few hand-picked visitors who were occasionally allowed past the main gate of the castle. Yes, visitors who might mistakenly presume that on the quiet she had a man in her life might otherwise just as incorrectly assume that she led a life of pure wanton excess. Therefore, the one and only odor that emanated from her many skin follicles to follow this painfully practical woman around the castle was the all-too-familiar smell that came from the excessive use of carbolic soap. Indeed, Polly conceded that there was not a frivolous bone to be found anywhere in this woman's odious body, and that was official!

Having found a suitably sharp knife in the drawer, Polly headed over toward the sink, which was filled with the potatoes that required her immediate attention. She carefully removed her precious ring from her finger and gently placed it down on the drainer for safety before picking up a knife to start peeling.

Polly found it hard to complete her tasks with Miss Scrimp, otherwise known to all as "Dragon's Breath," presiding over her like a fixated hawk anxious to swoop down on its prey. She could almost feel the woman's hot and foul-smelling breath on the nape of her neck, as well as the strong, stale whiff from sweaty armpits mixed with carbolic soap as she stood over Polly as she attempted to mop the floors before going on to polish a whole household of shoes.

"Go easy on the shoe polish, Polly. Do not use frivolous amounts. Remember, we're here to save when and wherever we can."

Finally, old Dragon's Breath left the room to check that the younger children were doing as they had been ordered and so were getting ready for bed.

As Polly continued on with her kitchen chores, she had one little pleasure that truly helped to keep her going, and this was when she was given the opportunity of listening to the radio, which sat on a high shelf, well out of reach of all the children. Polly loved listening in so much that it took much of the hardship out of the tasks as she sang along to all the new hits that made their way into the charts. It could be said that she knew the words to every hit song, and if she didn't, then she would not rest until she learned the words by heart.

That night she was really enjoying herself as she sang along to hit record after hit record while peeling an insurmountably large basinful of potatoes. The humorous disc jockeys always interspersed the music with personal witty stories, as well as many touching letters from listeners writing in to the show and other frivolous chitchat that never failed to make her tedious jobs feel lighter and more bearable. This night, like every other Friday night, disc jockey Tony Tictac had promised his best ever show.

"We even have a rare interview with Superstar Freddie Fruitless coming up in just five minutes, and we will be inviting you, the listeners, to phone in and express your feelings concerning his latest, very controversial single," the DJ excitedly told his audience of listeners. "I promise all of you out there listening in on my show that this is one interview you will surely not want to miss, because Freddie has agreed to come on the show to discuss his choice of lyrics on his latest released single, as well as his last album, which is causing quite a storm nationwide. So, mums and dads, you've just got time to put the kids to bed or pop the kettle on and make a quick cuppa while we play his latest single, 'Why Does Bad Feel So Good?' followed up by his last number one, 'I'm Real Wicked to the Core.'"

Polly's ears pricked up when she heard Freddie's name mentioned, and immediately her thoughts went back to their last awful meeting, when not only had he refused to help her and her seriously ill friend Toby, but he had taken things further by forcing her to kneel on the ground and beg forgiveness before pushing her face down into a muddy pool.

As those sad memories came flooding back, she had the distinct feeling that nothing much had changed in Freddie's notably narcissistic life. However, Polly felt compelled by a morbid fascination to listen in on the interview, which the DJ said would be taking place in just over five minutes. Polly had finished all the kitchen chores and knew the only way she would get to listen in on the interview was if she borrowed the radio while she was doing her shoe-cleaning chores. Having climbed onto a chair, she was able to grab hold of the radio and sneak it into the cold room, where normally with Cecilia's help she nightly polished all the shoes.

Just as he promised, two songs later the noticeably excited DJ began his interview.

"Well then, Freddie, it's great to have you here in our humble little studio in Merseyside. Do me a huge favor by reminding our listeners just how many number one hits you've had."

"Tony, it's great to have me on your show, and to be perfectly honest, I can't remember, but I think it's either thirteen or fourteen number one's when I last cared to count," he cheerfully stated. "Yep, I think it's safe to say it was fourteen at last count."

"You must be really pleased to hear that your latest, and I might add controversial, single, 'Why Does Bad Feel So Good?' which was only released two weeks ago, has just made it to number one in the British charts."

"Yeah, Tony. Now, how cool is that?" he laughed.

"Not cool at all, Freddie," Polly abruptly interjected. "When are you going to grow up and start behaving like a responsible adult?" she angrily sniffed.

"Well, Freddie, I hope you don't mind, but the question on a lot of parents' minds is, Quite what is behind your latest message?"

"Yes, you've got that one right, Tone, for we're all asking that one," Polly snorted.

"Sorry, Tony. I'm not exactly sure what you're getting at."

"Well, Freddie, allow me the privilege of spelling it out for you. The lyrics to many of your songs appear to flaunt and encourage rebellion, and they all seem to have a blatant disregard toward the monarchy, as well as being anti-establishment."

"Yeah, right. Well I happen to believe that we should scrap the monarchy, and while we're at it, let's scrap the government. Yeah, be done with the lot of them," he snorted. "They are, after all, nothing more than a financial drain on the British economy," he insisted.

"And so are you!" a very angry Polly shouted. "How dare you be so disgracefully rude about our dear queen and our government," she continued to cry out as, taking hold of a stiff brush, she began to exact her revenge on the shoe in her hand. Yes, in history past, the queen would have been perfectly entitled to shout, "Off with his head!" to such a horrible, rude person.

"Freddie, dare I suggest that your lyrics seem deliberately antagonistic, as they regularly criticize our society leaders and imply that it's all right for all of us to do exactly whatever we fancy, whenever we feel like doing it? Are you sure this is the message you want to get out there?"

"Yeah, sure, Tony. I understand where you're coming from and what you're getting at, but shouldn't it be all right for all of us to do whatever makes us happy and has us feeling great?"

"Well, pardon me for saying this, but that sounds absurdly selfish to me, for surely that can't be right if it is at the expense of others?"

"My sentiments exactly!" Polly loudly shouted at the radio as she furiously continued brushing the same shoe.

"Well, I can't answer for anyone else, can I?" Freddie sourly stated, his voice beginning to betray distinct signs of irritation.

"OK, but surely you can agree with me that there are some things that, although they seem or appear right, plainly are not right."

"Go on, Tone. Give it to him," Polly shouted at the radio.

"I dunno! Don't ask me, Tony. I'm just a regular London lad. I'm not Einstein! Admittedly, I do get drunk, and yeah, I do confess to taking a few drugs, mainly for health reasons, of course."

"Oh, yes. Of course," the DJ replied with an underlying note of sarcasm in his voice.

"But Tony, be a good bloke and give me a break here, for I do all these things because of the serious pressure that I'm constantly under. It's one of those things that just happens, probably because I'm constantly in the limelight," he tried to suggest.

"Freddie, I have to be blunt and say that it's you who puts yourself in the limelight when you do and say such blatantly crazy things."

"Quite right, Tone," Polly interjected.

"Yeah, I know that, Tony, but really underneath I'm just a lovable pop idol who girls dig so much they put my posters on their bedroom walls and go to sleep most nights dreaming of me. What is also true is that we all know that the kids love to get high as they dance to the hypnotic rhythm of my beat. So tell me, now what could possibly be wrong with any of that? What the world needs more of is love, sweet love, and I'm happy to oblige, for I love the chicks, and the chicks, well, they really love me."

On hearing all this nonsensical rubbish, Polly could hardly contain herself a moment longer.

"Right, Freddie, but that's only because they don't really know you. If they did, they'd know for sure that not only do you know nothing about true, unselfish love, but you're sadly nothing more than a callous, egotistical drunkard who'd sell your grandmother up the river for less than tuppence halfpenny," she continued to furiously yell at the radio.

"Well, that's why I'm asking you all these specific questions, Freddie, for you seem to be so proud of your drug-taking antics and wild parties, and so many of your songs, dare I say it, not only seem aimed at teenagers but in many ways appear to encourage kids to copy you in pulling off outrageous stunts or otherwise succumb to random acts of violence."

"What particular act of violence are we talking about here, Tony?" a now furious Freddie raged.

"Only last week you hit the headlines when you smashed up the hotel suite you were staying in."

"OK, hands up on that one. Maybe things did get a little out of control," he childishly sniggered. "Yeah, Tony, not too keen to do that one again, for that unfortunate little episode cost me an arm and a leg," he added. "The bill ran into the thousands."

"Shame on you, Freddie!" an indignant Polly continued to shout into the radio. "That money could have been put to much better use," she cried. "Instead you spend it all getting high and wrecking hotels, you stupid, dumb idiot."

"Well then, Freddie, there was also that girlfriend who claims you assaulted her. It was the main story selling papers a few weeks ago, and I think I am speaking on behalf of most of my listeners when I say that the whole nation was shocked by the severity of her injuries. I mean, you must have seen that the front page of most newspapers had pictures of her lying in a hospital bed covered in bruises with a severely fractured jaw."

"Tony, what can I say in my defense except to say, don't believe everything you see and read? She really didn't look half as bad as some of those pictures portrayed."

"Excuse me?" a shocked Tony interrupted.

"Go on, Tone. Go for the jugular, and give him what for," Polly shouted as she continued to butt in on the interview.

"Tony, you wanna know something? I believe the media are really out to get me, really I do. I mean, I feel framed. Yeah, the whole thing's a setup, for they definitely used theater makeup to make her injuries look a whole heap worse than what they really were," he mournfully bleated.

"But wait a minute, Freddie! You really don't get it, do you? No decent, thinking man would ever think to resort to any such violence. No woman deserves this, for may I say that at the end of the day they are the fairer and, so, the weaker sex. And I have to add that no right-minded man would ever think to do such a thing," the frustrated DJ cried out as he tried and failed to understand where his guest was coming from. "I mean, if it's all right for you, a star, to resort to such inhumane violence, then can you not see that you are giving the go-ahead for every troubled male teenager to do likewise? Surely you can clearly see that."

"No, I don't see things your way. Really I don't," Freddie angrily snorted.

"Unbelievable!"

"Look, believe you me, Tony. She had it coming to her. For one thing, she had far too much to drink that night, and so had I. I tell you now, hand on heart, that she swung the first punch, and I can't remember much after that," he guffawed.

"Laugh as much as you like, Freddie, for I believe she is now in the process of filing a major lawsuit against you."

THE TROUBLE WITH POLLY BROWN

"Well, she sure won't win," he grumbled.

"That's not for you to say, and this is why so many parents have written in to my show asking me to represent them and, in doing so, voice their concerns. After all, you are a superstar!"

"Yes, Freddie. Tone speaks for us all, and remember this: 'he who laughs last, laughs loudest,'" Polly fumed.

"Yeah, yeah. They can be as angry as they like, but to tell you the truth, Tony, right now I really don't give a monkey about anything they say."

"Freddie, you should, for my listeners feel they have every reason to be angry with you. They believe you to be an appalling role model for their children. Do you agree or disagree?"

"Of course I don't agree with them, Tony. And why should I? They are just jealous, and that's why they all want to stick the boot in! I mean, half the girls 'round here are actually asking for it anyway, if you get my drift," he huffed.

"That's your opinion, and I really don't agree with you."

"Suit yourself."

"Freddie, don't you think the parents have a point? Boys need to grow up respecting and protecting girls, not beating them up!"

"Come on, Tone. Tell it like it is. Speak up, and don't hold back; he needs to hear the truth from someone," Polly yelled out as she threw her polishing brush at the wall as a mark of protest.

"Come on, Tony, give me a break here. It's as though the whole world wants to place the blame on me for this girl's plight, as well as all the mess their own seriously dysfunctional kids are in," he angrily snorted. "Yes, mums and dads, I believe it's called *parental responsibility*," he scornfully sneered. "And as I haven't fathered any of your little blighters, I surely cannot be hung, drawn, and quartered for every imaginable and random act of violence from now to the end of Christendom!" he said, gnashing his teeth with rage.

"Calm down, Freddie!" the radio host intervened.

"No, I won't calm down until I've said what needs to be said. I feel I must yet again repeat that I am not the guilty party here!" he angrily shouted down the microphone.

"OK, mate, keep your knickers on," Tony ordered. "In fact, tell you what. Later on in the show we will be opening up the phone lines so that parents from all over the British Isles can have the rare opportunity of speaking directly with you. I hope you're up for it, mate, as it will be quite challenging. As of this moment there appears to be a growing number of upset, if not outraged, parents out there, and they are all dying to get their hands on you and then scalp you!"

"You bet there are!" Polly continued to yell at the radio. "I wish I was able to get my hands on a telephone, because I'd not hesitate to phone in and give you a small piece of my mind," she angrily sniffed.

Polly could tell from his silence that the strain of the interview was beginning to take its toll on Freddie. His long silence before responding to the DJ's announcement seemed to speak for itself that Freddie Fruitless was highly agitated by Tony's line of questioning. Polly was delighted.

"Yeah right, Tony. But as you so rightly stated earlier in the show, I am a superstar, and that in itself gives me rights and privileges that ordinary, undeserving people don't get, doesn't it? Before you answer that one, can I say that I only sing the songs, so I do not think I am in any way responsible if my fans take what I say literally and then go out there and do wild, crazy, if not downright illegal things."

"So you don't think you should take any responsibility or criticism whatsoever for any of the violent acts you so readily suggest in the lyrics of many of your songs?"

"Nope. None whatsoever, mate!" he huffed and puffed. "Mate, it's called *artistic expression*, and yeah, I know none of my songs will ever make it on Sunday night's *Songs of Praise*, but if, heaven forbid, they ever did, then you can bet your life something's gone real wrong."

"Right. Well, one of your lyrics says, and I quote, 'Dope is my coke and my reason for living. So live it up, live it up, and then you'll find your freedom.' Come on, Freddie. Get real. Are drugs really freedom?"

"Yes, Freddie, you right wally. Go into the prisons and mental hospitals, and then tell us if drugs bring freedom," Polly continued to yell at the radio.

"Yeah, Tony, my boy, I am being real. I think it's a great line in a great song."

"Well then, you are encouraging youngsters all over Great Britain to try out drugs using blatant lies, stating that in experimenting with downright dangerous drugs they will experience freedom."

"Yeah, well, it's a sort of inner freedom, really."

"Surely you of all people know that drug-taking only leads to immense misery, family breakdowns, prison sentences, and in some cases death. After all, you've lost two band members to drugs in the last year! Am I correct?"

"Yeah, pretty sad really. They were such nice blokes, and their kids and families aren't taking it at all well. Yeah, very sad."

"OK then, Freddie. Surely if you really did care about your band members and their families, you would warn of the dangers of drugs. Instead of which, you seem to sing their praises."

"No, not really, mate, so don't go putting words into my mouth," he sulkily sniffed.

"I am only asking you to explain to our listeners what you really mean, as many of them are most concerned that you are wrongly influencing their children, and so they wholeheartedly believe you are not what they want their sons and daughters to follow after."

"OK, that's it. I'm out of here. I am, after all, a superstar with more number ones under my belt than you've had cooked dinners, so I don't have to hang around this God-forsaken hole and listen to your moral-izing load of—" Freddie's microphone was suddenly cut off. Tony's voice quickly returned to fill the silence.

"Well, sorry, folks, but I guess that brings a very dramatic end to this interview. I therefore apologize, as sadly there will no longer be an opportunity to speak with the man himself, but we can only hope and pray that if nothing else, Freddie will consider the terrible heartache and misery that drug-taking and domestic violence causes. This is the *Tony Tictac Show*, so let's move on and play another great single that this week has taken the charts by storm."

"Nope. As the saying goes, 'a leper never changes his spots,'" Polly wearily stated as she finally placed down the now highly polished shoe she had so fervently been brushing all the while the interview had been taking place. In getting so caught up in the moment, Polly had spent the whole interview polishing one lone shoe. She knew she would have to race ahead if she was to have any chance of finishing this chore before Miss Scrimp appeared on the scene to examine each individual shoe and give her approval, and with Cecilia off sick yet again, it made the task very long and grueling.

Finally, Miss Scrimp poked her misshapen nose into the room. "Are we finished?" she snootily asked.

"Almost," Polly replied as she quickly hid the radio under the table out of sight.

She then stood to attention as Miss Scrimp, like a military general on parade, marched up and down beside the long table, stopping every now and then to snort and pick up a shoe or two to scrutinize. A tired and wilting Polly could only stand and inwardly sigh as Miss Scrimp appeared to deliberately take an excruciatingly long time, her inspections as thorough as a forensic scientist desperate for a breakthrough as she intensely scrutinized every single shoe, thoroughly determined and focused on finding some fault. "Give them all more spit and polish, girl, for none of these shoes are up to par," Miss Scrimp harshly ordered before turning on her heels to head back to the television room to once more put her feet up and watch the late-night news in peace over a mug of comforting, frothy hot chocolate.

Polly was extremely glad when she was finally dismissed and sent off to bed, for the hour was indeed very late. She was also relieved that she had managed to place the radio back on the top shelf without anyone having missed it. However, she felt very downcast and concerned that she had not managed to fulfill her promise to speak with her brother James, and so once again she had let him down. She worried that there might come a time when he no longer wished to confide or share anything with her, as quite rightly he would no longer trust or have any confidence in her. She could therefore only hope that with blood being thicker than water, he would always find it in his heart to forgive her for all failures, perceived or otherwise.

As Polly lay staring into the darkness wondering how to make it up to James, she suddenly had another thought that caused her to immediately begin panicking. The cause of this sudden distress was that she realized she no longer had her special ring on her finger. "Oh, no. I've lost my precious ring!" she cried. Polly sat bolt upright in bed as she struggled to think where she might have left it. She definitely still had the ring on at lunchtime. She remembered nervously twisting it 'round her finger as she spoke to Will, the new boy. She still had it on her finger as she traveled home from school on the train, because as usual she had twisted it 'round as she lay back on the head rest with her eyes closed. So where had she lost it?

Tears began to prick her eyes as she considered the possibility that she might never find the ring that meant so much to her. It had, after all, been given to her by dear Ralph along with the diary when she accepted the challenge to go to Piadora. He had gone to great lengths in warning her never to let it out of her sight, for without it she could not enter through the gates of Piadora. Now it was gone. Polly struggled to hold back the tears that were now burning her cheeks as she considered how every single time she had touched it, she had automatically found herself thinking back to Piadora and the Princesses' School of Training, as well as Mrs. O'Brien and Hodgekiss, and—oh dear, this loss was all too much for her to cope with.

The ring was, after all, her only link with all that had ever made her feel safe as well as happy. It helped her visualize dear, sweet Thomas, happy for the first time ever, and it never failed to produce a smile whenever she caught a sudden glimpse of Aazi. As she had yet to receive any news of him, she needed to be able to picture his little, most captivating features. No, this ring was such a major source of comfort to her that she felt incapable of facing up to the possibility that it might be lost forever. As the pain of her loss began to well up inside, it once again guaranteed her another restless night as she struggled to think where she had so absentmindedly left it.

In her latest bout of despair, she suddenly found herself thinking back to one of her last conversations with Hodgekiss before she chose to leave Piadora and return to the castle. He had told her that the Copper Kettle Tea Room was no longer in the hands of Mr. and Mrs. Greedol but had been taken over by dear friends of his who went by the name of Mr. and Mrs. Kindlyside. He had also told her that these nice people would be standing in the gap until she was old enough and capable enough to take on the tearoom. These friends of Hodgekiss could also be trusted to help and advise her if need be.

So that night in between lengthy bouts of beating herself up for being so stupid and careless in losing the ring, she intermittently closed her eyes to earnestly pray for its safe return whilst vowing to pay a visit to the tearoom to finally make their acquaintance.

"Nighty night, Polly Fester," came the unexpected but loud whisper from the next bed. "Polly Fester...Polly Brown...Polly Brown, the sickest psycho in our town. No, wait—the saddest loser in our town."

Polly took in a deep breath as a stray, ice-cold tear ran unchecked down her face. "Gailey, please stop," she begged. "It's the middle of the night, and we both need our sleep."

"Hey, girls. I forgot to give you some very interesting news," Gailey shouted down the dormitory. "Remember the Copper Kettle Tearoom in the High Street? Well, for some stupid, fat reason the new owners have decided to change its name, and you'll never guess in a month of Sundays what crazy name they've decided on!"

"Go on, Gailey. Do us all a favor and spill the beans," a lone voice rang out from the other end of the dormitory.

Gailey needed no further encouragement.

"They have chosen to call it Polly's Pantry. Can you believe it? What a disaster the place will now turn out to be. Yeah, who in a month of Sundays would be such a bloomin' idiot to choose to rename their tearoom by that sad, sick name?"

"Yep, that sure is hideous. It's doomed to failure, 'cos if anyone knows stinky Polly Brown, then they will surely never ever want to eat there!" another voice shouted out in the dark. "After all, everyone 'round here knows that Polly's got the lurgy!"

"Yes, with a name like that, mark my words, it will be closed within a month," another voice shouted out in the dark.

Polly, though deeply offended by their unfair and cruel words, wisely decided to keep her thoughts to herself. If truth be known, she had completely forgotten about the new owners, for in not having been allowed to leave the castle for quite a lengthy period of time, she had not pressed her nose up to the large window pane to get as much as a quick peek at what the new owners might look like.

Polly heard her cruel tormentor snigger under the covers, and then when Polly believed it was now safe to come out from under the blankets because the room was quiet, Gailey came up from under the sheets to begin another fresh round of humiliating and personal cruel insults. "Polly Brown, Polly Brown, the ugliest girl for miles around," she sneered.

Chapter Eight
THE LOST RING

*D*UE TO GREAT tiredness Polly found herself struggling to crawl out of bed the next morning, but as she headed toward the bathroom she surprised herself by suddenly having a mental flashback, which saw her taking off the ring before placing it down on the sink drainer. "Ahh, now I remember! Yes, that's where I left it," she gasped as renewed hope began to well up inside. "Yes, yes, I took it off when I was ordered to peel the potatoes. Oh, dear God, please let it still be where I left it," she said, momentarily closing her eyes while clasping her hands as though this act alone would serve to further endorse her fervent request of finding her precious and very sentimental lost ring.

That morning Polly found herself feeling very impatient as she lined up with the other children while waiting for the first available wash-basin. Before too long she was nearing the front of the line, and once there, she was forced to watch on as Gailey deliberately, slowly picked up the round tin that bore a small, hardened pink tablet of toothpaste in its center. The tin made its way to her mouth, whereupon she then spat into the tin to moisten the hard lump before taking her toothbrush to make the tablet bubble up into a frosty paste. Now with some of the pink stuff finally sticking the bristles, she stuffed the head of the toothbrush in her mouth and began an up-and-down motion as she set about cleaning her teeth.

No sooner had she placed the tin back down when Tommy Pulleyblank, who was standing in pants and vest at the next available sink, shouted out in her direction. "'Ere, Gailey girl. Hand me the toothpaste tin, 'cos we're clean out of it at this sink. All that's left at the bottom of this tin is a bit of Toby's disgusting, frothy spittle where he gobbed into the tin."

Gailey instantly obliged and lent over to pass the tin.

"Help yourself, Tommy. And while yer at it, you could do me a big favor by doing a really nice, big gob into the tin, 'cos there is only Polly McCavity left to clean her rotten old teeth."

"Sure thing, Gailey," Tommy snorted as he then delivered a giant-sized amount of frothy spittle into the tin before taking his toothbrush to furiously mix it up into a frothy lather.

Polly felt quite sickened. The foul-tasting toothpaste was disgusting enough before automatically being spat into by each and every child who, wishing to give their teeth a good scrub, needed to produce a decent amount of lather that would hopefully stick to the bristles of their toothbrush. She believed this regular practice to be terribly unhygienic, but in the eyes of most of the children, it was the only solution to the problem, as the tablet in the tin was always like a hardened, dried-up piece of soap. Boritz always bought this cheap tinned toothpaste for the foster children, as it went much further than all other brands on the market, and more importantly, it was only one-fifth of the price. After having a quick wash down, Polly deliberated whether to skip cleaning her teeth or just gargle with water. Moments later she made the decision to bite the bullet.

So, picking up her toothbrush, she made her way to where the round metal tin, minus its top, still lay abandoned on the side of the old, cracked basin. She momentarily found herself feeling quite distressed as she stared down at the contents of the tin, which still bore evidence of a revoltingly large amount of Tommy's frothy spittle, plus an excessive amount of bristles that had broken off the toothbrushes as the children viciously lathered up the paste with the head of their toothbrush. She therefore took a deep breath to sum up the courage before plunging the head of her toothbrush directly into the center of the hideously offensive matter.

After minimally swirling the brush around in the frothy paste she closed her eyes tight and proceeded to bring the toothbrush up to her mouth. Making one final gulp, her face momentarily locked in a deep grimace, she opened wide and began to brush. In that small instant she longed for the luxury of some minty flavored toothpaste that not only could be squeezed out of a tube but also could not be tampered with. The length of time Polly cleaned her teeth that morning was so unacceptably short that it would most surely have had most dentists reeling with shock, but then they weren't the ones forced to use this diabolical and disgracefully unhygienic method to clean their teeth.

As soon as Polly finished up, she grabbed her schoolbag and raced downstairs, hurriedly heading toward the kitchen door. It was still locked! "Oh, come on. Whoever is on duty, please, it must be time for breakfast," she mumbled as her sense of desperation began once more to heighten.

Finally she caught sight of Pitstop as he turned the corner and bared his teeth before approaching her in his usual menacing manner. Polly knew this could only mean one thing. Uncle Boritz would appear around the corner any second now, as master and dog were utterly inseparable.

She felt both awkward and nervous that she was standing alone by the door, as she would have felt happier and safer to be just one in a crowd of children whenever it came to any form of personal encounter with Uncle Boritz or Aunt Mildred, for her fear of both was equal. Polly took a deep breath as she waited for Uncle Boritz to find the right key from the large set that hung from his waist. It took three attempts before he found the correct one that opened the kitchen door. Luckily for Polly, she was not alone for long, for as soon as the key twisted in the lock, a barrage of children raced past her like a determined herd of wildebeest on the rampage as they fought to get through the kitchen door ahead of her. All the children began impatiently pushing and shoving as they bravely fought every obstacle and hindrance in order to get some food into their very hungry empty bellies.

Polly was pushed aside as the older children jumped the queue in their haste to get their breakfast first. None of the younger children ever dared complain at the unfairness of this ritual, for they knew better than that. Yes, they knew to do so would be most unwise, unless of course they did not mind a few heavy blows to their chest or a thick lip later in the day to remind them of the unspoken pecking order that at all times prevailed.

Upon opening the door, Boritz also very wisely moved to one side, managing to avoid being trampled to the ground as child fought child on their way into the kitchen. Without further adieu, he turned and headed back down the long corridor toward his private sitting room with Pitstop still faithfully at his side.

Polly, having finally made it through the door, raced directly over to the kitchen sink. As her eyes frantically scanned the drainer, it quickly became obvious to her that her precious ring was nowhere in sight. Polly felt panicky as she once more tried to retrace her steps in her desperate and futile bid to locate the lost ring. She upturned all the pots and pans that lay piled up high on the drainer. Nothing. She even tried to stick her smallest fingers down the plughole, but still she had no joy. She bent down to open the cupboard under the sink and then began furiously emptying the contents out onto the floor, trying all the while to remain as focused as possible in her sad and futile attempt to find her prized possession. Pretty soon she realized that she was fast running out of time, and so she raced up to the tables, begging all the latecomers to breakfast to assist her in finding the ring. But none among them were the remotest bit interested in helping her out, for they were all far too busy extracting the usual wriggly silverfish that regularly took early morning swimming lessons in their piled-up bowls of stale cornflakes.

She then noted that James had just finished his breakfast and was about to leave the table to take his empty bowl to the sink to be washed up. "James. Thank goodness you've finished. Please, I really need your help, for I've lost my precious ring, and—"

"Go away, Polly. Don't even think of asking for my help. Just leave me alone," James quietly sniffed as he abandoned the table, at the same time deliberately avoiding all eye contact with her as he hastily headed toward the sink to place his bowl down. He then turned and made his way toward the kitchen door in order to leave the house and catch the school bus.

Polly felt hurt and frustrated that James was not only unprepared to offer his help in her search but was now no longer speaking to her. She realized that once again she had let him down, and as a result he had quite understandably taken great offense. But what made it harder to bear was the sad realization that instead of standing together to face the many storms in their lives, their relationship was rapidly and very tragically deteriorating. She felt hopelessly incapable of finding the solution required to make things right between them.

It was not to long after James left for the bus stop that Polly was forced to abandon her search for the ring, as she needed to leave forthwith if she were to have any hope of making it to the bus stop in time to catch the bus. Grabbing hold of her schoolbag, she made her way to the front door, only to suddenly remember she still had one last port of call, and this was to go to the larder and collect the provisions that the night before she had carefully put to one side for today's cookery class. Today of all days was very important, for she had been moved up a class. Instead of having to please Mrs. Greaseball, she now had the new challenge of winning over Miss Strickneene, who not only took over any class that was a teacher down due to sickness, but she just happened to also be the deputy headmistress.

As she went to pick up the brown paper bag, a hand suddenly shot in front of her face and grabbed hold of the bag. Polly swung round, her eyes following after the bag. "Gailey, give it back," she gulped. "Please don't do this to me, for I was up extremely late last night weighing out all the ingredients," she wailed.

"Tough!" retorted Gailey with a wicked smirk. "You'll just have to weigh out some more, won't you, fish face? This 'ere bag now belongs to me. See you in class, Polyester Fester."

"I can't go to school without the ingredients. Uncle Boritz has the keys to the food cupboard, and I have no idea where to find him. So please, I beg of you, give me back my bag."

"Take a jump of a high cliff, Fester," Gailey smirked as she headed for the door. "Oh, and if you even dare to split on me by telling the teacher, then I swear I'll stuff your stinkin' head right down the bog till ye drown," she sneered.

On hearing this latest unpleasant threat, Polly realized she was wasting her breath. There was no way Gailey would ever consider doing the decent thing by rightfully returning the bag, as she too required them for today's cookery lesson.

So with no food in her stomach and no ingredients in her schoolbag, Polly made haste to race toward the bus stop to catch the bus that then dropped them off at the train station to make the last part of their journey to the school. To her utter horror, as she turned the last corner she could only watch helplessly as her school bus drove straight past with Gailey keenly parading the bag of ingredients up to the window, a fat, cheesy grin on her face as from her seat on the bus she waved good-bye to Polly.

Polly groaned deeply and dropped her schoolbag to the ground, feeling greatly discouraged by all the events of the morning. Already the black clouds that hung around just waiting for her appearance were making it their personal duty, as always, to haunt her, and it was only seven forty in the morning!

Eventually she picked up her bag and began the long, tedious walk to the train station, for the next bus was not due at the stop for another forty-five minutes and so would guarantee her a visit to the headmaster's office, for it would get her into school much too late.

As she walked the long distance to the train station with her head hung low and a heavy heart, she barely noticed a brand-new red bus pass by her before pulling up a few yards farther down the road. The bus driver then made several extremely loud honking noises as he attempted but failed to capture her attention. The loud honks continued, and eventually a couple of the children stuck their heads out of an open window and called out to her. Finally she looked up and realized they were calling her by name. She still made no effort to walk faster, preferring to watch on as the rear door of the bus opened and out popped a very familiar head.

"Polly, dear, is that you?" a very familiar and friendly Irish voice shouted out.

"Huh? I cannot believe it," a deliriously happy Polly cried out.

Polly immediately found her feet and began racing toward the vehicle as fast as her young legs could carry her, all the while excitedly yelling, "Mrs. O'Brien! Mrs. O'Brien! Mrs. O'Brien, I can't believe it's you. How wonderful and unexpected this is," Polly croaked as she struggled to catch her breath and smile at the same time. "I thought your school must have closed down, as I have not seen you or any of the girls from your school on the bus," she stuttered, suddenly feeling overwhelmed by such strong emotions of great joy and happiness that she immediately began to break down and cry.

Mrs. O'Brien grabbed hold of Polly's hand and pulled her toward her. "Close down! Heaven forbid that such a thing would ever happen, for the French would immediately shut down the ports and throw themselves a week-long party, and that, dear Polly, would never do."

Polly used her sleeve to wipe away the fresh tears that were now unashamedly racing down her cheeks.

"I'm so sorry, Mrs. O'Brien. I feel so ridiculous—in fact, a real idiot—to be acting in such a foolish manner, but I can't help myself, for I am so overwhelmed with happiness to see you again," Polly cried.

"Well, don't just stand on the steps fly-catching, dear. Hop on our new private bus. There's a good girl. Otherwise we'll all be jolly late for school and so find ourselves being sent to the headmaster's office. Come on, come on," she beckoned.

Polly hurriedly clambered up the steps, and then with gay abandon she flung herself into the arms of her adorable teacher to give her a long, hard embrace.

"Feel free to cry as much as you like Polly, my dear, but it won't get you to school any faster," Mrs. O'Brien stated as she returned the hug before wiping away a few of Polly's tears with a gentle sweep of her hand. "Well, Polly dear, if nothing else, you'll surely start this day with a nice, clean face. Now come along, dear, and find a seat, and then we can set off once more."

Polly obeyed and released her tense grip of Mrs. O'Brien as she then walked down the aisle of the bus, anxiously looking for a spare seat.

"Our school close down! No more cookery lessons? Oh, deary me! I cannot think that such a travesty should ever be allowed to take place, Polly dear. No, it must remain well beyond the realm of possibilities, for just imagine our dear French neighbors not only thinking but actually believing that they alone produce the world's most gastronomic victuals, as well as the most famous cooks," she pouted before overdramatically raising her eyes into her head to further emphasis her utter horror.

Polly stood for a while in the aisle, all the while drinking in all her teacher's amusing anecdotes.

"No, no, Polly dearest. Forget what I just said. Don't even begin to imagine it," she mumbled in her rich Irish brogue, shaking her head as if to make such terrible imaginations flee her thoughts immediately.

Polly's eyes continued to fill with tears, as just listening to Mrs. O'Brien and her delightfully playful intonations inexplicably reached deep into her broken, wounded heart, instantly ridding her of all despair as it replaced all doom and gloom with vibrant cheer and fresh optimism.

"Right then, Polly. You can't remain standing up in the aisle, so go and sit next to dear, sweet miss Vivienne Levine. I'll have you know this lass has just joined us from over the pond."

"Uhh," was all Polly managed to murmur as she moved slowly toward the vacant seat. Even after taking her seat, she still managed to have a ridiculously stupid grin plastered over her face as she continued to savor every amusing word and gesture that Mrs. O'Brien cared to conjure up and then deliver.

"America. Dearest America," she stated as she came behind their seats and gave the pretty young American girl a friendly pat on the back. "Yes, and she will be spending the next year learning how awfully well-groomed English ladies spend their days usefully. Now won't that be a lot of fun?" Mrs. O'Brien said with a giggle as she moved over to give young Polly a little dig in the ribs to wake her up from her dream-like state.

"And I have to tell you, Polly, this young American sweetheart is already giving the girls a run for their money. I do believe her spectacularly unusual desserts, as well as other interesting and varied creations, will in the years to come win her many an award and accolade as they find their way into a number of splendid cookery books. So make her acquaintance quickly before you get off this bus. There's a dear."

Polly happily did as she was told, and after introducing herself to the lovely Miss Levine she sat back, feeling thankful that the bus had stopped and saved her from much trouble.

Sadly for her, in no time at all the bus pulled up outside the train station. Polly stood up from her seat with the full intention of quickly disembarking, as she knew she could not afford to miss the next train, but as she turned to say a quick good-bye to Vivienne and the other girls, Mrs. O'Brien suddenly reached out and grabbed her by the hand.

"Polly, dear, you must understand me when I say you must never, ever forget Piadora."

"Yes, Mrs. O'Brien. I will try to remember."

"Oh, Polly, the word *try* is not good enough. You, my dear one, must seek to nurture and build on everything you learned there. Do you truly understand?" she said as her grip tightened in her bid to stress the point. "For whether you do or do not fully comprehend everything, your hidden strengths, Polly, are indeed the most potent weapons against all—I repeat, *all*—the forces of darkness that are now more determined than ever to pull you down and bring your spirit to its chasm of destruction."

Polly nodded once more, but Mrs. O'Brien had not yet finished.

"Polly, dear, are you really listening to me? For hell has no particular preference as to whom it slowly and surreptitiously sucks into its bowels. Oh, no. It just lies in wait, seeking to pounce most unmercifully on any available and unwitting victim. But *you*, my precious one, have a glorious future, so promise me here right now you will never compromise but will continue to fight the good fight. You must prevail to ensure that such a terrible thing will never happen."

Polly nodded her head as though she were in perfect agreement with Mrs. O'Brien, but deep inside she could already feel herself timidly fending off the first rumbles of very unwelcome murmurings that were mischievously seeking to re-invade her mind and emotions with their obsequious and sickeningly spiteful methods. They were, after all, expert strategists in the art of psychological warfare. These dark and subliminal forces thought nothing of continuously and viciously bombarding her mind with hideous, soul-destroying thoughts such as, "Nothing ever changes. I'm just a useless, festering, ugly blob. I'll never amount to anything. Nobody could ever love me. Everything in my life is just too painful. There's nowhere left to run. Nobody cares if I live or die. Life is unfair, and best of all, Polly Brown, you're a complete idiot if you believe your life will ever improve or get better. So do us all a favor and give up now, and then we can get back to the way things used to be. Yes, and this way you'll soon be feeling back to your good, old, very remorseful self. We, for our part, hereby promise to leave off all punishments usually meted out to those traitors who think they can abandon their lowly post, having the nerve to even consider that they can achieve great things, even believing they might one day become inspiring pioneers of one kind or another."

And so it went on and on as the wildly ecstatic but viciously cruel and sinister whisperings chanted, all the while regrouping and repositioning themselves. They were once more well on the way to taking back full control.

However, at present these evil whisperings had little choice but to hold back, for Polly hadn't exactly cracked and thrown in the towel. No, she was still winning her very personal battlefield of the mind and soul, but only just. Her wonderful experiences in Piadora still felt so fresh and alive, for they were indelibly written on the chords in her heart for safekeeping. So, at least for the present, she had triumphantly fought off all niggling and harmful thoughts that sought to hinder then suck her back down into the hellishly frightening pit of destruction where they could and would do with her as they wished, causing her to relinquish all rights to happiness.

As Polly sat on a bench waiting for the next train to arrive, she felt truly grateful for the lift but also saddened by the realization that with the arrival of the new bus, this would surely mean less opportunities than ever for her to accidentally bump into her dear, darling teacher. She would also miss the idle chit-chat of the well-heeled girls as they sat huddled on seats, heads touching as they shared, as all young girls do, their deepest, intimate secrets with each other. Her eyes brimmed with tears as she then thought that she might never again hear Mrs. O'Brien's loud and very amusing exhortations as she proudly sought to instill her good and very sensible values into the girls. She closed her eyes and gulped, giving serious consideration as to how on earth was she going to make it through another day, let alone the rest of her life!

Polly could just about see her train in the distance, but as it had yet to pull into the station, she decided to pull out her timetable from her schoolbag to remind herself what other lessons she had that day. She was instantly dismayed to discover that after domestic science with the deputy headmistress Miss Strickneene, she then had PE, better known as physical education with Miss Peligrano. Polly couldn't help but make a deep sigh, for she knew with much certainty that she did not have her PE kit in her bag either, as this too had rather mysteriously gone missing.

THE TROUBLE WITH POLLY BROWN

"Oh, no. I can't believe this!" she groaned as she wearily stood up from the bench and waited for the train to stop so she could open the door and climb into carriage.

———◆———

Of course, just as Polly had feared, Miss Strickneene was most annoyed.

"Polly Brown, I am not the least amused," she airily stated. She then dismissed Polly from her classroom and ordered her to go and fill up a bucket with soapy water.

"While the other girls make a deliciously fluffy Victoria sponge cake, you, my girl, can spend the time scrubbing out the shower block," the slightly dumpy Miss Strickneene told her in a dismissive tone of voice as she then held open the door to allow Polly to leave her classroom and head for the shower block.

"But wait. Before you go on your way, pray, tell me how it is that your foster sister Gailey has all the right ingredients, and yet you, Polly Brown, have failed to produce any. So don't stand there pretending to be dumb! Mrs. Greaseball warned me to expect nothing good from you, and from today's performance I can see that she was absolutely correct."

Polly shrugged her shoulders, though not out of defiance, more because she had firmly come to believe that nobody in the world cared one iota about getting to the truth of this or any other matter. At least this appeared to be the case regarding just about everything that concerned her miserably unfair and chaotic world.

Today of all days truth in its entirety mattered not a jot, for Polly had other, much more pressing things on her mind, namely the gut-wrenching loss of her precious and most prized ring, and the unexpected loss of this made all other problems pale into insignificance. However, much to her amazement, as she undertook the arduous task of cleaning the whole shower block and changing rooms, she quite unexpectedly found herself overtaken by intoxicatingly happy feelings that in no time at all had her feeling extremely light-headed and overwhelmed by irrepressible joy.

And so Polly Brown, professional cleaner and performer extraordinaire, found herself rather unexpectedly rising to the occasion, as with mop and bucket she single-handedly cleaned the entire shower block whilst singing "The Impossible Dream" at the top of her voice, the mop handle standing in for a microphone of course!

With no one standing over her to order her around, she also found herself dancing rather demurely around the shower block, and by flipping the handle, the mop now became a stand-in for her absent male suitor. "Well, Stanley, my good man, it appears that of all the pupils in this school, surprise, surprise, I've become the chosen one, with every teacher not only hating me more than ever but also wishing to hand me all your old cleaning tasks," she sniffed as she brought the mop head up close to her face in order to have a meaningful conversation with it.

"So do me a great favor, Stanley, and enjoy the break. Oh, and while you're at it, I would consider it a great honor if you would do just one more of those delightful cartwheels for me," she said, giving a light-hearted laugh. "Then you're free to make yourself a splendid cup of tea, although I must warn you that according to our dear headmaster, you, my dear man, have rather absentmindedly left your teapot and caddy in the school shed. So until we can find some way of getting it to you, may I take the liberty of suggesting that you use a teabag instead," she advised.

"Here's to you, Stanley Albert Horlicks, the kindest caretaker in all the land," she shouted, placing the mop to one side and raising her hand into the air as though she were holding up a bone china teacup. She then brought it down to her lips, pretending to sip some hot tea, extending her little pinky in the same manner that she had witnessed other very prim and proper ladies do in order to keep their composure whilst sipping hot tea from delicate bone china teacups.

With the shower block now pristine clean, Polly took the mop and cleaning agents back to the store cupboard and then reported back to Miss "Never One to Pussyfoot" Strickneene.

"There are still another twenty minutes until the lunch break," she stated as she looked down and observed her delicate gold wristwatch, which Polly duly noted was badly pinching her skin, as it was really too small and delicate for her generously plump wrist. "Time enough for you to start cleaning out this food cupboard. So fill up this bowl with warm soapy water, and then follow me," Miss Strickneene ordered, giving her chic and heavily lacquered hair the very important gentle pat. Polly knew this pat was most essential in case perchance she were to accidentally bump into any one of the many male teachers, whom Miss Strickneene had come to heavily rely on for daily compliments, as they never failed to subserviently express their greatest admiration toward her.

For some unfathomable reason, Polly didn't mind or fear the deputy headmistress, although it was plainly obvious that she posed some form of threat to all other female teachers, who failed to hide their annoyance at what they considered "disgracefully flirtatious behavior" that was "not becoming of a deputy headmistress, or a cookery teacher for that matter." However, as Miss Strickneene was the deputy head, her highness was allowed to get away with pretty much what she liked and still keep her throne and crown intact.

Despite being a little—how shall we say?—pudgy, she still managed a light and hearty spring in her step as she breezed down the lengthy corridors, pausing only for the odd lighthearted private joke with any male teacher who happened to pass by. Often she could be seen walking toward her classroom accompanied by a large plate in her outstretched hand.

"Did you really make this wonderful cake creation all by yourself?" the male teachers would stop and loudly gasp as they unwittingly drunk in her heady perfume.

"Why of course, Mr. Meakins," she would demurely reply through her cherubic, overly plastered lipstick lips, as she used her free hand to subtly adjust his tie, as well as stroke off that annoying and most unhygienic imaginary wisp of hair that seemed always to be stuck to his and every other male teacher's lapel as they happily stopped to converse with her.

"Well then, Miss Strickneene, you should consider sending your wonderful recipes to Mrs. Beeton, for I'm sure she would happily add them to her next cookbook."

"Oh, Mr. Meakins, don't flatter me in such a manner," she would softly purr as once more she gave her heavily lacquered and coiffure hair the now famous pat, which sent automated signals to her eyelashes, commanding them to begin fluttering so as to draw forth further compliments from the mouth of her latest admirer. This woman was undeniably queen bee of the school, with all the male drones subconsciously, if not consciously, following after her, her highly sensuous perfume, as it overwhelmingly drifted down the stale, sweat-smelling corridors of the school, seducing all males—teachers and pupils alike—to fall wildly and irrevocably in love with her.

As Polly took it upon herself to keenly observe all this seemingly irrational behavior, which only took place in Queen Bee's presence, she had some time before mistakenly began to believe that a bottle of perfume could well be the answer to all her prayers, especially as she was always desperately seeking untried ways in the hope of finding some meaningful friendships. Imagine her delight when on her way to school one day she happened to come upon what appeared to be an expensive bottle of exquisite perfume in the crack of the seat. Needless to say, Polly assumed that it must have fallen out of the handbag of some classy lady, especially as she thought the petite purple receptacle looked pretty expensive looking.

It came as no surprise that after breakfast one fine day, instead of leaving to catch the school bus, she made a small detour and headed back upstairs. With no one around she used the occasion to smother her hair and uniform with the entire contents, shaking it violently over her head until she was satisfied she had emptied the bottle of every single drop. First she was almost ordered off the bus, and then she found herself sitting quite alone in the normally crammed train compartment. This in itself would have been enough to have most normal people seriously questioning that something must be horribly wrong, but not Polly. No, apart from feeling happy and gloriously optimistic, she chose to keep her head firmly in the sand, as with a skip in her step she had headed toward the school with higher than usual expectations of having a great day.

When finally she was ordered to vacate the class and head for the shower block to rinse off what was not only making the whole class nauseous but also causing some pupils to have strange burning sensations at the back of their throats, well, only then did it finally dawn on her that something was clearly very wrong.

It would be many hours later when back at the castle she was finally enlightened by Bertha Banoffee, who, apart from being more clued up than Polly, unquestioningly had much clearer vision than her counterpart. "Polly, you dumb idiot. This was not a bottle of expensive Italian

Mozo Muzzichuzi! No, you dumb fool, if you had taken the time to read the label correctly, you would realize that according to the label you have been a stupid idiot, for you doused yourself from head to toe with a highly concentrated form of mosquito repellant! Yes, and according to this bottle, it is primarily used by soldiers for the prevention of malaria when facing combat in the African jungle or other equally high-ratio mosquito-ridden zones."

Polly was aghast and found it hard to believe that she had done such a stupid, idiotic thing.

"Give it back to me. Let me have a proper look," she yelled, grabbing the bottle back from Bertha. Sure enough, Bertha was absolutely correct, for despite being a small label, the word *warning* was not only written in red but also in block capitals. Then *highly concentrated* was written under the warning, and although this writing wasn't in capitals it was almost as clear. However, on a more positive note, it also meant that she couldn't entirely rule out further perfume trials, especially, as it had now been substantiated that all failure was down to her own incompetence; therefore, her life of pure loneliness and isolation could still be changed if only she could find the right bottle of highly desirable sweet-smelling perfume.

Polly would stand at Miss Strickneene's desk, and with eyes closed tight, she too would breathe in as deep as she felt able, for just like the male drones, she also delighted in her teacher's heady and sickly sweet aroma, which never failed to linger long after every mortal had left the classroom.

Chapter Nine
PLEASE TRY MY JAM ROLY-POLY

*T*T WAS ONLY a short while later that Polly heard the bell, indicating that morning lessons were finally over and it was now time for lunch, but still her teacher told her to ignore the bell and carry on cleaning out the cupboard. Finally Miss Strickneene relented and told her that she could finish some schoolwork in an after-school detention, so she was finally free to go. Polly thanked her teacher and then raced down the corridor toward the dining hall as fast as she was able.

As she was so late, there was only the teeniest piece of shriveled up toad in the hole lying abandoned on a plate, sadly accompanied only by a very creative-looking blob of lumpy mashed potatoes that some considerate pupil had adorned with a smiling face using leftover shriveled peas. But Polly didn't really care, for she was still mourning the loss of her precious and irreplaceable ring.

"Polly! Over here, Polly," came a booming voice, followed by a loud whistle. Polly looked up and could see Will beckoning her to come over and take a seat at his table. Polly quickly made her way across the seriously noisy dining hall toward his table before slumping down in a seat in a way that told all present she was clearly pretty fed up.

"I thought I'd really upset you and therefore this was the reason why you were nowhere to be found this lunch break. But judging by the look on your face I was clearly wrong," Will said, giving a wide, rather lopsided grin as he rather thoughtfully went on to pour her a glass of water.

"Oh, no, Will. Nothing like that," she glumly sniffed. "Not only do I have more detentions than anyone else in the school, but I have been in terrible trouble with Miss Strickneene for not having everything I needed for lessons. Then after shouting at me, she—"

"What, Miss Lovely Legs Strickneene? Oh, come on, Polly. She is, after all, an adorable darling of a teacher who would never hurt a fly." Will forcefully stated raising an eyebrow to further emphasize his pure disbelief.

"As I was saying, Miss Strickneene can and regularly does shout," a now offended Polly sniffed, raising her voice as she began to feel frustrated that "Miss Lovely Legs" had in no time at all succeeded in drawing yet another totally unsuspecting and innocent fly into her voracious, man-eating web. Truth be told, she was now feeling very peeved.

"Yes, Will, I'll have you know she never shouts at any of the males in the school, boys included! So can you not clearly see that's why every male from here to Dover is desperately and hopelessly in love with her? And I just happen to believe that it has much to do with the amount of expensive, heavy perfume she drenches herself in."

"Oh, right. Hey, calm down, Polly! Although I have to say you look so cute when you get this mad," he sniffed, giving her another lopsided grin.

Now she was really infuriated, as she felt he was not taking her seriously enough. "William Montgomery, I think you, just like every male in this school, are now under her spell, for she has utterly seduced you with her ruby red lips and heavy perfume. Ha! And what's cool about it is you don't know it has happened to you! So trust me when I say that before long you too will be telling her how delicious her Chelsea buns taste and how delightfully scrumptious and melt-in-the-mouth her stupid Eccles cakes are," she scornfully stated, her voice raised as she was now feeling maddened and furious with him.

"All right, Polly, do us both a favor by calming down, for I hear you," Will stated, as he tried and failed miserably to look serious.

"And so as I was saying before you so rudely interrupted me"—Polly sniffed, screwing up her eyes as she sought to prove her point—"your wonderful Miss Strickneene then gave me lots of cleaning jobs to do, and I've only just been allowed to leave the classroom." Polly breathed a deep sigh that indicated she had clean run out of wind and as a result had nothing further to say on the matter.

"Oh, dear, and it doesn't look like there was much dinner left for you either," Will commiserated. "Although the happy face looks very…"

"Happy?" Polly rather glumly interjected.

"Well, Polly, you beat me to it, although I was going to say 'rather enterprising.'"

"Even with the happy face it still looks a rather sad and pathetic meal, doesn't it? And worse still, they have completely run out of pudding. But if I'm honest, Will, I'm not the least bit hungry, for today I sadly discovered that I have lost my special ring that I treasured, and with it I have completely lost my appetite."

"I'm sorry to hear that, but would a rather sorry looking bowl of Jam Roly-Poly serve in anyway to make you feel better?" he asked as he considerately placed his uneaten sponge pudding in front of her. "And please don't pay any attention whatsoever to what it looks like, for I have it on the greatest authority that it tastes a whole heap better than it looks, honest! The creamy custard in particular," he said as he almost dipped his finger into the bowl.

"Thanks, Will. That's awfully kind of you, but you eat it, for nothing is going to make me feel better," she said, pushing the bowl back toward him.

"Want to bet on that?" Will quipped.

"Bet on what?" Polly queried.

"Well, you've just thrown down the gauntlet, so I quite rightly need to rise to the challenge."

"Challenge! What challenge? Will, do me a favor and help me out here, for I am in no mood for any of your impulsive craziness. What on this earth are you talking about?" she said with a distinct note of exasperation.

"Why, the challenge to make Polly Brown have a smile as wide as the happy-faced peas decorating your mash," he quipped. "So come on, Miss Spoilsport. Give me a chance. Say you'll come back to my place after school."

Polly was about to once more decline his kind offer when Will wisely leaned over to place a finger over her lips.

"Shh. It's not open for discussion," he said with a gentle firmness that secretly touched her. "It's my place after school, no ifs or buts."

Polly still tried to raise a hand in protest, but Will was having none of it. "Polly, I'm warning you now that I do not have the slightest intention of allowing you to leave my home until your hideously heavy heart is no longer as downcast as these seriously depressing shriveled-up peas—no, better still, until you beg me to help you stop laughing. End of story," he said as he pushed the pudding bowl back in front of her.

"Checkmate! Now enjoy this Jam Roly-Poly, or I will never again play Prince Charming by saving you a miserable, measly-looking school pud," he said as he gave her a small wink, followed closely by another lopsided grin. He then hastily grabbed his schoolbag and hurriedly left the dinner hall to get to his first afternoon lesson.

<hr />

The final bell of the day rang, and the classes quickly cleared as the pupils once more joined up with friends and made their way toward the school gates, heads down, as they took the opportunity to engage deeply in all sorts of frivolous, if not sometimes mind-boggling after-school conversation.

Polly held back and used the opportunity to empty out her tatty schoolbag to rid it of quite an assortment of unwanted rubbish. She then attempted to give her locker a thorough tidying up, stopping every once in a while to look out of the window as she waited for the playground to become completely deserted.

"Great, that large group is finally heading out the school gates. Oh, no. More latecomers. Come on, guys, leave the playground. Go on. You can kick that ball around when you get to the train station," she irately muttered, as with all her heart she willed the playground to be entirely rid of all pupils and so become deserted.

Polly let out a deep sigh and then headed back to her locker. "This spring clean is definitely seriously overdue," she murmured under her breath as she continued to busy herself with the task at hand. "Hmm. It was the best thing I could do. A clean and tidy locker, then a clear-thinking mind," she muttered, albeit rather unconvincingly, for the real truth lay somewhere else entirely! Yes, if nothing else, it meant that if Will was really only messing around and had no real intention of inviting her to his home, well, then no one else need know. She could not bear to be made a fool of, especially when most days did not draw to a close without some form of personal, very demoralizing humiliation. By staying behind to tidy up her locker, she had given herself the perfect excuse to slip out of the school late to quietly make her way home without any ridicule from other pupils. This way no one need know that she was wishing with all her heart that the new boy was genuine in his desire for real friendship. If he didn't show up, then no real and lasting harm had been done. All she would have to do was act really casual and maybe a bit off hand the next time she had occasion to bump into him.

Looking up at the clock on the wall, she decided it was time to pluck up the courage required and, like all other pupils beforehand, evacuate the building. So, picking up her schoolbag and without knowing what to expect, she headed down the stairs and then through a door that led directly into the playground and large playing field as she continued to head toward the school gates. Polly was truly pleased to see Will leaning heavily against one of the gates, his school jacket tossed casually over a shoulder as he waited patiently for her to appear.

"Are you always this much of a slowcoach?" he asked, giving her an overtly generous smile. "I was about to give up the ghost and wander home on my ownsome lonesome."

"I'm sorry," was all Polly felt capable of answering back as she began to cough nervously.

"Come on, Polly Brown. Allow me to lead the way," he said as he cheerfully linked his arm through hers to gently pull her in the direction he wished to take. "I hope you don't mind, but I have just one small errand, and that is to collect a meat pie from the grocer's shop in the village. Then we will go straight back to my place."

"That's fine by me, Will, so take your time," said Polly, giving his arm a quick and timid squeeze.

With the pie paid for, they then left the store and headed down a long lane toward Will's house. Some fifteen minutes later Will stopped outside an old, rickety gate.

"We're almost there," he breathlessly announced.

"Here? I can't see anything ahead except an overgrown, densely thick forest of shrubs and trees," she challenged, moving her head from side to side and shielding her eyes from the sun as she attempted to see into the distance.

"Polly, I assure you there is a large house hidden somewhere amongst these tall trees," Will replied rather sheepishly as his hand reached out to open an old, rusty wrought iron gate that had almost fallen off its hinges.

"Well, Will, what are we waiting for? Open the gate wide, for I cannot see any houses whatsoever from where I'm standing."

"Hmm. All right then."

Polly observed that for some unfathomable reason, Will, having finally opened the gate, now appeared somewhat reluctant to go through it.

"OK, Polly, now this is the bit where I ask you to accept me for who I truly am," he said, as with both hands bearing down on her shoulders he moved her to one side to then stand directly in front of her, staring meaningfully into her eyes.

"It might help if you dared speak in plain old English, Will, for what on earth do you mean? You are not making any sense, and now I'm feeling peculiarly puzzled." Polly sniffed, suddenly feeling quite anxious, as searching his eyes she looked for even the smallest clue that might give her a hint as to what was really going on.

Polly could not help but notice that he now appeared very twitched up and jumpy, and his new, very unexpected demeanor threw Polly somewhat, as up until this moment in time she had never experienced him in such an agitated state of nervousness. No, something was definitely wrong, for up until this moment he had always oozed remarkable self-confidence. "Will, is there something you're holding back? Please tell me now, because you're making me feel on edge."

"Well, Polly you're about to enter my world for the first time, and if I'm to be honest, it's a world that I rarely allow any outsider to see or become a part of. So forgive me, but I need to ask, Can I truly trust you with my private world?"

"Oh, Will, I am at the same time both touched and saddened— touched that you would consider me enough of a friend to invite me to your home and saddened that it would even cross your mind that I might one day betray you, as I know this would seriously threaten, if not end, our friendship once and for all."

"That's good to know, Polly. Forgive me, but I just needed a little reassurance."

⚬⋅✦⋅⚬

Will drew a deep breath and visibly relaxed as he debated how much more, if anything, he should say to Polly regarding his unusual family. He quickly decided that it was best to remain quiet and low key and thereby allow everything to take its natural course.

Chapter Ten
ARE YOU A FAN OF EARL GREY?

After making their way down a narrow trail that required the use of both hands to push back large amounts of bushy bracken, they finally found themselves in a large clearing. As Polly looked up, she let out a large gasp. "Wow, Will, is that really your house?" she said, pointing into the distance.

"Yep, afraid so," Will replied with a half-hearted grin.

"It's so huge. It's like a fairytale Gothic mansion."

"Hmm, a Gothic monstrosity, more like!" Will quietly conceded as he continued to give Polly another of his famous lopsided grins.

"How amazing that something as big and beautiful as this is so hidden out of sight that no one would ever know it is here."

"Polly, it might look great from a distance, but I assure you that when you get close up, you will see that, sadly, it's terribly run down and dilapidated."

"Oh, I'm sure it could do with a bit of tender loving care, but—"

"Couldn't we all?" Will interjected. "The house definitely needs a bit of attention. In fact, that's quite funny, as my house is even called Tumbledown Cottage. So come on, then. Let's go in," he said, as once more he grabbed her by the hand and then raced toward the house with great determination.

As they stood in the porch entrance while Will searched his trouser pocket for his door key, he had one final request. "Right now, do as I say, and close your eyes," he ordered as he attempted to turn the key in the lock.

"Why?" Polly dared to ask.

"Just do as I say, Polly," Will stated in little more than a whisper, at the same time gently putting his hand across her mouth to suggest that she should take a deep breath and for once do as she was told without questioning or murmuring.

Polly submitted to this gesture and obeyed by closing her eyes tightly, as she then allowed Will to guide her through the door.

She continued to hold Will's hand very tightly as he gently led her into a room. "Can I open my eyes yet?" Polly nervously asked.

"Not just yet," came the reply.

Suddenly Polly felt something warm brush up against her leg. She let out a small squeal. Then something furry touched her other leg, causing a shiver to run the full length of her spine. She let out another squeal and opened her eyes. The room was pitch black, causing Polly to squint as she struggled to get her eyesight back into full focus. Seconds later and she could see movement, lots of movement, as small, shadowy objects darted back and forth at great speed in front of her. Will let go of her hand and marched over to a large bay window. He then pulled back the dark, heavily draped curtains, giving the hot afternoon sun instant permission to penetrate the room with its abundantly generous and bedazzling streams of warm sunlight.

Polly winced and raised her hands up to her forehead to allow her eyes to once more adapt, as the flood of light continued to wheedle out all darkness in exchange for some most welcome and comforting warmth. And as Polly once more attempted to look around the enormous but dreadfully dilapidated room with its large, ancient-looking furniture, she was shocked to note that it was overrun with cats! Black cats, brown cats, Persian cats, and ginger cats by the dozen! They were everywhere!

"Goodness, Will! Are all these yours?" Polly dared to ask.

"Well, only Scoota belongs to me, and as you can clearly see, she is happily expecting some babies of her own," he said with a grin as, crouching down, he began to tickle her large tummy before allowing the pretty white cat to turn over to then begin licking his fingers.

"She's a real beauty, isn't she?" His voice betrayed a distinct note of tenderness.

"Tell me, Will. What possessed you to name her Scoota?" Polly asked, slightly bemused. "I mean, the name seems far more appropriate for a male cat."

Before he could answer, Polly heard the somewhat strangled voice of an old woman crying out. "William dearest, is that you? William dear, be a good boy and answer me. Are you there?"

"Yes, Mother. It's me, and I'm in the drawing room," he reticently replied. Polly was quick to notice that his voice appeared somewhat downhearted, maybe even a little embarrassed, yes, as though he was not too happy to be home.

Suddenly Polly turned to see an old, wizened woman enter the room in a wheelchair.

"I see we have a visitor. How rare and unexpected," she stated in a rather sinister but posh, upper-crust accent. "So, Will, do me the kindness of telling me the poor girl's name."

"It's Polly, Polly Brown, and she's a good friend from school."

"Oh pray, tell me, William, does your new friend like cats?" the old, white-haired woman rather snootily asked.

"I've no idea whatsoever!" Will replied, at the same time looking more than a little flustered.

Polly for a reason remained conspicuously silent, for as she normally put her foot right in it she was very unsure as to what, if anything, was the best way to answer the lady. And she really did want to be respectful.

"Does the girl have a voice?" the feeble old lady rather primly asked.

"Of course she does, Mother."

"Then would it be too much to ask for the girl to speak up for herself? Are you a friend or foe of the feline?"

Polly furrowed her brow, thereby suggesting that she felt incapable of answering the old lady's question, as she did not fully understand what she was being asked.

"My dear, do you like cats?"

"Well, I think so," Polly stuttered.

"You think so! What sort of reply is that? Are you not capable of giving a reasonable and thereby simple answer, for it's either a firm yes or no. So which is it to be?"

"Oh, Mother, stop scaring her," Will quickly interjected with a distinct note of resignation in his voice.

His mother raised her hand dismissively as she continued to ignore him. "Well, girl, I'm still waiting on your reply."

"Yes, I do like cats. Not that I know much about them, for I have never had the privilege of owning one. But as I love all animals alike, then it must surely include cats."

"Oh, good. I'm delighted to hear that, for it makes you a very welcome visitor under this roof. These little feline beauties are the love of my life. Aren't you, my little precious ones?" she said as she patted her lap, giving a clear invitation for one of her many cats to jump up into her lap.

"Come on, Lucretia dearest. Come to Mother. You see, Polly, unlike most humans, cats will never hurt or abandon you," she wistfully sniffed as she began to stroke the head of the cat who had jumped up and was now little more than a soft, purring ball in her lap. "Anyway, William, I do hope you remembered to pick up a meat pie on the way home from school. Otherwise there will be no supper, and that will really cause great upset to your brother."

"Yes, Mother, I did," Will stated as he lifted the bag that contained the pie into the air for her to see.

"Splendid! Now I propose that we all go through to the kitchen, and Will dearest, you can organize a nice pot of tea on a tray with some biscuits. Polly dear, I assume that just like the rest of us you too simply adore Earl Grey?"

Polly was confused. Will had never mentioned that he had a brother. Was he older or younger? Did Will get on with him? And finally, who on earth was Earl Grey? And why would this strange woman wrongly presume that Polly not only knew the man but also adored him? Oh, and merely out of interest, precisely how many cats lived in this dilapidated mansion? All these questions were buzzing 'round in Polly's young head as she followed Will, his mother, and twenty or more cats out of the drawing room, as like a most somber funeral procession, they quietly headed down the long corridor toward the kitchen.

Polly held back, allowing the old woman in the chair to get well ahead of them.

"Psst! Will, you've never told me that you had a brother," she whispered, giving him quite a rough nudge to express her annoyance.

"Hang on a minute, Polly. Up until this moment in time I have been more concerned about your home crisis than I have about giving out my family details. So give me a break. I assure you that you will, in due course, meet him."

"All right, but tell me quickly before we get to the kitchen, who exactly is Earl Grey? Is he another weird relative of yours? And why does your mother think I not only know him but actually adore him?"

"Oh, Polly, you daft little thing! Allow me to enlighten you, for Earl Grey is not a person! No, it's a rather splendid aromatic tea infused with bergamot that is usually served up with a nice twist of lemon."

"Right, well I'm glad you told me, although I'm now feeling like a prize idiot," she murmured as she continued to follow after the long line of cats and Will's mother in her wheelchair.

"Look, Polly, I'm going to make mother a pot of tea, and then I think we'll quickly excuse ourselves. That way we can talk about things more openly," he whispered in her ear.

Polly nodded her agreement, for she had hoped for a private moment with Will. Besides, she badly needed his help with a couple of tough pieces of English literature homework that she was well behind with and that had to be on her teacher's desk by 9:00 a.m. sharp, or else!

"Mother, if you'd like me to make you some tea and bring it on a tray to your boudoir, I think that would be the best idea. Since neither of us fancies hot tea, we'll just help ourselves to a glass of lemonade from the fridge and then excuse ourselves, if that's all right with you."

His mother stopped in her tracks and then very abruptly turned full circle in her wheelchair. "I understand, Will. You'd rather I disappear and leave you two alone. I see."

"No, Mother. It's just that, well, we have lots of homework and other things to talk about. Please understand."

"Oh, I understand all right. Yes, I wouldn't want to embarrass you in front of your delightful guest. Tut tut. Oh no, that would not do at all, would it?" she said in rather disparaging tones.

"Come on, Mother. Be fair. This is the first time in ages that I've brought anyone into the house. Normally it's Jack or Robert, and they converse with you for hours on end."

Will's mother pulled a long, surly face, then lifted her nose high in the air as if to emphasize her utter contempt toward her son. "William, I no longer require any form of refreshment, and if later I change my mind, well, then I will do it without the help of your services," she snorted, as without warning she abruptly turned her wheelchair to face in the opposite direction. Then without any further dialogue, friendly or otherwise, she wheeled her way down the hallway until she was well out of sight.

"Oh, Will. What on earth was all that about? She's really upset with you for bringing me here, isn't she? Look, I won't stay. I think it's best if I go, for I think I have already outstayed my welcome."

"You'll do no such thing, Polly. It was I who invited you here, and she has got to understand and come to terms with the fact that I need friends as well as a mother." Will then guided her into the kitchen and began to fill up two glass tumblers with lemonade when he was interrupted by another strange and booming voice that could not fail to alarm Polly further.

"William, where are you? Get up here immediately, for I am in dire need of a fresh glass of water."

Polly trembled as she hoarsely whispered, "Will, is that your father calling out to you?"

"Oh, no. He left years ago," Will stated, very matter-of-fact.

"Well, if it is not your father, then who on earth is it?"

"Polly, that noise that you've just heard, well, that is coming from upstairs, and it is coming from Edmund, my older brother, who, sadly, is bed ridden."

"Oh, right. Then shouldn't we go and find out what he wants?" Polly asked as she cautiously made her way over toward the kitchen door.

"Yes, I guess we'd better," Will quietly responded as he made his way toward her, clutching two rather over-filled glasses of lemonade. "Here, Polly. Take this, and you'd better sip some right away." Polly reached out and took one from him. "Make sure you don't spill any, or Mother will be most displeased," he warned.

Polly responded by quickly taking a large slurp to prevent such a catastrophe from ever happening.

"OK, Polly, just follow after me."

Polly obeyed, following after Will as he made his way down some rather stately looking corridors that bore huge, ornate pictures on the walls, pictures of haughty, pompous men, all with big noses, mind you, and bedecked in strange powdered wigs.

When they reached the end of this corridor and turned left, Polly's eyes nearly popped out of her head, for directly in front of her were some very wide and beautifully ornate stairs. "Wow, this staircase must have been handmade by a master craftsman," Polly exclaimed as she caressed the intricately ornate banister that she was holding on to for support as she quickly made her way to the top.

"Don't be deceived, Polly, for you'll quickly find out that, like everything else seemingly impressive in this house, this banister too is extremely wobbly. Be very careful not to lean too heavily on it."

He might as well have been talking to himself, for Polly was lost in wonderment as she continued climbing the stairs, at the same time taking in the surroundings.

"Wow, and look at that huge crystal chandelier. It's utterly fabulous. Oh, golly gosh, it looks as though it is only hanging by a thread or two. Will, aren't you the least bit afraid that if one of the brass links gives way it will crash to the ground and be forever ruined?"

Will did not care to answer her, as he seemed much more concerned with what lay ahead. As soon as their feet touched the top landing, he directed her to follow him down a very dimly lit corridor before coming to a halt outside a closed door.

With his ear close up to the door, Will timidly gave the door a gentle knock.

"Well, what are you waiting for? Come on in," a very aggressive and seemingly nasty voice shouted out from behind the other side of the closed door. Polly noticed that Will's hand was trembling slightly as he twisted the knob and pushed open the door. She then cautiously followed Will into the room. Once again, the room was in total darkness, and it felt distinctly cold, that is, until Will went over to the window and opened some large shutters. With the shutters now pulled to one side, the cold air quickly dispersed, as the powerful sun was given its first permission of the day to generously flood the room with its warmth, immediately eliminating the former chilly and most hostile atmosphere.

Polly looked over toward the big, old oak bed that dominated the room before taking a long, hard look at its angry occupant.

"Hi. You must be Edmund," Polly said as she breezed up to the bed and stuck out a hand for him to shake. "And before you ask, I'm Polly,

Polly Brown to be precise," she stated in her friendly but informative manner as she continued to hold out her hand in her bid to be warm.

The surly young man did not move a muscle in response to her friendly, outgoing gesture.

"Sorry, Polly, but he's in too much pain to move, so please don't be too offended."

Polly shot Will one of her "It's too late, for I'm already offended" looks, which had Will quickly covering up for his brother's sad and offensive behavior.

"Look, Polly. If, like Edmund, you'd broken just about every bone in your body, you might well struggle to give a handshake. He's in so much pain, and I'm sure you must realize that sickness makes most of us exceedingly grumpy," Will said as he went to great pains to ease the increasingly chilly atmosphere that had now turned into a very awkward silence.

Polly withdrew her hand, but despite Will's excuses, she still considered his brother to be a very rude if not obnoxious person, for she had made the rather clever observation that neither his mouth nor his face was bandaged up. Well then, there was nothing preventing him from giving a gentle and sincerely polite greeting.

"Did you remember my painkillers?" he sourly growled in Will's direction.

"Yes, I brought them yesterday. See, they are right here beside your book on the bedside locker. Did you not see them? Here, allow me to fetch you a glass of water, and then you can take some with your pills, as well as quench your thirst," Will tried to helpfully suggest.

"Yes, get me some water, and while you're at it, I've had nothing to eat all day, so run downstairs and make me a toasted sandwich. In fact, what I really fancy is a buck rabbit, so run along and make me something nice," he petulantly demanded. "And then I really need my pillows plumping up. Better still, I need to swap mine with yours. I'm certain yours are feather filled and therefore more comfortable than these old ones. Oh, and did you remember to buy the meat pie? Otherwise you'd better get back down to the village before the shop shuts," he said in a smoldering tone of voice.

Polly, who was quietly listening in, quite rightly thought Edmund was a very rude and offensive young man, for she had been painfully aware that there had not been one single "please" among his many requests, nor for that matter one measly "thank you." If it were left to her, she would refuse to obey a single order; well, at least until he showed a more gracious side to what otherwise seemed like very miserable and utterly deplorable behavior.

"Will, what an utterly cantankerous old sourpuss he is," Polly commented as she went back down to the kitchen to help him make his brother a buck rabbit.

Will remained silent concerning his brother's very sad and most troubling behavior.

"Tell me, Will, what exactly is a buck rabbit? Surely you don't intend to kill a baby rabbit and put him under the toaster just to satisfy your mean old brother, do you?" she said, feeling suitably horrified.

"Oh, Polly. There you go again. Buck rabbit has nothing whatsoever to do with rabbits."

"Well, if that's so, why then is it called buck rabbit?" she quizzed.

"Honestly, Polly, I have no idea, for it's simply cheese on toast, topped off with a poached egg. Trust me when I say it tastes even better if you add a smidgeon of English *moutard*."

Polly screwed up her nose. "*Moutard*?"

"Oops, sorry. That's French for *mustard*, of course. It's important that you put the thinnest scraping of English mustard on the toast, for this draws out the full flavor out of the cheese as it melts. You then pile on the grated cheese before popping it under a hot grill. You then leave it under the grill until the cheese sizzles and becomes a lovely golden brown. Add a lightly poached egg on top, and voila! You have a buck rabbit. I promise you, it tastes utterly scrumptious. And you can also make Welsh rabbit; this is melted cheese on toast without the—"

"Rabbit," Polly quickly interjected.

"No, silly. Without the poached egg. Don't ask me why such dishes have such unusual names. Call it 'the British way,' if you will."

"I know what you mean," said Polly, breaking into a smile. "I mean, who ever thought to call a lusciously light sponge pudding filled with juicy sultanas 'spotted dick'?"

"Exactly, Polly. It would appear that the English like weird and wonderful names for most things that are decidedly yummy."

"Will, I agree with you on just about everything, but tell me truthfully, has your brother always been such a grouchy old sourpuss?" Polly asked, trying to revert back to the subject of his brother and his extremely offensive behavior.

"Truthfully, no," Will was swift to respond. "Actually, he's got much worse over the years," he admitted, giving a heavy sigh that inadequately expressed just how concerned he truly felt for Edmund. "I don't think he ever recovered from Father leaving home. I think he took it badly, as he was the one walking up the drive at the time Dad left. As the car drove by, he realized that the occupant of the car was Dad, and he never even stopped to say his final good-byes or give as much as a small wave. That was the last time he, or I, for that matter, saw our father," he wearily sighed as he placed two thick slices of whole-grain bread under the grill to toast.

"Oh, gosh. How awful," were the only comments that spilled from her lips as she listened most intently to Will telling the story.

"As soon as Edmund was eighteen, he joined the army, mainly because he wanted to get out of here. I think he found everything about home life much too painful. Well, he was doing really well, that is, until one day during a military exercise he was terribly injured." Will went uncomfortably silent.

"Go on, Will. Tell me more," Polly urged as she spread butter on the warm toast before piling it high with a mountain of shredded cheese.

"Polly, wait a second. Have you put the *moutard* on the toast?"

Polly pulled a long face.

"Mustard, Polly. Here, catch."

Polly was very thankful, as well as relieved, to catch the mustard pot and made a mental note to tell Will as soon as it seemed right that she had an ongoing eye problem, so throwing things her way was, at the end of the day, pretty inadvisable!

"Well caught, Polly, but you will probably find everything I tell you from this moment in time very hard to believe."

"Try me," was Polly's simple reply as she turned the toast upside down to allow the cheese to drop off. This way she could add some mustard before placing the cheese back on the toast.

"Edmund was on a regular parachuting exercise. Everything was going to plan. He opened his parachute at the right time, but sadly, he bungled up, for he did not land in the manner he was trained. Despite being in agonizing pain, he got up and began the long hike back to base. It was not too long before he realized something was very wrong. For one thing, he could hardly breathe."

Polly let out a loud gasp as she stood by the cooker and slipped the metal grill pan that held the cheese on toast under the grill. "My goodness, this is becoming one of the worst stories I've ever heard," she exclaimed as she placed some water in a special pan, her full intention being to wait until the water boiled and to then poach an egg. Polly found herself feeling thoroughly repentant concerning all the ill feeling she had been experiencing toward Edmund.

"Well, my brother told his commanding officer that something was very wrong, but his pleas to rest went ignored, for he was ordered to carry on walking. Edmund struggled to walk for over eighteen miles, and all that time he was in the most hideous, excruciating pain. When he arrived back at base, he passed out and was immediately taken to hospital. It was only then that the full impact of his injuries was made known. Yes, Polly he had broken virtually every single bone in his body. In a procedure to try and repair some of the fractures, he became paralyzed from the waist down, and he can no longer walk."

"You couldn't see it, Polly, but he's still swathed in bandages from the chest down," Will went on to inform her. "And I guess he feels very bitter and frustrated that such a thing should happen to him. He was such an athlete before this. He lived and breathed sports, and now he feels his life is well and truly over. This is why he is so very hurt and bitter."

"My goodness, how simply dreadful," Polly gasped, suddenly feeling very overwhelmed by compassion on Edmund's behalf.

"Yes, he has been confined to his bed for nine long months, and I guess it's all taken a terrible toll on him."

"Oh, Will. I feel so sad for him. Is there anything I can do to make things easier for him?" she asked out of deep concern as she watched Will crack an egg into a special tray before placing it over the pan of boiling water.

"I don't think so, Polly. Goodness knows I have tried my best to be patient with him, so I guess he still needs time alone to work things out for himself. Oh my goodness! Quick, Polly! Remove the toast from under the grill, for the cheese has just caught fire!"

"Oops!" said Polly as she quickly grabbed hold of a kitchen towel and hurriedly pulled the rack down from the grill, throwing the cloth over the toast to put out the small flame. Seconds later she quickly whipped the cloth away to take a peek at what remained beneath it. "It's a bit burnt at the edges, but otherwise it looks fine," she over-optimistically stated.

Will made his way over to Polly to take a good look.

"Hmm. Well, I don't know if it will do, for Edmund has become very fussy these days, and he may get very upset if we place this burnt sacrificial offering in front of him."

"Really, Will? I dare to think otherwise, for I'm sure if he's as hungry as he says he is, then he will be fine with it. Besides, if we quickly scrape off all the burnt bits, he will never know any different," Polly confidently stated as she bent down and began scrutinizing the toast from every angle.

"You know, Polly, in my opinion it may be best to start all over again, yes, make it from scratch," Will stated, giving her a quick despairing look as he stood over the sorry-looking buck rabbit weighing up all his limited options. "Yes, we either risk all by just placing the egg on top, which will indeed hide some of the burnt bits, and then leave his room quickly without mentioning that it's a bit singed at the edges, or we start from scratch and once more face his wrath for having taken such a long time. Polly, which is it to be?"

"Let's just take it up to him and see," Polly very brightly suggested. "If it turns out that he doesn't want it, well then, I'd be more than happy to polish it off," she said.

Will turned around to take the poached egg out of the pan and slip it onto the cheese on toast. "Oh my goodness, I too have failed in my duty, for this egg is meant to be runny, not solid as a rock and frazzled at the edges," he lamented, as against his better judgment he then dropped it on top of the burnt cheese on toast to head up the stairs.

"Will, did you not see that the egg almost bounced off the plate?" Polly announced with a grimace.

"Oh, well. Let's get it over with," Will rather wistfully stated as he encouraged Polly to go ahead of him and open the door to let him through.

As it happened, Will turned out to be horribly correct.

"This poor cheese on toast was obviously hung, drawn, and quartered before being cremated," his brother yelled as he rather contemptuously held up the rubbery egg between his fingers to peer down at the slightly blackened cheese on toast, his furrowed brow furiously twitching with rage.

"I'm so sorry, Edmund. We honestly tried our best. We will go back down to the kitchen and start again," a remorseful Will hurriedly suggested in his desperate bid to put things right.

"Forget it! I will hang on until suppertime. But if that too gets positively incinerated, you're very life is then in jeopardy, dear brother. Do you hear me? I swear I will make it my sole objective to make your life as miserable as can be. Now get out of here, you absolute cretin. Yes, both of you. Yes, get out," he yelled. Then out of pure frustration, he threw a glass in their direction. Luckily the glass missed them, albeit by a few inches, as it smashed into the door. Polly instantly fell to her knees and began to pick up the large and dangerously sharp shards of glass that now littered the floor.

"Leave it alone, Polly. I'll clear it up later. Let's just get out of here while we can," Will ordered as he firmly grabbed hold of her elbow and pulled her to her feet. "Come on. It's time to go," he gently urged, pushing her out of the room before anything else untoward could happen.

As soon as they were back out on the landing and alone, Will invited Polly to ascend a further set of stairs. Polly held back.

"Will, I think I should go home, for my being here has caused enough upset to last a lifetime, don't you think?" she said, a very weary and forlorn look written all over her face.

"Nonsense. I just want you to come with me for a moment," he said as he held out his hand for her to take. "Come on, Polly. Trust me."

After they had climbed the next set of stairs, Will ushered her down another small corridor before opening a door that led into another large room. Polly stood with her mouth open wide, for in the corner of the room was the biggest and most elegant grand piano she had ever set eyes on.

"It's a Bechstein," Will hurriedly informed her in manner that might suggest that the name would mean something to her. Of course, it didn't, but that still didn't stop Polly from making further excitable sounds as she timidly stepped up to it.

"Can *you* play this?" she asked as she casually brushed the tips of her fingers over the keys.

"Why, of course," he swiftly replied. "Would you like to hear me play?"

"What, now?"

"Well, I think now might be considered the perfect moment, as I'm standing right on front of it. That is, unless you have some special concert in mind that as of yet I know nothing of," Will good-humoredly replied.

Polly smiled and then raced into the middle of the room to give a twirl. "Play on, dear maestro!" she shouted, as she overdramatically gestured for him to take his seat and begin.

Will stretched and wiggled his long fingers, doing some rather outlandish form of hand exercises that Polly presumed only experienced concert musicians would even care to do. Finally he allowed his long fingers to caress the keys before shouting out, "Prontissimo." He then began to play with much enthusiasm and energy as, lost in the music, he climbed into a higher stratosphere that most mere mortals know little of. How long he played is neither here nor there. What can be categorically stated is that this moment in time was the most magical event that Polly had ever been blessed with experiencing outside of her visit to Piadora. As Will continued to play whatever music his young heart dictated, an equally heady Polly danced around with the gay abandonment of a wind-up ballerina from a musical box that continues to twirl long after all music has stopped. Polly laughed and danced, then danced some more as her friend Will entranced and captivated her heart with his exceptional playing.

It did not come to a halt until Polly finally collapsed breathlessly to the floor. "Will, you really are the best!" she jubilantly cried.

Will broke into a smile as he got up from the piano to come over and join her. "Right, Polly, I think it's about time we got down to doing a bit of homework, don't you? So come on. Get out your books, and let me take a look," he gently ordered.

Polly responded by pulling a rather long and extremely childish face. "Oh, must we? I have been enjoying myself so much. It's a shame to spoil it all now by doing stupid, horrid homework," she sniffed rather churlishly.

"Yes, now! And allow me to tell you bluntly, homework is not—I repeat, not—stupid. Stupid is for those who fail to realize how important homework, and therefore an education, is. It's good to have fun, but we must also work; otherwise, your life will go nowhere, and that's a mathematical certainty!"

"You're beginning to sound as boring as many of my teachers," she moaned.

"Well, I'm glad to hear it! Sorry, Polly, but I'm not going to change my mind on this one. I've seen too many of my brother's friends who messed around in school and treated homework as something other lesser mortals did. And now they are paying for their sheer stupidity, for they are all struggling to find work that has any meaning or fulfillment, as they left school without any decent qualifications. So if all this means you consider me to be nothing short of a wet rag, then so be it."

"Sorry. I didn't mean to offend you," Polly mournfully sniffed.

"No offense taken. But Polly, please take the time to ask yourself this: Let's say you own a restaurant, and two students came for an interview. The first has completed school, and even though his or her grades are not straight As, all the reports talk of the student trying hard, being punctual, and always giving his best. The second student, however, has impressive grades, but if you read between the lines he or she put no effort into anything. Which of the two would you choose?"

Polly was convinced he was trying to catch her out. "I'm not answering you, Will, just in case you are trying to trick me," she glibly retorted.

"Polly, I promise that's truly not the case. I am just trying to make you see how important it is to do and give your best at school and why you should try to have a voracious appetite when it comes to learning. I want you to succeed, and if that means appearing hard and boorish, then so be it. So for the moment the fun's over, and now it's time to take a good look at your homework, or else I'll walk you straight home," he said in a most impressive voice of authority that all of a sudden had Polly feeling very submissive, although she had absolutely no intention whatsoever of showing it. She therefore remained with a downcast expression across her face, looking very glum, if not a little—dare I say it?—moody.

"Look, Polly. I want to help because I truly care. Neither of our home lives could be considered perfect. In truth, we have so many trials to overcome before we even hit the school gates each day. So if we do well at school, then it opens up so many possibilities for our future, for it finally gives us both something called *choice*."

"Choice? What precisely does that word mean?" Polly ruefully commented tongue in cheek as she thought of Uncle Boritz, the dictator controlling every minute of her life to the point where she felt as though she were nothing but a mere pawn on his private chessboard to be randomly shoved from square to square at his will.

"Right, then. Where is this homework? Let's get started, shall we?"

Polly suddenly felt very awkward and embarrassed.

Will noticed her silence and decided to push a little.

"Polly, I've upset and offended you, haven't I?" he suggested, showing great sensitivity.

"No, Will. Well maybe just a bit. It's just that, well, I'm seen as a bit of a dunce, a no-hoper, and therefore a waste of space by most of the teachers. It is the same with all of us that come from the castle. If I'm to be brutally honest, my brothers as well have always appeared to get the worst treatment, and I don't know why. I have tried to show the teachers that I am different, that I want to learn. Really, I have. But it feels completely hopeless." Polly felt so safe with Will that in no time at all she found herself sharing some of the most painful events of her life.

"Will, believe me when I tell you, if I ever go home having achieved anything, such as a certificate for poetry, there is never a single word of encouragement. No one is the slightest bit interested. So if I'm honest, I've completely given up, for why should I care when no one else does?"

Will remained silent, occasionally giving her hand a small squeeze to comfort her and let her know that he felt the depth of her pain.

"There are thirty-five of us at the orphanage, not counting their own five children," Polly informed him.

"I have not come across any pupil who goes by the surname of Scumberry yet," Will said as he furrowed his brow, an indication of his deep concern.

"No, and you wont. The youngest one, Jeremy, is less than a year old, and the oldest is sixteen. He lives away from home, as he is a boarder at a private school. The other, older children go to different fee-paying schools, and the youngest two are not yet ready for anything other than nursery school. Oh, yes, and in the castle they live their private lives on the other side of the bars from us. Theirs is the posh side."

"Posh side?"

"Yes, Will. You heard right. They have nice carpets and gas heaters and nice, comfortable furniture and every luxury imaginable, while our side is very sparsely furnished, and it is always freezing cold. No one who visits the castle is ever permitted to come and see our side, so they go on their way believing that we all live the same way. Even the Social Services remain ignorant of the differences, yet inside the castle there are big iron gates that divide their side from ours."

"What, gates inside the house?"

"Unbelievable as it may seem, there really are iron bars to divide us. We do see their children occasionally, but as they have a live-in granny who helps look after them and cooks for them, we do not see them that often. They often walk past us eating sweets and drinking soda, and so, for the most times it is very hard to bear." She sniffed as she volunteered information that she knew was strictly forbidden from ever being discussed outside the castle.

"The only way to help you understand is to ask you to imagine being in a crowd of people. You are all unbearably hungry and thirsty. Along comes a truck, and half of the crowd is given a wonderful meal, lots to drink, new clothes, and comfortable shoes for their feet. The others can do little but watch. The first group is then taken off somewhere wonderful for the day, leaving the others behind with nothing to look forward to. Imagine the tension that would exist between both groups on their return. Now, then. That's exactly how it is for us," she sighed.

"My brothers and I were the last ones to arrive at the castle, and so we have been hated ever since," she said, lowering her voice as she expressed something of the deep pain she was feeling. "Thomas never even made it. He felt so alone, so isolated," she softly said, her voice suddenly cracking with emotion.

"Who was Thomas?" Will gently dared to ask.

"He was my dear older brother, but sadly he has passed away," she stated in little more than a whisper. "They killed his spirit and soul first, and then he became ill. Will, I miss him so much," she confessed, tears hurtling unabashed down her cheeks as she felt the full impact of her deep and sad loss.

Will squeezed her hand even tighter. "Polly, I'm so sorry, really I am, and I feel honored that you feel safe enough to share these private and very painful things with me. I want you to know that I am and always will be a true friend," he mumbled as he let go of her hand to place a comforting arm around her shoulder. "And what's more, I have the broadest shoulders you'll ever get to see, so if you ever need a shoulder to cry on, then I'm your man," he commiserated. "But as time is marching on, we need to put all distractions aside and address this latest piece of homework."

Polly nodded her head in full agreement.

"Tell you what. Let's arrange to meet later in the week, and then we can talk longer about the things that are causing you such heartache," he suggested as he reached over with his free hand to wipe away a stray tear that was rolling down her cheek.

"You're so right, Will. I really need to get this piece of homework under my belt, so help me out if you can," she pleaded as she stuffed a book that had seen better days into his hands.

"Wow, Shakespeare's *Romeo and Juliet*. How come they are giving you such hard stuff at such a young age?"

"Oh, they are only wishing to give us an introduction to it in the vain hope that later we might even learn to love and appreciate such famous writers. They are at present organizing a school trip to take the class to visit his birthplace, which I believe is in Stratford-upon-Avon."

"Hey, that will be great," Will enthused.

"Yes, it would be wonderful, but I expect that I will be staying behind as usual, as I never have the money the school requires for any educational trips," she said wistfully.

"Hmm, that's so sad and unfair," Will dared to comment.

"Everything is unfair, Will. They are also hoping to take the class to the theater to see it live on stage. Again, I don't think I will be given that opportunity either," she mournfully stated as she reached out to grab her book back from out of his hand. "Oh, I wish I came from a rich family, and then I'd have none of these stupid troubles."

"Oh, Polly, don't be daft. Rich people still have their own trials and sorrows."

"Right, just like Uncle Boritz's snooty guests when he throws his lavish evening soirees. 'Oh dear. shall I opt for the duck confite, the lobster thermidore, or perhaps the filet mignon? This is so terribly trying, for I do believe the choice of sumptuous food to be simply overwhelming.'"

"Polly, please stop right now! I hate to hear you sounding so bitter and cynical, for you are too special a person to have such things brewing away like an overworked teapot from within you."

"Be fair, Will. Being a broke kid in care is no fun whatsoever. Let's face it. Wouldn't you like to be well off so you could live in a really plush house and buy whatsoever your heart desired?"

"Well, Polly, as you ask, my family was for many years considerably rich, but did this make us happy? The answer has to be a resounding no. Therefore, I would trade all the money in the world for a warm and loving home life, and that's the honest truth."

Polly couldn't argue this undeniable truth, no, not even for one moment, as she felt exactly the same.

"Also, you surely must realize that having money will not banish your problems. In fact, sometimes being disgustingly rich will only add to them," he said as he paused to take a breath.

Polly used this opportunity to pull a face to imply that she was not that easily blinkered, and therefore she was not entirely convinced.

"I mean, once you have riches, you spend the rest of your life worrying about trying to keep hold of them."

"Quite what do you mean by that?" she sniffed.

"OK, you buy a priceless piece of art, and you are then faced with putting it on a wall in your house or placing it in a vault. If you leave it on the wall, you might find yourself being burgled. So you now have a choice of having very costly insurance and expensive camera equipment installed in and around your property, or you place it for safekeeping in a vault. Truth is, do you ever really enjoy it? Left on the wall you worry about it. Stored in a vault you have little time to fully appreciate it. And this is but one small example, Polly. So tell me now, does that sound like a life of freedom?" he asked with more than a note of weariness in his tone of voice.

"Sounds just like Uncle Boritz, for making money, and lots of the stuff, is what makes the blood pump 'round his heart and course through his veins. I do believe that no one hates parting with it more than him. It's enough to give him a seizure," she commented with a sigh. "But even so, Will, being as poor as a church mouse isn't much fun either."

"Well then, that should give you even more reason and motivation to work hard at school so that you can have a future that's worth looking forward to," he said, jumping up from the floor. He then grabbed her hand to help her to her feet.

"So, Polly Brown, the smartest girl for miles around, let's start right here and right now to turn things round. You say that you will not be going to the theater due to lack of finances. Well then, Polly, we will have to create our very own private theater," he said as he raced across the floor and then began to drag a long table toward the center of the room. "Come on, Polly. Help me out. Grab the other end of the table. That's perfect. So you see, Cinders shall go to the ball after all."

"What precisely do you mean by that?"

"Exactly what I just said."

"Come on, Will. Speak plain English, for I fear you're beginning to sound a little crazy."

"No, Polly. On this occasion you're definitely wrong, for which of these is the more crazy: to lie down and accept defeat without doing everything within your power to change the things that are causing you such deep misery, or to fight with all your might to at least try and change the things you can?"

"So how do you propose to help things change for me, Will? I'd like to know, truly I would."

"Step by step, little by little, brick upon brick. Tell you what, Polly. How do you eat an elephant?"

"I've absolutely no idea," she innocently replied.

"One spoonful at a time," Will answered back before bursting into a fit of laughter.

"Ho ho ho," Polly sarcastically responded, as she was now beginning to feel a little annoyed with him.

"Seriously, though. That is how we will tackle the mountain of setbacks in your life—one small spoonful at a time. The good news, Polly, is it can begin here, today."

"What? Today? Come on, Will. Don't be so daft and naïve."

"Yes, right here, right now! So come on, Polly Brown, do me a huge favor and climb up onto the table," he ordered with a forcefulness she had not seen before. "We will turn the tables 'round by making up our own plays, yes, hundreds of them, all filled to overflowing with murder, mystery, great passion, and the like," he announced as he jumped up on the table to join her. "Who knows? We might write so many that one day, just like Shakespeare and Dickens, we might become so famous that schoolchildren all across the world will be acting out our plays."

"M'lud, ladies and gentleman, may I have your full attention, as for the first time ever I present to you the wonderful, awesome, indubitable talents of Miss Polly Brown, who, if you are not yet fully aware, is without a shadow of doubt the sweetest young lady this side of town."

Polly blushed and let out a giggle. "Oh, Will. You really are a bit crazy," she mused.

"No, just a bit different," he earnestly replied as he grabbed her hand and continued to hopelessly overact.

"So come, my lady, let us make haste to learn something of the tragic and sadly blighted lives of these star-crossed lovers named Romeo and Juliet," he shouted into the air as without warning he grabbed the book back from out of her hand, causing her to almost topple off the table, for she was so startled.

Will and Polly continued to make it a habit of spending time together whenever they could inside and out of school. Some weeks after Polly first accompanied him to his house, Will once again offered to chaperone her home from school. On the way, Polly turned to her new friend and told him that she really wanted to take him on a little detour.

A few minutes later they found themselves standing outside the entrance door of a big, old, beautiful church.

"Will, this is where I sing in the choir, so let me show you something that is my secret alone." After entering the church, Polly took Will through a small door that said "Private" and then up some stone steps until they came to a place where yet another set of steps meandered of on the right side. However, these steps were roped off, and so were presumably out of bounds. "Quick, Will, climb under this rope," Polly assertively ordered.

"But it says, 'Strictly no admittance.'"

"I know, but please trust me, for I want to show you my secret hiding place," she whispered.

As they continued climbing, the steps grew narrower and narrower. Soon they were both standing in a small bell tower.

"This is my special hiding place, Will," Polly breathlessly stated. "Don't you think it's funny that just like Quasimodo, I too have my own bell tower in which to hide away?"

"Polly, help me out here, for I really can't quite see the connection between you and Quasimodo."

"Oh, right," she nervously laughed.

"No, really."

"Well, he was so ugly he had to hide away in a bell tower, and as I am like him, then I too have my own bell tower in order to hide away."

Will shook his head as though taken by surprise by what she so nonchalantly stated as though it were fact.

"But Polly, what on earth is going on inside that mixed-up head of yours? You're nothing like Quasimodo!"

"Oh, but I am. He was an ugly monster that people made fun of, and so am I. So it is fitting that just like him I have my tower to hide away in," she said in a very matter-of-fact tone of voice.

Will was silent.

Polly moved across to the other side of the room and began to stare down at the street below. "Come over here, Will, for if you look down, you will see that all the people look like little ants from here," she brightly stated.

"Polly, I need to get you home," he very anxiously stated.

"Oh, Will. Don't be such a bore. Do we have to go?" she moaned.

"Yes, it's getting late. But we must talk more about this some time, because at times you really seem a little crazy to me, besides which, this bell tower is really very dangerous. Look, there are parts of the floor that have completely rotted away. You could easily fall to your death, and trust me when I say that nobody would ever find you."

"Maybe that would be a good thing, for no one would care if that happened," Polly rather sadly muttered under her breath.

"It really isn't safe for you to be up here at all," he remonstrated. "Besides, you could well be breaking the law."

"What law, Will? This is a church! As a rule of thumb, policemen don't tend to come up here, and as I'm not stealing the candles or the hymn books, I have done nothing wrong."

"Yes, but it's still not right," he emphatically stated.

"I know all that, Mr. Goody Two-Shoes, but this is the only place I know to come where I can hide away from all the sheer craziness of my life," she groaned.

"Come on, Polly. Let's not argue about who's right and who's wrong. Let's just get out of here now," he hastily suggested.

Polly simply shrugged her shoulders, as rather reluctantly she followed him down the steep steps and prepared to go home.

As they neared the castle, Polly felt all the old fear return. How crazy she was to have shown Will her secret hideout, and she also knew for certain that she was just as crazy to have agreed to go back to Will's house in the first place. She felt certain that she would be seriously rebuked for not making the tea on time, and even if she worked at a furious pace, her chores would take her well into the early hours of the next morning.

Will must have sensed her anxiety, as he directly asked what was troubling her.

"Nothing, Will. I'm just being stupid, really I am," was her very nervous reply.

Will did not look convinced, but he pushed no further.

"Look, Polly, I'm so sorry if at times I come over as a little stern. It's just that I really care about you, and the thought of you hiding away in that frightfully small and very dangerous bell tower is, quite frankly, very distressing."

"Thanks for even caring," she sighed.

"Same time tomorrow?" he asked.

"Oh, if only. Look, Will, I've had a great time, really I have, but for reasons that I cannot speak of at the moment, I am not sure when I will be allowed out to see you again," she said, her voice sounding frail and tinged with sadness.

"That's fine, but you now owe me," replied Will.

"Owe you for what?

"The challenge, of course."

"Oh, that. Yes, William Montgomery, you've won the challenge, hands down. You made me very happy, because for a short moment in history I actually forgot that I have so many problems to cope with."

"Ahh, so I did win? Therefore, Polly Brown, may I ask you to put all this down in writing?"

"Hmm. So I suppose this is the bit where you kneel down in front of me, and I'm meant to draw a sword and tap you on both shoulders as I most solemnly knight you 'Sir Galahad'?" she stated with a distinct air of pomposity.

"Oh no, my sweet, fair one. You can leave that honor till later, when I have shown thee that I am forever at thy side, ready to serve and protect thee, hereby rescuing thee from the tower in which thou are slavishly imprisoned, even if it means slaying a ferocious, demonical dragon or two."

Polly tried to stifle a giggle but failed miserably.

"So allow me the privilege of telling thee that I shall never, ever shy away from helping thee, for thou art truly a fair and most courageous maiden. And so, 'tis with this in mind, milady, that I must sadly bid thee farewell."

"Oh, my lord, 'tis not farewell, like it were forever. Oh no, my gallant and trustworthy knight, 'tis only a momentary, yes, a fleeting good-bye, though perchance, I pray, it will not be too long till we meet again on some distant shore, if not betwixt the shelves of the school's library for the most learned," she replied as she struggled to remain standing due to a serious fit of the giggles that had her wanting to collapse onto the ground and then perhaps roll around with uncontrollable laughter.

Will watched on with avid interest. Polly, for the first time, didn't shrink under his gaze. The joy within her in that moment gave her a new and unshakeable confidence, however fleeting.

"Well done, Polly. I can see you'll be loving every line of Shakespeare before too long," he warmly stated as he then looked down at his watch.

"Oh my goodness. I'm late! If I don't get home soon, I'll probably be burnt at the stake," he cried, a serious look appearing across his face as it dawned on him that he must hurry home immediately, for he had a pie that needed to be baked yesterday if he was to be spared the doghouse treatment.

"It only seems like five minutes has gone by since we left the school gates to go home. The trouble is, the days draw to a close so quickly in the winter months," Polly sighed.

"Once again, milady, I do bid thee farewell and dost hope that tomorrow I might catch more than a glimpse of thy fair face at thy school for the most studious and learned," he cried, making a lowly bow before turning on his heels to race back home.

Polly hugged herself tightly, her tender spirit continuing to soar, as for the first time ever outside of her experience in Piadora she felt valued for who she was. She also had to admit that her sides were aching terribly from all the laughter.

Alone, with only the evening stars for companionship, she shut her eyes tight and whispered into the darkness. "Dear God, please let Will be for real. Oh, and as a further afterthought, please allow me to slip back into the castle without any admonition. Thank You. Over and out, Polly Brown. "

Chapter Eleven
DELIVER US FROM GLUTTONY

*P*OLLY HEADED TOWARD the front door, all the time experiencing the keenest sense of dread, because she had knowingly stayed out late without having official permission. She also knew that as she was on ROPE and therefore confined to the castle, this could only mean further trouble for her. Polly dropped her bag in the hallway and went into the kitchen to immediately set about her tasks.

"Where have you been?" a nosy Bertha Banoffee quizzed.

"Oh, nowhere. Nowhere in particular. It's just that I needed to see a teacher about some homework that I haven't done," Polly replied, feeling very guilty that she was not being truthful.

"Yeah, right. Pull the other leg; it's got bells on it!" responded Bertha, as she remained totally unconvinced by Polly's weak explanation, but before Bertha had the chance to challenge her further, Gailey Gobbstopper entered the kitchen area.

On seeing Polly standing there, she sidled up and gave her a quick dig in the ribs to gain her full attention. "Here, Polyester Fester, try a spoonful of this very light, mouthwatering Victoria sponge cake that I made in school today," she said as she waved a plate under Polly's nose before quickly whisking it away. "When will you ever learn you're up against the best?" she scornfully hissed as she turned and walked away, laughing out loud.

Before Polly had any time to react to Gailey's usual spiteful behavior, there was an unexpected disturbance in the eating area of the kitchen. Polly turned on her heels just in time to see Uncle Boritz enter the kitchen area single-handedly clutching a huge silver machine that was dangerously weighing him down. Massive beads of sweat began pouring down his craggy, lined face as he continued to stagger along, desperately seeking a clear surface on which to rest the machine before he irretrievably collapsed from the physical strain. Reacting to the impending crisis, four of the boys raced over to give their help, becoming instant coffin bearers, as unburdening their struggling guardian of the monstrous machine they rested the machine on their young shoulders and slowly continued to shuffle along toward the nearest available surface.

Uncle Boritz, who was now miraculously freed from this over-whelming burden, continued his involvement by monitoring the boys' every movement. He stopped only to pull a large handkerchief from his pocket and began to mop his dripping brow with one hand while his other was used to direct the boys as to where to head with his new and very precious cargo. Finally the boys were able to off-load the huge mystery appliance onto a table that just seconds earlier had been quickly cleared of all clutter.

Polly observed that Uncle Boritz was so overcome with excite-ment at his new find that her absence had rather miraculously gone unnoticed. The next thirty minutes were then spent with all the foster children racing backward and forward to get whatever ingredient or implement he bellowed out as he tried hard to read from the tatty, yellowing instruction manual that appeared to accompany the huge mysterious contraption.

Polly chose to stand to one side watching on in amazement, at the same time feeling deeply liberated by her snatched time with Will and grateful that due to her uncle's latest acquisition, this gothic monstrosity had undoubtedly saved her from further punishment.

Finally Uncle Boritz produced a large brown cardboard box, which, once opened, revealed hundreds of stacked-up ice cream cornets that were shaped like large sea shells.

"My precious little poppets, I have just had the good fortune of being given this wonderful, magical ice cream machine, and I might add that as it was so generously donated, it has come at absolutely no cost to my good self."

"Ooh!" they all cried, their eyes out on stalks as they dreamed of what was about to happen.

"So for tonight, and tonight only, feel free to feast on as much ice cream as your young hearts desire and your bellies dictate."

Great gulps of sheer disbelief as well as gasps of delight circled the room as the children repeated his offer over and over, for they could hardly believe their ears. They rarely got to taste ice cream, as it was considered so expensive. And on the last count there had been more foster children than ever, so with more mouths to feed, ice cream was indeed rarely on the menu.

There had been an occasion near Easter when, as a treat, they were surprised to be taken to the cinema to see the latest biblical epic that had just made it to the box office. The drive to the cinema had been long, with all the children packed into the back of the van like sardines, so by the time they arrived at the cinema, they were already feeling hot and frazzled, as well as hungry and thirsty.

They begged over and over to be allowed a small drink or ice cream, but Uncle Boritz was having none of it. The excuse behind his blatant refusal was simple. It was Lent, and that, according to the Catholic calendar, was not a time for indulging the flesh with any form of earthly creature comfort. Oh no, for according to Uncle, as well as the saints in heaven but on standby, this time in the calendar was a rather splendid opportunity for the now-listless children to consider and then commit themselves to a torturous afternoon of self-denial and suffering. And so they were given no choice but to sit through three and a half hours of cinematic excellence with throats as parched as sandpaper seemingly peppered with brick dust as they witnessed all other children in the crowded theater dip into tubs of tantalizing toffee-laced ice cream and thickly covered chocolate ice cream bars. Even more aggravating was to be forced to listen to the sound of endless children slurping and burping as they guzzled down even larger volumes of fizzy soda, stopping only to lazily stretch over to fill the empty vacuum of their mouths with fistfuls of butter popcorn from large boxes that were conveniently situated on the arm rests for their immediate disposal.

Any attempts to be Christlike were immediately vanquished, as murderous jealously consumed the heart of each and every desperate child that day in the cinema. Try as they might, they found it nigh impossible to concentrate on the movie, or anything else for that matter, as they endured three or more hours of distressingly annoying noise that came from children undoing one irritating sweet wrapper after another, while their tongues had long been forced to cleave to the roofs of their mouths, so dire was their need for liquid refreshment. Polly could not speak on behalf of the others, but by the time the credits rolled, she felt totally ready for martyrdom or otherwise inclined to commit a murder or two!

So what they had all believed would be a wonderful impromptu visit to the cinema had quickly turned in to a most harrowing affair that did little to help Polly or any of the other children fully appreciate the deeper meaning of Easter.

As a result of that specific bygone occasion, as well as many other equally distressing events, she could easily be forgiven for seriously questioning whether she or any of the others had heard right. For was Uncle Boritz really handing out such an invitation, which actually encouraged them all to eat as much ice cream as they cared to? Polly stood amongst the small minority that chose to cautiously hold back. What was the hidden snag? There surely had to be a hidden price tag, for never, as a rule, did he willingly and freely give anything away for the pure joy of giving. So like many of the other children, she felt very unnerved and therefore cautious by this unexpected act of overwhelming generosity.

The younger children gave no serious thought to the matter, as they instantly responded by hurriedly placing themselves in a most orderly line; after all, they had little time for questioning anything when free ice cream was on the menu. Finally, the remaining children, against their better judgment, decided to throw all caution to the wind and so went forward to help themselves to a shell from the large box before returning to join the lineup of very exhilarated children as they too waited with bated breath for their turn to finally arrive.

Some of the more impatient children were unable to endure the lengthy wait, as the tap on the silver contraption filled up each cone with freezing ice far too slowly for their liking. So by the time they reached the machine of constantly flowing milky ice cream, their edible shells had long disappeared into their hungry bellies, forcing them to either lose their rightful place in the line or cup their hands in a desperate bid to still get their fair claim of a pile of thick, freezing liquid. Then with the ice cream swirled into mountainous peaks in the shell—or melting fast in the cupped but hot, sticky palms of grubby hands—they made their way to the back of the line to merrily demolish the ice cream. With the ice cream gone and white mustache lips, they once more impatiently waited for their turn to come around again.

Polly had never seen anything like it, but as she secretly admitted to feeling very hungry, she hoped it would be all right to help herself to a cone shell and join the end of the queue. She also prayed that, as Uncle Boritz appeared to be in a temporary state of euphoria, he would forget that she was on ROPE and that punishment meant she was exempt from all family treats. Luckily for Polly, he was so caught up with the moment that he failed to notice her standing alongside the other children as she waited for her turn to come 'round. The same applied where Gailey was concerned, for Polly knew that if Gailey even caught sight of Polly with a cornet in her hand, it was almost certain she would immediately alert Uncle Boritz and get her removed from the kitchen. Happily, Gailey was so overtaken with elation that she too failed to compute that Polly was surreptitiously joining in on the treat.

The large box of cones took an age to empty, as child after child, time after time, joyfully dipped their hand in the box, pulled out a cornet, and after a refill then made his or her way to the back to join the long line once more as they gobbled down this unexpected, luscious treat.

At approximately 9:00 p.m. Greenwich meantime, the overworked and thoroughly exhausted ice cream machine found itself struggling to continue on with any further demands as it forced out the last dollop of frozen milky ice before a flashing light signaled complete shutdown. Amazingly, there were no cries of despair to be heard, for if the truth be known, every child, who much earlier in the evening had been wildly elated, was now on the kitchen floor clutching his or her extended belly, facing the ordeal of coping with hideously agonizing stomach cramps. Many of the children were belching loudly before becoming physically sick as they rolled around on the floor curled up in pitifully tight balls as they sought desperately to minimize the intensely excruciating pain that comes from eating too much.

Uncle Boritz stood to one side, his arms folded soberly, a look of great consternation belying his true feelings as he stood watch over the poor, pathetic-looking creatures who now rather haphazardly littered the floor.

Sad as it may seem, young Polly was amongst those wretches lying facedown on the floor curled up in a tight ball as she writhed around in pure gut-wrenching agony. At one point she unexpectedly found herself looking up at the smug face of Uncle Boritz, only to find herself having disturbing flashes of Soogara, the wicked Candy Cotton Queen. "Oh my goodness," she cried, feeling completely overwhelmed by remorse. "How could I allow this to happen to me again? Wasn't the first time enough?' she cried as she curled into an even tighter ball, anguished tears squeezing through her tightly closed eyelids before escaping down her hot, burning cheeks. As the pain continued to intensify, she thought back to her horrendous ordeal in the dungeon and how, when she had given up all hope, darling and very brave Napoli Bonaparti had come to her rescue.

"Will I ever truly learn?" she whispered, all the while privately rebuking herself for being such a stupid fool while clutching herself tighter still as the griping pains grew steadily worse.

<hr/>

Uncle Boritz carefully stepped over the bodies of the children as they continued to roll around the floor racked by agonizing pain that was steadily becoming more unbearable by the minute. He then chose to hover in the midst of them as he fumbled about in his trouser pocket, jangling around some loose change. He then began to shake his head.

"Tut tut tut. Disgraceful! Oh, how beastly for all you little sugar lumps, for you really must learn to take control of your insatiable lust for food once and for all," he said as an amused look came to settle on his face. "For you would think that by now I would have successfully drummed it into your thick numbskulls that gluttony is considered one of the seven most deadly and wicked sins, one that inevitably has dire consequences, such as you all are now rather sadly experiencing," he admonished as he coldheartedly moved forward to crush the cardboard cone box underfoot. "Let's hope that the long night ahead will give you all adequate time to reflect on your gross and greedy behavior," he spat.

Two fierce stomps of his shoe were all that was needed to completely flatten the large, empty cornet box. He then gave it a contemptuously hearty kick across the floor. Pitstop followed at his master's heels, his tongue hanging down as he festooned both the floor as well as the severely pain-racked children with his usual trail of slithery, slimy drool.

"Good boy, Pitstop. Good boy," Uncle Boritz muttered as he patted his faithful beast on the head. "Now you too can see what happens when greedy, overindulgent little paupers allow their eyes to become much bigger than their bellies. They look so sad and so very pitiful, don't they?" he said as he patted the beast on the head, a wide grin forming on his face. "Bless their little cotton socks. This sad affair must surely work to purge them of all future desire to ever again eat ice cream. Yes, I don't believe they will be begging me for anything sweet for many long months to come," he chortled.

Pitstop gave a deep growl for his affirmation.

Aunt Mildred, who, due to a severe migraine and uncontrollable nosebleed, had been lying upstairs on her bed, entered the room only to be met by a scene of absolute carnage.

As she stood over the children, one hand on hip, the other pegging her nose due to the terrible stench of vomit, she too was completely out of mercy. She continued surveying the kitchen floor, a look of pure disgust written all over her face.

"Boritz, what the dickens has been going on behind my back?" she screamed.

"I hope you're well and truly satisfied, for look at them all; they are in the most distressed state, and all thanks to you," she forlornly cried. "I only have to be absent awhile due to a headache and utter exhaustion, and this is how you repay me! Pray, tell me now, who is going to clear up all this putrefying mess from the floor?" she angrily queried.

Boritz quick response was to childishly shrug his shoulders like a naughty boy caught with his fingers in the honey jar.

"You should never have allowed them to stuff their ugly little faces with so much ice cream, for not only is it a total waste of money, but there is also every possibility that none of them will be fit for school tomorrow," she raged. "And I, for one, have not the slightest intention of forfeiting my already planned shopping expedition to stay at home and nurse a nauseous bunch of children back to full health," she contemptuously spat in his direction. "Oh, no. Hear me now and hear me clearly: this affair is not going to scupper any of my plans," she snorted.

Uncle Boritz stood in an amused silence as he allowed Aunt Mildred to express all that was troubling her seemingly fragile and volatile heart.

"Calm down, dearest one. Calm down, or you'll get another of your terrible headaches that normally keep you bedridden for days on end," was all he could manage to mutter.

"I daresay all this has, as usual, done much to entertain and amuse you, but I, for one, am deeply upset," she sternly admitted as she struggled to contain the depth of anger she was truly experiencing.

"Come, come, my dear. Spare me the histrionics. Better still, do not distress your good self any further; otherwise, your migraine, as well as your unstoppable nosebleeds, will undoubtedly return with a vengeance," he muttered. "Try to see things from my perspective, Mildred dear, for the ice cream machine will be off our hands in the next couple of days, and at least we can have the joy of knowing that not only will we sell it for a rather splendid price, but it is also in perfect working order, so there will be no comeback this time 'round."

Aunt Mildred seemed to perk up as her husband explained the logic behind what had seemed, up until this moment in time, as nothing short of sheer lunacy.

"Yes, I daresay this experiment may have caused us some slight inconvenience," he said as he surveyed the children and the mess they had created all over the floor, "but it has also worked for the good, as we stand to make quite a killing when we sell it," he said as he reassuringly patted her hand in his feeble attempt to commiserate with her. "So come on, dear. Don't be so defeated. Just look on the bright side."

Poor Aunt Mildred failed dismally to appreciate his supposedly comforting words. "Pray, tell me, dear, how are we going to get them all upstairs and undressed for bed? Oh, I do believe this is all too much, truly it is," she cried as she broke down into desperate sobbing. Boritz quickly rummaged around in his pockets and finally produced a large, spotty red handkerchief, which upon sight, only encouraged her to bawl louder.

"Don't panic, my dear, we'll get Miss Scrimp to come down from her bedroom to lend a helping hand, and I'll also phone Cecilia and ask her to come quickly to our aid," he said calmly as he continued on with his patronizing words of comfort.

"Don't be so stupid and disrespectful, dear," Mildred rather aggressively snapped back. "May I use this moment to remind you that Cecilia is once more back under the professional care of Dr. Ninkumpoop, who says her prognosis is not looking good at all. And other than dear Miss Scrimp, who is having a few hours off from her tireless work in the laundry room, who else in your infinite wisdom might you readily suggest?"

"Well, sweet pea, since you care to mention it, at this precise moment in time I sadly find myself at a complete loss for words. I therefore find myself to be, as usual, entirely at your mercy," he muttered in his usual obsequious tones.

"And so you should be, Boritz my dear, for ever since Mr. Peawee was forced to leave the castle due to certain unmentionable events, we have not been the least fortunate in finding ourselves another helper even the remotest bit willing to work such long hours for such a paltry sum of money, even though it is combined with full board and lodging."

"Sadly, that is true," he morosely muttered.

"So, pray, tell me, my sovereign mastermind, what precisely do you intend to do now?"

Boritz shrugged his shoulders as he continued to play out the remorseful but desperately floundering man. Oh, he knew that, given time, she would eventually calm down; all he had to do was sit and wait it out and, in the meantime, try his utmost to look suitably repentant.

"Are you paying serious attention to all I am saying, Boritz? For I do believe you are also completely oblivious to the fact that there is a most severe gale brewing up, making the weather outside most inhospitable. Even if you made numerous calls asking for help, no one in their right mind is going to leave the warmth and comfort of their home to come over to the castle and then assist me in getting all these desperately sick children up from the floor and into their beds," she bitterly sniffed.

Suddenly, and much to Boritz's relief, the front doorbell rang, and so with Pitstop close at his side and with a thankful heart, he left the troubling scene to go and see who it was daring to call at this unearthly hour, when, as Mildred had just stated, all right-minded persons would never think to venture out on such a terrible evening as this.

Boritz stopped short of the door and then bent down to peer through the tiny spy glass that was intended to give some idea as to who was on the other side. He felt quite alarmed when he discovered that he could see very little, with the exception of a tall, dark shadow lurking under the porch light. So it was with great reserve and caution that he opened the heavy, creaking oak door to get a better look at the mysterious and up until now unidentified caller.

However, before he pulled back the large iron bolt, he turned to check that Pitstop was on standby, baring his razor-sharp teeth, ready and willing to pounce at a moment's notice if necessary. Confident that he was in full control, he pulled back the bolt, then placed his hand on the doorknob and opened the door wide. He happily breathed a deep sigh of relief before patting Pitstop on his head, sending him the message that all was well and therefore on this occasion so he was not required to sink his razor-sharp incisors deep into the flesh of this particular visitor. Even though Boritz was safely sheltered from the storm, he still managed to shudder as he heard the deafeningly loud crack of thunder as it ripped through the magnificently clouded skies with a vengeance. This was followed on quickly by brilliant streaks of lightning that were blinding in their intensity as they sought to strike out at any object that dared cross swords with them. The wind continued to howl mercilessly, as though it were mourning some sad souls lost at sea, and the sheet rain was equally relentless in its fury as it lashed down hard from the sorely angry and darkened skies above.

"Come in, come in," Boritz hurriedly urged the silent stranger. The tall, willowy man dressed in a long black raincoat nodded, then stooped as he sought to enter through the door before taking off his rain-drenched hat and making direct eye contact with Boritz. "I'm sorry it's so late, but I felt that I had to come immediately," said the croaky voice in barely a whisper as rainwater continued to drip from his forehead as well as from the end of his misshapen nose. Boritz nodded to suggest he understood and then moved to one side to allow the mysterious guest to dispense with his umbrella in the tall wrought iron stand.

"Dear sir, please do allow me the pleasure of taking your coat from you," Boritz sycophantically fawned in his usual and very sickening attempt to curry great favor. The distinguished looking old man hesitated, a concerned look darkening his long, scarred face. "Thank you, but I think it will not be necessary, for I have no intention of staying too long. Therefore, I think it best that I leave my coat on, for that way I can disappear quickly if conditions necessitate that I must," said the aged and mysterious silver-haired guest.

"Nonsense, my dear man. I won't hear of it. Oh, no, no, no. There is no one here to even take note of your visit, albeit very cloak and dagger. So pray, stay as long as need be," Uncle Boritz stated very matter-of-factly.

"Thank you, dear sir, and I apologize most profusely for turning up unannounced at such an hour as this, but I must stress that I would never have ventured out on such a night if I did not believe my errand to be of the utmost importance."

Boritz remained silent as he beckoned his guest to follow him down the long, highly polished hallway. They momentarily stopped halfway down as Boritz fumbled through his thick bunch of keys, struggling to find the right key to open the iron gate. With the small gate finally unlocked, he ushered the gentleman through the opening before quickly relocking it from the other side.

As they walked the remaining distance to Boritz's private sitting room, not a word passed between them. Finally they entered the sitting room, his private sanctuary, and then with the door firmly closed behind them, they took it in turns to breathe a sigh of relief, for they believed themselves to be finally safe—yes, safe from all snooping children with elephant-sized flapping ears and equally long, talkative tongues, which might bring great harm if they were to listen in and then pass on any of their uncle's personal and very private conversations.

"Please do feel free to take a seat, Professor Fossilize," Boritz said with the utmost charm as he beckoned the tall and elegantly dressed silver-haired gentleman toward a thick plush armchair.

"Mmm…forgive me, but before we get down to the reasons for this urgent visit, I feel the need to clarify something," the professor quickly said, his voice suddenly sounding a bit annoyed, if not a teeny bit strained. "It's Fossil, not Fossilize," he protested as he tried and desperately failed in his effort to take no offense.

"Oh, I'm so sorry, Professor Foosil," an extremely repentant Boritz replied, feeling slightly humiliated that he should inexcusably get the poor chap's name wrong, and, if I might add, on their second acquaintance.

"Apology accepted," said the professor as he sunk back into the chair and began to visibly relax.

Boritz, feeling mightily relieved, then walked a few paces and sat down on a large and very plush velvet sofa. Pitstop waited until his master was comfortably seated before crouching down at his side, his ears pricked, his long, razor-sharp tongue hanging out as he too waited with insatiable expectation to hear the reason behind this sudden and very unexpected late-night visitation.

Boritz moved forward in his seat and was about to break the awkward silence, but due to his bad nerves and an unexpected bout of uncontrollable gas, he was forced to feign a bad coughing fit to hide his embarrassment, and so he failed to notice that once again he further insulted his guest.

"Professor Fossilize, sadly, I am unable to offer you any form of refreshment, for even as we speak, there is a little ongoing crisis still panning out in the kitchen that unfortunately will not be alleviated until I return to assist my dear wife, Mildred. However, all is not entirely lost, for I do have some rather special vintage port, as well as some excellent reserve Napoleon brandy in my private cupboard if you would care for a drop."

Professor Fossil paused while he considered his colleague's thoughtful and kind offer.

"Thank you, but I feel I must decline your generous offer concerning any form of strong refreshment, but, dear sir, may I also remind you one final time that my surname is not Fossilize, but Professor *Fossil*," he abruptly stated. "And, my dear fellow, as I am one of the most respected archeological historians this country has to offer, it might pay you, sir, to remember this and so accord me both my correct name and title. Or pray, tell me now, am I asking too much?"

Poor Boritz couldn't show it, but he was now feeling utterly mortified, for how could he make the same mistake not once but twice—and all in the space of a few mere seconds? He needed Mildred by his side, and fast. Without her he was in danger of revealing himself to be little more than a bumbling idiot who had no idea which way to turn. Not that she knew this, of course. Oh no, she could never be allowed such a position of power, or she might use it to her advantage. Such deceit would be considered by him to be unacceptable if not utterly irreprehensible.

"Oh, that would never, never do," he muttered, shaking his head from side to side as though he were trying to release himself from the middle of some unbelievably frightful nightmare. "My darling Mildred running the show? Never in a month of Sundays!" he muttered under his breath as once again he tried hard to give the professor his full and most deserved attention

"Anyway, Mr. Skunkbelly, as my time is considered by most to be, well—what shall I say?—considerably expensive and therefore well out of the range of most mere mortals, it would, I believe, be most advisable if we got down to the brass tacks of why I have chosen such an earthly hour to pay you this clandestine visit."

Poor Boritz was now feeling utterly distraught by the professor's presumably unwitting error, but he felt far too demoralized to make any mention of it. "Skunkbelly! Fancy calling me Skunkbelly. That is much, much worse than Fossilize," he quietly murmured as he forced a weak smile, at the same time giving serious thought as to just how severe the damage to his personal coffers might become, as the professor had just reminded him he was no little cheapskate he could keep happy with a few pounds. Just thinking of the potential sums of money that might possibly be extracted from his bank account to pay the good professor's bill now made it almost impossible for him to even begin to relax.

"Right, now where were we?" the learned professor mumbled as he placed his expensive looking leather-bound briefcase on his lap and released the brass clasp. Then after a few moments spent fumbling around, he finally produced the item he was searching for. Opening up the slim yellow package, he then turned it upside down to give it a good shake, his objective being to reveal the contents of the mysterious package. In just a matter of seconds an ornate gold ring fell directly into the palm of his free hand. "I am here to return this ring to you in person. But before I do, I need to ask how perchance you came upon such a ring as this? Yes, where on earth did you find it?"

"Well, professor, I am not really too sure. You see, one of the children, Gailey Gobbstopper, to be precise, witnessed another of my unfortunate children remove the ring from her finger and place it for safekeeping by the soap while she peeled some potatoes. Of course, Gailey was quick to realize that it was valuable; she therefore waited for the perfect opportunity to present itself so that she could grab the ring and bring it straight to me. And that, in a nutshell, is how the ring came to be in my possession. We have come to believe that the child in question stumbled across it in a field close to some nearby fortress ruins. At least that's the story so far."

"Well, I have to say that despite my many years of expertise in this field, I have never to date come across such a beautifully exquisite ring—that unfortunately I have not been able to put a historical date to. This fact alone is troubling me greatly, nor, for that matter, can I even begin to tell you from what country it originated. All I can say is that I believe this ring to be of extraordinary value; yes, it is probably worth a small king's ransom."

Boritz's whole face suddenly lit up like candles on a birthday cake as enormous monetary signs popped up like an old-fashioned cash register in front of his bulbous eyes. His heart then began to hammer loudly, as this latest piece of magnificently good news caused his heart valves not only to expand but to pump harder, as they too found the urgent need to express their joy and liberation at this exceedingly marvelous and very unexpected development.

"Yes, the royal coat of arms in particular has such extraordinary detail, and as I placed it under my specialist microscope before subjecting it to a battery of tests I discovered..."

As the professor continued to assault poor Boritz's mind with detail after detail, all of which was far too technical for him to truly understand or cope with, the professor had little idea that his host had switched off completely.

"What I would suggest at this point is that you step up your investigative techniques and try your utmost to find out precisely where she found it, as this would help matters considerably. I, for one, have exhausted every reference book I could lay my hands on. I have also been in dialogue with a number of very well-respected fellow historians, as I sought their professional opinion and expertise on the matter in hand. To date, none of them have been able to be of any real assistance."

"Dear chap, I pray you did not reveal the source from which this ring came into your possession?" Boritz hoarsely enquired, an icy shudder suddenly going the full length of his spine as he found himself feeling most protective in his concern for the ongoing safety of his precious ring.

"Oh no, no, no. You have my utmost assurance that both the ring and your connection to it remain our secret alone, and I have gone to great pains to ensure that this will remain so. Yes, I would urge you to trust me implicitly, Mr. Shuffleberry, for at the end of the day you are paying me very handsomely not only for my expertise in this field but also for my professional discretion."

Uncle Boritz grimaced as he silently suffered yet a further aberration regarding his beloved family name.

"I'm very glad to hear that," Boritz mumbled as he took his handkerchief and began to wipe the sweat from his brow, great anxiety welling up within as he once again pondered the disturbing thought of just how much the professor's loyalty and silence might end up costing him.

"Well, I must say that as a last resort I took it upon myself to contact the British History Museum in the hope of getting some further form of enlightenment on this delicate matter. They cooperated fully by doing a most extensive search of the archives, but sadly they were still unable to come up with any historical document hidden away in the vaults that could shed further light as to the origin and therefore the authenticity of this ring. And so it is with great sadness of heart that I am unable to help you further in my professional capacity as a historian, that is, unless I am given much more information and considerable funds with which to work."

"Yes, yes, I fully understand," Boritz muttered as he struggled to come 'round from his dreamy, almost catatonic daze.

"So might I suggest that one way of following up on the ring would be to write or pay a visit to each and every castle in England, Scotland, and of course, let us not forget Ireland, as one of these remote castles might well hold the key to this mysterious ring. Of course, if you have no luck with any of these, then you might care to broaden your search to cover Europe as well."

"Oh, dear. To go so far afield would surely cost a king's ransom. I mean, this would involve trekking around much of the continent. No, no. This is all quite unthinkable, for amongst other things, where would I find the time to do all this?" Boritz exclaimed, shaking his head, for he was now feeling in a most beleaguered state.

"Mr. Skunkbe—"

"Scumberry! The correct name is Scumberry," Boritz quickly interjected, lest the good professor suffer another extraordinary bout of memory loss that resulted in his good name once more being rather disdainfully expressed incorrectly.

"Yes, well then, Mr. Scumberry, as I was saying, I am fully prepared to continue investigating further on your behalf, but you must realize that to do so would add considerably to my bill. I therefore leave it entirely in your fair hands as to where, if anywhere, we go from here."

"Yes, yes," was all Boritz could find to mutter as he rather glumly tried hard to consider his very limited options.

"So, Mr. Scum…um…yes, berry, the hour is indeed late, and so I must bid you farewell, for I must quickly head off back to London, as my colleagues are anxiously awaiting my arrival at Paddington. I'm not entirely sure whether I should allow you to be privy to this, but my colleagues have just unearthed a new and therefore very exciting Roman burial site, along with a number of priceless artifacts that require dating. As I have no wish to keep them waiting any longer than necessary, I must excuse myself and then rush to catch a train."

Professor Fossil got up from the chair, but sadly, poor Boritz felt glued to his seat, his forehead sweating profusely.

"I say, old chum, are you feeling all right? Do you need a physician? You look rather ashen," the now disturbed professor asked out of genuine concern as he continued to peer down at Boritz over his spectacles. Boritz still failed to move a muscle, leaving the dear professor still rather stupidly holding his hand out with the full expectation that as a matter of courtesy it would in due season be shaken.

"Uhh," moaned Boritz. The concerned professor gave up and removed his outstretched hand, which he then positioned inside his jacket, reaching into an inner pocket. He brought out a crisp white envelope he had placed there earlier for safekeeping. "If all is, indeed, well with you, and you therefore do not require the assistance of a doctor, may I leave you my bill for services rendered? Before you ask, I have documented every test that was done on the ring, as well as all my trips on your behalf, phone calls, time spent at the British History Museum, etc. Yes, every service has been individually itemized and then recorded on the account, just as you as requested," he said as he placed the cool, crisp white envelope in Boritz's open but seriously trembling right hand.

The request for money brought Boritz right back into the land of the living, as without warning he jumped to his feet as though he had just been shocked back to life with the help of an electric eel. Still feeling as shaky as wobbly jelly fresh out of the mold, Boritz limply took hold of the professor's hand to finally do the gentlemanly thing and shake it. "Professor Fossil, if this ring is, as you say, worth a fortune, can I have your word that this discovery will remain a secret between the two of us?" he croaked as he struggled to find the correct words of persuasion.

"Of course, Mr. Scuttlebug. Confidentiality is, after all, my middle name, and so it goes without saying that you have my word, which is my bond. However, I would be failing in my duty if I did not suitably warn you that should this ring turn out to be of great national importance to the history of our beloved country, then you, sir, are under some form of obligation from the authorities to report your priceless find."

"Oh, but if I were to do such a thing, not only would I lose the ring forever, but I know they will only offer me some small paltry amount of money, yes, a mere pittance in exchange for my parting with this priceless and most beautiful ring."

"This may be true, but you have to understand the importance of holding on to all archeological finds that must then be recorded and preserved, for they do, I believe, bear much witness and testimony to our distinctly noble heritage. So surely, dear sir, this matters far more than any financial recompense or personal gain."

"Financial what?" sniffed Boritz, as he refused to take heed to the gentle words of warning that came from the learned man.

"Money, Mr. Scullberry. Yes, I would sincerely like to think that for a gentleman of your caliber and social standing to have your name written down in history as the person who discovered this precious ring would, in itself, be reward enough."

"Oh, yes. Yes, of course," Boritz unconvincingly spluttered as he promptly placed a hand on the professor's arm before anxiously hurrying the ancient-looking historian toward the door of the drawing room. Pitstop, who had been taking a well-earned nap, leapt to his feet to dutifully follow after his master. As the three of them frantically rushed down the long corridor making their way toward the front door, a now very frazzled Boritz appeared to almost be pushing the poor learned gentleman along in his desperate bid to see him leave. The reason for this extraordinarily rude behavior was simply that he had no desire to hear another word from the professor that might even attempt to strike at his already seared conscience and thus find him handing over the priceless ring for the good of our great British heritage!

As they reached the front door, Boritz, as a gesture of good measure, placed a hand on the learned professor's arm and gave it a friendly pat. "Professor Fossil, I will have my secretary put your check in the post forthwith! And I thank you from the bottom of my heart for all your kind assistance," he said in his usual obsequious tones, as he still wished to appear both courteous and amicable toward the professor.

The professor, though looking deep in thought, took the time to politely thank him.

Still, Uncle Boritz felt uneasy and nervous. "Oh, and we are still in full agreement, are we not, that all of this shall, for the time being, remain wholly between us? For I am relying on the assumption that the rules regarding privileged information apply here," Uncle Boritz said, giving a wicked wink as he then gave the learned historian a friendly, hearty pat on the back.

"Let's just say for the time being that it's more of a gentlemen's agreement," the professor calmly replied as he motioned for Boritz to pass him both his hat and umbrella from the wrought iron stand. Placing his hat back on his head, he then waited patiently for Boritz to unchain the front door and thus allow him to leave.

Boritz opened the door with great gusto, but before he had time to move aside and allow his guest to depart, the sheet rain unexpectedly lashed out at him, instantly soaking him from head to foot and very nearly ruining his smart velveteen jacket. Boritz felt deeply humiliated as large beads of rainwater began to drip down his forehead, so he anxiously pulled out his handkerchief to wipe down his face.

The learned professor must have either not noticed or pretended to ignore what had just taken place, as he chose that moment to end his time with Boritz. "I bid you good night, Mr. Sherriberry."

"Yes, good night, professor."

"I guess one could be considered quite a fool to be out on such a night as this," the professor lightheartedly commented as he struggled to release the catch on his umbrella before heading off in the direction of the station, most determined to catch the next train to Paddington.

"Pompous old fart," Boritz muttered under his breath as, still dripping water from his forehead, he closed the door on the gentleman, stopping only to peer through the glass eye in order to check that the gentleman had truly departed to go on his merry way.

With the front door now firmly shut and the heavy link chain once more back in position, with Pitstop languishing at his side, they headed back to his private drawing room, for he wanted to further examine the ring, which for the time being was rightfully back in his possession. He also recognized that he needed to quickly dry off, as he was now feeling more than a little chilly from the disastrous impromptu soaking that he had just received.

Beaming from ear to ear with immense joy, he placed the ring in his jacket pocket before concluding that this might be an opportune moment to open Professor Fossil's envelope containing the invoice, as to be honest he had absolutely no idea as to the charges he might well have incurred.

Boritz's legs immediately began to quiver and shake like vast Roman columns fragmenting before they finally collapse during the midst of a terrible earthquake. He felt weak and drained as he continued to stare down at the figures in front of him. He chose to struggle on with his inspection until he reached the end of the statement, which showed the final amount owing in bright red ink.

Feeling very ill and panicked, he hastily attempted to adjust his glasses, sincere in the belief that a bout of double vision was more than likely behind this temporary optical illusion that had him seeing what he perceived to be little short of a ridiculously greedy and therefore grossly unwarranted financial settlement.

Sadly, even with his glasses readjusted, the final sum looked daunting, leaving dear Boritz feeling very distressed that he had unwittingly clocked up such a hideously huge bill, and in such a short space of time. He swallowed hard before allowing a deep groan to rise up from his very bowels and then escape from between his trembling lips. "Goodness gracious me, I must surely be dreaming, for this is most intolerable and outrageous," he hoarsely declared. "Nine thousand pounds, three shillings, and tuppence halfpenny! Oh, good grief. Where does this thoroughly dishonorable man get his figures from, for this is all absolutely disgraceful," he cried out in pure desperation.

By now he was feeling decidedly overheated, and he wiped away large beads of sweat from his brow before moving further down the page to examine the bill in more detail. "What? Am I seeing correctly? Tea and cream cakes at Harrods with Professor Pangaea and Professor Igneous? The man should be locked up! How dare he insult me in such a manner by using my hard-earned funds to live it up in London's most fashionable and expensive store," he roared. "Now then, what's this? Oh, no. This is equally preposterous!" he despairingly gasped as his eye caught hold of yet another further potential discrepancy, causing his hands to tremble more than ever.

"The man's an absolute lunatic to think he can extort money from me under the guise of purchasing four luxury Fortnum and Mason food basket as a goodwill gesture to say a big thank-you to all the staff at the Natural History Museum!" he gulped. "I really don't care that he thought this would be a most excellent gesture for their many unpaid hours spent digging through the museum's archives. I happen to believe that a tip of two pounds to share between them would have more than sufficed! This will undoubtedly be the last time I use the services of the professor, for I consider this man to be guilty of the most disgracefully wicked extortion," he lamented as he slumped back onto the comfy chair, closing his eyes tight as he considered this latest heavy and very painful financial burden that might possibly have brought him to the brink of financial ruination, had he continued to use the services of this most learned gentleman.

He let out a deep groan, for he was now experiencing symptoms of acute pain brought on by sudden, rather erratic heartbeats. In no time at all he was forced to begin his deep breathing exercises in the hope of relieving the immensely unpleasant symptoms this unwelcome bout of stress had brought on.

Then without warning he opened his eyes wide and cried out, "Oh my goodness! Mildred!" he spluttered. "The sick children! Oh, deary me! I completely forgot. Help for my poor and sad life is most assuredly over, for I'm most certainly in the doghouse now!" he loudly wailed.

On hearing the word *doghouse*, Pitstop's finely tuned ears pricked up, and with thick slobber still hanging like stalactites from his open jaws he abandoned all paw-licking activity to look deep into his master's excruciatingly pained, water-filled eyes to express a deep sense of empathy.

Boritz mopped his sweaty brow and then stood up, giving yet another huge, deep sigh of despair. Pitstop joined in by immediately giving one of his deepest and fiercest growls as he defiantly took his rightful place by his master's side, fully prepared and willing to escort him into the very bowels of hell to face the worst!

Chapter Twelve
RULE BRITANNIA

*U*NCLE BORITZ FINALLY took a firm grip of himself, and despite feeling the most tremendous sense of anxiety and dread, he hurriedly locked the door of his private sitting room before cautiously heading back toward the kitchen with Pitstop, as always, faithfully at his side. When he reached the kitchen door, he nervously stooped down to place his ear up against the keyhole, for he was anxious to hear if there were any voices or disturbing noises coming from the kitchen at such a late hour. He was pleasantly pleased to discover that everything was silent.

"Phew!" he whispered as he raised his eyes upward as if to say a thank-you.

He then drew in a deep breath as he went through his long self-help list of appropriate psychological preparations that would hopefully dispel all fear and if nothing else ply him with a humongous amount of courage, the prerequisite to entering the room.

"Good boy, Pitstop. I think the coast is clear."

He halted for one small further moment, for in the nick of time he suddenly remembered just how important it was that the drawbridge to his emotions be securely shut down tight in order to shield or fend off any choice and cutting words dear Mildred might unfairly wish to vent in her anger and frustration toward him. He deemed this to be of the utmost necessity, lest any of her stinging choice words quite inadvertently pierce his cold, steely heart or conscience. He knew from past experience that such unpleasant clashes could well cause him to suffer prolonged pangs of guilt or remorse, as well as any other equally confusing and most unwelcome symptoms that would certainly have him feeling at death's door in just a matter of minutes.

"Psst. Mildred, my dearest one, are you in here?" he hoarsely whispered as, with great trepidation, he cautiously made his way across the room in the dark, heading for the light switch. "Pitstop, stay and guard the door. There's a good boy," he ordered.

Boritz could just about hear the faint murmurings of someone, somewhere whimpering, but it was very difficult, if not impossible, to discern whose they were or where they might possibly be coming from.

"Come on, Mildred. Don't play your morose and very tiresome games with me," he muttered as he rather precariously continued in the dark to make his way across the room. "If you're still up, then please be a dear and say so," he said out loud as he then stood on something that felt immensely soft but unstable. Seconds later found him stumbling over something else long and lumpy that was also lying directly in his pathway. Poor Boritz was so overtaken by surprise that he found himself swaying back and forth like an overexuberant child in charge of a rocking chair, as he struggled to remain upright long enough to make it over to the wall with its elusive light switch. Immense relief flooded his entire being when his fat outstretched fingers finally made contact with the wall. The next few minutes were then spent anxiously fumbling around in the dark as he tried hard before finally succeeding in finding the switch.

The aging, dysfunctional fluorescent light repeatedly flickered on and off before finally conceding to light up the room, albeit dimly. Boritz then turned full circle and was immediately shocked to realize that those lumps that he had stood on as he searched his way in the dark were, in fact, the corpse-like bodies of some of the more cumbersome children, who lay out for the count and therefore immobilized as they continued to rather untidily litter the kitchen floor.

Boritz squinted as he finally caught sight of his dear, demoralized wife huddled in a corner, intermittently sniffing into the bright pink Chantilly lace hanky that she very shakily held up to her nose. He rushed over to where she sat in a very distressed, crumpled heap, and immediately did the most inspirationally gentlemanly thing he could think to do, which was to place a comforting arm on her shoulder. "Mildred, dearest, please stop all this unnecessary whining, for you appear utterly spent," he rather curtly ordered as he halfheartedly patted her arm. His attempt to give further comfort fell on deaf ears, as she continued on with both her wailing as well as her plentiful tears.

"Please, Boritz. Give me a break, for I really can't stop myself," she begrudgingly simpered.

"Dearest, might I take this opportunity to remind you that you alone are not responsible for replenishing the whole earth with water. It's been done before, so might I take this occasion to comment that as I have neither the time nor the inclination to follow after Noah by building myself an ark to save myself from drowning in a river of your overzealous self-pity, I would therefore strongly urge you to stop this ridiculous torrent, and now!"

Mildred began to bawl even louder.

"Besides, I cannot help but observe that your nose is beginning to look like that of a deeply depressed clown in mourning," he rather heartlessly continued.

"Boritz, how can you be so viciously cruel?" she forlornly cried.

Boritz wasn't listening. "*And*, I hasten to add, your eyes aren't faring much better either, for they do indeed look most puffed up and swollen. So try and help yourself, dear, sweet munchkin, by bringing your highly emotional state under control—there's a dear—before you give yourself another tiresome and troubling nosebleed. That's better. Now, tell me: where are all the other children? For as of now they are nowhere to be seen, which leads me to presume you must have found some sort of help after all."

"No, Boritz! None whatsoever!" Mildred snarled through gritted teeth. "Miss Scrimp, as well as my good self, have spent the entire evening struggling to get the children up the stairs and into their beds. We started with the younger, smaller children, as, being lighter, they were easier to carry. But I can tell you now it has been a nigh impossible feat, and this is why so many of the older and therefore heavier children are still lying in a comatose state on the kitchen floor," she simpered and snorted.

"There, there, dearest. I do believe that you have given yourself a most chronic case of the snuffles, so have another hard blow," he very helpfully suggested as he tried hard to commiserate with her.

"Yes, we tried to move them, but it was an impossible task from the start. We therefore had no other choice but to throw a blanket over each of them while we awaited your return to assist us," she hysterically wailed.

"Yes, dear. Do please go on." he urged.

"It was an impossible task from the start, even with Miss Scrimp clasping hold of their ankles while I tackled the job from the other end, holding each child under their armpits as we dragged their sickly, dazed bodies up the stairs and then along the corridor to their dormitory."

"Hmm. Continue on."

"But Boritz dearest, I'll have you know that it was still an almighty struggle from which I don't think I will ever fully recover," she sobbed as she reached into her pocket for an extra hanky on which to have a good blow.

"There, there, Mildred."

"Dearest, apart from feeling most angry with you, I am also—how shall I say?—feeling very delicate at this precise moment in time," she sobbed.

"My dearest, please do not take this as an insult, but may I remind you that you've always felt poorly and fragile. What more can I possibly say? Hands up, I am, as you so regularly and pitifully remind me, totally guilty of all aforesaid charges, for to leave you on your own to do such a wearisome task was, I understand, utterly indefensible. But I simply had no other choice," he stated, shaking his head as he continued to mutter, "I had no other choice. I had no other…"

Mildred momentarily stopped all wailing, until, scrambling about in her pocket, she managed to produce yet another handkerchief. This time the hanky was silky purple and polka dotted, with some very pretty violets embroidered on each corner, and after producing this fresh handkerchief, her wails began to get louder and louder.

"There, there, dearest. Give your nose a good blow and then have yourself another good and hearty cry if need be, for not only is it good for the soul, but it also saves on my already outrageous water bill. I have to say that the impressive amount of tears that you, my dear, manage to squeeze from those eensy-weensy, piddly little tear ducts is surely more than enough to sink even the *Titanic*!"

Mildred shook her head violently, as she now clearly felt even more hurt and misunderstood, and so she began to squall and bawl louder than ever.

Boritz, who was also in full flow, chose to ignore the noise and continued on. "Carry on with your latest challenging mission, dearest, for those tears that so generously cascade down your cheeks never fail in acting like windscreen wipers as they rather expertly manage to wash your entire face," he informed her in a most unkind and derogatory manner.

Mildred blew her nose and chose not to engage in any further argument. She continued on with her hardship story. "Even after we dragged and bumped their limp and sorely, sickly bodies up the staircase, we still managed to crack a few heads against the wall, for sadly we had little alternative but to swing each body back and forth, only letting go when we believed they would land in the center of the bed. If the truth be told, Boritz dear, some never even made it," she reluctantly confided.

"Quite what do you mean by that, dearest?" he hardly dared ask.

"Hmm. Exactly what I just said. Some of the children did not end up in their beds as expected, but due to Miss Scrimp's heavy-handed manner, after flying through the air they indeed landed on the floor on the other side of their beds. Without saying much more, they all, without exception, landed with a most terrible, heavy thump. I am praying that there are no broken bones to deal with tomorrow, although I have to try and encourage myself by saying they were *almost* in their beds," she volunteered in little more than a whisper.

"Almost in their beds?" a wide-eyed Boritz questioned as he then gave her another troubling and most judgmental look.

"Yes, almost. But don't you give me that somber and highly critical look, for not only am I advancing in years and so lacking the stamina, but alas I do not come from any highly disciplined athletic background."

"Hmm, but Miss Scrimp does."

"True, but may I also remind you that Miss Scrimp's Scottish log-throwing days were over many years ago. Therefore we are just normal simple people struggling to do our best in an most impossible situation. Yes, as I stated, we aimed for the target, and well…er…sometimes we just missed the mark. Simple as that, for that's how it is," she cried out.

Boritz was dumfounded and therefore lost for words.

"The truth is, I feel, well, mortified, if not utterly demoralized," she wept, as once more she allowed herself permission to feel the full extent of her martyrdom "And as I previously stated, dear, without you on board to help out, we were simply unable to complete the task. Needless to say, we are both utterly exhausted and therefore on the brink of despair," she said as she gave another loud snort into her purple polka-dotted hanky.

Boritz gave her another weary, half-hearted pat on the back as he mumbled a very trite, "There, there, dear," as he continued to conjure up a very sorry picture of those unfortunate children, who like the Highland fling had been flung so high they never actually made it to their intended destiny but sadly landed flat on the floor on the other side of their beds. He could not help but wonder just how bruised their poor, limp bodies would be feeling by the next morning.

"Also, dearest, you have just tripped over dear, oversized Bertha, who even with the combined efforts of both of us was much too heavy to even roll to one side for safety's sake while we awaited your return," she sniffed.

Upon realizing that Mildred had no intention of charitably dropping the subject, Boritz began to presume that this must lie with the fact that he was failing to show significant levels of remorse. He knew in that moment that he must act quickly, so without warning he began to clutch at his chest and cry out, "Mildred dearest, how can you ever forgive me for all the distress I have caused, what with my ice cream machine and then abandoning you in your most dire moment of need? My heart is racing, and I think I may well faint, if not collapse to the floor to die here in front of you," he gasped as he continued most dramatically to clutch his chest.

Mildred remained stoically unmoved. "May I suggest that this very belated drama could be considered most inappropriate, dearest? I will choose to ignore your latest offense as I continue on with my story. Right, where was I? Then as if all this was not bad enough, to add insult to injury we were to be further demoralized by having the extremely nauseating task of mopping up immeasurable amounts of the children's revolting stomach contents from the floor. And as all children had eaten a small portion of barbecue flavor baked beans for tea, followed by exorbitant amounts of slushy ice cream, you cannot begin to imagine how utterly repulsive this all was when mixed together," she angrily snorted. "I also happen to believe this was something Polly should have been doing and would have done, had she been suitably disposed, instead of which, just like the others, she continued to be horribly sick," she whimpered before finally adding, "*And* all this when I was led to believe that the miserable miscreant was still on ROPE!"

"She still is, my dear little chocolate truffle. She still is!" he commiserated.

"Well, if that is the case, Boritz dear, then please do me the small courtesy of explaining why she was ever allowed to be on the receiving end of such a generous treat, a treat which she believed entitled her to eat just as much ice cream as her miserable heart desired." Mildred sniffed in a most offended manner.

"Oh, no, no, no. Mildred, my tender little sweet pea, you, my dearest, have got it all wrong, for the wicked girl had no permission whatsoever!"

Boritz then stopped mid flow to give his dutiful wife the most tender of smiles, for she had inadvertently handed him the most unexpected and very welcome opt-out clause, which right up until this moment in time had, for some inexplicable reason, completely alluded him.

His chest cavity suddenly arose victorious, and with fresh, vibrant air in his lungs and new wind in his sails, he instantly went from a miserable, impotent wretch seeking forgiveness to his usual stature— that of a completely resurrected and fully restored demigod. Now all recrimination and blame could finally be removed from his shoulders, as they both joined ranks to give their undivided attention and judgment concerning Polly Brown and her latest show of impudent, if not downright abhorrently sneaky behavior.

"Oh, the endless trouble this selfish girl has always caused us," Boritz cried out as he threw his hands into the air as a gesture of his utter helplessness and displeasure.

"Yes, Boritz dearest, the girl is, as you so rightly dare to suggest, nothing but trouble. End of story," Mildred indignantly snorted. "Yes, always has been and always will be."

Boritz felt very encouraged to step things up a notch and, by doing so, take it to the next level. "Yes, Mildred, I am so glad we are finally on the same page, for the wicked girl has shown yet again just how corrupt she truly is by furtively joining the others in the ice cream line when she knew full well she was banned at this time from all such treats. And so, you, my dearest, precious one, can rest assured that I will see to it that Polly is further punished for flouting our rules and asserting herself in a most unacceptable manner, hereby challenging our supreme authority."

As Boritz went into one of his usual self-satisfying monologues, he truly believed he could hear the London Philharmonic Orchestra playing their superb rendition of "The Dambusters" as, like a military general, he went on to give his own rendition of Winston Churchill's most heroically famous speech.

"Yes, Mildred, never in the field of human conflict was so much owed by so many to so few. So we will never surrender. We will fight them on the beaches, and we will fight them all, Polly Brown included, on the shores and…"

He remained in full flow until Mildred forced him to stop by tactfully reminding him that World War II was a thing of the past, so they were no longer fighting on the beaches in northern France but here inside the castle discussing the fate of the very young and difficult foster child Polly Brown.

"Well, dearest, thank you for reminding me, but to tell you the truth, dealing with this young vagabond could easily be interpreted as being just as traumatic a task as anything we hardy Brits faced in World War II. So I assure you that just like the perpetrators of that most diabolical war, likewise she will not get off this one scot-free. You have my sincere word on this one."

On hearing that Polly would now definitely face punishment for her unruly conduct, Aunt Mildred's longsuffering and haunted face visibly relaxed, with Boritz even bearing witness to the faintest smile miraculously appearing from out of nowhere.

"Yes, dear. What was I thinking? At the end of the day, if Polly had done as she was instructed and been obedient—"

"Yes, yes, dearest. Keep going," Boritz rather rudely interrupted, as he was now feeling ecstatic that his missus was finally getting the picture.

"Yes, instead of being wickedly deceitful, well then, she would have been available to assist in putting the others to bed as well as cleaning up all the hazardous waste that the poorly children spewed up all over the floor as they continued to be sick throughout the night," Mildred stated with great clarity and vision, as it finally dawned on her who the real culprit truly was.

"Yes, I now see it very clearly, for at the end of the day it most surely is Polly who is wholly to blame for this rather unfortunate and positively ghastly episode," she beamed.

"Yes, yes," cried an elated Boritz, as raising his hands and his eyes toward heaven he mouthed a silent thank-you to God.

Boritz was overcome with delight that Mildred had finally come to her senses and was now placing the blame where for all intents and purposes it rightfully should be placed. And so he breathed a loud sigh of relief, deeply thankful that he was finally exonerated and so now completely off the hook.

"Trust me, Mildred, when I say that Polly Brown will be dealt with first thing tomorrow," he said as in a gentlemanly fashion he got down on bended knee to tenderly cup his wife's tender cheeks and then take hold of her small and trembling hands in his. "In the meantime, dearest, I am in receipt of some excellent news that would most certainly gladden and uplift even the heaviest of hearts," he said in barely a whisper. "Allow me to share with you that when I left your presence to go and answer the doorbell, I was most surprised to discover Professor Fossil on the other side of our door."

"Boritz, forgive me for asking, but quite who is Professor Fossil? I, for one, have never heard of him. And more to the point, what on earth was he doing at our door at such an unacceptably late calling hour of the night?"

"Shh, my dear. I am uncertain as to whether I told you this piece of information, dearest, but some weeks ago I took it upon myself to hire the man in his professional capacity to find out as much as he was able concerning the origins of Polly's rather exquisite-looking ring that we confiscated."

Mildred sniffed while continuing to nod her head in agreement.

"Well, he was unable to come up with any exact date, etc., or where the ring originated from, but he has assured me that this ring is, well—how shall I put it?—it's priceless! Therefore, my little peanut butter sandwich, I suggest you go and pack us a suitcase, for you and I are finally going to take a well-earned holiday."

"Holiday, Boritz!" Mildred queried, suddenly perking up. "Tell me, why and where?"

"Well, my precious little cupcake, *we* are going to travel the full length and breadth of the British Empire, living it up in the most opulent style and divine decadence until—"

"British Empire, Boritz? Need I remind you that sadly we are no longer 'this great empire' and haven't been for many long years, alas, not since Queen Victoria was on the throne and dear Gladstone was our prime minister? Yes, that was indeed a most glorious time in our history; however, since then it has been downhill all the way," she sorrowfully concluded.

"Yes, dear," he morosely muttered.

"You know something, Boritz dearest, if we were still an empire, well then, our trip could possibly take far longer than a couple of weeks as we crisscrossed the globe, heading for faraway lands that we once very considerately helped ourselves to."

"Yes, yes. Hush, my dearest. Stop interrupting me, and just listen," he cried with more than a hint of exasperation, for he had been feeling thoroughly intoxicated with excitement before she so rudely interrupted him with pious, if not corrective, behavior that could easily turn once more into an unpleasant altercation between the two of them, if he chose to allow it.

"As I was saying, pumpkin, we will spend the next few weeks traveling around our beloved country, and what with your voraciously unquenchable appetite for places of historical value, we shall be stopping at every castle and place of national interest in our pursuit to find out where this ring originated from. I, for one, fully intend to leave no stone, large or small, unturned until I get the answers I most certainly require."

"Ooh, Boritz dearest, speaking of large stones, does this mean we might be able to visit Stonehenge?"

"Yes, my dear. It most certainly can include Stonehenge if this will make you happy."

"Boritz dear, while I'm still thinking, I know we no longer own India, Australia, or the Bahamas, for that matter; even certain parts of Africa sadly no longer fly our Union Jack, heralding that they are no longer under our charge. But pray, perchance is there any possibility that we might just still own an itsy witsy, teeny weenie piece of South America?"

"Quite what exactly do you mean, Mildred?"

"Well, do we own a small piece of Brazil or Paraguay? Or anywhere else nice and warm, for I'm so very tired of the British weather, what with all its wintry, blustery wind, smog, and rain."

"Hmm. My dearest peach, I do believe Montserrat and the Cayman Islands might well still be under British sovereignty, and then of course there are the Falkland Islands. I'm more than sure they still fly the Union Jack."

"Well, I for one have never heard of them, Boritz, so where on heaven's earth are they situated?"

"Just off Argentina, my dearest."

"Oh, forgive me for asking, Boritz dearest, but before you go on to give me every historical fact dating back to Columbus, I fear that I have only one immediate concern."

"Oh, and what is that, my dearest chubby cheeks?"

"Do these so-called Fortlamb Islands have a nice stretch of sandy white beach for me to pitch my stripy deck chair and sun umbrella?"

"Well, I'm fairly sure we could find you a sandy beach, my dearest, and as these small islands are just off Argentina, I should imagine the weather would be extremely favorable."

"Wonderful. Wonderful!" Mildred cried, clapping her hands loudly, for she was finding it almost impossible to contain her newfound excitement. "So can I pack our bathing suits, dearest?" she perkily asked.

"Yes, my little pickled onion. Pack as many swimsuits as you care to," he replied.

"By the way, Boritz, where on God's precious earth is Argentina?"

"Well, I'm not too sure, my little cauliflower floret, but if you really want to know, then I will leave you for a moment to go in search of a book so that together we can take a quick peek," he chuckled as he quickly vacated the room to race toward his private library.

He returned minutes later with a large book that he had pulled down from a neatly arrayed line of books from off one of his very impressive library shelves. Back in the kitchen he hurried over to where Mildred was still crouched in the corner. As he opened the book, a small but thick piece of printed cardboard fluttered to the floor. Boritz hurriedly stooped down to pick it up. He then tore the ticket into tiny pieces before discreetly placing the bits in his breast pocket. If the truth be known, that small and seemingly insignificant piece of cardboard was indeed a library ticket, and so the book in question should rightfully have been returned to the school library some five years previous.

"Oh, dear, dear. As you can see, Mildred, it is much too far away for us to consider paying even the smallest of visits, given the short amount of time I have allocated for this entire trip. But never mind, dearest; I am sure you will be thrilled by Buckingham Palace, enraptured by Windsor Castle, enthralled by Warwick Castle, utterly captivated by Belvoir Castle, and suitably enamored by just about every other castle and palatial residence your sparkly little eyes get to feast upon."

Mildred took this rare opportunity to grab hold and tenderly squeeze his fat, sweaty hand, her eyes instantly glazing over, as filled with fresh wonderment she looked him directly in the eye. "Boritz, this trip sounds like heaven on earth, my dear. But with us gone, pray, have you taken into serious consideration the problem of the children?"

"Children? Problem? Quite what do you mean, Mildred?"

"Well, Boritz, who on earth could possibly take charge of such a large bunch of wild, out-of-control paupers as those we are so blessed to be raising?" Mildred very tongue in cheek snapped as she immediately came to her full senses.

Boritz shrugged his shoulders, for sadly she was right. He had not given even a moment's thought to this seemingly trivial problem. However, minutes later saw his mind in overload as he seriously began computing every imaginable possibility.

Mildred saw this sudden and most miraculous oratory abstinence as an opportunity to offer both her input and guidance. "Oh, Boritz dear, at this moment there appears to be no suitable answer, so it really looks pretty hopeless. I, for one, know of no suitably mature adult who could even begin to look after so many difficult children, for none have the years of experience that we have so faithfully racked up. And surely we can't leave the pitiful little mites alone to fend for themselves, can we? I mean, that would surely be considered by most to be disgracefully unconscionable!"

"Yes, if news of such a thing were to leak out, we might find ourselves being pilloried or, worse still, strapped into the ducking chair," a now sorely depressed Boritz muttered.

"Darling, don't be stupid! Ducking chairs haven't been used to punish people for many a year, in fact, if I'm correct, since the last century," she felt the need to remind him.

"Well, if we were to be caught out leaving them to fend for themselves, the courts of this land might well be forced into reinstating this intolerably inhumane punishment," he miserably sniffed.

"Yes, it really would be asking way too much to ask poor Miss Scrimp to single-handedly take care of the mischievous little blighters, for you know full well just how difficult they can at times be," she continued to spout.

"Hmm," Boritz continued to mutter as he gave careful thought to all these annoying little concerns that his dear wife was spouting on about.

"So tell me, my dear, have you really thought this one through? And if, my dearest, you have as usual taken all things into consideration, then it is time for you to share with me precisely what you have in mind if we are to successfully overcome this latest obstacle."

"Well, Mildred, as you've asked me so nicely, I will rise to the occasion and confer by sharing with you my exact intentions. Tomorrow before the sun rises I shall telephone both Mrs. Gumball and Mrs. Grimespot and request that both ladies do us a great kindness by stepping into our shoes for the duration of our proposed absence. You see, Mildred dear, it is imperative that we grab this opportunity while we can, for as you are well aware, the Christmas holidays are almost upon us."

"Quite what are you getting at, Boritz dearest?"

"Please do me the courtesy of paying attention, Mildred, and for once in your profoundly humdrum life, stop interrupting me. If we were to leave it until the holidays, we would find ourselves having to shell out more money, for as the children would be home from school, they would therefore require far more supervision. And without appearing brutally callous, dearest one, more supervision equals more pay for the ladies."

Mildred nodded her head. Boritz took this to mean that she fully understood and therefore now completely appreciated where he was coming from. "You're quite right, dear, for if our trip coincided with the school holidays, well, then it could easily become ridiculously expensive."

"Yes, but this way, if we time it just right, not only do the children spend a healthy amount of each day attending school, but add to this the tediously lengthy amount of time taken up with the traveling to and fro, and this leaves only the bare minimum of hours when the ladies will be required to be on hand and thus supervise the children."

"Keep going, my precious one, for I do believe you are now on the right track," cried a once more very excited Mildred, who was now clasping her hands tightly.

Needless to say, Boritz needed no further encouragement to continue sharing his latest rather ingenious plan. "Yes, they will only have to organize breakfast and supper, and what's more, the older children can get stuck in with helping when it comes to getting the younger ones ready for bed. Obviously the weekends will be a slightly different story, but I do believe that I have even those sorted out to my complete satisfaction."

"Well, go on, go on," Mildred encouraged.

"For starters, on both Saturdays the ladies can place all the younger children in front of the television after breakfast, and they will surely be very happy and content to remain glued to the box until bedtime, for they will certainly see it as something of a rare treat. If they need to use the loo, then the older ones will be on hand to take them up to the bathroom. And if the youngsters even begin to get grizzly, well then, the older ones can throw them packets of crisps and chocolate fingers in a manner similar to that of feeding chimps at the zoo."

"Oh, Boritz, my most magnificent star of the universe, you really do have such a perfectly wicked sense of humor," Mildred stated as she failed hopelessly to stifle an unexpectedly girlish giggle.

"Thank you, dearest. Now allow me the grace to continue. As for Sundays, the majority of the morning is usually taken up with getting ready for and then attending church. So I will take it upon myself to ask dear Father Constantinople to obligingly extend his already ridiculously overextended Bible readings, followed by an extra lengthy sermon. This will indeed go a long way to keeping their tender bottoms stuck to the wooden pews, and therefore out of trouble, until well into the afternoon. Once home from church, the ladies will be on standby to feed the little mites a small but satisfying lunchtime sandwich."

"Wonderful. Simply wonderful!" Mildred gleefully cried.

"Then with lunch over, they can once again all be plonked down in front of the television until teatime, when baked beans on toast, washed down with a milky cup of tea, will be served up at precisely 6:00 p.m. So before you can say, 'Bob's your uncle,' it will be time for bed and then up for school on Monday morning. How does all this sit with you, Mildred dearest?"

"Oh, my darling, you are indeed the brightest spangled star in the cosmos, for you, my wonderful dearest one, certainly think up an answer for everything," Mildred gasped as her upper lip involuntary curled upward into an extremely large smile. This was indeed a feat so radical that it was both hard and odd for her usually very down-trodden facial features to respond, as they were now using muscles that had rarely been called upon in the past.

"And as for the older children, we all know they are extraordinarily easy to bargain with," he sniffed, his brow holding a permanent furrowed state as he continued on with his attempts to work things out. "If they are promised that they will be allowed to stay up and watch some highly unsuitable and frightfully gory film undisturbed, helped on only by a succession of highly desirable snack treats, well then, they will cheerfully volunteer their services in helping get the younger children up the stairs and into bed as fast as you can say, 'Jack Robinson.' So, Mildred, my precious little petal, how am I doing so far?"

"You, my sweet jewel of the Nile, are doing rather splendidly," Mildred perkily encouraged.

Boritz instantaneously began to glow from ear to ear.

"So you see, Mildred dearest, with a bit of proper organization and the help of our old cleaning ladies, this venture is back on the table, as once again it becomes most viable."

Mildred began to clap her hands as an expression of her overwhelming feelings of joy, but then suddenly and without notice she once more stopped in her tracks, the elusive radiant smile slowly ebbing from her face until like the flame of a candle it was entirely snuffed out.

"Boritz, that's all well and good," Mildred sniffed as her overturned smile turned to a deep frown of great concern. She began to shake her head in pure disbelief, biting down on her trembling bottom lip at the same time. "Oh, Boritz dear, captain of my heart, this is positively ghastly; however, I feel you have failed to remember one very and most important factor—that it has only been a few months since *you*, dearest one, chose to dismiss not one but both ladies from our good service. And if you care to cast your mind back to that historic moment in time, you might well remember that both ladies were quite shocked and distraught to be dismissed from their humble posts with no formal notice whatsoever! So you see, dearest, we—or rather, you— were not exactly bountiful toward either party."

"Goodness gracious me! This most grievous situation had entirely slipped my memory," he mournfully gasped.

"Perhaps it is also good to also remember that we gave them no financial compensation whatsoever."

"Oh, good grief," was all Boritz was capable of muttering as sadly he realized that for once his beloved really did have a point of concern.

With her conniving husband surprisingly clean out of words, Mildred took this as a most excellent opportunity to stand in the gap and use his convenient lack of dialogue to continue her own monologue, much to his utter annoyance.

"Yes, Boritz dear. Normal practice would have required us to give at least a week, if not a whole month's notice—indeed, time enough to allow them both to seek out other employment. So taking all of this into consideration, why on earth would either lady ever consider helping us out in our time of need?" Mildred took it upon herself to ask, as she continued to search his face.

"Enough! Shut it, dear!" he abrasively demanded. "Your constant and most pedantic drones are indeed most tiresome. I need time alone to think, and your unworthy, pitiful babblings are not only very unhelpful, but they will indeed drive me to the edge of a high precipice if you do not hold in abeyance that over-exercised muscle contained in your facial orifice," he reminded in a most unpleasant, scornful tone of voice.

"You mean my tongue, dearest, don't you?" she sniffed, yet again feeling most hurt and offended.

A lengthy "hmm" was all that Boritz cared to comment regarding his latest mean and harsh communication toward his ever dutiful wife.

Even so, Mildred was right. He therefore secretly wished that in hindsight he had shown both ladies his more charitable side, but back then how was he to know that there would come a time when the tables would be turned, and he would need some charity shown him as he stooped as low as he felt capable to ask these lesser mortals for their help?

"Oh, dear Boritz, at the end of the day one is inclined to feel most tired and distraught, as one is left to debate as to whether there is really an acceptable solution to this fresh and most wearisome problem," she reassured in little more than a whisper.

Boritz was deep in thought and was therefore in no hurry to give her the immediate response that she required.

Mildred, having once more found her tongue, took his failure to reply as an excuse to continue on with yet more thought-provoking concerns that out of nowhere had just popped into her mind. "My very precious star of the universe, you must surely agree that the likelihood that one, if not both, women will by now have found themselves new positions remains well within the bounds of possibility. As both women have large families of their own to provide for, one might well imagine that they will have been forced to accept any position offered to them, if only out of sheer desperation and necessity. If this turns out to be the case, they would surely be most unwilling to turn their backs on their new employers to come back here and work for the mere pittance we considered ourselves so generous to bestow on them," she hastily reminded him.

Boritz appeared to give careful consideration to all that Mildred had to say, but then, to stop her rabbiting on any further, for it was giving him an almighty headache, he finally decided to take over.

"Well, my dearest, forgive me if I beg to differ, but I have it on the highest authority that since leaving the castle, neither lady has had the remotest piece of luck in finding any suitable employment. I am therefore more than confident that once I present our current situation to the dear ladies, they will, I believe, jump at the opportunity and even consider themselves most fortunate to find themselves once more in the employment of our good selves, even if it is only for the duration of our holiday. I will, of course, encourage them further by offering both ladies the once-in-a-lifetime opportunity of being in receipt of an excellent reference that will most certainly help them find other reasonable employment at some future date."

"Well, Boritz, if all this turns out to be true, then this is indeed wonderful news, for it must surely mean that both ladies will by now be in most urgent need of money. But dare I take this opportunity to ask how come you, my dear, are so up-to-date on such matters?"

"Because, my dearest, I make it a top priority to keep abreast of such things, and as every potential new employer contacts me asking for a written personal reference as to the credibility and worthiness of those lesser creatures that we have in the past employed, well then, my dear, I leave the rest for you to work out in your little, and often somewhat confused, head."

"Oh, Boritz, commander of our solar system and beyond, you, my dear, are such an overwhelmingly powerful man. What would I do, and where would I be without you at the helm?"

"And the rudder," Boritz whispered under his breath.

"Precisely, my dear! Now come along and let us head for the stairs and bed, as I, for one, am in urgent need of some serious shut-eye."

"Yes, dear."

"Tomorrow morning when I arise from my blissful slumber, I will purpose to make all essential phone calls, leaving you to content yourself with the more trivial things of life, such as packing the suitcase with the odd pair of underpants, toothbrush, razor, and all other essential paraphernalia that are necessary if one is wanting to experience a successful holiday."

The next morning came far too soon for the children, who were all desperately overtired and groggy, with many of them still suffering the very unpleasant symptoms and side effects from their ice cream binge. This day would be replayed many times in the head of each demoralized child, as there was not one among them who did not pathetically drop to his or her knees and beg permission to be allowed the day off school, for they were all without fail still feeling terrible queasy. However, neither their pale, limp bodies nor their heartfelt, pitiful pleas fell on fertile ground when it came to the cold, stony heart of Aunt Mildred. No, it all fell on completely deaf ears, for Aunt Mildred was having none of it, as she systematically marched like a sergeant major on patrol through each dormitory shouting out her orders at the top of her lungs.

"Wakey, wakey; rise and shine," she shrieked in ridiculously high decibels before most unfeelingly stripping the bedclothes off each bed, thereby forcing each poor and bewildered occupant to get up, as without the protection of bedclothes they quickly began to shiver from the cold in the draughty, sparsely furnished dormitories.

"Right, you messy, undisciplined bunch of wimps. You all have just five minutes to get dressed and make your beds. Failure to fulfill this task within the allotted time will spell immeasurable trouble. Do I make myself clear?" she yelled.

"Yes, Aunt Mildred," they stuttered as, shivering violently, they jumped up and down in a vain effort to keep warm.

Even poor Bertha Banoffee, who had spent the whole night lying on the cold flagstone floor of the kitchen, was shown no extra mercy, as she was ordered to get up from the floor and make haste to get washed and changed into her spare school uniform.

That ghastly morning all the children were impossibly slow as they dragged their sickened, fragile torsos in the general direction of the bathroom. So it came as no surprise that there was no time whatsoever for any child to sit down and even half fill his or her tummy with any nourishment that might aid them through the lengthy school day.

By the time every child had made it to the bathroom there were only minutes left to make a dash for the bus stop to catch the school bus.

However, if the truth be told, not one of the feeble, bleary-eyed children had the slightest desire to sit in front of the normal bowl of stale cereal, making the usual eye contact with the ridiculously lively silverfish, who thought nothing of flaunting themselves as they cheekily wriggled to and fro in the lukewarm, thick, lumpy-powdered milk.

Having made their weary way to the bottom of the stairs, the poor children showed not an atom of resistance, as they were then frog-marched to the front door by a very militant Aunt Mildred, who administered the usual threats by grabbing hold of an ear or two to dutifully remind each child of what possibly could befall them, should they dare miss the school bus.

Boritz, for once, also took a responsible parental position and stood by Mildred to wave the children off. Never one to miss an opportunity, he used the occasion to warn each and every poorly child to expect a family meeting to take place on their return from school.

———◦•◦◦———

With the children now out of the way, Mildred happily busied herself emptying out drawer after drawer as she scratched around for suitably classy clothing, as well as a swimming costume or two to pack for her impending holiday.

Boritz, in the meantime, set about making those urgent phone calls that were necessary if their trip was to go ahead as planned. Happily for Boritz, both ladies were, as he had so rightly stated, available to help out. Mrs. Gloria Gumball said she would go immediately and pack a suitcase and be at the castle as soon as she was required, and dear Gertrude Grimespot even volunteered the help of her younger sister, Hilda, who had traveled many miles to stay for an extended period of time with Gerty and the rest of her close-knit family.

Boritz then found himself with the embarrassing task of having to cancel the previously arranged round of golf with his dear friend and headmaster Edwood Batty, as well as his close friend, good old Dr. Glumchops. He knew they would completely understand and appreciate his explanation for canceling, especially when they heard that he had little choice as the trip was a matter of great urgency, and so he asked both friends to show charitable forgiveness toward dear Mildred, as well as his good self.

Also canceled was their pre-planned supper date at the Toad in the Hole. "Tell dear Agnes we will organize another date on our return, and likewise we will be contacting Egor and Ethel to inform them that the supper date is temporarily postponed," Boritz politely informed Edwood Batty.

Now all that was left to do was prepare a suitably hard-hitting sermon for the family meeting, which was to take place as soon as all the children returned from school. As he sat back in his chair in his dismal and abysmally untidy study, he considered that this meeting must essentially differ from all previous meetings, inasmuch as it must not take place in his study but elsewhere. This small change of plan would naturally have the children feeling very emotionally susceptible, for he knew that familiarity was extremely important to the insecure little urchins, and on this particular occasion he really believed he needed them to be feeling uncertain, queasy, and hopefully a little bit afraid. If this were to be the case, then it was absolutely necessary for him to challenge and overthrow their much-needed regular routine.

"Pattern, power. Nothing familiar. Nothing familiar. Pattern, power," he chanted over and over under his breath.

Without warning Boritz suddenly broke into a large, wicked smile as he came to believe that he had thought of the perfect place to hold this very special family meeting, and this was under the castle in the forbidden tunnel.

Chapter Thirteen
THE FORBIDDEN TUNNEL

*T*HE REASON THIS particular tunnel was forbidden had precious little to do with ghouls, ghosts, bloodstained walls, dismembered bodies, and those sort of unspeakably ghastly things that bring untold amounts of terror to the core of most normal, level-headed people. Simply, this underground tunnel or cellar held a lot of precious and very expensive tools that Boritz used as he busied himself with all his latest money-spinning ventures.

Boritz was, of course, well aware that in years gone by this tunnel might well have been used more as a prison dungeon, for its stone walls still contained suspicious-looking lumps of metal that presumably in past history had been used to chain up vile, monstrous criminals and insurgents of the king; but that was all in the past. Its present usage was more that of an underground bunker where Boritz worked on all sorts of crazy, half-baked schemes that in his egomaniacal mind he hoped might one day make him immensely rich, as well as famous.

His latest and most challenging invention to date was to design a trendy new box in which to bury the deceased. Now, these were no ordinary coffins but part of an ongoing project that Boritz had been working on for some time now. He regularly admitted to himself that this was his most exciting project to date, which, given time, would surely fill his coffers to overflowing and, in doing so, would rightfully make him his well-deserved millions. He believed that his idea of sweet-smelling coffins that decomposed along with the odiously rotting corpse would, given a reasonable amount of time, become most desirable, if not highly fashionable.

He reasoned that in the not-too-distant future there would indeed come a day when burial grounds would be so full to overflowing there would no longer be any space left in which to bury the freshly departed. Take, for instance, his very own deceased relatives Aunt Quantaloop, as well as dear Uncle Stickleberry. Both were sadly stacked up, box upon box, at some beastly, overcrowded church graveyard in London, and these were to name but a few of his dearly beloved departed friends and relatives. It was clearly a very distressing situation, which over a matter of time would only get much worse—that is, until the problem was properly and officially confronted.

It was also true to say that the problem of overcrowded graveyards had been the subject of great debate on a recent television documentary, and so Boritz thought he'd get in first; hence the first ever heavenly scented and biodegradable coffins.

The reason the children were going to be ordered down into the tunnel after school that day had little to do with him wishing to give the children a little peek at handcrafted coffins and thereby confirm their admiration toward his perfectionist skills; but simply, these coffins would serve him well when it came to getting them all to see things quickly from his perspective. After all, he considered that a modicum of fear in each child's tender heart was surely very healthy. It kept them alert, it prevented general unruliness, and it made them God fearing—and this was indeed very necessary if he alone was to lead the way in preserving good old-fashioned values, as well as continue to uphold discipline in the castle.

Up until now he had always held family meetings in his untidy, disheveled study, so this sudden and unexpected change of venue to this dark, dank cellar would surely scare them all witless, and even before a single word or threat dared tumble from his parted lips.

"Perfectissimo!" he joyously cried as he gloriously reveled at this latest mastermind of a thought.

As he continued to conjure up the order of things to come, he decided that it would serve him well if he were to lean against the stone wall and drum his fingers hard on the wood of a coffin lid, at the same time threatening severe punishments for all unruly behavior during his absence. If any chose to ignore his warnings, well then, they would indeed pay for it with their lives! Well, maybe not with their lives, but certainly with a very unpleasant and lengthy punishment that would have them immediately wishing for their lives to end.

Finally, he would administer all promised punishment to the despicably recalcitrant Polly Brown for her disgraceful disobedience with regard to the highly traumatic ice cream episode. Once all this was successfully handled, he would dismiss all the other children, with the exception of Polly. She would be forced to stay behind and explain how this ring mysteriously came to be in her possession. If, for once, she played ball by owning up and confessing everything, then this could save him wasting a large amount of time and money on hotel bills, restaurants, and other needless and exorbitant travel expenses as Mildred and his good self traveled the length and breadth of England in the hope of getting the answers they so desperately required. He privately conceded that this break was indeed long overdue, as she hadn't left the house for seemingly many a long year. However, setting all this to one side, if he could prize or wheedle all necessary information out of Polly without having to take this leisure break, then think of all the needless expense he would be saving them both.

He felt certain that Mildred would most likely burst into tears, and in her anger she would probably attempt to knock out his front teeth, or worse still, knock him to the ground with her suitcase and then give him a few bashes round the head. But that said, he also believed that, given time, she would indeed come 'round and see reason, especially if he were to suddenly produce a lovely gift-wrapped box of assorted chocolates accompanied by a dozen red roses. "Yes, chocolates are so very, very useful when one's hand is forced to resort to consoling a hysterical and very demanding woman trapped in the most dire emotional state of distress," he mused.

Of course, it also went without saying that if his talk turned out to be a thankless task, with Polly blatantly refusing to spill the beans despite many threats, well then, there was only one thing for it! She would spend the entire night locked in the tunnel along with his homemade coffins, and this would serve as a stark reminder of what might eventually befall her if she continued to be so, well, uncooperative.

However, if even a night of pure, unadulterated terror proved to be yet another thankless task, then sadly there was only one course of action left, and this was to take the wretched girl to see his esteemed friend and colleague, Dr. Nicholas Ninkumpoop. She would then have little choice but to undergo all medical treatments that the good doctor in his professional capacity recommended.

If he were forced into taking such drastic action, and he hoped things wouldn't come to that, well, he would use this opportunity to suggest to his fellow colleague that things were now well beyond all hope, so perhaps electroconvulsive therapy was the only serious way forward where the problematic and indefensibly arrogant Polly Brown was concerned.

He was so elated with the high level of brilliant ideas his private brainstorming had produced that in a matter of seconds irrepressible tears of joy began forming in the corners of his eyes. However, despite these unwelcome and most irritatingly inconvenient expressions of emotion, he could not help but jubilantly pat his stomach over and over as he continued to privately congratulate himself for being the intellectually superior man that God had quite rightly chosen to make him. Boritz leaned farther back on his seat, and after closing his eyes and breathing a deep sigh of self-satisfaction, he had himself a well-deserved cat nap while he waited the arrival of the children back at the castle. Pitstop finally alerted his master to the late hour by raising his head and making loud whimpering noises as he sought to stir his genius master from his fitful slumber.

And so it was that after school that unforgettable day, with all the children rounded up, they were given the order to quickly change out of their school uniforms and then follow after Uncle Boritz to an undisclosed meeting place. The children raced to get changed out of their uniforms, and it would not be too long before all the children would begin quaking with unspeakable fear as it dawned on them that they were not heading for the usual location of his study. Their panic and anguish only seemed to increase further as they headed out of the back door and down some concrete steps that led into the garden toward the underground tunnel.

It could have been a scene straight from the Pied Piper of Hamelin except for the distinct absence of singing and dancing, as the sad and heavy hearted children glumly followed both Uncle Boritz and Pitstop in single file as they trudged along a muddy trail heading toward the door of the tunnel. Uncle Boritz then spent quite some time rummaging through the mountain of keys that weighed heavily on his trouser pant belt until he finally selected what he believed to be the correct key to the lock. The children stood motionless in morbid silence, their bodies quietly quivering from cold as well as extreme fear as they watched on, feeling helpless, as Uncle Boritz struggled to open the thick, heavy, baronial door with the help of his large, rusty key.

Once it was open, he signaled for all the children to "without a fuss" follow after him in making their descent down some further steps. With all the children now inside and the heavy door then firmly shut behind him, he reached out his chubby fingers to search for the light switch. The bulb fizzled and spat as it struggled to perform its duty of lighting up the otherwise dark, dank room. Boritz winced as his eyes finally came to rest on the children all huddled together, their faces contorted by fear and confusion at all that was happening.

Some of the younger children started to shake with fear, and many began to whimper.

"Please, Uncle Boritz. Let us go back inside," little Sophie Shrimpbutton pleaded in little more than a whisper, her young body trembling with fear as she quickly clasped the first available hand. It belonged to the equally terrified little Sacha Shoesmith, who was also trembling in her boots.

Then another terrified and frail voice cried out, "Please, please let us go, Uncle," a teary eyed Thomasina Pitesky sobbed, her voice trailing off as Bertha Banoffee placed a hand over the young child's mouth, ordering her to shush.

"Please tell us you're not going to murder us all and then store us in those long boxes, Uncle Boritz, for we promise that we really will try even harder to be good," young, petrified Nora Nitpick whimpered as, bursting into tears, she held on to the left hand of Natalie, her older sister, as tightly as she possibly could.

"Children, children, stop all this unnecessary whining, for you really have no need whatsoever to fear," Uncle Boritz hauntingly reassured them, as slowly and deliberately he began to muzzle Pitstop's jaw with both hands in a manner that suggested he might easily choke the life out of the dumb animal. He then calmly released his grip and walked over to where his handmade coffins were leaning against the wall. Just as he had rehearsed over and over in his mind, with a mischievously crooked smile alighting his overblown, pockmarked face, he calmly began to drum his fingernails hard against the nearest wood coffin shored up against the wall.

The meeting that day was to be considered a complete success, because all the children were made to clearly understand that any unacceptable behavior, planned now or for the future, would be met with swift, if not very severe punishment. Every bleary eye remained glued on his hands as though their terror-filled hearts beat loudly to the drum of his fingers as he deliberately and cold-heartedly drummed down hard on the wooden coffin. That dark day Boritz was sure they knew with every fiber of their being that full cooperation was imperative, for he truly meant business.

Finally satisfied that nothing more need be said, he cried, "Enough! Now then, Polly, come and stand before me, because before anyone can leave this aforesaid meeting we still have a certain, rather ugly situation that needs to be resolved. Then and only then can we vacate this cellar to leave and go about our business."

All the children simultaneously began moaning and groaning.

"Yes, my little toasted toadies, we are sadly still required to concern ourselves with a very selfish act of rebellion that needs urgent addressing."

Polly took in a deep breath.

"Yes, Polly Brown, you are indeed a most rare and insolent girl. How dare you deceive us all by falsely assuming that you had any right or entitlement to discontinue your chores to join the rest of us in last night's gloriously jovial celebrations?"

Polly immediately bowed her head in shame.

"Are you listening to me? You knew full well that you were on ROPE, and still you chose to completely abandon your post to surreptitiously eat ice cream sundaes as you rather sneakily decided to join in all the festivities. What do you have to say for yourself, girl?" he snarled gnashing his teeth.

———◦—◦—◦———

Before Polly could open her mouth to answer the aforesaid charges—of which she alone was being accused—she was forced to shut up.

"Silence, you miserable miscreant! Everything you care to say will, as always, be nothing more than a tissue of lies, for we all know that you, my dear, think nothing of telling us one porky pie after another, lies that we will be expected to try our best to unravel, as you are something of a professional when it comes to fibbing and telling real porkies," he roared. Polly had little choice other than to cease from even beginning to explain herself, although she knew that this time she had no excuse whatsoever regarding her insubordinate behavior and all else that had taken place on the previous evening. Her uncle was absolutely correct when he said that she had abandoned her duties to join in the general merriment, something she knew full well she was prohibited from doing when on ROPE. To also be included in that heinous of deeds was the charge of unlawfully helping herself to ice cream whilst neglecting to obtain the full permission of either guardian, so she knew without question that she must submit and enter a guilty plea to all the charges. She realized that in doing so she must accept any punishment he chose to mete out that day, even if it meant a public hanging!

She would have cried out there and then, "I'm utterly guilty!" if she thought it would help bring the meeting to some form of closure, thereby ending all suffering for the rest of the children who were entirely innocent of any crime whatsoever, but she knew that would never happen, as Uncle Boritz would not be the least satisfied until he finally had his full pound of flesh.

There in that dank cellar on that dark and dreary day, there could be no mercifully quick absolution.

"Kiddiewinks, allow me to enlighten all present by informing you that if this case were to be tried in a British military court, then such a preposterous act as Polly's would no doubt find her facing a severe court-martial. Children, to help clarify this little matter, the term used by the military is *going AWOL*, 'absent without leave,' and I assure you, hand on heart, that if Polly were on trial this day and this hour, she could expect only the stiffest sentence imaginable. God's honor."

The look on each child's face was one of sheer contempt as they drunk in every utterance that fell from their uncle's thick lips. "So tell me what to do next, my precious little peanut butter sandwiches. Sadly, as usual, I feel utterly impotent regarding this latest Polly crisis. Yes, my hands feel thoroughly tied."

All the children immediately hung their heads low, for no one wanted to say anything that might further displease him, leaving

Uncle Boritz with little choice but to continue on until they gave him a response that was to his liking and satisfaction.

"Her mischief appears to know no bounds, and so I find myself feeling sick to the pit of my stomach and at a complete loss for words. I am forced yet again to cry out, 'What on earth should we do with her, for she is one almighty headache of a problem?'"

Finally, one of the children found the courage to reply.

"As she's such a bloomin' problem, why don't we stick 'er in a coffin and nail the lid down tight?" Cecil Bogswater helpfully suggested, giving a loud snigger. All the children quickly applauded his idea by spontaneously bursting into cheers of laughter as they loudly clapped their hands.

"Force her to eat mud pies for a whole week until all her innards rot with gangrene and mildew," Gailey Gobbstopper snarled. "Better still, string her up."

"Yes, there's plenty of rope over there. We could tie her up in no time at all. That way we can all get to leave this stinky old cellar to go inside and watch *Bonanza*," Toby Trotter helpfully chipped in as he picked up a long length of cord from the floor. After quickly making a sliding hangman's noose, he began to use it as a lasso while loudly humming the opening tune of *Bonanza*.

This little act made some of the younger children begin to cry, because they would much rather be watching *Bonanza* or *The Lone Ranger*, with dear, darling Silver, his wonderful horse. Instead, they were stuck down here in this horrible, dark cellar, and all because of stupid Polly Brown. Finally, Toby was ordered to stop his nonsense, so he reluctantly handed the noose over to Uncle Boritz.

"Yes, and as always, it's because of smelly old Polly Brown we are all going to miss not only *Bonanza* but *The Lone Ranger* too if we stay down here much longer," Natalie Nitpick furiously complained. "*And it's the final episode of the series*. Oh, how I hate her."

"Yep, we all hate her, so if we are going to hang her up, then let's do it quick, 'cos none of us want to miss the last episode of *The Lone Ranger*," Michael Muzzlecombe, an older boy, loudly complained as he then set about coaxing all other children to join forces so as to get the dastardly deed over and done with.

"Come on, then. Who's willing to put the cord around her neck?" he cried out as he searched for a potential volunteer. "Hey, Gailey, you hate her the most, so you do it," he cried.

"Na, she ain't worth it," Gailey spluttered. Polly was instantly grateful that Gailey lacked the courage to put her money where her mouth was and, in doing so, put the rope around "Esther Fester's" neck.

"No! Stop it, all of you! That's my sister. You leave her alone. She's done nothing to harm any of you," came the sudden brave and so unexpected forceful demand from James, Polly's younger brother.

"Aw, shut up, you little toe rag, or I'll give yer a bleeding lip," Billy Osgood sniffed as he squared up to James.

"You're heading for a hard thump, you little ignoramus misfit," Tommy Pulleyblank aggressively yelled out as the crowd automatically parted, allowing him the access to move forward and confront James, who was infinitely smaller and weaker. He then placed his hands around James's throat and began to squeeze tightly. "If yer know what's best for yer, you'll stay well out of this," he snarled menacingly before releasing James from his grip.

James went a bright red and then began to cough and splutter as, gripped with fear by this fresh intimidation, he moved aside to gracefully bow out of any further confrontation.

"Enough, my chubby little cherubs. Enough! As you can see, it is very hard and distressing for any of us to determine what punishment should be administered, but alas, we cannot leave this room until some form of unanimous decision has been reached and then executed. It must be unanimous, for have I need of reminding you all that a house divided will most certainly fall? Therefore it is imperative that we stand together as one. Now, say after me, 'United we stand; divided we fall.'"

"United we stand...united we stand; divided we fall," they all chanted over and over in unison.

"There, there, my little ones. You now have the right idea. Now then, James Brown, you, my impudent little whippersnapper, will certainly face punishment for putting your interfering, snotty little nose where it was not welcome in your pitiful attempt to obstruct justice from being done. So as the Lord gives, He also takes away; I therefore intend to confiscate your miserable collection of model airplanes and military tanks until you learn that all defiant behavior in this castle constitutes gross rebellion and will therefore be met with the swiftest of disciplinary measures."

Polly let out a loud gasp as she witnessed her younger brother crumple to the floor in a heap before pitifully begging his uncle's forgiveness in a manner more suited to someone who genuinely believes his very life hangs in the balance.

"Please, please, Uncle. Don't take away my model planes. I'm so-so–sorry," he stuttered. "I promise I won't do anything like that ever again, I promise. I spent hours making those planes, and they are all I have," James pathetically sobbed, as in a praying pose he continued foolishly to grovel. But he really was wasting his breath, for his heart-rending pleas sadly fell on very stony ground.

"Oh, stop all your blubbering, for are you a man or a mouse?" he snorted.

All the children standing by began to titter.

"He's nothing but a wimpy little dormouse," they roared.

"Please, please give me some other punishment. I beg you, Uncle."

"Well, boy, sad to say, but your arrogance is truly indefensible! You really should have thought about all this before you so unrighteously sprung to your wicked sister's worthless cause. So I'm sorry to tell you, but the answer is a firm no. These items will remain in my sole possession until I see fit to return them, and that, my insolent young man, may be never!"

James's chest visibly collapsed as, scrunched up like a ball on the hard stone floor, he tried hard to wipe away the tears that were now uncontrollably spilling down his face.

"Please, Uncle. Not my models," he hoarsely whispered.

"Oh, put a sock in it!" Uncle Boritz scornfully sneered, raising his eyes into his head to suggest that this drama was all too much to take.

"Please, please. I beg you," James tearfully continued to plead.

"Oh, grow up and be a man. Stop those ludicrously pathetic tears immediately, for your unimpressive melodramatics are really beginning to irritate me," a totally unsympathetic Boritz growled. "Right, children, please all ignore James, for we need to move on. As I previously stated, we cannot leave this room until we have come to some agreement with regard to Polly's punishment. So let's get on with it, shall we?"

"I don't have the slightest clue as to what punishment should be given Polly. All I know is that I'm missing The Lone Ranger," Polly heard one of the children whisper to another.

"I'm so cold and hungry, I don't even care about the TV program. I just want to get out of here," replied the other.

"Well I don't know about you, but I've just about had it with Polly and her stupid, ongoing problems," whispered Gailey as she sneered at Polly."

"Chop her into little pieces, then feed her to the pigs, for we don't care. We don't care," Percy Pillsbury suggested.

"Yes, chop her up, chop her up," Cecil Bogswater shouted out at the top of his lungs. "She's a dangerous disease that needs eliminating. That's why we call her Fester."

"Well, Cecil, it's strange that you should say such a thing, for if you were to familiarize yourself with any medical dictionary you will pretty soon discover that there are many serious diseases that start with Polly's name."

"Really, Uncle?"

"Yes, offhand I can only think of one terrible sickness called poly-cystic fibrosis, but if we were to scour a medical dictionary we would find plenty more."

"So she really is a disease?"

"Oh, absolutely!"

All too soon, with the exception of James, who was still curled up on the basement floor, they were all chanting, "Chop her up! Chop her up!" Then, "Feed her to the pigs and scavengers, for we don't care, we don't care! She's such a bloomin' misfit anyway, so Uncle, do with her whatever you want," they chanted in unison.

Boritz stood sanctimoniously watching, his arms crossed, as he smiled with delight.

"Children, children, let's not get so carried away," he stated as he pretended to shake his head in pure disbelief. "We must surely learn to be more charitable and merciful, mustn't we?"

The now dangerously confused and exhausted children all nodded.

"Yes, but this is Polly Brown, and we've clean run out of any mercy toward smelly, grotty Esther Fester," Michael Muzzlecombe snarled.

"Hmm. So, children, on reflection I am indeed most reluctant to leave Polly in your hands. No, I think it is best that as I am the only cool-headed one left amongst you, then I think it should ultimately be left for me to decide her fate."

Truth be known, he had no intention whatsoever of allowing the other children to do any such dastardly deed, but it was also true to say that their alarmingly overemotional response had truly pleased him, for it now allowed him the freedom to mete out any detestable form of punishment that he cared to. And better still, if any child dared to complain, well then, he could cheerfully play the outraged victim.

"Hold your horses, kiddiewinks! May I take this opportunity to remind all present that none of you were prepared to show Polly any mercy whatsoever, for if you rightly remember, it was you lot that advocated her punishment be death—*and*, may I remind, in such a gruesome manner!"

He would then take his thick glasses off his nose to slowly give them a wipe, all the while giving the children time to reevaluate their high moral stance regarding Polly's punishment.

"Yes, indeed. I for one was shocked to the core and grieved by your overwhelming and violent need for vengeance, and so it was I who prevented any of you from carrying out your proposed and, I might add, very inhumane punishment. My choice of discipline is nothing as severe, and so it should be perceived as considerably benevolent, all things considered."

Yes, happily he had his speech all worked out if they showed anything other than utter compliance with regard to his sentencing of Polly.

Needless to say, young Polly seemed nearly to faint as Uncle Boritz proceeded to pronounce the punishment.

"Sadly, nothing but the stiffest of sentences will work when it comes to you, Polly Brown," he sanctimoniously stated as he directed his right index finger firmly in Polly's direction. "Yes, girl, stand to attention when I talk to you.

Polly did as she was told.

"I am, therefore, obliged to propose that there be a further six months extension on ROPE and that your daily food allowance be halved. Also, any child seen talking to you will be presumed a traitor to the cause and therefore a collaborator. In such a case, they too will find themselves being punished in a most severe manner.

"Finally, Polly Brown, every evening you will run around the walled garden fifty times shouting, 'I am the dumbest, sickest problem this town has ever seen.' This discipline will continue on for a minimum of three months in the hope of reforming your disgracefully belligerent, unregenerate, and equally unrepentant character," he stated with an air of judiciary superiority before breaking into a warm, benevolent smile for the benefit of all the other children, who were now very reliable witnesses to his very moderate sentence.

"There, there. Members of the jury, I mean, children, does this sentence meet with your approval? If it does, well then, we can all finally go indoors."

———•❈•———

The children all ran forward to give Uncle Boritz an overwhelmingly demonstrative hug, for with Polly finally sentenced they believed their ordeal was happily over. Now they could leave this horribly dank, musty-smelling dungeon to quickly get back into the warmth and watch their dreadfully missed television shows.

They were also filled with the deepest admiration toward their uncle and benefactor, for how, when not one of them had any clue as to what punishment they should suggest for Polly, had Uncle Boritz so suddenly come up with such a brilliant sentence, and in no time at all? He really was a genius.

"Thank you, thank you, Uncle Boritz. Now can we go back indoors? Please, please say yes, 'cos not only are we starving, but we're also missing the last episode of *The Lone Ranger*," the children pathetically begged.

"Of course you can leave, my precious little whippersnappers," he stated as his fingers began to affectionately ruffle the blonde, disheveled hair of young, tearstained Thomasina Pitesky.

"And if you are all good as gold, well then, tell you what? You could be in receipt of a very nice treat, such as a delicious bar of chocolate, later on this evening," he said with a warm, endearing smile. "And maybe, yes, maybe some potato chips and fizzy soda to also look forward to."

"Ooh, ooh! Oh, Uncle, we love you so much," the children gasped, as many who were gathered 'round looked up at him adoringly and unanimously reached out to hug and cling to whatever part of his body they could easily reach, for without exception they were all suddenly feeling very weak and emotional.

"Thank you so very, very much, Uncle Boritz," they tearfully whispered, their voices choked with emotion and deep appreciation as they continued to embrace and cling to him as though their very lives depended on it.

Now, with the exception of Polly and James, there was not one child that terrible night that did not feel overwhelmed with immense gratitude toward dear Uncle Boritz. No words were necessary to express this truth, as every heart and mind experienced their own individual epiphany that confirmed once and for all that dear Uncle Boritz was indeed Superman and Spider-Man all rolled into one.

Did not the whole wide world know and agree that he was, indeed, master of the universe and therefore worthy of all praise? Not only had they come through this latest horribly unpleasant event alive and in one piece, but as if this was not enough, they might even find themselves in for a little treat later that evening. Uncle Boritz was way better than Superman, the Lone Ranger, or come to think of it, any other savior of the universe!

"My little winkle pickers, with the exception of Polly, you are all now officially dismissed," Uncle Boritz announced to the delight and relief of all present.

The children ran from the cellar yelling and screaming and shouting for joy, their young, tender hearts freed from all fear once more.

"Right then, Polly dear. The reason I've asked you to stay behind is because I think you and I need a little tête-à-tête."

Polly shrugged her shoulders, as she did not understand what he meant.

"We, my dear, are going to have our own private little chin wag, don't you think?" he said in a most sinister tone of voice.

Chapter Fourteen
HELP ME MAKE IT THROUGH THE NIGHT

*P*OLLY TRIED TO tell herself over and over not to panic, but this was a tall order for a young, defenseless girl who had every legitimate reason to fear the worst.

Uncle Boritz waited until the last child had high-tailed it out of the dank cellar before he once more slowly closed the door, twisting the large, rusty key in the lock in a meaningfully slow, precise manner. The only people left in the tunnel were Polly and himself; oh, and Pitstop.

Polly watched on as Uncle Boritz bent down to place an ear to the keyhole of the door, as if to confirm that there were no nosy stragglers attempting to listen in. Seemingly satisfied that all the children were now back inside the castle, he turned to her and began to get right down to the heart of the matter.

"All right, Polly, let's get down to business. You can make this easy or difficult; the choice is yours. I need answers to certain things, and if I don't get them, well then, I cannot be held responsible for what might ultimately happen to you, my dear," he said as he came right up to her face to stare directly into her eyes.

Polly blinked. She was alarmed, for at this moment in time she had absolutely no idea as to what he was referring to.

"Please, Uncle. What else have I done?" she innocently croaked.

"Oh, please don't play the 'Ooh, what have I done?' number on me," he said in a most unnatural high falsetto voice. "You should know by now that it will not work, as I find your ongoing stream of porkies quite, quite detestable."

"I truly don't know what I've said that really is a lie, so I really do need you to tell me," she stated, feeling both weak as well as exasperated.

"Well, girl, I need information," he snarled.

"Information about what, Uncle?" was Polly's innocent reply as she tried exceptionally hard not to feel intimidated.

"Information as to where this particular ring came from," he sneered as he proceeded to whisk her lost and most sacred ring from out of his pocket to then dangle it on a piece of string only inches away from her face.

"Ahh, my ring! My ring!" she cried in little more than a whisper, as she was now feeling very choked up with emotion.

"Finders keepers, losers weepers!" he mocked as he began swinging the ring back and forth like the pendulum on an old grandfather clock.

"Uncle Boritz, please give me back my ring, for it was given to me by someone very close to my heart," she cried.

"Liar," he yelled, going a deep purplish blue in the face. "Don't mess with me, girl, for you will live to regret it," he snapped, as once again he brought his face right up to hers in his desperate bid to intimidate her. "Tell me the truth, the whole truth, and nothing but the truth, you disgraceful little fibber," he continued to bark.

Polly was now shaking from head to toe. She felt like a frightened, wounded animal surrounded by bloodthirsty wolves with nowhere to run and hide. It was obvious that Uncle Boritz was on the verge of erupting, and this could mean anything might happen. Yes, anything!

"Please, Uncle Boritz, I am telling you the truth. I was given the ring by Ralph, who is one of the many homeless vagrants who every now and then rings the castle doorbell asking for a cup of tea and a cheese sandwich. He has, over time, become a good friend of mine, and one day he invited me to go to tea at a place called Piadora. Oh, Uncle, it really is the most magnificent kingdom imaginable. Ralph sent me the ring, along with a letter that stated that I must wear this ring at all times if I was to have any hope of entering the kingdom," she forlornly cried. "Uncle, I must tell you that Piadora is—"

Polly was unable to finish her sentence because she drew a deep breath to stifle the pain that came from an unexpected, sharp slap across her face.

"Bridle your rogue tongue, girl," he viperously roared, his volatile rage becoming more prevalent by the minute. "This time you have truly crossed the line. You have precisely five minutes to come clean and tell me exactly where you acquired this ring, or mark my words, you will find yourself shackled in irons and dragged off to the gallows. Otherwise you will serve the rest of your days down in the dungeons at the Tower of London, for I can no longer tolerate your continual fibs."

"Oh no, not the Tower of London."

"Yes, and then you will be terribly sorry that you were ever born," he sniffed as he drew a deep breath. "What a staggeringly ridiculous story! You are asking me to swallow a story that some penniless, smelly old vagabond would give you, of all people, a priceless ring? Well, if any of this turns out to be true, then I will surely be the first to eat my hat!" he muttered under his breath."

Polly began to rub her burning cheek, at the same time feeling sick to the pit of her stomach. She had been completely truthful, and still he did not believe her. What more could she do?

"Well, girl, what is it to be?" he sneered. "Are we on the same page? Where and from whom did you steal this valuable ring, you intolerable little thief?"

Polly instantly lowered her head, for the pain of being accused of such wickedness was, and always had been, very unbearable. True, she should have been used to it by now, but sadly the word *thief* still shot through her fragile heart like a jagged-edged knife.

"You can spare yourself a lot of pain and suffering by simply owning up right now," he grilled.

Polly lowered her head further still as she briefly considered telling a lie—a lie that might just get her out of this awful mess, but a lie all the same.

"I'm so sorry, Uncle, truly I am, for I don't know what else to tell you. This special ring really was given to me by a very precious friend. He is a tramp, and yes, from time to time he is a bit smelly, but he has a heart of gold. This ring that he gave me allows me to gain entry into the kingdom of Piadora," she said, flinching as she recoiled slightly so as to prevent herself from being on the receiving end of any further hard slaps.

Despite the room being very dimly lit, Polly was aware that Uncle Boritz's breathing was becoming heavier by the minute, a very clear indication that warned of impending danger.

"All right, Polly, you can stop all ridiculous babbling, for I can clearly see that as usual I'm plainly wasting my time," he snorted, his eyes blazing with rage. "You are, indeed, an insult to my intelligence, for you continue to talk such complete nonsensical gibberish."

"Oh, Uncle, it's not gibberish. I promise it's the truth."

"Hmm, sadly you leave me no other alternative than to leave you down here in the basement overnight. This way you will have plenty of time to reconsider your atrocious, pie-in-the-sky story. In the meantime, I believe there to be little hope for you, and so you leave me no choice but to place you under the care of my good friend and associate Dr. Ninkumpoop, who is, I believe, much better qualified than I in dealing with such reprobate nutcases as your good self."

Polly remained completely silent with her head hung low as she tried to take in all that he was threatening. Sadly, even her silence seemed to provoke him.

"Are you always this belligerent and insolent? Look at me when I'm talking to you," he snorted, showing a great deal of disgust toward her.

"Yes, sir."

"The trouble with you, Polly Brown, is that we—by this I mean everyone in authority—have all come to a complete standstill where you are concerned, and time is clearly running out for a little weasel like you," he stated.

Polly timidly raised her head and tried to look him directly in the eye as he continued to give her a hard dressing-down.

"However, I feel I would not be doing my duty properly if I did not solemnly warn you that at this specialized hospital they have numerous machines that, once plugged into your brain, will send high voltages of electricity throughout your body in an effort to turn you from the rebellious, recalcitrant individual that you are into a conforming and compliant model member of society.

"Sadly, I also need to add that it is a well-known fact that most people who find themselves admitted to these special asylums rarely ever get to leave," he stated in very convincing and menacing tones.

This new piece of information sent Polly an ice-cold shudder that traveled the whole length of her spine, and although she tried her hardest to remain brave, she could not help but allow a small, pitiful whimper to escape her trembling lips.

"Hmm. Whimper as much as you like, for the pain has only just begun," he snorted, raising his nose higher into the air as a show of his utter contempt toward her.

As Polly stood alone and afraid, she determined that as soon as she was able, she would go to her dictionary to look up some of the words that he had called her in his anger, words like *recalcitrant, impudent, unregenerate*. She had the distinct feeling that all the words meant bad things, but exactly what these long words truly meant she had little to no idea.

And so with all said and done and with Pitstop faithfully at this side, Uncle Boritz turned to climb the few steps that led up to the cellar door. He then paused for a moment by the door.

"Brrr. This cold is beginning to get to me. I can't wait to get back indoors to the warmth and a cup of Mildred's deliciously comforting hot cocoa," he muttered. "And this will surely go down a treat with a couple of shortbread fingers to dip into my cocoa."

"I hasten to remind you that this night will, I believe, feel like an eternity. Yes, the thermometer hanging on the wall is already displaying record low temperatures," he warned. "So I'm sure you will agree with me that this is indeed turning out to be one of the cruelest winters of recent years. And as if that were not enough, you, Polly dearest, will have to overcome the freezing torrent of icy winds that rage like delirious, demented demons throughout this underground tunnel," he malevolently spewed forth.

Once again young Polly took a deep gulp as she listened intently to his serious threats.

"So, my dear, even if you choose to spend the night pathetically crouched in a corner, the harsh, howling wind will gnaw and chew at your bones, and your blood will surely curdle before freezing up, if not from fright then most surely from cold," he said, giving a very sinister smile.

Polly began to openly shudder as she was forced to listen to his intimidating threats.

"Then the clawing darkness will begin to shroud your waif-like body like a claustrophobic and thick blanket, thus enabling your flesh to begin crawling with indescribable terror. And all because you will not allow your guilty conscience the rest it most surely deserves and own up."

Polly let out a loud gasp as once more she lowered her head and tried to calm down her racing heart.

"Yes, Polly dear, as you remain cloistered in this dank, musty cellar, you are indeed in for a long, dark night of the soul," he coldheartedly spat. "Hmm. It would pay you great dividends to remember the words of warning that many moons ago flowed from the pen of our own brilliant Charlotte Brontë: 'A ruffled mind makes a restless pillow.' So sleep well, Polly dear. Sleep well."

Polly remained with her head hung low, for she did not dare look up until she was quite sure that both master and beast had truly departed. When she finally dared raise her head and as her eyes came to settle on the heavy door, her only way of escape, she instantly heard the loud, ugly twist of the large, rusty key rattle in the lock. She knew without a doubt that just as Uncle had promised, her ordeal was about to begin.

Then, as if all this were not more than enough for her to deal with, the dim light that had continuously struggled to hold out throughout the entire, very unpleasant confrontation finally fizzled and died, leaving the dark and dank room shrouded in the thickest blanket of darkness. Feeling in the deepest despair, Polly crawled into a corner, and plunging her head into the palms of both hands, she wept bitterly.

"Dear God, yes, um, it's me, Polly Brown—back again like the great plague of London to bother You once more. And yes, I know it only seems like five minutes has passed since I last pestered You, but sadly I find myself yet again up a gum tree with no way down, and I assure You that this particular crisis is as bad as it gets. So if ever I needed Your assistance, it must surely be now," she whimpered as she blew into her cupped hands in her desperate and futile attempt to stay warm. "Oh, and might I just add that there is little to no doubt that my fingers and toes will freeze and then surely drop off if I don't get some help and quickly? So please, don't leave me waiting at the end of a long line of petitioners, for I don't think I have much time left to play with," came the strangled, anguished mutterings and moans of a young and terrified child frozen with fear and seemingly comfortless.

Polly began to shiver and shake violently, and with her teeth chattering loudly, she wondered how she could possibly make it through the night when she didn't even have the *SAS Survival Guide* on her being. This useful book was given to her, along with some much-needed advice, by the lovely and most concerned lanky Corporal Beanpod, because he felt that if anyone needed such a book, it had to be Polly!

"How right the lovely corporal was," she sniffed, "for I do declare that I get myself in more desperate pickles than anyone else I've ever known." That thought made her want to scream, but sadly she couldn't even begin to muster the necessary effort required. "How dumb I truly am, for how come when I need the help of that most important book, it is tucked away in my locker for purposes of safety?" she groaned, shaking her head in pure despair and disbelief.

Then quite out of the blue she remembered that Corporal Beanpod's survival book had given preeminence to the dangers surrounding hypothermia, and it had instructed that it was of the utmost importance to make sure she conserved as much heat as possible in her body if she were to have any hope of making it through the night. Failure to do so would bring on the first onset of terrifying hallucinations.

"What on earth can I do to help myself stay warm?" she muttered under her breath. She remembered that a hat or cap on her head was of the utmost importance, for this would conserve her energy levels and help keep in the heat. But where down here in this dark basement would she find herself a hat, of all things?

Before she had time to answer her own question, she found herself having a flashback of Morag and the other tramps camped around the bonfire. All her homeless friends were absolute experts when it came to keeping themselves warm, for they had little choice, as they were all homeless and therefore continuously exposed to the cruel elements. Night after freezing night as they battled high winds, sleet, ice, and fierce snowstorms, they were reminded of the dangers they faced from hypothermia if they remained lazy and therefore unprepared. She had watched on as they all stuffed thick wads of crumpled-up newspaper down their jumpers and trousers so as to conserve their body heat. Polly knew in that moment that she must do likewise; she must search for paper or material. But how was that possible, for since the light bulb had blown, the room was in total darkness?

Then once more quite out of the blue she had a brainwave. "Yes, I know what I can do," she cried as she leapt to her feet, and then with hands outstretched she gingerly tiptoed across the room in the general direction of uncle's handmade coffins, which were still resting against a far wall.

Finally her hands made contact with hard wood. "Bingo!" she victoriously cried as she heartily pushed one of the boxes to the ground. It landed with an almighty thump.

Oh my goodness. What trouble I will be in if this box is irretrievably damaged, she thought. She then quickly dismissed this thought as being quite irrelevant, for her survival was surely all that mattered here. She could only hope that Uncle Boritz, given time, would also see things from this perspective.

Polly then fell down on her knees beside the coffin, and with both hands she quickly began to feel around the inside. "Good, that's very good," she muttered as she hurriedly ripped out all the thickly padded satin material that was loosely stitched to the inside of the box. She then stuffed the material up her jumper, then up her long sleeves before pushing more down the front of her trousers. Finally she wound a long length of the material 'round and 'round her head as she attempted to improvise for lack of a real hat.

"I'm feeling a bit better already," she whispered as she intermittently blew a few hot breaths into her cupped hands before rubbing them together. "Hopefully I will soon begin feeling as warm as toast."

Experiencing a newfound courage, she quickly pushed another of her uncle's precious handmade boxes over.

"Oops. Tallyho," she shrieked as a further coffin made considerable noise as it crash-landed onto the floor beside her.

She then wasted no time clambering into the very plush satin lined box. Once inside she gently shifted the top lid so that it delicately balanced over the box. She knew not to close it tight, as she was not yet deceased and therefore still in need of fresh air if she were to keep breathing. Satisfied that the night's sleeping arrangements were the best she could do, she then curled up into a tight ball with her arms cradling her chest for added warmth.

As she lay immobilized with fright in the crippling darkness, she hoped with all her heart that with God now fully aware of her desperate situation, she might, with some hands-on help from Him, just make it through the night.

That night, as promised, the temperature plunged to new, unheard-of depths of unbearable cold, and the revengeful, howling wind did wickedly and viciously tear through the tunnel, terrorizing every timid, vulnerable creature that tried to hide away in the many nooks and crannies of the castle dungeons. Despite the newspaper stuffing and the added protection that came from sheltering inside the coffin, still Polly found herself shivering and trembling from head to toe as the temperature mercilessly continued to plummet until it was well below zero.

With her teeth chattering at a speed similar to that of a pneumatic drill, she once again made a dramatic cry for help. "Brrr. Dear God, please remember me! I'm the stupid, crazy girl who goes by the name Polly Brown. As usual, I have nowhere and no one else to turn to for help, so please, please help me make it through the night," she sadly whimpered as pain-filled tears sluggishly trickled down her ice-cold cheeks.

She brought her legs up farther to her chest in her vain bid to keep warm, but even this could not prevent the painful shivers that stabbed without mercy like freshly sharpened pencils into her soft flesh. When even this failed to keep her warm, she closed her eyes, and though her teeth were chattering loudly, she began to think of Piadora and dear sweet Mrs. O'Brien, her wonderful cookery teacher.

From there she turned her attention to Aazi, and she fleetingly allowed herself to feel hurt as she pondered why he had not taken the time to reply to even one of her many friendly letters. "Perhaps he took offense at my many chocolate-sealed letters," she mused, suddenly feeling very remorseful that she had used stale chocolate to make her own private seal of authority on each letter. Or perhaps he found her writings far too nosy and demanding to cope with. Otherwise, what if another one of her other letters had proved far too distasteful?

"There must be some stupid reason why he has refused to write back, although it is most probable that I will never find out," she sniffed, feeling even more miserable and disconsolate, as once more she felt the full spectrum of deep, painful emotions.

Then she thought of her special teachers Mrs. Bailey and Mr. Beloski, and it made her want to weep even more, for she desperately longed to hear their kind words of encouragement and comfort. Then what of her friend Ralph? Sadly, again she wondered if she would ever see him or any other of her friends in this lifetime.

Suddenly her ears pricked up, for she believed she had heard something, something very strange, something out of the ordinary. She timidly pushed aside the lid, and then she nervously sat upright in the box. Squinting her eyes, she tried hard to look around her, but she could see nothing whatsoever, as she was consumed in the thickest darkness.

Seconds later she once more heard another unidentified noise. It was coming from the other side of the room, and it continued on, as the sound got closer and closer to where she now sat rigid in the box.

"Who is there?" she fearfully cried out. "What do you want?"

Polly continued to stare into the darkness. Her heart was pounding loudly within her breast as she tried but hopelessly failed to remain calm. Seconds later she heard a strange but identifiable purring noise, and she breathed a sigh of relief, for she knew in that moment that she had nothing to be afraid of.

"Why, it must be a stray neighborhood cat," she contemplated.

Suddenly she felt the warm body of an animal as it sprang straight into her arms. She placed a hand on the breathing, furry lump and gently lowered the bundle into her lap. She was amazed to feel its warm heart beat as it snuggled up to her. Seconds later and she felt another similar creature jump into her lap and then curl up, then another and another.

Polly counted seven in all, and then once more she began to unnecessarily panic. What if they were not kittens but rather large rats? She wisely rebuked herself for being so fearful and stupid, for she reasoned that surely if they were rats, they would by now be tearing away at her flesh, just as they had when she had been tied up in the castle dungeons until dear, sweet Napoli had rescued her. Polly slowly and timidly placed her hands in her lap, and in seconds she could feel tiny little sticky tongues licking her fingers as they sought to make friendly contact with her.

Moments later a much larger creature jumped into the box and began to purr loudly. The creature made its way right up to her face before nuzzling into her neck. Polly reached out a hand to stroke the unidentified animal and immediately found her fingers making contact with a leather collar studded with little diamonds. In that moment it dawned on her that this was not a bunch of stray cats after all.

"Scoota, is that you?" she cried out. The gentle animal let out a large meow to identify herself. "And these sweet little balls are your kittens. Well done. You have seven precious and perfect little darlings," she tearfully cried.

Polly reached out for the lid and once more placed it over the box. In no time at all she felt both secure and warm, for the heat and love of all these friendly little furry balls as they nestled up together did much to fend off the coldhearted and frigidly chilling blizzard. Moments later, by some unforeseen miracle, Polly fell asleep, blissfully unaware that the raging storm was worsening by the moment.

As Polly and the kittens lay sound asleep, a strange, uninvited light came to hover over her. The mystical light began to sing the most beautiful, tenderly sweet lullaby, and it was so powerful in its brilliance that it instantly dispelled all darkness. It also became clear that the thermometer, which only minutes earlier had plunged to well below zero before finally freezing up with large jagged tentacles of ice, was once more on the move, only this time it raced upward, forcing the basement to become delightfully warm.

The magnificent light continued to hover over Polly, and it was clear to see that her face no longer held any fear, just a pure radiance.

Meanwhile, back indoors the only sound to be heard throughout the castle as well as its battlements was the painful sound that came from Mildred's horrendously loud snoring—and all this despite having a large peg firmly attached to the end of her nostrils.

Suddenly, out of nowhere there came a loud crack of thunder, followed closely by the largest flash of lightning, which whipped across the sky like a shining steel sword before slicing through their curtains and ricocheting off their bed.

"Argh. What was that?" Mildred screamed as both circular cucumber pieces fell from her eyes and tumbled into her lap as she hastily sat bolt upright in the bed. She then hurriedly removed the peg from the end of her nose, her whole body quaking with immeasurable terror.

"I have absolutely no idea," an equally scared Boritz was forced to admit as he too sat perfectly rigid in the bed.

"Well, I think I can still hear noises, so are you sure you locked all the doors?" Mildred asked out of concern, for she had retired to the bedroom much earlier than him due to an impending migraine.

"Yes, my dear, I most certainly did."

"And the children? I presume they are all safely tucked up in bed. And is the dog out patrolling the garden in order to protect us from all potential thieves and robbers?"

"No, dear. Pitstop is not outside on guard. I took the liberty of bringing him up to the bedroom, and so he is asleep at the end of our bed, for I could not find it in my heart to leave him out on such a night as this. And with regard all the children, well, with the exception of one they are all cozily tucked up tight in their beds."

"Excuse me, Boritz dear. Did I hear you right? Which of the children is still up at this unearthly hour of the night? Please don't tell me you've allowed a few of them to stay up to watch some ghastly and most gruesome horror film."

"Oh no, dearest. Would I do such a thing without first obtaining your approval and thus your consent?"

"Well, Boritz dear, I would sincerely hope not."

"Don't worry, dearest. There's actually no need for you to know or concern yourself, so please just place those limp pieces of cucumber back on both eyes, peg your nose, and then go back to sleep. There's a dear."

"Boritz, I'll do no such thing until you tell me all!" she furiously spat.

"Well, um…"

"Come on. Spit it out," she angrily demanded.

"Hmm. Well, I hardly need to tell you, for surely you can guess that it's Polly Brown who is still up."

"Why? What has she done this time 'round?" she cried, her eyes bulging from their sockets as she tried to take in this latest astonishing piece of information.

"Well, I decided that she should be punished, as she still refuses to come clean as to where and from whom she stole the ring."

"Boritz dear, tell me quickly: where on earth have you left her?"

"Oh, do I have to tell you?" he whined like a mischievous boy.

"Yes, of course you do, unless you wish for me to cancel our trip," she fumed as she deliberately folded her arms to send a clear message of her intentional defiance. "You know full well that I will not tolerate being left in the dark regarding such things."

"Well, um, I locked her down in the cellar. There, I've said it."

"Cellar?"

"Yes, you heard correct. The cellar, or tunnel, or basement—whatever you prefer to call it."

"Boritz, have you gone completely off your rocker? You miserable excuse for a man. I could cheerfully kill you for this. Listen to me right now! It's two thirty in the morning, and for all you know, the poor girl might well have frozen to death already. Oh, I could understand you leaving her down there on some perfectly warm and balmy night, but the temperature this night is seriously well below freezing, the wind is ferociously howling, and we are in the middle of a most tempestuous storm. So forgive me for pointing out that if anything untoward happens to her, we will be in horse dung right up to our scraggy little necks."

"Oh, sweet pea, don't be so melodramatic! There's really no need to get so horribly personal, for your neck might well resemble that of a seriously undernourished turkey, but mine is definitely not the least bit scraggy. In fact, it's quite firm considering my age," he snorted while stroking his neck to privately confirm that it was nothing as flabby as his wife's very unflattering rolls of flab that hung loosely round her aging neck.

"Boritz, are you even listening to me?"

"Yes, dear, I am, for in truth I have little to no choice in the matter, as you are painfully bellowing into my ear, which will surely suffer permanent damage if you don't calm right down and thus address me in more gentle, if not consolatory, tone of voice," he sulkily admonished.

"Listen, Boritz, this is an extremely bad time to be dishing out such a punishment, for you must surely realize that, heaven forbid, if anything bad were to happen to her—well, not only would we have to cancel the holiday, but you do realize we would lose most if not all our deposit?"

"And more," he quickly chipped in.

"Yes, and much more besides. Also, has it even crossed your feeble little mind that it could result in a police investigation that in no time at all could find the castle crawling with police officers as they determinedly search the castle for so-called evidence of some heinous crime?"

"You have made a good point, dear."

"Also, we surely would be forced to endure more frequent visits from nosy social workers, and you know how much we would hate for such a disagreeable thing to happen."

"Yes, you have another good point there," he miserably agreed.

"Also, we have managed to keep Thomas's death under wraps. Imagine for a minute what would happen if the truth concerning that young boy ever leaked out. Why, we'd never ever be able to hold our heads up high again. And try to think clearly when I say you have worked very hard to climb the social ladder, and at present you are highly thought of and esteemed by most in this town. Do you really want to lose all that over a stupid, mixed-up little brat?"

"No, dear. I don't believe I do."

"So in the light of all I have just said, it would pay you to stem your insatiable need for revenge and go get the girl before her fingers and toes fall off due to the bitter cold."

"Do I have to?" he very childishly moaned. "For even with my thick dressing gown wrapped around me tightly, as well as my scarf bound tightly round my neck, those icy winds will quickly bite straight through my vest, and I might surely suffer another catastrophic bout of pneumonia," he winged.

"Oh, Boritz, you can be such an irritating and feeble little wimp! You have never had anything more than a chesty little cough or cold in all the years I've known you," she harshly scolded.

"Well, that's not entirely true, dear, for I hasten to remind you that I did get a most terrible bout of influenza a few years back."

"Oh, yes, you did, and so did half the nation. And you survived and came through it, didn't you?" she scornfully reminded him.

"Yes, that's perfectly true, dearest, but I lost more than a few pounds due to my sudden loss of appetite, as well as my very high fever."

"Well, personally speaking, you could do with losing a few more pounds, so get your podgy and sweaty little body out of this bed, and go get her before I really lose my temper," she said through clenched teeth.

"All right, my dear. If you say so. But please do calm down, or I will be forced to spend the rest of the night in one of the guest bedrooms."

"Suit yourself," she angrily muttered as she struggled to place the cucumber slices back over her eyes. "And before you leave to go and release her, kindly pass me my bottle of pain relievers."

Boritz stumbled over to her dressing table in search of her pills.

"Dearest, the whole dressing table appears to resemble the medicine cabinet of the local pharmacy, for it is littered with a vast selection of medicine bottles and pills, many of which are considerably past their sell-by date. So you need to be more specific if I am to put my finger on the ones you are requesting I find."

"Specific? How specific do you need me to be?" she roared.

"Well, dearest, please advise me further as to which of these few hundred or so bottles you now so urgently require."

"Just find the one with the green label," she impatiently ordered.

"Very well, dear. And if against all odds I have the fortune to miraculously hit the jackpot, can I forget Polly altogether and just slip back under the sheets, as I am already feeling more than a little chilly?"

"Boritz, you pitiful little weasel, you'd best do as I say and go get her, or else!" were her last threatening words before securing the peg back on the end of her bright red nose as, in a state of frustration, she rolled over and proceeded to huffily pull the bedclothes up to her neck, a clear indication that all meaningful conversation was well and truly over.

After placing his dressing gown tightly 'round him, and with his thick scarf protecting his neck and chest, a bleary-eyed Boritz, with torch in hand, woke up Pitstop. The two of them were forced to trudge down the long corridors of the castle as they systematically checked every door and window to make sure they were properly locked, ensuring they were safe from intruders.

Finally they got 'round to addressing the matter of Polly, who needed to be released from his underground bunker and then regimentally escorted to her bed. Trudging slowly through the garden, his teeth began to furiously chatter, and his ears felt as though they were about to be savagely ripped from his head, such was the unbearable ferocity of the wind that harsh and very cruel winter's night.

After making his way across the garden, he stood outside the tunnel to once more fumble around for the right key to place into the lock "Brrr. It's so unbelievably cold." He winced as his breath visibly appeared to freeze right in front of his eyes.

Pitstop, who stood beside him, could only whimper his complete agreement.

Finally, the creaky door to the tunnel opened. Boritz thought he saw a faint light in the tunnel briefly, before it suddenly dispersed. Uncle Boritz, with Pitstop stalking in his shadow, carefully made his way down the narrow steps of the dank, dark room, only to be hit by the extreme warmth of the space. Seconds later saw him feeling thoroughly confused, as he began stripping off his scarf and dressing gown. He was convinced that he was about to pass out due to the intense heat. Feeling very unnerved, he slowly and cautiously made his way across the room, his torch light bouncing off the walls as he tried hard to get a feel of where everything was situated, Polly included.

Boritz blinked. He then took in a mighty sharp breath and blinked again, though this time around more through shock, as his torch light began to convey to him something of the destruction of his beloved handcrafted coffins. He began to sway back and forth as, feeling deeply mortified, he almost fainted, for with his own eyes he stood and witnessed his beloved prize project, his meticulous craftsmanship, his labor of love, strewn like discarded packaging all across the basement floor.

Shaken to the core of his being, he still managed to stagger like a desperately stricken man over to where the upturned coffins lay abandoned, and with a long stick he carefully pushed one of the lids over to one side. Looking down with his torch in his hand, he was once more visibly shocked to see the laid-out corpse of Polly Brown sound asleep and surrounded by many equally docile furry balls of fluff.

<hr />

With the full force of his torch light shining on her face, Polly gave a loud yawn, and then shaking her head, she opened her eyes, only to be met by an eyeful of Pitstop's slimy drool. As Polly wiped the slobber from her cheek, she then realized that the other face peering down at her was the distraught and ashen face of Uncle Boritz.

"Is it morning already?" she innocently asked, giving an almighty yawn.

"Quite what have you done to my beloved coffins?" he whispered in a hysterically high, strangled voice. As per usual, the question was rhetorical, for Polly was given no time at all in which to answer.

"Girl, this beggars belief. I'll have you know that the idea behind these coffins took me years to conceive before constructing, *and* all this was done with my own bare hands," he sorrowfully lamented. "Yes, these creations were intended to help make my fortune. So what took me years to create and then implement, you, girl, have intentionally destroyed in less than a night. What plausible explanation could you possibly come up with for such needless, unwarranted destruction?" he hoarsely whispered.

"I am so sorry, Uncle, but I had to do something, and quick; otherwise, I would not have survived the night, for I could well have died from the cold," she reasoned.

"Girl, I have little choice but to leave this matter for the present, but you can rest assured that I will give this latest atrocity my full attention, if not first thing tomorrow then as soon as I return from my holiday," he roared. "Hmm. This fact should surely have you quaking in your boots, for I intend to make you pay fully for all this absurdly senseless and intentionally destructive behavior, for these coffins were my babies and therefore very precious to me," he sorrowfully lamented.

"I'm truly sorry, really I am," Polly quietly sighed, but she could see that Uncle Boritz was indeed in no mood to listen, let alone forgive her.

"Now, get up, girl, and get to your bed quickly before I change my mind and leave you down here for the rest of the night," he snorted.

Polly obeyed, as she carefully picked up each kitten and gently placed each of them to one side before standing up to quietly step out of the damaged coffin. "Uncle Boritz, I am so sorry, truly I am," she muttered remorsefully, as with head down she attempted to pull out all the stuffing from her shirt and shirt sleeves before turning her attention to the stuffing that was still down her trousers.

"Now get out of my sight," he spat, his whole torso visibly shaking.

Polly obeyed, and after walking across the floor, she began climbing the steps that led to the open cellar door.

"Just one minute!" Uncle Boritz bellowed as he quickly shone the torch in her direction.

Polly stopped in her tracks and turned once more to face her enraged uncle.

"I do believe that you still have something on your odious body that belongs to me," he thundered.

Polly looked confused.

With his eyes raised toward the heavens and using his index finger, Uncle Boritz began tapping the side of his head repeatedly. Polly continued to look perplexed. It then dawned on her that she rather foolishly still had a long piece of the silky material tied around her forehead. She sheepishly unwound the band from her head and held out her hand to pass it directly back to him.

"Here, shall I bring it down to you?" she most innocently asked.

"No, girl, just drop it on the ground, and then do as I say and get out of my sight before I do something I might live to regret," he snarled through clenched teeth.

Polly wasted no time, as despite the cold and dark she raced full pelt across the garden in her desperate endeavor to get as far away from her uncle as she could. She did not even look to the left or to the right until she believed that she was safely out of harm's way, and that meant crawling, fully clothed, into her bed and then hiding away under the blanket for the remainder of the night.

Early the next morning Polly sat in her bed as she quietly and anxiously flicked through her dictionary trying to look up certain specific words. "Ah, here we are: *belligerent*. The dictionary says 'hostile, aggressive, ready to start a fight, or go to war.' Oh, dear. How can this be, for I have always hated anything and everything to do with war?" she wailed as she thought back to her many history lessons.

She then moved on as she tried looking up yet another of the many cruel words that in his anger her Uncle Boritz had called her. "Ahh, here it is: *impudent*. Right. This is the correct page; now where is it? Here we are. It says 'rude, showing a lack of respect.' Oh dear," she sighed. "Next, *recalcitrant*. Ahh, here it is: 'stubbornly resisting authority, hard to handle.' Oh, goodness. I am turning out to be such a problem to the whole wide world," she cried, slamming the dictionary shut before throwing it at the wall as she vented her overwhelming frustration. Luckily for her, the other girls in the room failed to be disturbed as, lost to the world, they remained deep in their slumber.

A now thoroughly inconsolable Polly threw her head back down on the pillow and pulled the thin blanket over her head as she then quietly sobbed into Langdon's soft, furry body, all the while lamenting as to just how troubling a nuisance she had become to the whole wide world.

THE TROUBLE WITH POLLY BROWN

Chapter Fifteen
WILL MEETS THE LIKELY LADS

*P*OLLY KNEW SHE would once more miss the bus if she did not hurry and get straight into her uniform. She made it down the stairs, only to bump straight into James, who was also running late if he were to catch the bus.

She immediately noticed that he had red rims around his eyes, and she needed little help to work out that her brother was still feeling very distraught that his precious models not only had been confiscated but most likely for an undetermined period of time.

"If you wanted to say good-bye to Uncle Boritz and Aunt Mildred, you're five minutes too late, for they've already left," James miserably confided as he sat on the stairs, his hands cupping his downtrodden face.

"James, if the truth be known, I'm very relieved to have missed them," Polly honestly admitted. "So let's head off together to the bus stop," she suggested as she attempted to put a friendly arm around his shoulder.

James shook his head. "No, Polly. You go on ahead, for if I miss the bus, then so what?"

"Come on, James. Remember that Uncle threatened terrible consequences for those who dared misbehave while he is away."

"I really don't care anymore," he briskly retorted, his face etched with pain. "There is nothing he could do that could hurt me more than taking away my model planes," he moaned, another anguished look washing over his young face.

"Look, James, maybe they'll have such a fantastic holiday that Uncle will want to be kind and give them back on his return," Polly stated, as she attempted to be more than a little over-optimistic in her forecast.

"I doubt that very much, for we all know that when he's mad, well then, he's out for blood," James glumly retorted.

Polly could clearly see that her brother was feeling very depressed, and in this sad moment in time she knew that any words of comfort that spilled from her lips would only seem trite and irrelevant. So, as usual, she had no choice but to remain helpless and, so, feel utterly useless.

"Come on. I'll race you to the bus," Polly yelled as she grabbed hold of his jacket and began to pull him in the general direction of the front door.

James was having none of it. "No, Polly. Go away. Please leave me alone. You go on ahead, for I meant what I said. I truly no longer care what happens to me."

All this left Polly with little choice than to leave him behind and head as quickly as she could to catch the school bus. After racing down the street as fast as her legs could carry her, she was relieved to see the bus was still in the parking bay with other school children still waiting to board, and this immediately lifted her spirits.

With both Aunt Mildred and Uncle Boritz away for the next two weeks, Polly felt like a huge weight had been lifted off her shoulders. She still had the long list of tedious chores that she had to get through every night, but somehow even these did not seem quite so tiresome.

She was also able to sneak out of the castle on numerous occasions, mostly to see her new friend, Will, but on one occasion it was for an entirely different and very personal reason.

Polly had promised herself for some time now that she must pay an impromptu visit to the tearoom, and that visit was now seriously long overdue. She needed to see for herself that the name of the tearoom really had been changed from The Copper Kettle to Polly's Pantry. She hated to admit that she was equally curious to see what the new owners, who went by the name of the Kindlysides, really looked like. After all, with a surname like that, they could hardly be as mean and mealy minded as the Greedols, could they?

"No, surely not," she mumbled under her breath as she hastily made her way down the road, heading for the tearoom.

As Polly stood outside the tearoom looking up, she had to admit that she felt tickled pink to see that the tearoom really had been

THE TROUBLE WITH POLLY BROWN

renamed and was now called Polly's Pantry. However, as she stood outside looking in, she felt a mixture of both fear as well as anticipation, because up until now she had never met the new owners. Oh, she had meant to pay them a visit, but getting time off from all her duties was a chore in itself. Looking through the large glass window, it was clear that little had been done to alter the tearoom. It still looked much the same as it had always done, quaint and old fashioned, with lots of teapots adorning the shelves, as well as endless brass and copper bric-a-brac, which all the tourists begged to purchase, the American ones in particular.

Polly took a deep breath as she then tried to muster up the necessary courage to enter the building. Once through the door, she was immediately greeted by an extremely cheerful-looking waitress.

"Hello, my dear. May I help you?" the pleasantly plump waitress politely asked, her voice betraying a very unusual accent that Polly instantly realized was extremely rare in these parts.

"I hope so, but before you help me, may I be so bold as to ask your name and where you are originally from?" Polly brazenly inquired.

The kindly waitress removed her thin-framed glasses in order to get a better look at Polly.

"My name is Mrs. Moira Muldoon, so pray, tell me, wee young lady, by what name do you like to be known?"

"Oh, me? Well, my name is Polly Esther Brown."

"Well, that's a lovely name, my dear."

"Oh, trust me, Mrs. Muldoon, when I say it isn't. Yes, it's horrible, and I so hate it. Yes, I hate it very much," Polly said, lowering her eyes as she spoke.

"Now the bright light has gone out of your eyes, deary. I suspect much has gone on in your young life for you to hate your name with such fervency."

"Yes, that's very true," Polly sadly admitted.

"Now, deary, you wished to know what part of Scotland I come from, did you not?"

"Yes, do please tell me," Polly said, perking up again.

"Well, as you asked so nicely, I am from a wee place in Scotland called Dundee."

"Oh, that sounds like such a lovely place to live, although I've never been there. Truth is, I've never been anywhere, and if I'm to be honest, anywhere sounds a whole heap better than where I am," Polly ruefully stated.

"Well, Polly dear, you're still very young, so you've got years ahead of you in which to travel. But don't make the mistake of thinking things will be better elsewhere, for remember this: wherever we go, we take ourselves with us; so make sure somewhere else is not just a badly thought-out escape plan."

Polly lowered her head as she considered the kind lady's wise words.

Mrs. Muldoon quickly moved on. "Well, Polly, I'm sure you'll get to Dundee sooner or later."

"Oh, I do hope so, but tell me, isn't that where they make Dundee cake, tartan cloth, and pots of marmalade?" Polly brightly asked.

"Oh, and a lot more," the delightful lady laughed. "But tell me, Polly, what brings you here, and how can I help you?"

"Well, a mutual friend told me that it was important to come and say hello to the new owners."

"You mean the Kindlysides, don't you, deary? But if you're hoping to fill in a job application form, then sadly you are much too late, for the extra waitress position has just been filled."

Polly continued to look past the kindly middle-aged lady, as she was not the least bit bothered by this latest piece of information.

"Yes, that's their name. But I am not looking for a job. I just need to know if they are available to speak with me," Polly sincerely stated.

"Well, sadly, you've just missed them, for they have only just popped out to do a few wee errands," the waitress informed Polly as she straightened her already smooth and pristine white lace apron. Polly noticed her skin was flawless skin and her hair was rinsed pink.

"Oh, dear. I was so hoping to meet with them," Polly sniffed, her voice betraying bitter disappointment. "You say both of them are out?"

"Yes, deary. I'm sorry to say they won't be back for quite a wee while, so they've left me in charge. 'Tis a shame you didn't think to make an appointment."

"Oh, yes. I know I should have, but I have no access to a phone and so very little time after school and..." Polly's voice trailed off. "Mrs.

Muldoon, at the risk of sounding very rude, are you really sure they both are out on urgent errands?"

"Oh yes, deary, for they do everything together, as they cannot bear to be apart, no, not for one minute. They really are joined at the hip, so to speak. Hmm. It's quite touching, really."

"Are you joking when you say they are never apart?" Polly asked as she broke into a girlish giggle.

"No, deary. Never, ever," the kind lady briskly replied, showing the teeniest hint of annoyance at her integrity being questioned, and by one so young as Polly.

"Oh," said Polly, "that's very nice. So I imagine they must be newly-weds then?"

"Well, not really, deary, unless of course you count being married for forty odd years as being newly wed," Mrs. Muldoon solemnly stated as once more she smoothed down her apron. "Yes, you can't miss them, for they walk around town arm in arm like newlyweds, greeting every passerby as though they were some long-lost acquaintance. It sometimes turns their 'popping out for errands' into quite lengthy procedures. Hmm. I believe that since this wonderful couple arrived in town, they have made such a difference. Yes, such a difference," she stated dreamily.

"What do you mean by 'difference,' Mrs. Muldoon?" a very wide-eyed Polly now dared to ask.

"Well, deary, everyone in this town seems so much happier and friendlier, and the customers who frequent this tearoom are now remarkably overgenerous with the tips they leave on the table. I've never known anything like it, and Polly dear, trust me when I say that I've worked in many a restaurant in my time. The customers coming in here are, without exception, so delightfully polite. There is never any conversation that is at the expense of others, and it has even been known for some kind customers to offer their help with the washing up!"

"Mrs. Muldoon, now I know for sure you're clowning around with me!" Polly retorted, as she allowed herself the freedom to break into a fit of the giggles.

"Laugh as much as you like, deary. All I know is that since this couple came to town, the sky is much bluer, the grass is greener, the flowers are blooming at double—no, triple—their usual speed. And as for the birds in the trees, well, they have not stopped singing, not even for a minute. So no, deary, I am not joking, for there is something very special about this couple. Hmm, something I can't quite put my finger on," she stated, her eyes moistening and welling up with tears as she continued to speak with such affection about her employers.

"I'm sorry I had a sudden fit of the giggles, Mrs. Muldoon, for I have no wish to upset you," Polly insisted.

"That's perfectly all right, Polly. Now don't tell anybody this, but sometimes I go home and sit down on my rocking chair just to have a good weep, because never in my life have I been treated with such thorough kindness."

All this made Polly most intrigued, as well as more desperate than ever to make their acquaintance.

"Hmm. It's as though they are not from around these parts."

"Mrs. Muldoon, please don't speak in riddles, but tell me plainly: quite what do you mean?"

"Well, don't repeat this deary, but it's as though they came from another planet far away in the heavens."

"Another planet! Mrs. Muldoon, have you been drinking?"

"Ooh, no, deary. I have not had a drop from the bottle for many a year. All I am suggesting is that this special couple is from somewhere else, although where that place might be at this moment in time I am not too sure!"

"Really?" Polly muttered.

"Yes, deary. There really is no earthly way to describe them, for I believe them to be simply perfect."

"Ooh," was all Polly now cared to comment, for she was feeling utterly enthralled by all she was hearing.

"You see, little one, they are so, so in love, and I, for one, have never worked for such kind people, people who have no need to daily remind me of my lowly position in life. No, in fact, Polly dear, they tell me every day how perfectly delighted they are to have found me. Now, answer me, Polly dearest, how wonderful is that?"

"Mrs. Muldoon, they do indeed sound absolutely wonderful—in fact, beyond perfection to me," Polly cried out. "Yes, so perfect that I can hardly bear to hear another word about them. And by giving me such a wonderful and vivid picture of how awfully nice they truly are, you have just made my need to meet with them more urgent than ever."

"Aye, my dear. Patience. You will surely meet them in time. For my part, I promise to let them know that you called."

"Promise me, Mrs. Muldoon, that you will not forget to tell them that I called, as I wished to make their acquaintance," Polly said with a heartfelt urgency as she grabbed hold of the poor and unsuspecting woman's hand to give it a hearty shake, similar to the one she had previously given to the equally unsuspecting, poor mailman.

"Promise me. Please promise me."

Mrs. Muldoon was forced on the spot to promise many times over before Polly finally loosened her ridiculously tight grip of the poor lady's right hand.

Despite the disappointment of having still not met the Kindlysides, Polly found herself feeling a strange sort of contentment as she raced home. She had just heard firsthand from the lovely Mrs. Muldoon that the new owners were extremely kind and considerate in all their dealings, so hopefully the next time she was able to call at the tearoom, the Kindlysides would be around and therefore available to speak with her.

With her guardians still away on holiday, Polly began to experience a new release of joy inside, as for the first time ever she knew what it felt like to feel carefree without having to fear what might lie ahead when she got home to the castle. It's true she still had to deal with the old battle-ax Miss Scrimp, but truth be told, she was nothing more than a pussycat when compared with Uncle Boritz. Polly even managed a new spring in her step as she went about her mundane evening chores.

Over the next couple of weeks Polly was also able to slip away after school to spend a small amount of time getting to know her new friend, Will, much better. As a result of all of this, she could now freely admit that finally something very good had turned up in her otherwise pitifully sad life. Will appeared not only to fully understand her, but he was also the only person on Planet Earth who seemed happy to want to spend the time to get to know her. Polly felt a new glow deep inside that mirrored her newfound hope.

Unbeknown to Polly, there was someone else who was equally interested in her relationship with Will. In fact, she was so interested she
was making it her personal duty to record the date and time of every
secretive meeting that took place between the two of them.

Being the perfect detective that she truly was, she even took covert
photographs of the pair together, not that they were doing anything
that could be considered unacceptable and untoward but purely
because the more information she would be able to pass on, then the
more handsome the reward. She freely admitted to hating Polly with
a passion, so to see Polly acting so footloose and fancy free was more
than enough to make her blood boil. She therefore considered it to be
her God-given duty to spy on Polly and report back all she saw and
heard, thereby personally seeing to it that Polly's newfound happiness
be very short lived.

Alarmingly, due to this unacknowledged inner rage, her hands
began shaking badly, as with a sharpened pencil she hurriedly scribbled down the time and date of this latest secret interlude between Will
and Polly. As she wrote down all she saw, she sadly considered this to
be an excellent opportunity to add some extra, very lurid details of
her own choosing; otherwise, she might not have enough compelling
evidence to get Uncle's blood to boiling point at the very least.

Sadly, even knowing that Polly would face punishment for this
secretive liaison was not enough, for it still left Gailey struggling to
understand quite what the attraction was. After all, why should smelly,
ugly, lice-ridden Polly "Fester" Brown have such a handsome older boy
paying her such attention, when she, Gailey Gobbstopper, had never
been shown such adoration by anyone? This most definitely had to be
stopped at all costs, and Polly should and would be severely punished
for having the temerity to sneak behind her guardians' backs to yet
again indulge in clandestine meetings with an unknown boy of highly
dubious origins, according to the latest gossip being bandied around
the school playground. That gossip not only spoke of a haunted
mansion overrun with thousands of viciously rabid cats but also spoke

of both murder and madness that ran amok throughout the new boy's family history.

With all this in mind, Gailey had made it her mission to find out as much as she could about the mysterious new boy, and she was delighted to report back that having left no stone unturned, nothing looked remotely good regarding his ancestral background or their recent move to the area.

Yes, Polly Brown would indeed pay very dearly for this latest breach of conduct, or so she hoped with all her jealous heart.

The final bell rang loudly down the long corridors, informing all pupils that the day had finally come to an end. Polly waited until the classroom had emptied before picking up her schoolbag to leave. This little procedure had become routine over the past two weeks, for she knew that Will would be aimlessly hanging about by the school gates, secretly hoping to catch her before she left for the train station and home. She knew he would sidle alongside and then beg her to come back to his place, and she also knew she would show some resistance or give some flimsy excuse for not going before finally caving in to his demands. Today would be no different.

"Hi, Polly. How was your day?" he said as he playfully danced around her, his school jacket casually slung over his shoulder.

"I'm so glad you asked, Will, because for once it has been a very good day, leaving me feeling happy and therefore surprisingly content," Polly replied, her glowing cheeks instantly betraying her, as they automatically went a ridiculous bright red as her eyes finally met Will's. Oh, how she wished that she would not blush so easily.

"Well, that's great, because you're obviously in a good mood. And when you're in a good mood, you never hesitate to say yes to all my very reasonable requests."

"Is that so?" Polly mused.

"Yes, so hopefully, without having to get down on both knees and beg, I would very much like it if you would quickly say yes to coming back to my place for a while."

"Hmm," was all that came forth from Polly as she played along with him.

"Look, Polly, *yes* is a very easy word to say. Quite simply, all you have to do is open your mouth and spell out *y-e-s*," he said as he playfully took hold of both her cheeks to squeeze as he attempted to force any form of agreement from her.

Polly laughed. "I daresay I could come back, Will, although I cannot be too late. Hmm. On the other hand, maybe it would be best if I said no this time 'round, for I am so behind on my household chores, as well as my homework," she complained.

"Oh, don't worry. I promise to help you with all your homework. So, come on; say you'll come. You won't regret it," he begged and pleaded.

"Oh, all right then, but I can only come for a short while," Polly firmly stated, as she then unexpectedly grabbed hold of his arm to link her arm through his.

Back at Will's house, they set about making a nice pot of Darjeeling tea for his overly demanding mother, as well as a ham and cheese sandwich for his equally angry, bedridden brother before walking up some further stairs with glass tumblers of lemonade in hand as they headed for their secret place in order to continue on with their exciting and new formed friendship in private.

On this occasion, Polly found herself to be in a very talkative mood.

"Will, I have never shared anything with you concerning a very special place called Piadora, but now I'd very much like to."

Will placed his glass of lemonade to one side and came to sit down beside her, as he showed great interest in all she had to say.

First she spoke of some of the unmentionable things that were taking place most days behind the castle walls, events such as the one she had just experienced when she was forced to spend most of the night sleeping in the homemade coffin. Will was naturally aghast that such things should ever take place. Polly was glad to finally have someone who listened to her. She was also relieved to see that he did not even attempt to justify her uncle's actions by suggesting they were in any way normal. Instead, he manifested genuine outrage that Polly and all the other children were being subjected to such harsh and cruel treatment.

"What about his own children? Does he punish them in the same way?"

"Don't be silly. Of course not!"

"You said once that his children live totally separate lives from all the foster children, and this included attending different schools. So do any of them ever step in and say anything?"

"Well, no. Sometimes they are not even around when things happen, but Will, you have to understand that the youngest one, Jeremy, is less than a year old. Then there's John, who is only seven. Now, Joseph, well, he is eleven. Then there's Jake, who is thirteen; Alan is fourteen, nearly fifteen; and the eldest is Andrew, and he is sixteen years old. He goes to a private school that is some distance from home, and so he only comes back for the odd weekend break, as well as the school holidays."

"All right, Polly, but what about the rest. Do they mingle with you?"

"Not really, because they live in a different wing of the castle, so their lives are very different from ours, even down to eating very different food at mealtimes. Yes, they are the really lucky ones," she sniffed.

"Polly, we need to get you and the others some help," he insisted, coughing out loud as his strained voice spasmodically began croaking with emotion.

Polly placed a hand over his. "Will, don't be daft. What I told you is for your ears only, and so must remain a secret, never to be shared. I have in the past been seriously punished for disloyalty, so if any of this ever got out...Trust me, Uncle Boritz is on the friendliest terms with the whole wide world."

"Now you're speaking crazy!"

"Well, anyone who is anybody," she said, giving a resigned sigh. "For sadly, anyone who reaches into our lives or has any connection with us immediately becomes his new best friend. This includes the police force, as well as the headmaster of both junior and senior schools. So Will, tell me straight: where in the world can I turn for help? Even Dr. Glumchops is his golfing partner, and he comes without fail to the castle once a week to socialize and enjoy a traditional afternoon tea with Uncle Boritz. So it goes without saying that anyone who cares to visit the castle will find their name and phone number written into his private address book pronto. That's always how it works," she rather despondently stated.

"What about the social services? They surely have a duty of care to you all."

"What social services? Believe me, Will, when I tell you that I have hardly ever seen anyone from their department. It's as if they have forgotten that we even exist."

———•••———

"Utterly disgraceful! In fact, it's deplorable," was all Will was capable of muttering to all he was being told.

There were times when, to be honest, he truly wanted to stop her in order to challenge her truthfulness and recollections, because much of what she spoke of seemed utterly beyond belief. However, something prevented him from going down this path, and this was surely because in the short time he had known Polly, he had come to believe that she was an unusual person of deep integrity. That is why he had chosen to invest in her alone; he knew with all his heart that she was very different from the crowd.

"Will, I want to leave the subject of the castle and go on to tell you about something else that you might find even more far-fetched, if not quite unbelievable."

Will nodded, as once more he picked up his glass to take a long sip of lemonade.

"Will, when I was truly at my lowest ebb, I met a couple of very likable tramps. One of the gentlemen was called Hodgekiss; the other, Ralph. They invited me to take a dangerous journey and come join them for tea in the most wonderful kingdom that you could ever imagine."

As Will availed himself to listen to tale after tale, he suddenly found himself feeling slightly uncomfortable, but even though it took everything he had, he knew he must remain calm and collected and give her the freedom to express all that she felt she needed to.

Finally, he interrupted her.

"Polly, if this so-called place truly exists, then how come no one has ever heard of it?"

"Oh, but they have. It's just that most who have been there keep it to themselves for the simple reason that it all seems so ridiculously implausible that such a place could truly exist," a wide-eyed Polly insisted as she placed her glass to her mouth to take a long sip of lemonade. "But listen to me, Will. I have two friends, Justin Kase and Justin Thyme, and if I was to introduce these lads to you, they would surely confirm most of what I am telling you, for the simple reason that they too tried to climb Piadora. However, they refused to go with our guide, preferring to make the dangerous expedition alone, without any professional help. As a result of their stupidity, they had a terrible accident that landed both of them in Hope in Your Heart Hospital."

Polly didn't even stop to catch her breath, as tripping over her words she raced on excitedly as she allowed her very dramatic story to continue unfolding. "And it was only because of Dr. Loveheart, as well as dear, sweet Dr. Darling, that the lads came through their terrible ordeal unscathed and—"

"Whoa there. Hold on, Polly, and for goodness sake do yourself a favor by taking a deep breath, will you?" Will demanded, as he was now finding it virtually impossible to keep a straight face.

"Dr. Darling? Dr. Loveheart? Are you kidding me? Next you'll be telling me about another doctor named Dr. Sweetheart!"

"No, Will, you're just not listening to me. There was no Dr. Sweetheart on the mountain; just Dr. Darling and Dr. Loveheart. I'm not kidding, for both doctors were absolutely wonderful and so awfully kind. Then there is Aazi. As soon as a letter finally arrives from him, you will know for certain that I am telling you the whole truth and nothing but the truth."

"Calm down, Polly. You really do have my undivided attention, but you must understand that when you tell me that your climb up Mount Everest was just the practice climb, you must surely realize that this is all getting very hard to swallow!" he stated, giving a small but very telling grimace.

"I know it is, Will, but I promise I would not lie to you. Our guide, who went by the name Sir Eggmond Hoolari, was quite the madman, and to be perfectly honest, this verbose gentleman almost drove me to the cliff of complete despair, for he was so unbelievably stupid and arrogant."

Will listened on without uttering another word because he felt physically sickened, as though he were sinking in quicksand. Therefore to interject and question her very absurd story any further would be utterly futile. She was, he believed, so convinced of her story that black could be white, and she'd readily and willingly believe it.

"Will, he even abandoned me on the mountain when he found there was not enough room for everyone in the helicopter and they needed to get Aazi to the hospital as quickly as they possibly could," she spluttered as once more she began tripping over her words.

"What? Polly, you cannot be serious! This professional climber, along with a bunch of nurses and doctors, left you, a child, to die alone in the freezing cold on a mountain?"

"Yes, he did, Will. And believe me when I say that I nearly did die. I mean, after he placed the stretcher with Aazi in the helicopter, there really was only room for a few more, and that's why he left me. I promise you with all my heart that all this is perfectly true."

Will swallowed hard. For the first time since he first set eyes on her in the school corridor, he was finding this latest incredulous story just far too difficult to digest, let alone believe.

"Polly, I long to believe you; really, I do. But your story gets more and more fanciful with each and every word you utter. So tell me you're just playing me for the fool, and I will understand."

"Stop it, Will, for I am being serious. I need you to believe me; really I do. Look, if I introduce you to the two Justins, who are such good friends—and Will, believe me when I say they are truly inseparable—I know that they will readily confirm and so validate my story. Then will you believe me?"

"Well, I guess I'll have no choice other than to try and believe you, and trust me, Polly, when I say that I really do want to believe you," Will nervously replied, feeling momentarily distracted as he tried and failed dismally to come to terms with all the craziness he was being asked to swallow down and fully believe.

If the truth were to be known, he sorely wished that today of all days he had not invited her back to his house. Then maybe, just maybe they could have carried on as normal. But now after her very disturbing revelations concerning Sir Eggmond Hoolari, Mrs. O'Brien with her school for princesses in training, Piadora itself—oh, as well as Hodgekiss and the lovable vagrant Ralph—well, he was left seriously wondering if there was even the slightest possibility of resuming their friendship with any sense of normality.

As he sat back and studied her facial features afresh, Will felt numbed, as well as lost for words, for he sincerely believed that she had unwittingly given him every reason under the sun to end their friendship, or at the very least put it on hold. He already had a slightly demented mother, as well as a seriously depressed brother; therefore, he felt in no position to take on any further heavy burdens. So, sadly, in that moment he felt incapable of dismissing these new concerns regarding Polly's credibility and, alas, her mental stability as well.

Polly excitedly rambled on with her remarkable story, all the while remaining completely innocent and therefore oblivious to this latest, fresh crisis she had just caused.

"That's settled, then. Tomorrow I will find both boys, and we can take it from there. But for now, Will, I need your complete attention, as we need to concentrate fully on my homework before I have to rush back to the castle," she stated brightly as she then hurriedly opened her exercise book to begin.

True to her word, the next day after school found Polly racing over toward Will, who was nervously standing alone by the school gates. The reason for his agitation was simple: should this be the occasion for him to tell Polly that their close friendship was over, or should he just leave for home and let Polly work out the reason for herself? The hideous turmoil he felt inside left him feeling both sad and confused.

"Will, I've finally located both boys, and as always, they are together in the café at the train station. So come on. Let's race over to the station and catch them before their train gets in."

Will, in his endeavor to bring this nonsense to its natural finality, nodded his head in agreement.

Minutes later and despite being out of breath, Polly and Will burst into the café. Polly rushed over to where two boys were seated, and, in spite of the fact that they were in the company of two females, she overexuberantly began to greet them and explain to Will which was Justin Kase and which was Justin Thyme.

Both boys were taken aback by her. However, Polly, never one to concern herself with small courtesies, continued to get straight to the point. "Hi there, guys. I need a quick word with you both."

Both Justins appeared pretty annoyed with her. "Not now. Can't you see we're busy? So buzz off," Justin Kase rudely whispered in a voice loud enough for her and Will to hear.

"Yes, all right. But boys, I need you to meet my good friend, Will," Polly anxiously continued.

"Yes, yes. We'll talk to you both later if we must, but for now leave us alone, for we've just met these lovely girls, so don't mess it up for us," Justin Thyme muttered through clenched teeth.

Will could clearly see that her sense of timing was drastically out and tried hard to coax Polly to leave the boys well alone and come with him, but Polly was having none of it.

"Boys, please tell Will about Sir Eggmond Hoolari and how you guys went ahead of us to climb Mount Piadora," she begged.

The boys continued to ignore Polly.

"If nothing else, please tell Will about your accident," she breathlessly pleaded. "Look, Justin, you've still got a scar from your terrible head wound," she stated, pointing at Justin's Kase's deeply scarred forehead.

Neither boy appeared the slightest bit amused by Polly's refusal to leave them alone, and they continued on chatting amongst themselves, oblivious to her. After all, Will thought, they had tried hard to be reasonable, and they had made it quite plain that they were too busy to talk, for they were at a very critical stage in their chat with two extremely gorgeous girls.

Both boys looked up, and Justin Thyme was the first to speak. "Look, I don't know who you are or why you are speaking such utter tosh! I, for one, have never met you or your friend Sir Egghead, or whatever his name is. So do us all a big favor and leave us alone."

Polly stood silent and dumbfounded, unable to hide the look of great shock that was clearly visible to all as Justin Thyme continued on.

"I can also categorically state that as I am very unfit, I've never as much as climbed a mole hill let alone a mountain. So, young lady, you are suffering from a case of mistaken identity, for you really do have the wrong people. Get it into your thick head that we don't want to talk to you, so push off," he exasperatedly expressed through gritted teeth.

Polly drew breath before letting out a gasp that genuinely conveyed her pure disbelief.

"Justin, don't be silly. Of course you know me," she cried as she quickly gave Will a friendly dig in the ribs, as if to convey that all this was just a friendly game that the boys were playing on her.

"Guys, come on now. Stop messing around, for you saved me and Jessica when we were lost in the desert. Come on. Tell Will here the truth," she cried out in desperation.

"Come on, Polly. Let's get out of here." Will sniffed, as he was now feeling very embarrassed by her.

But Polly refused to leave, even after he grabbed hold of her arm and gently attempted to pull her away from the group to head out of the door. "No, Will. Let go of me, for I'm not leaving until these lads finally admit the truth. Justin Kase, tell your friend off; for he is just fooling around, isn't he?"

Justin Kase looked up and shook his head. "Buzz off, for we've all had enough! We've tried to be nice, but for some reason you won't listen. Neither of us has ever met you before, and we have no reason to ever want to get to know you either, as you're obviously completely deranged. Also, this scar is from a biking accident that I had two years ago, so I would suggest that both you and your friend do the right thing by leaving this café to get the next train out of here."

"Yes, go back home to your silly little fantasies, for if you continue bothering us, I warn you now, things might just get ugly," Justin Thyme added.

Polly looked both boys directly in the eye, and both boys surreptitiously looked away. She then stood, arms folded, shaking her head to express her utter disbelief.

Will could tell she had really believed that the boys would help her out, and instead they had contributed to making a complete fool of her. As Polly turned to leave, she was finally forced to admit that it was she alone who had made a complete fool of herself.

"Will, I'm so sorry. I know I have been incredibly stupid. I feel so humiliated. Just take me home, please," she whispered through a mist of tears, her voice showing great strain. Will obliged by taking the same train and then walking her the distance to the castle.

As they continued the walk together but alone, neither uttered a single word to the other. The sky above them quickly turned the most oppressive dark gray, and the sun, which moments earlier had shone so gloriously, instantly disappeared completely behind thundering, rolling clouds, as though it were going into premature mourning for the loss of a unique and once beautiful friendship.

"Take care, Polly," was all Will felt capable of muttering as with a seriously burdened heart he left her at the castle gates to walk the long distance home.

"Will, I'm telling you the truth, really I am," she cried out after him.

Will pretended not to listen as he slunk away with his hands thrust deep into his trouser pockets and his head and upper torso stooped low as though he were carrying the weight of the whole world on his shoulders. With each sad and lonely step he took, he tried hard to give serious thought to all he had heard that night. As he went over and over all she had told him, it all had him feeling very perplexed and wondering quite where to go from here!

"Hey, Will. See you at school tomorrow. Perhaps we can meet up at lunchtime," a desperate Polly called out after him. "Please save me a seat in the dining hall."

Will made no attempt to turn around and reply. He just continued on walking.

Chapter Sixteen
NOTHING BUT THE TRUTH

*A*S POLLY OPENED the front door of the castle, she was caught off guard as she was greeted by much noise and excitement. "Polly, guess what? Aunt and Uncle are finally home, and they've brought us all a wonderful present of some strawberry-flavored candy. Aren't they the best?" a sticky-faced Bertha Banoffee ecstatically shouted.

"Great!" was all Polly managed to mutter, as Bertha then began dancing in circles around Polly before rather grossly plunging the end of her thick candy stick straight back into her strawberry-smeared mouth to continue on with the sucking.

Polly's heart sank as she considered how little it took to get all the children into a crazed, euphoric state. She also knew deep in her heart that in no time at all things would indeed be back to normal, and ten, twenty, or a hundred sugary candy sticks could never even begin to sweeten that bitter truth.

Polly wearily climbed the stairs and forlornly headed toward the dormitory to change from her uniform into her work clothes. In truth, she had no need of candy; all she hoped was that no one had missed her or realized she was late home. This time she was very fortunate.

As the evening drew to a close, she was pleasantly surprised to discover that she only had the shoes left to clean and then she could head off to bed. As she stood in a freezing cold room rubbing and polishing each pair of shoes until they shone, she found herself feeling quite concerned that Will had seemed so terribly tired and withdrawn on the way home. She could only hope to put things right the next day.

Suddenly the door opened, and she could hear the pitter-patter of feet as well as the heavy breathing that could only come from one source, and that was Pitstop!

"Well, good evening to you, Polly," Uncle Boritz snorted.

"Good evening, Uncle," Polly half-heartedly mumbled as she lowered her head and with a polish rag began to feverishly rub the shoe she held out.

"Most sadly, we have clean run out of candy, and therefore there is none available for James or your good self—not that you are entitled to any such treat, for may I remind that you, girl, are still on relinquishment of all privileges and enjoyments. With that in mind, may I use this opportunity to bring to your attention that we have yet to deal with the scene of utter carnage I encountered regarding my handmade coffins."

Polly lowered her eyelids as she continued vigorously rubbing the shoe she was still holding.

"I am therefore putting you on notice that you will be attending a meeting with Dr. Ninkumpoop to decide where we go from here. But before this happens, I need you to know that Mildred and I have spent the past two weeks running around the countryside like a couple of headless chickens in our attempt to find out anything concerning this ring. And I'm sorry to say that, no thanks to you, we have come back from this quest none the wiser as to where this valuable ring originated from.

"As you continue to refuse to cooperate with us, I have been left with little choice other than to go ahead and contact the Federal Bureau of Investigation, better known across the pond as the FBI. They are in the process of sending me two of their best men, who have truly spectacular skills when it comes to ousting the truth from people such as yourself, as well as many other potential or international terrorists.

"They land at Heathrow Airport tomorrow morning. Of course, they will need some time of refreshment in a London hotel, but then they will immediately make their way here. So it is very much in your interest to be as cooperative with these gentlemen as you are able; otherwise I cannot even begin to imagine the consequences."

Uncle Boritz plunged his hand deep into his pocket and pulled out a long stick of strawberry flavored candy. "Yes, this was the piece I was saving for you, but sadly, as you can see, Pitstop got to it first. Such a disgusting animal to have slobbered all over this candy treat, don't you think?" he smugly grinned. He then proceeded to bring the candy up to his own mouth to stick between his thick, generous lips to slowly suck on. "Hmm, lovely. Ooh, strawberry. Delish. Here, Pitstop. You can now dispose of the rest. There's a good boy," he said, patting the beast with one hand while holding the candy up to the beast's slimy, drooling jaws with his free hand to allow Pitstop to once more slobber all over the candy stick.

Polly continued to fervently polish the same shoe that was still in her hand as she tried hard not to show any emotion or distress that would encourage him to taunt her further.

"All the same, admit it: you would have so loved this treat, for it was a yummy strawberry flavor, and I do believe strawberries are your all-time favorite fruit, am I right?" he mischievously quizzed. "Speak up! Am I right?"

"Yes. Yes, Uncle Boritz, you are correct. They are my favorite, not that I ever get to eat any," she answered in little more than a whisper.

"Shame. Never mind. You wouldn't want to savor this one now, would you? It's now well and truly covered in his thick, slimy drool. Hmm, most unhygienic, if you ask me," he snorted as he quickly removed the candy from the jaws of the beast to wave in her direction.

Pitstop made a loud growl, that if interpreted would clearly express, "Give me back my treat, or you're dead meat."

"Ha ha. Polly dear, I, for one, am certain that one of the other children will give you a lick of theirs, that is, if you care to get down on both knees and beg them. Well, good night."

"Good night, Uncle." Polly finally placed the gleaming shoe back on the table next to the last pair of shoes on row two that still required polishing.

Polly instantly felt sad at the news that James had been denied the candy treat, for she believed it had everything to do with him standing up and trying to defend her at the last family meeting. She also knew that the other boys would make much of this, as all sweets tasted even better if they could be used as a weapon to taunt any child who had been denied the treat due to some punishment. For once, Polly was truly glad that dear Thomas was no longer around, for she felt sure he too would have been denied the candy and would therefore have been forced to face similar taunts and humiliation from some of the other bully boys, as well as Uncle Boritz, who simply relished the thought of children groveling at his feet as they wished with all their being to obtain something of his mercy.

She considered how James would be baited by the gloating boys as, sucking on candy, they sought to torture him further in any and every way they could. She wished with all her heart that she could save him from all further misery, but sadly, as always, she felt completely over-whelmed and powerless.

With all her chores finally completed, Polly quietly made her way to the stairs to head for bed. She knew it was very late, and there-fore assumed the other children would be fast asleep, so she was truly taken by surprise to find her younger brother, James, sitting hunched up in his dressing gown at the bottom of the staircase.

"How are things?" she asked as she sat down beside him and gently slipped her arm around his shoulder.

"Awful, just awful," he tearfully replied.

"James, I'm so sorry, for I know you didn't get any candy, and I bet the boys got a lot of pleasure out of seeing you suffer," she said, giving his hand a gentle squeeze. James nodded his head.

"But at the end of the day it's only candy, and we all know that it rots your teeth," she commiserated.

"Oh, Polly. It's not just the candy. I asked Uncle Boritz this evening if I could have my models back, and he said that he could not even remember where he put them. I don't believe him. He is so mean and spiteful. I hate him, I really do," he moaned.

"Hmm. James, I'm so sorry. I have no idea what to say to comfort you."

"You don't have to say anything, for I'm not staying here any longer. I am leaving this horrid castle, and I'm going to find somewhere else to live."

"James, don't be crazy. Where will you go? The streets are very dangerous, especially at nighttime. Please rethink before you do some-thing crazy that you may well live to regret," she pleaded, as she was now feeling very anxious and concerned for her younger brother.

"I don't know where I'm going, but to be honest I really don't care. I just want to get out of here for good," he adamantly cried.

"James, running away is no answer, trust me."

"Oh, Polly, don't you even dare to preach at me, for you of all people have no right to tell me what to do, especially as you've run away many times before."

"Yes, and look where it got me," she gently reminded him.

"Look, Polly, you don't have to worry, because Toby is coming with me, and he says his mum and sister live in London, so we are going to go and find them. So good-bye, dear sister." James got up from where he was sitting and walked toward the front door.

"No, wait! I can't let you go alone."

"I'm not on my own. I've already told you that Toby is coming with me. He knows his school report is so very bad that when Uncle gets to read it, he will almost certainly be on ROPE for the next few months, so he's not going to hang around long enough for him to find out. He's packed a bag, and he's waiting in his room for me to give him the signal to go."

"No, no, no. You are both far too young to run away, and at this ridiculously late hour. Please don't go," she begged as she attempted to grab hold of his arm in a final, desperate bid to make him see reason.

James pushed her away and then began to whistle, his signal to Toby that the time to leave had come. Seconds later and Toby was standing at the top of the stairs, ready and willing to leave.

"James, wait one minute, and I'll come with you," she anxiously cried. "I've already lost one brother, and I'm not about to lose another."

"Oh, you never told me she was comin'. That changes things. I ain't going nowhere if she's comin too," Toby groaned, dropping his bag to the floor as if to reemphasize his position on the matter.

"No, she's definitely not coming with us," James retorted. "Sorry, Polly. Two's company; three's a crowd. Just go to bed. We'll be fine. You'll see."

Polly realized that it was useless, for all her anxious pleas fell on deaf ears, so she continued to walk up the stairs, feeling very concerned for both boys. Before she reached the top stair she heard the front door click, and she turned around to see that both boys had gone.

Polly turned on the bathroom light and proceeded toward the basin to wash her face and clean her teeth. She caught a sudden glimpse of her wearied, troubled features in the mirror, and she felt she looked more like fifty in years rather than twelve going on thirteen.

As she stood silent at the basin with toothbrush in hand, her conscience began to make very loud noises as it warned of the perils both boys could face if they remained alone on the streets. She instantly felt awful as she agonized over whether she should go and report to her guardians that the boys had run away. As she considered her very limited options, she knew she could not face her brother hating her even more for splitting on them, so with great reluctance she decided against her better judgment that under no circumstances could she squeal on them.

With all this in mind, she also knew in her heart that she could not go to bed knowing both boys were not safely tucked up in their beds. She would never be able to live with herself if anything terrible or unforeseen were to happen to either of them. Thinking out loud, she suddenly surprised herself by saying, "Whether they like it or not, I am going with them." She threw her toothbrush back into the tooth mug and then turned to run down the stairs and out into the darkness, her only objective now being to find and join the boys.

Luckily, the boys hadn't gotten too far before she caught up with them. They were understandably pretty furious with her, but they had little choice other than to allow her to stay.

They had been walking for about an hour and were now feeling tired when Toby Trotter came up with what appeared to be a good idea to their tired legs. "I'm going to stick out my hand and hitchhike until someone stops and offers us a lift," Toby suddenly announced.

"Oh, no. Toby, listen to me. You must not do such a thing! Are you crazy? Think of the danger you are putting us into!"

"Aw, shut up, Polly. I'm tired of your fateful predictions. No one is going to harm us. You're such a pathetic scaredy-cat. Go home now if you're so afraid," he snorted.

"Yes, Toby, I am afraid, and so should you be, because many terrible things have happened to children who accepted lifts from perfect strangers."

"Yeah, right," he snarled back at her.

"Look, remember Abbey Shipton?"

"So?"

"Well, don't you remember the long months the police combed the woods before they found her?"

"Yeah, but just 'cos that happened to her doesn't mean it will happen to us, does it?"

"Toby, wake up. Are you really listening to me? Taking a lift from someone you've never met before is like playing Russian roulette, so please put your hand back down by your side, I beg—"

Before Polly had time to finish her sentence, a dark-colored car pulled off the road. "Where are you youngsters headed for?" a friendly voice called out.

"We wish to get to London," Toby hollered.

"Well, don't just stand there catching flies. Hop in," the kindly male voice shouted back.

Polly was left with little choice but to follow the boys into the back of the stranger's car. She could only pray that, unlike Abbey, they would come out of this unscathed to go on and make it to their destination.

As they made themselves comfortable in the back of the car, the gentleman driving turned to make his acquaintance. "Hi there. My name's Ern, and this 'ere is my luverly missus, Hannah. So what finds you young ones traveling at such a late hour?" the kindly man with the silver hair and matching silver mustache inquired.

Polly immediately spoke up. "Well, sir. We are on our way to London to find Toby's mother."

"Oh, did she invite you to come and stay then?"

"Well, not exactly. It's just that—"

Suddenly Polly felt her leg stinging, as Toby had just given her a very hard pinch, his private way of telling her to shut up. As Polly rubbed her leg and continued to engage in light conversation, she suddenly turned her head to one side to avoid being blinded by the flash of light coming from the beam of a car traveling in the opposite direction. As she turned her head to one side, she suddenly found herself looking over at James, and she was immediately shocked to realize that, unlike Toby or herself, he had well and truly given the game away!

Polly prodded James before discreetly pointing to his feet. Unbelievable as it may seem, James was sitting on the backseat still dressed in his nightclothes, his threadbare dressing gown wrapped around him and slippers on both feet. Oh, and a big, beaming smile on his face.

Polly inwardly groaned. She had been so taken up with trying to persuade her brother not to run away that she had given little thought to his attire. She knew in that desperate moment in time that the game was well and truly up!

Polly continued to ramble on in the forlorn hope that this nice elderly couple might well be visually impaired and that this impediment might hopefully prevent them from being aware of this acutely embarrassing situation, but deep inside she thought it highly unlikely that both parties would be on the road in the middle of a dark night and without their prescription glasses. Why, then, had neither party made any mention of it?

All too soon the gentleman in the driver's seat announced he would have to drop them off at the next convenient place, as they needed to head off in another direction. Polly felt sad but relieved. She also wondered what she was going to do concerning her younger brother, for she didn't believe they could continue on with James still dressed in his nightwear. Someone, somewhere was bound to start asking questions.

After waving their good-byes to the kindly couple, Polly turned to James to address their immediate problem.

"James, what on earth were you thinking of, you daft idiot? You should at least have got dressed."

"Yes, you stupid plonker! I wish I'd never agreed to come away with such a bloomin' couple of misfits. What are we going to do now?" Toby cried.

James put on an idiotic-looking face and shrugged his shoulders as he confessed he had absolutely no idea.

"Beats me. I know I've messed up, but perhaps—"

"Yes, you have, you stupid nitwit," Toby blazed.

They were still involved in a heated discussion when Polly became aware of two, no, three police cars heading in their direction.

"Look, guys. Maybe they are not after us, so keep your cool. Just continue to walk on as though you haven't noticed them," Polly sternly ordered both boys.

Sadly for Polly, the police cars pulled up with their lights flashing wildly and their sirens making that terrorizing, horribly unfriendly high-pitched noise that instantly gets your heart beating at twice its normal speed. Two officers got out of the first car, and after dramatically slamming their doors, they began to approach them.

"Excuse me, miss, but perhaps you would like to explain to us officers of the law as to why three young children, one dressed in his pajamas, are out walking in the middle of the night?"

Polly bowed her head in shame.

"Taking in the full moon, are we? Unless, of course, you're all on your way to a fancy dress party, in which case only the little fellow in his slippers and pajamas has got it right, and the other two of you look way too normal. Wouldn't you agree, PC Inkblot?"

The extremely tall officer standing next to him simply nodded his head in agreement, as with a grin on his face he pulled out his special notepad with the view to taking down an accurate account of all conversations that would now surely take place.

Quick-thinking Toby was the first to speak. "Well, as you asked us, officer, we were actually on our way home from a pajama party," he insisted.

"Just on their way home from a pajama party, with only one of the suspects actually wearing his pajamas..." PC Inkblot repeated aloud while furiously scribbling in his notebook. "Hmm. Very suspicious, if you ask me," he murmured.

"I see, young sir, and at what specific address might this party have taken place?"

"None of yer business," Toby curtly replied.

"And what might your name be?" the officious detective sniffed.

"Toby. Toby Neville Trotter. TNT to all my friends."

"Hmm. TNT. Now, I believe that to be very dangerous stuff," PC Inkblot wrote down in the comments column of his official notepad. "This night might not end very well at all with a name like that," he muttered.

"Yeah, and don't we have a bloomin' right to remain silent?" James interjected.

"Aw, shut up, James, you pinhead. He's still speakin' to me," Toby growled.

"Toby, young man. Listen to me. We can do this the easy way or the hard way," the stern officer known to all as Detective Constable Chickpea snarled.

"Easy or hard way; choice is all theirs," PC Inkblot most dutifully continued to record. "Yes, I do believe it's make-your-mind-up time."

"Yeah, we don't 'ave to say nufink if we don't want to, 'cos we ain't done nothing wrong yet," Toby rather impudently suggested.

"Well, young sir, we dare to disagree with you, because most pajama parties indisputably have the occupants of those pajamas sleeping under mounds of blankets in a warm bed, at least, until the cock cares to stretch his legs and crow. Am I correct in my thinking, young Inkblot?" Chickpea turned to ask his spotty, willowy fellow officer.

"Yes, DC Chickpea. You are, as usual, right on."

"And as this beat is on my side of the town, then I am entitled to ask these and any other choice questions that I care to. Is that also right on, PC Inkblot?"

"Yes, sir. You are indeed entitled to ask these here young people anything you care to. And I might use this here occasion to add that anything they do say can and will be taken down as material evidence," PC Inkblot rattled off in a most superior, if not somewhat officious manner as he continued to write down verbatim all that passed between them.

"Then am I to presume that these youngsters did not stay at the party because the breakfast was, sadly, not too their liking?"

"No, sir. I would imagine the breakfast was, as you suggest, obviously not to their liking. Maybe they didn't like the sausage and bacon and would have preferred something a bit more simple, like yogurt with honey and a nice bit of fresh fruit. I know my mum suffers with digestive problems, so she doesn't like a heavy breakfast and…"

"Pay attention, Inkblot! I was not asking you for your thoughts on this matter or your dotty mum's personal breakfast preferences, you insufferable excuse for an officer of the law," the red-haired, bloated faced detective yelled directly into his face.

PC Inkblot stood to attention looking very shamefaced at being shouted at, and in such an unexpectedly nasty and unpleasant manner.

The DC then turned on his heels to once more growl down at the terrified children.

"How rude!" PC Inkblot muttered under his breath. "Suit yourself, Chickpea, for my mum has always loved my personal thoughts and writings. Hmm. She says I've got real talent when it comes to giving heart to a real-life story," Polly overheard him quietly mutter.

DC Chickpea, with hands behind his back, then swiveled 'round once more to address the young constable.

"Inkblot, understand me when I say that I was merely trying to pick your brains for some sort of rational explanation as to why these youngsters are not safely tucked up in a warm bed. Against all odds, I was hoping for some light to be shed that might explain something of why they are out on the streets at this dangerous hour of the night. I repeat, I was therefore not expecting you to come up with some alternative but satisfying nutritional option for the breakfast menu. Are we clear on this one?"

"Perfectly, sir," Inkblot sniffed as he adjusted his hard hat and tried to look as suitably concerned as he was able. After all, this was indeed a most serious matter. "No personal opinions or comments required by my good self concerning helpful, fitness-conscious breakfast suggestions," the young and fresh faced PC then scribbled down on his thick notepad.

Polly chose this opportunity to step forward, as she had come to the firm conclusion that to tell the truth was the best thing to do in this difficult situation. She really didn't want the crisis to flare up into a worst-case scenario, and it seemed to be rapidly heading in that direction.

"I'm so sorry, officers. We are all from the children's home, and we have become so unhappy in the home that we decided to run away and go to London in search of a better life."

"Oh, so just like Dick Whittington and Oliver Twist, you miserable lot also believe that the streets of London are paved with gold, do you?" the red-haired detective sarcastically interjected.

"No, sir. I don't think any such thing. But as Toby has a mum who lives in Croydon just outside of London, so we were hoping—"

"Polly, you stupid prat. Shut yer gob now, or I'll shut it for yer!" Toby angrily shouted. "You'll get us in a whole heap of trouble."

"Young man, I think that's an understatement," the exasperated DC stated as he began to twirl his limp mustache between his fingertips.

"You're already in the muck up to your scrawny little necks," he chillingly stated.

Polly ignored Toby as she tried hard to continue explaining the real reasons behind their desperate actions.

By now Toby was so livid that he began to use very unacceptably expressive language as he further vented his utter contempt for all around him. The poor police officers, who believed they had seen and heard everything that life could throw at them when dealing with the criminal underworld, were completely taken back that one so young could speak such terribly foul language—and in front of adults!

Polly turned to Toby and begged him to calm down, but to no avail, as he then turned and began shouting extremely unpleasant expletives in her direction.

"Enough!" roared the shocked and enraged DC Chickpea. "I've just about had enough. Young man, I'll have you know that your disgracefully foul language has turned the air bluer then young PC Inkblot's uniform. I am therefore wholly unwilling to listen to anymore of your utterly disgraceful and most offensive barrage of abuse. PC Inkblot, I order you to handcuff these young villains. Then lock them all in the back of your police van and run them back to the police station for further questioning."

PC Inkblot gave a deep sigh as he placed his highly important and treasured notepad back into his breast pocket before urging the young, very disrespectful hooligans in the direction of his police van.

Polly felt like a violent criminal as, handcuffed, she was ordered to crawl like an animal into the back of PC Inkblot's van. Even the windows had wire in the glass to prevent them escaping. She could give a number of very deep sighs, as she knew for certain that this was going to be a very long night.

Back at the station, the handcuffs were removed, and they were placed in a cold, bleak cell, which was then locked. They were then left alone for a considerable, lengthy time—time deliberately given to allow them to come together and get their stories aligned and correct before they would be individually interrogated and then obliged to give written statements that they would be unable to retract at some later date.

With the children huddled on a bench in one of the jail's many cells, the only sound echoing throughout the building was that of PC Inkblot's old-fashioned typewriter as he methodically typed out every word of the unpleasant altercation that had taken place between the officers of the law and these young but hardened, thuggish criminals. After all, this potentially damning piece of evidence had to be faithfully and fervently recorded, as it might be required as evidence by Her Majesty's Courts Service at some future unknown date.

Who knows? Such a case as this might well bring the young PC a little local fame, with maybe the odd handsome picture or two of himself finding their way onto the front page of the local paper. He knew if this were to happen, his mum would be so proud of him. She would inevitably cut out the pictures and frame them so that every visitor to the house could be reminded of what a wonderful police officer her only son had become. "Aw, Mum, you really are the best," he sighed as he pictured her diligently framing the newspaper cuttings before placing them on the wall of every room in the house. Come to think of it, he might even find himself being considered for promotion.

The young, inexperienced officer gave himself a little slap on the wrist so as to remind himself not to get too carried away by future stardom, but he also smiled to himself as he considered how delighted his mum would also be when he showed her all he had recorded of this latest dynamic escapade. He knew for certain that, unlike DC Chickpea, she would want to swap her cookery or other gossip-filled magazine in preference for his latest thrilling piece of writing as she headed upstairs for some bedtime reading with a cup of hot cocoa in her other hand.

Chapter Seventeen
PC INKBLOT TO THE RESCUE

*A*T APPROXIMATELY FIVE thirty in the morning, the front doorbell of the castle rang. It was very quickly answered by a stupefied, half-comatose Boritz in dressing gown and slippers with a snarling Pitstop dutifully at his side.

"Argh. What time it?" he yawned as he struggled to stay awake.

"Good morning, sir. My name is PC Inkblot, and I do believe these young, bleary-eyed pipsqueaks are your personal property. Now, am I correct in my thinking?" he said, beaming from ear to ear as he reached down to give young James an affectionate pat on the head.

"Well, yes, Constable Inkblot, these little whippersnappers are mine. But out of courtesy, pray, tell me quickly, how did they come to be in your possession?" he inquired, his hands trembling as he fought to quell an overwhelming desire to explode into a rage.

"Well, sir, it is indeed quite a long but very interesting tale, so I would be most obliged if you would indulge my senses by allowing me to share this utterly riveting story—which does transcend most of my other stories—over a nice cuppa. How about it?"

"What? Oh, yes. Yes, very well then. Do please come on in," Boritz wearily sighed as he tried to keep himself in one piece, for in return for bottling up his rage, he was now feeling horribly nauseous. "Children, go upstairs and get into bed, for you still have a few hours left to sleep before you need to be up for school. So off you go, my little poppets, and Uncle will want to see you all in the morning."

With the weary children heading up the stairs to their beds, Boritz reluctantly ushered PC Inkblot to follow him to his private and very plush sitting room. "There, this is more comfortable. Now allow me a few minutes to go and brew a lovely pot of tea."

"Mercy me. Oh, mercy me," he anxiously squeaked over and over as he made the long way down the corridor toward the kitchen. Poor Boritz was relieved to be alone in the kitchen, as it allowed him the privilege of beating the walls with his bare fists before recognizing that he needed to do some of his deep breathing exercises, which had never failed to calm him down. It also gave him the vital extra time necessary to think of what to do and say, for at five thirty in the morning the scheming and conniving section of his brain had not had any reasonable length of time whatsoever to click into place.

Finally, after a number of deep breathing exercises, he began to feel a sense of peace and tranquility arising from within, so holding a tray bearing a pot of hot tea as well as a plateful of chocolate-covered biscuits, he headed back to the sitting room with fresh determination to come out of this acutely embarrassing situation as clean as a whistle. He was, after all, an expert in the field of management control, and this situation was no different, although he had to admit that this crisis topped the lot, for up until ten minutes ago he had known nothing about it whatsoever!

As Boritz was very used to playing the good host, he immediately began by pouring the tea.

"I'll play mother, then. Shall I?" he said, giving the young, fresh-faced officer a very generous smile. "Milk or lemon?" he squeaked as his throat once more closed up due to unexpected and very intense fear. Boritz, feeling horrified by the situation, quickly began to cough, as he believed this would help his throat and voice get back to normal.

"Thank you, good sir. I like my tea with a just a tad of milk, if that's all right by you."

"One lump or two?" Boritz politely asked with a sigh of relief, as the manly gruffness was once more present in his voice.

"Oh, two will be just fine, sir. Any more than that, and I'll get a dressing down from me mum, as I will begin putting on pounds," he said, giving his nonexistent belly a gentle, friendly pat.

Boritz obliged by putting not two, not even four, but six lumps into the young constable's tea, for he was beginning to feel quite light-headed if not somewhat delirious. He also firmly believed that adding more sugar might well be the antidote required to sweeten up this excuse for a young officer of the law.

"Oh, please do take one of my very delicious biscuits, officer," he said as he over-dramatically thrust the plate right up to the poor man's nose. "They are, after all, made from the finest Belgian chocolate, of this I assure you."

"Well, thank you, dear sir. I most certainly would love to try a couple," he replied as he then generously helped himself to at least five, if not six, biscuits.

Boritz watched on feeling hopelessly mortified as the young officer, having quickly polished off a number of biscuits, then rather greedily continued to help himself to a further large quantity of his preciously expensive biscuits. These biscuits were, after all, his favorite treat that he alone liked to binge on, and he was only doing his very best at being polite when he considerately placed the whole plate in front of the officer. He rather foolishly had not expected the young PC to brazenly help himself to so many. No wonder the young man had so many spots!

With the sudden revelation that the fresh, sincere-looking constable was without a conscience whatsoever when it came to eating someone else's biscuits, Boritz realized he would have to act quickly or risk losing the lot to the young, very greedy PC, who was clearly contemplating helping himself to further biscuits from the already half-emptied plate. Quick-thinking Boritz diplomatically whisked the plate away before the very impolite officer had the opportunity to help himself to anymore.

"Officer, I do believe you will put on some serious weight if you eat anymore. After all, they are extremely high in calories. My wife and I discovered these deliciously scrumptious biscuits in a little backstreet shop in London just after we had paid our respects at Buckingham Palace."

"Oh, so you're on close, friendly terms with our good queen, are you, sir?" the young and extremely naïve officer of the law dared to ask.

"Well, not exactly. No, we are not on first-name terms as of yet," Boritz hastily replied.

Had the young man not been an officer of the law, chances are extremely high that Boritz would have happily lied concerning his nonexistent relationship with the queen, but on this occasion he thought it unwise to embellish the truth, as it might well have future repercussions. Besides which, he felt he was already in up to his neck in water and believed he was just about to sink to the bottom of the canal.

"Now then, Constable Inkblot, I am all ears, so please enrich these little flappers by filling me in on all the details as to quite how my naughty little whippersnappers came to find themselves in your delightful custody."

"Well, sir, allow me the time to expediently run through this crisis one step at a time," the young and inexperienced PC suggested as he solemnly produced his notepad from his breast pocket to begin.

Boritz groaned from within, for he knew with assured certainty that this young officer would not be rushed, for he was clearly determined to give every fact as well as portray every nuance that had arisen during the very unpleasant altercation, as it was deemed imperative that Boritz be given a perfectly clear and vividly accurate picture of all that had taken place. Boritz therefore had little choice but to give the young, lanky constable the freedom of airspace he required to give a full and very detailed account while relaying every single second of that most dramatic evening.

As Boritz listened, he began to feel quite faint, especially when it came to the part where Polly felt obliged to explain their reasons for running away in the first place.

"Sir, it appears that the aforesaid children ran away due to various unpleasant and acrimonious events that have recently occurred inside these here walls."

"Now, come on, officer. We all know that these parentless children often suffer from serious psychological problems due to much trauma in their infant lives. Take Polly, for instance. Now, this young girl, along with her brothers, was abandoned by her seriously negligent mother and alcoholic father, both of whom had very checkered pasts. May I also take the liberty of informing you that she is now in the process of having professional assistance from none other than Dr. Ninkumpoop, who, may I remind you, is head of child psychiatric resources at our local mental hospital. This man is a recognized expert in his field who has a regular column in a national magazine, and I assure you that, having read the reports concerning this child, he is so concerned by the extent of her delusional behavior that he is about ready to have her committed to the hospital to undergo very radical therapy. Of this I assure you."

"Really? Is she that bad then?" the young and very naive officer asked as he swallowed every word that Boritz cared to utter.

"Worse!"

"Well, I never...You poor man," the extremely gullible constable gasped as, shaking his head, he continued sipping his hot tea.

"She is indeed a most suitable case for treatment, and if you have any doubts concerning all I say, then please feel free to contact the school's headmaster, Mr. Edwood Batty, whom you must surely be acquainted with."

"Yes, yes."

"Sadly, he has threatened many a time to have the girl removed, and I assure you, that it is only due to my constant intervention that she still remains in the school system."

"Golly gosh!" was all the troubled officer could then manage to splutter.

"I have literally had to beg Mr. Batty on bended knee, so to speak, to keep the poor girl in school, and up until recently he always set aside his own misgivings by caving in to my desperate pleas. However, a few days ago he phoned the castle to rather angrily inform me that enough was enough, and he would be putting in his own very chilling report regarding her poor mental condition."

"Oh, my goodness. So things are really that bad?"

"Unbelievably so, officer! You would have to live at the castle to see firsthand what we are regularly forced to endure. Poor Mildred, my darling wife, is on the verge of a nervous breakdown, and most of this can be attributed to young Polly's severe behavioral problems."

"Well, sir, in the light of all you are confiding in me, I believe it to be my moral duty to wrap this up in such a manner that we can all forget that any of this ever happened and thereby consider the case well and truly closed, " the generously warmhearted PC informed a now very jubilant Boritz.

"I would be so grateful, officer, if not deeply indebted, for if any of this were to get out, then just think of the negative impact it would have on the other young children we expend all our love and energy looking after. We do so rely on the immensely kind donations that are sent to us by very caring and charitable people, and such a story seeping out might well see this orphanage closing its doors for good."

"Trust me. Do not trouble yourself further with any such terrible thoughts, sir."

"Oh, and speaking of charities, before you leave, please do remind me to hand over a rather handsome check that I was intending to forward to the Officers' Retirement Fund. Tell me now, is my good friend "Gung ho" Rob Bobtail still on the force, or has he finally retired?"

"Oh, you're so behind the times, sir," the foolishly naïve young PC replied, "for sadly he retired from the force many months ago. Would you like me to send your greetings to him?"

"Well, that would be nice. I especially miss his little visits to the castle, for he did so love Mildred's very special brown bread and whisky pudding. But let us get back to the problem in hand, for the children will all be terribly fearful and afraid if they think there is even the remotest chance that we will be closed down due to some terrible misunderstanding, instigated yet again by our very own troubled Polly Brown. Yes, I assure you, hand on heart, that it would be such a travesty of justice, for there would be fountains of tears if the terrified youngsters were to be callously and coldheartedly informed that some uninformed judge had ordered that they be forcibly removed and taken elsewhere."

"Yes, sir. That would be terrible."

"They would indeed cling to us in a manner not too dissimilar to that of those poor and terrified folks on the *RMS Titanic* in its last desperate hours before it sank to the bottom of the ocean."

"Goodness, gracious me!" the wide-eyed officer of the law gasped as he began to conjure up pictures in his mind of such a painfully nightmarish event ever taking place.

"Sir, I've seen that old movie. Yes, it was called *A Night to Remember*. I saw it on the telly one night as I sat on the sofa eating fish 'n ' chips with me mum and sister, and hearing their haunting screams and cries as the ship went down into that freezing water was almost too much to bear," he dolefully admitted.

"Yes, the sinking of the *Titanic* is surely one of history's most terrible of tragedies, so I implore you, PC Inkblot, as our very future lies in your hands alone, please do not allow the closure of this home to become yet a further needless tragedy to rather shamefully go down in the annals of our history books."

"Oh, heaven forbid! That would be terribly unbearable."

"You must try to understand, officer, this is the only loving, secure home most of them have ever known. I therefore am of the opinion that such a kind, conscientious man as you so clearly are would struggle to ever forgive yourself if this were to happen as a mere result of a few inconsiderate children's self-gratuitous actions," he gushed.

"Goodness, gracious, you are right on that one, for I could never live with myself if I were to allow such a terrible thing to happen!" the innocent officer cried out loud.

On track, Boritz then tried to force a few crocodile tears to spring forth from his eyes. When the tears failed to appear, he quickly plunged his hand into his gold dressing gown pocket to whip out one of Mildred's spectacularly colorful handkerchiefs. Then, placing the handkerchief into the corner of his right eye, he began to squeeze down and pinch hard. Finally, due to the immense stinging sensation, a few desperate tears thankfully began to finally well up in the corners of both eyes.

"Pray, tell me, officer, if we were to turn our backs on these little, downtrodden mites, where on this forsaken earth would these poor, desperate creatures go?" he sobbed, as he deliberately allowed a tear to trickle unchecked down his bloated cheek.

PC Inkblot was, by this point, reaching into his pocket in search of his own handkerchief to wipe away the string of tears that were now positively streaming down his withdrawn but very reddened cheeks.

On seeing the profound impact his words were having on PC Inkblot, Boritz felt most encouraged to continue on drawing a hopelessly bleak picture of the youngsters' futures.

"It would forever weigh heavily on my already broken heart if we were to lose any of these infants and young children, all of whom have already suffered more than enough in this life," he sniffed as yet again he took his handkerchief to dab his once more dry eyes.

"I wholeheartedly agree with all you are saying, sir," sighed the young and very inexperienced police officer as he proceeded to wipe down his cheeks before noisily blowing his nose. "Sir, I truly cannot bear to hear anymore, so the matter in question is fully settled. I wholeheartedly agree with all you are saying, so there is no question in my mind that details concerning this event must never be allowed get out."

Moments later saw him take the pad that held all three children's statements, only to tear them up into little pieces in front of Boritz.

"There. And if my senior colleagues or my mother ever dare to challenge me as to how I lost all three statements, I will just throw my hands into the air and plead total ignorance."

"Ah, yes. Very commendable, PC Inkblot, but surely being an officer of the law and therefore fully conversant with the laws that govern our land, you of all people should surely know that you cannot plead such a thing, for ignorance of the law is no excuse."

"Sir, you're absolutely correct, but I'll worry about that later, for the thing uppermost in my mind is the welfare of these poor, dear children. Yes, I will gladly put my head on the block, if only to save them," he said as with a swelling breast he proudly continued to tear the evidence into tiny shreds.

"Allow me to dispose of your litter," Boritz said with a sly smile as he hurriedly removed the shredded statements from the constable's hand and then casually walked over to a nearby waste paper basket.

As the evidence tumbled into the basket, Boritz privately determined to come back and burn the paper trail at the first opportune moment, which hopefully would be as soon as this irritating and naively dumb constable left the building to go on his merry way.

"My lips are sealed, sir. It is as if this difficult situation never occurred. But before I take my leave and head back to the station, might I suggest that you give all the children a very stern talking-to on the dangers of taking lifts from complete strangers."

"Oh, absolutely, Inkblot. You have my word on that one. Trust me."

With the nuisance officer now on his way back to the station, Uncle Boritz headed back to his private sitting room to anxiously dispose of the evidence, which now lay in tatters at the bottom of the waste paper basket. He hastily dropped a lighted match into the basket and watched over it until he was thoroughly satisfied that all the evidence was nothing more than thoroughly irredeemable, charred remains. He then upturned a glass of water into the basket in order to douse the flames.

This done, and even though it was only nine thirty in the morning, he still decided to pour himself a glass of the finest Napoleon brandy and then went to find himself a comfortable chair. Once seated, he smugly placed his thick glasses back on his nose, then he took a quick slug of brandy from his glass before reaching over to pick up an envelope that sat waiting for his undivided attention. He then calmly opened up a large envelope and turned it upside down. Out spilled a number of suspicious-looking photographs, as well as a small pocket notebook. He opened the notebook, adjusted his thick glasses, and began to read.

"Well done, Gailey dear, for as usual you have really done your homework. I won't ask you how you managed to find out so much about the Montgomerys' murky private life,, but I know for sure it will assist me in what I have to do," he muttered loudly under his breath. "Now then, Pitstop, I need to make a few personal phone calls to confirm all this, and then after a little nap I believe it is high time I paid a little visit to make her acquaintance."

Pitstop instantly growled his approval.

At eleven thirty on the dot he made the promised call, and after placing the phone back on its receiver, he wasted no time putting on his old, heavy overcoat. He then placed his herringbone hat on his head for added warmth before tucking a thick, long scarf many times around his throat before leaving his private room to head toward the front door.

"Good boy. Now you stay here and look after Mildred for me. I won't be away too long, I promise," he said as he gave the beast a consolatory pat on the head.

Pitstop continued to whine and slobber as his master braced high winds to set out in the direction of the Montgomerys' house.

"I'm so glad she has agreed to see me, and at such short notice," he muttered as he tried to stop his teeth chattering from the cold. "Fancy living with a load of flea-infested cats," he continued to mutter as the harsh, cold wind tried its best to bite down hard into his flesh. "Now, a house filled with dogs, well, of course, that's an entirely different matter."

With the help of Gailey's simple directions, most of which were in the form of very basic drawings, Boritz soon found his way to the large, well-hidden house. He knocked hard on the door and then waited a considerable length of time for the door to be opened. Boritz blew his warm breath into his cupped hands as he attempted to keep warm.

"Brrr. It is so unbelievably cold," he miserably moaned.

Finally the creaky door opened, and as he dared to look down, he came face-to-face with a wizened, white-haired, fragile old lady strapped into a wheelchair. Boritz balked and stepped backward, as he was caught off guard as the amount of cats that had come to greet him at the door far exceeded his expectations.

"Don't stand at the door catching flies, Mr. Scumbrolly. Do come in. There's a good chap, for it is indeed a very cold and blustery day. So come on in, and I will make us a nice pot of Darjeeling tea. Then perhaps you can accord me the privilege of explaining why this meeting was of such urgency that it could not wait until later on in the week."

"Madam, before I enter your house I wish to point out that, like many before you, you too have my name entirely wrong."

"Oh!"

"It's Scumberry. S-c-u-m-b—"

"Yes, yes, all right," the lady impatiently replied.

"How appallingly discourteous of the old biddy," Boritz, feeling most annoyed, quietly mumbled under his breath as he entered the old lady's house.

As a matter of common courtesy, Boritz removed his hat and scarf and then subserviently followed after her and a hundred or so odd cats as they silently made their way down the long hall heading for her boudoir, where they could privately pour the tea as well as pour out all that was concerning their hearts and minds.

"Well, good lady, you certainly know how to set about making a most delicious and refreshing cup of tea."

"Why, thank you, Mr. Scumberry, for I truly believe in apportioning a set time of each day for the drinking of tea, as I am of the opinion that it is of the utmost importance."

"Oh, yes, I wholeheartedly agree with you, Mrs. Montgomery. Where would we be without our pot of tea?"

"Well, as one fine gentleman with a lot of common sense so rightly stated, 'There are few hours in life more agreeable than the hour dedicated to the ceremony of afternoon tea.'"

"I heartily agree, dear lady, although I must remind you that it is only a little after midday," he stated as he allowed her to top up his cup with further hot tea.

"Well, then on this occasion we will call it a late elevenses," she quickly retorted.

For well over an hour the two talked in secret whilst drinking vast volumes of calming tea, and then Mr. Scumberry announced he must make haste in getting back to the castle. Placing his empty tea cup to one side, he promptly placed his hat back on his head, wrapped his scarf tightly around his neck, and politely bid her farewell. As they stood in the doorway, he turned to say one final word.

"Madam, do I truly have your total agreement?" he asked.

"Oh, yes, Mr. Scumberry. I assure you now that you have my total, wholehearted approval and backing on this one."

<hr />

Will, who was descending the staircase with a book in his hand, caught a sudden glimpse of a stranger as he was leaving out the front door. He quickly closed his book.

"Tell me, Mother, who was your visitor? I do not recognize him," he curiously asked.

"No one of any interest to you," she harshly replied.

Later that day she demanded that her son follow her down to her private sitting room so that she could unburden herself of all the troubling things that the stranger had revealed concerning Will's close friendship with Polly. By the end of their bitter discussion, they were nowhere near any kind of amicable agreement.

"William, the girl is no longer welcome here. Do you understand?"

"That's truly ridiculous and unfair! Anyone would think she was a wicked criminal, yes, the next Lucrezia Borgia," he bitterly complained.

"Don't be so impudent, for I am suggesting no such thing. All I am saying is she appears to be a really troubled soul."

"Aren't we all?" Will angrily muttered under his breath.

"Are you paying attention, William, for there is absolutely no room whatsoever for compromise. You have no choice in this matter, for while you live under my roof, you will abide by my rules and adhere to all my wishes. I'll have you know that Mr. Scumberry is indeed a very powerful man, and he has made it most clear that failure to comply with his wishes will indubitably spell great trouble for us. And have we not already suffered enough, what with your brother and—"

"Yes, yes, Mother. Spare me the details."

"Well, son, I have no choice other than to remind you—"

"No, Mother, you really have no need to go through all that has happened, for alas, I believe I know it all by heart."

"Well, then."

"But come on, Mother, why should you allow such a ruthless and despicable man to intimidate us? Unless, of course, we have more terrible hidden family secrets that you might care to share?"

His mother began to murmur and mumble that there were indeed many skeletons in the family cupboard, secrets that she had always hoped against all odds would remain buried—that is, up until this untimely visit.

By the time his mother had finished sharing her concerns with Will, he was left with little choice other than to honor her and, in doing so, comply fully with her wishes. "Oh, all right then. In the light of all you have just revealed, I will end my friendship with her once and for all. There, Mother. You have my word on it. Now please do me a favor and leave the subject well alone."

"Yes, my dear, I will."

"Forgive me, but I think I will forgo lunch, as I wish to be left alone," he said as he quickly turned on his heels to head for the sanctity and solace of his bedroom. He also did not wish for her to witness that his eyes were unexpectedly smarting with tears.

Chapter Eighteen
THE MUCH-DREADED SCHOOL REPORT

A FEW DAYS LATER saw the last day of term before the Christmas holidays were once more upon them. As the school day came to its usual, timely end, Polly slowly emptied her desk, feeling equally empty inside. She could not help but feel deeply saddened, for she had endured a whole horrible day of watching as other pupils exchanged little precious gifts and gave each other long, meaningful hugs and kisses as they made plans to all meet up for cinema outings or shopping expeditions during the holidays. They also talked endlessly of what they were hoping to receive from other family members on Christmas Day. Polly had no such optimism, for tragically she just wished to make it through the holidays without further recriminations or punishments, for that wish alone to be fulfilled would most likely make her Christmas a reasonably pleasant and bearable one.

Having emptied her desk of all personal items, she stood in line to collect her school report, and once more she could only shudder as she considered what her teachers might well have written concerning her. She knew most of the report would not show her in a good light; after all, she did fall asleep in most of the lessons, and she never came to school with the necessary supplies to complete most tasks. This, in itself, was always enough to get her sent to the headmaster's office, ensuring she missed either the first half or the second half of most lessons, and with so much of her work remaining incomplete, she understandably continued to struggle to keep up with the rest of the class. She was always in hot water for unfinished homework, poor attendance, and for being ill prepared for lessons. Sadly for Polly, all this combined was really more than enough to make most of the teachers hate her.

Add to this the stark fact that Mr. Batty was on the friendliest terms with Uncle Boritz, as they regularly shared their love of golf, and this too had her believing that her report would not contain anything to commend her.

She also knew she would not be kept in the dark for too long, because Sunday lunch would be upon them in no time at all, and this was the favored time that Uncle Boritz loved to read out all the reports in front of everyone. This was his prime time, a time to address failures and admonish the wicked among them, as he relished and reveled in the demise of those children whose reports were simply not up to scratch. This was the time that most of the children, many of whom were serious underachievers, absolutely hated with a vengeance.

Polly looped a thick homemade scarf around her neck and gloomily headed for the school gate, hoping to meet up with Will, for if nothing else he could immediately put a smile on her face, but strangely, there was no sign of him. This disturbed her slightly, as she was now feeling very anxious as to how they could make any further plans to meet up during the Christmas break.

She sincerely hoped that the reason for his absence at the gate was solely due to the freezing weather conditions and not because she had in some way offended him. Truth was, she had not even caught as much as a glimpse of him for some time, and this was most disconcerting. Was he sick and therefore confined to his bed? Polly continued to head toward the train station, still anxiously clutching her school report tightly in her hand as she went over all potential possibilities concerning her now very dear and close friend Will.

When she arrived at the station, she headed straight for the waiting room with the full intention of standing in front of the stove fire to keep warm until her train pulled in. But as she opened the waiting room door, she was greeted by some of the children from the castle.

"Polly, if you're in here looking for Abigail, you'll have to wait a minute, for she's still in the bog."

"Oh, no. I wasn't looking for anyone in particular; I just wanted to get out of the cold until our train comes in."

"Well, do us all a favor and shut that door, for it's bloomin draughty in here!" Billy Osgood snarled.

"OK," she said as she closed the door behind her.

"Er, Polly, 'ave you opened your report yet?" Toby Trotter asked.

"No. Don't be stupid, Toby. You of all people should know that we aren't allowed to do such a terrible thing," Polly innocently replied.

"Oh, shut up, Polly, you stupid nitwit, for as usual you know nothin' about nothin'!" Abigail Crumble angrily sniped as she came out of the bathroom to join all the others in the waiting room.

"Look, we all ought to take a peek, 'cos at the end of the day we need to know if we're in big trouble on Sunday, don't we?" Bertha Banoffee fearfully interjected.

"We all know for sure that Toby here is in big trouble. Don't we, you stupid plonker?" Tommy Pulleyblank smugly stated with a big grin all over his freckle-filled face.

Some of the other children who were gathered around started to laugh.

"Look, I know a way we can get to read them and then seal them up again so that nobody, Uncle included, ever suspects a thing," Tommy said as he glanced around looking for moral support.

"Quite what do you mean?" Polly innocently asked.

"Well, we can steam them over this 'ere boiler and then carefully pry them open," said Tommy as he walked across the waiting room floor to stand over the boiler, which was blasting out a decent amount of heat. "Come on, you lot. Gather 'round. Then you can see for yourselves how to do it," he cheerfully stated.

All standing in the waiting room immediately obeyed and stood in awe and wonder as Tommy impressively took on the star role of tutor.

"Tommy, we might get into terrible trouble, for have you not noticed that on the outside of each envelope it says CONFIDENTIAL in big, unmistakable capital letters?" Polly politely pointed out as she looked on, feeling very unsure about all that was taking place.

"Oh, don't be such a sniveling little goody two-shoes," Tommy sneered as he pulled the report from the envelope as though he were a professional magician.

"Yes, Fester, go and take a long jump off a very short pier if you're going to act like such a little scaredy cat," Cecil Bogswater angrily snorted.

All those gathered 'round watching were tremendously impressed by his handling of the report and its envelope, so they did all they could to encourage him further.

Tommy, not one to avoid the limelight, instantly obliged by reading his report out loud. As he read out all the teachers' comments, those gathered 'round him began to laugh out loud. Finally Tommy reached the end of his two-page report, with only the headmaster's comments left unspoken.

"Go on then, Tommy. Don't leave us in the dark. What does thick-as-a-plank Batty have to say? Read it to us. Come on, don't hold back, for this is the good bit," Cordelia Simmonds goaded.

"Oh, all right then." He cleared his throat to continue on. "Well, here goes. 'If Pulleyblank could for even one minute stop playing the comedian and take his lessons seriously, then he might well begin to achieve some of his goals. Sadly, until he wakes up to this fact, he is going to continue failing in all his subjects. I would strongly suggest that he takes to heart all the teachers' advice and begins the next term by putting his head down to show more determination than ever to learn.'"

Tommy gave a nervous laugh that sounded more like a hyena and that gave all the other children the permission they needed to once again laugh out loud, as they then began prying open their school reports to read out loud.

"Look, any of you dimwits here got a blue pen?" Toby shouted.

"I have," shouted another as a blue pen was immediately passed around until it reached Toby.

"Look here, all of you. Watch carefully, and see what I can do. Right now D's can be changed to B's, and then you can add a plus. If you're careful, C's can also be turned to B's, and a minus requires only one upward stroke, and then that too becomes a plus. There, magic! I have saved my backside by turning all my D-minuses into B-pluses."

"Ooh, let us see," all the children cried as they anxiously gathered closer still to watch.

"Here, I'll show you all how to do it."

THE TROUBLE WITH POLLY BROWN

Each child, with the exception of Polly, took it in turn to disclose the confidential contents of their personal school report, and then with Tommy's helpful assistance, plus the magic stroke of a pen, they all dramatically improved their otherwise abysmally depressing grades. With all heads bowed, they concentrated hard on the task at hand, which was to use this time profitably by making those very important alterations to their grades.

Polly, however, chose this moment to quietly tiptoe out of the waiting room. She knew they would despise her further for not joining in, but she felt that in the light of all her present troubles, she could not face any further crisis, which might surely make things a whole heap worse than they already were.

———•◦•◦•———

Eventually, the much-dreaded Sunday lunchtime arrived. Polly sat alone to eat a pitifully small plate more suited to an inactive elderly person then an ever-growing, energetic child. Her plate bore just one thin slice of luncheon meat, one boiled potato cut into two, and three or four pieces of tinned carrots mixed with a tablespoon of peas. This was followed by a dessert of three slices of canned peaches with a dollop of canned sweetened cream. This meal had, as usual, only begun to touch on her hunger, but she had long learned to put up with the constant stomach pangs. She knew that there would be nothing else until suppertime, and this meal would also be equally sparse.

With the tables finally cleared of all dirty plates, it was time for Uncle Boritz to bring out his big black book, a book that quite understandably Polly truly detested. In a matter of minutes, all offenders were standing in the middle of the room, heads down, as they waited on Uncle Boritz's unmerciful wrath. However, as today was report day, it seemed he decided to leave all insults and grueling punishments until all the reports had been systematically read out and then openly discussed.

One by one he read each report out loud. Some of the reports did not seem so bad, while others, well, Uncle Boritz could only shake his head and make loud tutting noises.

However, on this occasion, when it came to Tommy Pulleyblank's report he had nothing but high praise.

"Well done, Tommy. Overall, this report is much better than expected, and your grades have so greatly improved that I must say I am most impressed."

The same could be said for all those who had remained in the train waiting room substantially altering the grades of their supposedly confidential school reports.

Finally, it was Polly's turn. As she was already on ROPE, she was amongst those unlucky ones already standing in the center of the room staring at the floor. The room went into a deathly hush as Uncle Boritz paused to adjust his thick glasses before tearing open the envelope to pull out the contents.

Uncle Boritz chose to mutter silently as he quickly skipped over her report. He then snorted loudly and began shaking his head like a puppet. Polly imagined he was thoroughly enjoying watching the children suffer in the center of the room.

"I feel stiff scared," a nervous Polly whispered to the child standing next to her.

"It's scared stiff, you stupid burk!" the other companion-in-misery petulantly retorted.

"Oh, sorry," Polly sighed.

"As per usual, your report appears to be far worse than all the others put together. What do you have to say about this?" he asked with the full pomposity of a high court judge, as over his thick glasses he glumly stared her directly in the eye, his true intention being to provoke some sort of reaction from her.

Polly said nothing, but she began to squirm all the same. Simply put, how could she say anything? He had not told her or anybody else in the room exactly what her report contained, good or bad!

"Hmm. All Ds and Fs. This, madam, is typical when it comes to you, but it is still totally unacceptable," he bristled.

"Now listen up, everybody, for according to the deputy head, not only is Polly extremely idle, often failing to bring any ingredients to her cookery lessons, but she has some choice comments to make. Ah, now let me see..."

In truth, it should have ended there, as the teacher had been in a hurry and had chosen not to add any further comments, but Uncle Boritz saw this as a golden opportunity to put his own spin on things.

"Yes, your teacher goes on to say, and I quote, 'What this girl considers witty, I consider insolence. I also believe there to be more intellectual vigor in a leftover bowl of soggy rice pudding.'"

All the children began to laugh hysterically at the thought of Polly being compared to a bowl of mushy rice pudding.

Boritz was so pleased at the children's hysterical response that it crossed his mind to continue on adding a few rather clever comments of his own wherever possible. After all, no one else would ever see the report, and besides, it was rather fun.

"Right, let's continue on. Mr. Warlord, your history teacher, says that much of this term has been taken up with a very comprehensive project on the Holocaust. He goes on to say that your overwhelming compulsion to be very argumentative and opinionated in group discussions is really quite extraordinary."

It was time again for Boritz to give additional spice to the history teacher's comments.

"Your teacher continues by adding, 'She lives to cause chaos in these discussions, while all other pupils meekly seek to divide historical fact from fiction.'"

"Well, I can't help myself, for some of the pupils really believe that the Holocaust never happened, and that's a downright lie. The terrible things that happened to those precious people must never be forgotten or removed from our history books; otherwise, it will surely happen again," Polly angrily piped up.

An angry Uncle Boritz paused to take off his thick glasses and give them a quick wipe over.

"There you go again, Miss Argumentative Know-It-All, giving your views when no one has asked for them or is particularly interested in them, for that matter. This, young madam, is why you get yourself in so—"

Suddenly he stopped addressing Polly, for he had good reason to look over in Mildred's direction with a show of great concern. If he wasn't mistaken, he felt sure he could hear the first rumbles of an emotional relapse about to take place, and so he began to shake his head slowly.

"Polly Brown lives to cause chaos. She lives to cause chaos. There, there, dear Mildred. Just take a long, deep breath. We are almost halfway through this very disturbing report," he stated as he sought to comfort her. Placing his glasses back on his nose, he then continued on.

Unbeknown to Polly, he dismissed many of the positive comments that some of the teachers had taken the time to write, as none of these concerned him the least. He was, after all, only interested in the comments that further blackened her already demonized character, and he had to admit he was thoroughly enjoying the response the other children were giving to this report. The raucous laughter caused many of the children to almost fall off their seats, so this factor alone encouraged him to seize the moment and really make up more humorous but insulting comments. He once more reminded himself that nobody present would ever consider challenging him or dare ask to review the report for themselves, for the reports were considered highly confidential and therefore intended for his eyes alone.

"Hmm. Other teachers report that you are surly and abrasive and very challenging when it comes to discussing anything you don't agree with, hmm, your math teacher, Mr. Snoggerhill in particular, for he complains that you are bone idle and that your grasp of long division can only be described as 'somewhat flimsy.'"

"I hate math because I can't understand any of it, and he won't take the time to even try to help me," she mumbled bitterly.

"Oh, deary, deary me! Of course, Polly. As usual, it's everybody else's fault. Today it's the turn of all your poor teachers to take the blame," he said, scratching his head as he continued mischievously to make up his own very uncharitable teachers' comments.

"Hmm, as for geography, Miss Dolagmite has this to say concerning the year's sad performance: 'This poor girl is profoundly socially inept, so much so that if I were called on to organize a school trip to the South Pole, I would indeed ensure that Polly join us, albeit one way!'"

Once more, all children present burst into hoots of laughter. Yes, with the exception of Polly and James, there was not one child listening in that day that didn't think this comment to be hysterically funny.

Boritz's lip began to curl with pleasure as he truly enjoyed playing the witty comedian, for he could see clearly that it made the children adore him even more. He even began to give great consideration to what he believed was yet another very good idea that might well one day come to fruition. "The South or North Pole. Hmm. What does it matter as long as it's a one-way ticket," he mumbled under his breath.

Boritz then took a moment to stare the poor girl out.

"Tut tut. Your poor biology teacher, Mrs. McGillicuddy, has left her box empty for the simple reason that she has not been at the school for the two weeks leading up to Christmas, and therefore she was unavailable for comment. However, we have been informed by the school that she is still totally distressed by the torturous and most harrowing eyeballs incident!

"And as for music? Well, I draw a complete blank on this one," he snorted, as he continued to make up more funny comments that would gain him top marks if this were ever to turn into a popularity contest. "Yes, as for Mr. Lapsongsushi, he complains that your singing is always so overly, boisterously loud and overbearing that he can hardly hear any of the other pupils, or their musical instruments for that matter. He also asks, 'Are you tone deaf?'"

The children now began screeching with laughter at this latest stinging indictment.

"You must agree that all of this is very, very disconcerting," he sniffed as he continued to shake his head to express his total disapproval. "Polly, stand to attention, you sniveling wretch! No, you're still slumping. I order you to stand up straight. Now do it!"

Polly instantly obeyed the command, but still Uncle Boritz wasn't the least bit satisfied.

Just then Boritz caught sight of Miss Scrimp. "Miss Scrimp, would you do me the great kindness of going to the cleaning cupboard to fetch a long-handled broom?"

Miss Scrimp nodded her agreement and immediately headed out of the door. She returned minutes later and walked directly over to where Polly still stood craning her neck in the air as though attempting to be extra obedient to his request. The broom handle was instantly forced down the back of Polly's dress in an attempt to make her stand up straighter.

All the children present once more began to laugh out loud.

"Thank you, Miss Scrimp. Right, that's much better, so let's carry on, shall we? Yes, it appears that even your grades are shamefully much lower than any of the other children's. This is all so hard to bear, don't you think?" he said with an air of pure disdain.

"Yes, Uncle Boritz," Polly muttered as once more she began to squirm before bowing her head further in disgrace. A lone tear splashed directly onto her right shoe.

"Speak up, girl, when you're being spoken to. You really do take the biscuit when it comes to sheer, unadulterated insolence," he snorted. "We only have the headmaster's comments left to read out, and judging by all we have heard so far, one can only imagine that his comments will be in keeping with the rest of this diabolical and most disappointing report," he said as he cleared his throat and tried hard to keep a straight face, for he was enjoying himself far too much.

One might imagine that as a child Boritz found immense pleasure and satisfaction in slowly and maliciously pulling the legs and wings off terrified insects as well as other small, unprotected animals. So it was well within the bounds of reason that he had carried this keen and warped sense of twisted pleasure into his adult life, although instead of frail insects, he now had the souls and minds of defenseless, vulnerable young children who remained thoroughly ill equipped to bear such extreme psychological torture, children with severely fragile hearts that he could emotionally dissect at his will. Happily for him, the pleasure was surely as equal as it had been way back then when he was a young boy.

Uncle Boritz took a long sip of tea from his cup before continuing on. Meanwhile, Aunt Mildred began sobbing most pitifully into an orange-and-cream striped handkerchief that bore her very initials in red embroidery on the left-hand corner of the handkerchief as she continued to tearfully moan out loud, "Oh, this is so very, very shameful that it is making me feel horribly ill, so much so that I can hardly bear to hear anymore."

"Oh, how I hate stinky Polly Fester, for she will most likely break up the family," Toby Trotter sniffed.

"Yeah, well I hate her much more then anybody else, for if Aunt Mildred has a breakdown and gets carted off to the funny farm, well then, it's all over for the lot of us," Gailey Gobstopper loudly commented. "It's time we got rid of the cross-eyed leper for good before she wrecks everything for the rest of us."

"I don't know about you, Gailey, but my buttocks are as numb as numb can be," Toby ruefully admitted as he wriggled back and forth.

"Mine too," Gailey whispered. "We've been sitting here for hours."

"Oh, do calm down, darling dearest one, for I am about to read Mr. Batty's personal comments, and then we can move on. So have patience, my dearest sweet pea, please," he begged. "Right. Here goes.

"'After reading all the teachers' comments, I can only come to one conclusion, and this is that Polly Brown is a very troubled soul who is in dire need of the sort of help that, alas, we at this school are not only unable but also quite unprepared to give. I am therefore of the opinion that she should be temporarily suspended until such a time as medical reports confirm that she has succumbed to a complete and very much needed reformation, which might allow her to join normal society again. I have to say that her exclusion gives me no satisfaction whatsoever, but I believe the warning bells have been ringing for some time, and therefore I feel it is my duty as headmaster of this school to act on behalf of all the other pupils and teaching staff, as well as for Polly's own benefit. I therefore wish Polly all the very best regarding her future.' Signed Mr. E. Batty, Headmaster. Hons. Dip. Dop. Dab. Dab. Dop."

Uncle Boritz then deliberately went silent as he very slowly laid the report to rest on the table in front of him in a manner that might suggest it were a very dangerous offensive weapon. He then carefully removed his glasses and produced a hanky to mop his sweaty brow before closing his eyes and sighing deeply, as if to express he had no idea whatsoever as to where to go from here. The tension in the room, which had been continually mounting, was now at an all-time high. Pitstop, clearly sensing the uncomfortably eerie mood, began to ferociously growl.

"Children, may I have your complete attention!" Uncle Boritz solemnly stated as he wearily got up from where he was seated and moved across the floor, heading for where Polly and a few other miserably loathsome miscreants still stood, all heads, without exception, hung low in the deepest shame.

"I was going to keep this one all to myself, but in the light of this cripplingly disgraceful report, I feel it would be best if instead I seek to share my heart and my deepest concerns with you all. There are certain things about to happen, and Mildred and I feel it is in the best interest that none of you are left in the dark. Sadly, I have completely run out of all reasonable options where Polly is concerned, for it appears that no amount of time spent on ROPE brings forth the changes one would hope for. It would also appear that no amount of harsh admonishments break her unruly spirit either, and so it seems pointless to extend her punishment by adding further weeks and months, for all this will indubitably take her well into next year."

There was an awkward, hushed silence as all the children listened intently to all Uncle Boritz had to say.

"As well as her expulsion from school, there is a little matter of a valuable ring that she has stolen from somewhere. If all this was not enough, she has been most careless with the truth when owning up to how this ring came to be in her possession, choosing instead to make up the most fanciful stories imaginable in her quest to keep the sordid truth hidden from us all, stories that would have us believing she has climbed some of the world's highest mountains with a gentleman going by the very suspicious name of Sir Eggmond Hoolari. She also claims to have climbed an unknown mountain that she wishes us all to believe leads directly to a magical kingdom named Piadora," Boritz stated while trying to keep a straight face. "One cannot even begin to consider what other stories she will come up with as she attempts to further nourish and embalm our already vivid imaginations.

"Yes, she even expects us to believe that she visited a princesses' school of training and then attended a banquet where she was encouraged to eat all that her heart desired."

Boritz suddenly broke out into a nervous titter that very quickly turned into loud, uncontrollable laughter, and this caused the nervous children to join in. Before long, they were all howling pitifully like a pack of extremely hungry wild dogs.

Polly still stood silently with her head hung low, the floor speckled with tearstained spots that belied her truest feelings, as Uncle Boritz did his usual best to incite and whip up the crowd of baying wolves into a deliberate frenzy.

"Tee hee hee. She also tells us that at this banquet she was invited to sing a song that she personally made up, titled 'Give, Give Me Love, 'Cos That's Just What I Need.' Ha ha." Uncle Boritz threw his head back as he continued to loudly laugh along with the children.

At this point Uncle Boritz produced his handkerchief to wipe away the first genuine tears he had shed in years, which were now streaming down his reddened face as he sought and failed to bring this sudden bout of hysterical laughter under some sort of reasonable control.

"And the worse lie of all must be that she says she was given a standing ovation and applause that continued for some time, and then—wait for it—they all rushed over to hug her. Ha ha ha. The girl is clearly a mental case, for her imagination has now completely run riot," he snorted as he wiped away more tears and struggled to bring some sense of order to the general hysteria that he was personally guilty of creating.

"Liar, liar, pants on fire," one of the younger ones shouted out.

"Polly Brown, Polly Brown, biggest liar for miles around," another young voice screamed in her direction.

"No, the biggest liar in this town," Gailey Gobbstopper bleated.

"Cut out her tongue," one of the children began to morbidly chant over and over.

"Children, children, do please calm down. Yes, we must all calm down," Boritz gently ordered, as he was now becoming less light-headed and therefore back to being more serious.

The children immediately stopped all chanting and laughter. Boritz had taught them better than to disobey him.

With the room once more in a deathly hush, he finally felt capable enough to continue on. "Now then, where was I? Ah, yes. As a result of her failure to come clean, we have been left with little choice other than to seek help from outside the usual sources. It is with this in mind that we chose to contact our American friends and brothers from the Federal Bureau of Investigation, better known as the FBI, to seek their assistance in this rather delicate matter. As a result, two men from this special bureau have hopped on a plane and are on their way here as we speak."

"Wow, all the way from America!" one overly excited child cried out.

"How amazing is that?" Hugo Huggins gasped.

"You are quite right, Hugo dear, for these men are specialists when it comes to getting people to reveal the whole sordid truth. I'll have you know that they have been involved in many top investigations that smelled very fishy."

Suddenly the telephone rang, and shortly thereafter Uncle Boritz was forced by Aunt Mildred to cease all conversation, as she needed him to take over and have a few words with the rather irate person on the other end of the line. This sudden, unexpected intermission allowed the children the freedom to wiggle around a little in their pitiful efforts to ease their numbed bottoms, oh, as well as start up a few conversations.

"Quite what is a 'fishy'?" Abigail Crumble asked, a confused look on her face, as she gave Tommy Pulleyblank a friendly dig in the ribs, for it was a well-known fact that if anyone could answer such a question, then it had to be Tommy. He was, after all, something of a genius, who knew everything about everything.

"Well, Abigail, I'm glad you asked, for it has a lot to do with someone trying to get away with something very devious, and when these special and very clever American detectives begin to delve deeper into the crime, they quickly realize that all is not well. So the whole thing smells very suspicious, if not just a little pongy."

"Then what does *pongy* mean?"

"Gosh, you girls are so unbelievably dumb. Just think of Bertha's sweaty socks in the wash basket on a hot summer's day, and then you'll understand what *pongy* really means," he sniffed.

"Oh, yes, her socks really do honk something terrible, but not as much as Toby's shoes, for they really reek high of rotten old cabbages."

"Hmm. Well, anyway, if there is a huge crime that is being covered up, the president calls in the FBI, and they will be ordered to leave no stone unturned in their determination to get to the bottom of it. They all leave the White House wearing dark pinstriped suits with matching dark glasses and pretend mustaches, as well as oversized trilby hats, and they drive 'round town in cars with blacked-out windows."

"Why are the windows blacked out?" a clearly mesmerized Cordelia interrupted.

"Come on, girls. That should be perfectly obvious to all, for it is of the utmost importance to go completely undercover in an operation such as theirs. And let me tell you now that what they don't know at the beginning of the investigation, they will certainly know by the end. Trust me on this one."

"Wow!" Cordelia muttered as she gave great consideration to all she was hearing.

"Yes, the FBI are so incredibly clever when it comes to finding out all sorts of things, in fact, everything. They bug telephone lines in hotel rooms, and they are like vicious little Rottweilers, who having bitten into the flesh of an ankle, hold on for their life and will not give up until they have the gotten all the answers they are searching for."

"What's a rotten-weeler?"

"It's called a Rottweiler, stupid! But as you ask, it is a very savage and snappy dog that lives and breathes to sink his razor-sharp gnashers deep into your ankle. Try as you may, even with all the agonized screaming in the world, you will not be able to shake him off, for once he has his razor-sharp teeth sunk deeply into your flesh, he will hold on forever."

"Golly gosh, how absolutely awful," Abigail Crumble exclaimed, her face now looking very pale and drawn as she pictured herself in a similar plight to the one being so dramatically and gruesomely depicted by Tommy.

"Please don't tell me any more, for I do declare that I am now feeling terribly queasy," she despairingly announced.

"All right, then. I'll say no more, for you're really nothing but a load of stupid old wimps. Anyway, I find your constant questions very irritating. So put a sock in it, and just understand when I say these men are really thorough. What they don't find out by their own determined efforts, well then, the aliens that are still held at Area 51 tell them the rest."

"Oh, golly gosh, how fantastic is that!" a very wide-eyed Cordelia gasped.

<hr />

Boritz, who was still arguing with the person at the other end of the line, was clearly on the verge of snapping.

"Mr. Brewster, what you're proposing here is absurd, if not utterly preposterous. Of course we will be going for punitive damages here, but may I hasten to remind you that what you, my man, are suggesting is utterly ridiculous to say the least, for I believe the defense intends to use *volenti non fit injuria* as the basis of their defense. Now, please don't interrupt me when I'm speaking, for I was about to say that I believe it is succinctly possible that the judge may well lean heavily in their favor if you don't allow me the space and time to consider all our necessary options. That is, if I am to continue to represent you…

"Mr. Brewster, please don't argue with me. You are completely misinterpreting what I am trying to suggest, for I didn't say I was resigning the case. I just said you need to back down so that I can do the best job I can on your behalf. So if you want my advice, go take an extended holiday, and please leave everything else to the professionals…

"Mr. Brewster, there's no need to insult me in such a manner…Mr. Brewster, are you listening to me? I am now feeling most offended. Please calm down, for I've had quite enough of your histrionics…Well, for goodness' sake, if nothing else consider taking a couple of anxiety pills, for your shouting is beginning to give me an almighty headache," Boritz loudly yelled down the phone.

On realizing that his sound advice was not going to be followed, Boritz made the snap decision to slam the phone back down on the receiver. He then took a deep breath, wiped the perspiration from his brow, and directed his attention back to the children.

"Good riddance!" he mumbled while using his index finger to push his spectacles to safety.

"Well, children, this is probably an inappropriate time to tell you, but when is there an appropriate time for such things? Hmm, well anyway, here goes: Polly's uncanny ability to tell ridiculously unbelievable lies has finally found its way across the pond, and as a result of her infamy and tale-bearing skills, they have even come to name their lie-detecting machine after her. Children, can you believe it?"

All the children took a long, drawn-out gasp, their eyes almost popping out of their small heads.

"Yes, after hearing all about Polly Brown, they deliberately chose to call their amazingly accurate lie detecting machine a 'polly-graph'!"

On hearing this news, some of the children began to hyperventilate as though completely shocked and aghast that Polly had found such notoriety—and all because of her wickedly disgraceful ability to tell lie upon lie.

"So, children, tomorrow Polly will be ordered to take this shameful and most degrading test. She will be forced to sit in a chair and be wired up, and then these American gentlemen will ask her all sorts of questions in their endeavor to get to the bottom of all this. And then what happens from there on is totally in her hands. She could still save herself all this embarrassment by telling us the truth while she still has time; otherwise, she will, I assure you, face being wired up to this unique contraption to be mercilessly quizzed for hour upon hour. Sadly, all I have left to say on this matter is, may God be with her!" he stated as he flippantly gestured a sign of the cross.

With his speech finally over, the great and masterful orator took one final sip of the remainder of his stone cold tea and then joyfully announced, "Kiddiewinks, if you're ready, please kindly make your way quietly to the drawing room, and before you can think to say, 'Bob's your uncle,' you will be delighted to hear that I will be coming around with packets of crisps, cans of fizzy soda, as well as scrumptious, yummy bars of chocolate—my little way of saying thank you and well done for having such wonderful and outstanding school reports."

"Hurray!" "Yes!" and "Ooh!" were the only three choice words shrieked into the air as the bleary-eyed but delighted children rejoiced in this latest brilliant piece of news.

"So with the exception of those children still standing awaiting their final sentencing, the rest of you are officially dismissed."

Chapter Nineteen
POLLY TAKES A POLYGRAPH

*T*HE ROOM WAS cleared in a matter of seconds as the grateful and eager children raced to get the best seats in the television lounge to watch the rest of *Bonanza* while they anxiously waited for the goodies their benevolent uncle had promised to bestow upon them.

The children who were still left standing in the center of the room looked morosely sullen as they were handed out sentences varying from one week to two months. James, along with Toby Trotter, were sadly amongst those now doing a long stint on ROPE for not only having the impudence to run away from the home but for also unnecessarily bringing the police to the doors of the castle. On this occasion Polly was spared any further sentencing, as Uncle Boritz had concluded that further punishments were indeed a waste of time, as she had already clocked up a massive nine months; therefore, it seemed pretty pointless to add any further sentence at this present time.

Finally satisfied that all wrongs had now been thoroughly righted, Uncle Boritz slammed shut his big, black book, which would not see the light of day until the following Sunday lunchtime. Then the wretched malcontents were quickly dismissed and ordered to head toward the kitchen, where Miss Scrimp had set up a roster of duties that required their immediate attention, menial chores that ranged from washing up and peeling hundreds of potatoes to scrubbing the garden steps and polishing the silver from his private sitting room, etc.

Meanwhile Boritz, along with Pitstop, retreated to his little private food cupboard to content himself counting out chocolate bars, packets of chips, and cans of soda, which he then placed in a large, open cardboard box. Then, armed to the teeth with all the goodies, he and

Pitstop hurriedly made their way down the long corridor toward the television lounge. Once through the door, Uncle Boritz made loud yelling noises, his way of announcing his arrival on the scene. He then began to throw down the treats in a manner more befitting a benevolent pop star. "Catch!" he joyfully cried out as he randomly threw the goodies into the open arms of the children, all the while absorbing the deep gratitude and adoration from his young, endearing fans as they jumped up and readily gushed all over him, hoping for as many sweets and cans of soda as they could possibly extricate from him.

By the time Polly made her way up the stairs and to her bed, she could only wonder what the next day would bring. Her mind went into overdrive as she imagined herself bound by thick rope to a chair and then wired up to some huge metal contraption that would have her head exploding into a million little fragments if she as much as hiccupped. Her only consolation was the thought that if such a terrible thing were to happen, at least all torment would forever cease, and her pain and shame would at last be finally over.

Polly climbed into bed, and after picking up Langdon to cuddle up to, she pulled the thin blanket up to her ears and earnestly prayed for sleep to come.

"Nighty night, Polly Fester, or should we now be saying, 'Let's all have a laugh at Polygraph! Tee hee," Gailey loudly sniggered as she began her usual round of very hateful, provocative taunts.

The next morning Polly had only managed to squash a few unwelcome silverfish as well as cram a couple of mouthfuls of stale cereal into her mouth when Uncle Boritz entered the kitchen and sternly ordered her to follow after him, the location, his private sitting room.

Polly obeyed instantly without a hint of complaint as she abandoned her stale breakfast cereal to hurriedly follow after him down the long corridor. But as soon as she entered his most private of rooms, she felt filled to bursting with fresh fear and anxiety.

"Polly, dearest, these gentleman are here to get to the bottom of where this ring truly came from," he said in a sugary sweet, sickly tone of voice that was quite unfamiliar to any way he had ever addressed her before. This fact alone had Polly feeling on edge as well as most bewildered and confused.

On noting her manifest fear, one of the gentlemen stepped forward and put out a hand for Polly to shake. "Hello there, young lady. Please do not be afraid. My name is Jack Treebalti, and my colleague here is Joseph Pizzani, and as you already know, we, young lady, are here to interview you. I expect your uncle has sat you down and told you a little bit about our very clever machine," he said, giving a friendly grin.

Polly declined to answer the tall man in the well-tailored suit or shake his thin, bony-fingered hand, as she was feeling so scared inside; instead, she chose to hang her head low in shame.

"Now then, Polly, dearest one, it is considered very bad manners not to shake the gentleman's hand when he is reaching out to you by being courteous and friendly," Uncle Boritz glowered.

"Yes, sir. I'm sorry," Polly mumbled as, feeling really nervous and jittery, she feebly stuck out her hand to then rather limply shake his.

"Right, then. Let's not waste any further time, shall we?" the nimble, bony-fingered man stated as he reached for pen and paper. "Polly, please do as I say, and go and sit on that chair nearest my colleague," he said, using his pen to generally direct her to where he wished her to be seated.

Polly moved very slowly toward the chair, all the time secretly rebuking herself for feeling so very afraid.

"Right, before we do this polygraph test, it is important that you become familiar with all that is about to take place. We will be asking you many different and varied questions, and it is important that you are as truthful as you can be. Do you understand everything we have said so far?"

Polly nodded her head. All the while her eyes fixated on the contraption in front of her. "Yes, sir," she stammered.

At this point she was wondering where on her torso these wires were going to be installed, and she hoped with all her heart that the wires were not going to be placed in her ears or up her nose to act like a vacuum cleaner as they sucked out her memory from within her brain.

Some straps were placed around Polly's small chest, and then a strange contraption was placed on the end of one of her fingers. Polly felt terrified.

"Polly, the wires that you are staring at will be connected to you, and the machine and these will be monitoring your heart rate and skin temperature. When you tell us something that may or may not be truthful, this machine is programmed to decipher the information and tell us whether you are lying or telling us the truth. Think of it like a graph that you might have in a geography lesson to record different changing climates; well, this is fairly similar. Polly, once more I need to ask, do you understand everything so far?"

"Yes, sir. I understand," Polly replied, giving a deep and heavy sigh as the gentlemen continued to wire her up to the machine.

"All right, then, Polly. For the machine to give us the correct readings it is necessary that you answer us with a simple yes or no. Do you understand me?"

"Yes, sir," Polly mumbled.

"Polly, please stop slouching. Do be a dear and sit up straight," Uncle Boritz kindly ordered.

"Mr. Scumberry, we think it best if we alone talk to Polly, so might I suggest that you leave the room. We will call you back when our interview is finished."

Boritz was both horrified and bewildered by their sudden request and failed to hide his offense. "Gentlemen, I would like to be present whilst this interview is conducted, for may I remind you that Polly is not only a juvenile, but she is also under my sole care. I therefore feel it is my duty to stay by her side and monitor everything that takes place to make sure it is in absolute accordance with our English judicial laws."

"Hmm."

"You must understand that I very much represent her interests in this matter," he snorted.

"Well, this interview will go much smoother if we were to have young Polly to ourselves," the tall man in the smart, tailored suit innocently stated. "Look, Mr. Scumberry, suffice it to say we know this is a very sensitive situation, but it requires a lot of concentration on our part. We cannot do our jobs to the best of our ability with you constantly breathing over our shoulders as well as interrupting us."

Boritz chose to remain undefeated.

"I'm sorry, gentlemen, but in accordance with the strict regulations of the Children's Act of 1897, I am thus forbidden to leave the room," he bluffed.

"Oh!" they replied in unison.

"Yes, I wonder, Are you technically fully conversant with this long and tediously thick judicial law?" he had the temerity to ask both gentlemen.

"No, sir. Sadly, we are not."

"Very well, gentlemen. Allow me the privilege of helping you out, for as a result of this act I am under the strictest legal obligation to send a very detailed report to the head offices of the social services. Failure to do so will find me standing in the docks, something that while I am in charge, I assure you, will never happen. Therefore, I insist that I stay to observe all that takes place and make sure that no rules are broken or slightly bent, so to speak."

With a show of annoyance, the gently spoken man in the immaculate suit had little choice other than to give in to Boritz's incessant demand to stay.

"Very well then, sir," the willowy and white-haired man sighed. "Although I have to say it is not normal to have any audience when we conduct interviews of such a highly sensitive nature."

The high-cheekboned man in the smart suit moved aside to allow his much-heavier colleague the space he needed in order for the test to begin.

"Right, then. Let's start. Are you Polly Esther Brown?"

"What sort of ridiculous question is that?" Polly queried, already feeling most offended.

"Please just answer the question," the corpulent, dark-haired man in the crumpled flamboyant purple suit ordered.

"Are you Polly Esther Brown?"

"Of course I am. Who else could I be? Besides, you are the ones who decided to do this, so if you think you have the wrong person, well then, just say so, for I won't rub your nose in it," she sniffed.

"Just answer the question."

"Yes."

"Do you live here at the castle?"

"Yes, sadly for both my brother as well as myself, we do," she mumbled almost under her breath.

"Look here, young lady, please do as I request and just answer with a simple yes or no," the rotund man with the disheveled hair and stubbly chin exasperatedly ordered.

"Yes."

Sadly the meeting had taken off to a very bad start due to Polly's serious misgivings as to the fairness of this strange and very disturbing interview. She had never been treated fairly before, and so naturally from the outset she was on the defensive.

Equally true was the sad fact that the two important-looking gentlemen could not fail but take offense, as they mistakenly mistook her over-the-top defensiveness for blatant rebellion and rudeness.

"I'm sorry, gentleman. As you can see, she really is an out-of-control rebel who, rather sadly, has always shown utter contempt toward those in authority. Truth be known, she is just like her mother, and I can tell you now that this mental madness runs throughout her family."

"Really!" said the shocked, overweight gentleman, who was recording all that was taking place.

"Oh, indeed. Her brother Thomas was a fine example of this. Hmm. Sadly, he was about to be assigned to a secure unit when he chose to run away. He is still on the national list of missing children."

On hearing all these lies, Polly inhaled sharply.

"Hmm, and most of them who run away to London are never ever seen again. Polly was caught running away just days ago, and the poor police officers who caught her and brought her back to the safety of our bosom, well, put bluntly, they were quite frankly very shocked by her outward aggression toward them."

"Don't worry, sir. We've seen her type before, so we know how to handle her." The overweight, oily-skinned gentleman with chin stubble sniffed as he began to wipe away continuous beads of sweat that were now forming on his forehead.

Polly continued to listen, feeling highly emotional and upset at the outrageous lies coming directly from the mouth of her so-called uncle, and once more she felt utterly powerless, so much so that she began to rock backward and forward in her chair in her sad effort to prevent herself from screaming and vomiting at the same time.

Why was Uncle Boritz saying such wickedly horrible things? she wondered. She refused outrightly to believe that her mother had been this terrible person he was making her out to be, and as for Thomas, he knew full well that Thomas had never been a runaway but had died from being sick because no one had cared or shown him any love or proper care.

As she considered these blatant lies and atrocious contradictions, Polly began to feel crazed inside her head, as strong, painful emotions began to well up inside and now threatened to engulf her. Quaking with fear, she began to quietly moan, her torso rocking back and forth as she tried to stifle the intense and mounting inner anguish. But in the space of a very short time, she could no longer hold back the black, ugly feelings that were threatening to overwhelm her as they sought to remind her of just how feeble and powerless she truly was when up against intimidating, powerful-looking strangers who cared nothing about truth and might even want to harm her.

Polly suddenly began to breathe too intensely and erratically, and then without warning she let out the most terrible, piercing scream, which seemed to spew forth from her deepest innermost parts. Boritz instantly rushed forward to restrain her.

"Polly, this is your uncle. Now please calm down," he ordered, using both arms to force her to stop rocking back and forth. He then quickly plunged his hand into his trouser pocket and produced a small bottle of pills. Quickly unscrewing the cap, he emptied a small quantity into the palm of his hand. "Here, take one of your calming down tranquilizers," he instructed, as he then forcibly pushed a number of pills into her mouth before placing his hand over her mouth to ensure that the pills were swallowed down.

"Sorry, gentleman. This may seem brutal, but I have to do this; otherwise, I assure you now, that she will spit them out."

"Polly, do I have to once more remind you that such rudeness and hostility is grossly unacceptable? You have always shown utter contempt toward those in authority, and I will not allow you to hijack this interview with any further displays of insolence. Do you hear me, young lady?"

"Yes, sir, I hear you," Polly limply replied, tears of inner rage and years of pent-up frustration hurtling down her burning cheeks like Roman chariots on the rampage.

"If you fail to comply with this order, then the rest of this week will be spent in splendid isolation, away from all your foster brothers and sisters, and I assure you now that James will certainly not be getting his model planes back until you begin to cooperate fully with these nice gentlemen."

Polly hung her head in shame, privately wishing for the floor to open up and swallow her. She knew that if nothing else, both gentlemen would be forgiven for thinking, if not fully believing, that she was a crazed lunatic who essentially needed to be locked away forever.

"You will therefore answer all questions without any further fuss; otherwise, young madam, I assure you now that you will pay dearly for your rebellion."

"Yes. All right, Uncle Boritz," Polly lamely whimpered as, with her head still hung low, she continued to experience the deepest sense of sadness. Once more she found herself mourning the loss of her mother, as well as her dear, sweet absent brother.

"I'm sorry to say this, Mr. Scumberry, but sadly, giving her those pills—even though it was done as an act of mercy to calm her down—was a mistake, for it has made it impossible to continue on with our test."

"You must be joking," Boritz rather rudely challenged.

"I'm sorry, but it would be a clear and most serious utter violation of her human as well as her legal rights."

"Well, gentlemen, I wasn't aware that she had any rights," a now furious Boritz raged.

"Oh, I assure you, Mr. Scumberry, she does, and so I warn you now that legally speaking, you, my dear man, are treading on our patch! I need to advise all parties concerned now that to carry on would be a blatant infringement of those rights. With Polly in such a highly charged and volatile state, we think it best that we adjourn for the day and start the test first thing tomorrow morning."

"Uh! Well, what about my rights?" Uncle Boritz angrily snorted.

"Sir, may I remind you that you are not the one being forced to take the test. With any drugs in her system, Polly is no longer allowed to take the test, so we will resume this test tomorrow. I hope this sits well with you, dear sir?" said the tall man with the kind and gentle smile.

"Oh, dear. Tut tut tut. This does not suit me at all, for this will surely mean further personal expense," Boritz moaned.

"Yes, I'm afraid so, but to continue on now would, I believe, be most futile and perfunctory, for it will also result in us being on the receiving end of very inaccurate information," the tall man firmly stated. "Besides which, may I once more remind you, Mr. Scumberry, that Polly has taken some form of tranquillizer, making it legally impossible to carry on with the test."

"Oh dear, I'm so sorry to hear that." Boritz lamented.

"Yes, Mr. Scumberry, I wonder if you are fully acquainted with our rather somewhat tedious judicial system," the tall man said, very tongue in cheek. "Oh, in many ways we have the same common law, but still it may well differ from that of the British judicial system. Yes, I do believe we have the nerve to most brazenly call it a system of justice," the American muttered under his breath, "And I would so hate to fall foul of our laws."

"Now, look here, gentlemen. I am certain that if Polly downs a nice cup of hot tea, she will immediately find herself feeling so much better. After all, was it not a famous gentleman of French persuasion who so aptly stated: 'There is no trouble so great or grave that cannot be much diminished by a nice cup of tea'? Gentlemen, if this be the case, then all we need do is add a nice couple of chocolate biscuits into the equation, and she will surely calm down to the point of obtaining enough newfound serenity that we will be able to move forward and thereby give things another try."

Boritz watched as both men quickly shot a most concerned glance at each other.

"Really, I do think we must give this one more shot before we surrender and give up the ghost. Don't you agree?" Boritz pleaded as he tried hard to hide his anger and disappointment at the thought of putting things off yet another day and of the horrific extra costs this would incur, which he alone would have to bear.

The men from the bureau were given no time to answer his question.

"Right. I will go to the kitchen and get Miss Scrimp to make us all a lovely pot of hot tea, accompanied by the finest Belgian biscuits as well as some fresh fruit scones and preserve."

"Well, sir, we think it best if we—"

"Now then, gentlemen, don't say another word, for you are most definitely going to have some well-deserved refreshments, and that is the end of the matter," Boritz forcefully stated as he then headed out of his private sitting room to go in search of Miss Scrimp and a highly desirable pot of tea, complete with sweet treats.

In no time at all Uncle Boritz returned to the sitting room with Miss Scrimp following on behind with a tea trolley filled to capacity with luxurious-looking refreshments.

"Miss Scrimp, kindly pour these gentlemen a nice cup of tea, and then take a glass of milk over to Polly," he calmly ordered. "Then please give the gentlemen a generous selection of scones and biscuits."

"Yes, sir," she quietly and graciously replied.

"Please do as I ask and pour the tea, Miss Scrimp."

Miss Scrimp nodded her compliance by quietly setting about doing all that her employer had commanded.

With everyone now served, Boritz quickly dismissed Miss Scrimp from the room to send her back to her cleaning tasks.

As for Polly, just as her uncle had suggested, she perked up considerably when she was offered some rather scrumptious-looking chocolate biscuits.

"Polly, dear, feel free to take as many as you like," Uncle Boritz chirpily stated as he placed the plate right under her nose. Polly cautiously picked one up and then quickly devoured it.

"Now, we all know that you like these biscuits, so Polly dear, don't hold back. Please take a couple more," Uncle Boritz so generous-heartedly ordered with a hearty smile, for it was of the utmost importance that he appear kind and benevolent.

However, much to his annoyance, Polly happily obliged by instantly helping herself to a large number of his favorite ones. Uncle Boritz immediately sent her a disapproving scowl as she readily helped herself to yet more biscuits, but Polly failed to notice anything untoward, as she was far too busy consuming the deliciously unexpected treat.

With all concerned suitably refreshed, Boritz believed it was now time for the polygraph to be resumed; however, the two gentleman stuck to their guns by still refusing to continue on. Boritz argued on for some time, but eventually he realized that he was getting nowhere, for these men were adamant that the polygraph would have to wait. Sadly for him, he was forced to yield to their wishes. As a result he was left with no choice but to pay for yet a further night's hotel accommodation for both gentlemen, with yet another three-course dinner and full English breakfast now being added to his ever-increasing bill.

The next day the test seemed to go on for hour after hour with the gentlemen endlessly asking the same questions over and over. They took a short break at lunchtime to take in some refreshments as well as a bit of exercise, and then in the early afternoon they met back in Boritz's private sitting room to once more resume this very important test. Finally they announced that all questioning was at an end, and Polly could now leave the room.

"Yes, Polly. Go and join all the other children. I believe they are all in the television lounge eagerly waiting the children's programs to start. Hurry up, or you'll miss them."

"But Uncle, you know full well that I'm not allowed to watch television or do anything other than chores when I'm on ROPE," Polly innocently but dutifully reminded him.

"Polly, don't be so silly. There you go again, child, speaking absolute mumbo jumbo and gobbledygook."

"But Uncle—"

"As per usual, you are speaking pure gobbledygook, so I really have no idea as to what you're talking about. Now, be a good dear and do as I say. Go on. Chop chop," he said with extreme jovialness. Then before she could mutter another word, he intentionally placed both hands on her young shoulders, bearing down hard as with the keenest sense of urgency he commandeered her toward the door of his private sitting room. As he closed the door on her, he felt the deepest sense of relief.

With Polly finally absent from the room, he was more than eager to hear the conclusions that the expert gentlemen had come to. So with hands in his trouser pockets, he shuffled back and forth behind both men as they eagerly poured over the graphs, attempting to decipher every little up and down movement that the highly sensitive needle had made on the graph paper. The moment Boritz had been waiting for finally arrived.

"Mr. Scumberry, we have been most tenacious in looking over all the graphs, and frightful as this may all seem, we can find no evidence that this pitifully sad young girl is lying. So where this all leaves us, we have absolutely no idea whatsoever!"

"What? You mean I've paid out all this money, and for nothing?" he cried.

"Well, sir, sadly this does seem to be the case, for when asked about the ring, she shows no signs at all of being deceitful. She truly believes this ring was given to her and that it acts like a key to a door that guarantees her safe passage into a land she has come to know as Piadora," the smart gentleman stated as he tried to draw Boritz's attention toward the graph.

"Look, sir, see these lines? Now pay attention, for if she were lying we would expect this to be indicated by a sudden sharp spiral, but as you can see for yourself, no spiral takes place. It is all still on an even keel."

"Hmm."

"Also, her description of both Ralph and Hodgekiss never altered once, despite being asked repetitively to describe them in intimate detail. Personally, I would have expected her to significantly alter some of the finer details, but alas, she did not," the tall gentleman in the smart suit continued to inform a now very disheartened Boritz.

"Really, how mighty peculiar!" was all an extremely disappointed Boritz could utter as it began to dawn on him that, sadly, all this time and expense had brought him nothing more than a much lighter bank account.

The tall, willowy man in the smart suit continued to sincerely share his thoughts and concerns with Boritz.

"Yes, to conclude, I think it's true to say that Polly did her absolute best to be as truthful as she could when recounting all her experiences. And when she finally related her harrowing climb up the mountain, well, I have to say that both my colleague as well as myself were truly moved to tears. This girl is extraordinarily tenacious and wholehearted in everything she says and does. It is therefore quite mystifying as to why she would even want to create an imaginary land such as Piadora."

"Hmm. Mystifying for us all," he lamented.

"So sadly, Mr. Scumberry, we have come to a sudden halt, and therefore we can go no further in our attempt to find out the origins of the ring. What is certain is that Polly did not steal the ring. It really was given to her as a present. Also, her friends, if imaginary, are as real to her as you and I. Therefore, she obviously needs the help that earlier on in the day you mentioned, yes, help from someone more suitably trained in the matters of the head and mind, experts such as your good friend and colleague Nick Ninkumpoop."

With his subservient canine growling dutifully at his side, Boritz bid both gentlemen farewell and quickly closed the door behind him. He then headed back to his private room with the full intention of reexamining the graphs as well as reevaluating the conclusions that both American gentlemen had come to. If even this failed to produce anything that might well have been overlooked, then at least he could sit all alone and contemplate not only his navel but his seriously diminished bank account! For truth be known, he had completely run out of ideas in terms of what, if anything, he could do next.

Pitstop, his ever faithful companion, quietly patted alongside him, his long, pink tongue limply poised over his front fangs as he left his usual thick, slimy trail of drool all along the highly polished corridor.

Once again in his sitting room, a profoundly desperate Boritz sunk heavily into a comfortable chair while experiencing the deepest sense of utter dismay, for despite spending a king's ransom on the polygraph affair as well as traveling the length and breadth of England with his good wife, Mildred, he was still none the wiser. Oh, he had to admit the holiday had been both educational as well as a lot of fun. They had eaten at some of the finest gourmet restaurants that England had to offer, and they had trudged over hill and dale as they visited one enchanting castle after another in their desperation to find out the real identity of the ring. However, it had all been to no avail, and this is why he had rather mistakenly hoped and believed that with these professionals on board, all would finally be revealed.

But he could not have gotten things more wrong. As he sat alone wallowing in the deepest self-pity, Boritz continued to muse about how else he could discover the source of this jolly old ring and its true value.

THE TROUBLE WITH POLLY BROWN

Chapter Twenty
GOOD-BYE, POLLY, GOOD-BYE

*L*ATER THAT SAME day Uncle Boritz invited Polly to join him in his comfortable and very plush sitting room, as he wished to have one final and very private audience with her.

"Well, Polly, how do you think you generally fared in terms of this unusual test?"

"I really have no idea," Polly quietly but politely mumbled.

"Hmm. Well, it is my sad duty to inform you that you were by no means exonerated, for not only did you fail the polygraph, but you failed it dramatically. As a result, these gentlemen were left with no alternative other than to agree with me that, whatever the reason, you, my dear, really have gone barking mad. Yes, sadly, as I have never failed to remind you and the other children, a leopard never, ever changes its spots!"

On hearing this latest piece of terrible news, Polly began reeling backward and forward, feeling sickened to the very core of her being. She closed her eyes tightly and let out a small exasperated gasp.

"There is nothing further to say except that in the morning after breakfast, Miss Scrimp will be ordered to pack a suitcase with a few of your personal belongings. You will then be taken by Mildred and my good self to the hospital. From tomorrow onward you will no longer be my problem but theirs. Until then, kindly get back to your duties."

Polly felt as though she had just been hit with a ten-ton hammer as she struggled to come to terms with failing the lie detector test when nothing she had relayed to the gentlemen had been as much as a small white lie—not that she believed in things such as white lies, as it was either the truth being told or it wasn't; at least, that's how she saw things.

Moments later, after being so brutally lied to and dismissed from her Uncle Boritz's presence, she sunk to her knees with a washcloth to clean the kitchen floor, and she felt paralyzed with a sadness so acute that it actually felt like the very life force had just been sucked out of her. In that lonely and very desperate moment in time, she felt she had no choice left other than to believe that she was, after all, in her uncle's own words, barking mad.

Had she really lost her marbles? Everyone else seemed to think so. She thought back to the boys at the train station, who had denied that they had ever known her. That little incident had left her feeling miserably confused. She then formally considered the sad and indisputable truth that Aazi had not even had the decency to reply to even one of her very friendly, chat-filled letters. This was yet more confirmation that she was, after all, in cuckoo land. Then surely the trump card was that she had failed the notoriously infallible lie detector test, and not just by a teeny bit but terribly.

No, enough was enough. She now had little choice but to face the harsh truth that all of this talk of Piadora had been little more than a figment of her wildly overactive imagination. Now she would have to face the terrible consequences of having been gullible enough to have fallen foul of such a ridiculous and unbelievable fantasy.

With Polly dismissed to go back to her punishment, Uncle Boritz then called all the other children to come to his private sitting room for a meeting. Once the children were comfortably seated, Boritz wasted no time at all at getting to the heart of the matter.

"Children, it probably comes as no surprise to any of you when I say that Polly has completely failed the polygraph."

"Who cares?" Tommy Pulleyblank murmured, as he chose to speak up for all present.

"I realize that none of you care, and why should you? However, still I need you to hear me out. It is now a matter of record, as she abysmally failed the polygraph, proving once and for all that she is a compulsive liar, and with this in mind, she will be leaving our tightly knit family to attend a specialist hospital that deals with children who are suffering from such appallingly severe diseases of the mind. It would therefore be best if you all keep your distance and stay well clear of her at this most difficult time. Please understand me when I give this order, for it is not my choice but hers alone. After all, good-byes can be very harrowing, and she needs time to herself consider her ways, as well as to reflect on the severity of all that has taken place."

Uncle Boritz inhaled deeply and, whilst doing so, took the time to observe how each child was digesting this latest piece of news. He still felt unsure as to whether a few might be inclined to want to say good-bye, if only because they genuinely felt sorry for her. He therefore decided he must try one more time to ensure that his express wishes were enforced.

"Children, let not any of your hearts be troubled or afraid, for this specific disease is not the least bit infectious or contagious; it there-fore cannot be caught by simply standing next to her. However, I must reinforce that as she is struggling with such a debilitating mental defi-ciency I sadly have to forbid you all from striking up even the smallest of conversations with her. Have I made myself clear?"

"Yes, Uncle," they quietly and unanimously agreed.

"Tomorrow, as soon as breakfast is over, Mildred and my good self will be escorting her to the hospital to begin her specialist treat-ment that will hopefully one day find her reconnecting with real life. Enough said. You are all officially dismissed."

<hr />

As the other children danced along the corridor as they headed back to the television lounge to continue watching their favorite western, James, who was still officially on ROPE, knew instinctively that there was now a greater urgency than ever to talk privately with his sister before she was taken away—and for all he knew it might well be forever!

James knew with the greatest of clarity that it was now or never. He needed to speak with his sister, and if he left it any longer, it could well prove to be too late. He quietly entered the kitchen, and immediately his eyes fell upon Polly as she furiously continued to scrub the kitchen floor down on all fours. James quietly knelt down beside her, feeling terribly overwhelmed with the thought that he might never see her again, and this moment in time might well be his last and only chance to ever say a proper good-bye to her. Polly stopped what she was doing and placed her brush back in the bucket before turning to face him.

"Listen to me, Polly. I now know that Piadora really does exist," he sniffed as he fought to hold back tears of anguish that his sister, the flesh of his flesh, was about to be taken from him, and maybe for good!

Polly shook her head, her eyes glistening with fresh tears.

"Oh, James, stop right now. Believe me when I say that Piadora is one big lie. It really doesn't exist. Even the polygraph has confirmed to everybody living within these walls that I am nothing more than a treacherous liar. So believe me when I say that I just made it all up as a way of getting through each day," she unconvincingly stated as she struggled to persuade her brother that everything she had told him and the others was entirely untrue.

"Please, Polly, listen to me. I beg you. Even though everyone in this place is calling you bonkers, I know you're not. Piadora really does exist, for I have finally met Hodgekiss, and Ralph too," he stated with the greatest sense of urgency.

"So tell me, James, precisely how long has all this been going on?" she coldheartedly quizzed, her eyes blazing.

"Look Polly, Ralph even gave me this book titled *The Prince and the Pauper*. Here, see for yourself."

Polly glanced over but then chose to close both her eyes as well as cover her ears in protest.

"Stop it, James! I'm not listening. Believing in all of this craziness has only made my pain a whole heap worse. Why, even Will has chosen to turn aside from me, and he of all people promised with his hand on his heart that he would always be my faithful friend who would see me through anything and everything. So go away and forget about it all. Promise me you will," she despairingly urged.

"No, I cannot do that, Polly. You are my sister, and I need you to leave this hateful castle and come with me, for I want us to go together to Piadora. If we steal away in the night, then you will not have to go to that awful hospital where they send horribly mad people."

"Stop it now!" she hissed. "If anyone hears us talking about any of this, then you will be joining me in the hospital, a hospital specially set up for lunatics like me! They even call it the loony bin. So, James, listen to me. Do you really want that for your life?" she cried out as she grabbed hold of both his arms out of sheer desperation.

"Polly, please stop it, for you're hurting me," he cried.

Polly instantly released him from her tight grip as once more she sunk to the floor in despair, her eyes brimming with fresh tears.

"Come with me. We can do this together. I beg you. You're my sister. You owe me this much, and as I cannot do this alone, I beg you to change your mind and say you'll come," he urged.

Sadly for him, all his strong pleading fell on stony ground.

"Sorry, James. I need you to drop this subject, for I'm most adamant when I say I'm not going," she sniffed, once more shaking her head to show him her utter disapproval.

James still wasn't about to give up. "Please, Polly. Please," he implored.

"James, please do me a favor and stop all this nonsensical rubbish. Go to bed, and forget about all of this, for as I've already told you, it can only bring you much sadness and misery," she angrily stated as she plunged her hand into the bucket to retrieve the scrubbing brush. Picking up the brush once more, she then threw it on the ground in frustration as she then began to wipe away the tears that were now furiously rolling down her cheeks.

"No, no, no. Polly, I cannot forget it, and shame on you for denying everything, because now that I have met Ralph and Hodgekiss, I no longer need any convincing."

"What? You've been secretly meeting with them?"

"Yes, Polly, I have. Ever since you were banned from making tea for the tramps, I have been called to take over, and that's how things started. So I don't care what that stupid polygraph read as true, for I now know in my heart that you didn't lie. Piadora does exist, as does the Hoolie Koolie and Hubber Blubber tree, and I promise, hand on heart, that at sometime in the future, in fact, as soon as I'm a bit older, then I am going to go on this journey, even if it means going it alone without you," he said as he unexpectedly lunged forward to give her an almighty embrace.

Polly's response was to ignore his sudden and very touching expression of affection as she wearily picked up the scrubbing brush to continue on with the cleaning.

However, a very determined James still chose to ignore her distressed pleas. "Polly, I'm so sorry that I've been moping around so much, and I'm just as sorry that I didn't believe you from the start," he stated, his arms still tightly clung 'round her shoulders as he continued to hang on to her and whisper in her ear. "You are, after all, my only sister, and at the end of the day you're very dear to me." He wept as he continued to hold her as though it would be for the last time ever.

James suddenly began to believe he finally was winning her over when Polly dropped the scrubbing brush back into the bucket of soapy water and reached to clasp his hands and hug him tightly.

"James, I insist that you listen to me. Please don't leave here. I beg of you. I promise you that Piadora is one fat, big lie that I made up, and it's just all got way out of control," she wept.

James jerked backward and then removed her arms from around his neck as he began to flounder. "Polly, I thought you of all people would tell me the truth. And now I see you've changed. You no longer care about right and wrong, truth and lies, and the like. Now I see you're no different from the rest of them," he contemptuously spat as he then quickly released himself from her grip to get up from the floor and make his way out of the room, for he too had punishment chores that he was expected to complete, and he knew he was running out of time.

"If you won't leave with me tonight, then I have no idea when, if ever, I'll see you again. But what I do know is that at some time in the future I will be ready and fully prepared to leave this hateful place, and when that time comes, trust me, I will know. I am not going to turn back, for I will do it with or without your help, that's for sure," he cried.

As he closed the kitchen door on his sister, bone of his bone, flesh of his flesh, he wiped away the tears that were now furiously and unashamedly running down both cheeks. For Uncle to have confiscated his model planes was one thing, but to take away his one and only precious sister by sending her to a hospital for nutty people when in his heart he knew she was innocent of all crimes was quite another. He was indeed justifiably completely heartbroken. In that anguished and forlorn moment he felt fueled with uncontrollable anger, for deep inside he believed that he might never see her again, and if this was based on all he had previously experienced, he felt just as sure her whereabouts would most certainly be forever withheld from him.

Therefore, in that small moment in time, he knew with every fiber of his being that he now had to use the time and be prepared to risk all to go down this never-before-trodden and so very scary path. It was now no longer just about him but also for the sake of his dear and very precious sister. He would now live every day of his life as though it were his last, as he secretly prepared himself for that day when he would leave. He would have to be mentally agile, and he needed to gain a bit of muscle on his arms. He felt determined to become physically strong, and if that meant using the lunchtime breaks to go to the school gym and get fit, then he would do whatever it took until finally he stopped looking so pathetically puny and malnourished. There would indeed come a time when he would face himself in the mirror and know that he was ready.

Polly continued on scrubbing the floor despite feeling fresh concerns regarding her younger brother. Later that night as she scrambled into her bed and cuddled Langdon tightly to her chest, she could only hope and pray that her younger brother would come to his senses and follow her advice by completely abandoning all ideas of heading off in hot pursuit of the elusive kingdom of Piadora. She sincerely hoped that if nothing else, she had put him off going alone, at least for the time being.

True to Uncle Boritz's word, after Polly had finished her painfully small bowl of cereal with the usual quota of silverfish struggling to stay alive as they floated to the surface in the lumpy substitute for milk, Polly was then ordered to go and brush her hair while Miss Scrimp dutifully headed upstairs to pack a light suitcase on behalf of the child. With this done, Polly was then ordered to go in a quiet and orderly fashion and sit in the car until he had finished reading his daily newspaper. Polly did as she was ordered, and so, without even being given the opportunity to say good-bye to her younger brother or any of the any of the other children, she was quickly and most efficiently escorted by Miss Scrimp to her guardians' car, which was parked outside under a large oak tree.

To her horror, Polly noticed that Miss Scrimp had her beloved Langdon scrunched up tightly under her right arm. He looked so limp and helpless that she could only hope that the unpleasantly strong odor emanating from under Miss Scrimp's armpits had caused the poor darling to pass out long ago. When they reached the car, Miss Scrimp demanded that Polly stand by the car door while she marched to the back of the car to place the small suitcase in the trunk. Then she ordered Polly to take a seat in the back and wait patiently for Aunt Mildred and Uncle Boritz, who planned to be with her as soon as they were able.

As Miss Scrimp brusquely slammed shut the side door of the car, she could have used this small opportunity to take hold of Polly's small, trembling hand to say a meaningful and maybe even tender-hearted good-bye, but sadly she was unable to rise to the occasion by giving even a morsel of human kindness, preferring to use the opportunity to give Polly one very sound and useful piece of advice. "Behave yourself, girl!" she growled, as she rather disdainfully thrust Langdon through the half-open window like he were some sort of unwanted and discarded rag doll. Polly immediately reached down to pick him up and stroke away his bruised feelings.

As she sat alone in the car feeling very scared for her future, a future that might well see her spending the rest of her days drugged up and hidden away in one of the many locked-up wards of the local loony bin, it made her hug Langdon even tighter.

She had heard so many terrifying stories about that place, stories that would make your blood run cold if they were only to be half believed. Polly also worried that she might never again set eyes on her younger brother to hold or hug him in times when he needed it most. As she continued to speculate on her very bleak future, she felt an inner urgency to send a small prayer upward, a prayer that asked God not only to take care of James on her behalf, something she would really appreciate His help with, but she also asked Him to remember to take care of her as well. Oh, and if it wasn't too much to ask, she would be really grateful if He would consider doing all within His power to make her considerably well in the head again.

As Polly innocently sat alone in the car waiting for her guardians to take her to the hospital, Boritz, having finished reading his daily paper, still found the time to merrily waltz into the kitchen, where all the other children still sat at the long tables, struggling to finish their most unappetizing breakfast cereal. He surreptitiously sidled up to Gailey and quietly whispered something in her ear.

"Go do your worst, Gailey," he muttered as he gave her a friendly pat of approval on the head.

He then stood in the center of the dining area of the large kitchen and called everyone to attention, for he had an important announcement to make. "Children, I know I gave you strict instructions to steer well clear of Polly. If I am correct, I also forbade you all to engage in any conversation with her whatsoever; well, I am about to release you from this obligation. Polly is due to leave for the hospital, and I think it would be appropriate if you were to all go out to the car and give her a final send-off."

"Oh, do we 'ave to? For I've only just started eating me breakfast," Tommy Pulleyblank sulked.

"Yes, you do. Look, I know that most of you have not yet finished your cereal, but as we are due to depart in about ten or so minutes, it would be good if you were to get up from your seats to go out and say your good-byes. I promise your breakfast will still be here when you return. So do as I say and go see her," he sternly ordered.

Seconds later saw all the children, minus one, gathering like a pack of out-of control-hoodlums as they quickly surrounded the car. Boritz, for his part, stood watching from a large window in the long corridor with Pitstop drooling by his side. As he stood in the hall looking out of the window, he casually jangled his big bunch of jailer keys, all the while callously observing all that was taking place outside by the car. His face betrayed nothing short of total amusement.

"Polly Brown, Polly Brown, the biggest loony's leavin' town," they chanted as they danced around the car like Indians on the warpath. The chanting got louder and more frenzied by the minute as they stuck their noses up to the window and pulled idiotic faces, wiggling their fingers in their ears and poking their tongues out like a brood of vipers.

Unbeknown to Boritz, a little farther down the hall, young James had taken it upon himself to stay behind and anxiously kneel on a window seat to watch out the window. He was therefore an extra witness to all the cruelty and vicious taunting that was taking place outside. However, unlike Boritz, he could only watch, feeling utterly powerless as well as sick to the pit of his stomach.

Soon James turned his attention from the window and tentatively peered down the passageway. James's heart began pounding loudly as he realized that Uncle Boritz had no idea that he was hiding away in one of the many window seats. He hoped and prayed that he would not be discovered, for he knew if he were caught, he would indeed be brutally punished.

While still gazing in Uncle Boritz's direction, in that briefest of moments James was flabbergasted to see just how much his guardian was thoroughly relishing and savoring every moment of this terrible scene. It was blatantly obvious to him that Uncle Boritz was the instigator behind this terrible event, as the children's heinous antics caused his uncle to chuckle out loud, at one point almost doubling him over with raucous laughter.

Finally Boritz stopped for long enough to look down at his watch, and he observed that the children had been out by the car for just over five minutes.

"This is giving me such pleasure," he loudly mused, "so let's say we give them another ten minutes or so," he muttered as he patted Pitstop on the head.

Pitstop made a loud whimper as if to express that this was all very boring for him, as he was unable to see a thing of what was going on as the window was well out of his reach.

"Oh, you poor thing. I didn't realize you were missing out on all the fun that is going on outside. So come on then, my big pooch. Jump up on this window seat. There's a good boy," he cried.

Outside, Gailey then began to sing a little ditty. "Come on, all of you, sing along," she cried as, picking up a fallen piece of branch from the ground, she then leaned into the car to poke and jab poor Polly.

Polly held her hands up to cover and protect her face.

"Oh, you're such a little scaredy cat," griped Gailey. "Come on, everyone. Now's yer last chance for payback," she bawled.

"Good-bye, Polly. Good-bye. Good-bye, Polly. Good-bye. Ha ha. We'll see you again, though we don't know or care when. Good-bye, Polly. Good-bye."

Gailey then reached in with her stick to give Polly another sharp jab in the ribs.

Polly curled into a small tight ball, her trembling hands now covering her ears as their screaming and howling felt overwhelmingly terrifying. She felt like an injured animal caught in a hunter's trap. She had nowhere to run or hide, and she even began to feel afraid for her life. She tried to crouch down on the floor of the car, as she mistakenly believed this might help protect her, as they would find it harder to reach in and hurt her. She was wrong.

"See yer, see yer, wouldn't wanna be yer," one of the older boys yelled out before picking up a small stone from the ground to lob at her. The stone hit her shoulder before bouncing off. He then threw another stone at her. "Bull's-eye," he screeched as the small stone hit her forehead, causing it to instantly begin bleeding.

"Loony, loony, the lunatic dipstick is off on the funny farm trip," they taunted.

"Yeah, she's off to the madhouse."

"No, it ain't the madhouse; it's the nutter's house, more like."

"Yeah, a one-way ticket with the barmy army."

"Yeah, she's off to la-la land, where, if they have any sense, they'll fry her brains," Gailey taunted.

"What brains? She ain't got any!" Toby Trotter sneered.

"Eh, rat bag. Take this," Gailey screamed as she reached in to give Polly a good, hard punch. In no time at all they were taking it in turns to reach in and punch, thump, scratch, or pull her hair.

Polly was helpless to do anything.

<hr />

James knelt on the window seat feeling completely paralyzed as he watched his precious sister cowering with fear on the backseat of the car with the frenzied mob of baying wolves attacking her with whatever came to hand, which included sticks, stones, and shoes.

Shaking violently from head to toe, he was forced into placing a timely hand over his mouth to muzzle the desperately painful whimpers that were coming from deep inside and were threatening to escape, for he determined that his presence in the corridor must remain a secret from Uncle Boritz.

"Someone, please help her," he croaked.

Seconds later what had been nothing more than a light, breezy wind noticeably began to pick up. Then within a matter of seconds, dark clouds quickly began to roll in. Soon the wind was howling and moaning in low-pitched tones as though it were preparing to go into the deepest fit of mourning. Large spots of rain began to hit the window panes with great force, their intensity increasing with each second that passed by.

"Oh, dear. I'd better call them in soon, for it looks like we're heading for an almighty downpour," Boritz gloomily informed his highly favored canine beast. "There was no mention whatsoever of this on the forecast this morning. How could they get it this so wrong?" he muttered.

Before he had even finished his sentence, an almighty boom, followed by a terrifyingly loud crack, rang through the sky as the enraged heavens finally burst forth, pouring down their vial of liquid fury on the earth below. Flashing, fiery lights swiftly cut through the veiled, dark skies like menacingly sharpened swords dividing asunder the surly, slothful clouds as in some deranged and frenzied stupor they dramatically lit up the heavens with their sheer brilliance.

"Oh, my goodness. Pitstop, I do believe the children will by now be soaked to the skin," he sniffed. "Yes, I think they've had long enough," he stated as once more he observed the time on his watch. "Yes, they've had a good fifteen minutes. Time enough, wouldn't you say, Pitstop? We'd better call them in quickly before they either drown or catch pneumonia. Yes, Mildred, would certainly give me much grief if that were to happen."

Pitstop growled his approval.

On Boritz's supreme orders, the children were reluctantly forced to back off and stop their childish games. As they reached the front door, it was clear that they were indeed dripping from head to toe. "Goodness me, you're all absolutely drenched. Now, do as I say and go upstairs and dry off and change, and make sure you put your wet clothes in the wash bin before Aunt Mildred gets to see you all in this terrible state," he commanded.

"Yes, Uncle Boritz," they simpered.

"Right, my little whippersnappers, I appeal to the lot of you to calm down. Yes, calm down. That's better. Now, you older ones do as I say and help the younger ones to get dried down, for they are soaked to the skin," he sternly ordered.

It was only a matter of a few seconds later that Mildred appeared on the scene, only to brightly announce that she was finally ready to go with her husband and Polly to the hospital.

"Boritz dear, please tell me, where are all the children?" she innocently asked.

"Oh, they all got a little bit wet," he quickly replied.

"All of them?"

"Yes, you heard right. All of them."

"What on earth were they all doing to get themselves wet? Oh, Boritz dear, please don't tell me you allowed them to go outside in the rain without their mackintoshes and Wellington boots?" she despairingly cried.

"Well, they were all thoughtfully wishing to say their last goodbyes to Polly when, without any warning, the heavens decided to send unexpected judgment by opening up. I tell you, my dear one, it took only a matter of seconds for vast torrents of rain to come down. Anyway, Mildred, I've got it all under control, so please don't worry your pretty head about a thing. As we speak, the children are upstairs drying off, and they will be down any moment now, for most of them are still wishing to finish up their breakfast cereal."

"Yes, but wet clothes means extra washing for Miss Scrimp and myself to do," she bitterly moaned.

"Yes, but you, my dear, will be with me all day, so it's Miss Scrimp who by all accounts should be complaining."

True to his word, the children appeared one by one and immediately headed back to the dining area of the kitchen to quickly polish off what remained of the cereal in their breakfast bowls.

"Children, behave yourselves, and let me warn you now, if any of you dare to give Miss Scrimp even the teeniest amount of trouble or strife, you'll be in for the high jump when I return. Do I make myself clear?"

"Yes, Uncle Boritz."

Meanwhile James, who had been hiding behind some curtains for some time now, finally found the courage to slide cautiously down from the window seat. On discovering that he was alone in the corridor, he slowly made his way toward the kitchen, his legs feeling like lead weights and his vexed heart equally heavy. He felt terribly confused inside, as he anxiously wondered what, if anything, he should do next. He reasoned that he had tried to say good-bye the night before, so Polly might well understand why he had not joined the others when they came out of the house to supposedly say good-bye. He also realized that to try and help her by fending the others off would have proved to be seriously futile, for sadly he was much younger as well as much weaker than most of the other boys. All the same, his conscience was already beginning to prick him.

No sooner had he determined that it was now safe for him to go outside and say a proper last good-bye, but he was confronted by his guardians as they left the kitchen to head out of the front door.

"James, what are you doing in the corridor?" Uncle Boritz demanded to know.

"Nothing, Uncle," James hesitantly replied.

"Well, go and join the others in the kitchen, and if nothing else, you can help with the washing up," Mildred barked.

James remained silent, preferring just to nod his head as he opened the kitchen door and pretended to go in.

James waited until he heard the loud, abrasive click of the front door before he turned on his heels to once more head back out into the corridor. He waited a few more minutes and then determined to make one last desperate dash outside to say even a fleeting good-bye to his dear sister. On the way to the front door he quickly glanced out of one of the many windows. He could just about see the head of Polly in the back of the car.

"Oh, no. I think I've left it too late," he cried in a deeply anguished voice.

"Goodness, girl, sit up straight," Mildred angrily demanded as she handed Boritz the collapsed but still dripping umbrella for him to throw down on the backseat. "And you can stop all that ridiculous whimpering and sobbing right now, for I simply refuse to sit here and listen to that wearisome racket all the way to the hospital. Do as I order and sit up straight. And tell me, girl, how come when we only leave you alone for a mere ten minutes I come to find you in this terrible state with blood dripping profusely down your face? Here, take this handkerchief and wipe your bleeding forehead, as well as your snotty little nose, before you spoil or stain the interior of our car. Do it now, you sniveling little wretch!" she growled as she dispassionately dropped a spare handkerchief over her shoulder and onto Polly's lap.

"My dear, may I step in here and suggest that Polly has done this to herself? As I watched from a window I could clearly see her banging her head on the back of the driver's seat headrest."

"Good gracious. What will the girl think to do next?" Mildred said, shaking her head to show her absolute disgust.

"Yes, Mildred, these are just more attention-seeking antics on her part, and so we'd do best to ignore them entirely."

"That's all well and good, Boritz, but think of the implications if we were to turn up at the hospital with her looking this way. Why, people might mistakenly believe that we had something to do with it, and that would never do. No, Bortiz dear, if she believes this pity party will get her more sympathy at the hospital, well, she can jolly well think again. I, for one, am having none of it," Mildred angrily snorted. "Yes, child, once we arrive at the hospital I will if necessary escort you into the women's bathroom and hold your head under a running tap while you will rinse your face. Is that clear? Until then hold the handkerchief to your forehead to stem the bleeding," she once again growled. "Boritz, dearest, please remember to drive with great care, for this weather has indeed turned most foul."

◆◆◆

James watched from the window as Aunt Mildred attempted to make her self comfortable in the front passenger seat and tossed a handkerchief in Polly's direction. He then listened as Uncle Boritz got into the driver's side of the car before slamming the door shut.

He then heard the familiar whirr as Uncle Boritz turned the ignition key. He made a loud gasp.

At the time he had no idea whatsoever that this final noise would haunt him night and day for sometime to come.

"Oh no! I cannot let her leave without telling her once more that despite everything I really do love her," he anxiously cried as he ran toward the front door and struggled to open it. His heart was once more pounding loudly within his breast as he tried his hardest to unbolt the door and then get to the car before it drove off. But it really was too late. By the time he got to where the car had previously stood under the large oak tree, he could only watch on helplessly as the car with Polly in the backseat swept through the black gates and immediately disappeared from view.

He hardly noticed that he was soaked through to the skin as the mischievous wind howled menacingly in his ears and the sheet rain continued to ferociously harass and bombard him from all sides. "Oh no!" was all the distraught young boy could mournfully cry as he crumpled to the ground, the small but sharp gravel stones piercing deep into the flesh of his knees, causing him to wince and cry out loud with the excruciatingly fierce pain.

Flashes of unbridled lightning continued to wreak havoc as they ripped across the listless, brooding sky before reaching down to angrily strike at any object in their path, and the aggressive thunder defiantly boomed, as if wishing to provoke him yet further with its restless and most terrifying noise. James felt wild. He felt bereft. He felt like an emptied chasm sorely grieved and bewildered. He felt numbed to the core of his being, yet burdened with the deepest anguish he had ever known. Momentarily stripped of all dignity, he suddenly reached over, and using both hands he scooped up a mixture of muddy earth and gravel. In an unthinkable and crazed state of emotion, he crammed the muddy gravel deep into his open mouth. Then, still down on his bloodied knees, with both fists tightly clenched, his contorted, tearstained face reaching upward toward the still-weeping heavens, he roared the deepest, most gut-wrenching noise that a deeply distressed soul could ever think to make. It was a cry so loud and grievously pitiful that the nearby trees were instantly stripped of all birds.

He then hung his head in sorrowful silence as in a state of abject brokenness he solemnly began to grieve both his brother, Thomas, who had gone to an early grave, and now his dearly departed sister, who though very much alive might as well be dead, for in that agonizing moment he firmly believed he would never see her again.

Chapter Twenty-One
IT'S A MAD WORLD

Meanwhile, back in Piadora a most urgent meeting had been called.

Hodgekiss shook his head in seeming consternation as he experienced Ralph in a most peculiar if not highly emotional state, as he feverishly shared with Hodgekiss and all the other angelic beings all that had befallen young Polly.

"Enough is enough! She needs an intervention! Surely it is time for us do something to help her?" he cried with an air of extreme exasperation. "Also, I believe it would not be in James's best interest to go on this journey at this particular moment in time. He's much too distraught by all that is happening around him, and this would only serve to adversely affect his judgment skills. So again, would it not be wise for us to encourage him to wait a little longer?"

Hodgekiss remained silent as he considered all that was being shared with him.

"Hodgekiss, if nothing else, I implore you to send a few of us down there with a view to intervene."

"Yes, on the subject of her younger brother I am in full agreement that James should be encouraged to persevere at the castle a little longer. His frame is so tiny. He needs to be encouraged to get into some kind of sport, yes, a sport that will toughen him up and see to it that he gets a few hairs on his chest."

"Oh, surely he's much too young to be sporting a hairy chest?" Mrs. O'Brien piped up.

"Mrs. O'Brien, it was merely a figure of speech," Hodgekiss tried to reassure her.

"Oh, good. But clearly he is still too young and gullible, if not a teensy bit puny, if you don't mind me saying."

"Well, he has a little time on his hands before we give him a proper invite, and so by a wealth of means we are going to encourage him to begin using the school gym."

"Simply splendid."

"I also understand entirely how awful you must feel, Ralph, for I too feel very troubled by all I see. But I must take the time to ask you, Is it right for us to continually interfere in the very messy affairs of mankind?"

"To answer correctly, I feel that most times it is best to leave mere mortals to sort things out amongst themselves, but—"

"I know you're right, Ralph, but answer this one honestly: Do mortals really do all within their power to sort things out amongst themselves? If so, why are there so many broken families and so many crazed and bleeding soldiers, dazed and destroyed as they stumble off the latest battlefield?" he asked, his eyes blazing with the deepest compassion.

"You are quite right, Hodgekiss, for humans suffer so much with stupid pride, and they appear to have so little ability to forgive. But Hodgekiss, this situation is very different from anything we have yet come up against. Look, she has even cried out for help. So can we really stand by and do nothing? And what about dear James? With Polly gone he might well become the next scapegoat. You know as well as I do that bullies always need a victim to feed off."

"Yes, I am considering what we can do to help James. But setting James aside, at least for the time being, pray, tell me, Ralph, if you could do anything you wished, what precisely would you care to do?"

Ralph shut his eyes momentarily before answering decisively. "Please allow me the privilege of at least paying Polly a visit in the hospital."

"Oh, and how do you propose to get past security in order to see her? It's well known that this particular hospital is as secure as any prison."

"Well, that's the easy part, for I shall visit the hospital as Lady Ralphella Butterkist, and I will attend the official ward opening ceremony as the highly honored guest whose duty it is to cut through the ribbon. I have always wanted to be the chosen one to cut through the ribbon with oversized scissors."

"Wait a minute, Ralph! What new ward? They have had to penny pinch for years."

"Ah, yes. Well, Hodgekiss, I do believe that's where we fit in, for Lady Ralphella Butterkist is such a delightfully charitable philanthropist, and believe it or not, she is about to donate a handsomely generous check to the hospital that will more than pay for this new ward to be built."

"Hmm. Go on, Ralph."

"Well, naturally, having been so generous, she will then be the obvious choice as the celebrity invited to cut the ribbon, don't you think?"

Hodgekiss shook his head and smiled as he pictured his extraordinarily passionate friend now suspiciously impersonating a high-society lady going by the very dubious name of Lady Ralphella Butterkist.

"Hodgekiss, may I also take Giles Blenkinsopp along with me, for if I am to appear like the very wealthy lady that I am, well then, I will need somebody to play the part of my devoted but downtrodden butler. And if you rightly remember, he was a butler for real when he lived and worked down there at Madhatterly Manor, so he wouldn't be a fish out of water."

"He might not be, but what of you, Ralph? I hope you really do know what you're getting yourself into."

"Yes, I do. And besides, this will be the most exciting adventure I have ever gone on," he stated as he gave Hodgekiss a ridiculously impish grin.

"Very well, Ralph, my good friend. I do believe you have come up with a bright and very pertinent idea, and it is good that Giles gets to see firsthand how we get things done when we dare to cross paths with members of the human race. Oh, and while we are at it, I would also like to suggest that a number of us who know and love young Polly write her a few thoughtful little messages of encouragement—not too many words, just something helpful that will pierce her soul and help her once more to believe in herself, as well as Piadora."

"Yes, yes, I will immediately get the word out. Oh, this is all so very exciting!" Ralph ecstatically shouted as he turned on his heels to go and get others involved in writing small letters of encouragement to Polly as well as go in search of Giles to get his consent to join him on this latest expedition to Planet Earth.

As Ralph was leaving, Hodgekiss stopped him in his tracks to give him one final word of advice.

"Oh, and Ralph, for this new adventure to have any hope of success, might I suggest that you take the time to exchange your smelly old boots for a more glamorous pair of high heels! Remember, you aroused a lot of suspicion and almost gave the game away last time."

Ralph immediately went a bright shade of pink.

"Oh, and Ralph, might I also suggest that you consider paying dear Mrs. O'Brien a quick visit to rummage through her extensive wardrobe of clothes. When she hears of your latest mission, as she most certainly will, I think she will want to loan you some of her makeup, as well as a decent looking hairpiece, a very much-needed fashion accessory where you are concerned!"

Ralph nodded his assent as he gave his bald head a quick, friendly pat.

"She may even wish to give you a few etiquette lessons that will teach you to walk and talk in the manner and pedigree of a refined society lady."

Ralph continued to feverishly nod his agreement.

"Ralph, I demand that you keep still while I apply this pink lipstick," Mrs. O'Brien sternly ordered. "It's as though you've got ants in your pants, you are wiggling around so much. Try to help yourself by calming down a tad," she groaned.

"I would if I could, but at this moment I can't help myself, for I am so very excited," Ralph quickly admitted.

THE TROUBLE WITH POLLY BROWN

"There we go; a superb pair of butterfly lips." Mrs. O'Brien giggled as she stood back to fully admire her workmanship. "Now Ralph, pay attention, for pretty soon you, my dear, will have to apply this delightful shade of lipstick to your voluptuous lips without any help whatsoever from me," she said, thrusting a small hand mirror in front of him so that he could take a good look at himself.

"Hmm. I look rather gorgeous, don't I?" he exclaimed as with both hands he puffed up his new, bouffant-styled hair.

"Don't get too carried away," Mrs. O'Brien pretended to sharply rebuke. "Another thing, Ralph: it is of the utmost importance that you learn everything there is to know about tea."

"Uh, tea, Mrs. O'Brien?"

"Yes, you heard me correctly, Ralph dearest, for it is widely known that every high society lady frequents tea parties, for not only are they a socially fashionable affairs, but it is the perfect occasion for these demure ladies to secretively munch through endless divinely decadent slices of cream cake whilst sharing the latest important gossip over an even more heavenly tasting cup of aromatic tea. It is therefore important that you know your teas, as well as your Ps and Qs, so to speak. Also, I think it might be a good idea if I were to lend you my two little Shih Tzu pups, Precious and Peaches, for many a refined lady has a dog or two, if merely for companionship."

"Oh, Mrs. O'Brien, that would be so kind of you, and I really will take great care of your sweet little dogs. That's a promise."

Ralph chuckled away to himself, as for the first time ever he tried to walk a straight line in a very smart and delicate pair of women's high-heeled shoes that Mrs. O'Brien had moments earlier picked out for him.

"My goodness. What pure discomfort ladies so willingly put themselves through just for the sake of looking fashionable!" he giggled before suddenly tripping over to fall flat on his face.

Mrs. O'Brien let out a loud gasp as she rushed over to where he now lay sprawled out on the floor.

"Ouch," he cried, rubbing his poor squashed nose as with her help he pulled himself up from the floor.

"There, there, Ralph. Or should I be calling you Ralphella?" She broke out into a smile just watching him abandon his painfully sore nose to now rub his equally sore knees. "Now you can see firsthand just how difficult being a real lady truly is," she said, bringing out a tissue to wipe clean some smudged lipstick that was now halfway up his left cheek.

Ralph grunted as once more he tried to walk with an air of grace. "If only women could be more like men, then all this would be a whole lot easier," he moaned.

"You're going to make a lovely lady eventually, but if I'm to be perfectly honest, Ralphella dear, as things stand, you will arouse plenty of suspicion. For one thing, you are so heavy handed and cumbersome! You have no choice but to put in a few weeks of continuous practice if you are to have any hope whatsoever of pulling off this one," Mrs. O'Brien stated.

Ralph made a deep groan at this latest news.

"Does this include some sort of a diet?" he asked, screwing up his face as he braced himself for an answer that he was most certain he did not wish to hear.

"I'm afraid it most certainly does. But cheer up, my dear, for I do declare that I just love your rose pink butterfly lips, for they are most becoming! So come this way, for we have got to spend more time training you up for tea parties, and then it's straight on to master the catwalk!" she said as she linked her arm through his and gave his hand a friendly and encouraging pat.

This time 'round Ralph was more determined than ever to conquer the virtually impossible art of walking tall and straight whilst in delicate high heels. Yes, he would master it for sure, even if it killed him! And looking at his feeble attempts, the chances were extremely high that it might!

———⬩✦⬩———

As the car made its merry way toward the hospital, the tension inside the car was palpable, causing Polly's stomach to begin churning over and over. Polly was therefore very relieved when Aunt Mildred opened her mouth to speak, even if it was only to ask Boritz to confirm the agreed time of their appointment with Dr. Ninkumpoop.

"Ah, I believe we are almost there," Mildred stated with a distinct sigh of relief.

The huge black wrought iron gates to the hospital slowly and gradually opened, allowing their car to pull into the car park. Once parked, Polly was ordered by her uncle to step out of the car. Uncle Boritz then grabbed a hold of her suitcase, and with Aunt Mildred close at her side, Polly was frog-marched up some steps to the front entrance of the medieval-looking facility.

Boritz dropped her suitcase to the ground and reached out to press the doorbell. Polly used the moment to take in the building and its surroundings. To her way of thinking, the hospital appeared to be nothing short of a gothic monstrosity that had not only been built in centuries gone by but quite clearly needed pulling down. It looked so old and decrepit with all the stone walls thickly clad with insect-filled ivy and other climbing vegetation, which just added to making the hospital feel morbidly ancient.

She momentarily moved her head to one side to take in the landscape, and as she did, she caught sight of an old bearded man trying hard to catch an imaginary butterfly or something. If the occasion had been anything other than it was that sad day, she would have had little choice but to break into fits of laughter, but as today of all days was to be no ordinary day, she chose not to.

Suddenly the front door opened, and an old hard-nosed nurse with horrid winklepicker shoes and gaping, rotten teeth grabbed hold of Polly's suitcase before brashly ordering them all to follow after her.

"Oh, nurse, may I trouble you to lead us in the direction of the nearest available bathroom, as this dear girl has had a sudden most unexpected fall?" Mildred sweetly went on to inform, "Yes, we are anxious to get her cleaned up before she meets with the good doctor."

The steely faced nurse obliged by directing them down a narrow hallway.

"You'll see it half way down on the right hand side," the miserable-looking nurse shouted after them. "I'll wait here until you return."

Polly felt like she'd walked for miles as in complete silence they headed down one dimly lit corridor after another. The only noise to be heard as they walked came from the passionless nurse as her shoes clicked and clacked along the harsh flagstone flooring as she continued briskly marching them down the lengthy, gloom-filled corridors. There were occasions when Polly thought she heard some distant muffled moans and cries of despair, but she quickly dismissed all this as being part of her overactive imagination.

Polly tried to keep up with the others while at the same time taking in some of her surroundings. She could not fail to notice that there was a distinct absence of windows, which would surely have brightened the corridors with their natural light, making the long trek much more pleasant. She also noted that what appeared to be all that was left of the peeling paint on the walls looked the most horrible, rancid green and murky yellow, and there was a distinct absence of any colorful pictures, which might surely give patients and visitors alike a little lift in their otherwise dampened spirits.

So, as she continued to follow after the cold, unfeeling nurse as they made their way down the bleak and soulless corridors of doom, she felt as empty and gloomy on the inside as the walls surrounding her portrayed on the outside.

Finally, like a locomotive train fresh out of steam, the stony-faced nurse came to an abrupt halt outside an unmarked door. With no word of warning she dropped Polly's suitcase to the floor and then knocked loudly on the door.

Seconds later, and with the help of a large key, it was opened from the inside by yet another drab, worn-out-looking nurse who, having picked up the suitcase, ordered in yet another passionless, monotone voice that they follow after her. They went down yet more lengthy corridors. After walking through what seemed like a maze, they found themselves being ordered to take a seat in a very drab waiting room.

After making her way to the center of the room, the nurse then stood still with an expressionless look on her face as in chillingly, monosyllabic tones she went on to inform them that Dr. Ninkumpoop had been told of their arrival at the hospital and was now on his way down to personally greet them. The nurse, having done her legal and moral duty, then grunted something pretty inaudible before turning on her heels to disappear, leaving them alone in the sparsely furnished waiting room.

They all remained seated, with not one friendly, comforting word of conversation passing between them. At one point, with little else to do but wait, Aunt Mildred opened her handbag in search of a handkerchief. The next five minutes seemed both endless and embarrassing for Polly, as her aunt then loudly and frequently blew into her spotted pink-and-white handkerchief, which bore an embroidered rose emblem on one corner. Polly, who was feeling very uncomfortable in her surroundings, felt visibly relieved when Aunt Mildred finally deigned to pop her favorite handkerchief back into her purse.

Out of boredom, Polly continued to gaze around the sparse room until her eyes fell on a coffee table stacked high with interesting, well-thumbed magazines, but she knew better than to stray over toward them, so she just sat and jiggled about as she tried and failed most miserably to get even the teeniest bit comfortable.

Seconds later the door burst open, and in marched the almost famous and much talked about Dr. Nick Ninkumpoop.

"Boritz, so awfully good to see you," the old and wizened doctor with the hysterical-sounding voice cried out as he generously held out a very decrepit, wrinkled hand to greet his friend.

Polly looked up, and her eyes immediately became fixated by his most peculiar and shockingly overgrown eyebrows, which notably took on the appearance of wings about to take flight. Polly continued to stare directly at him, for not only was his graying hair standing up on end, leaving her with the presumption that he must have recently survived a severe electrocution, but both ears were also nicely sprouting an overabundance of unrecognizable flora or fauna.

"Nick, likewise it is so good to see you," Boritz replied as he leaned forward to give his esteemed friend a warm and hearty shake of the hand. "You know Mildred, my wife, don't you?"

"Yes, yes, of course. I have had that pleasure on many occasions, although it must be quite some time since we last bumped into one another. Hmm. I think the occasion in question was probably some formal luncheon or dinner, although I'm ashamed to say that I can't think quite where this event took place," the doctor remarked, rubbing his chin thoughtfully as if this act alone would bring to the forefront the remembrance required, for this event was still quite clearly alluding him.

"Oh, deary me, this is quite, quite distressing to say the least!"

"No, no, Dr. Ninkumpoop, or may I call you Nick? Don't you remember that we met up at last year's hospital fete when you asked me to be involved in the prize-giving ceremony!" she meekly informed the doctor, her eyes never leaving his for one second as she meltingly went on to give him a lingering handshake as though it were the hand of some famous celebrity or king.

"Gosh, well then, that was some time ago, Mildred," he stated, looking a trifle embarrassed. "You, my dear, clearly have a much better memory than my good self," he said, giving her a warm, affectionate smile.

Mildred seemed to suck up his last comment as though it was some extremely rare compliment.

As Polly continued to listen to the slightly hysterical ramblings of the quirky doctor, she began to feel quite concerned and could only hope that his seeming hysteria was borne more out of immense personal happiness, as opposed to extreme madness. She hoped with all her heart that it was the former, as he was now the one person in the universe to which both her soul and mind—albeit against her will—was about to be entrusted.

As Polly attempted to show some interest in their polite but meaninglessly trite conversation, which was constantly filled with uninspiring social pleasantries, her eyes were suddenly drawn to a blackboard that up until this moment in time she had completely failed to notice. As her eyes scrutinized the message written in pink chalk, she began to feel quite alarmed, for someone had rather cheekily scrawled, "You don't have to be mad to work here, but it helps."

"Oh, goodness gracious me. I really am in the crazy house," she wearily mused.

"Now then, this must be the young whippersnapper, am I correct?" the doctor stated as through his thick glasses he observed her as though she were some rather vulgar-looking species of maggot under a microscope.

"Yes, sir," Polly mumbled.

"Well, girl, don't just sit there like a wilting cabbage going through the early stages of decomposition. Stand to attention when the good doctor is addressing you," Mildred sharply rebuked.

Polly, in an effort to be obedient, instantly jumped up from her seat, but with her head hung low she still only managed to whisper a very limp, deflated hello.

"Goodness gracious, girl, you are so socially ill bred. You'll have to do a lot better than that," Mildred scornfully reprimanded.

"It's all right. I quite understand if the girl is feeling a little bit nervous and afraid. So let's all go up to the hospital canteen and get a nice, hot cup of tea, shall we? After all is said and done, tea most surely is the priceless cup of life. Afterward I will take her up to the ward and introduce her to the staff that will be taking care of her."

On the way down to the canteen Boritz gave his wife a sly, hard dig in the ribs before mouthing a timely reminder that she was being most negligent in showing off her warm, maternal side. After all, it had over the years been a mutual agreement by both parties concerned that they would always behave in a certain manner and show great displays of affection toward the children and each other whenever they appeared in the public eye.

The next five minutes saw a sulking Mildred walking along huffing and puffing as she expressed deep hurt at his harsh rebuke, for at the end of the day he obviously needed to be reminded that she was truly at the end of her tether where the young, socially maladjusted Polly Brown was concerned.

As they sat at one of many plastic coated tables in the large, uninspiring, and almost empty canteen, the sounds dominating the entire air space were that of the kitchen staff yelling and shouting orders at each other as they prepared food and washed up large metal vats and other large bulky miscellaneous restaurant equipment.

Conversation was kept to a minimum as, savoring tea that looked and tasted more like filthy soapy dishwater, they continued to endure the constant crashing around of pots and pans made by uncouth kitchen staff. However, none of this could even begin to quench the spirit of Dr. Ninkumpoop as he continued enthusiastically to blow his own trumpet concerning all his latest treatments, which were taking him across the globe and winning him top awards in the medical field. "I do believe I am the talk of the town at this moment. In fact, my ears are burning even as we speak," he said, beaming from ear to ear.

Polly looked over and began to imagine a forest fire burning away due to the amount of undesirable plumage sticking out from both ears.

"Oh, I'm sure you're being far too modest, doctor. You are surely well on your way to becoming world famous," a sickly servile Mildred purred.

Both Mildred's and Boritz's faces shone with pride as they listened intently to the scatty, egotistical doctor droning on and on about all the accolades he now had under his belt.

"Please, somebody execute me now," Polly groaned under her breath, as she was forced to sit still and pretend to show some sort of polite interest in their entirely sycophantic three-way conversation while she continued to be completely ignored, something she had grown quite used to.

"Oh, Boritz old chum, while I'm at it I have just had some more very good news. Some darling old countess dowager who I had never heard of before but who, I'm told, has a most desirable and pala-tial residence somewhere just outside of Scunthorpe called me this morning to inform me that she wishes to pay for a brand new wing to be built onto the hospital. She gave me the address of her solicitor and suggested I call them, and they will then release the check."

"Goodness, Nick, that's marvelous, but are you going to disclose how much the check will be for?"

"Well, at this precise moment I am unprepared to disclose the amount, but let me tell you now it is an exceedingly large donation, in fact, the biggest we have ever received," he ecstatically cried.

"Unbelievable!" a very jealous Boritz muttered.

"The reason she gave is simply that she is so concerned for many of our teenage children, many of whom are falling by the wayside and therefore in urgent need of specialist help."

"Yes, yes."

"Now, if Polly is still residing with us when this brand new wing is finally finished, then naturally she will be transferred to this new section of the hospital. If the whole operation goes smoothly we are confident we will be able to open this new wing in perhaps the next twelve to eighteen months. Naturally, we will be inviting her to come and celebrate with us, and perhaps after downing a couple of glasses of champers she can then do the honor of cutting the ribbon."

"Nick, old boy, you have failed to reveal this generous-hearted lady's name."

"Oh, forgive me, old boy, her name is Lady Ralphella Butterkist."

"By the way, Boritz old chap, there must be an overabundance of philanthropists and other charitable people in the circles you move in, so are you at all familiar or acquainted with this particularly generous-hearted dowager?"

"No, Nick, sad to say I don't believe I've ever even heard of her, but I rather wish I had," he soulfully sniffed, his voice trailing off. "Perhaps you might consider inviting both Mildred and my good self to your opening ceremony, and naturally this could be seen as the perfect excuse for you to introduce us over a small liquid lunch. If, as you suggest, she has such a heart for young people, then she might wish to show us the benevolent side of her nature, for our home is always looking for extra financial assistance, as our monthly expenditure runs well into the thousands!"

"Hmm. I bet it does—and that doesn't even begin to take into account your love of fine antiques, as well as all the private golf and yacht club expenses. Oh, and we mustn't forget your passion for fine wines and restaurants either, old boy," Dr. Ninkumpoop playfully suggested as he gave his good friend a hearty pat on the back. "Yes, you've always had a natural inclination for the finer things in life."

"Never a truer word spoken in jest, Nick, for I do have to take the odd bit of time off, as working with such problematic, dysfunctional children is, to say the least, very, very exhausting."

"Hmm. Perhaps it is."

"So how about it, old boy? Will you send us an invite to attend the grand occasion?" Boritz grinned as he now gave the doctor a number of equally hearty slaps on the back as if to fully seal the gentleman's agreement.

"Yes, of course, old chap. Count yourself in," was the doctor's friendly and swift response to Boritz's very direct request.

Much to Polly's appreciation, the conversation eventually drew to a natural close. After placing his cup and saucer to one side, Dr. Ninkumpoop suggested that it was high time to take "the girl" up to the ward.

Boritz used this latest announcement to remind the good doctor that he had agreed to a meeting with them. "Nick, old boy, don't forget that we made an appointment with your secretary, for we felt the urgent need to have a quiet word in your ear before we leave to go home, or had you forgotten?"

The absent-minded doctor once more looked more than a trifle embarrassed that he had, as they so rightly suggested, quite forgotten he had given his agreement for this meeting to take place. Therefore, he called for one of his nurses to take Polly and her sorry-looking, battered suitcase up to the ward. Polly stood up to leave with another haggardly, mature-looking nurse, and the doctor assured her that he would come up shortly to make sure she was comfortably settled in.

As Polly was about to leave the room, she went over to where Aunt Mildred still sat nervously holding on to her almost-drained teacup to give her one last lingering hug and maybe a quick kiss good-bye.

Mildred visibly stiffened to something of a rigid waxwork manne-quin. She then quickly turned her head to one side to fend off the kiss that Polly intended to place on her right cheek. Squirming in her seat, Mildred finally placed her cup down and then suddenly lashed out, "Enough of this ridiculous nonsense, child. Just say your good-byes and be gone with you," she cried.

On being repelled in a manner not too dissimilar to that of some offen-sively vicious flesh-biting mosquito, Polly hurriedly removed her arms from around her aunt's neck. She momentarily hesitated, then moved away to stand in the center of the waiting area, all the while wondering whether in the light of Aunt Mildred's rejection it was even right to try and say good-bye to Uncle Boritz, for she was feeling seriously confused as to what should reasonably be expected of her. If she left the room failing to say a proper good-bye with a friendly hug or quick kiss, this surely would be perceived as her being disgracefully rude, and yet it was obvious that neither of her guardians really cared for even the smallest, most minimal amount of physical contact with her. Sadly for Polly, this latest occasion yet again deepened her plight of knowing with great certainty she was little more than a horrible stench under their continuously offended nostrils, and so everything she did or said caused their utter revulsion toward her to worsen. This sad little truth never failed to cause Polly unimaginable anguish, for to be abandoned by her mother felt practically impossible to overcome, but to then be hated and despised by the replacement mother, well, that made life truly unbearable.

She therefore willingly allowed the withering, taut-faced nurse to take her hand and lead her away, leaving the doctor and her guardians to discuss her behind her back, as she knew they would. How Polly hated leaving that room, like many other rooms beforehand, because she feared the talk would not be good. She knew she had nobody in the whole wide world even remotely willing to represent her and maybe present some kinder aspects regarding her character, so she anticipated that her character would be brutishly ripped to shreds and sickeningly assassinated in her absence. She would have loved for someone, anyone, to question her guardians' truthfulness when it came to telling the many grim Polly Brown horror stories that they both considered excellent tea time material.

———◆◆◆◆◆———

With Polly now making her way up to the ward, Dr. Ninkumpoop suggested that the Scumberrys follow after him to his office, where they could talk freely and unburden themselves of just about everything that might still be troubling their deeply concerned hearts.

It was well over an hour before they stepped out of his office to head for home.

"Well, Boritz, old chap, this private little chat has been, to say the least, most enlightening and informative, and so it will surely be of considerable help when it comes to constructing a mental hygiene plan for her to follow through. Knowing all this will also be crucial regarding what type of treatment we should opt for when dealing with her. I also promise to give great thought to all your helpful suggestions concerning the girl. Therefore, if it comes to the crunch, with all other avenues having been thoroughly exhausted, well then, I am certainly more than willing to consider giving her a round of electroconvulsive therapy."

"Thank you, Nick. We are deeply and profoundly indebted to you."

"I must say that though there have been a few alarming cases where certain patients have ended up as little more than catatonic dummies, there are many patients reporting great benefits from this alternative treatment. Why, I recently heard of one gentleman who, after many years of living as a recluse in a vegetative state of mourning, had the therapy, and his recovery was so incredibly successful that he recently opened up his own school of Latino dancing. Can you believe it?"

"Quite, quite unbelievable!" Boritz sniffed as he gave Mildred's hand a short, affirmative squeeze.

"However, I must warn that if we were to go down this avenue, there are many even within the profession who see it as the most senseless and barbaric form of therapy and believe that it should be dispensed with forthwith. With the girl being as young as she is, it might well cause something of an outcry," he stated as he contorted his facial expressions to add more weight to his concerns.

"Well, they should try living with her, for they wouldn't last a week," Boritz rudely interrupted, his bottom lip drooping like that of a surly child.

"Hmm. Quite! I therefore think that should we be forced to proceed down this path, we would be well advised to keep all this under our hats, yes, under wraps, so to speak."

"Mum's the word," Boritz cheerfully agreed, as he abandoned holding Mildred's hand to take a hold of the doctor's hand and give it a hearty shake and thereby make another informal gentleman's agreement.

"However, to my way of thinking, we should err on the side of caution and start with conventional methods, at least for the time being," the doctor thoughtfully mused.

"While I'm at it, Boritz, old chap, this might be as good a time as any to privately tell you that there is much talk about my moving on."

"Moving on?" a shocked Boritz queried.

"Yes, for I, old chap, have been offered a wonderful teaching post in Geneva, and although I have yet to fully make up my mind, the terms of the contract are, to say the least, highly favorable. If all this were to happen, there are two rather splendid candidates in the offing, Dr. Jellibone and Dr. Herringbone. Both, it appears, are originally from

Trinity College and so are of immaculate pedigree; therefore, either candidate is perfectly suited for the job."

"Oh, but Nick, we would be so terribly sorry to see you go," Mildred rather impertinently interjected, pulling a long, sad-looking face.

"Well, thank you, Mildred, but I'm not gone yet. However, if I do take up the post, it will be left to the hospital board's discretion as to which of these two potential candidates gets to take over for my good self. Anyway, old chum, you must understand that all this is at present highly confidential, so I would ask you to keep this little secret under your hat as well; there's a good chap."

"Affirmative, Nick, old chum. As with everything else, mum's the word. Thank you for entrusting us with your secret plans. Our lips are indeed thoroughly sealed, and so we will leave everything in your capable hands. Oh, and before we leave, please understand that we both feel it would be best if we stayed well away for the time being, as we really do need the break. We do trust that you will fully understand our position on this matter."

"Yes, yes, Boritz, although I have to suggest that if this proposed lack of involvement were to be for any lengthy amount of time, it might well affect the girl most adversely," he solemnly stated, as he then strategically placed a finger to the bridge of his nose to prevent his spectacles from sliding down any further, for they were in imminent danger of slipping off the end of his long, irregular-shaped nose.

On hearing this latest piece of private information, Boritz rather churlishly chose to pull another long, sullenly childish face, which the doctor, due to their longstanding friendship, once again chose to ignore.

"Friends, do not allow yourselves the privilege of taking great offense, for please try to remember that you represent family to the girl, and so it is important that you do not thoroughly neglect your responsibilities toward her. May I be bold enough to state that you are all she has in this world," he said over his thin-framed glasses.

"Oh, Nick, my good friend, trust me when I say it will only be for a short season. Let's leave it until after the new year."

"So do I take it that neither of you will be visiting Polly any time over the Christmas period?"

"No, Nick, for to be honest I have late January or early February in mind, yes, just long enough for us to have a well-earned rest in order to replenish and restore our bleeding and considerably battered emotions," he nervously insisted.

Doctor Ninkumpoop walked the couple to the main exit door and quickly said his polite good-byes. Then, as promised, he made his weary way up to the ward in which the girl, along with her small, battered suitcase, had been sent. Hopefully by now the nurse would have had plenty of time to unpack the noticeably tatty-looking case of her few personal possessions, placing them all into the small bedside locker. He also hoped that Polly would be willingly submissive to the hospital regimen as the ward staff ordered her to swallow down her first handful of "mother's little helpers," a cocktail of pleasantly assorted colorful pills that would, indeed, wash down very nicely with the further liquid medication he'd prescribed to jump-start the healing process. This would, in time, see her well on the way to a complete restoration of her seemingly very troubled young mind.

As the tall, impressively overeducated doctor stood ominously over the bed watching down on the small, frail figure curled up in a ball holding tightly on to a raggedy blue elephant, he could not fail but murmur.

"Tragic, so very tragic." He had little choice but to admit that he felt both baffled and concerned by the thought of how the same girl who could portray such angelic sweetness when fast asleep could supposedly cause such merry mayhem when awake. He would have many months to ponder the question and maybe, just maybe find the answer.

Chapter Twenty-Two
JINGLE ALL THE WAY

*C*HRISTMAS CAME AND went, and nobody seemed either to care or notice that Polly's locker was among only a few that was absent of a cheery Christmas greeting card or two. Neither did any of the staff think to query the sad fact that Polly had no Christmas stocking filled with little goodies and treats to excitedly unwrap on Christmas Day. And while other patients received visitor after visitor, most of whom wished to overcompensate their troubled friend or close relative by showering them with many small, kind Christmas gifts followed up by overly extended hugs and kisses, Polly, on the other hand, received no visitors, no gifts, in fact, nothing whatsoever! She did not even receive a bar of sweet-smelling soap or wooly socks or maybe some nice, yummy chocolates to make her feel even the teeniest bit loved at this special time of the year, and yet she was still expected by all to act as though she were full to overflowing with festive cheer.

Christmas Day saw Polly hide away under her bedclothes for the whole day, and Boxing Day was a repeat performance that saw her with her head hidden under the blankets, as once more she slept the entire day, only leaving the solace of her bed to use the bathroom or to get herself something to eat from the cold, generously unappetizing buffet that, due to staff shortages, was left out for the patients to help themselves to.

With Christmas finally over, the new year held very little promise either for young Polly, as over the next few months her outlook on life seemed as sludgy, gray, and dismal as the bleak and ferocious winter sleet that uncompromisingly held the hospital hostage as it constantly barraged the ancient building, seriously weighing down on the roof with heavy snow. If a patient or staff member even cared to look out of a locked window in search of some unexpected solace, his or her eyes would meet nothing but fields of white as well as endless, struggling trees mercilessly stripped of their leaves, their fragile boughs threatening to snap due to the weight of the snow that overnight turned to ice.

With each and every lonely day that passed, Polly, like those spindly, frail trees, felt equally on the verge of snapping, as she found herself sinking into a worsening depression that no amount of brightly colored pills could even begin to tackle. All too soon Polly was hardly recognizable as the perky, chat-filled young girl who had been sent there from the castle with a view to getting the help they believed she desperately needed.

She therefore had little choice than to attend the group therapy sessions, as well as face regular private interviews with Dr. Ninkumpoop. He used these private meetings to continuously grill her to the point of extreme exhaustion. Sadly, these meetings did very little to enlighten either Polly or the doctor as to the root cause of her so-called extreme and bizarre behavioral problems, problems, I might add, that the doctor had yet to witness for himself.

If the doctor for one moment had been able to get inside of Polly's head, he would have realized that she felt fearful and afraid to speak up and disclose anything that would undoubtedly be repeated to her guardians and would therefore find her in further deep water. She knew full well that the doctor was a close friend of Uncle Boritz, so she fully expected that he would report everything back to him. There was no way she was ever going to share anything of real significance with him. No, never in a month of Sundays!

Besides, what would this well-groomed man, dressed daily in expensive Armani suits, know of the fears and troubles she continually faced? After all, he presumably had a lovely home that came kitted out with an enticingly beautiful wife to balance on his arm. And, Polly imagined, he had at least two, if not three, adorable children waiting in earnest every night just to hear his key in the lock so they could rush to greet him. He would sit back patiently in a comfy chair while one of his beloved children gently placed slippers on his sore, aching feet while his dutiful wife busied herself making him a strong cup of tea. She would then sit at his side while he unburdened himself of all problems that persisted to perplex his troubled mind.

Then when all was said and done, they would head for the dining room to sit down for a family dinner. During this meal they would go on to enjoy the biggest luxury imaginable, which had nothing whatsoever to do with fine food, for this much-desired luxury was to bask in the warm fellowship and genuinely rich laughter that being a closely knit family brings. Oh, how Polly longed for such precious things as family with all her heart.

He surely never had to live with the fear of being removed and sent elsewhere time and time again. Did he know anything of the bullying she and others were regularly subjected to in the children's home? What's more, could he even begin to imagine what it was like to dread facing even one more horrendous day of school? No! Polly firmly believed that all Dr. Ninkumpoop's experiences of loss and suffering were simply gained from the extensive overreading of textbook upon textbook as he filled his mind to capacity with the doctrines of the learned. So what did he really know of her agonizing and consistently high levels of anxiety? Diddly squat, to be precise!

Every hideous and miserable day of her life was a cruel reminder that there would come a day in the not too distant future when, with her time finally up, she would then be mercilessly spewed up from the care system and left abandoned in the cruel, harsh world with no financial support whatsoever, just the challenge to make it if she could. Polly had one day taken the time to write out a list of some of the terrifying fears surrounding this eventuality that regularly managed to taunt her.

1. How would she manage to survive when she had no real family for support or any home with as much as a bed to call her own? She shuddered when she considered these things, for she felt she had little to no ability to cope with all that life was throwing at her now, let alone when she was forced to leave. Then what? She truly believed that to be left abandoned to fend for herself was no different to that of being thrown into the lion's den.

2. Heaven forbid, but would she land up like many of the other children in being sent to one of Her Majesty's prisons? She

believed that she would rather end her life than allow herself to be locked up and forgotten as though the key was then thrown away. She could not bear for everyone who once knew her to think, "Good riddance," as they remembered her only as some nasty, wicked criminal who at the end of the day got exactly what she deserved!

3. With the fear of being alone terrifying her on a daily basis, what would she do to survive?

4. Where would she go? She could not even imagine living on the streets at the mercy of other homeless ragamuffins, and with nowhere to lay her head at night, would she just die of cold under the stars?

5. So where do you go when there's nowhere to go and you absolutely hate being just where you are?

6. Could she pass enough school exams to have some sort of meaningful career? Well, that fear had now been fulfilled, as she had all too recently been expelled from school. So, next question?

7. Would she ever be capable of holding down any sort of decent job?

8. Would she ever even begin to feel normal or be normal enough to have a boyfriend when she was older? She put a large "no" against that question.

9. What about one day getting married? She could not imagine anyone ever wanting to marry someone as ugly and messed up in the head as she believed herself to be.

10. Would she ever have a key to her own door? Yes, would she ever have a place of her own where she could hide away undisturbed, for that would be more than a dream come true?

11. Come to think of it, would she ever know a time in her life when she would finally feel really safe and secure? A place where she could just be herself, warts and all? A place where she could take a day of her life to just lie tucked up in warm bed listening to her kind of music, eating whatever comfort food she fancied from an unlocked fridge while watching a sad movie with a box of hankies and luxury chocolates at her side? Would there ever come a day when such immense privileges would be hers for the taking? She very much doubted it.

Polly shuddered some more as she gave serious thought to all these questions that constantly plagued and tormented her. She struggled daily to ward off the constant, nagging array of issues that stalked her miserable, overactive mind, as they filled her with constant fear for her future. And this was just the daytime! At night there was even less to look forward to, other than a continuation of even more extreme anxieties as she wrestled and beat her pillow to a pulp while silently begging for sleep to come and put an end to yet another round of harrowing, nightly tortured thoughts.

So as Polly observed the quirky, portentous self-satisfied doctor sitting with his feet up on his desk as he alternated his frequent tea drinking with the smoking of a pipe, all the while bombarding her with question after irrelevant question, he gave her no reason for hope. Sadly for him, he was wasting his precious time, for she knew with the greatest assurance that he had nothing whatsoever in common with "Patient 579," for this particular specimen could receive no consolation, for she considered herself to be way beyond all help. She was, indeed, a most broken, battle-wearied patient.

To be fair, the learned doctor, for his part, put Polly through a battery of his more favored psychological tests, none of which provided him with even the smallest glimmer of encouragement, so much so that there came a time when he privately began to despair he would ever get the breakthrough he had promised not only the Scumberrys but also, and more importantly, a number of very influential medical journals. The temporary solution to the problem was to once more hike up the dosage of her medication. But surprise, surprise! All this additional medication only made her more docile than ever.

The Journal of Dr. N. Ninkumpoop

Feb. 3

Having sat in the room in total silence for well over half an hour, I decided to ask Patient 579 about any friends she might have in her life.

At first she looked at me, and with eyes blazing she sadly announced, "Nobody, for you, doctor, are looking at a real Billy-No-Mates." As she spoke of her extreme loneliness I felt pierced to the heart by her seemingly ruthless yet tragic honesty. Finally, after much coercion, I got her to talk about her brothers and about a new school friend called Will, although I have to say she was reluctant to share anything of importance regarding any of them. She did, however, care to speak of two boys named Justin Kase and Justin Thyme, who she had once trusted and believed to be friends, that is, until they had let her down so badly; although once again she was unwilling to specify anything or enlighten me as to what these specific wrongs were that had been done to her.

There came a point in this meeting where I believed I was utterly wasting my time when suddenly, quite out of the blue, she started talking about so-called friends she had met on her journey to an imaginary place she liked to call Piadora. These extraordinary strangers had names such as Captain Codswallop and Captain Humdinger as well as Captain Plimsol, a pilot who befriended her when she last traveled the world on Concorde! Apparently Captain Plimsol was not only very handsome but also a very good tennis player who invited the patient to accompany him to the yearly Wimbledon Tournament at some future date.

Patient 579 also informed me that both air hostesses Amanda and Annabel had both fancied him so terribly much that they often fought over who would make and then serve him his next cup of tea. Apparently they even tried to outwit one and other as they plied him with extra delicious chocolate biscuits. Patient 579 casually remarked that she was of the opinion

THE TROUBLE WITH POLLY BROWN

that by the end of the trip the handsome pilot had put on more than a few extra, unwanted pounds.

Then add a lanky SAS soldier named Corporal Beanpod to the private party going on in her head, and one is left wondering, Where on earth do we go from here? This likable soldier apparently gave her a survival book as a present, as he felt so concerned on her behalf.

Next in line was a savvy French soldier who went by the mystifying title of Napoli Bonaparti. Oh, I almost forgot to add that this unusual and wacky French soldier was on a mission of his own, which was to come to England with the express desire being to give Lord Nelson a jolly good beating. As we all know, Lord Nelson has long departed this earth, but my patient did not hesitate or even question this—or anything else nonsensical that this gentleman cared to tell her with regard to his mission to the shores of Great Britain.

As I listened on, my therapeutic ears on full alert, I attempted to decipher what really was going on inside her head, for I knew without a shadow of a doubt that we were on a one-way ticket heading straight for la-la land, better known in my circles as "the land of no return." This is, indeed, one of the most remarkable and fascinating cases I have ever had the pleasure of being involved in, in the many years I have worked at this hospital.

When at a later appointment I dared suggest that these people were definitely little more than figments of her illustrious imagination, she shook her head and whimpered that I was terribly wrong. She remained adamant that Napoli, the delightfully boastful Frenchman, had saved her from a wicked witch named Soogara when both she and Langdon were held hostage in some murky dungeon of a castle that no one I know has ever heard of.

She also shed many tears when she talked about meeting a young, poor Brazilian boy named Pedro when she found herself being imprisoned in his country. Sadly, it all left me questioning, Is their any end to this young girl's seriously potent imagination?

Feb. 28

Over the months that I have gotten to examine Patient 579, both her character and her disconcerting behavior have seriously led me to believe that she may well be suffering from the most severe case of multiple personalities that I have ever had the privilege of seeing, with each of the characters being played out. This is just one of many individual compartments within her seriously disturbed mind.

I find it most interesting that almost all these people she met on her journey have responded most sympathetically to her extremely dire and openly manifest need to be loved, and all have found their way into her heart by so gallantly coming to her rescue. She therefore feels an immense sense of appreciation and gratitude toward each and every one of these imaginary characters.

Yet we need to stop here and become mindful of what those adults who to date have raised her have to say, and sadly, with regard to her guardians' experiences of her, they would suggest that she knows very little about love and kindness. They would also contend that she openly displays nothing but hostility toward everyone she meets. So perhaps when all is said and done, the girl is indeed grappling with some

THE TROUBLE WITH POLLY BROWN

serious identity issues.

I also find it very interesting that most of the characters she mentions are people in authority. Take, for instance, Captain Codswallop, Captain Humdinger, and Captain Plimsol, to mention just a few.

All these male figures represent power, control, and stability, and so I firmly believe that Polly is crying out for some kind of solid father figure to come into her life, a somewhat mature, disciplined man who would ultimately help bring her actively spiraling-downward life under some form of control.

March 6

Today when Patient 579 came to have her individual session with me, she surprised me by bringing with her a large number of handwritten notes.

She told me that for some time now these letters had rather inexplicably appeared from out of the belly of her blue elephant, named Langdon. Naturally I was very suspicious, and therefore I asked to see some of the notes. At first she was reluctant to hand them over, as she said they were for her eyes only, but eventually after much coercion she finally agreed to allow me to be privy to a small selection of them.

As I read through the small pile she had brought down to my office I was taken by complete surprise to see that each and every note contained words of immense encouragement that were clearly designed to lift the girl's otherwise melancholic spirit.

Of course, I challenged her honesty by saying that I did not believe the notes to be real, and so I was just as certain that she had made them all up. Her immediate response to my very direct accusation was to stare me directly in the eye, and with the most haunting look of deep sadness she quietly insisted that not only had she never seen any these notes before, but since coming to this hospital she had not written as much as her name at the top of a piece of paper, let alone a chat-filled letter to anybody. Her story certainly checked out with the nurses, who confirmed that not only did she lie in the bed like a corpse every day with a sheet covering her head, but no one had ever borne witness to her ever sitting upright with pen and paper in hand. She had never asked a member of staff for an envelope, or a postage stamp for that matter.

I have to say here that it is quite plain that as each and every note has entirely different handwriting I am therefore left feeling inexplicably baffled and seriously unnerved by Patient 579.

March 16

Today on my usual ward rounds I asked one of the nurses to let me know when Patient 579 was out of the ward using the bathroom, for I wanted to see for myself if there was any truth to her story that Langdon, her elephant, was giving birth to one affirmation note after another. As soon as I had the signal I raced down the ward toward her bed, but even after stripping off the bedclothes it was abundantly clear that her elephant was nowhere to be found. Apparently, according to the ward sister, it appears that Langdon needs to use the bathroom as well! I felt like a prize idiot sent on a fool's errand!

I therefore decided to sit by her bedside and wait for them to return. Of course, all this had me feeling ridiculously stupid, as all the nurses appeared to know that I was only waiting around as I wished to check out Langdon's stomach contents.

When Patient 579 finally returned to her bed she did not seem the least perturbed when I asked if I could give Langdon a quick, on-the-spot medical examination. On checking over the blue elephant I discovered a small, shiny zipper deep into his stomach but well hidden by his fur. I smiled, as I now felt I finally had half the answer to this rather extraordinary puzzle. Now all that remained to be discovered was quite how many of the patients were in cahoots with her by agreeing to write the notes, and, if so, at what point of the day or night was this unashamedly magnanimous letter-writing class taking place?

However, when I informed her that I believed I knew what was really taking place, she immediately became most indignant. She went to great lengths to assure me that she had only recently discovered the secret zipper in his belly, and it certainly wasn't there before she came to this hospital. She then stated just as categorically that none of the patients had helped her out by writing any of the notes, for she did not really talk to anyone on the ward. She admitted that she had tried to make friends with some of them, but she claimed they were all so doped up with hospital medication that in the end she gave up even trying to converse with any of them. Once again I was left with no rhyme or reason, because having satisfied myself that I had just solved the mystery puzzle, I was once more left feeling more mystified then ever.

June 24

Today the patient came to down my office holding
a small basket of strawberries that she insisted I
take home to my family. I asked her who gave her
the strawberries, and she said that when she woke
up, they were already on her locker. She said that
she had no use of them, and that is why she had
brought them down to my office.

As I was in no frame of mind to believe such a wild
story, I tongue in cheek suggested that next time
she should offer them to the nurses on her ward.
Her immediate response had me reeling with shock.

Patient 579 informed me that the nurses had been
eating the strawberries nonstop for the past few
weeks, as every day a fresh supply was left sitting
on her bedside locker.

She then supplied me with the evidence I sorely
needed if I was to even begin to believe her story.
I eagerly snatched the note from her outstretched
hand, and once again I was seriously disconcerted
by its contents.

Dear [Patient 579; I have replaced the girl's name
with her patient number, as her true identity must
remain confidential],

Wimbledon is once more upon us, and still there is no word
of you. I recently heard, albeit through the grapevine, that
you have been hospitalized and so are considered by some
to be very sick in the head. May I tell you now that this sad
news is thoroughly disconcerting, for I only met a wonderful,
thoroughly inspiring young lady, who despite endless tough
trials yearned to love and be loved, as well as spread a little
more happiness in the world. Call that an illness if you must.

So I have been left with little choice but to sit through another year of Wimbledon tennis with a vacant seat at my right side.

As a result of all of this I feel I need to tell you that you are constantly in my heart and prayers, and so throughout the strawberry season, which happens to be the month of June, I will send you small baskets of strawberries every single day. And before you ask yourself why, it is because I know for sure that you need more persuading than most when it comes to believing in yourself. So, bearing the knowledge that straw-berries are your all-time favorite fruit to demolish, it seemed the perfect and most splendid thing to do. So, my little prin-cess, I hope you enjoy them. The sugar and thick cream will have to wait another year, as maybe next June we will finally get together at Wimbledon.

—Your good friend Captain Plimsol, xxx

PS: Amanda and Annabel both expressly asked me to send you their love.

I lay the letter to one side as she continued to explain her very unusual situation.

She told me that the first few punnets just sat on the locker until they rotted, as she had no appetite and therefore no interest in eating them. Eventually a few nurses tried to encourage her to eat a few, but still she refused. Finally, one of the nurses said, "Oh well, deary; waste not, want not," as she popped a large strawberry in her mouth, and so the patient instructed the member of staff to take away the rest of the punnet of strawberries to share with the other nurses. Now not a day goes by without the nurses on the ward collecting the punnets of strawberries from her bedside locker. They are then shared around the ward.

Surprisingly, her story checked out. The nurses cheerfully confirmed that despite Polly never receiving any visitors whatsoever, for the past month four or five punnets of fresh strawberries have mysteriously appeared on her bedside locker every day without fail. Each delivery just had a small note attached that called Polly a princess and ordered her to enjoy them.

The nurses assured me that they had been extremely vigilant in keeping watch, as they were convinced somebody was deliberately playing tricks. Naturally, they were desperate to catch them, but despite keeping a watchful eye, no one had ever seen a mysterious-looking stranger on the ward, let alone one bringing mountains of strawberries hidden away under his or her coat. This case is certainly getting more mysterious by the minute.

July 8

As usual, after Patient 579 once again handed me a number of freshly written notes of encouragement from her unidentified source, I decided to give her a large sheet of white paper. I then requested that while I read her latest batch of letters, she could help me by drawing an imaginary house. She was incredibly slow in responding to my order, but finally she picked up the crayons. After giving a deep sigh of dismay, she halfheartedly began to draw. With my pipe lit, I sat back in my chair, and after reading a few of the letters, I placed my feet up on the desk as I puffed away at my pipe, all the while dreaming that I was back on the golf course with all my good chums.

It must have been some twenty minutes before the girl placed her hands back in her lap, and with her head down she quietly announced that she had finished.

I glanced over at her drawing and realized straightaway that her house differed very dramatically from most drawings young patients had in the past obliged me by drawing.

I asked her to explain why the windows had thick, black bars, and she just shrugged her shoulders. There was also a distinct absence of any pretty floral curtains hanging from any of the windows, making the house feel very bleak and unwelcoming. In fact, if I'm to be perfectly honest, it made the house appear somewhat hostile.

Yet again, when I asked her to explain this peculiarity, she just shrugged her shoulders. It was at this point that I noticed that one of the upstairs bedrooms had been completely blacked out. When I asked her why she had decided to blacken out the room, her only response was to quietly moan, "What happens in the castle stays in the castle." I have to say that this all felt most disquieting to me.

I would go on to duly note that there was the absence of any chimney on the roof, which to me would signify warmth and coziness, so I took the liberty of asking her, "Why no chimney?" Yet again she could give me no satisfactory answer. However, there was still worse to come, for I suddenly realized I was staring at a house that had no front door whatsoever! When I asked her why there was no front door when all houses have front doors, she just looked up and quietly kept repeating over and over, "Doors are built to hide all the nasty things

inside. Doors are meant to hide all..." She then immediately clammed up and refused to disclose or explain
further what any of this truly meant.

By this point in the exercise I have to concede to
feeling thoroughly exasperated with her. We therefore sat in complete silence as I waited for her
to tell me something, anything, that might bring me
a little closer to understanding her private, most
secretive world.

At this pivotal point in the procedure I have to
confess that with my throat feeling decidedly
parched and my nerves also a little jangled, I made
the decision to leave the room with my teapot in
hand to head for the canteen in search of some
boiling water, as I wished to make myself a delicious
pot of Assam tea. I also wished to see if while I
was gone she might decide to once more pick up the
crayons to make some last-minute alterations to her
existing drawing. When ten minutes later I reentered
the room I could clearly see that the picture had
not been altered one iota. The girl still sat droopily
and expressionless, as suffering from this ridiculously diabolical inertia like a sleeping beauty; she
appeared as though she might just slide off the
chair onto the floor to sleep for the next hundred
or so years.

After pouring myself another rather delicious cup
of delicately blended, orange-spiced Assam tea, I
decided to continue on with my list of questions,
questions like, "Why have you colored the sky a deep
red instead of blue?" I followed this by, "Why have
you forgotten to draw the sun into your picture?"
After all, most young girls love a nice, bright, glowing
sun in the sky above their houses, don't they? Her
response to this was quite disconcerting to say the
least: "Sir, the reason for its absence is simple,

for maybe I did not want to draw something that for me does not exist. After all, there is no sunshine in my life, just dark clouds—and lots of them." I found this particular response to be of the utmost interest. I therefore made myself a personal note to follow up on this one at some later date.

I have to say that on this particularly enlightening session I went over the official time allocated, as I very much wanted to bring this meeting to a healthy conclusion. I also have to admit that I rather desired a further cup of wonderfully delicious tea, and so while my fresh tea leaves were happily infusing, I found the time to ask her why the sky in her drawing was absent of any birds. I then asked why her garden was absent of any pretty flowers, something I thought most unusual, as normally there would be an abundance of flowers on view in most English gardens.

Surprisingly enough, her reply to this question was instant: "Please, sir, if you care to look more closely, you will see that my red sky is covered in a thick, cloying smog that would surely have most birds dropping out of the sky, for without fresh air they would choke to death. As for the garden, you are sadly very mistaken, for if you cared to look harder, there are some flowers of sorts, although you might recognize them as stinging nettles. However, to my way of thinking they are still flowers."

"Flowers?" I questioned.

"Yes, they are flowers, although they are not pretty, and they rather horridly choose to hide amongst the brambles, ready to sting and bring pain to my bare legs as rather stupidly I attempt to strip the bushes of all their berries."

I hasten to add that all this left me again feeling very flustered and unnerved, as well as in dire need of another cup of choice blend aromatic tea to provide me with more much-needed liquid wisdom. In hindsight, perhaps I should have stopped this session there and then and not gone over the allocated time, as I was now feeling as disturbed by her drawings as I was her answers. However, being the caring and dutiful servant of all troubled minds that I hold myself to be, I chose to bravely soldier on.

After placing my cup down on its saucer I resumed my questioning, asking her why she had built such an extraordinarily high garden fence around her house.

At first she was very reluctant to give me any sort of answer. So, never one to give up, I continued to press and press her some more. In truth, when she did reply to my question, I have to be honest and say that her answer still haunts me to this very hour. She sat up straight and with a look of sheer exasperation, she stared me directly in the eye. "Doctor, you of all people must surely know that just as fences and high walls keep nosy, inquisitive intruders out, they are also built to keep prisoners in, aren't they?" I began to get a little overexcited, as I saw this as a golden opportunity to ask her which of the two she believed herself to be. Her response was to once more drop her head, and then in a barely audible voice she asked, "Prisoner or intruder, which of these two do you truly believe I am?"

I have to say all this left me feeling utterly flabbergasted, for incredible as it might seem, I felt that it was she who seemed to be playing me, and so it naturally left me, her therapist, feeling most uneasy. I therefore made the rapid decision to end this debatably highly enlightening but also very disturbing session immediately!

Chapter Twenty-Three
HELP! I NEED SOMEBODY

*T*HE COLD AND mind numbing winter had finally drawn to a close, taking with it the harsh, cruel winds and long, claustrophobically dark nights. Before too long the sound of restless, chirping birds could be heard as they brightly perched on leaf-filled branches to sing and announce the beginning of spring with its new and fresh, joy-filled days.

Polly, who up until now had kept herself to herself, finally made the decision to go over and talk to the only other patient on the ward who just happened to be of a similar age. She had noticed the young pretty girl when she first arrived on the ward on Boxing Day, but Polly had kept her distance, as she had been feeling far too depressed and downcast to make any effort to say even as much as a polite hello.

At the group therapy sessions, neither girl had ever cared to share any thoughts or feelings concerning anything, preferring to sit back and let others rant and rail about all that made their heads and hearts hurt so very badly. Occasionally, when they thought nobody was looking, they admittedly gave each other a furtive glance, but that was the limit both girls placed regarding any further, tiresome communication between themselves.

Just like Polly, the new girl with the pretty features had apparently chosen to keep very much to herself, but that would soon change, as Polly was now beginning to feel very desperate for real friendship in an otherwise hostile environment.

It was still well into summer before Polly finally plucked up the courage to go over and introduce herself.

"Hi, Lucinda. My name's Polly, but I guess you already know that, don't you?" she said as she invited herself to sit down on the end of the young girl's bed.

"Yes, I know who you are from those stupid group therapy sessions," the young girl replied, making a mockingly long, sullen face as she took hold of a hairbrush to brush her long golden locks.

"I figured you must hate those sessions almost as much as I do," Polly quipped.

"Yes, well, that's because the rest of them really are a load of fruit-cakes!" Lucinda said, breaking into a wide smile.

"Well, Lucinda, you've got really lovely long hair. I wish I had such beautiful hair like yours," Polly wistfully stated.

"Oh, you wouldn't, for it gets so horribly tangled with knots," the young, blue-eyed girl playfully retorted. "Anyway Polly, my mother calls me Luchea, especially when she's angry with me, all my friends call me Lucy, and the rest of the world calls me Lucinda. So I give you full permission to call me Lucy, as I feel we are about to become good friends."

"Here, Lucy, let me brush your hair for you. I promise to get all the tangles out without hurting you further," Polly insisted.

With all formalities quickly laid to one side, it took no time at all for the girls to become firm friends, and with that friendship came the obvious sharing of precious past and present secrets that up until now they had held dear and therefore locked away. Polly felt terribly saddened by all Lucy privately cared to share with her, secrets like the time she attempted to end everything and her reasons behind doing such a terrible thing. Likewise Lucy seemed equally saddened by all that had befallen Polly. In time, they vowed to stand by each other and, in doing so, never, ever betray each other to anyone, even under the threat of death. "True sisters guard their hearts and mouths from all idle and careless gossip, and they will never share with others what has been entrusted in confidence to their ears alone," became their constant verbal pledge.

<hr />

Of course, Doctor Ninkumpoop, on hearing of Polly and Lucinda's new but very close friendship, thought otherwise, and so he quickly determined that Lucinda could be the perfect vehicle to get inside Polly's mind and thereby learn all he needed to know. However, despite many meetings with Lucinda, meetings where he proposed all sorts of extra hospital privileges if she were prepared to open up and reveal all Polly had confided, she blatantly refused to cooperate. Lucinda could not be bought. It would finally dawn on him that those close bonds of true friendship that are wrought in times of great hardship are indeed the toughest and, so, are nigh impossible to destroy. He was now back at square one and therefore none the wiser when it came to learning anything new about hospital Patient 579, whose name in full was Polly Esther Brown.

Finally out of great frustration, oh, as well as unbelievable meanness, the doctor did something that to most decent, thinking people would seem inconceivable: he decided it was high time to break up their special friendship once and for all by having Polly transferred to a high-security ward where others of a similar ilk were locked away for their own protection, as well as for the good of mankind. Here in these wards there would be no ability for any kind of friendship to develop, let alone blossom, as all inpatients were utterly locked away in their own personal nightmares.

Once again Polly found herself alone, without a friend in the world. She quickly learned that other patients contented themselves by walking around in circles or wandering the long corridors back and forth as they shouted and yelled at hateful but imaginary people. Still others chose a more calm approach, such as sitting in the television lounge, passively staring into the blank screen in front of them.

At first Polly did attempt to open up the odd conversation or two, just as she had tried on the last ward. There was a day quite early on when she took it upon herself to walk up to a gentleman who was repeatedly banging his head against the wall, and typical of Polly, she dared to ask him why he was doing such a harmful thing to himself. The poor man was visibly shocked by her line of questioning, and so he looked her directly in the eye as he angrily informed her that what he was doing should be perfectly clear and therefore obvious to all. "I am doing my duty," he indignantly informed her before turning back to continue banging his bloodied forehead against the wall in front of him. Polly walked away feeling very perplexed, and so it would be a number of weeks before she plucked up the courage to once more give it another try.

This time she innocently came to sit down beside a patient in the hope of striking up a friendly conversation.

"Hello, Jasmine. My name is Polly."

"Go away. Leave me alone, for I am working very hard," Jasmine cried.

"Working hard at what?" Polly innocently requested to know.

"Can't you see that I'm concentrating my mind to stop every horrid war that is going on in this crazy, mixed-up world?" she screamed.

This response was more than enough to persuade Polly to completely give up trying to make polite conversation with any of the patients on Ward 707, as she had no desire whatsoever to join in with any of their deeply disturbing and most personal recreational activities. So, yet again, she resorted to hiding away under the bed covers while still trying as desperately hard as she was able to hold on to her fast-fading memories of Piadora.

<hr />

Despite keeping a diary of Polly's progress, Dr. Ninkumpoop was to remain in a permanent state of confused bewilderment as to the root cause of Polly's deep melancholy, especially when he was forced to accept that Polly was failing to respond to even one of his many internationally recognized and profoundly groundbreaking treatments.

All this left him feeling extremely frustrated and angry, and so he recommended that her medication be further increased in an effort to free her from this most disturbing malady, which took the form of a deeply penetrating melancholy, as well as eyes that now appeared permanently glazed over. Sadly, like everything else, this too failed dismally.

July 27

Latest entry regarding "the girl"

It would appear that Patient 579, who must continue to remain nameless, has lost all reason to live. Her bed and bedclothes have literally become her sanctuary and womb, far away from the hostile world she believes she experiences. Very occasionally she still presents me with little mysterious, hand-written notes that she says are sent from Piadora to encourage her, but now it has come to the point where I am no longer interested in either her notes or her little games. I am therefore going to ask her to keep all future notes to herself.

This morning after I confronted her and made my request known, she withdrew even further.

She appeared very confused by my refusal to read any more of them but shrugged her shoulders when I told her that she was obviously still hiding the truth from me, for freshly written notes of encour-agement don't just suddenly appear every day from the navel of an oversized elephant!

Of course, she was equally adamant that in this special case they did.

So, for the time being, she appears to have completely closed down, and therefore she has little to say of any meaning to anyone.

I have scrapped her involvement in group therapy sessions, as she made little to no effort to join in, opting to sullenly sit holding on for dear life to that very irritating blue elephant with a larger-than-average belly.

At mealtimes she sits alone, hurriedly eating up every tiny morsel on her plate as though it were a last supper.

With her plate thoroughly cleaned of all food, she heads back to the dormitory to climb back under the *sheets and hide away from the rest of the world. It also means she spends much of the day sleeping.*

I have to add that apart from the odd, sporadic moment of resistance, there is little opposition when she is forced to take her large volume of medications, and to date I have seen little that would suggest that the girl is an out-and-out rebel who needs reining in. However, as I observe her lying scrunched up in a tight ball with only her elephant for comfort, oh, as well as an increasing pile of darned notes, I am left wondering if, with everything else having failed, this might be the perfect time to consider giving electroconvulsive therapy a try. However, if the response from the medical community happens to be a resounding no to my otherwise bold sugges- tion, then from where, might I take the trouble to ask, will her very essential and most necessary cure possibly come from?

It did not seem like a whole year had passed before it was time to get the festive decorations and the battered Christmas tree out of storage once more. Sadly, once up and in position, it looked tattier than ever, even when covered by the sparse, ever-fading decorations that as a rule brighten up a Christmas tree. Equally sad was the truth that Polly had received hardly a visitor in all this time.

Oh, Uncle Boritz and Aunt Mildred had visited Polly twice throughout the year. The first time they left after only twenty minutes, as Aunt Mildred rather unfortunately had one of her troubling nosebleeds. As for the second time, they accidentally bumped into dear Dr. Ninkumpoop doing his ward rounds, so the majority of this otherwise short and therefore sacred visit was not spent with Polly but with all other parties fawning over each other as they tried hard to outdo each other with as much personal adulation and praise as they could think of.

So, Christmas Eve found Polly watching on as over-chummy nurses and doctors mischievously used this glorious annual occasion as the perfect excuse to kiss and hug each other for longer than they should—under the mistletoe, of course! Some even deigned to take things further by planting one wet kiss after another on every available rosy cheek as, filled with unabashed, festive cheer, they gathered around the Christmas tree to sing joyful carols intended to lift even the saddest spirits on the ward. Secretly, Polly could only feel great concern for the spindly, wilting tree, which due to hospital cutbacks appeared bereft of almost any pretty and precious decorations, save a battered-looking, one-armed fairy precariously dangling from the top branch that, just like her, appeared to be losing the battle to cling on for its very life.

She shook her head in disbelief as she viewed the straggly, fading tinsel that someone had so generously and randomly flung 'round a few of the scrawny branches along with some seriously dilapidated lights, most of which had near given up the ghost and so needed urgent replacing. As she stood sorrowfully looking up at the near naked symbol of festive generosity that was clearly meant to fill the empty palace of her soul to overflowing with unspeakable joy, or at the very least to the brim, she sadly felt nothing but paralyzed by pain and emptiness.

Polly was about to head back to her bed with its empty bedside locker but was prevented from doing so by the many overly excited staff who urged her to come and join in the singing, and so it was with great reluctance that she took her place alongside the other anxious patients in standing around the tree to bite their fingernails as, completely out of key, they bravely attempted to sing along to the heartwarming Christmas carols.

While other troubled souls sang out loud and with great gusto, Polly felt as though every word stuck like sandpaper to the back of her throat. After all, carols, as a rule of thumb, were the verbal expression of abiding hope, joy, and other good tidings that, in truth, all patients on this ward appeared to know absolutely nothing of. Polly could only bring herself to stand quiet and helpless as she forced herself to quietly mutter the words of *Silent Night*, which in times past had been her all-time favorite carol.

As she continued half-heartedly to mouth the words, she found herself looking back on many a Christmas past when she had casually wandered past frozen, red-nosed carolers jubilantly singing by the bedecked tree in the town center. She had often stopped to watch and wonder how their Christmas holiday might just differ from hers, and as she pressed her nose against the pane glass of a tearoom and watched families lovingly celebrating this festive occasion, once again she could only feel the intense anguish and loneliness that being a child in care brings. Many times she had quietly whispered into the dead of night, "Father Christmas, if you really do love giving children presents, then please give me the best present ever by bringing me and my brothers a loving, caring family to forever cherish."

This year was now her second Christmas spent in the hospital and was therefore another year where she entirely failed to even consider, let alone pray, this much dreamed-of request. So as she melancholically continued to stare up at the poor tree, it was a stark reminder that heartwarming Christmas carols were no longer enough, for they neither warmed the cockles of her heart, bringing a smile to her countenance, nor did they bring any form of internal relief. Now, just like this tree, she was in dire need of some tender care and attention. Or, if nothing else, a strong, loving hug would not only be warmly reciprocated, but it would also be considered the most special and much-appreciated Christmas gift that anyone could even think to give her.

Soon the evening drew to its natural close, and the patients were ordered to line up for their routine dosage of medication. Patient 579, as per usual, gulped hers down quickly and then immediately turned on her heels to head back to bed to once more hide away under the bedclothes and anxiously hope for Christmas to go as quickly as it came.

<hr />

Unbeknown to Polly, she did have a mysterious visitor that festive night, yes, a tall, dark, handsome visitor who had finally plucked up the necessary courage to pay her a very long overdue visit.

Just like Polly, he had found the miserably long walk down the dark, dingy corridors extremely unpleasant. He had also felt startled, if not shocked when he was informed by a most miserable-looking nurse that Polly had been removed from the general ward and was now being cared for in a high-security, locked ward.

As he walked along, he tried very hard not to imagine just how crazy she must surely be if she was now forcibly hidden away under lock and key in one of the worst wards in the hospital. Perhaps to see her this way would turn out to be far too much for him to bear, he nervously pondered. His anxiety was to be further heightened as, climbing the stairs, he was to find himself startled by a number of blood-curdling screams.

"Don't worry, luv. They're all safely locked away for their own good," one of the nurses grinned, her open and gummy mouth noticeably betraying an absence of any healthy-looking teeth.

He had obediently followed the nurse up many flights of stairs, his heart racing within his breast as he wondered what he might possibly say in his opening line to her, although there really was no way of telling if she would agree to or refuse an audience with him. At the last minute, the nurse, having placed her key in the lock, then opened the door wide.

His eyes instantly fell on Polly standing alone by the Christmas tree, and in that instant he panicked. In that panic he knew all he needed to know. He immediately found himself hearing his mother's very chilling warnings to stay away reverberating loudly through his head, and in that tragic moment in time he sincerely felt he had no other choice other than to hold back, for if his mother were to find out, she would be most infuriated with him. He could face that if it were to happen, but if Polly's guardians were to ever find out, well then, the repercussions would be far more catastrophic, for Mr. Scumberry had as good as promised that he would see to it that their family name be ruined forever.

"I'm so sorry, nurse, but I no longer wish to see her. I have to go, yes, for I've changed my mind," he hastily blurted out. "Yes, perhaps it's for the best, the best. I would so hate to see her looking so terribly ill, for that would be utterly unbearable, if not altogether intolerable," he loudly muttered as, stumbling over his words, he then went on to push something into her open hand.

"Please give her this little gift and card and tell her that I miss her so very much, and that is why I came here to see her today of all days," he miserably mumbled.

"Yes, luv, I most certainly will, for I happen to know that she'll really appreciate the card and gift, for to date she does not have as much as a single card on her bedside locker. God bless her, for it's as if she never existed before she came here."

"Oh really?"

"Yes, luv. If you ask me, she's as sad and hopeless a case if ever there was one," she remarked.

"Well then, that makes it of even more importance that she receives this special card and gift from me. So promise me, nurse, that you'll take it straight too her."

The old dear nodded and placed her hand on his arm. "It's probably for the best that you don't get to see her as she is now, luv," the old and withered nurse sniffed as she once more placed a decrepit hand on his to give it a reassuring and comforting pat.

"And tell her also that I hope and pray she is feeling better with each new day that passes," he hoarsely whispered, his voice cracking, as he was now feeling stirred to the very seat of his emotions. "I am feeling both contrite and broken," he whispered under his breath as he rebuked himself that, having come this far, he was now backing out.

Will quickly turned his face away from the nurse, as he did not wish for her to see how difficult and painful this all really was.

"All right, luv. You hurry on back home and leave it with me, for I'll tell her," the haggard-looking nurse answered.

Will turned back to look her directly in the eye.

"Promise?"

"I promise, hand on me heart," she reassured him as she gave him another toothless grin before firmly closing the door on him.

———◦◦◦◦◦———

As the nurse hurriedly marched down the long ward, her shoes still making their harsh, clickety-clack noise, from out of nowhere a young doctor bedecked with decorations more suited to the Christmas tree grabbed hold of her arm and beckoned her to join all the other staff in the office for the usual and very traditional glass of sherry.

The old nurse barely resisted, especially when she heard that not only had they saved her a couple of mince pies, but there was also a glass or two of sherry in the offing.

"Ooh, doctor. What a naughty but nice little treat," she foolishly giggled.

As soon as she stepped into the office, she immediately placed the card and gift to one side, as rather too quickly she accepted a glass of the heartwarming, festive liquid. She was then ordered to join everyone else present in raising a toast to dear friends and family. Sadly, from that moment on, she was never again to think of or remind herself concerning either the beautifully gift-wrapped present or the promise she had given to the nervous young man who had anxiously wished to visit Patient 579, formerly known as Polly Esther Brown.

A few glasses of sherry later, and Nurse Battersea, as she was known to all, was called down to another ward and another equally lively Christmas party. One thing was certain: by the next morning not only would she be nursing a sore head that would quickly have her feeling most repentant and wretched, but she would also be unable to recollect a single memory of anything that had taken place the night before.

———◦•◦———

With all the festive merriment going on in the tiny ward office, the card was in no time separated from the gift, as it quietly slid onto the floor. And as the card was the only clue as to whom the kind gift was from or to whom it was intended, the gift remained unclaimed for most of that distinctly melodious evening; that is, until one very merry and inquisitive doctor just happened to catch sight of it.

"I say, old chap, does anyone have the slightest idea as to whom this delightfully wrapped gift is meant for?" he cried out as his paper Christmas hat suddenly slid down his forehead to then completely cover his eyes.

"No idea, old boy, but it's so exquisitely wrapped that it must surely be intended for you, old boy."

"Yes, doctor, by one of the many nurses who secretly have the hots for you," another overly boisterous doctor laughed as he turned on his heels to once more pick up the now half-empty sherry bottle.

"I say, old chap, anyone in need of a quick refill?" he shouted as he moved around the small office, haphazardly pouring the celebratory drink into every available glass.

"Well, gentlemen. Bottoms up!" shrieked another slightly inebriated doctor as he lifted the glass to his lips and then proceeded to consume the whole glass in one hit.

"Chin chin!" shouted another equally intoxicated doctor as he proceeded to swig it down as though it were water.

"Well, don't keep us all in limbo. Open it up, old boy!" one of the doctors loudly suggested, referring back to the mystery gift.

The young and foolish doctor adjusted his paper Christmas hat so that he could once again see, and with everyone in the room egging him on, he felt he had little choice other than to find out what exactly lay beneath the extravagantly wrapped Christmas gift. He hurriedly pulled off the beautiful decorative ribbon before quickly stripping the gift of its exquisitely beautiful wrapping paper.

"Oh, yummy mummy. My favorite ever chocolates!" he euphorically cried.

"Mine too, old chap, so don't think for one minute you're keeping all those to yourself, for you're fat and ugly enough as it is," another doctor cried out, a little worse for wear.

It took less than five minutes for the whole box to be entirely consumed.

"Hey, doc, do me a favor and hand me another one of those rather scrumptious chocs, for I need some food in my stomach to help me sober up," another heavier-set doctor ordered the young doctor in the once more disheveled paper Christmas hat.

"Sorry, doc, but you're clean out of luck. Yes, rather sadly there appears to be none left," he sniffed as he then dismissively lopped the discarded chocolate box into a nearby waste paper basket. "But Merry Christmas anyway."

Before another festive word could pass between them, Patient 336 appeared at the office door looking severely stricken and panicked, as he believed his nighttime medication to be long overdue.

<hr/>

He agitatedly stood in the doorway in his pajamas waiting to be reassured that he had not been forgotten. Suddenly he caught sight of a white envelope lying abandoned on the floor. He discreetly bent down, and after picking it up, he surreptitiously slid the envelope into the pocket of his open dressing gown.

"Mr. Oddbin, please do as you're told. Go back to your bed, and we promise that we will bring the medication to you. Nurse Bickerstaff is halfway through the medicine round, and if you're not by your bed or waiting in line by the Christmas tree, then you'll miss out on your medication altogether," the cute young nurse warned, as she quickly slid off the lap of one of the younger doctors.

"Yes, so be a good boy and go and wait for her to come to you," a slightly intoxicated doctor jovially cried out. "And a very merry Christmas to you, dear Mr. Oddbin," he shouted as he raised his glass into the air before guzzling the contents down in a matter of seconds.

Mr. Oddbin was clearly not amused. He made a loud snort and began muttering about the absurdity under his breath as most reluctantly he made his way back to his bed. As per usual he did not believe one single word of what he was hearing. No ward nurse was going to give him his rightful medication that night, for he knew without a shadow of doubt that those wickedly unscrupulous aliens known as Orkamedians had vowed to withhold his medication this Christmas as well as every other Christmas, that is, until he agreed to return with them to become ruler of their dying planet Zodka. Or was it Vodka? Either way, it didn't matter, because his mind was made up; he wasn't going with them, and this was his final word on the matter!

As he sat on the bed grumbling and mumbling with nothing to do but wait for the nurse to come along with his desperately needed medication, he fumbled around in his dressing gown pocket and was suddenly overcome with shock as he pulled out a mysterious, never-before-seen white envelope.

"Hmm. Now I know for sure they're on to me," he coughed and spluttered as, feeling horribly sickened, he frantically pulled the card from its pristine envelope.

"Ahh. They have sent me yet another secretly coded message," he despairingly cried.

For the next hour or so he sat motionless on the bed and, like an innocent child, he found himself completely mesmerized by the beautiful, sparkly Christmas card, which portrayed the birth of a precious infant on a bright, star-filled night. Rather sadly for Mr. Oddbin, instead of just appreciating the card with its message of hope, each minute that passed found him becoming increasingly more convinced than ever that this card really was a timely last-minute warning from those nasty, suspicious little Orks, telling him his time to leave Earth had once more come 'round.

"Absolutely nothing they say will persuade me to go back with them this time 'round—or ever," he most miserably muttered.

Hopping down from his bed, his eyes quickly scanned up and down the long dormitory. Before leaving his bedside to quickly check out the bathroom stalls, he was very pleased to say that as of yet he could see no sign of them. Feeling greatly relieved, he carefully placed the aliens' secretive calling card alongside all other festive cards sent to him that week by very concerned, caring friends and relatives, and then he nervously climbed back into the bed to hide under the covers. As he hid in darkness under the blankets, only coming out when he needed fresh air, he hoped with all his might that the pestering little blighters would once more fail to discover his rather clever hiding place and so decide to leave it a further year before coming back to have another try at abducting him.

Chapter Twenty-Four
GOODWILL TO ALL MEN

ITH CHRISTMAS FINALLY over, New Year also came and went with yet more festive merriment, and all too soon it was time for the dilapidated tree to once more be packed away. The paltry decorations were also boxed up and taken, along with the tree, back into storage, for it was now time for the ward to get back to some sense of so-called normality.

Like all the other staff, Dr. Ninkumpoop returned from the Christmas holidays feeling thoroughly refreshed and rejuvenated and therefore ready to face any amount of fresh challenges that this new year would most certainly bring. For several months more he valiantly struggled on with his one-to-one counseling of Polly, and he also continued to diligently log his very sad and sensitive observations in his most private journal, which he hoped would, in the fullness of time, become a published work, a work so challenging that it would undoubtedly earn him millions, if not in monetary terms then certainly in accolades. This wily man knew that it was quite plausible that a case such as this could become a showcase and therefore the inspiration behind many groundbreaking techniques. It would also hopefully cause innumerable doctors and students of the mind and soul to specifically marvel for many a year to come at the rather engrossing study of Patient 579.

With all this in mind, Dr. Ninkumpoop tried harder than ever to persuade Polly to resume talking, but still she refused to comply and spill the beans. He even promised her that if she began to fully cooperate, she could easily find herself back on the old ward, where she could once again pick up her close friendship with Lucinda. Like everything else, this bribe too failed to convince Polly to open up and begin to tell the doctor all he wished to know.

This was a definite stalemate situation, which finally forced the doctor to take things into his own hands. On a warm day in July the doctor finished a closed-door meeting with the ward staff, having discussed Patient 579's sad lack of progress. She was effectively penciled in for her first electroconvulsive therapy, known in medical circles as ECT, to take place at 9:00 a.m. the following Wednesday morning.

Meanwhile, back in Piadora Ralph had been working extremely hard at trying to become an impressively high-class society lady. He was therefore very pleased to hear that his hard work had finally paid off, as Mrs. O'Brien took it upon herself to announce that he really was close to conquering the art of walking and talking in the manner of a real lady.

"Ralph, my good man, what more can I say? You look utterly gorgeous. Yes, you really do look the part, for you look so, well, tasteful," she radiantly cried as she gave him a quick peck on the cheek as an expression of her delight.

Ralph instantly blushed.

"Yes, I think so too! I look like a real cutie pie, don't I?" he announced, breaking into a smile.

"Yes, and remember not to get too carried away with this hoity-toily, toffee-nosed lifestyle," she warned, "or we'll be forced into doing something rather drastic to bring you back down to earth with a rude awakening," she cheerfully exclaimed. "Besides which, I'll have you know there is a long queue forming, as there are now many amongst us who are very anxious to get involved in this particular case."

"Really?"

"Yes, really. Many up here are most eager to get involved in the rescue of Polly, and Hodgekiss is doing his best to give them all similar tasks, for he has told them all to be patient, as there are so many more Polly Browns out there with no one to wipe away a tear or give them cause to

hope. So promise to behave yourself, or you'll lose this mission to someone else if you're not careful."

Ralph furrowed his brow as he tried to show her he was taking her playful threats most seriously, but still he could not dispense with the ridiculously fat, cheesy grin written all over his face.

"Oh, and before you leave, Ralph, please do me the great honor of explaining why you are in such a hurry, as the hospital extravaganza with its ribbon-cutting ceremony is two, if not three, days away from taking place?" she asked.

"Well, believe it or not, I thought I would visit the hospital early to prune back all the rhododendrons and lupines on the hospital grounds that need urgent attention if they are to survive the heat of the summer."

"Hmm. Ralph, your explanation is somewhat hard to swallow. Come on, don't hold back on me. Tell me the truth. What, my good man, is the real urgency?"

"Well, if I'm to be perfectly honest, I think time is fast running out for young Polly, and if this is so, then an intervention must take place, and pretty soon. If I don't move in fast, young Polly will be forced to have this absolutely terrible therapy known in medical circles as ECT where they literally fry your brains. There, Mrs. O'Brien; you now know the terrible, sordid truth," he deeply sighed.

"Oh my goodness! Poor Polly! This really all sounds too awful— so utterly incomprehensible, if not thoroughly reprehensible," Mrs. O'Brien gasped as she clasped her hands tightly. "Tell me the truth, Ralph. Have none of our letters of encouragement done anything to help?"

"Mrs. O'Brien, I am sure they have, but you must also remember the dark side has been equally busy. And remember she has been given so many pills that she cannot tell the difference between night and day. We must therefore be patient and continue on with our little letters of encouragement as we consider other, more direct strategies."

"Ralph, you must waste no further time, for in the light of what you have just shared with me, I think you are more than ready to go on this high adventure. I will anxiously be waiting back here for you, dying to know how everything pans out," she wistfully stated.

"Yes, well, before we meet up with Polly, there are a few other little errands that need my immediate attention."

"Really? And pray, tell me, what might those little errands involve?"

"Well, for one I need to catch up with those two likely lads."

"Oh, you mean Justin Kase and Justin Thyme."

"Oh, yes, for those likely lads have quite a lot of explaining to do. Then, of course, there's the great need to challenge Will, for he has truly backed off. I must see to it that he immediately comes back on board. Of course, I will keep you and everyone else informed," he tenderheartedly stated. "Remember this, Mrs. O'Brien, when all is said and done, do not despair, for we are most certainly on the winning team."

"Oh, please keep reminding me. But tell me, Ralph, is our own very dear Giles Blenkinsopp still happy to accompany you on this trip?"

"Oh, yes indeed. Young Blenkinsopp is just as excited about this special trip. You should see him in his handsome butler's outfit; he really looks like a distinguished gentleman. So perfect, yes, so very dapper."

"Yes, I bet he looks a proper gentleman. Now be off with you," she said as she gave him a gentle pat on his rear.

"Ooh, Mrs. O'Brien. Please behave yourself, for remember I am now considered a lady of much distinction," he stated as he began to walk away with his nose stuck high in the air.

Mrs. O'Brien could not fail but retort, "Oh, Ralphella, dearest one, remember what I said about not getting too caught up in the moment, yes, a little too toffee-nosed? Oh, and I think you're forgetting something."

Ralph spun 'round on his heels just in time to catch something small that was now flying through the air at great speed.

"Gotcha!" he cried as he then opened up his hand to view what he had only just managed to catch. "Ahh, my very essential pink lipstick.

Thank you so much, Mrs. O'Brien," he said as he playfully blew her a friendly kiss good-bye.

"Go, and don't you dare come back until you have rescued our dear Polly from that terribly disgraceful place," she anxiously cried out after him.

"Mrs. O'Brien, trust me when I say that I have absolutely no intention whatsoever of doing anything else," he shouted back.

"Blenkinsopp, do as I request and turn in here. Then pull over and park over there in between the marked-out lines," Lady Butterkist sharply ordered.

"Very well, madam," Blenkinsopp grumpily replied as, doing as he was told, he parked their old jalopy into a marked-out parking bay just outside the train station.

"Madam, since when have you resorted to traveling anywhere by train?" he mournfully muttered.

"Blenkinsopp, this truly is a first," she retorted.

"Well, madam, it is a well-known fact that British Rail is at present failing to get any of its passengers to their desired destinations on time, something to do with too much snow settling on the track or fallen branches on the line. Please do me the small courtesy and kindly explain why you have chosen to risk taking a train rather than to entrust me to get you to your destination on time," her very offended butler with a touch of the sniffles remarked.

"Blenkinsopp, trust me when I say that I have not the slightest wish to board any train now or in the near future. So be a dear and just wait for me, for I have a most important, itsy witsy, teeny weenie errand that I must urgently attend to."

"All right then, madam. I will do as you request and remain here awaiting your return," he sighed as he opened the passenger door to let her out.

"If I'm not back in twenty minutes, do feel free to come and find me," she said with an engaging smile.

"Madam, pray, tell me now, where will I start looking?"

"Try the station cafeteria, Blenkinsopp, for this is where I am almost certain to be found."

"Madam, if you are in need of some suitable refreshments, I must warn you now that railway cafes are not the least bit famous for their tea-making abilities or their nibbles."

"I know, Blenkinsopp, truly I do, but trust me when I say that this has naught to do with tea and more to do with suitably chastising a couple of seriously foolhardy teenage boys. So until I next require your services, please, will you kindly take Piddles and Tiddles for their usual walkies, for they are badly in need of some exercise after the long drive."

"Very well, Lady B."

"Oh, and Blenkinsopp, I cannot be entirely certain, but I do suspect that one of my precious pups has left a small, undesirable sample of her cargo on the backseat," she said, craning her head into the back portion of the car as her eyes then scanned the backseat in search of the offending item or items.

"I suspect you mean a 'whoopsie,' madam?"

"Exactly, Blenkinsopp, for there's definitely a most overwhelming and unpleasant odor coming directly from the back. Have a whiff and tell me if I'm correct."

"I believe you to be correct in your assumption, madam, for even though I was in the driving seat, there was a moment in time where my nose became most offended," he said, sniffing hard. "Yes, there is quite a strong pong, if you don't mind me saying. So while you are away, I will do my best to track down and then rid the car of the offending items, as well as its equally offensive odor."

"Oh, good. But Blenkinsopp, promise me now that you will in no way discipline my pups, for it was indeed a very long and emotionally arduous journey for the two of them."

"Very well, madam. I will refrain from giving either pup any form of disciplinary rebuke."

"Why, thank you, Blenkinsopp. Your agreement in this otherwise unpleasant matter is most appreciated, really it is."

Minutes later found Lady Butterkist marching toward the station buffet. As she stood at the counter she glanced around and immediately observed both boys sitting in a corner as they happily chatted up a couple of pretty-looking girls.

The young and very spotty server who stood behind the counter seemed in no particular hurry to serve the lady.

"I say, young man, what does one have to do to get a nice cup of tea around here?" Lady Butterkist loudly announced.

"I'm so sorry, madam, but I did not notice you standing at the counter. What can I get for you?"

"Young man, I would very much appreciate a nice spot of hot, calming tea."

"Certainly, madam. It will be with you in a jiffy."

Moments later the young boy returned and placed a hot paper cup filled to the brim with tea on the counter.

"That will be sixpence halfpenny, madam," he announced.

A shocked and surprised Lady Butterkist placed her hand around the scalding cup of tea. "I say, young man, what on earth do you call this?"

"It's a cup of tea, madam, for I'm more than certain that's exactly what you ordered."

"Young man, I know precisely what's in the cup, but what is this?" she indignantly asked as she gently tapped the side of the lightweight receptacle.

"It's a cup, madam."

"Wrong! It's certainly not a cup, young man, for a cup most certainly has a handle to secure one's fingers around in order to safely bring the beverage up to one's mouth. This receptacle has no handle whatsoever. So pray, tell me, how on earth am I supposed to drink my tea from this?" she challenged.

"Well, you're supposed to clasp both sides and…sort of cup—"

"Clasp both sides?" she gasped, shaking her head in supposed horror.

"Madam, it's a disposable cup that you clasp between your fingers."

"I see, but I don't see, for tell me, young man, has British Rail suffered a major robbery? What has become of the good, old-fashioned china cup and saucer that one used to enjoy sipping one's tea from?"

"They have been replaced, madam."

"Replaced?"

"Yes, madam. By these disposable cups."

"Young man, this is indeed a grievous travesty, an insidious crime if ever there was one, for there is no respectable way to drink precious tea other than from a china teacup. Has British Rail simply gone irretrievably mad, or have they just temporarily lost the plot?" she scolded.

"It would appear they've gone quite mad, madam, for every cup of tea is now served in these disposable cups, and I'll have you know that this is considered standard practice at every station café in Britain, as well as on every train buffet carriage."

"Well then, they should be thoroughly ashamed of themselves for sinking to such deplorable, low depths," she snorted as she begrudgingly took a sip of the tea from the foam cup. "To be forced to drink from this cumbersome monstrosity is indeed a most gross assault on one's senses," she wearily muttered.

"I'm sorry you are so disgruntled, madam, for these lightweight, disposable cups are not only considered cost effective, but they are also the latest in new technology."

"So you wish me to believe that for the sake of new technology I am sadly forced to drink heaven's most pleasurable gift to humanity from out of one of these whimsical and atrociously designed paper cups?"

"Yes, madam. It would appear so."

"Hmm. Blenkinsopp was right after all, for sadly their standards have indeed dropped as far down as the very bowels of hell itself," she loudly announced as, taking hold of the cup, she then headed for the table nearest where the boys sat, still preoccupied with chatting up a couple of lovely looking-ladies.

Lady Butterkist took a further few sips of tea and grimaced. "What I do in the name of love," she muttered as she began to listen in on the boys' conversation with their female guests.

"Er, Trace, I need the loo," one of the girls with the blonde, heavily backcombed hair and thick makeup suddenly announced.

"Sure thing, Shar. 'Ere, wait a minute and I'll come with yer, for I too need to touch up me makeup," the other young girl with dark, shoulder-length hair chirped up.

Lady Butterkist watched, feeling most amused as the giggling girls picked up their bulging handbags and then casually linked arms before making their way to the bathroom.

She smiled as she considered just how long they might spend away from the table as, once in the bathroom, they stood in front of a large mirror to set about touching up their lips with yet more ruby red lipstick before reapplying their already overloaded eye lashes with yet more thick mascara, all the while discussing what they liked and disliked about both boys. Yes, if she were not mistaken, they would surely be gone at least fifteen minutes, if not twenty. Time enough for Lady Butterkist to set to work.

"I say, boys, do either of you have the correct time?" Lady Butterkist loudly shouted in their direction.

"Yeah, it's just gone four in the afternoon," Justin Thyme replied as he anxiously looked down at his watch.

"Thank you so much, young man. Now, tell me, please, I have just been to the local school, as I am trying my very best to locate a certain person, and because I am not a relative, sad to say, they were not the least bit helpful."

"Oh, and who might you be looking for?" Justin Kase nonchalantly asked.

"Well, her name happens to be Polly, Polly Brown, to be precise."

"Oh, madam, you won't find her here or at any school, for a long time ago she was sent away to the nuthouse," Justin Kase informed the lady.

"Nuthouse?"

"Yeah, the asylum for lunatics."

"Well, I never!" she gasped, her face conveying enormous shock.

"Yeah, sadly she began talking about weird places, so they said she was a deranged lunatic who needed to be locked away—for the safety of others, of course."

"Oh, of course," Lady Butterkist replied, very tongue in cheek. "But allow me the silly pleasure of asking both you boys, was she really a lunatic?"

"Well, of sorts!" Justin Kase stated, wrinkling his nose as he spoke up.

"I see. So you knew her well then?"

"Yeah, we did. She was one of the orphans from the castle," he added.

"Well then, have either of you any idea as to how she might be doing?"

"None whatsoever," both boys said in unison as they slowly shook their heads.

"So, rather regrettably, although you knew her, she wasn't really a friend of yours?"

"Well, in a funny way she was. I mean, she could act a bit crazy, but looking back, she had a really big heart," both boys agreed.

"So help me out here. Neither of you have thought of visiting her to see how she's doing?"

"Well, no we haven't, 'cos we don't think it's our place to go and see her."

"Yeah, people might misunderstand our intentions."

"By 'people,' I presume you mean school chums, girlfriends, and family?"

"Yeah, it could be harmful to our—how shall I put it?—our image."

"I see. So what you are really saying is that both of you are greatly influenced by what others think of you. Sounds a pretty dangerous cocktail to me," she stated, raising a concerned eyebrow.

"Lady, what precisely do you mean?" Justin Kase innocently asked.

"Well, if you cannot dare follow your heart and do what is right due to the high risk of exposure or otherwise from offending the crowd, then clearly something is very wrong. Wouldn't you say so?"

"Yes, dear lady, but if you are trying to suggest that we should risk our reputations and in doing so choose to visit Polly in the local loony bin, then you're quite right, for we have no intention of risking our reputations," an offended Justin Kase quickly retorted.

"Ahh. How very interesting. For reputations are such dangerously flimsy things."

"Uhh?" Justin Kase mumbled.

"Well, allow me to explain. One minute we can be sailing high on the praises of others. Then in the wink of an eye our reputation can be forever stained or tarnished by one idle, misplaced word or by the cruel, deceptive words of another holding some pitiful grudge. It's both sad and funny that we come to place such high value on something so elusive that by the flip of a coin can so easily and readily be crushed and forever destroyed. Faithfulness, loyalty, and integrity of character are so much lower down the unspoken list of important attributes one can only hope to aspire to and thus obtain."

"Dear lady, are you suggesting that we are all seriously wrong and therefore deluded in our beliefs and thinking?" a very heated Justin Kase demanded to know.

"Oh, young man, don't be so presumptuous, for that is not an indulgence to which I am privy or otherwise allowed to judge. Time alone will judge you, as in later years you look back over your life and come to the sad realization that there were many mistakes made that could so easily have been corrected."

"Well, lady, I have to confess to feeling most sorry for Polly."

"Not sorry enough to pay Polly a small visit, and not sorry enough to once and for all set a certain record straight."

"What record?"

"Why, the record with her good friend, Will, of course! For surely you are not impervious to the fact that he still believes Polly has gone quite mad, especially with regard to her most provocative and creative story regarding Piadora."

"Oh, that!"

"Yes, that! You know something, boys. I would like to believe that both of you are sincere, decent-minded young men, and if you knew you could put things right, well then, I like to think that you would. So, I would like to humbly suggest that the next time you bump into her friend, William, you tell him the whole truth of what happened that day on the mountain, for at the end of the day you have nothing to lose, save your shame," she stated, giving both the boys a long and penetrating gaze.

"Shame?" an awkward and confused Justin Kase queried.

"Yes, shame. It's not exactly a popular word these days, but it certainly fits the crime."

"Crime?" he once again queried.

"Yes, the crime of not admitting the truth when a very desperate Polly begged and pleaded with you both to confirm her story to Will. You boys should be ashamed of yourselves, for you know full well you behaved very badly that day."

"How do you, a complete stranger, know any of this?" the now very shaken boys quickly wanted to know.

Of course, Lady Butterkist declined to answer the question.

"So you think we should go and find Will and then admit to him that we lied to save our own necks?"

"Yes, and in doing so you will indeed cleanse your hearts and minds of the guilt that you young men have been carrying around for a considerable length of time. After all, a clean conscience is a desirably healthy and most welcome asset to have, I assure you, for you can once more breathe deeply and enjoy a peaceful night's rest, free from agitation and the ghastly nightmares a disturbed conscience most surely brings."

"Lady, I do believe you're right on target, for neither Justin Thyme nor myself sleep well these days, and up until this moment we had no idea as to why this was the case."

"Well then, Justin, it is a good thing we bumped into each other this fair day, for today can mark the time to make amends, which, I promise, will certainly have far-reaching consequences."

"We will put it right, we promise," Justin Kase stated. "But I am still not sure we could face seeing her in that awful hospital."

"Well, take each day as it comes, for there may come a time when you feel you have the courage to pay her that visit. Until then I bid you farewell, for sadly my cup is drained, and I need to go on my way."

"Good-bye, er, Lady—" Justin Thyme stated, feeling most awkward, as he still had absolutely no idea by what name she answered to.

"Lady Butterkist, but please feel free to call me Ralphella, as after this pleasant and encouraging discourse I do believe we are now firm friends." Satisfied that she had finished what she came to do, she then stood up to leave. "Also, please allow me to leave the money for you to purchase further refreshments, for I do believe your throats will surely once more feel thoroughly parched before those young ladies believe themselves to be groomed enough to finally leave the bathroom and come back to join you."

"Yes, already they have been away a ridiculously long time," Justin Kase glumly stated as he looked down at his watch.

"Well, that's because both young ladies still have much to privately discuss in connection with you two lads. But let me assure you now that both young girls are apt to believe that they are head over heels in love. So take it easy, boys, won't you? And I beg of you, please don't lead them down the garden path, for the tender heart of a teenage girl is indeed precariously fragile and therefore easily wounded."

"We'll treat them right. That's a promise," they both happily assured the lady.

"Oh, and by the way, boys, please accept this personal invitation card to come on a journey to Piadora."

"Oh, we have already tried and failed," Justin Kase reluctantly admitted.

"Hence the head wound," his friend interjected as he quickly pointed to the large scar that ran the length of his friend's forehead.

"Well, maybe it's because you intended to gate-crash the party. Not such a good idea at the end of the day."

"How on earth did you know that?" a very confused and bewildered Justin Kase asked.

"This time I am giving you an open-ended invitation," Lady Butterkist warmly stated as she deliberately ignored this latest question.

"Thank you, Lady Butterkist. Maybe one day in the not-too-distant future we will take you up on your very kind offer."

"Oh, I'm sure you will," she calmly stated as with a deep smile on her face she made her way toward the exit door of the café.

"Oh, and boys, good luck with the dating," were her final parting words before she closed the café door to head back to her old jalopy and Giles Blenkinsopp, her devoted butler and part-time chauffeur.

"Absolutely exhilarating," she chuckled to herself as she privately considered the success of her exciting little rendezvous at the station café.

"Lady B., the offending items have been hunted down and disposed of, and the dogs have also been exercised."

"Wonderful."

"Oh, and I'm delighted to report that the car is once more smelling as fresh as a daisy."

"Splendid, Blenkinsopp. Simply splendid."

Chapter Twenty-Five
LADY BUTTERKIST TO THE RESCUE

*I*T WOULD NOT be too long before Blenkinsopp and Lady Ralphella Butterkist were driving way too fast down some of the longest and most winding country roads of picturesque Great Britain.

"Giles Blenkinsopp, I do declare this to be a most glorious day to stop and have ourselves a little picnic, so do be a dear and slow down so that we can pick a nice, pleasant spot to lay down the tartan rug and picnic basket."

"Very well, madam."

"Also, Piddles and Tiddles, my imperial little Shih Tzu pups, are in dire need of doing another little 'whoopsie' in the woods, so we cannot leave it too long in finding ourselves that perfect little oasis," she firmly stated as she caressed the little heads of both young pups.

It would only be a matter of minutes before Giles looked out of the window and observed a large clearing that he believed might well keep her ladyship happy.

"Would this particular site be to your ladyship's particular liking?" he inquired.

"Absolutely perfect, so you can stop the car now, Blenkinsopp," she beamed.

Giles brought the car to a total standstill then got out to go and open the rear door for her ladyship and her cute little dogs.

The pups immediately headed toward a little copse to do their private business, and Blenkinsopp obliged her ladyship by staggering into the middle of a poppy-filled meadow laden down with a large wicker hamper of goodies and a tartan rug draped over his shoulder.

"Wonderful, Blenkinsopp. I do believe we have a feast fit for a king."

Once they were settled down, Giles brought out the silver flagon of tea and began pouring. "Well done, Blenkinsopp. You've remembered to bring a couple of my best bone china tea cups, for this heavenly elixir tastes most disgusting when drunk from any other alternative receptacle, don't you agree?"

"Yes, madam. Plastic is gross, pottery just about bearable, but have you seen the latest invention that they are making drinking cups from? I believe it's called polystyrene foam. I wonder, madam, are you familiar with this new technology and therefore the latest trend from which to sip your beverage?"

"Allow me to say that before today's events I remained blissfully indisposed to such man-made creations, but all that has now changed, for disgraceful as it might seem, I found myself being forced against my will to drink from such a receptacle when I ordered tea in the station buffet. However, I will now adamantly state that I will never again choose to familiarize myself with such a vulgar creation, for the end of civilization will surely be nigh before I ever again allow myself to drink wonderful tea infusions from out of those ghastly polystyrene cups."

"Oh, madam."

"Yes, it was all very trying to say the least."

"Poor madam."

"Oh no, Giles, trust me when I say that disposable, lightweight cups for tea or other equally desirous beverages will never, ever catch on."

"Of course. Anything you say, madam. Oh, and does madam require her serviette at this present moment in time?"

"Why, thank you, Blenkinsopp. Do kindly pass it to me, and then do be a dear and sit down so we can begin our little picnic without further hesitation."

No sooner had the faithful butler dropped to his knees when suddenly a young man stepped out of the wooded area and began to aimlessly walk, hands in his pockets, a path that was in direct line with where they had just set up for their picnic and so were resting while enjoying the simple pleasure of drinking tea.

Before Giles could point him out, Lady Butterkist immediately caught sight of him, and after quickly placing her cup down on her saucer, she beckoned for him to come and join them.

"I say there, young man, would you care to join us in having a delightful cup of divine tea?"

"Well, thank you, dear lady, but I think I will refrain from your terribly gracious offer," he politely responded.

"Now then, young man, we will not take no for an answer. Besides, your eyes betray much sadness and regret. So don't be an insufferable spoilsport. Sit down, and allow us to pour you tea with a large dollop of sympathy, for we have both to running over, don't we, Blenkinsopp?" she merrily stated as she patted at an empty space on her tartan rug.

"Yes, madam, I do believe we have a chronic excess of both," he wearily agreed.

The handsome boy with the deeply melancholic eyes shrugged his shoulders as if to surrender before gently falling to his knees to join them.

"I'm afraid we're clean out of bone china cups, as there were only two rather lonely souls invited to picnic on this particular expedition, but I am sure my faithful butler will hand over his cup in exchange for a more modest plastic mug, which from time to time we are forced to use."

"Oh, please don't go to any bother on my behalf, for I am used to drinking from just about anything. Believe you me when I say that if I can drink from the deeply scarred plastic cups in the school dinner hall, then I can drink from anything."

"Nonsense, my dear man. You will indeed sip tea from my best bone china, end of story. Speaking of which, a short time ago I just happened to find myself in the station café, as I was in dire need of some refreshment. When I finally got some service, I was horrified to discover they were no longer serving the tea in proper china cups accompanied by a saucer but rather in a most vulgar, lightweight cup that I was informed went by the name polystyrene.

"As it is many years since I had taken the train, I found it all really quite extraordinary, if not disturbing. I have to say that I cannot imagine these new receptacles ever catching on, for to serve tea from anything other than china, bone china being the more preferable, is simply quite preposterous.

"Trust me when I feel compelled to say that in no time at all this weird and dastardly new product will soon become history, for I cannot ever imagine it catching on, as tea-drinking is surely a most serious British occupation."

"Yes, Lady B., but maybe British Rail has been forced against its will to make specific cutbacks," Blenkinsopp helpfully suggested,

"Blenkinsopp, I quite understand cutbacks, except when it comes to the customary ritual of serving good tea. I also find it hard to believe that they have managed to ruin a perfectly delightful name like Polly—and on such a vulgar and modern item—by calling it 'polystyrene.' What do you think of all of this, young man?"

"Yes, you're quite right, for Polly is indeed a wonderful name," Will readily agreed.

"Yes, if not somewhat magical, like that little old rhyme 'Polly, Put the Kettle On.' I always remember singing that when I was a young girl. Yes, such a special name, and I have to say that without exception every Polly I have ever met has been a most special and delightful individual," she sighed as she took a further sip of hot tea from her cup.

"So tell, young man, and don't be too modest: are you acquainted with any young lady who might go by that name?"

"Well, dear lady—"

"Oh, let us not dwell on social pleasantries. Please call me Lady B., and these here are Tiddles and Piddles, my royal little pooches."

"Yes, Lady B. I have no idea how to properly answer your question except to say that it is most unfortunate that by just mentioning that particular name in passing, it has yet served to further deepen my misery, for strange though it must seem, I have lost a very good friend who goes by that name."

"Lost! Quite what do you mean by *lost*? I mean, lost in France, lost in the woods, lost at sea...?"

"Oh, nothing so dramatic. I merely meant that I no longer see her."

"I thought as much, for I saw it in your eyes. Pray, tell me, young man, what is your name?"

"William. Will for short."

"I see, and pray, tell me, William, what were you doing out walking alone in this neck of the woods?"

"Oh, my lady, I just live a short distance from here. See that wooded copse liberally sprinkled with bluebells and daffodils?"

"Yes, I do see."

"Well, my house lies just behind it, so I often walk alone when I need to gather my thoughts. Life seems to crowd in on me, and out here I just walk for miles and then stand in awe at all the beauty surrounding me."

"Hmm, and tell me straight, William, does your particular house have a name?" Lady Butterkist politely asked.

"Yes, it does. But why all the questions?" he openly asked while taking a large gulp of tea from his cup.

"Oh, I'm just an inquisitive old lady. So don't hold back on me, Will. Just blurt it all out. There's a good fellow."

Will laughed. "My house is very aptly named Tumbledown Cottage."

"What an extraordinarily delightful name! I think on my return I will indeed change the name of my house to something quite similar. I like the sound of 'Tumbledown' or 'Tumbleweed Cottage.' Giles, pray tell me now, what do you think?"

"Madam, you live in such a palatial residence that I believe most people assume it to be a castle, so perhaps 'Tumbledown' or 'Tumble-weed Cottage' is simply not appropriate," Blenkinsopp felt it his duty to remind her.

"Well, Giles Blenkinsopp, I do declare 'Tumbledown Castle' sounds pretty perfect to me, for it suggests that many wars, as well as a few crimes of passion, might well have taken place in times gone by. So what do you think, Will?"

Once more Will shrugged his shoulders as if to suggest he had absolutely no thoughts on such a matter.

"Well, William dear, I could not fail to hear you murmur something about the name being most suitable. In fact, I believe the word you used was *apt*. So please enlighten us further as to why 'Tumble-down Cottage' is so appropriate."

"Must I?" he groaned.

"Oh, absolutely, for I don't have time for the problems of people who don't have problems. So please; I insist that at the very least you stay and share your cares and burdens with us, and as you do so, Blen-kinsopp will pour us all another fresh cup of tea. I also believe this to be a most splendid occasion to bring out the salmon and cucumber finger sandwiches. What do you think? Needless to say, all the crusts have been most thoughtfully and therefore carefully removed. There are also bite-sized asparagus and cream cheese sandwiches if these are more to your preference."

"Madam, may I interrupt by saying I do believe we are shy of a napkin for this fine young gentleman's immediate use."

"Napkin, Blenkinsopp? Pray, tell me now, what on God's earth is a napkin?"

"I'm so sorry, milady. What I meant and therefore intended to say was *serviette*."

"I should say so, Blenkinsopp, for you, my dear, are spending far too much time with that American friend of yours. What's his name?"

"You mean Sam, Lady Arrabella's butler?"

"Yes, precisely, and has he not just freshly arrived on these shores straight from America?"

"You are perfectly correct, madam. He is indeed from Boston."

"Well, Blenkinsopp, imagine if you will that if it hadn't been for the jolly old French sticking their noses in where it wasn't wanted, these good American people would all be speaking just like you and I, yes, perfectly good Queen's English!"

"Oh, madam, I apologize most profusely, so therefore I feel suitably chastised. But before you remonstrate further, I need you to address the problem at hand."

"What problem, Blenkinsopp?"

"Madam, we have no spare *serviette* for immediate use by our guest."

"Nonsense, Blenkinsopp. He is our guest after all, so don't just stand there being such a rotten spoilsport; just hand over your starched serviette. There's a dear."

"But madam, this specific serviette is most personal to me. It even has my initials sewn onto the corner," he quietly complained.

"Giles, now is not the time to throw a wobbly! Here, use this instead," she fussed. "It's one of my finest cotton handkerchiefs, and I assure you it is perfectly clean, for it has never been used and so is quite clear of all ghastly little germs," she insisted as she tried and failed to reassure him.

Poor Giles was aghast, as he was humiliatingly forced to part with his personal, starched white linen serviette in exchange for a handkerchief dotted all over with little smiling teddy bears with bright pink bows on their heads.

Will immediately tucked in to all the delights he was being offered, and he was quick to nod his approval. "Oh, this food is simply overwhelmingly delicious," he declared, giving her ladyship a warm smile. And so he stayed to savor these delights, as well as every other delight that Blenkinsopp cared to place in front of him.

"William, would you care to try a little caviar?" Blenkinsopp politely asked him. "It indeed washes down very nicely with a nice, cool glass of home made lemonade." Will quickly declined the black, glistening caviar. Blenkinsopp thought he noticed the boy turn a little squeamish as he looked at the caviar offered him.

After the delicate finger sandwiches they went on to enjoy scones and preserves, served with up with overly generous portions of wickedly scrumptious Devonshire clotted cream.

"Wow, it's perfectly delicious, but tell me, Lady B., why have I never heard of this type of cream before?"

"Well, William, as you ask, it's deemed to be so delicious that the upper aristocracy likes to keep it as their little secret. Besides, it is called clotted cream, because it does exactly what it says on the label."

"What's that?"

"It clots your arteries, well, at least if you eat too much of it," she laughed as she then added a further spoonful of the thick cream onto her already overladen scone.

The scones were followed by deliciously decadent chocolate-covered cake, and then as if all this was not enough, Will was handed a plate of freshly peeled fruit. It was indeed a picnic fit for a king or queen!

While Will enjoyed the tea and company, he chose to unburden himself of all that had befallen him since he had moved to the area. Will completely surprised himself by talking so openly and honestly to a couple of unusual and complete strangers. In truth, he could never have imagined himself doing such a thing, as he was normally a very private and most loyal individual, so when it came to sharing about his sick mother and brother, he did all within his power to speak well of them. He shared just as much of the detail as he believed wise and always kept to the forefront that he must honor his mother by not sharing anything that might lead to her demise or have anyone thinking the worst where she was concerned.

"So that's it in a nutshell, Lady B., for I have shared more than I ought with regard to my family's personal and somewhat tragic misfortunes."

"Will, I know that now is probably not the time, but certainly at some future date I would love to meet with your mother and your brother. It sounds to me as though your family has suffered much over the years, and this could well explain your dear mother's bitter spirit. I think it would be a very nice gesture if you were to, say, buy your mother a delightful bouquet of flowers and then sit down with her and talk over a nice cup of tea."

"Talk?"

"Yes, William. Talk. Most parents these days are estranged from their children because no one has the time anymore to listen and then understand. I do declare that we are all in far too much of a hurry. It sounds to me as though your mother has nobody to talk to, and she needs to know that underneath everything, you still love and care for her. May I be so bold to remind you that just as your father abandoned you boys, she too is a spurned wife and mother, hence her extreme and bitter spirit."

"Yes, that's true, Lady B., although at times it is very difficult, for she seems fairly determined to become England's next honorary martyr. Besides which, I am as poor as a church mouse, so I not have the wherewithal to buy her some of the finer things in life, like flowers and chocolates."

"William, I hear you, so you need to find less extravagant ways that cost nothing but will mean everything to her. For instance, you could try picking her a lovely bunch of wildflowers and then putting them in a vase by her bedside, or try baking her a small cake. I don't know if my suggestions are helpful, but I know you will think of something innovative, because the truth here is that you, William, are such a good and talented young man."

"Thank you for being so kind."

THE TROUBLE WITH POLLY BROWN

"Well, William, no matter how hard things seem at present, you must keep trying. There's a dear, for I believe it is in your hands alone as to whether your family comes together or falls apart. Yes, I believe you are the glue that will keep things going, and allow me to suggest that honoring your mother is a very good thing indeed. If you do not grow weary, you will in time reap due benefits. Trust me on this one."

"Oh, Lady B., believe me when I say that I so long to feel part of a happy, healthy family again."

"Trust me, Will. If you follow my advice to the letter, given time, it will happen; you have my word on it. As for your brother, I think nothing short of a miracle will do, so I believe you should start hoping and praying for one, for what has happened to this dear young man is, as you suggest, nothing short of a complete travesty."

"It certainly is," William sniffed as he tried but failed to remain composed. "He was my bigger brother who I used to look up to and believed in, and now all I see is a man full of hate and bitter, twisted rage." William immediately found himself feeling a little embarrassed, as he was now fighting hard to hold back the tears. He was, after all, a man, and men don't cry, do they?

As if she had heard his thoughts, Lady Butterkist suddenly told him, "Cry if you must." Then she continued, "Tell me, Blenkinsopp, why is it men supposedly aren't allowed to cry? For they are almost always allowed to get angry, and they most certainly are inclined toward laughter, but heaven forbid that a man should dare release his troubled heart and mind of some frightful burden by the shedding of tears that spring directly from the wounded palace of his soul. It's plainly ridiculous, don't you agree?"

"Absolutely, madam. Absolutely."

Will privately agreed with her assessment, but still he continued to fight back the tears, and so Lady Butterkist produced a further spare handkerchief.

"Here, blow into this, dear boy. And then abandon yourself entirely to getting drunk in your innermost soul with yet more hot tea, for as some ancient Chinese proverb goes, 'Tea is most surely drunk in order to forget the din of the world.' Well, it goes something like that anyway. Besides, it is most assuredly the British way. Yes, the perfect antidote to all sadness and melancholy is usually the simple making of a seriously strong pot of hot tea, tea that is then ultimately shared with as many participants as one can bear to involve whilst faithfully and sorrowfully shedding light on all of one's mishaps and misfortunes."

"True, perfectly true," Blenkinsopp muttered.

"Yes, and as the saying goes, 'A problem shared is indeed a problem halved,'" Lady Dutterkist mused. "So, I suggest you motivate yourself to find plenty of ideal tea-drinking companions, and you will see for yourself that as the problem is pleasantly mulled over between sips of hot sweet tea, a favorable solution will almost certainly be found. Isn't that so, Blenkinsopp?"

"Yes, madam. As usual you are indeed entirely correct."

"Thank you, Blenkinsopp. I do so like it when you agree with me," she said with a wide smile. "Now, Will dear. As I said, I would very much like to meet with your mother and your brother on some more appropriate occasion, so I would very much like for you to invite me over to your house for tea and some hot, buttered crumpets. How does that sound?"

"Why, yes, that would be so nice, Lady B., for you might not fully believe this, but my housebound mother is almost as passionate about tea as she is about cats. I must warn you now that the house is completely overrun with cats."

"Cats! How very interesting. Well, I had better leave Tiddles and Piddles at home for this future occasion. But I most assuredly will be in touch, and this engaging date will most certainly materialize, for I do believe your mother is in dire need of a good friend, and you know how women like to, well, gossip about life's ups and downs, as well as every other conceivably interesting topic."

"Yes, Lady B., I believe I know precisely what you mean," Will replied as he flashed her an all-knowing smile.

"Well, William, I do perceive that the poor lady has nobody in her private and very anguished world to turn to. May I also be as rude to suggest that your dear and very broken brother is sorely frustrated with everything in his life and so is in much need of a big chest on which to hammer his clenched fists without any fear of retribution? Now I'm not proposing that I am the one for such a thing, for as you can clearly see, I am a lady, and so it would be deemed most unbecoming."

"We all agree with you on that one, madam," Blenkinsopp quickly interjected.

"Thank you, Blenkinsopp. Now, allow me to tell you that our very dear Blenkinsopp spent many years in the British army, and he has a son who has followed in his footsteps. So, if anybody can understand something of the pain and anguish that these worn, torn soldiers experience, then it is surely he, and I assure you, hand on heart, that he has a most impressively broad chest. Don't you, Blenkinsopp?"

"Yes, madam. I believe I do."

"Well, Blenkinsopp, don't just stand their nodding and grinning like a Cheshire cat. Show him!"

"Show him what, madam?"

"Why, your lovely broad chest, of course!"

Blenkinsopp instantly looked horrified.

"Madam, what are you thinking?"

"Well, I would have thought that was obvious! I was thinking that you have such a wonderfully broad chest that I do so admire, so I thought you might just expose it a little for all to see."

"Madam, I advise you now that my unclothed chest is for my eyes only, or otherwise that of my bathroom mirror," he snorted.

"Oh, well. Suit yourself, but William's brother indisputably still needs our help regardless of your very shy and, might I say, touchy disposition."

Will immediately began to laugh. "No, really, Lady B., spare poor Blenkinsopp the embarrassment, for it really is not necessary for the poor man to disrobe himself. I thoroughly get the picture, really I do."

"Oh, all right then, for as dear Blenkinsopp will most sadly confirm, these brave soldiers might return in body, but their wounded and broken souls and spirits remain firmly back on the battlefield. Yes, I believe it to be such a tragedy that these dear men find themselves hardly able to vocalize anything meaningful; such is the extent of their personal trauma," she sniffed as she continued to sip from her china cup. "Ahh. This particular blend of tea has most certainly been sent from above, for it is indeed liquefied heaven."

Will, who was listening most intently, felt strangely reassured by all that Lady Butterkist shared in that strange moment in time, for he felt he had never met anyone who not only understood but also fully appreciated his private home crisis in the manner that she did. He therefore felt secretly relieved that he had finally been given the opportunity to bare his soul and share all that was vexing his mind.

"Now, tell me truthfully, Will, dear thing. I am more than inclined to believe that you, my dear, are holding something back from me, yes, concealing something of considerable importance that most urgently needs to be addressed forthwith."

Will, who was in the process of consoling his dry throat with further gulps of sumptuous tea, immediately began furiously spluttering, for how on earth did she know he was holding something back?

"Yes, I do declare there is definitely much more going on here than meets the eye," she thoughtfully mused.

"All right. There is more, and it has much to do with a young friend whose name you so casually and unwittingly mentioned much earlier in our conversation."

"Well, William, please enlighten me further, for I am not aware of mentioning anyone unfamiliar during our most pleasant discourse."

"Well, her name is Polly, Polly Brown, to be precise."

"Hmm. Much as I thought! Go on, young man. Spill the beans, and remember, leave nothing out!" Lady Butterkist anxiously ordered.

"Do I have to, for I believe it to be nothing short of a real can of worms?" he moaned.

"Oh, I'm afraid so, William, for those monstrously dark secrets you hide inside will, in time, most assuredly eat you up. That, my dear boy, is a mathematical certainty!"

Will finally caved in, and through misty, tear-filled eyes, he told the story of the strange, unpretentious young girl he had met on his first day at the new school.

"At first I had no idea as to why I was so attracted to her, for as she herself told me, she was considered the school's bumbling idiot or, rather, the patsy who appeared to take the blame for everything. Still, I felt this urgent and deep need to get to know everything about her. She seemed so scared and yet so defiantly defensive, so it was difficult, if not impossible, at first to make her see me as a friend and not foe. Before long I invited her to my house, and after much persuasion, she agreed. Sadly, it was not too long before my mother did her usual thing, which was to insult her and make her wish she had never come.

As for my brother, he too was no better, for he raged on and even hurled things at her. What was I to do?" he lamented.

"Go on, young man," Lady Butterkist urged as she reached over with her serviette to wipe a stray tear that was racing headlong down his cheek as he continued to unravel his story.

"Well, finally she opened up and told me something of the terrible things that were happening to her and others in the children's home, and then she begged me not to say anything to anybody. Of course, I gave her my word. But then, quite out of the blue, she began telling me the most wildly fanciful stories about a ridiculous place that could not possibly exist, and I have to admit it was at this point that I felt I could bear no more."

By now a deluge of hot tears were streaming down his ruddy cheeks, and Lady Butterkist tried her very best to catch all that were visibly running down his face, but to no avail, for she could not keep up.

"Polly asked me if I would be willing to meet up with the two boys who had joined her on the adventure, for she truly believed they would fully back up her story." Will began to feel all choked up.

"Carry on, William, for I am all ears," she gently urged.

"Well, Lady B., the meeting with them was little short of totally embarrassing. Polly was talking like a crazy person. The boys were intent on chatting up two young ladies who were having refreshments in the station café, and they did everything they could to get Polly to leave them alone. It was so incredibly horrible and painful to watch."

"Hmm."

"Then, as if all this was not enough, my mother called me into her private boudoir to inform me that Polly's guardian, Mr. Scumberry, had paid her a timely visit—yes, a very threatening visit, if truth be known," he sighed. "My mother insisted I was to have nothing more to do with the girl, for Mr. Scumberry sincerely believed it to be his moral duty to inform her that many years previous Polly had been diagnosed with something called schizophrenia, and therefore she was considered to be something of a danger to herself and others. The next thing I knew, Polly had been placed within the confines of the local mental hospital. I never even had the opportunity to say my good-byes. I miss her so much. I doubted her for too long, but now I have come to realize that she is just about the most wonderful, caring girl I have ever met," he pathetically wailed.

"There, there, dear. Please continue," Lady Butterkist said as she gave him a comforting pat on his shoulder.

"I seriously considered visiting her the Christmas before last, but as she had only been at the hospital for a matter of weeks, I thought that it might not be to wise, as she hadn't had an adequate amount of time to settle in."

"As if one can be left to settle into such a place!" Lady Butterkist snorted, at the same time shaking her head as a show of her absolute disapproval.

"Well, anyway. I decided against the idea, lest paying a visit proved to be more disruptive than helpful."

"Plainly."

"When Easter came 'round I once more found myself pining after her and therefore desperate to see her, but then I got cold feet. I then considered paying her a visit during the summer holidays, but once more I turned—"

"Chicken!"

"Thank you, but no thank you, Lady B., for I have had more than enough to eat. In fact, I'm pretty stuffed," he admitted, patting his stomach as if to emphasize the point.

"Oh, William, I wasn't offering you anymore to eat! Oh, no. I was merely suggesting that the word you required was, in fact, *chicken*. Yes, put bluntly, you, young man, chickened out entirely. And that is surely quite indefensible, is it not?" she stated quite abrasively.

"Well, yes, I guess it is," he lamely agreed, for he was plainly caught off guard by her bluntness.

"Oh, young man, please forgive my unintentional rudeness, but I don't ever stand on ceremony. Trust me, when something needs to be said, I do not hold back," she stated in her very matter-of-fact way.

"No, that's fine, because in truth you're absolutely right. Sadly, I did find myself yet again having cold feet," he admitted.

Giles interjected, "Yes, cold feet, madam. And have we not all found ourselves in that difficult position at some time or another in our life? We surely need to lay aside all harsh criticism and judgment, for I feel we must be a bit more charitable here."

"Yes, yes. So do be quiet, Blenkinsopp, for I need to hear more."

"Well, this last Christmas Eve I finally plucked up the courage to pay a visit to the hospital, and then, just as I got to her ward, I yet again chickened out, to use your words," he croaked, his face turning a bright scarlet. "I mean, I had heard the most terrible screams and cries as I approached her ward, and then as the nurse went ahead of me and opened the door, I caught a sudden glimpse of her standing in front of a Christmas tree. It was as though she was not really there. I mean, there was a girl who looked like Polly, but it certainly wasn't a Polly I had ever seen before, for this ghost of a girl appeared to me to be very broken down and vacant." Will began to break down as he tried and failed to continue on.

Lady Butterkist gently placed her arm around the distraught young man's shoulder. "Will, allow me to say that you, I believe, are the only real friend she has, so stop licking your wounds and try attending to hers," she gently advised. "Just get up, brush yourself down, and then get back into the arena. If I am allowed to be frank with you, I have to say that I am of the opinion that she never once lied to you, and she really trusted that you would be her friend through thick and thin, yes, through the ups and downs of life, through the wind and rain, over the hills and dales; yes, over the lumps and bumps and—"

"Madam, enough said! I think young Will gets the big picture. Don't you, young man?" Blenkinsopp quickly and sharply interjected before Lady Butterkist got too carried away.

"Oh, I know I have completely let her down. I mean, only yesterday I found myself unexpectedly running into both boys Polly took me to meet at the train station café. They were meeting up with a friend who attends my school. I was very surprised when they asked to speak alone with me, and in doing so they finally admitted to all that had happened. I have to say, I was very heartened to know that Polly had not been lying, and this has made me more determined than ever to pay her a visit, even though it is against my mother's express wishes. However, I still feel so torn, if not thoroughly miserable."

"Yes, that's how *you* feel, but what of dear Polly? How miserable do you think this darling, fractured soul feels, locked away with only the dark whisperings of the insanely mad for comfort and with no one even remotely willing to place an arm around her shoulder to console or wipe away a tear? Yes, dear boy, think again, for she has absolutely nobody to stroke her forehead and tell her everything will one day turn out all right."

"I know, I know," he cried as he hugged his head with both hands, utterly desperate.

"Yes, William, she has nothing and nobody. Would you believe it if I said that she has spent two Christmases without a single hug to reassure her that she is the slightest bit precious to anybody? So try as you may, William dear, but you only deceive yourself further if you as much as attempt to trivialize or worm your way out of this one."

"Oh, dear lady. Everything you say is true," he anxiously cried. "So what can I do?"

"Well, one thing's for certain. You can't leave things as they are, can you?"

"Yes, but your ladyship, I really did try. Honest! I went to the hospital, and I left a present and a Christmas card with the nurse on duty. And let me tell you that to date there has been not a single word of thank you regarding my thoughtful gift, and so I presume—"

"Oh, William Montgomery, how dare you presume anything! Come on, young man, you are only suffering from a bruised ego, for do you really think a card and present would be enough? I mean, did you not promise her that you would never abandon her? Come to think of it, do you even remember that promise?"

"Yes, now that you mention it, I do," he hoarsely whispered.

"Well then, young man, you are guilty of doing the same irresponsible and utterly irreprehensible actions as have always been done to her in the past."

"And what is that?" he loudly moaned.

"You, young man, broke your promise, and in doing so you joined the long list of heartless people who over the years have completely failed her and have badly let her down."

"Oh, but I never meant to," he cried.

"Few people ever do," Lady Butterkist murmured. "Oh, yes. I believe we are all full to overflowing with good intentions, but may I remind you, young man, that the very road to hell is indeed paved with good intentions."

"Oh, dear," he groaned.

"It is indeed better never to promise than to promise and never fulfill. Our word should indeed be our bond. Although I am fully aware that to say such a thing is not exactly popular these days."

"Yes, I wholeheartedly agree with you, Lady B. I have totally let her down. Yes, at the end of the day I've been such a blind and callous fool," he whimpered, a look of deep remorse written all over his face.

"Yes, you have. But don't be so hard on yourself, William, for at least you finally have the courage and honesty of heart to admit such things," she said in her bid to console him.

"And, speaking of such things, what of your gift and card? Do you even know that she received them?"

"No, that's true. I have absolutely no idea."

"Then come on, William. Forgive her also for imagined failures. Get up from the ground and go be her man. Be her hero, her Sir Galahad, her gladiator. Yes, stand and fight for her, as I know she would surely fight for you," she cried as, emotionally stirred, she stood to her feet and began to march around her tartan blanket.

Blenkinsopp, also clearly feeling very emotionally moved by her passionate and most rousing speech, jumped up from where he was seated and began to do likewise. "Go get her," he excitedly cried as he joined in and expressed his approval and agreement with both Will and her ladyship.

Moments later they were all shouting "yes, yes" at the top of their lungs as they marched 'round and 'round the large wicker basket. Finally, in a state of utter exhaustion, they all collapsed back down on the tartan rug. Will was fully determined to get his breath back.

"Well then, I take it that we're all unanimous in our verdict," a heavily breathing Lady Butterkist announced. "Therefore, our new and very dear friend William must immediately leave us to go and become Polly's most valiant knight in shining armor, ready and willing to slay any amount of ferocious dragons that dare cross his path, if he must, in his desperate and chivalrous bid to rescue her."

By this point Will felt so fired up he was ready to charge at anything and everything, if only he knew how.

"Lady B., please help me out, for I don't how or where to go from here," he cried.

"Well, my dear boy, remember that where there's a will, there's—"

"Usually a dead body," Blenkinsopp quickly chipped in.

"My, my...Blenkinsopp, up until this moment in time I was quite unaware of your razor-sharp wit. You have clearly hidden it from me all this time."

"Well, madam, it is my humble opinion that some things are best kept to oneself," he quietly suggested as he stared down at his feet.

"Well, as I was saying before I was so rudely interrupted, where there's a will, there's usually a way, and therefore you, William, must pursue every avenue until you find a meaningful way back into her life. Is that understood?"

"Oh, completely!" he uttered, his heart bursting and his eyes now radiant with hope as he quickly got to his feet to go on his way.

"Lady B., not only has it been an absolute honor to meet you, but this whole chance meeting has changed everything," he said as he took hold of her hand to give it a gentlemanly old-fashioned kiss. "Had this meeting been just a consummation of tea and friendship, well, that would have been enough in itself, but to come away with sound advice and a heart filled with fresh vigor and determination, well, that is most surely the icing on the cake."

"Why, thank you for the wonderful compliment," Lady Butterkist said with a smile. "It is very much appreciated," she said, her wide smile showing that she was bursting with pride.

"Yes, my lady, the tea has been simply splendid, but my sorrowful heart has indeed been rid of many a deep burden. I must leave immediately to go and do all within my power to sort things out. I shall start with my mother and then take it from there. Lady B., trust me when I say that I will go to the ends of the earth if necessary to find and help Polly. This I promise."

"Oh, William dear, a quick word of warning: take heed of careless words."

"What do you mean by that?"

"I mean be careful what you promise, for one day you might well find yourself eating your words."

"What do you mean?"

"Exactly what I just said, for it's terribly easy to get caught up in the heat of the moment and make promises that later, when things have cooled down, you cannot or simply do not intend to fulfill. You've let her down once, so I ask just one thing of you: make sure it doesn't happen again."

"Oh, Lady B., I assure you now that I am adamant in all I state, and so in front of witnesses I am more than prepared to declare that for Polly's sake I will go to the ends of the earth if need be. Such is my determination."

"Splendid."

"So thank you once more for all your graciousness, and promise me right here and now that you will indeed keep in touch," he said as he heartily shook her hand.

"William, I assure you, hand on heart, that my word is indeed my bond, and therefore I will be in touch in the very near future."

"Giles, thank you also, for it has also been a real pleasure meeting you too," Will said as he stuck out his hand for the butler to shake.

"I believe the pleasure to have been all mine," Blenkinsopp humbly stated. "But before you leave to go pursue this mission of righting the whole world's wrongs and rescuing troubled princesses from high towers, I happen to believe that you still have something on your person that rightfully belongs to me."

Will found himself struggling to understand the meaning behind Blenkinsopp's last and surprisingly surreptitious comment. He was inclined to think it was obviously "a man thing"; otherwise, surely he would just come out and say what he needed to say.

"Hmm," was all that Blenkinsopp cared to mutter as his eyes furtively moved away from Will's eyes to come to a sudden halt somewhere near his midriff.

Will followed his eyes but still failed to understand the butler's strangely covert message.

Blenkinsopp coughed. "My personalized serviette, sir."

"Oops!" Will burst into laughter as he immediately looked down and realized he was adding insult to injury, for he was about to leave and go home with the poor man's prized serviette still dangling from his trouser belt.

"So sorry, old chap. Do forgive me," he said as he released the serviette from his belt and handed it over.

"Sorry to even have to ask for it back, sir, but there's a limit to how many intolerable pink hankies patterned with smiling teddy bears

I will gladly endure for Queen and country," he said, giving Will a warm, hearty smile.

That same night as Will removed his shirt to get into the shower, he was alarmed to discover many white feathers fluttering onto the bathroom floor. He stooped down to pick one up, and as he held it in front of his eyes to examine it further, he could not even begin to understand quite where these feathers had originated from and, more to the point, how they had come to get inside his shirt.

"How perfectly strange," he muttered as he lathered up his hair with an excessive amount of shampoo.

Chapter Twenty-Six
THE TROUBLE WITH TEA

D R. NINKUMPOOP WAS thoroughly enjoying his early morning cup of classic Earl Grey tea as with his feet propped up on the table he continued to do the daily crossword in his favorite newspaper. He undeniably had to admit that rather atrociously he had spent far too long making up his mind as to which tea he should try out today from his personally imported private stash of exclusive teas, which remained hidden away for his use only in a locked drawer of his filing cabinet. But as he continued to sip away, the delicious aroma not only permeating the room but also reaching deep into his nostrils, he knew he needed no further persuasion that he had indeed made the correct decision with regard to his choice of tea for this particular morning. He also knew with much certainty that just as some well-known author had cared to remark, tea should indeed be taken in solitude, and therefore he had not been the least bit negligent in fully appropriating this most profound piece of wisdom. Yes, tea should be enjoyed in splendid isolation and not in the presence of some fidgety and tiresome old nurse indefinitely prattling away in his ear, for this would indeed have been most wearisome and would definitely have spoiled, if not entirely destroyed, this superbly heady moment of supreme indulgence.

He momentarily stopped what he was doing to glance down at his watch and was delighted to discover he had at least another fifteen minutes of pure, unadulterated leisure time left before he was required to join the nurses for his routine and very mundane tour of all the wards, with their mishmash of deeply troubled patients.

"Wonderful. I have almost finished my crossword, for I have only one clue left to answer before I am obliged to call it a day and head up to the wards," he murmured as with an air of immense satisfaction he began rubbing his chin as he tried to give great thought to the clue printed on the page in front of him.

"Right. Hmm. It has eight letters, and the first letter is an *A*. Oh, humbug! What is the word I'm looking for? Hmm. Let me go back and see if this word fits. Oh, how annoying. This word has one too many letters to fit into the column," he said, feeling most perplexed with himself.

Eventually he was forced to go back and read the clue one more time in the forlorn hope of coming up with the correct word to fit in the eight small boxes. "Ah, here we are: 'contempt or disregard for others,' and it begins with an *A*. Oh, dear. What is the word I am looking for? No, for once I can't think what it could be, and usually I am so proficient when it comes to doing these little crossword puzzles."

Suddenly there was a frantic knock on his office door.

"Go away, whoever you are," he cried out, as he made little to no attempt to hide his utter annoyance at being bothered in this manner.

Still the knocking continued.

"Please, may I remind you that as of this moment I am still off duty for another fifteen or so minutes, so do me the courtesy of coming back later."

"Doctor, doctor, this is Nurse Shufflebottom, and I urgently need to speak with you."

"Later, nurse. Later. Don't you understand that this is my precious and most private time of the day? Please do not provoke me into saying anything unkind in my attempt to get you to leave me well alone," he angrily shouted out in her direction.

"Doctor, I am fully aware that you're still off duty, and so I apologize profusely for this infringement on your time. I would not consider bothering you if it were not important, for I have someone with me who urgently requires a private audience with you," she shouted through the closed door.

"Oh, don't bother me now. Take whoever it is up to the canteen and ply them with as many revolting cups of hospital drain water, I mean, tea, as their delicate and tender stomachs can possibly withstand. Oh, and then do tell them that I will be up there to meet with them as soon as I am able."

"But doctor, I believe this visitor to be no ordinary visitor, and she informs me that she has come such a long way to see you. So can I persuade you to change your mind?"

"Oh, Nurse Shufflebottom, I hardly think so, for who on earth could be of such importance that I would wish to forfeit my perfectly good cup of tea and abandon my near complete crossword to go play the perfect host? Pray, tell me now: has our good Queen decided to pay an impromptu visit, as she is in dire need of a bit of tea and sympathy, or perhaps the president of the United States of America has decided to pop by for a cuppa and a round of golf?" he stated, very annoyed.

"No, doctor, you're right; it is none of these," she mumbled.

"Well then, maybe the pope has deigned to pay us a short visitation to pray for the hearts and minds of the many poor souls that wander the wards of this hospital feeling lost and forlorn? Which is it to be, Nurse Shufflebottom?" he sneered.

"Ahh. Well, it's not the darling pope either. It's actually a woman," she hesitantly replied as she began to stumble over her words.

"Precisely. Just a woman! Now, Nurse Shufflebottom, I do believe you are beginning to seriously irritate and therefore exasperate me, so kindly follow my direct orders and take my surprise visitors up to the canteen, and then do as I have already suggested by plying them with endless cups of disgustingly, insidious hospital tea," he furiously stated as he began chewing the end of his pen out of sheer frustration.

"Yes, doctor, but I think you are doing the wrong—"

"Enough, Shufflebottom! When I have need of your impertinent advice and wisdom, I will not hesitate to ask for it. Until such a time, I would urge you to do as I bid and take my guest or guests up to the canteen, pronto," he roared.

"Very well, doctor," she gently replied, her sorrowful voice trailing off.

———•••———

As the poor nurse did her duty by leading the visitors up to the canteen, she did all she was able to protect and therefore cover up this most awkward and embarrassing situation by apologizing on behalf of Dr. Ninkumpoop.

"Lady Butterkist, I feel so terribly embarrassed. Please accept my profuse apologies, for it's quite obvious to all and sundry that our very dear Dr. Ninkumpoop got out of his bed on the wrong side this morning, and I can only hope that when he realizes the full extent of his error, he will most certainly want to apologize in full for being such a...." She stopped mid-sentence, all the while struggling to find a suitably inoffensive word.

"Insufferable prat," Lady Butterkist quickly suggested.

"Excuse me!" the nurse mumbled, her eyes instantly widening. She could feel the heat rising to her face. "Madam, did I hear you correctly?"

"Yes, nurse, you did indeed hear correctly. I just helped out a little by filling in the little blank on your behalf," she said, giving a warm smile.

Nurse Shufflebottom, unaccustomed to such brutal honesty, took a step backward as if to express deep shock, but she could not stifle a visible smile.

"Well, I wasn't exactly going to use such strong, distasteful language in the presence of such a prominent lady as your good self, but as you are the one to be suggesting it, then yes, Lady Butterkist, *prat* certainly seems to be most appropriate, for it most surely hits the nail on the head where the doctor's misguided and rude actions are concerned," she said with a smile as she wholeheartedly agreed with the ever-so-posh lady standing in front of her.

"Oh, and Lady Butterkist, please do not take offense, but as a rule we do not allow any dogs to be brought into the hospital, something to do with the hygiene rules of this facility, but as you are something of a VIP and to date you have been offended by disgracefully rude behavior, well, I think this calls for a little bending of the rules. Don't you think?"

"Oh absolutely, my dear nurse."

"Yes, I think we should definitely turn a blind eye on this occasion."

"Why, thank you, nurse. Both Tiddles and Piddles are very glad to hear that they are not going to be mercilessly shunned, and instead they are to be welcomed. Yes, you are delighted, aren't you, my little pooches?" she said as, moving nearer, she allowed them to lick her cheeks.

THE TROUBLE WITH POLLY BROWN

The nurse took Lady Butterkist and her pups, along with Giles Blenkinsopp, her faithful and attentive butler, up to the draughty and equally dreary canteen, and just as the doctor ordered, she supplied both of them with a lukewarm cup of hospital tea, along with an overly generous slice of shriveled-up Dundee cake. She then considerately brought the pooches some much-needed liquid refreshment.

"I thought the pups might well appreciate a nice and refreshing bowl of water," she stated, placing the bowl on the ground.

"Thank you, nurse. That is so thoroughly kind and thoughtful of you," Lady Butterkist generously commented as she allowed both dogs to slip off her lap to go and drink from the bowl of water.

"Don't mention it. But, Lady Butterkist, please do try and make yourself and your butler as comfortable as possible while you wait for the good doctor to appear. However, I urgently need to get back to my ward duties, so if you require more tea, then our kitchen staff, who at present are setting up behind that counter, will gladly oblige by giving your cup as many refills as you so desire."

"Thank you, Nurse Shufflebottom. We are indeed most grateful for all that you have done for us," Lady Butterkist said, giving the old and very wearied nurse the first appreciative smile she had received in the many long months she had been working in this hospital.

———

As soon as the old nurse disappeared from sight, Ralph, or rather, Lady Ralphella Butterkist, picked up her cup of tea to contemptuously pour it into the nearby flower arrangement. "Who in their right mind would dare to drink this disgustingly offensive stuff, for it truly tastes like rat poison!" she loudly verbalized in the direction of Blenkinsopp, her trustworthy butler, who, after agreeing with her verdict, chose to do likewise and follow his mistress in dispensing with his cup of dishwatery tea into the same flower bowl.

"Madam, I am of the opinion that you are being far too kind, for it tastes more like old gnat's pee, to be precise," he snootily sniffed before placing his drained cup back on the saucer.

"Giles dearest, grant me the pleasure of verbalizing as to how you, of all people, would even begin to know what gnat's pee tastes like."

"Madam, I have about as much an idea on that one as you have at sampling rat poison. I therefore believe to date we are both equal in our personal ramblings."

"Hmm. I understand, Blenkinsopp, for it's perfectly true to say that I have never once tasted rat poison, but mark my words when I say that this rather splendid flower arrangement will surely be dead, if not within a matter of minutes, then certainly a few hours," she disdainfully whispered in his direction.

She then picked up the plate holding the uninvitingly stale lump of Dundee cake. "Fascinating," she mumbled as using her fingers she raised it to eye level for the distinct purpose of examining it before loudly exclaiming, "Utterly disgraceful!"

Letting go of the cake, it instantly became the next casualty as it crashed back down on the plate, crumbling into many pieces at the moment of impact. "I do declare this moldy, dried-up excuse for a piece of cake would break most, if not all, my teeth, for not only is this cake at least a month out of date, but it is not fit for consumption by either man or beast," she haughtily informed Blenkinsopp as she contemptuously pushed the plate to one side. "I think I'd be in danger of going quite mad if I were forced to eat all my meals in this canteen."

"Yes, I believe you would quite quickly go off your rocker," Giles quietly commented.

"Now then, Blenkinsopp, be a good man and find me a suitable glossy magazine to browse through while we await for his most royal highness to get off his narcissistic—"

"Bottom?"

"No, Giles. I was about to say 'throne.'"

"Oh yes, madam."

"Yes, anyway, until he takes the trouble to come to find us."

"Yes, madam."

"Ahh, yes. *English Heritage Magazine.* Hmm. I rather like the look of that manor house on the front cover. Blenkinsopp, be a dear and kindly bring that magazine over to me," she politely ordered.

"Why, I do believe it is our home being depicted on the front cover. Well, I never! Here, Blenkinsopp, take a look, for it really is our very own magnificent Blenkinsopp Castle," she excitedly cried. "Now haven't they done a most splendid job of showing it looking its absolute best? Wouldn't you agree?"

<hr />

It would be well over thirty-five minutes before Dr. Ninkumpoop finally had the courage to pull himself away from his precious crossword puzzle to then head up to the canteen in search of his mystery visitors.

Before he opened the door leading into canteen, he deliberately began to breathe louder and faster, only stopping a little short of hyperventilating. Finally he burst through the door and rushed over to where they were still perched whilst browsing through a stack of magazines and newspapers.

As he approached them he was both annoyed and horrified to see that these insubordinate visitors had entirely broken the rules by bringing dogs into the facility, and so he determined to address this situation as quickly as possible.

"Greetings. I am Dr. Ninkumpoop," he breathlessly stated as he held out his hand for the widely proportioned but well-heeled lady in the wide-brimmed hat to shake. "I most profusely apologize for keeping you waiting this long, but may I also remind you that, sadly, no animals are allowed in this hospital. It clearly states so on a large sign at the front entrance, so I'm afraid I will have to ask you to take your dogs back to your car as soon as is reasonably possible."

Lady Butterkist was clearly not amused. She showed her frustration by choosing to ignore his outstretched hand, snubbing him further by turning her head to one side in a show of utter disgust. She then slowly and deliberately placed the magazine down on the coffee table before getting to her feet to formally shake his outstretched hand, a displeased frown betraying her displeasure, her mouth as tightly closed as a walnut desperate to be cracked open.

"Awfully sorry to have kept you waiting, but I have so much to do and so little time in which to do it," he breathlessly cried. "So, may I be so bold as to inquire as to who might I be speaking with?" he quizzed.

"Sir, to answer the question, my name is Lady Ralphella Butterkist, and this here is my trustworthy butler, who answers to the name of

Giles, although I almost always prefer to call him Blenkinsopp after my recently deceased husband's stately home."

Dr. Ninkumpoop felt the blood suddenly drain from his face, and before long he began to flounder most pitifully. He then began having erratic heart palpitations as it dawned on him that standing in front of him was the generous-hearted lady who had sent him the magnificently humongous donation and whom he had deliberately kept waiting as he enjoyed his special tea and crossword. And to add insult to injury, he had rather stupidly rebuked her for bringing her dogs into the hospital! Oh, how could he be such a dumb idiot? He took a deep gulp, and then he began to sway a little.

"Goodness gracious me. So you, madam, are *the* Lady Butterkist? Well, I never," he cried, instantly feeling acutely embarrassed by his hideously undiplomatic error. "Dear, sweet lady, forgive me for saying this, but you have much need of checking your calendar, for I am afraid to inform that you must have your days somewhat confused. The ribbon-cutting ceremony to which you are so cordially invited is not happening today, nor tomorrow, but the day after. Therefore it is my humble opinion that you have mistakenly arrived on entirely the wrong day," he declared as his vexed heart continued to race most erratically.

"Dr. Ninkumpoop, pray, tell me now: are you feeling all right? You clearly seem out of breath, almost to the point of hyperventilating, and I cannot help but note and feel most disconcerted, as you, my dear, are swaying back and forth in a manner not dissimilar to that of a very drunken sailor," Lady Butterkist declared in a most innocent intonation of voice.

"Lady Butterkist, please forgive me, but sadly I am deeply offended by your very offhand suggestion, for I am not the least bit intoxicated, and I hardly believe that endless cups of Assam tea could have me behaving in such a visual state of disorder that you would consider alcohol to be the root cause of my apparent distress. Put simply, I am in a suitable state of shock at finding you here in this hospital a few days before the jolly celebrations even begin!"

"Oh!"

"So I can only continue to apologize most profusely, for I am indeed mortified for having been so negligent as to keep you waiting all this time, but I had no idea that my visitor was none other than your good self," he remorsefully stated as he tried hard to hide the full extent of just how upset he was truly feeling.

"Also, please accept my humble apologies with regard to your two little frisky pups, for the least I can do to put things right is to waive the rules entirely on this occasion."

"Well, Dr. Ninkumpoop, that is more than generous of you, and I am sure that Piddles and Tiddles, my little imperial Shih Tzus, would like to show you the full extent of their appreciation by giving you a little schmaltzy kiss," she said as, whisking them up into her arms, she pushed them headlong into his face. "Doctor, tell me now: did you know these precious little dogs come in teacup size also?"

"Ah, Lady Butterkist, I did not, but I must warn you that I am extremely allergic to all dogs," he cried as he hurriedly stepped backward to avoid any further contact with them.

"Really, doctor! Oh dear, how perfectly sad, for dogs are considered to be a most wonderful way to give and receive warmth and affection," Lady Butterkist commented as she cuddled both dogs to her ample bosom.

"There, there, Tiddles, my darling. Now don't be too upset with the good doctor, for your little wet kisses, though innocent enough, are most likely to cause his dimpled cheeks to come out in a most ghastly and unsightly rash, and we can't allow that to happen, can we?" she stated, slightly tongue in cheek.

The poor doctor, who was already feeling acutely embarrassed by his stupid error, was now plunged into feeling more anxious than ever.

"Well, dear doctor, I am sure you had many more pressing things to do besides pay us humble patrons the courtesy of a few minutes of your very precious time," she gently stated as she leaned over to give his arm a friendly but condescendingly reassuring pat.

"Yes, Lady Butterkist, you are quite right, for believe me when I say that every day in this hospital is a race against time," he chortled.

"I wholeheartedly agree. I, for one, do believe crossword puzzles can be most exhausting as well as extremely time-consuming," Lady Butterkist deliberately announced as she rather mischievously continued to play him at his own game.

"Sorry, what did you say? I don't believe I heard you correctly," the confused doctor mumbled as he scratched his head.

"Oh nothing, Ninkumpoop. Nothing at all. I merely commented that crosswords can be so very troubling, especially when we've so diligently applied ourselves to the task of finding a specific word that, rather regretfully, continues to allude us and yet is so necessary if we are to complete the crossword puzzle within a specified time frame."

Still the doctor was hopelessly confused, for he could not understand why she was making any sort of reference to crosswords when surely she had no idea that this was the very reason she had been forced to endure the long wait in the miserable hospital canteen.

"Dear doctor, I've been doing this crossword while we've been waiting so patiently for the pleasure of your company," Lady Butterkist stated as she stooped to pick up the newspaper before placing the open page right up to his nose. This seemingly innocent action completely served to startle the now very beleaguered doctor. "Yes, one of your kitchen staff very kindly offered to lend us his newspaper, as we had completely run out things to do while we waited for you so graciously to appear."

"Huh!"

"Yes, and I have only one word left to find, and then, I'm delighted to say, it will be completely finished. I have to say that both Blenkinsopp as well as my good self have spent an entire fifteen or so minutes trying to work out what this last word might possibly be, but to tell you the truth, up until this moment we have remained absolutely mystified, for the correct word has certainly eluded us both. Hasn't it, Blenkinsopp?"

"Completely, madam," he sniffed.

"Here, Dr. Ninkumpoop, please do us the kindness by taking a good look. Now, it starts with an *A* and has eight letters. Look closer, doctor, if you will, and if you have any idea whatsoever as to what that silly little word could possibly be, then do be a dear and do not keep us in the dark a moment longer than need be. Yes, kindly put us out of our abject misery by revealing all to us."

The defenseless and severely frazzled doctor was now completely speechless.

Still, Lady Butterkist relentlessly continued to press him for the correct answer.

"Here, doctor, the clue to this one reads, 'Contempt or disregard for others.' Now, Blenkinsopp here seems to think that the word required to fill in all the blanks is *arrogant*, but to be perfectly honest I'm not so sure. So pray, tell me now: being a specialist of the mind and the intellectual wizard that you most obviously are, what, perchance, do you think, my good man?"

"Yes, yes. Lady Butterkist, your butler most surely has come up with the correct answer," the doctor rather pathetically croaked.

"All right, if you believe *arrogant* to be the correct word, then let it be so. Blenkinsopp, my man, here is a pen. Please grant me the honor by of filling it in. Splendid, puzzle solved!" she cried as she then loudly clapped her hands in the manner of an overexcited child.

"Oh, and while we're at it, doctor dear," she whispered loudly in his ear, "I don't know if you are fully aware, but the tea served up to us in this canteen is not only very suspect, but I assure you, hand on heart, it is simply ghastly," she announced, shaking her head as if to fully emphasize her utter disgust.

"Oh, dear Lady Butterkist, I am so terribly sorry," he limply stated.

"Apology accepted, but all the same, I wonder, doctor, are you at all familiar with the historical events pertaining to a certain Boston Tea Party? If you are, I would very much appreciate it if you would do me the honor of casting your mind back to that most famous occasion and then do me the courtesy of telling me what, if anything, you might remember concerning that specific historical event."

"Hmm. As I wasn't there in person, I believe myself to be at a distinct disadvantage, for I don't believe I know anything whatsoever about the Boston Tea Party," he muttered.

"Hmm. I didn't think so. Well then, Ninkumpoop, allow me to give you an itsy witsy, teeny bitsy history lesson," she said as she turned to concentrate all her efforts into pulling off her long gloves, which she then dismissively presented to Blenkinsopp for safekeeping.

"Now then, Ninkumpoop, hear me out when I say that this particular tea party was no pleasant gathering between two generous-hearted nations but rather a most unhappy affair between us Brits and the Americans, and it all took place off the shores in Boston. It has, therefore, been written down in the annals of history in the hope that it might never again be repeated."

"Hmm, really?" he muttered in a most disinterested tone of voice.

"Yes, really. So please allow me the privilege of enlightening you, for not only did the Americans throw our tea chests overboard as they quite rightly chose to revolt against our unjustly high taxes, but alarming as this might seem, it was also discovered that some unscrupulous and very greedy English tea merchants were adding a certain portion of your name to the tea in order to make more profits. Yes, as the saying goes, where there's muck, there's money."

"Pray, what on earth are you implying, Lady Butterkist?" he cried aloud, feeling most alarmed. "Yes, precisely what do you mean by that?"

"Poop, dear doctor. Those greedy guzzlers were adding poop to the tea."

"Poop?" quizzed the now very confused doctor.

"Yes, Dr. Ninkumpoop. Just as the latter half of your surname suggests, to make more profit, these most wicked embezzlers were adding poop to the tea, thus turning it into a most foul and, might I add, bitter-tasting beverage."

"Goodness, Lady Butterkist! Trust me when I say that I had absolutely no idea. I hope those thieving men were shot at dawn for their utterly irreprehensible greed. However, pray, tell me: what has all this got to do with me?" he wearily sighed.

" Plenty!" she quickly retorted.

"Uh!"

"Yes, for unfortunately I would very much like to suggest that much of that pungent, poop-filled tea, having failed to find its way to the bottom of the ocean, has rather surprisingly found its way into this hospital canteen. Would you not agree?"

"Unbelievable!" was all he could muster in response to her unexpected and surprising accusation.

"In fact, I'm quite surprised you have not had a number of unexplained deaths on your hands due to patients and visitors alike being forced to drink this undeniably revolting concoction," she loudly declared.

"Oh, deary me!" he quietly muttered.

"Now, grant me a favor, doctor, by taking a good, hard look at this wilting flower arrangement," she snootily ordered as, picking up the bowl of flowers, she then proceeded to wave it right under his nose.

"Uhh!" he cried as he quickly moved his head to one side, for watching her wave the pot around so overdramatically had him thoroughly convinced that there was at least a 90 percent chance that his glasses would accidentally be knocked right off the end of his nose.

"Now, don't be such an old sourpuss. There's a dear. Please take a hard look. Why, it must be less than half an hour ago that these flowers were utterly lost in their moment of glory, as they positively bloomed and scented the room with their heavenly perfume, and now look at them, completely shriveled up and wilted!"

"Incredible!"

"I should say so! But, dear doctor, the correct word we are looking for here is *unbelievable*, for they are so beyond hope they are no longer even worthy of bedecking an abandoned shrine on some suitably remote Greek island."

"Yes, dear lady. Yes, I entirely agree with you," he most miserably spluttered in the hope of finally shutting her up, but sadly, similar to an overfilled teapot, she still continued to spout on.

"For since I fed this dear plant a spot of your hospital tea, you can see for yourself it is positively in the most advanced stages of dying, not too good an advertisement for any sort of hospital, wouldn't you agree?"

"Yes, yes," he mumbled.

"Thank you!" she snorted as she rather harshly placed the arrangement back down on the wooden coffee table.

Before the seriously confused doctor could once more draw breath and make any further helpful comment, she was off again. "Now then, Ninkumpoop, in light of all I have shown you, if I were you, I would certainly wish to exonerate my good name by making it my top priority to ensure that this hospital immediately changes its tea-drinking policy, do you not agree?"

"Yes, fully."

"Good. I believe we are finally on the same page."

"Yes, Lady Butterkist, I do believe we are," he wearily stated as he reluctantly gave his full agreement.

"So we must attempt to dispense with this cheap, rancid muck in preference for a nice, subtle, classic Chinese green tea scented with jasmine, or may I be so foolishly impertinent as to suggest a mellow Ceylon blend, for this, I believe, will go a long way in keeping patients and visitors alive for so much longer, oh, as well as deliriously happy."

"Yes, yes, Lady Butterkist."

"Hmm. I would also like to see you bring in some wonderful Darjeeling, as this really is the champagne of teas, which, once drunk, would certainly ensure that the palace of every confused and troubled soul finds a new sense of purpose and serenity."

"Yes, yes," he continued to weakly mutter.

"After all, the aim of this hospital must surely be to keep patients and visitors alike not only alive but also feeling thoroughly restored and back in their right mind. Am I correct in my thinking?"

"Yes, yes, my dear. You are quite right," he deeply sighed.

"Well then, dear sir, as we are a tea-drinking nation, I believe it behooves us to abandon all compromise and thus serve up only the very best in deliciously rich tasting tea."

"Yes, yes."

"Not bucket loads of what appears to be the foulest-smelling pee water I have ever had the misfortune to have placed under my nose. Do I make myself clear?"

"Abundantly!"

"Oh, I'm so blessed to know that finally we are of one accord," she joyfully cried.

"Lady Butterkist, you have my word that I will take it upon myself to look into this situation as a matter of great urgency," he subserviently whimpered.

"Well, I'm sure we would all appreciate your kind and much needed help in this little matter," she said. She then turned back toward the doctor to give him a warm, most appreciative smile while attempting to straighten his already perfectly straight tie in a manner more suited to that of a little boy about to take his first Communion.

"There. Sorted," she gleefully cried.

Chapter Twenty-Seven
PIDDLES PROVIDES A MIRACLE

Meanwhile, back in Piadora Hodgekiss had summoned Mrs. O'Brien to his side, as he desired to give her an up-to-the-minute report on Ralph's progress.

"Mrs. O'Brien, I have to tell you I could hardly believe the mountain of notes filled with words of encouragement that have been piling up here over the past few days. There were so many sacks full to overflowing that it will be utterly impossible for Polly to get through them all. Having combed through them, I have just picked out the ones I consider most appropriate at this specific time of need."

"Oh, Hodgekiss, that's wonderful, for if Polly were to see just how many of us really love and care about her, then she would instantly rise from the ashes of despair to once more become the wonderful and affectionate girl that she truly is," she said as she picked up one of the notes to read the contents.

"Hmm, you are so right about that. In fact, she would indeed be utterly overwhelmed by the amount of love we all have for her," he said as he reflected back on their last conversation.

"All these wonderful, touching letters make me feel so very weepy," Mrs. O'Brien confessed as she quickly placed a handkerchief up to her eyes.

"Mrs. O'Brien, please don't upset yourself, for you have yet to see the end of this matter. I also think that Ralph should immediately be given a job in the theater, as you have more than excelled in doing a most wonderful job on him. I, for one, firmly believe that no one would even begin to suspect a thing," he stated, giving a deep smile.

"Yes, but I have to confess that I am a more than a little shocked to hear that he has renamed my poor little imperial Shih Tzus 'Piddles' and 'Tiddles'! What is he playing at? Oh, poor Peaches and Precious. My little darlings must surely be feeling so confused by now, bless their little cotton bed socks."

"Mrs. O'Brien, please don't get too carried away, for I can't ever remember seeing any dog clothed in bed socks! But what has become of poor Dr. Ninkumpoop? Oh, how the mighty have fallen. The poor man has really gotten himself into such a beastly jam, as he finds himself being so mischievously bossed about by Ralph."

"Yes, Ralph is doing an amazing takeover bid," she enthused.

"Totally inspiring! I, for one, have not laughed so much in a long time. But watching his theatrics has me a tad concerned, for he seems to be enjoying the part of Lady Ralphella Butterkist a little too much for his own good. I fear he has clearly forgotten the main purpose of this mission."

"Trust me on this one, Hodgekiss. There is no way Ralph, or rather, Ralphella, will leave that hospital unless he has absolutely secured Polly's release, for not only has he been appointed guardian over her, but he feels strongly committed to helping her in every way that he possibly can."

"Well, that's good to hear, and by the way, Mrs. O'Brien, I just love the butterfly lips, and I have to say that he certainly has that walk down to perfection," Hodgekiss further stated, his smile getting wider as he continued to observe Ralph's stunningly brilliant performance.

"I daresay he'll get a large number of highly desirable cinematic awards for this one," Mrs. O'Brien cheekily commented.

"Yes, but if that were to happen, would we ever hear the last of it?" Hodgekiss mused as he continued to admire his dear friend's outstanding performance.

"I'm afraid not," Mrs. O'Brien speedily retorted.

Back at the hospital, Dr. Ninkumpoop was beginning to feel extremely anxious to get on with his day, and so he politely asked Lady Butterkist the true purpose behind her very impromptu visit.

"Well, as you ask, I am fully aware that the opening of the ward is still a few days away, but as Blenkinsopp and my good self were driving around enjoying the splendid English countryside with its gloriously divine summer weather, we just happened to find ourselves in this little neck of the woods, so to speak. Dear doctor, do you know that lovely wooded patch just off Primrose Lane?"

"Yes, yes, I do."

"Well, perhaps one fine day we could have ourselves a little picnic in those woods. Now wouldn't that be a lovely treat?"

"Yes, yes," he spluttered, scratching his chin as he secretly wished she would skip all this benignly casual conversation and just get to the point.

"Well, as soon as Blenkinsopp informed me that Hellingsbury Hospital lay just a little to the east of where we were going to lay our tartan rug down to have ourselves a little picnic, well, I made the bold decision to do a little detour and pop by in the hope that you might willingly and cheerfully give me my own very exclusive tour of your wonderful facility. Of course, if I am clearly out of order in making such a demanding request, then pray, tell me now, and we will be on our merry way long before you can say, 'Is there any mustard in this custard?'" she purred, giving the doctor a sweet, lingering smile. "So, doctor, is it at all possible?"

"Oh, absolutely, Lady Butterkist. I am completely at your service, so where would you like to start?" the doctor earnestly inquired as privately he attempted to pull himself together.

Having made a tour of virtually all the wards, the doctor then politely turned to ask Lady Butterkist if she had seen enough.

"Well, Dr. Ninkumpoop, I certainly cannot leave yet, as I have still to tour the locked wards."

"Locked wards?" he loudly queried, for suddenly he was feeling very shocked.

"Yes, doctor, the locked wards. Now don't pretend that, like Area 51, they don't exist, for I may be a little old in the tooth, and maybe I'm no longer the sharpest knife in the drawer, but I am fully aware of their existence. Please do not waste my time further by denying it."

"Oh, I wouldn't dream of doing such a thing," he stammered.

"Well then, without further adieu, kindly do me the courtesy of escorting us up to the locked wards."

The doctor was given little choice other than to obey her every wish.

In no time at all Lady Butterkist found herself standing at the end of young Polly's bed. She could clearly see that someone or something was lying hidden away under the bed clothing, so she knew that now was the perfect time to get the ball rolling, so to speak.

"Doctor, pray, tell me, by what name does this young hidden-away child go by?"

"Oh, her name is Polly Brown."

"Firstly, tell me now, why is she hidden away on a locked ward? And secondly why, when most children are outside taking in the fresh air whilst scrumping apples from orchards or playing endless games of conkers, meantime this particular child is still cocooned in her bed sheets at this extraordinarily late hour of the day?"

"Dear Lady Butterkist, forgive me for saying this, but this is one of my most troubling cases, in as much as—"

"Troubling? Now tell me straight, doctor, what has this poor young girl done that has forced you to take such drastic action as to lock her away with such old and seriously ill patients as are generally known to be on this ward?"

"Well, put plainly, according to her guardians she really is not right in the head. I have been working very hard day and night in my effort to get to the root of all her problems, for trust me when I say that she really is a very troubled soul."

"Aren't we all?" Lady Butterkist mumbled.

"Sorry, Lady Butterkist, I didn't quite hear you," he snorted.

"Oh really! Well, I wonder if you could see your way to allowing me to have a private little word with her?"

"Well, as long as I am in the near vicinity I suppose it would all right."

"I said in private!"

"Hmm. That's all very well, my dear lady, but the chances are high that she will not come up from under the bedclothes, for other than mealtimes she rarely pops out from under the blankets, and it's even rarer to find her speaking with anyone. So, believe me when I say that to have any form of reasonable conversation with her may well prove very unfruitful, if not nigh impossible!"

"Really?"

"Therefore, for all these reasons, as well as that of your personal safety, I am not too happy to oblige you in your otherwise seemingly innocent request."

"Dear doctor, this is not a request but rather a demand, for I would still very much like to try. I therefore insist that I be given a few moments alone with her."

The doctor had little choice but to succumb to her express wish. Therefore, albeit with great reluctance, he left the room, promising to return promptly.

With the doctor now well out of earshot, Lady Butterkist ordered Blenkinsopp to be vigilant in keeping a watchful eye on the office while she attempted to sort things out with Polly.

"Blenkinsopp, do as I ask, and stand over there and keep watch. Make sure the coast is clear at all times."

"Very well, madam."

"Polly dearest, please do come up from under the bedclothes," Lady Butterkist gently ordered.

She would go on to repeat her request a number of times, but still there was no movement, as a clinically depressed Polly continued to passively remain completely hidden away under the bedding.

"Polly dear, do make us all blissfully happy by arising from under the bed linen." Still there was no movement whatsoever.

"Polly dear, you are beginning to resemble that of a very dead corpse ready to undergo the knife of the local mortician," she loudly declared. Still nothing!

"Madam, do you not fully realize that we are getting nowhere, for trying to get Polly to cooperate is like trying to raise a pharaoh or two from his ancient tomb!"

"Giles, don't be so impatient. Give me a few more minutes, for I have something else up my sleeve that I believe may work to our advantage," she gently rebuked, as she decided to turn the temperature up by making things a tad more personal.

"Polly dear, how are you coping since leaving Piadora to return back to that horrid, hate-filled castle? Not too good, I presume. I wonder also if you have heard from our very dear Aazi, for he too seems to be going through similar very difficult trials."

As Lady Butterkist stood at the end of her bed, she began to see small, hopeful signs of movement under the bedclothes. This greatly encouraged her to continue on.

"Come on, sweetheart, for it is most difficult to have any form of meaningful conversation whilst you remain hidden under those heavy hospital blankets," she sniffed as she encouragingly continued to see something stir under the bedclothes.

"Now, tell me also, Polly, how is dear, young James doing these days? I have to admit that I and others have been most concerned for him since his model airplanes and other assortment of military models were so meanly confiscated. I mean, all he did was speak up for you, and as for that most unfortunate episode which had the two of you, along with one of the other children, running away from the home, yes, that was such a ghastly affair. Poor James really did feel like a prize idiot, so stupidly forgetting to change out of his pajamas. Hmm, and PC Inkblot, well, he really was quite a sweetheart, and he—"

Suddenly the covers were rolled back to finally reveal Polly's sad, long face lying on the pillow alongside Langdon's long trunk.

"Well, hello there, Polly. Thank you so much for finally agreeing to come out from under the bedclothes. I am also exceedingly glad to see that Langdon is still looking as clean as a whistle," Lady Butterkist commented. "Now then, young lady, before we have a good, hearty chin-wag, Christmas has come very late for you this year, but Blenkinsopp, my very dear and devoted butler, has brought you lots of lovely goodies, such as delicious chocolate and sweet-smelling bubble bath, some nice, wooly socks, and lots more things that young girls so love. So come on, Polly, be a good dear and sit up," she said with an air of great firmness tinged with kindness as she removed her wide-brimmed hat and, without looking, handed it over to Blenkinsopp for safekeeping.

Blenkinsopp could not fail but look terribly confused, as he already had a pup safely tucked away under each arm. "Madam," he said loudly as he began clearing his throat, "if God above would be so kind as to apportion me a third hand, I would thank Him most profusely from the bottom of my heart, truly I would. But until such times, I apologize that I am unable to release you from the heavy burden of your hat, as I would have you take note that I am already responsible for securing a pup under each arm."

"Nonsense, Blenkinsopp. As you have a very active mouth at your disposal, might I suggest we consider the use of your teeth in order to fully secure my hat?"

"My teeth, madam?"

"Oh, Blenkinsopp, please don't get stroppy with me. Now, just do as you're told, and open your mouth just wide enough to allow me to insert the brim of my hat between your upper and lower chompers," she mischievously ordered.

"There, that's it. Just a teeny bit wider. Splendid! Now just drop down those very sharp incisors!"

Blenkinsopp impassively moved forward and then bent over just enough to allow her ladyship the privilege of placing the brim of her hat between his teeth. "Now do as I say and bite down hard, Blenkinsopp. That way there will be no chance of you accidentally dropping my very expensive hat," she firmly ordered.

A wide-eyed Polly, who was watching the whole affair with a look of pure disbelief written all over her face, was left with little choice but to hold her hand to her mouth in order to stifle the first giggle that had perchance escaped since her arrival at the hospital.

All too soon she was chuckling away as the strange lady's poor butler was forced to have her hat hanging from his mouth while desperately trying to hold on to two very frisky dogs.

With the hat finally gripped between his teeth, Blenkinsopp straightened himself up, and in doing so he accidentally loosened his firm grip on the dogs. In a matter of seconds one of the pups leapt out from under his arm and then proceeded to race full pelt down the ward as fast as its little legs could go.

"Oh, goodness gracious me! Piddles, come back, come back," her ladyship alarmingly cried out. "Blenkinsopp, don't just stand there like a wet drip catching flies. Go get him, my man," she loudly ordered.

Lady Butterkist was delighted to hear Polly giggle as she watched this latest drama unfold before her very eyes.

"Yes, madam," Blenkinsopp mumbled as he tried hard to hold on to her hat whilst answering. Then, with her hat still clenched between his teeth and Tiddles safely tucked under his other arm, he began racing down the ward as he chased after Piddles the pup.

Suddenly, Piddles stopped in her tracks and pattered over toward a man sitting absolutely motionless in a chair as he stared into space.

On noticing her dog's reaction to the sad and tragic man, Lady Butterkist cried out an order to Blenkinsopp to stop in his tracks and leave Piddles well alone.

"I believe we may be about to witness a small miracle," she muttered under her breath as her curving lips broke into the warmest of smiles.

Piddles casually looked up at the severely withdrawn man, and the man stared back at Piddles. Piddles then licked her lips before making the cutest little noises as she moved her confused head to one side as though she were trying in her mind to weigh up this very sad patient. The wizened, pain-filled man, for his part, never moved as much as an inch. His soulful eyes remained focused on the dog as they continued to stare at each other as though they were desperately locked in some very intimate and most private game. Then without warning, Piddles leapt straight onto the man's lap and immediately began snuffling then licking his scarred, ravaged face with her tiny pink tongue. At first the man with the soulful, liquid eyes remained like a garden statue, not moving a muscle while a contented Piddles expressed herself by licking him all over. It started with his eyes, then his ears. She then moved down to his nose, followed by his mouth. Still, the man remained completely expressionless as Piddles continued in her own way to manifest great affection.

There was soon great hysteria in the ward, as patients began to crowd around.

Suddenly and without warning, huge tears billowed from the man's eyes before rolling uncontrollably down his hollow, sunken cheeks. However, none made it past his chin, as Piddles chose to lick them all up as they freely raced down his pained face. Seconds later, he slowly and cautiously placed a doddery arm around the dog. Moments later, and to Lady Butterkist's great joy, he cautiously placed both arms tightly around the dog as he slowly began to cuddle the warm, excitable body. Piddles's immediate response was to give the mournful gentleman considerably more affectionate licks. In the space of just a few minutes, the patient was then passionately hugging and kissing the pup in a manner that might suggest they had been inseparable, best friends for many years.

Eventually the nurses raced down the ward toward the large crowd that had formed around the bedside of Patient 333. What they discovered would not only shock them but stay with each of them for the rest of their lives, for Patient 333, who had never been anything more than a useless cabbage to arduously spoon-feed and wash and who had never once spoken a single word in the twenty years he had been at the hospital, was now rolling 'round the floor liberally laughing and crying as, cradling the precious pup in his arms, he continued to hug him tightly to his chest.

The anxious nursing staff quickly ordered all patients to go back to their own beds or alternatively head to the television lounge, as they wished to give the patient a very thorough medical examination before bleeping the on-call doctor to come and see for himself.

In turn, Lady Butterkist ordered Blenkinsopp to quietly advise the patient that if he were to choose to leave the hospital this very day, then she would be more than delighted to give Piddles the pup to him as her very special gift.

Blenkinsopp did as he was ordered and passed this information to the now deliriously happy patient, who wasted no time whatsoever in changing out of his worn-out striped pajamas to get back into the clothes he had arrived in some previous twenty or so years.

As ex-Patient 333 walked down the ward toward the door and freedom with Piddles safely tucked under one arm, Lady Butterkist, as usual, could not control her runaway tongue.

"Goodness gracious, Blenkinsopp. Can you believe it? The man is expelling feather after feather from the bottom of his most dated trousers," she gasped.

In a matter of seconds, many of the patients were to be found picking up the long, white feathers, then holding them up to their faces as they stared in wonder at them. Many patients then chose to run up and down the ward like young, innocent children as they placed a feather or two in the palm of their hands and then blew them into the air before chasing after them. Other, less energetic souls peered at the feathers and then began tickling themselves until they fell off their chairs due to too much uncontrollable laughter, and more still just walked back and forth with the feathers inserted behind their ears or strategically stuck in locks of their hair as they chose to become something of a fearless Indian warrior.

In truth, the ward was in complete pandemonium, with patients running after feathers and nurses running after patients and doctors running after nurses and patients.

"Madam, are you now happy? Indisputably this ward is now in complete bedlam."

"Yes, Blenkinsopp, but rather than 'bedlam' I prefer to call it 'splendid chaos.'"

"Madam, is it not amazing how much undeniable joy and pleasure the introduction of something as simple and pure as a feather has suddenly brought to this cold, unfeeling place."

"Yes, but goodness gracious, Giles, our poor man is leaving this ward looking simply ridiculous!" she gasped. "He needs to rather urgently shop around for a smart new suit that fits him properly, for I do believe he's not only shrunk a foot or two since he last wore that ridiculously dated outfit, but alas, he's also shed at least a hundred pounds or more. So much for hospital food, eh, Blenkinsopp?" She immediately opened her purse, and after dipping down deep she handed her faithful butler an envelope.

"Blenkinsopp, do be a poppet and run after him, for this gentleman thoroughly deserves some form of financial restitution after all he has endured. Kindly see to it that he gets this."

"Yes, madam."

"Oh, and please give him my calling card, and inform him that if he needs any help whatsoever in the future, then I'm his man, I mean, woman."

Blenkinsopp did all that he was ordered. The thin and gentle man turned, and with a smile so large it would melt any gracious heart, he waved his thanks. Then with Piddles tucked safely under his arm, he turned to leave the ward and the hospital forever.

"Madam, he cannot express enough gratitude for your kind and very gracious gift, and he promises to love Piddles as much as you have. He also said that he trusts that you won't mind too much if he chooses to spend the money on something entirely different that all his life he has yearned for."

"Blenkinsopp, what on earth do you mean?"

"Well, madam, would you believe it if I said that he desperately desires a new pair of swimming shorts, as well as a wet suit?"

"Oh goodness gracious, Giles! He won't stay out of this hospital for any length of time if he intends to prance down the High Street looking like Rudolph the Red-Nosed Reindeer, dressed only in swimming trunks and a snorkel!" she warily stated.

"No, madam. I am inclined to believe that you are totally misunderstanding the situation here."

"Really, Giles? Well, I'm all ears, so what are you waiting for? Please, keep me in the picture," she earnestly requested.

"Well, madam, he told me that after spending many years in a straitjacket, his biggest desire now is to dive into the deepest ocean and swim with the whales and dolphins. Once he has built up the confidence, he then intends to do a spot of deep-sea diving, hopefully off the Great Barrier Reef."

"The Great Barrier Reef?"

"Yes, Down Under, as he yearns once more to wonder and stand in awe of all the beauty he has missed out on by being cooped up in this dungeon all these long years. Excuse me, for they were his precise words, not mine," an embarrassed Giles mumbled.

"My sentiments entirely! Well, thank you for sharing all this with me, Blenkinsopp, for I feel deeply stirred to the seat of my emotions by this dear man. It is also wonderful to think just how much he will thoroughly appreciate every new and extraordinary experience that his new life will hopefully now bring."

"To use a few of your choice words, my sentiments exactly, madam."

"You know something, Blenkinsopp I think I might well consider joining him Down Under, although I feel certain my old swimming costume will seriously struggle to fit over my now very ample portions."

"Hmm. A word of caution, Mrs. B.: perhaps madam is more suited to land and therefore should stick to what she knows best, at least for the time being."

"You are right, Blenkinsopp. What was I thinking? I believe I have been swept away on a tide of emotion. Although I must say that it was very delightful watching the interaction between my Piddles and that dear ghost of a man, for it cannot fail to show all within these walls what a mere touch of unconditional love can do."

"As usual, you're absolutely correct, madam."

"Yes, if I'm honest, we are all in dire need of a bit of unfailing love, and sadly, that is the only medicine most here know nothing of and yet are in urgent need of. Quite frankly, I wonder how many patients would be left on these wards if they were to experience such a transcending love, if only for a small moment, in their sad, pitiful lives."

"Very few, madam, if any."

"Yes, Giles Blenkinsopp, I do believe you to be perfectly correct in your latest assumption. Now then, with all that excitement out of the way, let us return to our more immediate problem, and that is young Polly."

Chapter Twenty-Eight
POLLY'S MIRACULOUS RECOVERY

*N*ow, do be a dear and sit up, young lady, and allow me to make you more comfortable. There's a dear. Now, Polly, have we not just witnessed something rather extraordinary unfold before our very eyes?"

"Yes, it was pretty amazing and really touching to watch," Polly admitted, as she began brightening up with every minute that passed.

"Right, well, I do believe that now it is time for your special miracle, young lady."

Polly immediately responded to the request by allowing Lady Butterkist to puff up her pillows for her. She then sat back, clutching Langdon very tightly to her chest.

"There, now that's much better, for at last I can now see your pretty little face."

Polly instantly flinched on hearing the word *pretty*.

"What's the matter, dear? Have I said something wrong?" Lady Butterkist innocently asked.

"Oh, nothing, nothing at all, Lady Butterkist, although I am curious at to why you have come here to see me, when by even standing near my bed you may be in danger of catching something very nasty from me," she quietly stated.

"Call me Lady B., dear. Well, Polly, it's all absolute twaddle, really it is, for the only thing I fear I am in danger of catching around this bedside is a depressingly large dose of misery and melancholy," she snorted. "So quite what do you mean by that?"

"Well, Lady B., I'm supposed to be infectious and therefore very dangerous, for don't you know I've got the lurgy?"

"Hmm, is that so? You really don't look very dangerous to me."

"Well, Uncle Boritz told all the children that the American CIA have named their lying machine after me, and worse still, many dangerous diseases now bear my name," she mumbled.

"Absolute poppycock! Oh, Polly dear, are you always going to believe that you are responsible for all the world's wrongs?"

"I guess so, for Uncle tells me—"

"Polly, please listen carefully, for if you are referring to the polygraph, let me assure you now that this machine has been in since existence long before you were even a twinkle in your mother's eye. And as for these diseases that start with *poly-*, they too have been around for a very long time."

"Really?"

"Yes, really. Polly, you have been lied to, so unless you rather foolishly intend to live the remainder of your life believing that you alone are wholly responsible for every war, famine, and pestilence on this earth, I think it's high time you discharged yourself of all this ridiculous guilt that weighs so heavily on your young shoulders."

"I'll try," Polly timidly promised.

"Personally speaking, I'd find it quite an honor to have a disease, any disease, named after me," Lady B. quipped. "And I have to say that there a number of very fascinating diseases flying around the globe at this precise moment that have yet to be named, so we could always put our names forward in the hope of getting some liver, or better still, brain disease named after us," she said, beaming from ear to ear as she reached over to give Polly's small hand the first friendly, gentle squeeze she'd had in years.

"Well, all right then. I will try my utmost, Lady B.," she muttered as she then dropped her head down to avoid further eye contact.

Lady Butterkist could tell that being nice or kind to Polly no longer worked its usual magic, but she was up for the challenge.

"Now then, dearest one. Perhaps you would like Blenkinsopp to pour you a nice, refreshing glass of water, or maybe some orange squash?" she gently suggested.

Polly readily agreed to a glass of water.

As Blenkinsopp passed the glass to her, Lady Butterkist found it very difficult to keep her thoughts quietly to herself.

"What on God's earth have they done to the poor girl?" she angrily muttered under her breath before quickly rebuking herself, for she was meant to be acting the part of a well-bred and gentile aristocratic lady.

"Now then, dear, let's do a swap, shall we? Allow me the privilege of having a good look at Langdon, while you take ownership of this large bag of belated Christmas presents and begin opening them," the friendly lady with the very funny butterfly lips politely requested as she motioned for Polly to hand over her blue elephant.

"Go on, Polly dear. Do start unwrapping all these gifts, but do be careful, because there is a baked appletude pie at the bottom of the bag, and we wouldn't want that to crumble and get mashed up, would we now?"

Polly once again flinched as she heard the weird but kind lady refer to the pie as 'appletude,' not apple, for the only place she had ever heard it called by such a name was at the Princesses' School in Piadora. It instantly sent chilling tingles down her spine.

"Goodness gracious me, he really is a very dashing and hand-some little thing," the funny lady declared. "You know, I once knew a bright young girl whose elephant secretly carried all her brokenness and tears," the lady with the peculiar pink butterfly lips sniffed as she pointed directly at Langdon's exceedingly large tummy. "There must have been a whole lot of heartbreak and tears to make his stomach expand this much," she loudly mused as she playfully tickled Lang-don's exposed tummy.

Polly finally broke into a small smile.

"And that brave young lady embarked on an amazing journey to a secret kingdom called Piadora. Have you ever heard of such a land, dear?"

Polly bit down hard on her lip and shook her head, for although she hated lying, she believed she could no longer trust anyone when it came to talking about such traumatic things.

"Hmm. I didn't think so. This special land has lots of wonderful trees, such as the Hoolie Koolie tree, as well as the Hubber Blubber tree—beautiful, visually stunning trees whose sap can heal any frac-tured mind or soul for that matter."

On hearing the word *Piadora* followed by *Hoolie Koolie*, Polly found herself rather abruptly coming to, as though she were finally waking from some very bad dream. "Lady B., did you just say 'Hoolie Koolie'?" Polly quizzed.

"Yes, dear. I most certainly did."

"Well, how can you talk to me of such things? Have you been there and seen these things for yourself? Or is this just some new, horrible trick playing itself out as it messes with my feeble mind and imagination?" she tragically whimpered.

"Polly, I refuse to answer such a ridiculous and impertinent question, for of course I have been there."

"Oh, right. Well, believing in such things has caused me even more misery. My uncle regularly reminds me that I am nothing but a deceitful liar. He also tells me that a leper never changes its spots."

"Oh, Polly dear, not only are you misinformed, but you are indeed turning out to be a real Mrs. Malaprop! It is not a leper but a *leopard* that cannot change its spots."

"Whatever! Anyway, unless you have been to Piadora—which I doubt very much you have—you have absolutely no right to talk of such things."

"Have I been there?" Lady Butterkist muttered as though she was struggling with the very daftness of the question. "Now, please don't interrupt me again, as I wish to talk more of my recollections of this truly magnificent place. Now, dear, hurry along and unwrap those presents, for they took me and others an imaginably long length of time to gift wrap."

Polly gave a deep sigh as she picked up the next gift-wrapped present.

"Well, don't keep us all in suspenders. Who is it from, dear?" Lady Butterkist demanded to know.

"The gift tag on this box of chocolates says it's from the lovely Captain Humdinger," she cried, placing it to one side, for she was now feeling terribly mixed up and emotional.

Polly then picked up the next gift and read the label out loud. "Oh my goodness. This is getting crazier by the minute, for this one is from dear darling Captain Codswallop and his crew," she said, as upon opening the gift she was overwhelmed to see that it was a beautiful, hand-knitted nautical jumper that had her name sewn in gold on the front. "And the next gift is from dear Corporal Beanpod!"

Lady Butterkist pretended to ignore Polly and her comments as she continued on with her story.

"Funnily enough, that amazingly courageous young lady went by the same very special name. Yes, her name was also Polly, and speaking personally, I have never met a young girl with such a pure heart who put others before herself and risked everything to pursue what was right," Lady Butterkist casually stated as she then chose to stare Polly directly in the eye.

"Yes, that young girl had such a good nature, and she truly believed that love really was the answer to every prayer."

"How and when did you meet her?" Polly quietly asked.

Still the lady with the butterfly lips chose not to answer the question as she continued on with her story. "Yes, that lovely young girl was just so special and precious."

Tears suddenly began to flow down Polly's cheeks as she continued to listen to the strange but reassuringly kind lady with the weird butterfly lips.

"Here, Polly. Take him back," the expensively clothed lady ordered as she handed Langdon back over to its owner. She then sat down beside her on the bed, and after making herself comfortable, she went on with her story.

"Take another sip of water, dear. It will surely find a way to refresh the dehydrated parts of you and help make you feel a whole heap better," she ordered as she deliberately went on with her story telling. "Then continue on opening the presents, as you still have many more to unwrap."

"Yes, of course," Polly sniffed.

"This special young lady gave up everything to follow after what can only be termed the impossible dream, and I, for one, do so miss her," Lady Butterkist announced as she turned to Blenkinsopp to request that he immediately produce the most important vial of medicine from his trouser pocket, as well as a clean handkerchief from his breast pocket.

She then moved over to tenderly wipe away the tears that were now gently rolling down Polly's face. "I understand that all this must be terribly overwhelming for you, Polly my dear, but please understand this is not the best moment in time to question me. Just do as I say and drink this down, dear," she urged.

Polly naturally felt very reluctant to obey this latest very strange request. "But I don't know what it is, and all this hospital medicine is making me feel so horribly groggy and strangely sick," she confessed.

"I know, Polly dear. It is all truly tiresome, but despite all you have gone through, you have no choice but to now place your full trust in me." She reached over to whisper in her ear, "Piadora most certainly does exist. Ralph and Hodgekiss are also real, and as for dear, sweet Mrs. O'Brien, well, she sends you oodles and poodles of love. She says that this afternoon the girls will be thinking of you as they make yet another fresh batch of delicious appletude pies. So, Polly dear, it is high time we got you out of this ghastly place. So be a good girl, and please do as I request and take a sip of this drink that I have specially prepared for you."

Polly still showed the greatest reluctance in following this latest order.

"Polly, if you don't take this drink, then I must warn that the chances are extremely high that you will remain in this hospital for a considerably long length of time, if not forever. But drink it down now, and I promise you that not only will you be out of here in less than a day, but you will also walk out clothed in your right mind."

Polly took hold of the vial and placed it up to her trembling lips. Closing her eyes, she took a deep breath and opened her mouth to allow the sweet nectar to trickle slowly down her throat.

"Polly dearest, allow me to tell you that this medicine has come straight from the bark of the Hoolie Koolie tree, and not only will it immediately heal your soul, giving you much-needed clarity of mind, but it will also give you the strength and courage you so earnestly seek. It is therefore necessary for you to be able to continue on in your personal journey. So polish off every single tiny drop. There's a dear. And when you awake from this slumber, you will once more be fighting fit and ready to face anything and everything that might be thrown at you."

Polly dutifully continued to pour the sweet-tasting nectar into her mouth until it was completely gone. "Hmm. I could drink this all day, for it really does taste lusciously yummy," she dreamily stated. Then after licking her lips she closed her eyes, and with Langdon tucked under her arm, she once more slipped back under the covers to instantaneously fall into a deeply healing, peaceful slumber.

❖

Seconds later saw the doctor purposefully striding back up the ward toward them.

"Madam, he's on the move," Blenkinsopp dutifully alerted.

"That's fine, Giles, because we're finished and sorted," Lady Butterkist called out as she immediately got up from where she had been sitting on the bed.

"Hmm. Some challenges are so much harder than others," she muttered under her breath while playing with the string of pearls that hung around her neck. She then gave a deep, knowing sigh.

"Doctor, tell me, have you heard the wonderful news concerning your ex-Patient 333?"

"I have, indeed, Lady Butterkist, and I can only say that my colleagues and I, as well as the rest of the staff on this ward, are absolutely mystified as to how all this could possibly have taken place."

"Well, it is something of a miracle, that's for sure," she mused.

"Well, whatever. I, for one, am totally amazed, for I must confess that I gave up on the man many moons ago," he said, scratching his chin.

"Now, doctor, when we find ourselves in that hard place where everything seems lost and hopeless, that's surely the place where miracles are most likely to happen. Don't you think?" she rather poignantly suggested.

"Hmm. I'm not in any position to really answer that one," the doctor casually remarked as he glanced down at Polly fast asleep in her bed.

"Doctor, how perfectly sad it is to see her lying there like Sleeping Beauty waiting for that seemingly elusive miracle to not only wake her but then rid her completely of this make-believe world she seems happy to believe in."

"Yes, yes, Lady Butterkist, but please remember I did all I could to warn you," he mumbled. "Believe you me when I say that at this hospital we all hope and pray every day for that special miracle to take place where this young girl is concerned."

"Oh really, Dr. Ninkumpoop! So answer me truthfully, doctor, do you really believe in miracles?" Lady Butterkist innocently quizzed.

"What? Me…personally?"

"Yes, you! It's a straight question, doctor, no frills or hidden meanings, so do feel at liberty to fill in the blanks."

"Well, I can't say I've ever witnessed a miracle, or had one for that matter," he halfheartedly muttered.

"Well, then how can you pray for a miracle where Polly is concerned when clearly you don't even believe in their existence?" she dared to suggest.

"Madam, quite what do you mean by that?" he snorted.

"Well, you just said you are hoping and praying that Polly receives her miracle, and yet in the next breath you clearly admit to not believing in the existence of such inexplicably wonderful happenings. So which is it to be?" she challenged.

"Well, to be honest, madam, until your unexpected arrival on the scene, I haven't ever given it much thought, for I prefer to see myself as more of an intellectual, thinking man with mathematical and science-based thought processes. So, if I am to be absolutely honest with you, I believe miracles are more for those whose lives are mainly dictated by superficial and emotionally charged, thoroughly illogical feelings."

"Oh, by that you mean mushy, ooey-gooey feelings, rather than by solid and sound reason?" she interjected.

"Precisely."

"Well, I only have two words to reveal my thoughts regarding your thoughts on this matter."

"Oh, and pray, tell me what those two words might be."

"*Absolute bunkum!* Yes, total twaddle, Poopy, my boy! Miracles are not only timeless, but they are for everybody," she exasperatedly lashed out. "Yes, miracles care nothing for class or creed, or intellect for that matter. They just happen for those who expectantly watch and wait for them, which must surely mean they are not for the fainthearted or those who refuse to believe or give up hope that their miracle will ever come."

"I have to confess to knowing nothing of such things," he reluctantly admitted.

"Well, doctor, maybe, just maybe, you've had a few miracles in the past, but like many others, you have failed to recognize them for what they truly were," she gently dared to suggest.

"Well, no, madam. But without wishing to cause any offense—"

"None taken," she mischievously interrupted.

"Well, as I was about to say, I think I'd be the first to know if I had ever witnessed something one might rightly term supernatural or otherwise a miracle," he said, looking more than a little concerned. "I mean, I'm not exactly a religious-thinking man."

"Who said anything about religion? I am talking about certain wonderful, unexplainable events that defy all reason and logic."

"Hmm. I'm still not entirely sure I like where all this conversation is headed," he furiously muttered.

"Well, can you give me any reasonable explanation as to why the patient who occupied that bed for the past twenty years and who by all accounts sat motionless, staring into space, has just minutes ago left this institution perfectly clothed in his right min? Now, explain that one if you dare."

"Well, to be perfectly honest, Lady Butterkist, I have absolutely no idea what is going on around here at present, for in truth since I got out of bed this morning, my otherwise well-ordered and preserved world has become quite topsy-turvy, and against all rhyme and reason it seems to be quickly spiraling hideously out of control. Also, as I am not at liberty to discuss any patient's medical history, then sadly I am also unable to give a satisfactory answer to any of your seemingly impertinent questions."

"Look, Poopy, dear boy, stop being so evasive and thoroughly disagreeable," she remonstrated. "I am well aware that you are bound by ethics to withhold information regarding your patients, and I understand that today has been very trying to say the least. But can you not just agree with me that for the patient who has responded to absolutely nothing for over twenty years—that is, until Piddles, my precious little pooch, turned up and shows him some love and affection—well, surely this in itself is something of a special miracle?"

"Well, I guess...."

"Don't just guess, Ninkumpoop. Tell me straight whether you see this as a miracle."

"I can't say for sure," Dr. Ninkumpoop cautiously replied, as for the first time in his long life he found himself stammering like an awkward child.

"Well, putting your thoroughly belligerent attitude to one side, let's take the case of your dear brother Andrew. Now then, answer me this: did he not fall into a river when he was a small boy? And even though you did all within your power to rescue him, you sadly were not strong enough to drag him from the river."

The doctor was so thoroughly shocked by all she was saying that he remained tongue-tied with only the occasional and barely audible gasps escaping out through his visibly trembling lips.

"Hmm. And, doctor, I believe he was eventually fished out of the river by a very kind gentleman who, I believe, went by the name of Captain Codswallop, or something similar sounding." The poor doctor was now so paralyzed with shock that he felt incapable of responding to her question.

"Cat got your tongue, Poopy, my boy? Well, never mind. Just feel free to nod your head if all I am saying is irrevocably the truth, the whole truth, and nothing but the truth. There, that's good," she cheerfully encouraged. "See, a little nod of the head requires very little in the way of effort."

"Yes, Captain Codswallop did all in his power to resuscitate Andrew."

"And is it true to say, dear doctor, that your dear younger brother was, sadly, pronounced dead on arrival at Hope in Your Heart Hospital?"

The perplexed doctor was now looking extremely ashen, for quite rightly he was left seriously wondering as to how she could possibly know anything regarding this very private and personal tragedy that had taken place some previous forty or so years ago.

"Remember how stunned you were when a few hours later a Dr. Loveheart came running down the ward to say that Andrew had somewhat miraculously come back to life?" she reminded.

The poor doctor could do nothing but nod his head up and down as a show of affirmation.

"There, this nodding business is getting easier by the minute, isn't it, Poppy, my boy? Well then, I do believe that today of all days you may well be in for another treat, as you will have the honor of sitting in the front seat to witness the third miracle of your lifetime."

"Third?"

"Yes, doctor, your third. Now, lift up your fingers, and we will count together. Now, remember that the first was your brother; the second was your former patient, who has now gone off to swim with the dolphins, taking my precious pooch with him; and I do believe you are about to be fortunate enough in witnessing your third miracle, for when Polly wakes up in an hour or so, you, my dear, will be in for a mighty big surprise," she confidently stated as she stood directly in front of him, playfully pretending once more to formally straighten his already dead-straight tie.

"Uh?"

"So let's wait and see, shall we?" she mischievously whispered in his ear as she then patted his chest in a friendly, if not all too familiar manner that took him completely off guard.

All this talk left the now poorly fragile doctor firmly believing that he was on the verge of an extreme nervous collapse, as from the moment he left his crossword to innocently make his way up to the canteen and shake hands with this unusual lady his safe, introspective little world had been severely turned upside down, leaving him feeling more like most of his patients, yes, something of a nervous, jangled train wreck.

"Forgive me, Lady Butterkist, but I am suddenly feeling extraordinarily queasy and unwell."

"I'm not the least bit surprised, doctor dear. After all, miracles are supposed to turn our little cocooned lives upside down, and today has been a very unusual and most demanding day for you. Here, take one of these pills. I call them 'Mother's little helpers,' because just like a nice cup of tea, they quickly perk you up. I'm told that film stars like to take them all the time," she said, taking a small bottle from her purse to hand over to him.

The doctor looked horrified, as he immediately declined her offer. Failing to hide his utter disgust, he quickly handed the bottle back, shaking his head as if to say pills were designed for everybody else to blindly take but were certainly not meant for him. Oh, no. He only wrote out endless prescriptions for medication; he did not believe in actually taking any form of medication himself, and even if due to unexplainable sickness he were forced to resort to some form of medication, well, even then he would err on the side of caution until he was suitably informed as to all harmful side effects that might well occur as a result of swallowing down the medication in question.

"Madam, the only medication I ever care to digest comes directly from the herbs that are placed in fine teas."

An unphased Lady Butterkist placed the bottle back in her purse and then came up with another bright suggestion.

"Now, then. Speaking of tea, all this talk has made my throat as seriously arid and parched as the Arabian Desert at noon, so I don't suppose you, old boy, have a morsel of quality loose tea secretly stashed away in your office? I happen to believe that a strong and rich cup of Assam would not only moisten my lips but would most willingly slide down my dry throat a treat."

Chapter Twenty-Nine
BLENKINSOPP TO THE RESCUE

*A*S THEY WERE still standing by the bedside discussing many of the therapeutic qualities of tea, one of the nurses anxiously rushed down the ward toward the doctor.

"Forgive me for interrupting, Dr. Ninkumpoop, but we have a most unusual situation developing. We urgently need your sound advice to deal with it."

"Yes, nurse. I'm all ears."

"Well, doctor, you might find this hard to believe, but a coach load of lovely old dears has just broken down right outside the front gates of the hospital."

"Really?"

"Yes, really, doctor! Apparently, having been on the road for quite a number of hours, many of them found themselves in dire need of an urgent visit to the small room, if you get my drift, and with most garages closed due to this being a holiday weekend, the driver was forced to find some alternative but appropriate place that he could safely take them to. Having studied his map, he decided that we were the closest place en route that would surely have a number of male and female toilets that they could all happily use."

"Hmm. Yes, nurse. Go on."

"But, doctor, the drama continues, for as the coach approached the hospital gates, the engine mysteriously cut out."

"Oh, deary me!" sighed the doctor, giving his head a good scratch.

"Doctor, it doesn't finish there either, for there's more to tell."

"More?"

"Yes, more," the nurse sheepishly stated.

"Then I would be extremely obliged if you would fill me in on everything else. There's a dear," he ordered, his voice cracking due to severe strain.

"Well, Dr. Ninkumpoop, I hate to be the messenger of more bad news, but where the coach broke down is unbelievably inconvenient, for you'll never believe it, but it is now blocking the entire main entrance in and out of the hospital and is therefore causing a major problem for staff wishing to go home, as well as visitors, who are feeling most disgruntled as they find themselves prisoners in the hospital grounds."

"Oh, no. I cannot believe it!" the poor doctor gasped.

"I said you wouldn't," the nurse quickly retorted. "And doctor, I believe if we don't do something, and soon, we may find ourselves with a full-blown riot on our hands."

"Goodness gracious me! Could this crisis get any worse?" he cried out, as he was now really feeling the full pressure of this latest, rather extraordinary situation, which was becoming more complex by the minute.

"Yes, doctor, it most certainly could get worse, for there is still more."

"More, nurse? Tell me, how could there possibly be more to this story than you have already shared?"

"Well, doctor, the coach was on a direct route to the castle, as your good friends Mr. and Mrs. Scumberry are due to host their annual old people's tea party this very afternoon. Remember, you and your wife were officially invited to the event."

"Oh, yes, though I must admit I had completely forgotten. But quite what all this has to do with me, I'll never know."

"Well, doctor, as you ask, Mr. Scumberry telephoned the hospital a short while ago specifically asking for your help and assistance in managing this desperate crisis."

"How crazy is that? Does the wretched, ignoramus idiot of a man not recognize that I am a skilled surgeon of the mind and not some greasy little mechanic swathed entirely in oil-drenched clothes? There is little I can do to help in this most unfortunate crisis," he snarled.

"I'm so sorry, doctor," the nurse sighed, witnessing the extent of the poor doctor's distress.

"Unless, of course, he expects me to exchange my pristine white coat for a grease-covered wrench and a pair of soiled and baggy over-sized denim dungarees before allowing my manicured hands to get messed up as I resort to rolling under the undercarriage of the coach to take a jolly good look," he snorted.

"Well, doctor, sadly Mr. Scumberry has clean run out of ideas, for apparently he has telephoned every coachwork shop in the area, and due to this being the Easter holiday weekend, they are either closed or seriously booked up and therefore cannot afford the time nor spare a man to come out to investigate the problem."

"Oh, deary me," he pathetically wailed. "Then please tell me, nurse, does all this mean that this eyesore of a coach will be blocking both the exit and the entrance to the hospital until the problem is finally sorted and the coach can be towed away?"

"I'm afraid so, doctor."

"Then their little problem has indeed just become ours," the hope-lessly wearied and indignant doctor cried.

"Now what on earth can we do to rectify this most trying and down-right ridiculous situation?" he said as, throwing all dignity to one side, he pitifully threw his hands into the air in a rarely seen before display of great despair.

"Dr. Ninkumpoop, please do calm down. There is little point in getting your knickers in such a twist! For not only does rage both quench and seriously wound the palace of your soul, but I believe it will do very little to solve the problem or make it go away. What we need here is a touch of the old British way," interjected Lady Butter-kist, much to the doctor's further bewilderment.

"Uh?"

"Yes, we all need a nice, strong cup of sencha tea, for as the calming vapors begin to invade our heads and pervade our souls, it will indeed momentarily heal our jangled nerves as well as grant us the presence of mind, the very necessary prerequisite to coming up with the right answer to the problem. And you, dear doctor, of all people should know that this is indeed the British way of dealing with any unique crisis that attempts to beset and thus distress us."

"Oh, right."

"Yes, the many benefits that come from tea are truly incalculable, for may I dare to remind you that many a war has been won due to the British stiff upper lip that I believe comes directly from the clear thinking that a nice cup of tea undoubtedly incites. So, I suggest that once you've calmed right down, we then go in search of a kettle to make ourselves a pot of delicious, sweet tea, and If you are clean out of sencha, then without making any fuss whatsoever I will happily settle for a spot of delicious Darjeeling, if accompanied by a twist of lemon."

The poor doctor's face turned a very bright red, as like a naughty boy being found with his fingers in the cookie jar he'd been forced to bear a stern telling-off from Lady Butterfly Lips.

"Huh! My knickers in a twist? How dare she proceed to demoralize me in front of my staff," he miserably muttered under his breath. Normally he would have never conceded to allowing anyone to speak down to him in such a derogatory manner, but once more he had to quickly remind himself that she was indeed the money behind this brand-new hospital wing. So he forced himself to take a few deep breaths instead.

Once more Lady Butterkist took it upon herself to help and thus encourage the poor doctor. "There, doctor, you must resolve to breathe in more deeply. Yes, fill those flabby, underexercised little lungs of yours with yet more oxygen. Now, do as I say and take a deep breath. There. Wonderful. Now you can see that it calms the soul quite nicely and thus restores it to its natural serenity. So while you do a few more breathing exercises, do try and imagine yourself soaring up in the heavens, and as you look down toward Earth, please be a good boy and begin by seeing this crisis for what it is—just some little piece of trivia, yes, a little blot on the canvass of life that at the end of the day will most surely have a happy ending. There, there, dear doctor. Now come on, don't be such a little spoilsport, for you need to breathe a little deeper. There, that's much better."

The poor doctor had little choice other than to obey, but deep inside he was beginning to feel utterly humiliated, as rather unwittingly he had submitted himself to the role of the patient, with Lady Butterkist administering her own brand of holistic, mind-control therapy. It all left him feeling thoroughly impotent and inconsolable when it came to dealing with this latest ridiculous crisis.

"Now, if I may be so bold or perhaps seemingly impertinent as to make what I believe to be some very helpful suggestions—"Lady Butterkist brightly chirped up as once more she prepared to take over the situation before things could even begin to go further downhill than they already were—"I think our first duty is to the old dears still stuck on the coach. Yes, we need to quickly off-load the little darlings, and once they've all been for a quick pee—I can't believe I just said that," she mischievously gasped. "What I meant to say was, when they've all used the bathroom, we should escort them down to the canteen for some light refreshments, although as previously stated they cannot be allowed to drink the canteen tea; otherwise we might well see the poor little darlings one by one prematurely popping their clogs, and that would never do, would it, Poopy, my dear boy?"

"No, you're so very right, Lady Butterkist, but I do wish you would refrain from calling me 'Poopy dear,' for it's so belittling. I would also be equally grateful if you would refrain from suggesting that the hospital tea might actually kill the lot of them, for I believe you are being a tad overdramatic, don't you think?"

"Well, that's true, for I've not actually seen anyone drop down dead, but may I remind you, doctor, that I've only been here a matter of hours, and judging by the look of that once-flourishing flower arrangement, then forgive me, but there is every reason to believe that if nothing else, the patients are probably suffering from some very unpleasant symptoms associated with drinking beverages from this atrocious canteen."

"Quite unbelievable!" he angrily muttered.

"So, dear doctor, I don't suppose you could find it in your heart to generously donate a box of choice loose tea from your private stash so that the hardworking coach driver and his precious cargo of pensioners might get to enjoy a relaxing cup of tea with a digestive biscuit or two on the side? After all, they are already deeply traumatized by the breakdown, what with its most unfortunate delay. We simply cannot afford to further traumatize them with the disgraceful lack of wholesome refreshments on offer in the hospital canteen, can we?"

Once again the doctor was left with little choice, for how could he deny Lady Butterkist tea from his most private and exclusive hidden stash when she had shown his hospital such overwhelming unconditional generosity? He reluctantly caved in to her unusual request.

As the poor doctor sat back feeling thoroughly confused and distraught, he cast his mind back to the start of his perfect day, drinking quality tea and solving the clues of today's crossword puzzle. He could never have imagined that a day such as this, which had started in relative calm and tranquility, would in a mere matter of hours go into such rapid decline.

"Quite, quite remarkable!" he muttered most miserably under his breath.

"Now then, Ninkumpoop, listen to me carefully, old boy, for I have much more to say on this as well as many other matters."

"I'm sure you have," the deeply distressed doctor inwardly groaned.

"Blenkinsopp here is most familiar with automobile engines, coaches included, and so he will be more than delighted to get the tools from the boot of our old jalopy and then get down to work."

Pure relief washed over the fraught doctor as he drank in and savored the first good piece of news he'd heard all day.

"However, before any of this can take place, I do have another rather unusual request to make."

"Oh, no. Not another demand?" he queried as for the first time in his life he began furiously biting his nails.

"Now, doctor, I beg you to stop biting your nails. It's really most unbecoming, and trust me when I say that it's a disgracefully bad habit that you obviously need to seek some sort of professional help to combat."

"Uh?"

"Yes, you really need to ask yourself what is behind all your inner conflict and turmoil."

"What?"

"Anyway, doctor, back to my request—see it as sort of a barter if you must, for just like you need something from me, I too need something from you. So, it is time for us to negotiate."

"Yes, yes anything! Your wish is my command," he cried, for he was now feeling great anxiety with regard to an unpreventable riot taking place if the visitors were forced to abandon their vehicles and walk many miles to the nearest town to get a bus or train back to their respective homes.

"Well, doctor dear, at the risk of shocking the pants off you, I require you to fill in some important legal paperwork for me."

"Right. Just hand it over, and I'll do all I can."

"Oh, no. This is very specific paperwork, which I believe you alone have in your office filing cabinet."

"Uh?"

"Yes, Dr. Ninkumpoop, I wish for you to sign the release papers for young Polly, allowing her to leave here with me, for I wish to become something of a…mmm…guardian to the young lady."

"Madam, what you are proposing is absolutely preposterous!"

"Really?"

"Madam, are you barking mad?"

"No, I don't think so," she quickly replied. "Blenkinsopp, be a dear and answer me this, do my facial features instantly remind you of some poor, indisposed dog?"

"No, madam. They most certainly do not."

"Good. Well, I'm glad that one's settled. Next question that requires an immediate answer: Blenkinsopp, in your capacity as my butler and chauffeur, have you ever once heard me bark?"

"The answer is an affirmative no, madam."

"Well, then, would you consider me to verge on the side of madness?"

"Madam, as you ask, I believe you to be the sanest individual that it has ever been my privilege to work for, and I would like to use this occasion—"

"Yes, yes. All right. Thank you, Blenkinsopp, you have said quite enough," she said in her most usual, dismissive tone of voice. "So doctor, now that we have established that I am neither a dog, nor do I bark, I therefore have no immediate need to be put away in some dog sanctuary. Pray, tell me then, quite where do we go from here?"

"Madam, I apologize profusely for using such disrespectful and offensive language with regard your good self, but forgive me when I say that I was so caught up in the moment that I clearly forgot who I was speaking with. I also profess to not feeling quite myself at this precise moment in time. Put bluntly, I fear I am altogether losing either the plot or, at worse, my mind."

"My sentiments exactly," Lady Butterkist interjected.

"Well, madam, please allow me to express my own thoughts and concerns regarding the girl."

"You mean Polly," she quickly retorted.

"Yes, yes. I believe that is her name." he wearily replied.

"Well, then use it, Poopy, for she is neither an embarrassing itch that urgently needs to be scratched away, nor is she a vulgar blob on some scenic landscape that needs painting over. She is not a thing that you can freely and so dispassionately discuss. No, she is a wonderful, caring, considerate child who, despite all you seem to believe, truly deserves to be treated with utter respect and some kind and thoughtful consideration. Don't you think?"

"Yes, yes. Well, as I was just saying, Polly is in here for her own good, as well as for the safety of the public in general. No court in this land would even consider granting you custodial rights over such a sick child as she."

"Oh, I was not seeking custody of the child. I just want to become involved and help her in any positive way that I can," Lady Butterkist stated, raising her eyebrows to show a very timely sense of annoyance.

"Well, madam, I still cannot imagine why you are asking such a thing of me."

As the heated discussion continued on, another nurse needing his full attention gently resorted to tapping him on the shoulder. Alarmed, he quickly swung 'round to see who it was touching him in such a manner.

"I'm awfully sorry, doctor, but a number of very upset visitors are demanding to see you immediately, as they personally wish to hear from your mouth alone what you are currently doing to tackle this serious, ongoing problem."

"Yes, yes, nurse. Tell them to stay in the waiting area, and I will be down shortly."

"Well, please come quickly, doctor, before the situation worsens itself further."

Dr. Ninkumpoop sheepishly turned back to face Lady Butterkist. "Madam, my crisis appears to be ever deepening."

"So it would appear."

"Well, as a result I am entirely in your hands and therefore at your mercy. But please understand me when I say that I can do nothing without first speaking to Mr. Scumberry, for he is, after all, her legal guardian, and therefore his permission is most certainly required."

"I don't believe we will have much of a problem with that one," Lady Butterkist snorted. "But doctor, before that call to the castle is made, may I suggest that if you wish to have my continued financial support, you would be well advised to assure Mr. Scumberry that as her doctor you are more than satisfied that you have done all you can for her. Do I make myself clear?"

"Abundantly, Lady Butterkist. Abundantly!"

"Splendid."

"Well, if you would like to follow me down to my office, we can send some of my fine loose tea up to the canteen and then telephone the castle. And if, after speaking with Mr. Scumberry, he is in perfect agreement, well, then we will take it from there."

"Then let us waste no further time," she stated as she broke into a warm smile.

Dr. Ninkumpoop hurriedly rushed down the ward and into the office. Behind closed door he announced to his troubled staff that they should do all they could to appease all distraught visitors by assuring them that the problem was in hand and therefore would soon be sorted. "Offer them all as much free tea and cake as they desire," he hurriedly advised.

He also informed the nurses that he was taking Lady Butterkist down to his office, and he did not wish to be disturbed. He then informed his staff that Blenkinsopp, her trustworthy butler, had offered his expert services, and so in a matter of minutes he would undertake the work of a mechanic and hopefully sort out the problem. He then wished the nurses lots of good luck and left the office to head back down the ward toward Lady Butterkist.

As he walked back he was shocked to discover that a now rather disheveled Blenkinsopp had paid a quick visit to the bathroom to replace his immaculately smart butler's suit for that of a greasy, oil-stained pair of white dungarees, complete with oiled rags hanging from both side pockets. Holding a large wrench in one hand and a bag of tools in the other, he stood rather snootily beside Lady Butterkist to await her further orders.

At seeing the surprised doctor, Lady Butterkist broke into a smile.

"Dr. Ninkumpoop, you are looking a bit flushed. Are you all right, my good man?" she said, showing great concern.

"I'm perfectly fine," he mumbled.

"Oh, good. You know, I feel compelled to share that when I was a young girl guide our motto was 'Be prepared.' It was so instilled into me throughout my childhood that as an adult I have always made proper contingency plans to meet any unexpected event or catastrophe. Therefore, I have everything I might need on hand stashed away in the boot of our old jalopy. Yes, we carry a filled water canister, military ration packs—provided by Her Majesty's Military, of course—oh, as well as a lovely tartan rug for occasional picnics, a medical kit, and last but not least, a full tool kit for use if we break down."

"Hmm. Amazing!" the exasperated doctor muttered.

"Well, I'm also equally sure you would agree that Giles's butler's outfit would be most inappropriate for working under the bonnet or undercarriage of our old car, so he always ensures he has some old dungarees to change into in the event that he should be required to sort out any potential mechanical problems."

The doctor listened on, feeling most foolish, if not a little repentant, as he thought back to his earlier somewhat heartless and unruly comments regarding oily mechanics.

"Madam, do you wish for me to proceed down to the hospital entrance and begin the coach repairs?" Blenkinsopp politely asked.

"Definitely. Now, don't forget we need you to do your absolute best and get this coach back on the road as soon as possible, so no dillydallying."

"Of course, madam. Of course, for I will never fail in my duty toward mistress and Crown," he conscientiously retorted.

"Oh, and Blenkinsopp, just one more little thing."

"Madam?"

"I hope you don't mind me saying this, but I think you look a real darling in those rather racy oil-covered dungarees," she said, giving a warm smile.

"Why thank you, madam," he replied utterly straight faced as he turned on his heels to exit the ward.

"Right then, Lady Butterkist. Let us now retreat to my private office."

"Oh, good. And doctor dear, I do hope you intend to put the kettle on before we get down to the business in question, for I could well and truly murder a nice hot cup of tea!"

The doctor unlocked his office door and was immediately overwhelmed by a flurry of feathers, which mischievously began fluttering in front of his face.

"Where on God's earth did these pesky little things come from?" he cried out, feeling most alarmed.

"Heaven only knows," Lady Butterkist quickly retorted.

Tilting his head downward to avoid the feathers, he politely motioned for his wealthy guest to go ahead of him and take a seat. As the doctor then made his way around the desk to sit down, Lady Butterkist immediately reached across the desk and picked up his temporarily abandoned newspaper. "Poopy, old boy, I do believe you were filling in the same crossword as Blenkinsopp and my good self were attempting this morning. Tut tut. Yes, you naughty little man, for this crossword clearly shows that you, my dear, knew all along what the word was that we were all furiously searching for," she said as with a mischievous grin she casually tossed the paper back in his direction.

The poor and desperately confused doctor looked most distraught as, glancing down at the paper, he was horrified to discover that the last word, which he knew for sure he had left blank, had now rather mysteriously been filled in. And to add insult to injury, whoever had taken the shocking liberty of filling it in—and, I might add, without his personal authorization—had also deliberately used a ghastly red felt-tip pen when fitting the word *arrogant* into the eight small boxes. How could any of this have taken place, when as a matter of security his office was always and without fail double-locked?

Could this day get any worse or bizarre for that matter? he privately wondered.

Chapter Thirty
THE TEA PARTY

G OOD AFTERNOON. BORITZ speaking."

"Ahh, Boritz, my good man. This is Nick speaking."

"Dr. Ninkumpoop?"

"Oh, Boritz. Please call me Nick."

"Oh, Nick, thank goodness you've phoned. Please believe me when I say that I am so very embarrassed by all that has taken place today," he cried.

"Calm down, Boritz, old boy! Let me assure you now that we are doing all we can to make your coach load of pensioners as comfortable as we are able. At present we are also trying to sort out the problem of the coach, which you must be well aware has not only broken down right outside our gates but is blocking the exit as well as the entrance. Rather sadly, it has turned into something of a fiasco."

"Oh, Nick, I feel so personally responsible," he cried. "And as for those poor, old darlings, their wonderful tea that Mildred and the children spent many hours preparing will surely be spoiled and go to waste if they don't come shortly. I can only hope we can quickly come up with a favorable solution to this current and most embarrassing crisis."

"Well, Boritz, this is one of the reasons I am ringing you, for there is every chance that we may have found the answer to the problem."

"Wonderful!" he gleefully cried.

"Well, Boritz, wait until you hear what I have say before you get too carried away with excitement."

"Go on, doctor. Go on."

"I have someone here in my office who I am sure you will be most anxious to speak with, if not meet in person."

"Yes, yes. Carry on."

"Well, it's none other than Lady Ralphella Butterkist, the dowager countess of Scunthorpe. Remember when we last met up I spoke with you and told you all there is to tell with regard to this delightful lady?"

"Unbelievable, old boy! Tell me truthfully that you are joking around with me, for she is not expected at the hospital until later on this week—or so your personal invite led me to believe."

"Ah, yes. This is all perfectly true, but by some strange violation between the moon and the stars, she has surprised us all by turning up unannounced at the hospital a few days earlier than expected."

"Really?"

"Yes, to pay me an unofficial courtesy visit that, alas, I am not the least bit worthy of," he said rather tongue in cheek.

"Amazing!"

"Yes, and by some miracle Giles Blenkinsopp, her trustworthy butler and chauffeur, just happens to be something of a jack-of-all-trades, and therefore he is supremely confident that he can have the coach back on the road in no time at all."

"Well, Nick, this really is the best news I've heard all day," Boritz excitedly cried.

"Yes, I thought you'd think that. But, Boritz, my good man, please bear with me and listen hard, for there are a few minor conditions attached."

"Conditions?"

"Yes, Boritz. You heard me right, for this fine lady is something of a mean negotiator. Here, before I put my foot in it further, I think it best that I pass the phone over to her so that she can explain quite what this all means."

"Oh, all right then, Nick. Put her on," he anxiously cried.

"Good day, Lady Butterkist," Boritz heartily shouted down the phone.

"And a good day to you too, Mr. Scumbag," Lady Butterkist just as merrily responded.

The poor doctor, having just passed the phone over, was now innocently sipping his tea, and he was so horrified and shocked by her significant and most terrible blunder that without warning, he suddenly spurted a large mouthful of tea in the direction of Lady Butterkist.

"How gross!" Lady Butterkist muttered as she attempted to wipe the tea off her dress with one hand while at the same time continuing on with her conversation with Mr. Scumberry.

The poor doctor, having spoiled her outfit, could not be feeling more mortified than he was now feeling.

And worse still, he could only begin to imagine how his dear friend was feeling, as she had so obviously misheard his name.

"Lady Butterkist...Oh, dear. I fear you are so mistaken, for I have never once referred to him as Mr. Scumbag. Oh no, no, no. It's Scumberry, S-c-u-m-b-e-r-r-y," the shocked doctor attempted to advise as he quickly leaned over the desk to whisper in her ear.

"I think I know all my alphabet, doctor dear," her ladyship quickly retorted before turning to once more speak into the phone and rectify the situation as best as she could. "Awfully sorry, Scumbug! Tell me what I can do to put this right, as rather embarrassingly the good doctor has just dutifully informed me that I have entirely misheard, and so I've got my knickers in something of a twist with regard to your surname. Alas, it is not Scumbag or Scumbug, but Scum-something, with the word *berry* attached. I apologize most profusely, but as you can well imagine, it all sounds much the same to a little doddery old lady such as I am. So pray forgive me for this most unfortunate and terribly unseemly error."

———

Poor old Boritz felt thoroughly miserable and dejected, for as if life were not already treating him badly enough, he had just heard the supposedly charitable lady horrifically mispronounce his family name and call him "Scumbag." And if this wasn't enough, to add insult to injury, she had gone on to further insult his good name by calling him "Scumbug." Yes, she had indeed unwittingly called him nasty, horribly mean names, names that would surely pierce if not mortally wound the heart and mind of any decent, delicate mortal soul, he rather dolefully concluded.

Boritz, despite feeling emotionally choked up, willingly chose to lay this terrible blunder to one side, as he urgently wished to form a close and abiding friendship with this particular financially well-off lady.

"Dear Lady Butterkist, I humbly accept your apology in full, and I assure you now that no offense has or ever will be taken. In truth, I am exceedingly glad to get this rare opportunity to speak with you, albeit by telephone, although I have to add that my dearest wish is to one day meet with you face-to-face."

"Ditto."

"Well, that's wonderful to hear, Lady Butterkist."

"Yes, I too am most pleased to make your acquaintance, Mr. Scumbelli, but as the good doctor stated, I have some things of the utmost importance that I really feel the need to discuss with you alone. I hope I have chosen a choice time to unburden my heavily ladened chest of all these troublesome matters."

"Now is as good a time as any, so feel free, Lady Butterkist, for I am all ears."

"Well, thank you, Mr. Skunkberry."

"Boritz, please," he exasperatedly pleaded.

"All right, Mr. Boritz. Before you say anything else, I wish for you to consider granting me five very express wishes."

"Five!" he said, almost choking, as great beads of sweat began to pour from his deeply concerned brow.

"Yes, I do believe it was just five at last count, if that's all right with your good self."

"Oh, yes, yes, madam. Please tell me what these five special requests are, and I will do all within my power to see that they are fulfilled to your utmost liking," he fawned.

"Ah, that's all well and good, but while being entertained at this hospital, the good doctor escorted me around the wards. It was during this time that I happened to come upon a young girl named Polly Brown."

Poor Boritz's heart instantly sunk at the very mention of her name.

"Good grief. I so hoped not to hear that dreadful name for quite a while," he quietly muttered to himself.

"Speak up, Mr. Skunkberry. I couldn't quite catch what you just said, for this phone line is exceptionally poor."

"Yes, yes, Lady Butterkist. Do please go on," the further demoralized man urged.

"Well, you must forgive me for saying this, but I do believe that this hospital is not the place for such a young girl as Polly."

"I hear. I see."

"Well, I'm not too sure you really do, Mr. Skunkbelli, for she truly does not belong in such a place as this."

"Well, madam, may I firstly remind you once more that my family name is Scumberry. And I don't know what she has told you, but trust me when I say I feel obligated to tell you that Polly is just about one of the most profound liars that has ever been entrusted to my care."

"Really, Mr. Scumberry? Well, I feel just as obligated to inform you that the dear girl has said absolutely nothing to me! Oh, no; it is merely my own much-trusted perception. Call it female intuition or womanly instinct, if you must. And as it is so often stated, women are indeed the most perceptive of the two sexes. Will you not join me in wholeheartedly agreeing that this undeniably is the case?" she abruptly stated.

"Madam, do I really have any choice in this matter? You are, after all, a lady of much caliber and breeding, and therefore my immediate desire is to see to it that all your petitions are utterly fulfilled. So allow me the privilege and pleasure of knowing what your first wish might possible be."

"Well, the first wish is simply that Polly be allowed to leave this most dreadful institution this very day."

"What, today?" an utterly shocked Boritz queried.

"Wonderful, Boritz. So we have immediate agreement? For today, as any day goes, is a very, very good day. Now, I have already spoken with Dr. Ninkumpoop, and he is of the opinion that both he and his staff have done all they can for darling Polly. I therefore propose that you find it in your heart to sign your section of the release papers. I promise you, sir, that you will be greatly rewarded for your full cooperation in this otherwise delicate matter. As we speak, the dear doctor is most cheerfully filling in his section of the papers. Aren't you, Poopy, my dear?" she called out to the now thoroughly inconsolable professor of the mind.

"How priceless!" a confused and dumbfounded Boritz quietly muttered, shaking his head in pure disbelief as he tried and failed to imagine what on earth must be going on at the hospital for the good doctor to allow this woman to already be on such familiar and intimate terms that she could get away with calling him 'Poopy'! He quickly came to the wrong conclusion that the dear lady must have parted company with yet another overly generous check. Why else would he allow himself to be called 'Poopy' in such a disparaging fashion?

Meanwhile, a feeble and thoroughly demoralized Dr. Ninkumpoop grabbed hold of his teacup and began to furiously gulp down the remainder of its contents, his chosen way of attempting to drown all his sorrows. However, having taken a number of very large gulps, he suddenly found himself in the middle of the most frightful choking fit imaginable, which all too soon found him seriously struggling to take his last breath. Lady Butterkist seemed totally oblivious to this fresh crisis that had transpired in just a matter of a few seconds, as with her back turned she remained on the line, deep in serious discourse with Mr. Scumberry.

Now doubled over, Dr. Ninkumpoop quickly began to go purple in the face as he desperately tried to gasp for air. Still struggling to breathe, he then shot up from where he was seated, choking, coughing, and heaving violently as he continued to struggle for air.

All the while her ladyship continued to remain utterly oblivious to the life-threatening crisis going on behind her back as she stoically carried on her very intense negotiations with his very dear and close friend.

Moments later, with hot tears streaming furiously down his face and with the help of two of his long, nimble fingers, the visibly shaken, discombobulated doctor finally managed to extract a large, white feather that rather mysteriously had lodged itself at the very back of his throat.

Feeling feeble and thoroughly confused, he stood staring at the feather in disbelief as he realized that this stupid, insignificant white feather had in a matter of minutes almost brought his life to a horrid and most abrupt end. Now feeling seriously weak and in a turbulently homicidal mood, he stumbled like a crazed man back toward his desk and chair, wishing with his whole heart for this day, if not the whole world, to end—and sometime soon would be much preferred.

With impeccable timing, Lady Butterkist turned around just in time to witness the forlorn doctor slumped over his desk in the manner of a limp lettuce considerably beyond all hope of revival. Catching his eye, she quickly placed her hand over the receiver.

"How's the tea?" she innocently mouthed in his direction, flashing him the sweetest smile before turning back to carry on with her serious bargaining.

The poor, bewildered doctor was on the verge of physically tearing out his hair. However, as he had not been overly blessed with a decent enough crop of hair to take up this latest challenge, he therefore opted to give his forehead a couple of hard bangs on the desk. He felt forced into these extreme actions, as he could no longer control an inner compulsion to begin venting some of his most potent pent-up feelings of pure rage and anger, which he no longer wished to contain or disguise for as much as one more miserable moment.

———◦•◦•◦———

Now, to be perfectly honest, Boritz wasn't faring much better either, as he too was now feeling considerably vexed, for up until this moment in time he had not the faintest clue that this difficult request was going to be the first demand on her long list of requests. *What on earth would be coming next?* he anxiously deliberated.

He knew instantly that Mildred would be furious with him, but what else could he do? At the end of the day he really was no fool, and he knew for certain that if he did not show himself both eager and willing to comply with all her seemingly innocent requests, then she would most certainly decline his invitation to join them for tea and cakes at the castle. This could never be allowed to happen, no, not in a month of Sundays, as with all his heart he believed that in terms of financial support this meeting was vitally crucial.

"All right, Lady Butterkist. You have my humble and sincere word on this one. So pray, tell me something of your second request."

"Hmm. Mr. Scumberry, strange as this might seem, I wish to become something of a guardian to young Polly."

"Guardian! Madam, please grant me the pleasure of fully explaining yourself, for I am now most confused as to what possibly you mean by all of this, as she already has a legal guardian, who, I might add, just happens to be me."

"Oh, if only that were truly so, Mr. Skunkbelli, then she would not have been abandoned to the confines of this painfully pitiful institution. But setting this aside for the present, I am just after some form of loose involvement. Yes, I would like to be considered something of a guardian, although in this special case there would be no involvement whatsoever with the courts. Call it an honorable agreement amongst ourselves if you must."

"No judicial involvement?"

"None whatsoever! Mr. Skunkbelly, there wouldn't be any sort of legally binding contract or obligation. Oh, no. This would merely be a pact between friends, so to speak, and I take it we are now friends?"

"Yes, yes."

"This way, whenever I am passing by I can hopefully consider popping in to the castle to see how Polly is doing and at the same time hand over another check. I mean, would the scenario I have just described fit comfortably with you and your good wife?"

"Who, Mildred?"

"Well, I cannot say categorically that she is your good wife, for only you two know if you truly ever tied the knot and thus have a marriage that is legally binding and recognized by the church. But if I'm not mistaken she is your other half, is she not?"

"Yes, yes, Lady Butterkist. We are indeed well and truly joined at the hip. But I assure you now that Mildred will do exactly as I say, for in truth she has absolutely no other choice."

"Splendid! You know something, Mr. Scumberry? I like a man who is bold and fearless and knows how to keep a woman in her place."

"Really, Lady Butterkist?"

"Yes, really. There are not nearly enough men of such flawless moral caliber around these days," she said.

"Why thank you, Lady Butterkist, for it is well known in these parts that I keep my dear wife-in-strife exactly where she truly belongs, and that is rigidly under my thumb," he stated as he began to glow from head to foot.

"Yes, under your fat thumb and squashed to a seedless pulp," Lady Butterkist murmured under her breath.

"I think I am beginning to like this woman," he muttered, at the same time placing his hand over the receiver to ensure his furtive comment remained private.

"Oh, Mr. Scumberry, I am so very pleased that we are seeing things eye to eye like this, for this shows that we are on track for a very long and rewarding relationship, and I just happen to believe that, like most young, vulnerable children, Polly is a wonderful and very gifted child. I'm sure, as with everything else, you will readily agree with me on this one too."

"Yes, yes." He coughed and spluttered.

"Good. Then do I have your full cooperation on this one also?"

"Oh, absolutely, dear woman. Absolutely!"

"Oh, good. Now I am already halfway through, so almost nearing my last request. I do believe that I'm already up to number three. Am I correct in my thinking?"

"Yes, Lady Butterkist. This next request will indeed count as your third."

"Good, because sometimes I get a little confused when it comes down to numbers, or so my faithful butler, Blenkinsopp, tells me."

"Yes, well we all get to that stage in life where we momentarily begin to struggle. I think we rather aptly call them 'senior moments.'"

"Yes, Mr. Scumberry, I happen to think you're absolutely right on that one. Trouble is, my senior moments seem more and more to be joining up," she said, giving a deep, very resigned sigh.

"Well, madam, you seem perfectly clear in the head as far as I'm concerned," he consoled. "So pray, tell me, what might your third request be?"

"Well, now that you ask, I am more than hoping that you will happily succumb to my splendid idea of taking Polly away on a little adventure."

"Adventure?"

"Oh, don't sound so surprised, Mr. Scumberry, for I am more than a little inclined to believe that dear Polly is in desperate need of some sort of holiday break to recoup after her very ghastly and most elongated stay in this dreadful hospital. Yes, months of interrogation under the guise of therapy has, I believe, left the child utterly broken and demoralized, so I was thinking of taking her down to the west country for the next few months. I promise you, hand on heart, that she will keep up with her schoolwork, so you need not be the slightest bit worried or concerned about that."

"Oh, homework! Oh yes, yes."

"You know, Boritz, I am inclined to believe that she will need this length of time if she is to have any hope of making a full recovery from this very painful time in her life," she mused.

"Oh, help me. How much worse can this get?" he cried as the now very shocked Doctor Ninkumpoop momentarily stopped filling in Polly's release forms to rather petulantly throw down his pen. "How can this inexcusably rude and abhorrently abrasive lady be so dismissive of all my selfless, pioneering work," he mournfully muttered. "The cheek of the woman!"

"Uh!" sniffed Boritz, as talk of a holiday instantly produced large monetary signs that immediately began flashing in front of his eyes. "Lady Butterkist, please understand me when I say that we'd love to give Polly and all the other pitiful paupers, I mean children, a well-deserved holiday. But sadly, I happen to believe that at this present time it is quite out of the question, for there is simply not enough money in the coffers. Sadly, we are all having to endure certain hardships back here at the castle. I hate to admit this, but we are not exactly flush with money at present."

"Oh no, good sir, you have me wrong, for I am in no way requesting any monetary contribution from your good self. Oh, no, no, no," she tutted. "This would be coming entirely out of my own purse strings. I would very much like it if Polly were allowed to accompany me down to the west country. There is a most wonderful daffodil farm down there that I believe Polly will simply love and adore."

"What? A daffodil farm?"

"Oh, don't worry your pretty little head about a thing, Mr. Scumbelly, for rest assured it will be a working holiday."

"A working holiday? I'm glad to hear it!"

"Yes, for I believe hard, physical work is not only extremely gratifying, but it is also very good for the soul. She will work alongside many other youngsters, and by the end of the day she will indeed flop into bed exhausted but very happy. Trust me on this one."

"Oh, trust me too, dear lady, when I say that I also favor hard, physical work."

"Oh, Mr. Skunkbelli, I have no problem believing you on that that one! So Polly will be working very hard alongside other youngsters as they plant vegetables, groom horses, feed chickens, climb trees to pick apples, and take a scythe to the corn harvest. I wonder, have you ever had that most wonderful experience that comes from being 'lord of the applecart,' Mr. Scumberry? For it is a most exhilarating feeling, I assure you now."

"No, no, Lady Butterkist. Trust me when I say that I have never felt the need for such things. Such affirmations are for other lesser, struggling mortals, for I already enjoy the pleasure of being lord of the manor, so to speak."

"Ahh, well, what is truly wonderful is that Polly will be blessed with the opportunity of working in the fields, as well as with a variety of animals, and their gentile influence will be most beneficial in allowing her the necessary length of time required if we are to believe for a full recovery."

"Hmm. Fair enough, although I'm still not sure I entirely understand where you're coming from," he mumbled under his breath.

"Besides, if she were to have this little break, Boritz—may I still call you Boritz?"

"Oh, Lady Butterkist, I would be so delighted if you would," he fawned.

"Well, think of it this way then, Boritz dear: if Polly were to come away with me, it would then allow Mildred the space she might well need to come to terms with Polly returning home at such short notice. So can you not see a certain sense of rightness about my proposed plan?"

Poor Boritz could clearly see that this would give him the much-needed extra time required, for he knew for sure that when his good wife heard this latest piece of unsavory news, she was likely to explode to a degree not witnessed by man since the catastrophic eruption of Mount Vesuvius many moons ago. He therefore had no difficulty believing that the next few weeks at the castle would be an intolerably miserable affair as she spoiled handkerchief after handkerchief in her urgent and most dire need to vent a large amount of deeply rooted frustration from her most inconsolably wounded spirit.

"Yes, Lady Butterkist. I am beginning to think that your admirable plan would be most advantageous to all parties concerned."

"Splendid! Now let's quickly move on to my fourth request, and this is that I require you to contact the school's formidable headmaster, Mr. Batty, and confirm that Polly will be back at the school in a little over two months' time, yes, just in time to start the new school term, which, if I am correct, starts on September the seventh?"

"Oh, goodness gracious me! I don't think he will be happy to oblige with regard to this most specific request," he said, reeling back from her latest proposal.

"Oh, rest assured, Mr. Scumbelly, he will! I hope you don't mind, but I have already taken the liberty of speaking with him earlier this morning, and he has assured me that as long as you are in perfect agreement, then he will willingly take her back. I have also assured him that despite Polly being out of school for almost eighteen long months, she will be up to the task by the time she is ready to return."

Poor Boritz felt like a mutilated animal that was now completely cornered, and so he was left with little choice other than to concede fully to her fourth demand.

"Finally we arrive at my very last request, and this is, quite simply, that I would very much like to escort Polly home today. I was thinking if we, meaning Giles Blenkinsopp as well as my good self, were to board the coach along with the other ladies and gentlemen that you've already invited to tea, then perhaps you would allow me the privilege of joining you and your good wife for this special and most splendid occasion."

Boritz could hardly believe his ears, for ever since Dr. Ninkumpoop had first made mention of her, he had spent a considerable length of time trying to mastermind ways that would have her agreeing to pay a timely visit. Now, out of the blue and of her own volition, she was the one requesting permission to come to his castle, and he had not even had to put pen to paper to send out one of his usual begging letters. How amazing was that! He mouthed a silent thank-you to the heavens before responding.

"Mr. Scumbelly, or rather, Boritz, I do believe you have gone deathly silent on me, so is there a problem with my last request? Speak up, my good man. I strongly urge you."

"Oh, not at all, not at all, Lady Butterkist. I can safely speak for both Mildred as well as my good self when I say that we would consider it a truly great honor for you to pay us a little visit."

"Splendid, then lay a further two places at the table, for Giles Blenkinsopp, my trustworthy butler, and my good self will be with you before you can say, 'Is there any mustard in this custard?'"

"Yes, madam. Rest assured, you will be treated in a manner befitting a queen."

"Oh, Boritz, please see to it that you don't treat me any differently from any of the other guests, that is, unless we are all to be treated like royalty."

"Oh, yes, madam. That goes without saying. They will all be given royal treatment, but you, my dear, well, this special day you will be our queen of hearts," he obsequiously fawned.

"How touching, for whether you know it or not, I am all about hearts, changes of heart in particular," she muttered.

"Pardon me, madam. I didn't quite understand what you meant by that last statement."

"Oh, nothing to worry your very ambitious little head about. You know something, Boritz? It's amazing how easily things work out when we all get our heads together and then concede to bow to each other's expansive ideas," she wearily sighed as she placed the receiver down.

"Now then, Poopy, my boy, have you almost finished the paperwork? Wonderful. Then let us head back to the ward."

The doctor readily agreed, as he was feeling terribly broken if not a trifle nauseated by her conversation with Boritz, mainly due to her continual references that associated him with dung. After all, poop and dung were very much in the same category, if not the same thing, were they not? This day, this moment, there was nothing more he wanted to do other than go home to bed and have a good old bawl into his pillow.

Chapter Thirty-One
NOW EVERYONE WANTS A PIECE OF THE ACTION

Meanwhile, back in Piadora there was much talk of throwing a grand-scale impromptu party, for word had spread like wildfire that Ralph had succeeded in his mission, and as a result Polly was on the verge of leaving the hospital. As a result of this truly wonderful story circulating Piadora, a large number of angelic beings began to congregate, as they desired to hear more.

"Is it really true?" they all cried.

"Yes, it is absolutely true," Hodgekiss was happy to confirm.

"Then can we go and tell Mrs. O'Brien the good news?" some of them eagerly asked.

"By all means do, as you all are well aware she has been praying and waiting patiently for some good news regarding Polly, and at last it has come."

"Then can we throw a party?" one of the angelic beings asked, producing a large box of streamers and party whistles from out of nowhere. He then quickly began handing them around.

"Well, of course! You know me well enough to know any good news is the perfect excuse to throw a party," Hodgekiss said, giving one of his deep, reassuring smiles.

"Go spread the good news, and then tell Mrs. O'Brien to stoke up the fire in her stove, for this is the sort of splendid occasion that demands plenty of appletude pies to be baked."

A number of overexcited angelic beings departed to go and find Mrs. O'Brien, but some stayed behind, as they had further, very unexpected requests. They were indeed full of grace as they very politely made their requests known.

"After you, dear Gabriella."

"No, after you, dear Marcus."

"Oh, please—you speak first, dear Horatio."

"No, I think it would be respectful if I were to allow Demetrius to speak first, as—"

"Please, though your kind manners are most touching, I do fear we will be standing here for many a century if one of you does not take the plunge and go first," Hodgekiss interrupted. "So will someone just tell me something of what you so anxiously desire?"

One of the angelic beings named Habakkuk chose to step up to the task.

"Dear master, we are all exceedingly delighted that Ralph has succeeded in his most ambitious mission to get Polly released from the hospital, but as we all know everything, even events that have yet to take place, we very much wish to offer our services and in doing so become partakers in the next assignment."

"Hmm, I am truly deeply touched by your concern and affection for the young girl," Hodgekiss admitted.

Suddenly, before he could give a reply, there was a furor that had all the angelic beings looking around as an overly excited Mrs. O'Brien burst through the doors.

"I knew he could do it!" she cried. "Good old Ralph. He has been superbly outstanding in this mission," she continued to enthuse.

"He most certainly has," Hodgekiss happily agreed. "But it all has me wondering if he will be happy to go back to being a gentleman of the road again?"

"I very much doubt it," Mrs. O'Brien stated, as she too seriously pondered the question, "for he's now had a taste of the good life. Besides, he is so good at this role. Who could have known he would give the performance of a lifetime? Not only has he managed to get Polly released, but two other broken victims have also been given their freedom and the right to a new life. Now, how amazing is that!" she cried as she tightly clasped her hands together, as though this little endeavor would help contain if not restrain some of her excessive emotion on hearing this latest rather splendid piece of news. "I sincerely think this calls for some extra baking," she joyfully cried.

"Hmm. Believe me when I tell you, Mrs. O'Brien, that the audition line to get involved in Polly's young life has become unbelievably staggering in its magnitude. It's as if everybody in Piadora has abandoned all pleasures, as they are all very anxious and excited to become involved," Hodgekiss happily confided.

"You know, it's so ridiculously funny to think that when most humans stop their everyday activities and dare to think of the possibility that there might be some sort of afterlife, they inevitably have us sitting around on clouds all day. Oh, how utterly wrong they all are," she mused.

"Yes, I think they would be very touched and staggered if they could even have a tiny glimpse of what lengths we go to, to intervene when we try to warn, help, or rescue them from one disaster after another."

"And it's such fun, isn't it?" Mrs. O'Brien mischievously interrupted. "I, for one, never imagined that the afterlife could be so exciting. It makes everything else seem very drab and boring."

"Well, it has to remain this way, for ultimately it is up to them to decide if heaven even exists, and if so, if angelic beings really exist," Hodgekiss reminded.

"Yes, it is their choice alone," she sighed.

Suddenly Habikuk, who had been standing by, waiting most patiently for an answer to his original request, once more stepped in. "Anyway, Hodgekiss, getting back to Polly and her ongoing crises, can we all become involved in saving her? For, as we all see into the future, we know full well that she is about to head out on another dangerous and very precarious mission that will once more have her fighting for her life, oh, as well as that of her younger brother, James."

"I promise all here that there will be plenty of opportunity for all of you to play your part, if not in Polly's ongoing crisis then certainly in that of other poor, helpless humans who are living every day of their lives feeling abandoned and empty of all hope. Now, I think it is perfectly apparent to all that Ralph is enjoying the role of Lady Butterkist so much that I am sure I will be needing another tramp or vagrant to accompany me on my earthly travels. If the truth be known, on her next journey many of you will need to hone your expert warrior skills, for you must by now realize she will be heading for the Valley of Leviathan!"

There were loud gasps of disbelief, as the word leviathan echoed around the room, causing a great stir. Hodgekiss watched many began to tremble at the word.

"Oh goodness!" all in unison cried. "She will need great tenacity, as well as all available help if she is to have any hope of making it through that most shocking and terrible valley to come out not only alive but in one piece!"

"That is true. But I also need to remind you that she will also have to make her way across the Valley of Long-Dead Bones."

On hearing this latest piece of news, the sound of loud gasps continued to ripple throughout the land.

"However, let me reassure you all that Napoli Bonaparti will once again be playing a leading role, as will some of the other captains she met with on her first journey. I know for certain that Captain Humdinger has put his name down, as has dear Captain Codswallop.

"Let me also dare to share that on this next journey she will at some point find herself at the mercy of the very Rev. Mumbo-Jumbo."

"Oh, surely not! Oh, how can this be? Oh, goodness. The Reverend Mumbo-Jumbo?" many of those listening cried out.

"Hmm. I'm afraid so. She will therefore need much wisdom and guidance if she is to come through this particular ghastly episode unscathed," Hodgekiss confided.

"Oh, she most certainly will," they all agreed. "And Hodgekiss, we all are aware that there is much more to tell, yes, more terribly unnerving events that will surely find her literally quaking in her boots with fear."

"This is true, for yet again her home life is going to test her to the limit. But trust me when I say she is a real fighter with a passionate warrior spirit within her. Many believe it is tough trials that make us who we are, but I would like to humbly suggest that those dark nights of the soul just help to reveal the strength of character that was placed within at birth and has always been hidden deep within us."

"Yes, I suppose like nuggets of gold they need to be forcibly dug out of us," an angelic being named Malachi interrupted.

"Malachi, as always, I believe you're quite right," Hodgekiss responded. "Anyway, putting all this to one side, she still needs our continued support, as does her new best friend Lucinda, or Lucy, as she is now known, for this dear and very special young lady is also about to hit the darkest and most frightening time of her young life. We need to assign a number of you to make sure she gets the help and support she requires if she is to hang on in there.

"And then there is Will to consider. We all know that at times he can be a bit foolhardy, but I love his loyalty and integrity, as well as his earnest and sincere desire to be a true friend to dear Polly. He really is refreshingly kind, and he is such a decent, outstanding young gentleman with the sort of values that we all love and fondly appreciate. Yes, I think it is true to say that he is the very best we could ask for," Hodgekiss informed all those standing by.

"I also have to add that I find their friendship utterly compelling, for it is both interesting and touching to watch the ups and downs of their somewhat troubled relationship," he very forthrightly admitted. "At the end of the day, William Montgomery is one of a very rare breed, and so he is most worthy of this monumental task.

"His angry and very desperate brother is, I believe, way overdue for a visit from us, so trust me, dear friends, when I say that in the months ahead all of you will be approached and asked to begin rehearsing for some part or another, for we really do have our work cut out. This I promise."

"Oh, Hodgekiss, I believe her next adventure will not only be a nail-biting cliffhanger, but we'll all need our handkerchiefs at the ready, for it's certain to be a real weepy. That's for sure," Mrs. O'Brien thoughtfully concluded.

"Yes, Mrs. O'Brien. I have no doubt that you are right. But remember, we are on the winning side, and the best films are those where good ultimately overthrows evil."

"Oh, I just love it," Habikuk cried as he clapped his hands with joy.

"Yes, well, it would do us well to remember that this is not a movie but the life of a real young girl hanging in the balance, a girl who is regularly subjected to the most cruel and hideous wickedness and who has nowhere to turn. It is also more than apparent that there are many deserving people out there whose intolerable lives are just as dire and therefore seemingly beyond all hope. It is our prime task to do all within our power to comfort and guide them as best we can, so let us consider what vital role we can play, and in doing so, let's always give our very best to as many desperate and troubled people as choose to accept our help and support."

Chapter Thirty-Two
PLEASE RELEASE ME, LET ME GO

*B*ACK ON THE ward, Dr. Ninkumpoop and Lady Butterkist immediately headed toward Polly's bed, which, much to their surprise, was surrounded by patients as well as nurses. "Doctor, come quickly," the nurses anxiously cried.

The doctor raced toward the bed and was instantly shocked to see a fully dressed Polly playing with Lady Butterkist's other pooch.

"Hello, doctor. I hope you don't mind, but I am feeling so incredibly wonderful and overflowing with joy that I had little choice left but to get up so as not to waste another precious minute of this glorious day. I wonder if I'd be allowed permission to take this gorgeous little thing for a long walk in the hospital gardens, for I would love to get a bit of fresh air."

The poor doctor was speechless and totally flabbergasted. He had never seen anything like it, for not only was she up and dressed, but her face, well, it looked so unbelievably radiant. Why, only yesterday he had cared to comment in his private journal just how tortured a being she had over the months become and that the dark circles due to lack of sleep had appeared under her eyes, giving her a most terrifying and haunting look that, if he were to be totally honest, absolutely repulsed him. Now as he looked her directly in the eye, he could see no signs whatsoever that she had ever in her young life experienced as much as one sleepless night.

"Polly, are you sure you're feeling all right?"

"Oh, doctor, I have never felt better in my life," she cried. "Here, take this pup. He is so cute, isn't he?" she cried as she dumped the dog into the forlorn-looking doctor's arms.

As the doctor was seriously struggling to digest this latest, most mystifying happening, as well as hold on to the yappy dog, her ladyship's oil-drenched butler strolled down the ward toward them.

"Madam, may I take a moment of your time?"

"What is it, Blenkinsopp?"

"Well, madam, I need to speak with you in private," he said in little more than a whisper.

"Come on, Blenkinsopp, do be a dear and stop all this—how shall I say it?—temperamental shilly-shallying, for it really is quite unnecessary. Do be a dear and just say what you need to say."

"Madam, I truly believe this is for your ears alone," he whispered, a justifiably concerned frown now appearing on his seriously lined forehead.

"Nonsense, Blenkinsopp. Just go ahead and state your business," she insisted.

A very nervous Blenkinsopp started to clear his throat.

"What's up, my dear man? For you appear to have a frog in your throat."

"No, madam, just a slight tickle."

"Well, what are you waiting for? Go ahead and spit it out," she impatiently requested.

"Oh, very well then, madam. Here goes. I need your stockings."

"My stockings, Blenkinsopp?"

"Yes, madam, I need you to remove your stockings and then hand them over to me."

"Blenkinsopp, I'm not sure I understand."

"Forgive me, madam. It has more to do with needing a temporary fan belt in order to get the broken-down coach once more back on the road."

"Oh, forgive me, my dear man, for now I clearly see where you're coming from."

"May I remind your ladyship that this has always worked for us in the past when the old jalopy has broken down? Alas, I also did everything in my power to insist that this little conversation be just between our good selves and therefore in private so as to dispense with any confusion or embarrassment."

"You're quite right, Blenkinsopp, so I now feel suitably chastised, for you did all in your power to warn me. I am not the least bit flustered by this latest unusual request."

"Thank you, madam," a most relieved Blenkinsopp replied.

Moments later, her ladyship left for the bathroom, and then minutes later she once more headed back down the ward toward the doctor and Blenkinsopp.

"Here, take them," she ordered. "I've done you the small courtesy of placing them in this little paper bag that I always carry in my purse just in case Piddles or Tiddles do an inappropriately managed little whoopsie that requires me, their guardian, to scoop up and then suitably dispose of."

"Thank you, madam, and I trust that en route to the castle we will be able to find a shop where we can hopefully replace them."

"Thank you for your very touching concern, Blenkinsopp, for the weather is beginning to get a little nippy to say the least," her ladyship commented, giving a most mischievous smile.

"Yes, madam. It's amazing what one can achieve with a hammer, a pair of nylons, and a bit of ingenuity," he stated with a wink as he then turned to head out of the ward to go and get back under the coach.

"Now, doctor, while we wait for Blenkinsopp to fix the problem of the fan belt, I would very much like to suggest that Polly is given some special time to say her good-byes to her dear and close friend Lucinda."

"Well, Lady Butterkist, I will see what I can do, but I have to warn you now that Lucinda has not been very well recently, and without wishing to say too much, she has spent these past few weeks within the confines of a padded cell—for her own good, you must understand," the doctor reluctantly confided.

"Oh, I understand, doctor. Really I do. But it is absolutely vital that the two girls be allowed to say their good-byes."

"All right then, dear lady. Without further adieu, let us head down to the ward," he heavily sighed.

"Polly, you need to get up from the floor, for we are going to see Lucinda. Please bring that appletude pie with you, as I'm sure she would really appreciate a slice or two," Lady Butterkist brightly suggested.

When they finally reached the ward, Lady Butterkist suggested that Polly go ahead, and she would join them a bit later. The door was opened from the inside, and after a few words from the doctor, Polly was ordered to follow a nurse down the ward.

Doctor Ninkumpoop then turned to inform his wealthy guest that he needed to leave for a short while to go and personally check on the pensioners.

"Oh, just leave me here. I will find the powder room and have myself a very necessary freshen-up," she stated.

"All right then, Lady Butterkist. I will catch up with you later," the relieved doctor stated.

"Oh, doctor. Before you leave, I have just one more teeny little request."

Dr. Ninkumpoop drew a deep breath, for he could only begin to wonder what more he could do for this extremely demanding lady.

"Are you sure it's small?"

"Oh, I promise you, hand on heart. It's really teeny weenie. Honest!"

"Go on then."

"Well, you may well think that this a most strange request, but I was wondering if you would allow me to take away that floral arrangement."

"What floral arrangement?"

"Why, the one from the hospital canteen that earlier on in the day was officially pronounced dead."

"Well, if it's dead as you say..."

"Dead as a doorpost." she interjected.

"Then why on earth would you even want it?" he asked.

"Oh, never you mind. But am I to take it?"

"Yes, feel free to take it, as well as anything else you might care for," the wearied doctor replied.

"Splendid."

"Yes, I will get one of the nurses to immediately bring it down to you," he once more sighed.

"Oh, thank you, kindly doctor. You're such a peach."

———————

THE TROUBLE WITH POLLY BROWN

As Polly stood by Lucinda's bed, she could not fail to hide her shock, for she believed she had never seen her friend in such a terrible state. Although Lucy's eyes were closed, she could see that they had dark circles around them, and her normally rosy cheeks were now a ghostly white, as though the very blood had been drained from them. Even her normally beautiful, glossy hair was lank and seriously matted.

"Oh, Lucy. You look absolutely awful, yes, like a whitewashed tomb," she shakily muttered under her breath. "Lucy, it's me, Polly. I've come to say good-bye."

Lucinda appeared to be asleep.

"Lucy, please wake up. I beg you, for I urgently wish to speak with you," Polly whispered in her ear, at the same time removing some limp strands of hair away from over her friend's eyes. Still there was no movement.

"Lucy, please talk to me. I'm begging you."

Lucy finally rolled over and opened her eyes. Polly immediately noticed that both her trembling wrists were tightly bandaged.

"Lucy, please tell me this is not what I think it is," Polly cried out loud.

Lucy refused to reply as she lay on her back looking vacant with a lone tear rolling down her cheek.

"Forget the celebration with apple pie, Lucy, for I cannot bear to leave you in this way," Polly whispered as she wiped away Lucinda's tear before planting a small kiss on her forehead. "I'll be back in a jiff," she sniffed, as she then turned to race up the ward toward the door.

A nurse caught hold of her arm as she fled down the ward.

"What's wrong, deary?" she asked out of polite concern.

"Leave me alone, for I just need to get out of here," a distraught Polly cried as she continued to race down the ward toward the exit door.

Polly burst through the exit door and was immediately met by Lady Butterkist, who was on her way in search of her.

"Polly dear, what on earth is the matter?" she quizzed as Polly quite unexpectedly threw herself into the arms of the lady.

With tears in her eyes, Polly looked up and at first found herself unable to speak, such was her distress.

"Now take a deep breath, Polly. There's a dear," Lady Butterkist gently ordered. "There, take one more. Yes, breathe in deeply, and then come and sit down on this bench beside me," she ordered as she gently directed Polly toward a long bench in the hospital corridor. "There. That's much better. Now we can talk."

"Oh, Lady B., as much as I want to come with you and go on this holiday to the west country, I simply cannot even think to leave Lucy behind, and so, put plainly, I am unable to go with you."

"Now, hang on a moment, Polly."

"No, Lady B., I cannot hang on, for dear Lucy's poor life is just about hanging on by a thread, and she is in the worst crisis I have ever seen her in. As I am her only lifeline in that I am the only true friend she has, then I must remain close at hand, for right now she needs me more than ever," she wept as she stumbled to get the words out.

"Right then, Polly dear. I must also go and see what I can do for her. So do as I say and go back into the ward and await my return," she sternly ordered.

Lady Butterkist then marched determinedly down the long corridor as though she were on a serious mission, and Polly obeyed by making her way back to Lucinda's bed.

Once there, she immediately resumed consoling her friend. "Lucy, please take Langdon and look after him for me, will you? He will keep you warm, and he will hold all your tears, for he is a truly faithful elephant. I have told the good lady who has come to visit me that I will not leave without you. As usual, this might well get me into tons of trouble. Who knows? They may decide to lock me up for quite a long time for being such a nuisance and rebel. If they do, I will not see you for a long time, but I want you to know that I am near you, and I will be sending my love to you every single minute of the day," she simpered.

Another lone tear rolled down one of Lucy's sunken, hollow cheeks as she still lay staring up into space.

Polly took hold of her hand and continued to promise to be there for her and do all she could for her close friend.

"Lucy, we really are in this together. We are more than friends; we are sisters, and so you mean everything to me," she whimpered.

Suddenly Polly was forced to look up, for there was quite a commotion going on at the door entrance. A sorely fueled-up Lady Butterkist had once more returned to the scene.

"Nurse, do your job and take me immediately to Lucinda's bed," she sharply ordered.

The nurse dutifully obeyed, and seconds later Lady Butterkist found herself standing at the end of bed as an anxious Polly sat holding Lucinda's pale, thin hand.

"Right, Polly. Everything is sorted. You, young lady, are definitely coming with me to the west country."

"I'm so sorry, Lady B., but without wishing to offend you further, I don't think you quite understand my position, for there is no way I'm leaving here today without Lucy," she glumly cried.

"Well, Polly dear, that's very good to hear, for I assure you that dear Lucinda is now coming with us too."

On hearing the surprisingly good news, Polly instantly burst into tears.

"Now then, Polly, don't you dare throw a wobbly on me, for there's been more than enough emotions expressed throughout this day."

"Are you sure? Answer me truthfully and tell me this is not some stupid, mindless joke."

"Hand on heart, this is no joke, Polly, for I would not do such a thing to you of all people. Lucinda really is coming on holiday with us," Lady Butterkist confirmed. "Yes, girls, it will be nothing but fun and frolics for the next four weeks, I will see to that."

"Frolics?"

"Oh, that's an old-fashioned word for 'constant laughter,' or something like that. We, my dears, are going to have ourselves a simply glorious time," she triumphantly stated.

"That's all well and good, but can you not see for yourself that Lucy is looking so pale and poorly that I cannot imagine ever seeing a smile light up her pretty face again?" Polly ruefully observed.

"Well, let's get on the road, shall we? Then we will see what can be done to help dear Lucinda."

"Lady B., tell me straight: how can we leave to go on holiday when the news circulating around the wards is that you are the celebrity expected to cut the ribbon at the official ward-opening ceremony, which I am told is less than two days away?"

"Well, Polly, believe it or not, I've already sorted out that little problem, for I do indeed have friends in high places."

"High places?"

"Polly, do be a dear and stop repeating my every word, for it's very irritating to say the least. When I say 'high places,' that's precisely what I mean. Yes, my dear, I have arranged for one of England's latest and biggest celebrities to take my place and, so, cut the ribbon."

"Really, who is that then?" a surprised Polly quizzed.

"Well, someone who has a real thirst for champagne and who cannot bear to be out of the limelight for any length of time."

"Don't speak in riddles. Tell me now, for I'm dying to know," Polly wistfully groaned.

"Well, don't get too excited Polly, but it is none other than Freddie Fruitless! How's that for a spectacular event?" she cried, clasping her hands as she savored her sheer brilliance.

"What? Freddie Fruitless?" an alarmed Polly cried.

"Polly dear, I hate to say this, but you're doing it again by repeating my words. So yes, dear, you heard right the first time. Freddie Fruitless is taking over from me. Now, if you wish to stay behind because, like every other teenage girl, you too secretly adore the man, then I will try my best to understand and come to terms with it."

"Oh, Lady B., I fear you have made one terribly big mistake, for please don't be offended when I say out loud that the man is a real slimy toad—and I know this firsthand!"

"Hmm. I had hoped that might be your reaction, for in all fairness, if the man keeps on going down this most destructive path, well, he might as well get an early preview of where he is almost certain to end," she stated very tongue in cheek.

"Are you saying that he may well find himself incarcerated behind the walls of a mental institution?"

"Yes, Polly, I do, but time alone will tell. It is all up to him, for fame and fortune most certainly come with a heavy price tag."

"So is Dr. Ninkumpoop happy to be getting Freddie?"

"Oh, absolutely! Dear Dr. Ninkumpoop really brightened up, well, momentarily anyway, and he became most ecstatic at the news, especially when I told him that I had already settled things in terms of financial reimbursement, for, as you are probably aware, these stars do not come cheap."

"Oh, Lady B.," Polly giggled.

"Yes, and he is not a totally stupid man, for he knows that such a big name like that will most certainly pull bigger crowds than some rustic old dame—minus her nylon stockings," she said, giving Polly a most mischievous wink.

"Oh, Lady B., you really are becoming a bit of a scallywag."

"Well, I don't know about that, but if I could predict anything of tomorrow's events, then certainly, I believe, by the time the official ceremony is well under way, many a tongue will indeed be wagging. Anyway, enough said. Let us concentrate all our efforts on getting dear Lucinda back to normal, as she really needs a lot of tender, loving care."

"Oh, Lucy, this is the best treat that has happened to either of us in a very long time. I promise you we will have such fun and friendship," she cried as she squeezed Lucy's pale hand tightly. "So let's get you up and dressed and ready to go," Polly excitedly cried.

"Yes, Lucinda dear. I am not at liberty to divulge all that has taken place, but I can say that I had the good doctor ring your parents at their home and suggest that this special vacation would be most be most beneficial in nursing you back to full health. The poor darlings are so anxious to see you whole and happy that they were more than willing to agree to this trip. So let's waste no further time. We will get a nurse to help you get dressed into more suitable clothing, as well as pack your belongings, and then we must head down to the good doctor's office to say our final good-byes."

"Thank you so much, Lady B. In fact, thank you for everything, for you are such a miracle worker," Polly sniffed as she fought back tears of great joy.

"Don't mention it, dear, but do please wipe away those tears, or we will all begin boo-hooing, and that will most likely panic and upset many of the other emotionally fragile patients. Don't you think?"

"Yes, Lady B. I'm sure you're right. It's just I am feeling so overwhelmed with gratitude for all the unearned kindness you have shown me."

"Well, thank you, Polly, for a grateful heart is a very healthy thing, for it is indeed good that we all try to daily count our blessings. Now, let's go and say our good-byes and thank the wonderful, hard-working nurses for all the good and sacrificial work that they do. Then when Lucinda is ready, we must quickly head down to the dear doctor's office to sign ourselves out of this ghastly facility."

As they entered the ward office they were met by a nurse holding a severely drooping floral arrangement.

"Milady, Dr. Ninkumpoop told me to give you these, but I can't for the life of me imagine why, as they look as dead as a doorpost," she sniffed.

"Well, I'm a dab hand at bringing things back to life, so thank you, nurse," Lady Butterkist replied as she took charge of the flower arrangement.

On the way down the stairs, Polly continued on with their conversation. "Why would the doctor even think to give you a bunch of dead flowers?" a very inquisitive Polly asked.

"Well, Polly, this might surprise you, but I actually asked to be allowed to take them away, as it appears to me that nothing has much chance of surviving in here. Yes, let the dead bury the dead. But trust me when I say a little bit of fresh air, coupled with a bit of nurturing care, will see these flowers once more blooming, and in no time at all," she enthused.

"Well, they look way beyond all hope to me," Polly rather openly and rudely declared.

"Well, that's what they said about you, dear, but that certainly did not turn out to be the case, did it?" Lady Butterkist gently reminded Polly.

"Oh, Lady B., you really do have an answer for everything."

"Hmm. It certainly appears that way, but I prefer to think of myself as simply a thoroughly charming, efficacious old lady."

"Efficacious! Is that really a word, or have you simply made it up?"

"My dear, I truly resent such a spurious allegation being pointed at me," she stated as she gave the pretence of being truly offended.

"Well then, don't hold out, for what does *efficacious* really mean?"

"Well, Polly, I'll leave that for you to find out for yourself—with the help of your little dictionary, of course!"

"Oh, of course, and I promise to report back once I have the answer."

"Want to know something, Polly? I believe even my nylons have managed to play their little part in one of today's many small but precious miracles," she said as she quickly changed the subject. "Yes, for with their help Blenkinsopp was able to temporarily mend the fan belt and so get the coach back on the road."

"That's very true," Polly interjected.

"Therefore, the darling little pensioners will, happily, not go home hungry and disappointed, as we can all finally head off for some tea and crumpets at the castle," she informed Polly in a very matter-of-fact tone of voice.

"Oh, the castle," Polly sniffed, giving a sigh as deep as a deflating air balloon. "I don't know how ready I am for that."

"Polly dear, stop yourself now, for you really will worry yourself into an early grave. Remember that you are not going back there alone, for I will be alongside you every step of the way to give you all necessary support. And let's face it—before you can say, 'Is there any mustard in this custard?' we will all be heading off to the land of the tiddy oggy."

"Oh, no. Lady B., please no more strange lands or kingdoms, for I'm still desperately trying to get over Piadora," Polly dared to confess.

"Polly, stop right there! Do not say another word! For one thing, you must never even consider allowing yourself to get over Piadora. Oh, no. It must course through your veins like blood on its way back to the heart in search of fresh oxygen. Polly, believe me when I say that Piadora is your lifeline and your comfort in times of trouble. Piadora is your hope and confidence, so under no circumstances—and I repeat, under no circumstances—must you ever forget this."

"Yes, Lady B. Forgive me for ever saying such a terrible thing."

"I do, Polly. I do. Secondly, please don't fret, for my reference to the tiddy oggy is merely a different way of saying that we, my dear, will be traveling down to the delightful coast of Cornwall, home of the famous Cornish pasty, better known in more informed circles as the good old tiddy oggy."

"Oh, now I remember, for my good friend Ralph introduced me to those lovely pies that the wives of the Cornish tin miners used to bake and give their husbands to take down into the tin mines for their lunch."

"Tell me, Polly dear. This Ralph fellow, was he nice and kind to you? I mean, did he become something of a true and close friend?" Lady Butterkist asked.

"Oh, Lady B., come to think of it, now that you mention it, he had the same color eyes as you and, come to think of it, a very similar shaped nose."

"Oh really!"

"Yes, but the similarities really do end there, for if I tell you this, you really must keep it to yourself," she said in a most adult fashion.

"Go on, Polly, spill the beans, and please leave nothing out," she demanded, as she was very eager to know what Polly really thought about Ralph.

"Well, I hate to speak ill of anyone."

"Go on, go on," Lady Butterkist urged.

"Well, if I'm to be perfectly frank, there were times when he stank to high heavens," she said, pinching the end of her nose to truly emphasize the point.

"Really! That bad?"

"Yes, really."

"Oh my goodness!"

"Well, in his defense, he might have been a bit of a stinky Pete, but his terrible circumstances sadly dictated that he live on the streets. At times that meant rummaging through filthy, smelly hotel dustbins as he went in search of food. That is why at times he truly ponged. But to be really honest, milady, I have to say that he had a wonderful, generous, and kind heart. Yes, he would share his last crust of bread with you if he had to, and I truly miss him," she confessed.

"In fact, we shared many a hot tiddy oggy as we sat and talked about all my inner struggles, as well as the many overwhelming challenges I regularly faced. So it will seem terribly strange to once more swallow down a tiddy oggy without that sweet and kind gentleman being at my side," she sighed.

"Well dear, I'm told that absence makes the heart grow fonder."

"Yes, I'm sure that's true, but I would really love to speak and share with him once more, especially over a few rather yummy tiddy oggies," Polly once more sighed.

"Personally speaking, I can't wait to sink my teeth into a deliciously scrumptious tiddy oggy," Lady Butterkist brightly declared.

"Sounds good to me," Polly laughed. "So let's quickly say good-bye to the doctor and then hightail it out of here."

"Yes, but what of poor, beleaguered Dr. Ninkumpoop? This day started off so well for him; that is, until he met me," Lady Butterkist sniffed, shrugging her shoulders as if to express her total bewilderment. "Now suddenly he's three patients down and minus a considerable amount of his stash of much prized and ridiculously expensive choice tea."

"Yes, and from what I hear, he's also nursing a very sore throat," Polly interrupted.

"Yes, it's hard to imagine just how poorly the dear man is at present feeling or what will transpire next, for his confusion is such that I imagine in his present condition he would be perfectly incapable of even finding his way out of a paper bag," she said. "I hate to be the harbinger of terrible tidings, but one cannot even begin to speculate as to what might happen next," she mischievously sighed.

On listening to the dear lady, Polly suddenly broke into a ridiculously huge smile. "Oh, you really are something of an angel," she cried, as out of the blue she gave Lady Butterfly Lips one of her almighty rib-cracking Polly Brown hugs.

"Ouch. I try to be, Polly, really I try."

Chapter Thirty-Three
GEORGE'S GURGLING GUTS

*O*NCE OUTSIDE, POLLY and Lucy stood patiently by the coach as, knowing their manners, they politely and graciously waited for the elderly people to board the coach first. Polly, feeling a little curious, watched on as the good lady went over to have a private audience with her butler and give her remaining precious pup a final kiss and cuddle. She watched on as Lady Butterkist then handed the wilted floral arrangement to Giles to hold on to while she scoured her purse for some mysterious item that she appeared to need. In no time at all she produced a small vial from her handbag, and some of the miscellaneous concoction was then poured directly into the pot of the floral arrangement.

Polly's eyes sprang out on stalks, and she shook her head in disbelief as in a matter of seconds the floral arrangement burst back into life and appeared to bloom bigger and brighter with each moment that passed. In no time at all the arrangement was so unbelievably huge that Giles then had quite a struggle as he attempted to fit it into the rear seat of their large jalopy. A very pleased Lady Butterkist then took a pen and a piece of card from her purse, and after scribbling a little message, she duly handed the card to her butler before waving him off.

"Wow, she really is no ordinary lady!" Polly gasped before pretending not to have noticed as she quickly turned to finally board the coach.

"Girls, head toward the back of the coach," Lady Butterkist shouted as she made her way over to where the girls still stood about to board the coach.

"Lady B., why is Giles not coming with us?" Polly politely asked.

"Oh, don't worry. Most of the journey he will be following on behind in our old jalopy, besides which he has dear Piddles to take care of as well, for my young pup would get coach sick if he were to accompany us."

"Do dogs get travel sick?"

"Oh, my pooch gets travel sick, seasick, homesick, lovesick, yes, the whole caboodle!" Lady Butterkist replied. "However, Giles has also been ordered to make a little detour on my behalf."

"Oh, is that why you left the floral arrangement with him?"

"Polly, how observant you are, my dear. Right. Let's sit down here, and then we can finally begin to relax. Also, Polly, if you would like to hand this special drink to Lucinda, then I am sure she will quickly begin feeling a whole heap better."

"What's in it?" a curious Polly ventured to ask as she cast her mind back to a few minutes previous when she witnessed the floral arrangement so miraculously spring back to life.

"Never you mind, dear. But believe me when I say this elixir has the sap of the Hoolie Koolie tree and the Hubber Blubber tree, so combined it will indubitably work wonders."

A tired and thirsty Lucinda readily took hold of the drink and wasted no time emptying the entire bottle.

"I think now would be the perfect time to release your wrists of those dreadful bandages, my dear," Lady Butterkist helpfully suggested.

"Oh, absolutely," Polly cried.

"Polly, can you help out by unwinding the bandages?" Lucinda asked as she held out both hands.

"Wow, that drink was the most delicious-tasting drink I think I've ever had. But Polly, I feel so awfully tired, so would you mind if I just close my eyes and go to sleep for the journey?" Lucinda pitifully requested.

"Go ahead, Lucy, and I will wake you up when we finally arrive at the castle."

With Lucinda fast asleep and all the old folks excitedly chattering away, Lady Butterkist suggested that this seemed the perfect time for a little sing-song—that is, if the pensioners were up to it.

"What do you mean 'if we're up to it'?" an offended, fiery old man shouted back down the aisle. "We're always up for it. We'll give you a run for your money, I'll say!"

"Yes, I bet my old missus could sing you and the girls under the table," another high-spirited man roared as he waved his cane in the air.

"Quite a stroppy little bunch, aren't they?" Lady Butterkist leaned over to whisper in Polly's ear.

In no time at all everyone on board was having themselves the time of their lives as going on a trip down memory lane they sang one old song after another. They sang loud, and they sang bold—sometimes a little shrill, but always with their whole heart and soul.

Polly smiled, as up until now she had no idea whatsoever that older folks could have so much feisty life in them.

About twenty minutes into the sing-song another doddery old man sporting a brown checked cap stood up and requested that the next song be "Knees Up, Mother Brown." In no time at all the whole coach was shaking rather violently as the sprightly pensioners sang out loud and began stamping their feet on the floor of the coach. It is true to say that many even managed to wave their scrawny legs high into the air, as they got completely carried away with the song. Why, even the wheelchairs that had been securely parked and then strapped into a special bay began jumping up and down as the high-spirited pensioners' intense feet-stomping created immensely strong vibrations.

Suddenly Polly looked down and momentarily caught sight of Lady Butterkist's very muscular, hair-covered calves.

"Oh my goodness, Lady B.!" Polly cried, her eyes out on stalks as she dealt with this very sudden shock. Her eyes remained fixated on the lady's surprising-looking legs.

A very mortified Ralphella Butterkist stopped in her tracks and quickly pulled her dress down as far over her knobby knees as it could reach.

"Lady B., forgive me for saying this, but you certainly have the most incredibly thick, hairy legs I've ever seen on a lady of means."

"Oh my!" was all Lady Butterkist could manage to utter. "Oh yes, Polly. It would be no lie to tell you it's been quite a problem for all the females in my ancestral line, something to do with being of Scottish thoroughbred, I believe, or so my private physician assures me."

"Well, Lady B., help is at hand, for have you ever considered waxing?" Polly, eager to help, whispered in the good lady's ear.

"Wax, Polly? Quite what sort of wax are we talking about here? Ear wax? Beeswax? Candle wax?"

"Well, sort of. But it is the very latest method that ladies of distinction are using to remove all unwanted and unsightly hair. And it must work, for Miss Scrimp, who works at the castle, well, she used to have quite a lot of excess facial hair, as well as a mustache—that is, until Aunt Mildred insisted that she give waxing a try," Polly stated in all earnest.

"Oh really!"

"I mean, she still acts like a member of the Gestapo, but trust me when I say that she no longer bears such a strong resemblance their leader, and it's all down to the removal of her otherwise frightful mustache."

"Thank you, Polly, for your concern and thus your helpful contribution. I might just have a dabble at it if and when the right moment arises."

"Yes, Lady B., that's a jolly good idea, for I'm told it can be quite a painful procedure, as would you believe the wax strips literally rip the hair right out of the skin follicle?"

"How ghastly!"

"Yes, but given your awful condition, I still I think it would be worthwhile for you to give it a try," Polly, in all her profound innocence, continued to helpfully suggest.

"Well, if I'm to be honest, it all sounds simply frightful to me, Polly. So shall we leave all talk of such women's issues for a more suitably appropriate time?"

"Oh, as usual I've really put my foot in it, haven't I? Oh, Lady Butterkist, I didn't mean to offend you, really I didn't. Please forgive me. My stupid mouth gets me into all sorts of trouble," a very panicked Polly asked.

"Oh, no, my dear. You have not offended me the slightest. On the contrary, you have reminded me that it would be most advisable to purchase another pair of nylons as soon as possible or until such a time as I am able to try my hand at a bit of follicle-ripping and waxing."

Lady Butterkist then stood up, and with the coach thundering along the highway she bravely fought her way to the front of the coach to have a little word in the ear of George, the friendly and ever-so-helpful coach driver.

"Good news, Polly. Darling George is going to stop en route to the castle in order to allow me to quickly nip into a shop and purchase some new nylons."

It was only a mere ten minutes later when, as promised, George, the kind coach driver, dutifully stopped outside a general store on a village green to allow her ladyship to disembark the coach and go in search of this urgently required personal item.

Many of the party also used the opportunity to leave the coach. What with the large amount of tea most of them had drunk back at the hospital, many of the dears were once more in urgent need of a bathroom.

Polly giggled to overhear George use the occasion to kindly ask her ladyship to purchase a cheese-and-pickle sandwich on his behalf, as he chose to confide in her that rather mysteriously his stomach was churning over like a washing machine indefinitely stuck on the spin cycle.

Ten to fifteen minutes later found Lady Butterkist reboarding the coach, and Polly noted that judging by the amount of carrier bags she was now struggling to hold on to with both hands, she had either brought up the whole store of stockings or she had made a large number of other presumably unnecessary purchases.

After wearily climbing the steep steps, she dutifully handed over a brown paper bag to the coach driver.

"Thank you, my good lady. Now, tell me quickly, how much dosh do I owe yer?" he said as he struggled to get his wallet out of his back pocket.

"Nothing whatsoever, my good man! This sandwich is on the house, and let's all hope and pray that the combination of cheddar cheese with pickle finally does the trick in bringing to a halt those awful gurgling sound effects," she said, giving him a friendly tap on the shoulder before heading back down the aisle toward her seat.

As she collapsed onto the backseat, dropping down the bags filled with her purchases, she turned to speak to Polly.

"Polly, be a good girl. Close your eyes and then turn away while I discreetly attempt to put on these new nylons," she firmly ordered.

With her eyes tightly shut, Polly listened to endless moans, groans, and gasps as the dear lady struggled to put on the nylons without bringing adverse attention to herself.

"Goodness gracious, these hose sincerely cannot be large, and yet that is what it says on the packaging," the good lady loudly mumbled, causing Polly to stifle a giggle or two.

"Ahh, finally. There. That's good. Now I'm feeling comfortable. Right. Polly dear, you can now open your eyes. "

"Lady B., I know it is none of my business, so forgive my seeming impertinence or overinquisitiveness, but I thought you only went shopping for stockings, and yet, in just a matter of minutes it appears as though you've bought up the whole store."

"Polly dear, please don't exaggerate! It was only half the store, and I might take the liberty of adding that the owners are most delighted to have done business with me."

"Oh, that's good to know," Polly quipped.

"And you're absolutely right, young lady, when you say that it is none of your business. But with that said, I will share my well-kept secret to successful shopping expeditions. Being a lady of means, I have indeed learned to shop at great speed. I merely point toward any item my tender heart desires, and an assistant races behind me, dropping all my purchases into a shopping cart. By the time I make my merry way to the front of the store, my goods are not only packed but gift wrapped, and I need only stop long enough to sign the check, simple as that. Although needless to say, these days I find shopping less exhilarating and therefore far more exhausting," she said, giving a very deep sigh.

"Oh!" said Polly as she wisely decided it was perhaps time to drop the subject.

Moments later, a calm and fully restored Lady Butterkist produced a large bar of chocolate from one of her many bags, which she immediately passed on to Polly.

"While shopping I got a little waylaid. Yes, I was feeling a bit naughty, so I bought this scrumptious-looking chocolate bar, telling myself I would only have a square or two, for I do so love chocolate.

But who am I kidding? If I popped just one square into my mouth, it would not stop there. Oh, no. I would not be content until I had polished off the whole jolly bar. Oh, well. Such is life," she stated, a look of deep resignation written on her face.

"Who doesn't love chocolate" Polly helpfully commiserated.

"Well, yes, but sadly those unseen calories are no longer very kind to me," she admitted as she shook her head. "So until doctors find a way to suck out the fat without any pain whatsoever, I am sad to say that it's on my forbidden list of no-nos. So the bar's all yours, dear."

"Gosh, thank you, for I'm absolutely famished," Polly admitted as she quickly ripped off the wrapper and began to chomp into the chocolate bar in a most frenzied and therefore gluttonous manner.

"Polly dearest, please do me an almighty favor."

"Uh, what's that?" Polly asked as she continued in a most unladylike fashion to cram the chocolate into her open mouth.

"Gobbling down your food in that manner is so unseemly, unless, of course, you believe yourself to be a turkey having its last supper before Thanksgiving dinner," she cheerfully reprimanded.

"Oops. Sorry."

"Besides which, may I care to remind you that it's good to share, so you should consider saving some of the chocolate for your dear friend Lucinda."

Polly smiled as she wiped her mouth and then placed the remainder of the chocolate bar in her pocket with the full intention of handing the rest over to Lucy when she finally woke up.

"You've missed a bit," Lady Butterkist quickly pointed out as she drew attention to a large chocolate smudge on the left side of Polly's mouth.

"Thank you," Polly chirpily replied.

"I'll make a lady out of you somehow, although only heaven knows precisely how long that is going to take, my dear," Lady Butterkist quipped as shaking her head in pretend dismay she chose to firmly squeeze Polly's hand.

Twenty or so minutes later the coach pulled off the road, and Polly found her heart pounding faster and louder with a huge sense of foreboding at the familiar sight of the castle. The coach came to a juddering halt as it waited for the huge black gates to slowly open up in front of them. Moments later the coach came to rest under the large oak tree.

As the driver used the air brakes, Polly joined in by giving a hopelessly large sigh that expressed the immense inner defeat she felt. "Oh, Lady B., I'd rather stay behind in the coach and keep George company, so do I really have to go in?" she cried in a fresh state of anguish.

"Oh absolutely, dear, for facing our innermost fears head-on is the prerequisite to inner peace and wholeness. Now, take a long, deep breath, and then do as you promised by waking dear Lucinda up. There's a good girl."

"Lucy, it's time for you to wake up, for we have arrived," Polly cried.

To Polly's amazement, Lucinda immediately opened her eyes, and then without warning, she jumped to her feet. "Oh, Polly. This is turning into a wonderful day, for I feel absolutely fabulous. Wow, that sleep has done me so much good. I feel as bright as a new button, yes, like a brand-new person. Really, I do," she excitedly cried.

"There, Polly. What did I tell you?" Lady Butterkist said as she gave Polly a friendly I-told-you-so nudge with her elbow.

"Lady B., this really is a miracle," Polly excitedly cried.

"Shh. Well, girls, let's keep it to ourselves for the present time, shall we? It's time to look ahead to our forthcoming vacation."

"Yes, Lady B. I am so exci—"

Before Polly could mutter another word, the doors of the coach opened, and a large, corpulent figure arose from the steps to then rush headlong down the aisle, a dribbling beast of a hound following close at his heels.

"Lady Butterkist, may I say your timing's matchless, for as we speak the tables are all laid out with the silverware, and the teapot is being warmed under the tea cozy. May I also say what an honor it is to finally meet you. We are indeed deeply and utterly privileged to have you attend our annual tea party event," he sycophantically enthused. "Yes, we are all over the moon with excitement. Now please follow after me, and I will take you directly to my private sitting room, as my dear darling wife, Mildred, is just dying to meet with you."

"Thank you kindly, Mr. Scumberry, but before I follow after you, perhaps it would be nice if you were to acknowledge dear Polly here, as I am led to believe that the child has not seen you for some considerable time."

"Oh, yes, yes. How extraordinarily careless of me," he stuttered. "Forgive me, Polly, for in all the excitement I simply forgot my manners."

"Yes, and we all know for sure that 'manners maketh the man,'" Lady Butterkist quickly and most mischievously interjected.

Boritz carried on undeterred. "So, Polly dear, allow me to tell you how wonderful it is to have you back in the bosom of our large but close-knit family. We have all missed you so very much," he anxiously stuttered and spluttered.

Polly nervously clung to Lady Butterkist for emotional support as she refused to make any eye contact.

Boritz tried to keep up the pretence of being a loving and concerned father figure. "My, Polly, you really are looking very well," he said, while as a gesture of his sincerity he reached over to give her a most awkward half-hearted hug, which due to her bewildered state was not the least reciprocated.

"Mr. Scumberry, please..."

"Dear lady, I thought after our recent telephone conversation that we were now on friendly first-name terms, so do please call me Boritz," he wearily insisted, as with much relief he turned his full attention back on the lady.

"All right then, Boritz. I need to warn you that as well as my precious little pooch, who is at present being taken care of by my chauffeur, we have also brought along an extra young guest who goes by the name of Lucinda. I do hope this extra addition will not be too much of an inconvenience or problem to either you or your dear wife, for I will willingly forgo a buttered crumpet or two if there is now simply not enough to go 'round."

"Nonsense, dear lady. You will do no such thing, for there is always plenty to go 'round at this castle. Please let me assure you now that any guest of yours is a most welcome addition to this party. Let us waste no further time, for you have already spent far too long aboard this incredibly stuffy coach, so please do as I say and follow after me."

As they exited the coach Lady Butterkist handed a number of carrier bags to both Polly and Lucy, which she asked them to temporarily take care of for her. Boritz also stopped by the steps to inform the driver that at some point in the afternoon a cup of refreshing tea would be bought out to him.

"Oh, dear, sweet Boritz, let us not start the afternoon off by being so unscrupulously parsimonious," Lady Butterkist gently remonstrated.

"Uh?"

"Well, surely we can do better than that."

"Please don't speak in riddles, for quite what do you mean by that last comment, Lady Butterkist?" Boritz asked very defensively.

"Well, would it not be considered a decent and most generous-hearted action on your part if you were to invite the poor man to join us all at the castle tea party?" she loudly declared as she stared him out in a manner not dissimilar to that of a beady-eyed bald eagle eager to swoop down on its prey. "For not only will he feel terribly sad and lonely left out here on his tod, but I submit that his parched throat is not his only problem. Oh, no, for throughout this lengthy journey his belly has persistently rumbled louder than a frenziedly, famished humpback whale heading off to feast at the annual family fish fiesta."

"Uh!"

"So arguably I believe I am definite in my assumption that both tea and cakes would be most agreeable with this fine gentleman. Speak up, my good man. For isn't this so?"

"Quite true, milady," piped up the driver. "Firstly I apologize profusely for my disgracefully loud, gurgling guts. I had hoped that the cheese 'n pickle sarny you so kindly bought me might happily bring an abrupt end to my noisy and offensive digestive problems."

"My good man, quite clearly it has not!" Lady Butterkist loudly commented.

"Well, ma'am, I think is true to say that a slice of cake or two would cheerfully put an end to this otherwise very embarrassing little problem," he said, giving a sly wink followed by a seriously lopsided grin. "But first I need to sweep through this coach, for as you can plainly see for yourself, the floor of this coach has been overwhelmed by a blanket of mysterious white feathers. I can only think that in all the excitement one of the old dears accidentally burst a pillow she was using as a headrest," he said, scratching his head in total bewilderment as he tried to fully appreciate the immense clearing-up task that lay ahead.

"Anyway, where was I? Ahh, yes. After the sweep-up I would very much appreciate a nice cuppa char, as well as a plate of whatever's on the menu."

"There, Boritz. What did I say?" Lady Butterkist interjected.

"Plus a bit of company would be much appreciated, if it were not too much trouble. It would, after all, be such a pleasure to be allowed to join in all the merriment."

"Well, I do believe I've hit the nail right on the head, so let's all agree now that once the dear man has swept up all these rather annoying and very suspect feathers, he should then be allowed to join us, for as the old saying goes, the more the merrier. Eh, Boritz?"

"Very well, dear lady. Have it your own way," he reluctantly sighed.

Only Polly heard Lady Butterkist mutter under her breath, "I normally do, Boritz, as to your peril you, my good man, are only just about to discover!" Then she grabbed hold of both Polly's and Lucinda's available hands and began to stride purposefully toward the main door of the castle.

Chapter Thirty-Four
LET'S GET ON WITH THE SHOW

*M*INUTES LATER FOUND Lady Butterkist and the girls being directed into Boritz's private sitting room.

"Lady Butterkist, how simply wonderful it is to finally meet with you," Mildred warmly stated as she quickly got up from her seat to shake the good lady's gloved hand. "We have heard so much about you, and now finally we are getting the privilege of meeting with you face-to-face," Mildred sweetly said as she continued to gently shake Lady Butterkist's gloved hand. "Now tell me truthfully, where is your devoted butler hiding? I was firmly led to believe that he too would be joining us."

"Oh, he will be here before you can say, 'Is there any mustard in this custard?' for I am the reason behind his late arrival, as I ordered him to make a slight detour on my behalf, yes, to visit some very dear, wonderful friends of mine, the Montgomerys. I wonder, do you know of them? Of course, you probably don't, as they only moved to this area recently."

"No, I don't think we do know them. I am right, Boritz, am I not?" Mildred queried in all sincerity.

"Well, they've only been in the area for, let's say, two years at the most, and they have two truly delightful sons, William and Edmund. Anyway, I ordered Blenkinsopp to slip by their house bearing good tidings, as well as a small floral arrangement. Dear Mrs. Montgomery has become something of a close friend and confidante during these past months, and so I hope to drop by and have afternoon tea with her in the not-too-distant future."

Polly's mouth dropped open at this latest, wonderful revelation, for she could hardly believe her ears that dear Lady Butterkist not only knew Will but was also on familiar terms with the whole family.

Uncle Boritz suddenly began a lengthy bout of coughing and spluttering.

"Boritz dearest, are you all right? Would you care for a spot of water?" Mildred asked out of genuine concern.

"No, thank you, my dear. I shall be fine. It's nothing more than a surprise little tickle that has rather disgracefully found its sorry little way to the back of my throat," he coughed.

"Well, by now all the old folks will hopefully have found themselves a comfortable seat, and so they will certainly be waiting on us. Perhaps we should make haste and join them all in the baronial hall," Mildred brightly suggested.

"That would be most wonderful, Mrs. Scumberry. But surely you too would like to welcome Polly home before we all sit down for this special tea?" Lady Butterkist rather poignantly suggested.

"Oh, my! What was I thinking?" Mildred stuttered, at the same time going distinctly beetroot in the face.

"Quite!" her ladyship quickly interjected.

"Hello, Polly. It's so nice to see you," she half-heartedly muttered as she then turned to head for the door. "Oh, and by the way, James is not very well, so sadly he will not be in today's performance. At present he is holed up in the boys' dormitory."

"Oh no! He is going to be all right, isn't he? I have so missed him. When can I see him?" Polly anxiously interrupted.

"Well, Polly, I will take you up to his room later on when I take his tea, as he is equally keen to see you," Aunt Mildred sniffed.

"Can't I just slip up to his room and see him, for I have not seen him for such a long time," she desperately pleaded.

"I'm sorry, Polly, but the answer is a firm no. All our guests have been kept waiting long enough. As soon as the concert is over, I will personally see to it that you are taken up the boys' dormitory. That's a promise. Now, do as I say by leaving the subject well alone. There's a good girl. Right, then. Everybody, it's time for tea, so please follow after me."

Lady Butterkist immediately took hold of Polly's hand and squeezed it tightly. Somehow Polly felt that despite appearances Lady Butterkist really understood all that was going on.

On their way to the baronial hall, Aunt Mildred excitedly chatted away. "Lady Butterkist, we have worked extraordinarily hard to put together a rather delicious tea, and the children have also worked terribly hard at rehearsals, for they are very eager to put on a little show for your benefit, as well as the very delightful pensioners."

"Mrs. Scumberry, it all sounds positively wonderful to me," Lady Butterkist keenly replied.

"Yes, well, when you think that they all struggle with fairly severe emotional impediments, as well as very troublesome learning disabilities, then it makes their efforts all the more amazing, for when it comes to putting on a little show, somehow and against all odds they have managed to excel. Yes, we have some imaginative little dancers amongst them, as well as some delightful singers. And a couple of the boys have great potential if in the future they should ever wish to become magicians. So as soon as the tea is over, then the children's performance will begin.

"Polly, would you like to join with the others and be a part of today's performance? You always sang so well in the past," Mildred cared to comment.

Polly gave her answer by shaking her head from side to side to give a decisive no.

"Oh, please cooperate and change your mind. There's a dear. For I'm certain it would give Lady Butterkist much pleasure, for you sound so much like a nightingale on a sweet and warm April night," Mildred continued to urge.

Still Polly adamantly refused to agree to the request.

"Why ever not, Polly dear? I, for one, would dearly love to hear you sing," Lady Butterkist gently coaxed.

"Yes, Uncle Boritz thinks your choice of song should be 'Without Your Help I'm All Alone in This World,' for you sing that song so beautifully. So please, for all our sakes, tell us that you will," Aunt Mildred pleaded.

Eventually, and not because of the pressure put on her by Aunt Mildred but for the sake of Lady Butterkist, Polly finally agreed, albeit very reluctantly.

"That's wonderful news, Polly. So hurry off to go find the other children, and they will help you find a costume from the dressing-up box," Mildred breezily suggested. "As we speak, they are all in the back room rummaging through the dressing-up trunk, so it would be advisable if you were to hurry up, or there might not be much left in the way of costumes."

———————

Lady Butterkist once again spoke up. "I know it is not my place to interfere, but…"

"Dead right it isn't your place to speak out," an acid-tongued Mildred accidentally blurted out. She then quickly covered her mouth to prevent any further insults from spewing forth, for she knew to say anything further might well have very damaging financial repercussions.

She was grateful that Lady Butterkist chose to ignore her very disgraceful behavior as she continued on. "As I was saying, might I suggest that Polly be allowed to stay and share a table with my party? I am also waiting on my little coach butler, who will hopefully turn up any time now, along with my precious pooch."

"Oh, dear. Lady Butterkist, forgive me, but alas, I'm not too sure that this would be a good idea. I mean, if—"

Much to Mildred's utter annoyance, Lady Butterkist did not allow her to finish her sentence before rather rudely chipping in. "Mrs. Scumberry, may I remind you that Polly has spent an awfully long time on the coach, and so, like us all, she is ravenously hungry. Once she has eaten, she can then quickly disappear to join the others in the back room."

"Very well then, Lady Butterkist. Polly can stay a while with her good friend, but you'll need to keep a sturdy eye on her table manners—or lack of them," she quietly mumbled under her breath.

Mildred turned to anxiously head over toward another table, for she was once more struggling to hold back her fury at being overruled—

and by a mere guest at a special function that she was throwing—but she knew better than to show it.

"Who does she think she is, bloomin' Lady Muck from O'Dirt Castle," she quietly but angrily fumed. As she walked away, she heard the lady calling after her, so she put on a bright face before turning 'round to head back to her table.

"Lady Butterkist, I believe you called?"

"Mrs. Scumberry, before you leave again and while I think of it, a good friend of mine has baked a rather large number of very delicious appletude, I mean, apple pies, and she was most insistent that all the children be given the opportunity to try a little piece. I would like to submit the idea of introducing myself to the children and allowing them a taste of this fine apple pie. Naturally, this would all take place after the show."

"Well, if I'm to be honest, I'm not too sure about that. Most of the children very quickly become undisciplined, and at any given opportunity they are liable to become disgracefully greedy. So perhaps you could allow me to store the pies for another, more suitable occasion."

"Mildred—may I call you Mildred?"

"Oh, please do, Lady Butterkist."

"Well, Mildred, these apple pies have been specially baked with the children in mind. I am sure that if we were to confine each child to just a small slither of the pie, I don't think it could do them too much harm. So what do you say?"

Mildred, in trembling high-pitched tones, responded, as she unhappily found herself yet again being forced to comply with the good lady's perfectly unreasonable request.

"Well then, Mildred, that's settled. Now then, Polly, do please come and take a seat betwixt Lucinda and myself while we wait for that little slowcoach Giles to appear. There's a dear," she said, gently patting the chair to indicate that this was the particular chair she wished Polly to park herself down on.

"Oh, and Mildred dear, one small but final request."

"Yes, Lady Butterkist. What more can I do for you?" Mildred asked, trying with all her might to restrain herself.

"Well, I would be most appreciative if you could get me a small bowl of water for little Tiddles, for it is certain that by the time she arrives here she will undoubtedly be in dire need of liquid refreshment."

"I will see to it. And is there anything else that her ladyship could possibly require before I leave to serve all my other equally hungry and thirsty guests?" Mildred asked through gritted teeth.

"No, Mildred dear, but thank you for asking. I think that will be all, at least for the present."

Chapter Thirty-Five
BEAUTY IS IN THE EYE OF THE BEHOLDER

*T*HE TEA PARTY was truly superb. Mildred had gone to much trouble to make sure that only the finest delicacies were served. The baked ham and asparagus quiche was mouthwateringly decadent, and the scones and preserves were utterly outstanding. The champagne sorbet reached new heights in terms of tasting simply divine, and the melt-in-the-mouth Victoria sponge cake had all the guests in pure ecstasy, for it was indeed the lightest and fluffiest cake they had demolished in many a year.

And to top it all, Lady Butterkist watched on with both astonishment and amusement as a subservient, gushing Boritz willingly rushed from table to table refilling empty tea cups with more English breakfast tea than most of the old dears could possibly handle. All too soon there was a seriously long line of impatient old folks holding on as best they could as they waited in desperation for the little room to once more become available.

"Lady Butterkist, was my homemade Victoria sponge cake to your liking? For I'll have you know that even the raspberry jam filling was made by my own fair hands," Mildred gushed. "Yes, the raspberries came straight from our private garden and were handpicked by myself," Mildred informed Lady Butterkist, as ingratiating herself further she without asking went on to pour more tea into the good lady's half-drained teacup.

Lady Butterkist quickly placed her hand over the cup. "Oh, my dear Mildred, sadly I must refuse all further refreshments, for as I have not been blessed with the retentive capabilities of a desert camel, I fear if I were to drink any more tea, it would indeed be most unwise of me."

"I'm so sorry, milady. It was indeed most presumptuous on my part not to ask before I moved to refill your teacup. But please tell me, has everything else been to your ladyship's complete satisfaction?"

"Oh, Mildred, how sweet of you to ask, for I have to admit that as soon as that heavenly sponge cake came directly in contact with the sensors on my tongue, I could clearly hear the sound of angels singing the "Hallelujah Chorus" from *Handel's Messiah*, for in a nutshell it was all superbly divine. Yes, it was indeed utterly spondelicious," she said, closing her eyes to reflect on all she had eaten as she continued on with her most charitable appraisal.

"Thank you so much, Lady Butterkist. You are so very kind," Mildred delightedly gasped.

Giles, who had finally turned up halfway through the tea, quickly turned to whisper in her ladyship's free ear. "Madam, forgive me for mentioning this, but put bluntly, I believe *spondelicious* not to be a genuine word."

"Well, Giles, I beg to differ, but at the end of the day, what does it matter? Mildred is so full of herself, she has failed to even notice. Now then, Polly dear, have you eaten your fill?"

"Yes, in fact, if I'm honest, I'm feeling more than a little bloated," Polly dared admit.

"Then, dearest, perhaps it would be considered wise if you were to stop eating and go and get yourself ready for the upcoming show."

A very nervous and unsure Polly got up from her seat, and after excusing herself, she quickly disappeared from the hall. Lady Butterkist paused for a few moments, and when she thought no one was looking, she picked up a few of her shopping bags and then discreetly got up from her seat to follow after Polly, her main intention being to see firsthand how Polly's arrival back at the castle would affect all the other children.

She felt like a stalker as she trailed behind the young girl, but all too soon it became apparent as to why Polly was as fearful as she was.

———⋆⋅⋆———

"Hey, everybody. Guess what? The fruit- and nutcase is back from the funny farm," Gailey Gobbstopper shouted.

"Yeah, Fester, how was life for yer in the loony bin?" Toby Trotter snarled. "Treat yer well in the madhouse, did they?"

Polly remained as silent as a lamb as she quietly walked over to the dressing-up chest in the hope of finding an unclaimed yet suitable dressing-up outfit left that she could wear. However, as she walked past Gailey, their eyes momentarily locked.

"Hey, are you lookin' at me or chewin' bricks? Either way you'll lose yer teeth," Gailey menacingly threatened. "Yeah, look at me again, and I'll punch yer lights out."

Polly flinched and dropped her head, as she expected to be hit or punched by Gailey as she walked past.

"Yeah, Loopy Lou, as you can see, we did yer proud by saving the very best for you," Toby Trotter sneered.

"Yeah, there's a bright green dunce cap, a really grotty-looking banana costume, oh, and a rather drab rat's costume that, just like you, is falling apart at the seams. So take yer pick, Polygraph," Gailey viperously sneered.

Polly swallowed hard before biting down on her lip as she tried to prevent herself from retorting, for despite feeling horribly hurt and intimidated by their terribly cruel and unfair goading, she had no wish whatsoever to provoke her tormentors into taking things further. With her head hung low, she dropped to her knees beside the trunk and then halfheartedly began to rummage through the chest in order to see for herself what, if anything, was left of the costumes that might be considered suitable enough for her to wear.

"Cat got a hold of yer tongue, eh, Fester?" Gailey continued to taunt.

"Yeah, spaz, are yer listenin'?" Toby Trotter snorted as he sidled up to her and gave her a quick thump.

"Yeah, Fester, they told us you had to be strung up in chains in the madhouse 'cos you went so crazy," Gailey continued to provoke. "Although heaven knows and everyone else on Planet Earth knows that madness and mayhem runs in yer bloomin' family. Yer dad was off his rocker, as well as yer mum, who according to official records was just as bonkers. And as for Thomas, well, we all know that he was a right lunatic. So it all goes to show that madness and maladies run in your genes, eh, Fester?" she cried as she reached over to give her a hard jab in the arm.

"Yeah, and just 'cos you were allowed to eat cream cakes and hobnob with that snootily posh lady don't mean we now have to bow down and crawl to yer," Toby Trotter sneered.

"Yeah, and we've all just been told that today you are gonna sing that pathetic song you've always sung at the old folks' party. What a joke that will be!" Tommy Pulleyblank sniggered.

"Yes, but I am only singing it because Aunt Mildred has specifically requested that I sing it today," a very subdued Polly reluctantly replied.

"Yeah, right. Pull the other leg; it's got bells on it!" Toby Totter menacingly sneered.

"Please, leave me alone, I beg you, for I'm telling the truth. I really don't want to sing in this stupid concert, but I have no choice because Aunt Mildred has requested that not only do I sing, but she specifically wants me to sing this song."

"Oh, do us a big favor; go jump in the lake and drown yourself, for I don't believe Aunt Mildred would ever ask you to sing anything, you miserable loser," Gailey Gobbstopper contemptuously spat.

"Yeah, take a long walk off a short plank, you spaz," one of the other older boys hatefully snorted.

"'Ere, everybody gather 'round, 'cos loathsome Fester here is gonna sing her stupid favorite song, 'I'm All Alone in This World,'" Gailey loudly announced.

"Aw, now ain't that a shame?" Tommy Pulleyblank shouted out as he rubbed his eyes as he took on the pretense of crying.

"Boo hoo hoo, Fester's in a stew. She's singing out loud to please the stinkin' crowd, but nobody anywhere cares a jolly hoot," Gailey Gobbstopper started to chant, trying to provoke a wild response from Polly.

All the children quickly gathered 'round, and in no time at all they were all painfully howling the tune of "I'm All Alone in this World" like a pack of desperately injured wolf cubs crying out for their mother to urgently attend them.

"Goodness gracious me, how grotesque!" a horrified Lady Butterkist mumbled. "If they are going to make this sort of atrocious noise, at the very least they should be standing in front of the Wailing Wall," she muttered as she tried hard to hide her outrage.

Before she could mutter another word, from out of nowhere Boritz and Pitstop appeared on the scene. Of course, unbeknown to him or the children, a now very shaken Lady Butterkist remained hidden from view, feeling thoroughly saddened as well as disgusted by all she was witnessing.

"Children, children, what on earth do you think you are you doing? That terrible and most penetrating noise could surely raise even the morbidly dead from their tombs. I assure you now with great authority that none of you have any hope of making it into the Westminster Cathedral Choir if you continue howling like a bunch of stray cats whose tails got stuck in a mangle," he chortled.

"Uncle Boritz, is it true that Polly Fester is gonna sing that pathetic song that she always gets to sing?" Gailey Gobbstopper dared to ask.

Boritz started to laugh. "Yes, Gailey, you heard right, but listen up, everybody, before you make Polly's life more miserable than it already is: remember this, for the past two years due to her mental malady, she has been unavailable to participate in our annual concerts. It is also true to say that these past two years have seen far less money in the coffers than in previous years. So do your sums, boys and girls, for this leads me to assume that Polly and her sad song are what is needed if we are to end this day with a thoroughly healthy bank balance."

"Oh, Uncle, give us a break, for we all know she can't sing a miserable note in tune," Toby Trotter sneered.

"No ifs or buts. Leave her alone for now."

"Oh, Uncle, don't be so mean, for we really don't need smelly Polly in this show."

"Tut tut. How wrong you all are, for she sings her sad song with such unique conviction that the old dears desperately struggle to hold back the tears, and then without fail they quickly bring out their checkbooks to write extremely generous donations. So with this in mind, I ask that you give her a break, at least for the time being," he gruffly ordered.

"Oh, Uncle, I still think you're barking up the wrong tree. We really 'ave no need of Polly Poo-face, and we wos only 'avin ourselves a bit of fun," Toby Trotter moaned.

"Well, all right then, Toby. But try to keep the noise level down, because we wouldn't want any of the miserable old blighters to unintentionally hear you, would we now?"

Once more the children began to mock Polly as they outrageously continued to howl the words of the song, and Boritz did nothing to quash their mindless and most misguided cruelty, as he appeared to encourage them further with their merciless and inappropriately cruel teasing.

"Children, children, if you are going to sing along with her, at the very least try to hit the right key, for your horrendously hideous howling is about to give me, as well as Pitstop here, an almighty and insufferable headache," he laughingly roared as, jangling the bunch of keys hanging from his belt, he moved toward the dressing-up box to directly confront Polly.

"Oh, Polly, ignore their unkind banter, for you will as usual melt the hearts of the old dears as you sing your so very sad song and with such timing and mesmerizing conviction. But allow me to illuminate you further by confirming that you are very alone in this world, for I know of no one who cares a jot or tittle about you," he hatefully sneered. "Yes, may I use this apt moment to remind you that from headmaster to Dr. Ninkumpoop, all were on the verge of completely giving up on you, that is, until this beastly and brazen lady turned up to rescue you. But when she's long gone, then pray, tell me if you dare, who then will be left to protect you?" he challenged as he then motioned for the children to continue on.

"Good gracious, this wickedly heinous and most malicious man could certainly do with a serious dose of his own medicine," Lady Butterkist whispered as she struggled to prevent tears from forming in the corner of her eyes. "And I'm going to do all in my power to make sure that he gets it," she mumbled as she continued to hold back the tears on young Polly's behalf.

Egged on by their uncle, the children mercilessly began howling the tune even louder.

A horrified Lady Butterkist decided she could take no more. "Enough is enough, you bunch of indefensible whitewashed tombs," she quietly and distressingly cried. It was indeed more than time to make her presence known.

"Oh, Polly, trust me when I say that one day they will pay dearly for every idle and cruel word arising from their pretentiously cold and miserable hearts," she muttered, as with the pretense of being lost she suddenly stumbled into the room.

"I say, everybody, I am looking for the throne room, but I seem to have entirely lost my bearings," she very theatrically announced as she then continued on with the pretense of looking dazed and slightly confused.

Boritz drew in a very sharp breath.

"I'm so sorry, Lady Butterkist, but you've come through the wrong door. The bathroom that you require is through the other door and then halfway down the corridor on the right," a very flustered Boritz stuttered.

"Well, I sincerely and most profusely apologize if I have disturbed you in the middle of a most private matter," Lady Butterkist said, raising her eyebrow to suggest that she was most concerned by what was taking place behind closed doors.

"Yes, we were all just having ourselves a bit of fun as we try hard to encourage Polly to practice her song for today's performance," he went on to add. "Yes, it was just a little bit of silly fun. Really it was," he miserably muttered.

"Well, I'm sure you were, but let me say clearly that I frown on such behavior, for if all the fun is at someone else's expense, and thus their demise, then it is surely quite indefensible."

"Oh, no, Lady Butterkist. We assure you right now that we were all just having a good, hearty laugh, weren't we, children?"

"Yes, Uncle."

"All the same, I am very glad to have once more found Polly, as I very absentmindedly forgot to give this little gift I intended for her. So Polly dear, please do get up from the floor and try this on," she insisted. "I bought this when George, our lovely coach driver, briefly allowed me the occasion to do a quick spot of shopping. So go and quickly find a bathroom and then come back to show me," she gently ordered.

Moments later found Polly dressed in the most beautiful pink dress she had seen since her time at the Princesses' School of Training in Piadora.

"Oh, Polly. You look perfectly gorgeous, yes, most becoming in that exquisite dress! You are indeed quite the debutante," an overexhilarated Lady B. gleefully cried.

All the children stood by watching, speechless. Polly was dumbstuck herself.

"Polly dear, do delight us all by giving a little twirl," she continued to enthuse. "Simply enchanting! Now, all that is missing are some matching shoes, most crucial if you are to look your best. And then, wait for it, no princess should wear this dress without the addition of a very special jewel-encrusted crown," she cried, clasping her hands together tightly as she expressed her unbridled excitement. "So, Polly dear, please take ownership of this bag also, for in it are the shoes to match the outfit as well as a most stunning diamante tiara."

"Lady Butterk…thank you so very much," was all a seriously overwhelmed Polly could possibly even begin to stutter.

"Of course, in years to come, the diamonds will indeed be genuine, for I have no doubt whatsoever that a real prince will one day surely wish to get down on one knee and then propose to you, my girl," she quickly added.

"Yeah, he'll have to be a really slimy frog or mangy toad to ever want to kiss 'er rotten old lips," Gailey angrily mumbled. The lady's choice of powerfully affectionate words was obviously having a devastating effect on Gailey Gobbstopper's dark and devious emotions. "Oh, yuck! Must we be forced to stand here and listen to any more of this sickeningly namby-pamby load of garbage? I really can't take much more," she muttered through clenched teeth in Toby Trotter's ear but loud enough for Polly to hear.

"Me neither. I can't stand here twiddling my thumbs as I'm forced to listen to this cringe-worthy load of old bunkum," he furtively confessed as he joined ranks with Gailey. "Anyway, I don't know which of the two of them is more gaga, Polly or Lady Loopy Lou!"

"Shh, or the old boot will hear you," Gailey whispered as she began to crease up with laughter at Toby's very rude name-calling.

Polly hung her head low. In addition to hearing Gailey's cruel commentary, Polly was feeling very uncomfortable and self-conscious. She failed to appreciate the lady's very generous gifts, as well as her kind but seemingly inappropriate appraisal.

"Thank you so kindly for this lovely dress, Lady B., but I'm not sure that I am the right one to be wearing it," she muttered, her face hot with embarrassment.

"What on earth do you mean, child?"

"Well, I hardly think that I of all people deserve this kind of attention or this pretty dress," Polly feebly mumbled.

"Absolute twaddle! Let me assure you now, Polly Brown, that you of all people definitely do deserve this, and much more!" she said with a distinct air of authority. "So if you really want to thank me, you can start by lifting your head up, as I can see nothing worthy of your attention on this disgracefully dusty old floor. There, that's better. Now we can all see your pretty face. Right. Now come and stand by this tall mirror and allow me to brush your hair, and then we can finally crown your head with this delightfully sparkling tiara."

Polly, with her head lowered, meekly obeyed and came over to stand in front of the long gilded mirror.

"I think I'm gonna be sick if this carries on much longer," Gailey quietly moaned.

"Polly, we'll brush your soft hair until it shines," the kind lady declared. "Now look in the mirror and tell yourself out loud that you look simply lovely," she sternly ordered.

"I can't," Polly choked.

"What do you mean, you can't?"

"I feel so terribly ugly," she anxiously whispered, as through a mist of tears she once more hung her head as though in deep shame.

You could have heard a pin drop in the room, as all eyes were now firmly fixed on both the lady and Polly.

"Ugly? What absolute poppycock! Who has told you such wicked things? Polly, please lift up your head, for you're yet again playing the avoidance game by looking at your feet instead of in the mirror. Now, please open your eyes, for I assure you, hand on heart, that you genuinely are a beautiful girl with a tremendously kind and effervescent spirit," the lady stated, seeming suitably shocked by Polly's tragically sad admission.

"Why, your skin is as soft as peaches and cream, and as for your beautiful brown eyes, not only are they crystal clear, but their sparkle is like a million newly formed stars lighting up the sky at night. Need I go on?"

At this point most, if not all, the children present felt thoroughly sick to the pit of their unbearably empty stomachs, for it was becoming something of an excruciating ordeal for them to both watch and listen as Polly had such ridiculously touching words of appraisal heaped on her head.

At the end of the day, was the lady legally blind? Or was she, like Polly, slightly cuckoo in the head? In urgent need of assurance, they quickly reminded themselves that both parties had suspiciously made each other's acquaintance back at the local loony bin, so the only healthy conclusion must surely be that Polly Brown, as well as the lady in question, were both stark raving bonkers. Yes, that was it. It was very apparent to everybody else in the room, Uncle Boritz included, that Polly was nothing more than a sad and pathetic miscreant, although they weren't entirely sure what the true meaning of the word *miscreant* was, but at the end of the day, it didn't much matter, for the general consensus of opinion was that she was nothing but a miserable outcast who deserved absolutely nothing. No, not now or ever!

"Lady B., when I look in the mirror I can only see the most hideous monster looking back," she quietly admitted as a few tears trickled aimlessly down the side of her cheeks. She then shook her head from side to side. "Yes, most people see me as nothing but an ugly monster with straggly hair, muddy brown eyes, crooked teeth, and eyes so terribly wonky that, just like the hunchback, I am jeered and spat upon by others. So, please don't force me to look at myself for even a moment longer," she begged, a deeply haunting expression now enveloping her entire sorrow-filled face.

"I cannot imagine for one moment where this cruel and most distorted image of yourself has come from," the kind lady sniffed, "for

I tell you now, Polly, it's all absolute twaddle. Really, it is," she said as she too now held back the tears.

"Lady B., please. This is all too hard and painful for me to bear," she replied in little more than a croaky whisper.

"Oh, Polly dear. Forgive me, but I'm afraid I cannot leave it. I'll have you know that you have a lovely, very friendly little face. Come on, children. Please help me out here by telling Polly that she does have a lovely face."

At first there was a ghostly, eerie silence, as tragically the children were at a complete loss as to what they were now supposed to do, think, or feel, for that matter. Normally their uncle would go first and very helpfully show them, and then all they had to do was copy everything he did and said. But even he was standing with his mouth open, and to date no words or new orders had come forth. What was his problem? This whole unpleasant situation was getting very uncomfortable, if not a little creepy. The air was now so thick with tension that you could cut through it with a knife. Still, the awkward and embarrassing silence continued on and on as the children waited to be told or at the very least be given some sort of guidance by their uncle as to what they should all do next. It never came.

<hr />

Finally, without warning and much to Boritz's utter horror, one of the boys took it upon himself to break the awkward silence, and so he began to chant, "Pretty Polly. Pretty Polly," over and over.

All too soon the other younger children, in similar parrot fashion, automatically joined in. "Pretty Polly. Caw caw. Pretty Polly," they continued to squawk and squall in high-pitched tones as finally they fell back into their usual very comfortably and automatic patterns of ridiculing her.

A shocked and infuriated Lady Butterkist immediately stopped brushing Polly's hair and abruptly swung 'round.

However, on witnessing the intensity of her fury, Boritz quickly stepped in to take charge. "Children, stop all this wickedly inappropriate behavior right now!" he very abrasively snapped.

All the children instantly obeyed, but not before Lady Butterkist had the opportunity of seeing for herself that every face appeared to be totally confused by this latest strange order.

"That's better. Now the lot of you must immediately apologize and say you're terribly sorry, for you have really upset poor Polly by being so unkind."

The children all stood in a stupefied silence, a look of total bewilderment betraying their underlying feelings.

"Children, if I have to repeat myself once more, I warn you now, there will be trouble ahead. So, do as I have ordered and immediately apologize for your very inappropriate and insulting behavior," he angrily remonstrated.

"Sorry, Polly," they bitterly and reluctantly chanted in unison.

"There, Lady Butterkist. Everything is now sorted."

"Sir, I beg to differ," she angrily snorted. "I have seen quite enough, for such raw and savage meanness to be at the hands of such young children is utterly inexcusable, and I, for one, have rarely ever witnessed such wicked behavior from children as young as these."

Lady B. proceeded to hand back the hairbrush to Polly and then quickly excused herself from the room muttering something about needing the bathroom, as she was suddenly experiencing moments of extreme nausea.

A now deeply concerned Boritz was left feeling most infuriated, and so he turned to vent some of his fury at the children.

"What on earth were you all thinking?" he roared.

"What's the problem, Uncle? We were only making fun of Polly like we always do," came Gailey Gobbstopper's immediate and very surly reply.

"Fun? You stupid imbeciles! Don't you realize that this eminent lady is a prominent and very important person? You load of heathens may well have ruined everything. I promise you now that if she leaves here never to return, I'll have your guts for garters," he raged. "And some of you may well find yourselves out on the streets hungry and without a warm bed to sleep in."

"We're very sorry, Uncle. Really we are," the now very lost and contrite children subserviently whimpered.

"Well, kindly be on your best behavior from now until the lady finally decides to leave us," he sternly instructed.

"Well, it's not fair, 'cos I want Polly's dress, as it would look much nicer on me," Gailey Gobbstopper moaned.

"Gailey, please be reasonable! I can hardly strip it off her, now can I?" Uncle Boritz roared.

"Why not? You gave me her swimsuit that special day when we went to the beach."

"Well, that was an entirely different situation. You were needlessly crying and making a fool of yourself by begging me, and all because you thought her swimsuit was nicer than yours. I only gave in because Mildred and I felt entitled to some peace and quiet as we sunbathed."

"Well, why can't you do it this time?" Gailey huffed.

"Allow me to continue without further interruptions," he barked. "I repeat: I only gave in, as I didn't want you ruining the entire day for poor Mildred, and so I decided on that occasion it would be much easier for everybody if I gave in to you. That was the one and only reason it was immediately stripped from her waiflike body to be handed over to you. And, if I rightly remember, you didn't even have the manners to say thank you to us. So this time 'round you need to be much more patient."

"Patient?" Gailey queried.

"Yes, remember that patience is a virtue, and virtue is a grace," he impatiently snapped.

"And Grace is a little girl who never washed her face," Gailey sulkily sniped.

"Oh, grow up, Gailey. You're not five years old anymore, so stop being such a prima donna," he angrily chastised. "Get it into your thick head that you will have to jolly well wait until Lady Moneybags has finally left the building to go on her way. Then, and only then, can you have the dress. Until such a time, Gailey dear, it would behoove you to stay well out of the way and keep your lips tightly buttoned. Do you fully understand me?"

"Yes, Uncle Boritz, but promise me that the dress and the tiara will eventually become mine."

"Yes, Gailey dear, I promise," he wearily stated. "Now it's time to get back into the baronial hall, for the old dears have just about finished their tea, and I need you all to play the desperately pitiful orphan card to the best of your ability. Do you all hear me?"

"Yes, Uncle, loud and clear," they all pathetically groaned.

"Toby, are you ready with your magic act? And Gailey dear, are you and the girls ready to sing the usual sad songs? Good. And Tommy, are the boys ready for your chimney sweep dance routine to go ahead?"

"Yes, Uncle. We've just finished blackening our faces with the lump of coal you gave us earlier."

"Splendid! Right then, children, you all know the procedure, so please form a disciplined line and then quietly make your way to the baronial hall. However, before you dare to leave my presence to get on with the show, allow me to forewarn you all that if today we fail to bring in the necessary funds, then I assure you there will be less food on the table and therefore many more miserable, Moaning Minnies hugging their hopelessly hungry bellies tight as they rock themselves to sleep at night. So go onto that stage and be sure to do your absolute best for Uncle."

"Yes, Uncle Boritz," came the lame reply as they halfheartedly filed out of the room heading toward the hall to begin the much-awaited show.

Chapter Thirty-Six
SHOW ME THE WAY TO GO HOME

*B*ORITZ WAS QUITE pleased that the whole audience, without exception, truly enjoyed the show from start to finish, despite its many imperfections, which included Toby Trotter losing his footing and accidentally falling off the stage during the final moments of his magic act. Looking a little stunned, he quickly got up from the floor, and while profusely rubbing his sore elbow, he hurriedly made his way up the steps and back on stage to continue on with his performance. This rather unfortunate little faux pas worked for the good, as it had the old dears rocking back and forth with laughter. Happily for him, he only suffered a couple of minor bruises. And yes, it's true, the stage set did completely collapse as three of the girls were halfway through their song and dancing routine. But all things considered, the show was deemed to be a success, and the old dears gladly showed their approval by their thunderous applause and hand clapping.

The finale began with Polly standing alone under a small spotlight singing her pitiful song out loud with all her heart and soul. The rest of the children, under great sufferance, were forced to stand in the background and produce large, glowing smiles as they all mouthed the words, at the same time linking arms as united in love and friendship they swayed to and fro to the music. It was less than a minute into her performance before Polly had all the old dears sniffling and reaching for a tissue, and by the time she reached the last verse, there was no longer a dry eye in the place. Oh, that is, with the exception of Boritz, Pitstop, as well as Mildred and all the other children from the castle, who found the whole thing a most painful and ghastly ordeal but who had little choice but to endure it.

The pensioners were so moved by her touching performance that they immediately rose or staggered to their feet to give her a standing ovation. Polly gave a quick curtsey before hurriedly exiting the stage. It was now time for Boritz to take over and thus bring the show, as well as the day, to a suitably satisfactory close.

"Right then, kiddiewinks. Please come back up on the stage to take one final bow," he ordered. The children reluctantly did as they were told, and after endless bows from the boys and cute curtsies from the girls, he then instructed them to make their way down from the stage and then go and politely shake the hand of a pensioner or two.

"All right, children. Your time is up. Say a quick good-bye to our guests, and then you must head back to the changing room to get out of your costumes. Now do as I say, and immediately go and get changed."

Satisfied that they were all well and truly out of earshot, he once more walked to the center of the stage, and after clearing his throat, he began, "Ladies and gentlemen, may I have your complete, undivided attention? Thank you," he said as he tapped the microphone to check that it was still working properly. "It has been our great privilege to invite you here today. Mildred and I hope that you have really enjoyed the tea that we laid on for you, but more importantly we hope that you were touched and delighted by the variety of performances given by the children. It is true to say that these wonderful children may not have given the most professional performance you've ever had the pleasure of attending, but they certainly put everything, their hearts included, into giving a thoroughly engaging little concert. I think you'll all readily agree with me when I say they did a truly memorable and outstanding job."

The pensioners once more began clapping loudly to show their full appreciation.

"Yes, ladies and gentlemen, continue on with your warm-hearted clapping for as long as you wish, for each and every one of these darling children are precious beyond words," he fawned, pausing only to take another deep breath.

"As many of you are surely well aware, a large number of these children came to us from very unfortunate backgrounds, and so their lives have been plagued with trauma upon trauma—that is, until they finally found safe refuge within the four walls of this castle. Here we devote a considerable amount of time and effort into restoring and healing their very damaged, tender hearts, and it goes without saying that time and effort costs money," he stated as he continued, as usual, to pontificate. This went on for well over half an hour before he finally brought things to a close.

"I can only hope that having heard something of what these children have been through, it has reached deep inside and touched the cockles of your heart. I would therefore urge you to consider becoming a patron and friend of the castle and in doing so bestow a charitable donation that will go a long way in enabling these poor children to get the love and help that they so desperately need and deserve. So please, if you have in any way felt touched by these children, then I would urge you to delve deep into your pockets, as we would be delighted to receive both cash as well as checks. If you are writing a check, please make it payable to 'The Castle Orphans Fund.' We cannot thank you enough for your overwhelmingly kind generosity.

"Also, before I leave this stage to go be with the children, I wish to say that we have been highly honored in having a very special guest in our midst. Yes, ladies and gentlemen, may I present the dowager countess of Scunthorpe."

He paused to allow everyone present to give another thunderous round of applause. "Yes, I wish to say a special thank-you to this most delightfully charming lady for making the effort to join us here today, and also to her butler, who joined the tea party very late but to whom we are deeply indebted, for without his help and mechanical expertise none of this would have taken place today. So we thank you kindly from the very bottom of our hearts," he said as he then began furiously clapping to show his full appreciation. "Remember now, if any of you need help with writing out your checks or are simply in need of a pen, Mildred, my dear wife, is on hand to assist you in any useful way that she can."

He was about to leave the stage when he remembered he still had one thing that he had quite unwittingly forgotten to address.

"Oh, and on one final note: please do remember to use the bathroom before you reboard the coach, as the driver insists that the next stop will not take place until you have been back on the road for at least a couple of hours. Thank you, and have a pleasant and safe trip home. Oh, and God willing, we hope to see you all again next year."

Boritz's heart was racing, and his eyeballs were bulging out their sockets as, thrilled to the core of his being, he witnessed a large number of the pensioners still sitting in their seats as with severely shaky hands they struggled to write out their personalized checks. Boritz saw it as his solemn duty to go up to each individual, and standing over them with tears smarting his eyes, he personally thanked each and every one of them for their extraordinary kindness and outstanding generosity.

Finally he made his way over to where Lady Butterkist and her party still sat as Giles continued to drink endless cups of tea.

<hr />

Lady Butterkist, now feeling very tired of waiting around, picked up Tiddles from the floor and began playing little kissing games with her.

"Lady Butterkist, I do hope you have enjoyed this special occasion," he beamed.

"Oh, thoroughly! It has been a most wonderful and most interesting experience to say the least," she said as she playfully patted her pooch on the head.

"Well, Lady Butterkist, Mildred and my good self would be more than delighted if you were to agree to come and join us in our private sitting room for further refreshments before you take to the road. Quite frankly, it would also be good to talk with you some more before you leave."

"Well, Boritz, that would be fine, but before I agree to such a thing, I would very much like to see the children and offer them all some of my delicious appletude pie. Also, I am most concerned that young Polly should be allowed to see her younger brother and spend a short amount of time with him before she joins us to head off down to the west country."

"Oh, Lady Butterkist, consider it done. First we will round up all the children, and once they have met with you, we will then share around your pies. You may also, if you wish, accompany Polly up to the dormitory to meet her brother. In the meantime I will organize for a fresh pot of tea to be brought down to my private sitting room."

"Well, Boritz, I fear to turn down your kind offer of more tea, as sadly for me I have a bladder more consistent with the size of a shelled peanut," she mischievously commented. "But thank you all the same."

Mildred dutifully escorted Lady Butterkist down many corridors until they finally reached the television and game room. The room they entered was in complete darkness with the exception of the light coming out of the television screen. Mildred turned and switched on the light.

"Aw, turn that bloomin' light off now," an irate voice boomed out.

"Yeah, we like watchin' the TV in the dark, so quit messin' about, will yer?"

Mildred marched over and immediately switched the off button on the television.

"Children, forgive the interruption, but Lady Butterkist has requested to meet with you all. So, kindly stop complaining, and be good enough to get up from where you're seated to come and introduce yourselves and shake the good lady's hand."

Once again, the tension was palpable.

"Aw, do we 'ave to? We've already done as you asked by entertaining that load of old codgers, and now we are in the middle of watchin' one of our favorite programs," one boy bitterly complained.

"Shucks, why do we 'ave to meet the old dear? After all, she's your bloomin' friend, not ours," another older child moaned.

"Silence, all of you!" Mildred quickly snapped. "Stop being a load of Moaning Minnies, and just do as you are told by getting off your idle backsides to come and pay your respects. Lady Butterkist has, after all, come a long way today, and what's more, she has a special little teatime treat in store for you all."

"Oh, great. I hope it's a bar of chocolate," Natalie Nitpick excitedly suggested as she quickly jumped to her feet.

"Nah, I bet it isn't," one of the other girls sulkily joined in.

"Well, maybe it's a whole bag of sweets for each of us," another hopeful child stated, giving a toothy grin.

Lady B. decided that was as good a time as any to begin. "Children, firstly: well done, all of you, on giving a first-class show. My guests and I were highly entertained and therefore very delighted to be given the opportunity of watching you all. And Toby, I have to admire you for carrying on despite your obvious injuries. I do so hope you have fully recovered without too many bruises," she said with a warm smile. "Now, I have brought a few delicious apple pies with me that, once you have tried them, I am sure you will agree they taste simply heavenly. So, gather around and try some. I have already cut the pies into small, serviceable slithers, and Mildred is over there putting the delicate portions of pie onto some small plates. So go and grab one now. What are you waiting for?"

None of the children needed to be given this order for a second time, as they raced over toward Aunt Mildred and the table covered with small disposable plates of apple pie.

What took place next had Lady Butterkist feeling thoroughly shocked, as she bore witness to the children not only pushing each other but viciously grabbing hold of one another's hair and clothing in order to get ahead of the person in front of them.

"'Ere, maggot face. I was 'ere first," one boy snarled as he grabbed hold of a plate and almost pushed it into face of the boy standing beside him.

"Get your filthy 'ands off me, or I'll punch yer in the kisser," another ferociously threatened.

A now speechless Lady Butterkist, already shocked by the high levels of animosity between them all, stood in amazement as her eyes followed after a plate of pie as it flew at great speed through the air before crash-landing at Pitstop's feet. Showing no manners or politeness whatsoever, Pitstop dropped his head and savagely demolished the pie in less than a couple of seconds. Then, with slimy, thick saliva drooling from his ferocious jaws, he inched nearer the table desperate to get his teeth into more of the pie. In no time at all the scene became little more than a bun-fight, with the children jostling and hurling every imaginable insult at each other as, stopping at nothing, they did all within their power to obtain what they considered to be their fair share of the pie.

"Oy! Give it back to me," an angry voice yelled.

"No chance, mate. I got 'er first," came the quick and abrasive reply.

"Grr. I swear you'll pay for this later when you get the fat lip you deserve, moron," the other boy gruffly hissed. "Yeah, I'll punch yer lights out, really I will."

"Yeah? You and whose army?" the other boy spat back.

The younger ones wisely and therefore cautiously held back while the older children carried on.

"'Ere, don't shove me out the way!" another boy yelled as he put up his fists to show he was more than ready for a fight if need be.

Lady Butterkist watched and waited to see if Mildred would take charge and use some much-needed discipline, but it was not to be. It was as though she were either blind to the deep, underlying frustration of the children or she didn't care. Either way, Lady Butterkist felt she was left with little choice but to try and intervene before things got a whole lot uglier than they already were.

"Children, shame on the lot of you!" she loudly and abruptly cried. "Please do us all a favor by stopping all this nonsensical squabbling immediately!"

All the children stopped in their tracks as though they were in the middle of a game of musical statues. The older ones stood with their mouth wide open, looking utterly dumbstruck as they tried and failed to comprehend quite what was going on. Their anger showed itself in their bright red faces and quivering lips, as they now struggled to hold back their outrage.

"Come along, children. It is time to show some manners," Mildred brusquely intervened, her motive clear to all. This was her domain and so therefore her problem alone to address if need be.

Lady Butterkist ignored this as she continued to speak her mind. "Surely you could at least show some kindness to one another. And as for the older ones amongst you, would it not be considerate to let the younger ones help themselves to some pie first? In fact, some of you older children should surely help the younger ones by kindly bringing a plate of pie to them," she dared to suggest.

<hr />

Mildred stopped serving the pie, as she also was now desperately struggling to hide her anger at the continued actions of the impudent Lady Butterkist, who by taking over and challenging the way things were done, was, in her eyes, completely out of order!

So, Lady Muck now thinks she can step in and become Lady Bloomin' Bountiful, does she? And without my express permission! Mildred fumed. How dare this cantankerous old biddy even begin to think she can override my authority in such a despicable manner. I've had more than a bellyful of this so-called lady.

"Mildred, I profusely apologize for interfering in matters that ordinarily should not concern me."

"You're quite right there!" Mildred replied as she failed miserably to hide her annoyance.

"However, this is not the first but the second time today that I have borne witness to the most unbelievably hostile and extremely unpleasant manners and attitudes; therefore, I can no longer remain silent as a lamb, as I am most incensed by all I've seen. These children are, I believe, in very short supply of kindness toward each other, and it cannot fail but make me wonder quite what else goes on behind these castle walls."

Mildred stiffened as she tried hard to swallow her pride and show some humility in her answer.

"Lady Butterkist, please try hard to forgive us all our sinful weaknesses, for there are mitigating circumstances here, I assure you. The children are very exhausted, for they have stayed up extremely late the entire week, as they wished to properly rehearse for this event. None of them are usually this grumpy and mean with one another. I fear they are all just a trifle overtired," she said as she tried hard to excuse all that had taken place.

"I should say so," Lady B quickly interjected.

"Well, to be perfectly honest, the play also got them all a little overexcited, and when they are anxious, they do indeed become more aggressive. But much of that has to do with their unfortunate childhoods, so the blame for the majority of today's bad behavior, I believe, primarily lies elsewhere. Anyway, these are small, insignificant details; the bigger picture is surely what matters. Don't you agree?" she said as, smarting from the criticism, she felt an urgent need to justify herself.

"Mildred, I quite understand that the children are overtired, but it still does not excuse all I have witnessed, and if I am in any way to offer financial assistance—for I believe that is what you are hoping for—well then, these so-called small details require your full and immediate attention."

"Oh, yes indeed, Lady Butterkist. We will certainly do our best to sort things out, for at the end of the day we are a warm and very close-knit family. Aren't we, children?"

There was a deathly hush in the room, so much so you could easily have heard a pin drop.

"Children, must I repeat myself again? We *are* a close-knit family, aren't we?" a now very demoralized Aunt Mildred demanded to know. "Children, answer me when I speak, for I do require an answer."

"Yes, Aunt Mildred," they morosely replied.

<hr />

"Those appletude pies had better begin their good work, and soon," a very agitated Lady B. managed to mumble under her breath.

"Mildred, pray, tell me, has Polly already gone up to her brother's room, or otherwise where is she?"

"Oh, Lady Butterkist, after she changed she was then whisked away by Boritz to go and join her friend Lucinda. As we speak, Boritz is probably amusing them all with one wild cock-'n'-bull story after another. Such is his forte," she halfheartedly laughed.

"Very well. Then please lead the way, for it will be dark before we know it, and we must soon get on the road."

However, before she could leave, Lady Butterkist felt she could not leave without addressing the children one final time. "Children, forgive my involvement in this situation, but I have found it most grievous and perplexing to stand and watch. If I can leave you with one small but sound piece of advice, it would be this: I assure you now that all your lives would feel a lot richer and happier if you were to think of showing each other a little more courtesy and consideration. Is that not true, Mildred?"

"Oh, yes, yes—perfectly true, Lady Butterkist."

"After all, I happen to believe that all you handsome young boys are fine gentlemen in the making, so it is inconceivable that such decent, self-respecting boys would stoop so low as to be both foul-mouthed and quarrelsome by threatening each other with fat lips and bleeding noses at the drop of a hat, in this case over a small, insignificant amount of apple pie," she sadly stated as she witnessed a large piece of pie on the floor that had clearly been overlooked by Pitstop.

"And as for you lovely young ladies, well, it is pretty clear to me that you are certainly princesses in training, and every princess I've ever had the good fortune to meet has been a most gentle and gracious creature and certainly not given to aggressive acts such as hair-pulling and hurtful name-calling. So think on these things, will you?"

"Yes, ma'am," the younger children happily responded.

"So no hard feelings, eh, children?" she said as she persisted to give them all a cheerful and friendly smile. "Now go and enjoy the remainder of the delicious apple pie," she gently ordered.

The older children manifested great resilience to her command by not twitching or budging an inch. Instead, they chose to stand perfectly still looking intensely tight-lipped and strained, for clearly they were not the slightest bit amused by her severe reprimand.

The younger ones, however, were of an entirely different mind and so reciprocated by breaking into beautiful smiles that very nicely showed off their irregular and gappy teeth as they lifted their hands to brightly and warmly wave good-bye to the very nice lady. They then wasted no time at all in heading off toward the table to do just as the kind lady had suggested, and that was to get their fair share of the pie before the older ones finally came to their senses and once again adopted their previous bullying positions by roughly pushing them aside so that they alone could quickly gobble down every last crumb.

"Oh, by the way, Mildred. One last thing. Can you explain to me why that child over there, Gailey, I believe her name to be, is wearing the dress, shoes, and tiara that only a matter of a few hours ago I gave as a personal gift to Polly?"

"Oh, dear. I had not noticed. Perhaps Polly allowed Gailey to try the dress on. Yes, that will be it," she unconvincingly stuttered and spluttered, her face going a deep scarlet.

"Well, forgive me, but I would be most pleased if you were to ask Gailey to kindly hand it back to me, as Polly will be needing to take this dress away with her on holiday. You see, I am planning the odd surprise party or two."

"Oh, right."

"So kindly see to it that everything is back in her possession before we take our leave."

"Yes, Lady Butterkist. I will go and speak with Gailey right now and order her to immediately take off the dress," a very embarrassed Mildred miserably mumbled. "So please wait here, and as soon as the dress is back in your possession, we will go and find Polly and the others."

"And the tiara."

"Yes, of course. The tiara as well."

"Oh, I'd be most delighted if the shoes too were also to be returned, as I'm sure you will wholeheartedly agree with me that they do much to complete the ensemble."

"Yes, yes."

Mildred left Lady Butterkist and marched like a poker-faced drill sergeant over to where Gailey still stood to whisper sweet nothings directly in her ear.

"Gailey, get that bloomin' dress off right now," she muttered.

"Why?" Gailey loudly moaned.

"Shh. Don't argue with me. Just do as you're told, girl," Mildred ordered through clenched teeth.

"It's not fair. The dress is now mine. Uncle Boritz told me—"

"Gailey, shut up and just do as you're told, or else I'll be forced to rip it off you myself. Do you understand me?" she growled.

Gailey's face dropped a mile as with her nose now completely out of joint she turned to sulkily make her way out of the room to change out of the dress.

"Oh, and she wants the shoes and tiara as well," Mildred called out after her.

"If I can't have this rotten old dress then neither can she," she raged as she tore the dress from her body, deliberately ripping it at the seams. Kicking off the shoes, she then angrily picked them up, only to throw them hard against the wall.

"Stupid, stinky shoes. Who wants them anyway?" she cried.

After walking over to pick up them up from where they were strewn, she then rather spitefully proceeded to dig out the little diamond sequins that made a delightfully pretty pattern on the front section of both shoes. Not quite finished, she then willfully threw the tiara to the floor and began to crush it underfoot until she was thoroughly satisfied that the tiara was irretrievably damaged.

"There, Fester. You are now officially deposed," she sniggered. "Yep, Polyester, all's fair in love and war."

With a big smile finally alighting her otherwise forlorn face, she willfully scrunched the torn dress into a tight ball before tossing it, along with the shoes and desecrated tiara back, into its original bag. Then, reaching for the folded pink tissue that earlier had played its part in keeping the gift a hidden surprise, she used that same tissue paper to hide her latest mean and foul crime.

<hr />

All meaningful conversation between Mildred and Lady Butterkist was utterly depleted due to the sheer awkwardness of this latest inexcusable and most embarrassing situation.

Gailey quickly handed over the bag to Aunt Mildred before racing off to join the other older children.

"My profuse apologies, Lady Butterkist," Mildred forced herself to mutter as she dutifully handed the bag over.

"Apology accepted," Lady B quickly responded.

"Now, I think without further adieu we should make haste in finding our way back to the sitting room," Mildred tersely announced.

Mildred chose to keep all her thoughts to herself as she efficiently escorted Lady Butterkist back to their private sitting room to collect Polly. "Who on earth does holier-than-thou Lady Mucktruck think she is?" she angrily mumbled under her breath. "I don't know how much more of this impossible woman I can reasonably be expected to tolerate. Really I don't," she quietly moaned.

Chapter Thirty-Seven
JAMES AND POLLY GET REACQUAINTED

*H*AVING FINALLY COME to rescue Polly from Uncle Boritz's very oppressive charms, Mildred and Lady Butterkist left the rest of the party, and taking Polly with them, they headed up the heavy oak staircase to make their way to the boys' dormitory. They walked in complete silence as they turned down one long corridor after another before finally reaching the closed door of the dormitory that held the sick child.

"Mildred, before we head in, forgive me for asking, but what exactly is young James's malady?"

"Well, as you ask, Dr. Glumchops, the family practitioner, says he has unluckily suffered from a spot of very distressing pneumonia. But mark my words, he's well on his way to a full recovery," she said very taut-lipped.

"Well, I daresay Polly must be most relieved to hear that her brother is finally on the mend," Lady Butterkist casually remarked as she followed Mildred into the room.

"James, how good it is to get to see you at last," Polly joyfully cried as she rushed over to his bed to greet him with one of her overpoweringly humongous hugs. "I'm so happy to see you. Oh, you'll never know just how happy just seeing you makes me feel. I feel as though I could explode with joy and excitement," she shouted as she once again threw herself into his arms.

"Polly, if you hug me any tighter, I swear I'll suffer more than a few cracked ribs," James half joked as he began to cough and wheeze.

"James, you still look so poorly to me. Are you eating enough?" Polly asked out of deep concern as she drew back to stare him directly in the eye.

James tilted his face downward and chose to completely ignore the question.

"Polly, it is so good to see you. I am so glad you are finally home, and I am at a loss for words because you look so—"

"Positively glowing! I think they're the two words you're looking for," Lady Butterkist quickly interjected.

"You're bang on, for she looks really great," James replied, breaking into a big smile.

"Well, James, I'm actually feeling pretty good right now, as well as ridiculously excited, for I need to let you know that I am going away, although only for a short while, as dear Lady B. feels the break will do me a lot of good. We are heading down to the west country, and apparently the scenery down there is magnificently splendid."

"Polly, I'm very glad for you, for it all sounds very wonderful," James said with a caring smile.

"Well, to be perfectly honest, I would so love for you to come along with us, and I would also love for you to meet dear, sweet Lucy, for she has become such a close friend to me. Imagine what fun we would all have if you were able to join us," she cried.

"That's really nice, Polly," James croaked. "You go and have a good time for both of us, and remember to bring me back a whopping big stick of pink sugary rock," he said as he tried to laugh.

Lady Butterkist was greatly troubled to see that he then stopped as he clutched his chest. All sudden movement, laughter included, seemed still much too painful for him to bear.

"James, I'll not only bring you the biggest stick of rock candy that I can find, but I'll also send you a dozen or more postcards too," she said brightly as she continued to clutch his small hand ever so tightly.

"By the way, have you any new model planes for me to admire?"

James once more tilted his head down and seemed a bit distracted and therefore most reluctant to answer her.

"Come on, James. It's not too difficult a question to answer, is it?"

"No, Polly, sadly I haven't," he quietly admitted.

"Well, have you had the others returned?" she brazenly dared to ask as she quickly made a mental note of the fact that his bedside locker was completely bare.

"Uh, hmm…well, not yet."

"What do you mean by 'not yet'? Remember I have been gone nearly a whole two years!" she cried.

James hesitated before answering. "Well, I think Uncle Boritz has had a lot of trouble remembering just where he hid them," James feebly mumbled.

"Nonsense! That's just another one of his very lame and mean excuses," Polly lashed out. "It's just not right."

"Polly, please try hard not to upset James or your good self. Try to keep things on a more positive note. There's a dear," Mildred, who was hovering nearby listening in, curtly interrupted.

However, Polly wasn't in any mind to listen.

"Anyway, if you don't mind me asking, how on earth did you manage to catch pneumonia?" Polly dared to ask.

James once more dropped his head as if to say that due to present company, he was unable to give specifics.

This seemingly insignificant event did not go unnoticed by Lady Butterkist.

—•—••—•—

An anxious Mildred quickly moved forward, as she was quite unprepared for Polly to continue on in this unacceptable vein by alluding to certain unwarranted and therefore outrageous questions. She was therefore very glad as well as relieved by her decision to remain present while they had their first conversation since Polly left for the hospital some two years previous.

"Give Polly an inch, and she takes a jolly mile," she muttered through clenched teeth before determining to take back control—and quickly!

"OK, Polly dear. You are asking the poor boy far too many questions, and as far as I know, James is not on trial, nor will he be in the foreseeable future!" she said as she tried hard to turn it into something of a joke. "So I think you've overstayed your welcome, for as you can certainly see, your younger brother is very tired and needs his rest if he is to have any hope of making a full and speedy recovery. So Polly, be a dear and quickly say your good-byes."

She therefore reluctantly leaned over the bed to give James one final, prolonged sisterly hug.

"I'm so sorry that I never came to see you, but I had no way of getting to the hospital, and I was forbidden to even write you a letter. Please forgive me, for I promise that not a day has gone by without me missing you so terribly," he whispered.

"James, I truly understand, and so I forgive you everything. But listen to me: I also promise we will get to the bottom of what's happened to your models. Trust me when I say I am not going to let this one go without a fight," she whispered in his ear as she gave his hand one final squeeze.

Aunt Mildred had no time to react to Polly's dubious warning before Polly then brazenly turned to face her.

"Aunt Mildred, I hope you don't mind me asking, but when is James going to get anything to eat for tea? I'm sure he must be very hungry by now," she bravely asked.

Mildred was once more taken back by her outspokenness.

"Well, there are plenty of leftovers from the tea party that can be put on a tray and brought up to James. But don't worry your pretty little head over it, for I will see to it later when everyone has left to go on their way," she stuttered.

"Well, I'm really sorry to say this, as I have no wish to offend you, but I do not want to leave here until I know that James has eaten something," she stated in her very outspoken manner, folding her arms at the same time as if to convey that she really meant business.

"Well, quite frankly, I don't think you of all people should be speaking to me in that disgracefully high-minded tone of voice," a very unhappy Mildred sharply rebuked. "Didn't your stay at the hospital teach you anything?"

"Come, Mildred dear, I thought—"

"Lady Butterkist, 'I thought' simply doesn't work for me, no, not in this castle anyway," she abruptly stated, smarting at the thought of yet again being forced to bow the knee to this thoroughly obnoxious lady. "It would pay you great dividends to keep all your thoughts—kind or otherwise—exclusively to yourself," she quickly and harshly rebuked, for she felt angry that the old bat was once again overstepping the mark by interfering where she was neither welcome nor invited.

Sadly for Mildred, her harsh words fell on deaf ears and therefore did not deter Lady Butterkist from continuing on with her helpful suggestions.

"I'm sorry, Mildred, but I still need to point out that Polly was not intentionally meaning to be rude, for surely it is quite understandable that she is most anxious to see her younger brother once more fit and healthy. So, why don't we give them a further few precious moments alone while you and I go and prepare a little platter of goodies for him. And may I remind you that there is still plenty of my apple pie just crying out to be gobbled up, so what if we were to head down to the kitchen to quickly rustle up a couple of boiled eggs with toasted fingers or a couple of cheese-and-ham toasties. This will only take us a matter of minutes. If we then add a nice cup of warm milk and some of my rather scrumptious apple pie, we will then have a substantial feast fit for any young prince on the mend. So come on, let us leave together and go to the kitchen to get things sorted," she suggested.

"Very well then," Mildred rather begrudgingly replied.

"All right then, Mildred dear. You lead the way."

Mildred could only subserviently nod her head in apparent agreement. But if the truth be known, she was now absolutely seething with rage. However, she knew better than to let the full extent of her anger show, so she was forced to keep all remaining ill feeling safely tucked away from view. She still managed to march way ahead of Lady Butterkist, smarting with humiliation at the way she perceived Polly had so deliberately and willfully undermined her. In fact, come to think of it, she had been feeling very disturbed and threatened from the outstart. Yes, if she were to be honest and reflect back, things had felt mighty peculiar from the very moment this strange lady had cared to set foot on the property. She also began to seriously wonder just how much more she could take of this outspoken and very dominating battle-axe before she finally exploded and gave her a large piece of her mind.

In no time at all a tray with comforting food was on its merry way up to James. As they climbed the stairs together, Lady Butterkist broke the uncomfortably awkward silence, and so she gave Mildred a warm and friendly tap on her arm.

"There, Mildred, between the two of us I do believe we have put together such a splendid tea that James will be back on his feet before we can say, 'Jack Robinson.'"

"Yes, I'm sure you're absolutely right," Mildred wearily agreed. "Also, Lady Butterkist, as soon as we have dispensed with this tray of food, I think it would be right and proper if we insist Polly says a quick good-bye, and then we must quickly head back to the sitting room, for your guests have been holed up now for some considerable time, and Boritz does get more than a little carried away with all his stories and rhetoric."

"Is that so?"

"Oh, very much so, for please understand, what with dear Boritz being a lawyer, he naturally has a real gift of the gab. I would imagine that by now your guests might well be chomping at the bit as they implore someone, if not anyone, to release them before they go away feeling most depleted, if not utterly drained."

"Oh, dear."

"Yes, he is an eminent lawyer who spends his life championing the causes of the underprivileged and victimized. I have to say his beating around the bush is quite clearly an asset in court, for by the time he has expounded the case on behalf of his client, I have it on good authority that many a judge is ready to put a gun to his head. Such is their sheer desperation for a speedy end to the trial."

"Oh, deary me!"

"Sad to say, he has no idea whatsoever as to when to take a break or end a conversation for that matter," she adamantly stated, for it was now very much in her vested interest to confide such things, the underlying reason being that she sorely wanted them off her property, and sooner rather than later.

"Oh, yes. Of course, Mildred. If this surely is the case, then we would do well to hurry along and rescue the rest of our party, who not only must be bored to tears by now but praying desperately for the Fifth Cavalry to arrive."

"Yes, dear lady. It would be most advisable to hurry along."

"James, sadly I have to leave, but promise me you'll stay in bed until you feel a whole heap better," Polly said as she reached over to give him a final sisterly kiss on the forehead.

"Yes, but only if you promise to write, and soon," he quickly retorted as he gave her hand a tight squeeze. "Please hurry back. I miss you so very much," he quickly added as he watched her walk across the room, heading for the door.

Mildred then, quite forgetting herself, marched down the long corridor well ahead of Polly and Lady Butterkist in a manner more befitting a military general being summoned to his war cabinet for a crisis meeting. As she approached the closed sitting room door, she faltered just long enough to take a long, deep breath. This done, she abruptly opened the door and loudly announced that they were back.

"Boritz, it is high time we released these good people and let them be on their way," Mildred cheerfully stated.

"Absolutely, Mildred dearest. We were just about to round things up here anyway, so as usual, your timing is impeccable."

"Giles, please, will you go ahead of us all and take Tiddles out to the car, for she must be allowed to spend a penny before we leave," Lady Butterkist asked.

"Very well, madam."

"Oh, and Mildred, I cannot thank you enough for your gracious hospitality. I do believe that I am forever indebted to you," Lady Butterkist sweetly stated. "If I had more time, I would like to stay and discuss giving your orphanage my utmost support, in financial terms, that is. Sad to say, the hour is desperately late, and we must depart as soon as possible. I would therefore like to suggest that on our return I will allow enough time to address your ongoing needs before I take out my checkbook in order to make a handsome donation."

<hr />

Boritz's heart leapt for joy within his breast as he gloried in her kind and very charitable offer. He then sat motionless for a moment as he went on to envision her writing many naughts after the comma. *Will it be fifty thousand pounds? Will it be one hundred and fifty thousand pounds? Perhaps even more besides*, he happily pondered. He waited a moment until his churning bowels had the decency to calm down, and then he arose from the comfort of his chair and walked toward her to gently shake or maybe even kiss her gloved hand in his obsequious but gentlemanly manner.

"Most magnanimously kind lady, what more can I say? It has been nothing short of a real pleasure to make your acquaintance, and I assure you, hand on heart, that nothing you care to give to such a needy cause as ours will, in any way, be squandered. Let me assure you now that every single penny will be put to good use in making these poor and desperate children's lives just that little bit more bearable. And let me—"

"Thank you, Boritz, for your heart-wrenching words cannot fail but bring tears to my eyes," Lady Butterkist interrupted.

"But please, dear lady, you must leave now. Otherwise, it will be dark before you arrive at your destination," he keenly stated. "So allow me the great privilege of escorting you all to your car."

"How very noble of you, Boritz," Mildred muttered through clenched teeth.

"Why, thank you again, Boritz, for I am deeply touched by your concern, although I have to say that dear Blenkinsopp was a bit of a rally driver in his time, and therefore he knows these roads like the back of his hand."

"Oh, Lady Butterkist, I have no doubt that he is the best money can buy! But all the same, the tight curves make these roads quite dangerous, and rather absurdly many youths who have barely abandoned their school ties and geometry sets are disposed to challenge the universe as well as their own mortality as they race each other down them at nothing but top speeds. In all sincerity I am left with no other alternative but to advise that you and your party take even greater measures than normal to stay safe."

"Sir, we will indeed take great heed of your kind and thoughtful warning," Giles interrupted.

"Well, in view of all this, it would seem most unreasonable to keep you here a moment longer. Yes, it would be most inconsiderate and ungentlemanly of me, to say the least," he fawned.

"You are quite right, Boritz, so without further adieu we will say our pleasant good-byes and then be on our way. I will keep in constant touch regarding Polly's progress, and on my return I will do as promised by giving you a most generous donation to help with the running of this home."

"Lady Butterkist, what can I say? You are indeed a wonderful and most charitable woman," he stated, beaming from ear to ear. "So come on, Polly dear. Hurry up and finish your milk, and then you and your young friend must prepare to leave by putting on your coats and scarves before you go on your way."

As Boritz and Mildred stood at the front porch to see the party off on their way, Boritz then followed them to the car and attempted to give Polly one final hug.

"Well, Polly, we expect you to be on your very best behavior. And don't forget to write, as we will all be eagerly longing to hear news of you," he brightly chirped as he anxiously waited for Polly and Lucinda to climb into the backseat of the car before slamming the door shut.

"Au revoir and safe journey," he loudly cried as their car revved up and then proceeded to leave the driveway. Pitstop dutifully stood alongside his master, his long, miserable tongue despairingly hanging from his mean and droopy face.

"What an intolerable old trollop she turned out to be," Mildred snorted. "Yes, 'good-bye and good riddance to the lot of them' is all I can bring myself to say," Mildred meanly muttered under her breath as, forcing herself, she continued to apply herself to the task by outwardly waving them off with plentiful, overly generous kisses into the air.

"Mildred, if I may say so, you seem a bit down in the doldrums, dear."

"Well, trust me when I say that it's not been that easy," she admitted.

"Well, now that the day has finally drawn to a close, let us waste no time in heading back inside to reap the full benefits of the warmth before I go to my desk to do a final count of all today has brought us," Boritz suggested as, feeling all nice and fuzzy inside, he placed a loving arm around Mildred's miniscule waist.

"Yes, let's. And if you would care to see to it that Pitstop gets his belated dinner, I for my part will go and check on the children before we retire early."

Boritz was in the middle of feeding Pitstop his long-overdue dinner when Mildred anxiously rushed back into the room.

"Oh, dearest one, never in a month of Sundays are you going to believe this one!"

"Well, just try me, for after all we've been put through this day I am sorely inclined to believe just about anything and everything, dearest."

"Well, I went to check on the children, and what I saw beggars all belief. Yes, it has shocked me rigid to the very core of my being."

"Tell me truthfully, holding nothing back: what precisely is going on?"

"Well, as I turned on the light, I was shocked to discover that the room was literally littered with hundreds of small white feathers. I asked the children to explain themselves, and, in a nutshell, they couldn't. But as I stood, hand on hip, refusing to budge until I had an answer that suitably satisfied me, I suddenly realized that this was by no means the only strange thing that had gone on in my absence."

"Quite what do you mean by that, Mildred?"

"Well, earlier on this afternoon the older ones had begged to be allowed to watch a most unsuitably violent film they were all very eager to see. I, of course, quickly caved in to their request, mainly due to the fact that they all did their bit today in helping bring in the funds."

"Go on," he urged.

"Well, as I stood in the center of the room I quickly realized they had changed channels from the violent movie, and now they were all watching a sickeningly schmaltzy family film, yes, one far more suited to the younger children's needs."

"Hmm. And what of the older children? Surely they weren't the least bit happy with this state of affairs?"

"Well, that's what one would imagine…"

"Yes, one would, so do be a dear and get on with the story," he urged, giving her a most disconsolate frown.

"Oh, all right, dear. Well, the strange thing is this: not only were they all happier than I've ever before witnessed, but the younger children were settled comfortably on the older children's laps, with the older ones feeding the younger ones large spoonfuls of that over-bearing lady's apple pie! I've never seen anything like it, no, never in a month of Sundays!" she said, scratching her head as she felt she had need of reemphasizing her considerable disbelief.

"Oh, pull the other one; it's got bells on it!" he scornfully remarked as he continued to empty the tin of dog meat into Pitstop's empty bowl.

"You don't believe me, do you?" she furiously challenged. "But if I'd come in here to tell you I'd just swallowed a whole camel along with its entrails, you'd probably find that much easier to believe."

"That's probably true, dearest," he apathetically responded.

"Well, so much for your great ability to judge!" she sneered.

"Forgive me, Mildred dearest, but this is truly one of your wildest stories to date. It certainly beggars all belief," he quickly retaliated.

"Well, if you truly believe this to be just some fanciful, made-up story, then please feel free to come see for yourself," she chided before turning on her heels to quickly leave the room.

"Oh, trust me, as soon as I'm done feeding Pitstop, we most surely will come down to their playroom to see for ourselves," he needlessly replied, for the now very disgruntled Mildred was long gone!

Chapter Thirty-Eight
THE LAND OF THE TIDDY OGGY

Meanwhile, back in Piadora the noise of great laughter was heard resounding throughout the entire kingdom as all in the land continued to enjoy Ralph's, or rather Lady Butterkist's, effortlessly eloquent yet absolutely riveting performance.

"Hodgekiss, Ralph really is superb at playing Lady Butterkist. He really has found his niche," one person cried out.

"Yes, and he is getting better by the minute," another member of the crowd shouted out.

"His antics are little short of hysterical," another voice joined in.

"Yes, you are all absolutely correct, for he has certainly become something of an all-around entertainer," Hodgekiss beamed. "But come, gather 'round and listen, for it is almost time for the next round of auditions to take place. Remember, we are still looking for someone to play the part of a very wise man. He will be required to speak with a believable cockney, yes, a real East End accent. He should be short and dumpy, and I think he should almost be bald. He also needs to be quick thinking, witty, yes, good with words, and given to cracking endless, very irritating jokes at the drop of a hat—yes, a bit of a wisecrack, really. And so, I think at the end of the day he should bear the title 'Mr. Wiseman.'"

The crowd was in uproar as they listened to the credentials that were necessary if they were to have any hope of getting the part.

"According to Mrs. O'Brien, who is standing right next to me, we have well over five thousand persons of interest who have put their name down for a chance to star in this interesting role. She also tells me that some

of you are feeling a trifle despondent, as this character will surely take many months to fully master. So let me encourage you by saying that you still have plenty time, as the final auditions are still many months away. Let me also just add that if you fail to get chosen for this part, there are still many other absorbing characters that have yet to be disclosed, characters such as the very Rev. Mumbo-Jumbo. Now, if after reading up on this character you believe yourself to be worthy of a tryout, then kindly put your name down, along with the briefest of comments as to why you think you are the perfect applicant for this special role. So, everybody, please keep up the rehearsals, for remember, practice makes perfect."

"Yes, we most surely will," the crowd gleefully roared.

"Oh, and before I forget, there is another wonderful role that I am about to cast."

"Ooh, tell us more," the delighted crowd cried.

"Well, I have the forms right in front of me for anyone wishing to audition for the part of Mr. Madgewick, the happiest man on Earth."

There was a great rumble, as the whole crowd moved forward to take a form as well as beg for the part.

"Much as I guessed, there is not one among you who could not easily play this particular role, for I need no reminding that you are all deliriously happy all of the time. Anyway, even though this particular audition might be considered by some as being perfunctory, we would still like to see who amongst you very happy people will play the part to its absolute best. I also promise these auditions will continue on until we have seen to it that everybody gets their moment of opportunity to shine and perhaps win a part in the next stage of Polly's very unpredictable, topsy-turvy life," Hodgekiss cheerfully informed his very attentive mixed bag of hopefuls.

"Oh, Hodgekiss, we are all so excited, for it is plainly obvious to all that we are in for a wealth of fun in the up-and-coming months," Mrs. O'Brien said, giving one of her deep and generous smiles.

"We certainly do have a lot to look forward to, Mrs. O'Brien. That we certainly do."

"Well, I'd best get back to my wonderful cookery class. The darling princesses are eager to get on with today's lesson, for they are all very excited about making their very first ever plum puddings."

"Before you go on your merry way, I have rarely seen such excitement at being a part of young Polly's next journey, so I have to warn now that as there are more applicants than ever wishing for a small part in this next, most critical intervention, we really do have our work cut out in choosing the perfect ones for the different roles," Hodgekiss quietly commented in Mrs. O'Brien's attentive ear.

"I agree, but we do have a number of months before she once again heads on another journey. So, there's time enough to practice, and up here we all love a hearty challenge, don't we? It also tickles me pink to think that most earthlings too readily believe that we sit around all day playing our harps so as not to die of boredom."

"Well, won't they be in for a big surprise when they finally depart Earth, only to discover the truth," Hodgekiss cheerfully commented, breaking into a warm smile. "All the same, it might be good for you to learn to play the harp."

"I very much doubt that! For Hodgekiss, as you well know, I have little spare time on my hands to even consider learning to play such a beautiful instrument," she mused. "Besides which, I've always been such a slow learner that it would be quite painful for anyone to listen as I practice."

"Well, that may be true, Mrs. O'Brien, but consider this: you do have the rest of eternity at your disposal to become an expert in this particular field of music."

"Trust me when I say that in my case, I don't believe even that time frame would nearly be long enough," she playfully retorted.

As soon as they were hurtling down the long and very winding lanes, Polly decided that this was an opportune moment to let out a deep sigh of relief.

"Well, Polly, my girl, you braved and mastered that ordeal and came through it triumphant, so well done. Now let us forget your guardians and the castle, and distance ourselves from every sorely unpleasant memory so that we can thoroughly enjoy and thus appreciate this unexpected gift of a holiday. So, sit back and enjoy the ride. Is Tiddles sitting comfortably?"

"Yes, she's safe and happy," the girls replied.

Giles also breathed the deepest sigh. "I thought you'd never come back and rescue us from that insufferable hedonistic and hideously smarmy man," Giles cheerfully confessed. "I feel so soiled that I find myself with the urgent need to throw myself into the shower and scrub myself down, as well as throw my clothes into a washing machine, for I feel so terribly soiled by my time in his presence."

"Well, Giles dear, I understand fully and so share your sentiments. I cannot thank you enough for escorting me. You are such a wonderful support and companion. When we arrive at our destiny, there will be plenty of opportunity for a shower and change of clothes. And, in light of all you have just shared, let me remind you that we only paid a short visit, but Polly and the other children, they live under his regime every day of their lives—and I might add, with no relief. So we must count our blessings and do all we can to find a way into the other children's young but atrociously dark lives."

"You're absolutely right, madam."

"Right. Allow me to tell both you girls that our journey will be long, so I have taken the trouble of booking us into a very nice bed-and-breakfast for the night," she stated as she turned her head to address the girls, who were sitting stretched-out, looking very relaxed and happy on the backseat of the car.

"As Boritz cared to hint, the roads are too dangerous and narrow, so I think we should be mindful of all this. Hmm, yes, we would do well to err on the side of caution," she advised.

It would be less than an hour before they pulled off the road, and after going down a short, very bumpy lane, they arrived outside the bed-and-breakfast.

"Oh, Lucy, take a good look, for the house is all lit up with beautiful outside lights," a wide-eyed Polly cried.

"Ahh, yes. Girls, here we are at Mistletoe Cottage. Oh, how I love this gorgeous and so special place. So come on, girls. Hop out of the car, and let's go inside and introduce ourselves, shall we?"

In no time at all they were comfortably settled in, with the girls extremely happy to discover they were sharing a bedroom all to themselves. Giles headed down the corridor toward his room, and Lady Butterkist informed both girls that she would be in the room right next to them.

"I am just a hair's breadth away if you need me. But kindly remember that these walls are astonishingly paper thin, so no girlish giggling or pillow fights tonight, for we are all in dire need of some beauty sleep. Yes, girls, may I take the time to remind that lack of sleep produces spots. I will give you both a whole twenty minutes to quickly freshen up, and then we must head downstairs to the dining hall for a spot of supper before we head back upstairs to retire for the night. Here, Tiddles. You come with me," she cried.

After tucking into a hearty roast chicken dinner followed by strawberry trifle covered with thick whipped cream, they all said their weary good-nights and headed off to bed.

The next morning, as requested by Lady B., they all arose early, and after a very satisfying full English breakfast, they made plans to continue on with their journey.

Giles, with a red pen in hand, considerately began marking a few places on his laid-out map that would appear to be excellent places to stop for refreshments. Lady Butterkist then got up and quietly disappeared, as she wished to hand back the bedroom keys and settle up the bill with the head receptionist before continuing on with their journey—heading toward the Devon Coast and then farther down toward delightful Cornwall.

By midmorning the sun was shining so brightly that Lady Butterkist demanded that Blenkinsopp pull over in order to pull down the roof.

"Simply splendid! That's much better. Now we can breathe in the fresh country air and at the same time fully engage ourselves in God's creation as we further delight in the glorious countryside while listening to the birds singing in the trees and hedgerows. Oh, I know I say it every time, but I will surely never tire of the breathtaking beauty of our wonderful English countryside," she very contentedly sighed.

On the way down to the west country they all joined in to play I Spy, and when they grew tired of that game, they chose to sing their heart out with every single song that came to mind. Polly was very surprised to discover that dear Giles, or Blenkinsopp, as he was often called by her ladyship, had an extremely good voice. She was also equally surprised to discover that he was very up to date when it came to who was in and who was out where pop songs were concerned. Yes, amazing as it might sound, he knew which group was number one in the charts; in fact, he was more than able to recite the whole top twenty!

Polly and Lucy sang and giggled, then giggled and sang as they sat huddled together in the back with Tiddles, and cranking along, the old jalopy slowly made its journey down one picturesque country lane after another.

Early afternoon came, and Lady Butterkist confirmed to all that they were well over halfway toward arriving at their destination. She also announced that despite her hearty breakfast, she was once more feeling pretty famished, and so she suggested that they make a quick stop at a pretty English teahouse. In no time at all they were munching their way through thickly buttered crumpets, followed by hot scones smothered with warm lemon curd or strawberry jam and then piled high with tablespoons of thick clotted cream. This was happily washed down with endless cups of steaming tea.

An excited Polly took hold of her serviette and immediately tucked it under her chin like an infant's bib.

"Child, what are you doing?" Lady Butterkist asked, a look of horror written all over her face.

"Why, I'm tucking in my serviette to prevent any spillages from ruining my clothes," Polly innocently replied.

"Well, child, kindly remove the serviette from under your chin, and delicately place it on your lap, for that is where it belongs."

"Oh!"

"That is, unless you're something of a swarthy, string-vested Italian about to launch into a bowl of meat sauce and spaghetti, in which case, to place your serviette under your chin becomes almost forgivable."

"Yes, Lady B."

"There. That's much better. I do believe you, my little princess, are in urgent need of some useful etiquette lessons, or you'll never get to go to the ball," Lady B. sniffed.

Polly secretly smiled as, after placing the serviette on her lap, it promptly slid down onto the floor and came to rest by her feet. At first she pretended not to notice, but minutes later found her giving the serviette a quick kick under the table. Luckily for her, Lady Butterkist was well away with the stars reveling in the joys that an English high tea brings.

"Oh, these walnut and raspberry scones are absolutely *spondelicious*," her ladyship loudly announced. Everyone at the table quickly agreed.

"Lady Butterkist, do be an angel and pass me the sugar bowl," Giles politely requested. "Oh, and while I'm at it, madam, I've said it before, but I promise that *spondelicious* is not a genuine word."

"Oh really?"

"Yes, I know, for I have taken the liberty of checking with my English dictionary."

"Oh, Blenkinsopp, don't be such a mischievously analytical heretic; there is simply no other word I know that can go anywhere near describing these wonderful scones. So *spondelicious* might not be a word in your books, but it is in mine. So there," she snorted as she then munched into another scone piled mountain high with clotted cream.

With a mouthful of scone still not swallowed, Polly began to laugh and giggle at Lady Butterkist's playful dispute with Giles, at the same time inadvertently spraying the table with crumbs from her mouth.

She then turned to Lucy to announce that for the first time in her life she was feeling as free as a bird.

"Polly, do be a dear and close your mouth while you're eating, for it's not very ladylike to have glimpses of your half-eaten food churning around in a manner much similar to that of your smalls spinning in the washtub."

"Oops! Forgive me," Polly cried, accidentally spraying the table with yet more crumbs of her half-eaten scone.

"Me too, Polly!" Lucy cried. "I know this break has only just begun, but already I am wishing that it would never come to an end."

"All right, young ladies. If you're finished, then I propose that we all pay a quick trip to the little girls' room to freshen up. Oh, and Blenkinsopp, would you then be a dear by escorting both girls and Tiddles here back to the car, and I will follow on shortly?"

"Yes, madam."

"I have just one teeny weenie but all the same urgent phone call that I need to make, and then we can be on our merry way."

"All well and good, madam."

"Girls, the good news is that we are less than two hours away from our final destination, so go with Giles, and I will be back before you can say, 'Is there any mustard in this custard?'"

Chapter Thirty-Nine
POOR, POOR DR. NINKUMPOOP

WITH DEEPLY CONTENTED hearts and thoroughly satisfied stomachs, the girls happily rested in the back of the car, closing their eyes and allowing the fresh breeze to playfully caress their hair while the mellow sun preferred to kiss and taunt their fair, dimpled cheeks with its gentle, comforting rays of warmth.

Moments later found both girls fast asleep.

"Bless their little cotton socks. They look like a pair of angels out for the count after arriving back from some roller-coaster assignment," Giles cheerfully commented.

"Sounds more like us," her ladyship replied very tongue in cheek. "Personally, I think it is good for both of them to have this little opportunity for a cat nap, as I am a firm believer that sleep does much to restore our minds and bodies, and the poor darlings have gone through much tribulation these past months."

"That's very true," Giles commiserated. "So tell me straight, Lady B., am I correct in my presumption that your little phone call had much to do with finding out firsthand how the ribbon-cutting event panned out at the hospital gala?" he asked, turning to deliberately look her directly in the eye.

"Oh, Giles Blenkinsopp, you don't miss a thing! You're a naughty little rascal for asking me such things; however, as the girls are sound asleep, I suppose that now is as good a time as any to reveal all."

"Oh, please do!" he cried with the keenest sense of urgency.

"Well, much as I suspected, I'm afraid things did not go that well at all."

"Quite what do you mean? Come along, don't lead me up a blind alley, for it's time to spill all the beans," he cried. "Did Freddie fail to turn up?"

"Oh, no. He turned up all right, but sadly he was legless before he even got out of his car."

"What do you mean by 'legless'?"

"Oh, far too much drinky-poohs, Giles."

"You mean he was inebriated, madam? As in, worse for the wear?"

"Yes, Giles, as drunk as a skunk on a pirate's ship, to be more precise! For, sad to say, there was nothing whatsoever redeemable about him that day. He was sadly very much worse for the wear, as well as high as a kite on every imaginable and highly suspect medication."

"Goodness gracious me! Well, in light of all you have cared to share, did he even manage to stand up straight long enough to cut the ribbon?"

"Well, I believe he did, but there was a lot of upset and commotion surrounding the whole ghastly event."

"Oh, deary me. How unbelievably atrocious! Lady B., perhaps at the end of the day we were wrong to back out of this special ceremony," Giles woefully commented.

"No, Giles. We were perfectly within our rights to cancel our attendance, for sometimes there are other, more important things that need to be exposed."

"Yes, I'm sure you're right, madam."

"For one thing, Freddie needs to face some frightfully critical issues before it becomes far too late, as do certain others who only out of respect I do not care to name or mention. So if nothing else, this day should surely encourage many of those in attendance to take a hard and honest look at themselves."

"I'm sure they will, madam."

"Hmm. Rather sadly for all concerned, there was a great deal of camera footage gathered. Apparently it will all be aired as one of tonight's main news items, which, I might add, in view of all that has taken place, they have now decided to extend with a view to giving this top story the extra coverage they believe it deserves."

"Gosh! For if this is the case, then I suspect that you, madam, are holding things back and so have not finished revealing everything that you know. So break with tradition by telling me, your devoted butler, the whole gruesome story, and this time leave nothing out. Let me start by asking, Did Freddie go on to wreck the whole event?"

"Hmm. Sadly, he did, for outrageous as it all may seem, he went on to further disgrace himself by swearing at the town's delightful mayor. He then threw a full glass of Don Pérignon champagne over two most innocent and unsuspecting bystanders."

"Good grief! That stuff's so terribly expensive!"

"I should say so, for *grief* does not even begin to sum up the sheer horror concerning the events of that day, as—wait for it—he then went on to manhandle and assault a photographer, and in the fracas an empty bottle accidentally hit Mr. Scumberry's poor, sensitive wife, Mildred, leaving her nursing the most terrible bleeding nose."

"Shocking. Absolutely shocking!" Giles warily muttered.

"Oh, it was indeed most brutal, for according to the nurse that I spoke with, she bled so badly down her clothing that the dry cleaning shop has sadly reported back that her heavily sequined dress is quite beyond any form of salvation. Yes, as unbelievable as all this must seem, the dress is entirely ruined."

"Poor, poor Mildred!"

"My sentiments entirely, for to have a bad nosebleed is one thing, but to allow it to utterly ruin your most expensive posh party dress can only be considered preposterously disastrous!"

"Madam, this is all so utterly absurd!" Giles heavily sighed as he dutifully raised his eyes to the heavens as though he were seeking a divine answer to the question now uppermost in his thoughts. "Where will it all end?"

"Who knows, Giles dear? Who knows?" she loudly tutted, shaking her head at the same time.

"Oh, and then to crown it all, I'll have you know that he left poor Dr. Ninkumpoop nursing an almighty black eye."

"Oh my goodness! All this in the space of just a couple of hours?"

"Oh, no. This all transpired within the first twenty minutes or so! Yes, Freddie staggered into the hospital with a very unfortunate-looking girl on his arm, one who I might dare suggest was not at all appropriately dressed for such an important occasion as this."

Giles shook his head violently as he tried hard to hurriedly vacate his mind of his personal interpretation of what the poor girl might, or rather might not, have been wearing!

"Giles, are you still listening?

"Oh absolutely, madam. Absolutely."

"Well, he then rather outrageously demanded a couple of glasses of champers before the ceremony even got underway. Hmm, and while trying to cut the ribbon with those ridiculously huge scissors, he crashed to the floor, taking a poor, innocent nurse down with him."

"Goodness gracious me. How utterly distressing for all concerned!"

"Yes, dreadful. And to cap it all, throughout the whole terrible incident his language was both crass and unbelievably foul, to say the least."

"Good grief," was all Giles now cared to comment.

"Well, according to the nurse I spoke with this morning, no word has yet been created that could even begin to express the level of anxiety and disruption this man has unfortunately caused.

"Sadly for Freddie, he was taken away in handcuffs to spend the night in a cell, and as far as I am aware, he will remain locked away behind bars until he faces the full wrath of a circuit judge, next Tuesday, I believe."

"Not the best way to end the day," Blenkinsopp muttered.

"I should say so, for he will surely need that dear judge not only to be very understanding but also in excellent humor if he is to even consider extending an unwarranted amount of mercy toward him."

"Well, let's hope that the judge has a good wife who on Tuesday morning lovingly decides to bless him with a hearty cooked breakfast, for a filled belly surely makes for a full heart, and if so, he might well be far more lenient in his sentencing."

"But Giles, my man, it doesn't even end there, for there is still more to tell."

"More! Tell me how possibly could there be more to this already very disturbing story?" he asked, shaking his head to convey his total and utter disbelief.

"Trust me when I say there is always more," she said in a very smug tone of voice. "During my phone conversation, the distraught nurse dared to confide that for his part, poor Dr. Ninkumpoop has chosen to lock himself away in one of the hospital's many padded cells with only his professional diaries and personal memoirs for comfort."

"Well then, shame on the man," a shocked Giles muttered, "for at the very least he too is guilty of gross professional misconduct."

"Giles, be a dear and try not to be so hard on him."

"Madam, it's hard not to be critical, for things really couldn't get much worse!"

"Oh, Giles dear, don't be so irresponsibly trite, for sadly, things can get much worse, and often do, although I'm not entirely sure whether this is the right time to reveal anything further of this incredible but seriously ghastly story."

"Madam, I beg you now, please do. It is not the least bit fair to leave me hanging on like this, for the suspense alone is almost killing me."

"Oh, very well then. If you insist."

"I do, madam. I must insist you reveal all."

"Well, at the time of my phone conversation, and mind, this is all according to the nigh hysterical nurse on the other end of the telephone..."

"Keep going!"

"Well, as a direct result of all that has taken place..."

"Yes, yes. Go on."

"He has rather inexplicably chosen to abandon his expensive suit, as well as—dare I say it?—all undergarments!" she revealed in little more than a prudish whisper, closing her eyes at the same time in order to fully express the seriousness of this latest, very unpredictable action.

"What? He has removed all his clothing?"

"Yes. Every single stitch!"

"Madam, are you serious?"

"Very!"

"You mean, he's entirely...utterly naked."

"Absolutely!"

"Socks as well?"

"Giles, what difference would it make if he were or were not still wearing his socks?"

"Nothing, madam, except I would like to humbly suggest that, were his socks still covering his feet, his nakedness wouldn't seem quite so entire, would it?"

"Well, whether he has socks on his little tootsies or not, he's now as footloose and fancy free as the day he came into the world. So I have no choice but to conclude that something has gone seriously wrong for the poor man, for to not only shun those around him by locking himself away but to then discard every single item of his clothing, socks included, well, that is something else entirely!"

"Then he's clearly gone cuckoo!" Blenkinsopp added.

"That is not for you or I to judge. But sadly there is much cause for concern, as between bouts of incoherent mutterings and hysterical laughter he is still adamantly refusing to unlock the door or speak with anyone. Such is his demise. It is all rather unfortunate. Really it is," she mumbled. "Especially when you hear that there is already talk of using ECT in an attempt to quickly and forcibly shock him back to reality."

"Hmm. How utterly awful! Although, tell me truthfully, madam, if the hospital's top psychiatrist has finally lost his marbles, then pray, tell me, who is left to help him—or anyone else, for that matter?"

"Quite!"

"Well, this is surely one of the most sad and thoroughly disturbing stories I have heard in a long while."

"Yes, Blenkinsopp, one can only begin to imagine the catastrophic damage to many a distinguished reputation such a tragic and unfortunate day as this will almost certainly bring."

"Madam, are you sure that all of this rather unfortunate saga was caught on camera?"

"Yes, and sadly we all know that a camera rarely lies."

Chapter Forty
LET'S GET SAND BETWEEN OUR TOES

*T*HE GIRLS REMAINED fast asleep as the car slowly made its way along the glorious Devonshire coastline.

"The calm, blue sea looks so impressively inviting, so I would so love to dip a toe or two in those waters," Lady Butterkist brightly commented.

"So would I, madam, but that little pleasure will have to wait a while, as we need to plod on toward our goal, so to speak."

"Yes, I know. But still it would be so awfully nice," she sighed.

Moments later found the car precariously perched on a cliff top, as Lady Butterkist was absolutely insistent in her belief that she had espied a less trodden route that would have her safely down on the beach in no time at all.

"Giles, I will only be gone for a teeny weenie amount of time. Yes, just five minutes or so," she readily assured him.

Giles, who knew better, agreed to remain by the car and keep a constant vigil over the car and the two sleeping beauties, who continued to remain lost to the world on the backseat.

Twenty-five minutes later found a windswept Lady Butterkist struggling hard to make it back up the path due to a fully laden bucket of shells that prevented her from using both hands in order to keep her balance.

"I'm back. I'm back," she shouted as she suddenly appeared over the horizon.

"So I can see, dear lady. So I can see," Giles muttered as he moved forward to rescue her ladyship in case she accidentally lost her footing and toppled over the cliff, which, he could see, would be quite imminent if he failed in his duty to give immediate assistance.

"I thought the girls would like these very pretty seashells," she breathlessly cried.

"Yes, but from where and from whom did you manage to obtain that rather snazzy holiday bucket?"

"Well, rather lucky for me it lay abandoned by a large fortress sand-castle. I assure you, I waited and waited, but there was nobody in sight. So, eventually I decided to help myself. I thought it to be the perfect receptacle for placing these very delightful shells. Here, Blenkinsopp, would you like some?"

"That's most thoughtful of you, madam, but unbelievable as this may seem, seashells really aren't my thing, at least not at the moment."

"Oh, so you never stick them on cards, paint them bright colors, place them 'round the bathtub, or—"

"No, madam. Do I really need to repeat myself? Seashells are not my thing," he firmly stated, quite exasperated. "Now, golf balls, well, that's an entirely different matter."

"Well, I'm sorry, Giles, but try as I may, I can't for one minute imagine what a load of golf balls strategically placed around a bathtub would even begin to look like," she snorted.

Giles raised his eyes to the heavens and very wisely chose to keep his lips tightly buttoned.

With her ladyship safely back in her seat, Giles started up the car, and they continued on their journey.

"There must have been something in that drink you gave the girls earlier, for they look like heavily sedated babes in the wood."

"Well, Blenkinsopp, now you come to mention it, I did pop a bit of sap from the Hubber Blubber tree in their early morning cup of tea."

"Madam, I thought as much."

"Yes, but I was much more careful how much I put in this time 'round."

"Huh!"

"Yes, the last time I used this potion I think I got a little bit carried away. Yes, it was back at the castle when I needed to sedate Pitstop, that vicious pit bull of a dog, and if I'm to be honest I think I put a bit too much in his dog food, for I hear they had to use a crane to lift the poor dog from off poor Boritz. Hmm. Another rather unfortunate episode," she declared, drawing in her breath.

"Oh, madam, what were we thinking?"

"Precisely, Blenkinsopp, although it was necessary to sedate both girls to ensure that our secret hideout remains just that—yes, a complete secret. It would be most unfortunate if any of them were to ever be discovered, for it would indeed hinder our work down here and make it all the more difficult than it already is."

"Yes, I agree. This way we are on call to help and heal, and happily nobody suspects a thing."

"Precisely, Blenkinsopp. Precisely."

"Well, milady, as the girls are still deep in the land of nod, may I be so bold as to ask you about something that is bothering me so terribly?"

"I'm all ears, Giles."

"Well, we have seen dear Dr. Ninkumpoop's terribly sad demise."

"Indeed we have, for as that little saying goes, 'Oh, how the mighty have fallen.'"

"Yes, but what of the disgracefully avaricious Scumberrys? Surely their wickedness and deceit far exceed anything the poor doctor might or might not have done."

"You're absolutely correct, but there you go again, Giles, making hasty judgments as though you alone are the officially recognized barometer that decides just how bad an action truly is and therefore who deserves the most punishment. We were never given this task, and so it never ceases to amaze me as to just how easily as well as quickly we take it upon ourselves to become the lawful adjudicators of all we meet. Anyway, where the Scumberrys are concerned, I would ask you to trust me when I say I know my onions!"

"But, milady, how can you ever justify defending that couple of extraordinarily wicked buffoons?" he snorted.

"Well, Blenkinsopp, my dear, after all is said and done, this is the most classic case of *folie à deux* I've witnessed in many a year."

"*Folie a what*, madam?"

"Really, Giles, sometimes I think you're quite an ignoramus when it comes to the more refined things in life," she snorted.

"Well, madam, you of all people would know."

"Well, Giles, simply put, *folie à deux* is French for 'a madness shared by two people'!"

"My goodness, Lady B. You leave me utterly speechless, for this must surely be the perfect way to describe this dreadful couple, although, I have to add, when you use French, it does make you sound unbelievably hoity-toity!"

"Why, thank you, Blenkinsopp. I shall indeed take that as a compliment. I also feel that I must remind you once again that ours is not to judge; all we can do is watch and wait and see how this, as well as other matters, will lie. But I beg you to understand me when I say there really is method in my madness, for I promise you that despite all appearances to the contrary, I am absolutely on top of this one."

"Really?"

"Yes, really. I will take this occasion to also remark that there are those amongst us that cannot face any form of mild correction, so it would not matter how far they fell; they would still fail take heed or change their ways, for they have no conscience whatsoever. They have renegade spirits, as well as a seared conscience. Take Freddie, for instance. He might well fall into that category; however, time alone will tell all," she counseled.

"Yes, but in some ways Freddie is little more than a harmless, self-destructive old fool who is mainly hurting himself, but that is surely not the case where those awful, sycophantic scavengers the Scumberrys are concerned," he mournfully sighed.

"Now, now, Blenkinsopp. Your words are not only condemning but are beginning to sound most uncharitable. So I must once again remind you it is not for us to judge, for only heaven knows the answer to this one," she commiserated.

"Well, it all leaves me utterly flummoxed as to why in the light of all you know and have observed you still insist on offering financial assistance when it is obvious to all that the only ones who will benefit from the money will be that rather beastly couple. Yes, as none of those poor, deprived children are likely to gain anything from your kindness; it really makes absolutely no sense at all to me," he loudly murmured.

"Giles, clearly it doesn't, but answer me this, have I parted with any money yet? Did you see me write out a check?"

"No, but…"

"No buts. Did you or did you not see me place a signed check directly into his greedy and grubby little paws?"

"No, but you did promise to do so on your return."

"How observant you are, for indeed I did promise just that."

"Well then, as you are not prone or given to lying, you will of course keep your word, for may I have occasion to remind you that a man's word is indeed his bond."

"Oh, and I fully intend to," she quickly retorted.

"Milady, you are once more fooling with my mind, for I might not be the sharpest knife in the drawer, but am I to believe that you still fully intend to give great financial assistance to one of the most corrupt and unmerciful couples I have ever had the misfortune of meeting?"

"Oh, Giles. Have a little more faith in me. Do not presume anything! Yes, it is true I will always honor my word, and if in this case it means writing out a very substantial check, then so be it."

"Uh!"

"Yes, but as to what becomes of that check, well, that is an entirely different matter."

"Milady, are you suggesting he might well lose or mislay it?"

"Enough said! Just wait and see how this matter will lie, and know this, Giles: we might live our lives thinking we can get away with wicked and unlawful things, but at the end of the day, time alone has an uncanny way of catching up with us. Believe you me."

"Madam, I believe I do," he lightheartedly chuckled.

"Now, I do believe I recognize that little church with its pretty steeple, and if so, then happily we are just a matter of minutes away from our desired destination."

Chapter Forty-One
YOU NEVER MESS WITH DEAR AUNT BESS

*T*HE CAR SWERVED up the long, winding drive and came to a halt outside a very large thatch-roofed cottage.

"Ahh. Finally we have arrived. Oh, how I simply adore this very special place," Lady Butterkist gleefully cried.

As she waited for Giles to come around the car to open her side of the car, a large, very buxom lady dressed in a long apron that went way past her knees rushed down some steps to greet them.

"Ralph, I mean, Lady Ralphella, how lovely to see you, for it's been such a long time since you were last here," she joyfully cried as Lady Butterkist stepped out of the car and then moved forward to greet her.

"I believe you're quite right, Aunt Bessie," she said, giving her a friendly hug. "It's been a long time, and I have really missed you, as well as this wonderful place."

"Now, then. Are these two darlin' little sleeping beauties the ones you told me about?" she said, placing her head right up to the window to take a quick peek.

"They are indeed."

"Oh, they look like such angelic little cherubs," the rosy-cheeked lady declared.

"Well, I hope you will still be seeing them in the same light by the end of their stay," Lady Butterkist playfully commented.

"Needless to say, but I'm sure I will, for we normally get all the fight out of them in a matter of days," Aunt Bessie retorted.

"Yes, I for one wouldn't want to square up against you, Aunt Bessie. That's for sure," Giles cheekily commented.

"Giles, forgive me, for I didn't mean to ignore you. How are you doing?" the kindly lady with the rosy cheeks and graying, silver hair asked as she pushed an extra grip into the bun on the back of her head to ensure that it remained secure before reaching out to give him a firm hug.

"Well, Aunt Bessie, I have to concede to really enjoying being a chauffeur and butler, but there are times when Ralph, or rather, Lady Butterkist, can and regularly does overstep the mark, if you know what I mean."

"You bet I do," she replied, giving a loud, hearty laugh. "But don't you worry or fret, luv, because if she gets too big for her boots, come and find me, for I have a number of large rolling pins at the ready," she quipped, her deep voice betraying her Cornish heritage.

"I might just take you up on that," he quickly retorted.

As the girls were still sound asleep, they were carried up to their bedroom by staff members of the household and quickly tucked into their beds.

Lady B. watched on as Aunt Bessie gave both of them a light kiss on the forehead before switching off the bedside lamp.

"Bless their little cotton socks, they are so out for the count that to tell truth, you'd be forgiven for thinking they'd really kicked the bucket," she rather wickedly remarked.

"Really, Aunt Bessie!" Lady B. giggled.

"Well, they are so sound asleep that they will probably not wake till the cock crows in the morn'," she sighed as she closed the door of their room.

As Lady Butterkist joined Aunt Bessie in heading down the stairs toward the kitchen, she used this moment in time to fill her in on everything she thought might be helpful regarding both girls.

"Aunt Bessie, they have both been through an awful lot, and so I imagine in the days to come there might, well, be a few tantrums and tears."

"Oh, I'm quite sure there will be, and don't worry, 'cos I'm quite used to that."

"Well, allow me to also inform you that the girls are suffering from a hideous lack of self-worth. Both girls believe they are useless and ugly, and as for dear Polly, why, she recently confessed to me that if she looks in the mirror, she sees nothing but a hoary monster looking back at her."

"Goodness gracious me! We certainly have our work cut out for us, don't we?"

"Lucinda is not much better, and it is only thanks to the sap of the Hoolie Koolie and Hubber Blubber that her wrist wounds are entirely healed. I fear her mind and heart will take considerably longer."

"Well, you've certainly brought them to the right place, for I intend to love on both girls," the large, bubbly lady with the silver bun and kind wrinkles cried.

"Yes, let me assure you, Aunt Bessie, that both girls have a real propensity toward becoming proper young ladies, and they truly do deserve our help."

"Trust me, Lady B., by the time they leave here, they will believe themselves to be princesses. We will work really hard to give them a new image of themselves," she reassured.

"Splendid! Now let me ask you, Aunt Bessie, how many other girls and boys are staying at the house at present?"

"Well, let's see. At last count we had eight boys ranging from thirteen to sixteen and nine girls, Polly and Lucy included."

"Wonderful, then they will have plenty of time to make other friendships," Lady Butterkist commented.

"Oh, yes. Definitely. Mind, we do work them hard, school work included, but we also play hard too. By the time the sun goes down, there are no arguments about bedtimes, for by the end of each workday they are all ready and eager to just flop into bed," she said, giving a quirky smile. "At present we are bringing in the daffodils. Then we'll be pickin' the apples and cherries down in orchards. Then there's the barley and wheat harvest, and so it goes on."

"Good."

"Yes, I'm glad to say that God's fertile earth just keeps on giving us an overabundance of crops, and all He requires is for us to show up to sow and then till the land," she said in her deep Cornish accent.

"Tell me, Aunt Bessie, how is the animal sanctuary doing?"

"Well, it's as full as the house, for sadly, just like these children, animals are equally at the mercy of humans, who can be so intolerably cruel."

"Yes, it really does beggar belief," Lady B. sighed.

"Come see our latest addition. He's a wonderful ol' horse named Boxer who has been here for nigh on three weeks. His scars, mind, are more than visible to the naked eye, and if you look him straight in eye, it is clear he has been through much. I figure it may well be a good thing to allow Polly to befriend and nurture him."

"Sounds good to me."

"Then we have a wonderful Scotch border collie we've renamed Lassie who also is severely traumatized, and so I thought it would be good to entrust her to the care of dear Lucinda."

"Aunt Bessie, it all makes my heart bleed, truly it does, for it is so very sad."

"Yes, but want to know something? As they care for and nurture these poor, darling animals, it quietly does a tremendous healing work on all parties concerned."

"I couldn't agree more, and Aunt Bessie, I would be eternally grateful if you could find the time to once again show me around the animal sanctuary so that I can familiarize myself with all the new animals that have recently been rescued and brought here."

"Oh absolutely, Lady B., but before I take you 'round, I would like for us to find Giles and the rest of my staff. We can all sit down for a hearty supper of steak and mushroom pie served with tatties and other fresh vegetables and also plentiful crusty, home-baked bread. This will be followed on by apple and black currant crumble with thick, creamy custard. Oh, and a large dollop of clotted cream."

"Oh, it all sounds simply splendid to me," Lady Butterkist enthused, "and I have always loved your homemade bread in particular."

"Why, thank you, Lady B. Mind it's probably 'cos it's full of healthy goodness with naught taken out."

That night Aunt Bessie could easily have served up anything she cared to, boiled beetle stew and slithering snake fritters included. I'm happy to say that on this occasion neither of these grotesque and unfamiliar dishes were on the menu, but if they had been, then they would probably have been enjoyed by everybody present as they believed it to be yet further evidence of Aunt Bessie's highly imaginative and very creative cookery skills at work.

I think it is also true to say that much more than the sumptuous food was the glorious and intimate fellowship of likeminded hearts and souls whose abundant laughter, like heady perfume, thronged the air above, for no price tag could ever be put on that. They therefore sat at the table for hours on end while all participants were given their fair share of airspace to talk of anything they cared. They lucidly shared personal stories of heartache and, likewise, stories of great joy, and it was as though none at the long table wished to spoil the magical atmosphere by being first to bid good night and leave to head off in the direction of bed.

Finally, with the hour bending nearer toward dawn, they reached an agreement that all remaining stories still needing to be told should be stored away until the next evening, and they should all, without further delay, quickly head off to their bedchambers.

On the way up the stairs Lady Butterkist turned to ask a great favor of Aunt Bessie.

"Aunt Bessie, I need your help."

"Doesn't everybody?" she replied, giving a wry smile.

"Yes, but I know that that you were once a very gifted seamstress."

"So I am most humbly led to believe, although in all fairness I have to add that most who bestow on me such gracious words of affection usually need my help with something they are unable to restitch, adjust, or sew," she very good-humoredly stated.

"Well, I would really appreciate your kind help regarding my little problem. I brought this special dress, along with the shoes and tiara, for dear Polly. However, to my utter amazement, later on that same day I witnessed another child wearing the whole attire. I was very troubled and asked their guardian for the whole ensemble to be returned. It came as no surprise when perusing the bag I quickly discovered that the child, in a jealous fit of rage, had tried hard to destroy the outfit. As a result of this tantrum, the dress needs serious attention, as do the shoes. Luckily I bought an extra identical tiara, so hopefully Polly can still remain blissfully unaware of the horrible damage that has willfully been done to her prized possessions."

"All right, Mrs. B. If you care to leave the contents of the bag with me, then the first spare moment I get I will take a good look for myself. Hmm. I can probably do wonders with the dress, and I believe I can also save the shoes. So leave them with me, and you'll have them back well before the first of many parties takes place."

"Aunt Bessie, you are a real godsend."

"Keep telling me, my dear. Keep telling me."

"Oh, rest assured I will, and I bid you a well-earned peaceful night. Good night, and God bless," Lady Butterkist whispered, as with her shoes in her hand she tiptoed down the corridor toward her room.

"God bless you too, dear. I hope your bed feels real comfy, and I'll see you sometime after cock crows in morn'," Aunt Bessie whispered back.

<hr />

The next morning the girls were gently awoken by reams of glorious sunlight streaming across their pillows.

"Lucy, get up and come and look out of this window. Quick, make haste, for the view is really indescribably beautiful."

Lucy leapt from her bed and raced over to join Polly at the window. "Gosh, you're right, Polly. It looks so absolutely gorgeous that I just want to run wild and free through those meadows and pick as many wildflowers as I possibly can."

As they stood by the window savoring the view, Aunt Bessie gave a hard knock and then poked her head around the door.

"Well, me luvies, as of yet you don't know me, but the name by which I answer is Aunt Bessie, and I'll be the one looking after both you lovely lasses," she said with a hearty, warm grin. "You were both fast asleep when you arrived here in the dead of night, so I didn't get the opportunity to introduce myself or my small team of staff. But if after getting washed and dressed you'll come with me, I will take you downstairs for breakfast and introduce you to all the other youngsters, as well as the rest of my wonderful staff. How does that sound?"

Both girls broke into a smile and readily agreed.

"So chop chop. The bathroom is through that door, and there are some fresh clothes, as well as a soft 'n' fluffy bath towel, on the end of both beds. I'll be back before you can say, 'Jack Robinson,' so you'd best get yourselves bathed straight away," she drawled as she then quietly closed the door behind her.

"She seems awfully nice, although I do declare that she is most difficult to understand," Lucy stated as she picked up a thick, fluffy towel and demurely waltzed toward the bathroom.

"Yes, I know her accent is so thick that you have to listen really hard. They also say words quite differently. I suppose it's the Cornish way. Hmm. But setting that aside, you're absolutely right, Lucy; I do believe we are going to like it here—very much, yes, very much," she mused.

With both girls washed and dressed, they had less than a spare minute before Aunt Bessie, true to her word, returned to the room to collect them.

"Well, luvies, you both look as pretty as a picture, and I hope you've given your teeth a good scrub as well as brushed your hair."

"Yes, we have," they both grinned.

"Then both of you's smell mighty fine to me," she said, sniffing the air. "So, no more time for idle chitchat. You'd best follow after me."

Having gone down a steep flight of stairs, they turned a corner, and then Aunt Bessie pushed open a door and beckoned for both girls to follow her into the kitchen.

As they stood in the large kitchen, Polly's attention immediately fell on the huge cooking stove that had numerous pots boiling and bubbling away. Her eyes then fell onto a sea of unrecognizable children's faces as they sat around two or three long farmhouse tables. Polly was immediately relieved to see Lady Butterkist sitting at the end of one of the long pine tables with Giles to her left and Tiddles to her right, as the pooch was securely strapped into an infant high chair with a bib around her neck as she too waited impatiently for her breakfast to come.

"Polly and Lucinda, I insist that you come over here and join us," Lady Butterkist beckoned as she pointed to two vacant seats.

"Lady B., behave yourself, for you're in my kitchen now, so I give the orders," Aunt Bessie said very lightheartedly. "I need to introduce them to all my staff, as well as the other children before they sit down," Aunt Bessie said as she continued to show who was boss of this establishment by overruling her ladyship.

"Right. Listen up, everybody! Please allow me to introduce our two newest members of the family. Everybody, this is Polly, and this is Lucinda. Both girls will be with us till there's naught left in fields to harvest. Then they will leave to return home in time for the new school year, so I believe that time to be early September. Am I correct, Lady B.?"

"Indeed you are, Aunt Bessie."

"Well then, girls and boys, please make Polly and Lucinda feel at home by coming up after breakfast to quickly introduce yourselves. Also, as they are new here, they probably feel a little nervous and unsure as to quite what is expected of them. This is where you all fit in, for they might well need your help on some things. I ask you kindly to please do all within your power to make them feel as welcome as you yourselves were made to feel when you first set a foot in this here place."

Polly chose this moment to give all the children a friendly wave, and they all broke into clapping their hands before waving back at the girls.

"Oh, Lucy, I already feel so at home in this place," Polly quietly whispered in Lucy's available ear.

"Me too, Polly. Me too."

The girls were introduced to Aunt Bessie's friendly and very lively team of helpers—Tim, Tom, Tessa, and Molly. Polly could not fail to discern that each and every one of them not only had a truly caring manner, but they all had just as healthy an appetite for good, old-fashioned fun.

———

Over the next few months, Polly and Lucy would work hard as they joined other youngsters in gathering and preparing daffodils to be sold at the local market in the old town square. When they needed a rest, they would simply upturn their metal buckets and sit watching the old women with their deeply lined, sun-scorched faces, their heads covered with scarves, as they came up to the storehouse laden down with huge bunches of beautiful, bright, freshly cut golden daffodils.

And when the daffodils were no more, they turned their attention to feeding chickens, milking cows and goats, as well as a large assortment of other farm jobs that were safe enough for all the young people to learn to do. More importantly, they learned to laugh again. Many a lunchtime found the pair of them lazing on their backs in the middle of a cornfield as they brazenly dared the sun to kiss and warm their freckled cheeks and foreheads as, chewing on long grasses, they intimately shared whatever their young hearts dictated.

When the season to pick apples finally came 'round, they and others battled long ladders into the orchards and climbed high into the trees to pick the rosiest and juiciest apples, which were simply crying out to be eaten. Best of all, they were granted permission to ride at the front of the applecart, holding the reins as they guided the horses that pulled the heavy load.

On more than one occasion, Lucy and Polly deliberately let go of the reins to stand up and shout into the warm summer breeze, "We are now the lords of the applecart," as, soaring high, they burst into fits of glorious laughter before collapsing back down into their seats to once more grab hold of the reins.

When they were not needed on the farm or in the orchards, they could normally be found hovering over the stove in Aunt Bessie's large kitchen, holding long wooden spoons as they waited to be asked to taste the dish in question.

"Royal tasters, grab your wooden spoons and come and taste this," Aunt Bessie would yell out. Both girls needed no further encouragement, as they raced each other to be the first one to dip a spoon into her cauldron of soup—or stew or bowl of fruit trifle. Aunt Bessie would stand by pretending to be anxious as she waited for the official verdict. It was always the same.

"Truly scrumptious. Absolutely delicious. Ten out of ten every time," they would cry as they licked their lips and dunked their spoon for the second time 'round. They often hovered over Aunt Bessie, their eyes wide as saucers as they studiously watched her turn the apples into a swirl of sweet, delicious nectar known to the locals as cider, and they were even encouraged to try their hand at making sweet and gooey apple and blackberry jam. Better still, Aunt Bessie was even prepared to turn a blind eye as they enjoyed the simple pleasure of licking out all her used pans of the leftover jams and jellies made by her fair hands.

Oh, and let's not forget the sweet honey they regularly collected from the bee farm. Unlike anything they had ever known, Aunt Bessie's face never had a shadow or trace of anger when the foolish girls mischievously dipped their fingers into the sweet-smelling, thick honey time and time again as their craving for pleasurably sweet things intensified.

The next few months saw the girls grow in natural grace and wisdom. They also used the time wisely by catching up with all their nagging schoolwork. Both girls worked so hard that in no time at all they rather miraculously discovered the true joy of learning. From then on they loved all schoolwork, math included, and they also loved their teacher, Mrs. Pickletree, so very much that both girls began to have a most voracious appetite to know more than ever of the big world about them.

"Please, please, Mrs. Pickletree. We earnestly beg you to give us much more homework," they often cried. Needless to say, Mrs. Pickletree always responded by sticking both fingers in her ears, as she absolutely refused to listen to such things, her main objection being that too much homework would make the girls both boring and dull. She remained totally adamant that both girls were to expend all excess energy in developing other recreational skills. Although her refusal to oblige quite clearly flummoxed both girls, it still did nothing to prevent them from regularly imploring dear, sweet Mrs. Penelope Pickletree for lots of extra homework to be given to each of them.

The girls would often see Giles around the large thatched cottage as he happily busied himself doing the more menial jobs of a handyman. He would often stop what he was doing to offer them a treacle toffee or other boiled sweet or two. Here at this special house, even Lady Butterkist managed to make herself useful by popping a pinny 'round her ample waist before she plunged her hands into the washing-up bowl or flew 'round the kitchen with a drying-up cloth as, like a busy bee, she helped other staff with the clearing up.

It seemed that no task was considered too lowly or too mighty that it could not be done by anyone and everyone living on the farm. Polly quickly became aware that every person she had occasion to work with had learned to give honor and respect where it was due, and that really meant to everyone they had occasion to meet or work with. The evidence of this mainly unspoken belief was the ease and friendship that freely flowed between all.

It was true that each morning before they sat down to eat breakfast, Aunt Bessie's voice could be heard above all others, as with the same message each day she called out across the tables. "Good morn' to all you luverly people, and let's remember to treat everyone we meet with the same patience and grace that we would hope for them to treat us. So with that said, let us now start the day by thanking the good Lord for the food spread before us, and may I remind the golden oldies amongst us to thank Him with much gratitude for the privilege of having a few teeth left in our gobs so as to enable us to chew on this good food."

Polly never failed to hide a hysterical giggle as time after time Aunt Bessie made it her business to remind the more mature among them to even be grateful for all remaining teeth.

Polly would, over time, learn much of the private sufferings of others, and she became very friendly with three delightful girls from southern Ireland. She listened, feeling most intrigued as the girls, with their delightful accents, spoke so lovingly about their homeland. These girls may well have had their personal struggles to overcome, but they also had the biggest hearts Polly had ever known. They were always laughing and giggling and telling strange Irish tales. Polly could never quite decide if they were true or whether they were simply concocting stories as they playfully messed with her. Once Polly and Lucy had mastered these girls' unusual accents, they wasted no time whatsoever in joining up with them.

During their stay there seemed to be at least one birthday a week, if not more, and as every birthday was considered most important, it was seen as completely natural for a party to take place. Before long, Polly had been invited to so many birthday parties that it did much to make up for all the ones she'd missed out on over the years due to her penny-pinching guardians' total abhorrence at parting with money under any circumstances. Also, at these parties it was decreed that all in the house should exchange gifts, so yet again everybody went away feeling as though it had been their party as they reveled in some most desirable gift they would now treasure forever.

Many weeks into her stay, while she sat at the dining table, she came to the realization that she loved each and every one of the other children, as well as the staff who regularly worked alongside to help restore and rebuild their confidence. The staff, many of whom were quite young in years, were so kind and remarkably patient, especially if one of the youngsters found himself or herself struggling with some unfamiliar task they believed themselves to be totally worthless or otherwise incapable of undertaking or fulfilling. No one here mocked and jeered, pulled hair, or did anything threatening. No, never! For none among them would even think of being so wickedly mean.

Polly came to believe that concerning the young people who shared the house, most, if not all, had suffered deeply shattered lives that included a wealth of cruelty, so none in the tiny community wished for a continuation of such things. They had indeed replaced all forms of hate with love and affection and bitterness with kindness, anger with tolerance, and so forth. Therefore, the atmosphere permeating throughout the farmhouse was, in Polly's own words, "deliciously warm and squidgy."

For her part, Lady Butterkist kept a beady eye on both girls until she was satisfied that they no longer had any real need of her.

One day in mid July she took it upon herself to call Polly into the drawing room, as she wished to talk most privately with her.

"Polly dear, I asked you here with a specific reason in mind, for today you will not be working in the orchards or on the farm. I hope you don't mind, but I took it upon myself to invite someone very special to come and pay you a timely visit."

Polly immediately looked extremely anxious and concerned.

"Oh, Lady B., who on earth could this be?" she cried. "So please don't hold back, or else I will surely die from anxiety, if not from intrigue."

No sooner had those words passed from her lips than she made a loud gasp.

"Will, is that really you?" she cried, her eyes immediately misting over as she looked over in the direction of the door.

"Indeed it is, Polly," he answered as he raced over to give her a warm, friendly hug.

"Oh, Polly. Forgive me everything, for now I know the truth. I am so thoroughly ashamed of myself, and—"

Polly placed a finger over his lips. "Enough, Will. Enough! For it is just so wonderful to see you once more, and I have to say, you're looking more, well, how shall I put it? Hmm, more gorgeous than ever," she giggled, turning a deep scarlet. "I can't believe I just said that!" she gasped as she turned to Lady Butterkist for additional help.

"Well, Polly, as we all know, you've always been one for wearing the whole of your heart on your sleeve, so I for one would hesitate before joining any secret society with you, my dear," she quipped.

"Too right!" Will interjected.

"Yes, they'd have no need to interrogate you, for you'd offer up everything before they even had the temerity to ask," she mused. "Anyway, I am going to leave you two alone for a while, as I am certain you have much catching up to do. Oh, and William dear, there is an extra place at the table for both lunch and supper, and then Giles will do the decent thing and drive you home."

"Thank you, Lady B. I am forever indebted to you."

"Nonsense, young man, for I believe it to be my utmost privilege to finally bring together what others have most wickedly sought to divide asunder. Now then, Polly, my dear one, I will bring you both some hot tea, as well as a slice of Aunt Bessie's homemade fruitcake, and then perhaps you might like to take a stroll around this wonderful manor house and show William all there is to see. I think he will particularly take a liking to the farmyard, and maybe you could consider going on something of an apple scrumping expedition in the orchard and bring back some deliciously ripe apples for William to take home to his mother and brother. Perhaps later on today we could pop out and get ourselves a scrumptious, hot tiddy oggy," she brightly suggested.

"Yes, Lady B. I think that's a grand idea."

<hr />

The hours seemed more like minutes to Polly as she talked with Will as they slowly strolled down to the orchard. "Go on, Will. You climb the tree and throw down the apples for me to catch," she suggested, "for my stomach is full of butterflies, so I really don't feel up to the task."

"Nonsense, Polly! If we're going to have the audacity to scrump at all, then at least have the decency to come up here and join me. That way we can scrump properly," he roguishly demanded. This left Polly with no choice but to climb up the tree to join him as she then set about doing her fair share of the apple scrumping.

They continued to share as they made their way back toward the thatched farmhouse to get ready for a little outing with her ladyship. On the way back to the house Polly could not help but feel sad when he finally got around to confessing that he had tried to visit her at the hospital.

"I'm so sorry, Polly. When the nurse opened the door and I caught sight of you standing all alone in front of that disgracefully straggly Christmas tree, it was more than I could bear. Really, it was."

"Please, Will. You don't have to explain," she consoled.

"Oh, but I do, Polly, for when you didn't write to thank me for my gift and card, well, I presumed that due to everything that had happened between us you had now deliberately come to the conclusion that it was in your best interest to cut me out of your life for good."

"What? Will, I promise you I never received anything from you, or anyone else for that matter, so I had no idea that you still cared about me."

"Oh, Polly, of course I care. I promise, hand on heart, that I sent some beautifully gift-wrapped chocolates, and they were very expensive, I'll have you know."

"Oh, thank you, Will. I know I would have truly appreciated them."

"Don't mention it. And as for the card, well, I spent over an hour in the store as I deliberated which card to send, for it was of the utmost importance to find the perfect card with the right greeting inside that would truly touch you as well as represent me."

"Well, I promise you, Will, I never received the card or the gift, so in the end, like everything else I guess, if I'm to be perfectly honest, yes, I gave up on you."

"I thought as much."

"I guess that makes us quits, don't you think?"

"I believe it does."

"Well then, no more reminiscing and punishing ourselves. Let's lay every stupid little niggle and misunderstanding aside and just enjoy this most precious moment in time, shall we?"

"Yes, Polly. I wholeheartedly agree," he said, looking visibly relieved. "Come on, Polly. You'll have to walk a lot faster, for I can see both

Giles and Lady B. impatiently standing by their old jalopy as they wait on us."

The outing was wonderful as they took in the picturesque countryside on that warm and hazy summer afternoon. Lady Butterkist made sure that Will finally got to taste his first genuine Cornish tiddy oggy, and his verdict was the same as everyone else's, for he declared that they were indeed truly scrumptious!

That magical day seemed far too short for both Polly and Will, and after saying their good-byes, Will promised not only to keep in touch but also to save her a seat in the dining room on their first day back at school.

"Will, at present I have no idea as to when the first day back at school is," Polly freely admitted.

"Oh, if I'm right, I do believe it's the ninth of September."

"Good, then I'll see you on the ninth, William Montgomery, and on fear of death by means most foul and unpleasant, please remember to save me some treacle pud!"

"You bet!" he happily responded as, giving her a long and final wave, he slid into the backseat of Lady Butterkist's old jalopy to then hurriedly close the door.

"Giles, please put your foot down hard on the pedal," Will hurriedly demanded. "Yes, drive away quickly, for I would hate for her to see me shedding tears."

Chapter Forty-Two
LETTERS OF HOPE

A FEW MORE WEEKS passed, and once again Lady Butterkist invited Polly to abandon her household tasks to join her in the drawing room.

"Polly dear, I am very much hoping this won't become something of a habit, but I have another very important visitor who is dying for the opportunity to see you."

"Who could it be this time 'round?" Polly anxiously cried.

Suddenly the door burst open, and in rushed her younger brother, James.

Polly immediately burst into tears. James followed suit. Seconds later found them in a deep, meaningful embrace.

"Oh, James. This is so extraordinarily wonderful that I feel like bursting into a million little fragments," she cried.

"Well, don't do it in here, dear, for Aunt Bessie would be most annoyed, and I'd hate to have to clear up the mess," Lady Butterkist quickly chipped in.

"Oh, Lady B., once more I can think of no way to thank you for this day. Yet again you have made me the happiest person on earth."

"Thank you, my dear, for I must again remind you that I delight to put back together that which others most maliciously and deceitfully seek to divide asunder. Now then, you two have much to catch up on, so I will go away and only come back when I am bearing a tray heaped with Aunt Bessie's chocolate-smothered cookies and a jug of homemade lemonade. Oh, and Polly, if I were you, I'd put on my party dress, for everybody here is taking the afternoon off, as we believe this visit calls for a serious party to take place," she said as she quickly tossed a few streamers in Polly's direction for her to catch hold of.

Polly laughed. "Oh, Lady B., you really do think of every little detail."

"Of course, my dear, for that is where my true talents lie. Now get wonderfully reacquainted while I go and make some lemonade," she cried as she waltzed toward the open door and disappeared.

"Oh, James, this is so unexpected and therefore so wonderful," she cried. "Did you get any of my postcards?"

"Well, I got one," he admitted.

"Oh, no! I've sent at least five or six," she said, giving him a disturbed look.

"Well, you know our guardians as well as I do, so I was lucky to get even one," he sighed.

"I know," she commiserated. "So thank goodness you are no longer ill. I was so shocked to see you lying in bed with pneumonia. How did you catch it?"

"Well, I'd rather not say, except it was due to a punishment."

"I thought as much," she sighed.

"Anyway, let's not dwell on such things, for I'm much better now."

"Oh, James. This is so very precious; you have no idea what this means to me."

"To tell you the truth, Polly, I was so surprised when Aunt Mildred told me to go and change into something respectable, as Giles would be picking me up and bringing me to see you—which leads me to believe that Lady Butterkist has secrets and ammunition that as of yet we know nothing of!"

"You can say that again, for she definitely treads where others fear to tread, except in Lady B.'s case I feel should exchange the word *tread* for *tramples*," Polly quipped. "Yes, I cannot even begin to imagine the conversation that must have taken place to get our guardians to agree to this," she quite rightly mused.

Polly had the time of her life showing James around the farmhouse and the animal sanctuary.

"Let's go and see what Aunt Bessie's cooking us all for lunch," Polly brightly suggested.

"Hmm. Whatever you're cooking in that big oven of yours, Aunt Bessie, it smells real good," Polly sighed as she stopped in her tracks and then breathed in deep.

"Well, Polly me luver, as you ask, it's your very favorite snake and pygmy pie."

"Snake and pygmy pie! Pray, what on earth is that?" James asked, looking extremely shocked.

"Well, we place a few pygmies in a pot, add a few carrots and onions, and then bring to the boil—"

"Aunt Bessie, stop playing around!" Polly giggled. "James, what Aunt Bessie really means is that she's serving up my favorite dinner of steak and kidney pie!"

"Same thing to me," Aunt Bessie roared, her plump cheeks blushing redder than ever. "And I'd be right in thinking that this here must be your younger brother?"

"Yes, Aunt Bessie, and I am thrilled to have him pay me this surprise visit."

"Well, best sit down and try some of my homemade bread with this luverly gooseberry jam. Come on, then. Don't stand about sucking eggs, me little sunshine. We don't stand on ceremony down in these parts, so sit down here and get tucked in right away," she playfully ordered them both. "But remember to save some room for the party that's taking place later on this very afternoon," she dutifully reminded.

"Oh, we surely will," Polly chirped back.

"Polly, I hope coming here today makes things better between us," he anxiously sniffed.

"Yes, of course it does, you silly old thing," she replied as she placed a sisterly arm around his neck.

"Oh, Polly. I promise that I cried myself to sleep every single night that you were in that horrible hospital. I imagined all sorts of terrible things, and many times I dreamt of sneaking out and coming to find you, but I had no way of getting to the hospital."

"Please, James. I truly understand."

"I begged to be allowed to write, but they refused to give me the stationery or the stamp. They even refused to pass on the correct address, and so I was up a gum tree without a paddle."

"Yes, James, but forgive me for saying this, but I don't think you've got that quirky little saying right, for giving it some serious thought, would you be in need of a paddle if you're stuck up a gum tree? No, I think not."

"Oh, but I only said that, Polly, because I've heard you say that same thing many times over."

"Yes, James, I'm sure you're right, for I often get my words and phrases entirely mixed up, as well as the wrong way round. In fact, Lady Butterkist tells me regularly that I'm a real Miss Malaprop."

"Oh, so who's she?"

"Oh, never you mind."

"No, tell me please."

"Well, she's a lady who used to get her words all mixed up and around the wrong way."

"Oh. Anyway, I tell you now, Polly, these past two years have felt really terrible and so lonely for me."

"I believe you. Really, I do. But come on, James, eat up, for I want to show you one of my best friends. His name is Boxer, and he came here a few weeks ahead of me."

After lunch Polly and James took a gentle stroll down to the animal sanctuary. "Look, James, there are dogs, cats, goats, turtles, in fact, an unimaginable array of animals that people bought as pets and even cruelly hurt before thoughtlessly abandoning them with about as much conscience as comes with discarding an ice cream wrapper."

"I know. It's awful."

"Come. Don't be afraid. He will not hurt you," she said, beckoning James to come and stand beside her.

James resisted a little before nervously walking toward her.

"Here, Boxer loves to be stroked, so come over and touch his long, silky mane."

"Polly, what are those awful marks all down his neck and back?"

"Oh, they are the scars from where he has been constantly beaten," she quietly explained.

Tears instantly welled in her brother's eyes.

"Oh, the poor thing. How beastly. How could anyone do such a thing?"

"James, I really have no idea at all," she sighed. "How do half the terrible things that go on in this world happen? Why do people drop bombs? I have always had the torment of such hideous questions terrorizing me night after night as I wrestle with my pillow, and at least for the present I have stopped asking, for there appears to be no answer that could ever begin to satisfy me. I am learning just to do what my conscience tells me is right and not worry about what others chose to do or not do."

"Hmm."

"Here, keep stroking him. That's it. Yes, James, as I was saying, I can't allow my life to be plunged into the doldrums because others choose wickedness over goodness and hate over love. As Shakespeare himself once wrote, at least I think it was him, and therefore I quote: 'Ours is not to question why. Ours—'"

"OK, clever clogs. Don't get too brainy on me, for I think I get your drift," he said as he gently began to stroke Boxer.

To quote Lady B., the surprise party that afternoon was an absolute blast.

So once more the day came to an end long before either James or Polly wished for. As she stood by the old jalopy still in her party dress as she waited to see him on his way, he turned, and with a serious and solemn face he looked her directly in the eye.

"James, what is it?" she politely asked

James began to stutter and tremble.

"James, come on. You're beginning to really frighten me."

Still he stood in an awkward silence, a look of high anxiety splashed all over his young features.

"Please don't hold back from me. After all, I'm your sister, so spit it out," she cried.

James still said nothing, as he sheepishly chose the moment to thrust his hand deep into his trouser pocket.

"This is all very mysterious. What are you hiding away in your pocket?" she nervously asked.

James reluctantly removed his hand from his pocket, bringing with him a small bundle of what looked like scrunched up notes.

"Here, Polly. I believe these rightfully belong to you, so therefore they should be in your possession," he quietly announced.

"For me?"

"Yes, you."

"James, tell me, what are they?" she quizzed.

"See for yourself," he once again quietly responded.

"Oh my goodness. These are letters from Aazi! Tell me, James, where on earth did you find them?"

James hung his head low. "Promise you won't tell?" he mumbled.

"Don't be so daft! You know I'd never do anything like blow the whistle to get you in trouble. But all the same, you must come clean and tell me right away. Where on earth did you find them?"

"Well, remember when I was so upset that time Uncle Boritz told me he was unable to remember where he had placed all my models for safekeeping?"

"Yes, I remember, so go on," she urged.

"Well, I eventually decided to do a bit of my own detective work."

"Yes, go on."

"Well, one day I waited until he was saying his usual good-byes to fat old Dr. Glumchops, and you know how boorishly longwinded and ridiculously verbose his good-byes always are," he said as he then went on to reenact his sycophantic guardian.

"Dear boy, we simply cannot afford to leave it so long till we next meet, for our times together stretch both my imagination as well as my extraordinarily meticulous and virile wit. So good-bye to you, my good man, and please send my express regards and undying wishes to your awfully wonderful and most deserving wife, whatever her name might be."

"Yes, yes. Oh, James, you're so funny. I had no idea that you could imitate him so well," she said as she broke into a laugh.

"Well, Polly, allow me to continue, for as his study door was partially open and his vicious guard dog was absent from guard patrol, I used the opportunity to sneak into his study to take a good look for myself."

"Yes, go on," she impatiently urged.

"Well, when I saw my models in his locked glass-fronted cabinet alongside all his awards and trophies, I decided there and then that it was now or never. I was going to take back what rightfully belonged to me—yes, my property."

"Goodness, you are really brave!"

"No, Polly. *Brave* isn't the right word. *Angry* and *desperate* best describe how I felt at the time, for I'd had just about a bellyful of his lame excuses."

"Or rather, his downright lies," Polly quickly interjected.

"Yes, well anyway, using a small screwdriver I managed to pry opened the door to the glass cabinet, and that was when I found them. I was really shocked when I realized that the bundle of letters had been kept from you, and so I decided there and then that it was right to take just a few of them. The reason I only helped myself to a few was so as not to arouse unnecessary suspicion."

"But what of your precious models, James?"

"Well, I made the decision to just leave them where they were, as I thought retrieving some of your letters was far more important," he quietly commented.

"Oh, James, how caring and unselfish you are. You are such a wonderful brother. I cannot thank you enough," she cried.

The two of them stood for many minutes locked in a meaningful embrace.

"Oh, and before you leave, James, I too have something for you," Polly said.

She suddenly produced a paper bag she had deliberately kept hidden away in her canvas shoulder bag that she had carried around all day, except during the party.

"Here, James. These are for you."

"What's in the bag?"

"Take a quick nose and see for yourself."

"Luverly jubbly! Wow, six sticks of sugary rock to get my teeth into!"

"Well, mind you clean your teeth thoroughly after eating them, else you'll have plenty of new cavities to deal with."

"There you go again being my over-bossy sister."

"Oh, I'm sorry. It's just force of habit," she said, breaking into a generous smile.

"I know it means you truly care, so thank you, Polly. It's really kind and thoughtful of you."

"Well, I promised you I'd get you some rock, didn't I?"

"Yes, and this time you kept your word," he reminded.

"I have never once intended to do otherwise," she quipped.

"Well, once again, thank you, Polly," he said as he reached over to give her a tender, brotherly hug.

Lady Butterkist, who had been standing to one side stroking her pooch, moved forward and quietly announced that it was time for

James to get in the car, as she had promised his guardians that he would not be late getting back.

"Polly, you need to let go of James. There's a dear, for Giles has to get him home at the agreed time. Otherwise I'm amply sure there will be fireworks, and lots of them!" she gently reminded.

Polly was reluctant to let go of her younger brother.

"James, please hold in there, for I will be back soon, and this time we are going to stand together. All right?" James nodded his head and then tried to break free of her clasp.

"Polly, I've got to go," he said, looking more than a little downcast.

"Take care," Polly quietly whispered as James made himself comfortable in the backseat of the old jalopy. The car began to slowly move down the gravel path, and James quickly stuck his head out of the back window to give her a final wave.

"Polly, please come home soon," he loudly shouted as he then sat back on the seat. Polly could see him wipe tears from his eyes as they pulled away.

She watched until the car had completely disappeared from sight, and then she went back into the manor house to find a quiet corner, a place where she could privately read the handful of letters she had desperately longed for and had taken what seemed like an eternity for her to finally receive.

Finding herself that highly desired quiet corner, she slunk down onto the floor and tightly closed her eyes, as over and over she promised herself that she must not shed a further tear this day. So much for promises, for as she read letter after letter she could only resort to shedding more tears, for the letters made her laugh, and they also made her cry.

So, she determined to write him another letter the very next day. In this letter she would try her best to explain all that had taken place and why suddenly she had stopped all meaningful correspondence.

She was most happy to hear that he had done as she had specifically requested by licking off the splodge of chocolate on the bottom of each letter she'd sent, for he confirmed the chocolate to be truly delicious. He then went on to tell her that he had considered doing likewise; only as chocolate was in short supply in his region of the country, he was intending to end each letter by squashing a tasty roasted beetle or grasshopper perfectly cooked on an open fire, but then knowing Polly as he did, he wisely came to his senses and concluded that she would feel far to squeamish to even give these little African delicacies a try. He also felt concerned by a certain letter sent by her that assumed he wore no clothes. He went on to inform Polly that in some ways she was correct in her thinking, for indeed, there were many tribes in the forest that wore very little in the way of garments, but his tribe wasn't one of them.

Polly, of course, was very relieved to hear this.

She allowed the tears to flow freely as he privately shared a large number of heartaches he had been forced to face since returning from Piadora, and he freely admitted that there had been many times that, like her, he had wanted to give up, for they had him no longer believing in Piadora or anything else associated with it. He also broke the news to her that since arriving back at the village, his eyesight was now deteriorating rapidly with each and every month that passed by. There was some talk of taking him to see a specialist eye doctor in a nearby town, but they needed to save a lot of money first if this was ever to happen.

"I need another miracle," he wrote.

Polly wept at that sad piece of news. "Oh, Aazi, why do I ever complain about my life when you too have the most unbearable struggles to overcome?" she sobbed.

Polly slipped the letters back into the envelopes, and with her eyes closed, she held them close to her heart.

"Aazi, I will always love you. And we will see other again, and you will know immediately who I am, blind or not blind," she whispered as she stayed for a while in the darkened room to calm her restless spirit and dream once more of Piadora.

Chapter Forty-Three
ALL GOOD THINGS MUST COME TO AN END

*M*ANY WEEKS LATER and Polly was once more called to go and see Lady Butterkist in the drawing room, this time with Lucinda.

"Girls, come and sit down, and then make yourselves comfortable," she said as she patted the comfortable sofa beside her.

With the girls both seated she began. "I have nothing but the deepest admiration for the both of you."

"Thank you, Lady B.," they happily replied.

"Both you girls have exceeded all my expectations in just about everything you have put your hand to. And, judging by the way you relate to the staff, as well as all the other young adults, I perceive that both of you are developing some very close and abiding friendships. This is most touching and rewarding for me to observe. I cannot even begin to tell you just how proud I am of both of you. Aunt Bessie also informs me that both of you have caught up with schoolwork, and so you are on target, proving my theory that you not only have pretty faces but you're both highly intelligent as well.

"However, that said, I feel this is the perfect time to tell you that I will be going away for a week or so, as I have a few very important things to which I must attend. When I return, it will almost be time to bring this holiday to a close, and then sadly for all, we must head back home. Polly, you, my dear, will be returning to the castle. And as for Lucinda, well, you, my dearest, will have to be ever so patient with me. I have spoken with your parents this very morning, and as of yet they have not come to any decision as to whether they are able to have you home. If at the end of the day their answer is a firm no, then Lucinda dear, you are going to need to be very brave, as I will be left with no other choice but to deposit you back at Hellingsbury Hospital."

On hearing this latest ghastly piece of news, Lucinda immediately collapsed to the floor. "Oh no, Lady B. Please don't send me back there. I beg of you," she cried.

Polly instantly dropped down beside her, and with an arm around her friend and tears in her eyes, she looked up and begged Lady Butterkist to go and visit Lucinda's parents and persuade them to have her back.

"Lady B., don't they realize how awful that hospital is? Please don't let this happen. There must be something you can do," she wailed.

"I'm sorry, Polly. I promise you that I am doing all I can on Lucinda's behalf. I too will be bitterly frustrated if I am forced to take her back, but I will have no other option, other than to fulfill my original obligation."

"Obligation!" Polly cried in utter dismay.

"Yes, obligation, and watch yourself, Polly dear, for once more you're repeating me, something I find rather irritating to say the least."

"Oops. Sorry."

"Apology accepted. Now, listen to me. I promised to ensure that on Lucinda's return she would be brought back to the safety of the hospital with its specialist team of doctors, although having been introduced to some of them, I personally am left completely at a loss as to where some of their so-called specialist skills truly lie," she muttered. "And in Dr. Ninkumpoop's case, I believe it to have been more on the golf course!"

"Lady B., you of all people are able to do anything and everything! So please think of something," Polly begged.

"Look, girls. I will continue to put pressure on Lucinda's parents, but in the meantime I need both of you to keep on track and have some faith. Believe me when I say that nothing is set in concrete, so you need to keep your hopes up by not allowing yourselves to go downhill," she wearily cautioned.

"Yes, Lady B. We promise that we will try our utmost," Polly assured her.

"Yes, remember, it's not over until the fat lady sings, besides which, I still have a few undisclosed cards up my sleeve. So, I will leave you girls alone while I go to make some tea," she quietly stated as she reached for the door handle and quickly disappeared.

"Oh, Polly. What am I to do?" Lucinda despairingly bleated.

"Honestly! At this exact moment I have no idea, except to say we must do as Lady B. instructed and hang on in there." Polly tried her best to encourage her friend as she remained on the floor hugging Lucy as she attempted to comfort her.

"Polly, you know that they will lock me away forever in one of those awful padded cells, and then I will go horribly mad," she wept.

"No you won't, Lucy. I'm certain Lady B. will never allow that to happen to you again," Polly said as she tried to reassure her very dear friend.

"Polly, I know at present you want to help, but you wait, in a few months' time you too will surely have completely forgotten me. And then what?"

"Don't say such things, Lucy! How could I ever forget or abandon you? It's never going to happen. Look, Lucy, I promise if the worst comes to the worst, and you are sent back to the hospital, I will sneak out and come visit you as often as I am able. If when we meet up you're down in the doldrums, I will do all within my power to once more make you laugh. I will also bring you special little treats. You have my word."

"Promise?"

"Yes, I promise, Lucy, but we are getting a little carried away with ourselves, for as of yet we know nothing of how the matter will fall, and Lady B. has given us her assurance that she will keep on trying."

"I hope she will," Lucy moaned.

"Lucy, although at the moment everything seems hopelessly bleak, I know for sure that Lady B. will not leave things as they are, for it's simply not in her nature, if you know what I mean. So let's try and trust her, shall we? Surely you agree that she is much too stubborn and bighearted to just walk away from this latest problem."

"Hmm, never a truer word spoken," Lucy said as she quickly began to brighten up.

"So Lucy, let's just try and enjoy the remainder of our time together," she enthused as she gave her dear friend an encouraging hug.

The next several days turned out to be very precious, as both girls sought to make their last days together really count. They raced each other up hills, and then with arms spread out like the wings of an eagle, they pushed against the wind as they soared and then swooped downhill toward the valleys below. They also paid regular visits to dear Boxer to whisper endless sweet nothings in his ear, as well as shower him with tasty pieces of apple and carrot and occasional sugar lumps they had sneaked from Aunt Bessie's kitchen storehouse. They also took Lassie the Scottish border collie for plenty of long walks over hill and dale as they took it in turns to throw large sticks for him to chase after. They also saw to it that Lassie got her fair share of cuddles, as well as the odd terribly nice treat.

Many a day they chose to walk barefoot through cold, rippling waters as they chased scores of minnows and tadpoles on their journey downstream, and they made each other fragile daisy chain necklaces and weaved colorful flowers into each other's hair. Lucy seemed obsessed with picking posy after posy of wild woodland flowers, which she would then conscientiously arrange in small glass vases before placing on top of Polly's bedside locker.

Polly, in turn (with Aunt Bessie's blessing), sneaked upstairs with plate after plate of gooey chocolate cake for them to secretly share as they tried to ignore all nagging and cumbersome burdens, preferring only to bask and wallow in their gloriously deep and intimate friendship.

"Oh Polly, remember that the day after tomorrow is the day that Lady Butterkist will return bearing either good or terribly bad news, and in truth I can hardly bear it, really I can't," Lucy wailed.

"I know, Lucy. Then shortly after that we will be saying our final good-byes. I, for one, can hardly handle that," Polly admitted.

"Me too, Polly. But just knowing I have a real sister and friend like you really helps me face my tomorrows. I love you loads and feel proud to have you in my life. I can't say any more at present," she croaked as a lone tear slowly trickled down her forlorn face.

"Yes, we are sisters forever," Polly quipped. "Anyway, Lucy, are you going to eat that last bit of cake or what?" Polly chipped in, eager to quickly change the subject, as she did not feel it would be helpful for Lucy to dwell on such things. "Because if you don't wolf it down right now, I will," she threatened, quickly moving forward toward the plate with her spoon. Both girls then playfully fought off each other as they made a final, desperate grab for the very last spoonful of Aunt Bessie's hot chocolate fudge cake.

"I win," Lucy yelled, her mouth full of cake, as she cheekily waved her now empty spoon in the air. She then impishly licked her lips of all residual cake crumbs. "Here, Polly. As the loser you can lick the plate clean," she cried.

A few nights later found them sitting at the table enjoying one of Aunt Bessie's most delicious dinners when Lady Butterkist, back from her travels, burst through the kitchen door before hurriedly making her way toward both girls, who were seated at a dining table.

"Lucinda! Polly! Never, ever underestimate me!" she cheerfully cried. "For Lucinda, you, my dear, are not going back to the hospital after all! Yes, you, dearest, are finally going home!"

"Oh, Lady B., you're a real brick. Truly you are!" Polly cried as she jumped up from her seat and raced over to give her an overwhelmingly gigantic hug in the style to which increasingly she was becoming accustomed, at least when the bearer of the hug was young Polly.

"I'll do this far more often if this is the response I get," Lady Butterkist laughed.

Both girls then hugged each other, shrieking loudly as they began to dance for joy, as due to the sudden, most welcome onset of irrepressible happiness they were unwilling to contain their excitable emotions a moment longer.

All too soon everyone present had abandoned their supper plates as they joined the girls dancing around the kitchen as well as—dare I say it?—lots of dancing on the tables. Aunt Bessie chose to turn a blind eye to this very excessive outburst, preferring, of course, to join in.

"Well, if you can't beat them, you might as well join them, I say," she said as she threw off her shoes and began to dance around the kitchen.

"Oh, I think this calls for extra chocolate cake and hot cocoa," Aunt Bessie roared loudly as she then danced into the center of the room with a large, thickly covered chocolate cake balanced on her outstretched hand, the other hand hitching up her long apron as though it were a skirt as she continued prancing around the kitchen in the manner of a deliriously happy cook having just received notice of a substantial pay increase!

The party was in full swing until very late, when rather reluctantly, both girls were forced by their elders to call it a day.

"'Tis more than time to hit the sack, girls, for tomorrow morn' you'll be up at dawn and then down in orchards for most of day," Aunt Bessie took it upon herself to remind. "So say your brief good nights, and then please head up them stairs to your beds," she insisted.

"Yes, Aunt Bessie," they happily replied.

"Oh, Aunt Bessie, I have written a letter to a good friend of mine who lives in Africa, and I need a stamp and some help getting it posted. If I give it to you tomorrow, will you be able to help?" Polly asked.

"Of course, me darlin', just leave it with me, and I'll see to it that it gets posted. Oh and girls, may I also remind you both not to forget to properly brush your little toothy pegs," she gently coaxed.

"Yes, Aunt Bessie. We'll brush our teeth till they sparkle. That's a promise. Good night, everybody," they cried out as they gave a final wave before heading up the stairs to head toward their bedroom.

Both girls immediately obeyed, and once they were changed into their pajamas, they flopped like limp, over-mollycoddled rag dolls into their beds to fall into a deeply satisfying slumber.

<hr />

There came a time when all in the house were forced to acknowledge that this particular party was well and truly over. Sadly for all, it was time for Polly and Lucy to leave and head for home. Both girls spent ages swapping addresses and saying their good-byes to staff, as well as all others left behind. There were tears and long hugs, and then more long hugs followed closely by yet further tears as both girls struggled to terminate this most glorious holiday that had brought much ease and healing to their young and tender souls.

They then stood silently and somberly by the car, a small suitcase by each girl's side as they anxiously waited for Giles and Lady Butterkist to appear.

Eventually the door of the thatched cottage opened, and both Aunt Bessie and Lady Butterkist could be seen sprightly making their way down the steps as, deep in conversation, they headed toward the parked car.

"Ahh, there you are, girls. Oh, dear. I see Giles is not yet with us. Really, there are times when that dear man appears as slow as a semi-conscious constipated tortoise nearing the end of a month-long marathon," she huffed. "I hear from Aunt Bessie and I see by your sorrowfully glum faces that you've said all your good-byes, so let's place your suitcases by the boot of the car, and then we can get in the car and make ourselves comfortable while we wait for that little slow-coach of a chauffeur to abandon his precious cup of tea to come and drive us home. Ah, here he comes. Giles, please place their suitcases in the boot, for we must be on our way."

"Very well, madam."

Both Polly and Lucy turned to simultaneously give Aunt Bessie a ridiculously long and lengthy hug. "Oh, Aunt Bessie, tell us now, why do we have to leave here?" they both cried out.

"Well, me little darlins, it's because life has to go on. You both are extraordinary young girls, and you have your whole lives before you. Livin' here may seem like heaven, but it's only a fore-taster of the real thing, truly it is."

"Oh, please let us stay. I promise to do all the washing up till my hands wrinkle up for good and I've lost as many teeth as you, Aunt Bess, for I don't ever want to leave here," Lucy cried as she clung tightly to Aunt Bessie's ample waist.

"It's not fair," Polly cried.

"That's right, Polly dear. Life is not fair, and the bad news is, however hard you try, you don't get to make it out alive," she said tongue in cheek as she sought to bring a smile to their tearstained faces.

"Now then, Lucy, wipe your eyes, and then listen to me! Both you girls must go climb your own mountains and dig your own paths. But woe betide either of you if you so much as dare err off the straight and narrow road, for you can bet your sorry little lives that I'll be right behind you with me rolling pin," she choked, as she tried hard and lost the fight to hold back the tears.

"Now you girls have got me all misty eyed, and I daresay if I allow you to hug me much longer, then in no time at all you'll have me blub-bering and squalling like a newborn baby," she said, her voice choked with emotion as she lifted the hem of her apron to wipe away tears that were now threatening to cascade down her cheeks.

"Please, Aunt Bess, will you say good-bye to Mrs. Pickletree and tell her that not only will we miss all her wonderful lessons, but we will truly miss her too? We looked all over the house for her this morning, and we were left feeling very distressed, for sadly for us she was nowhere to be found," Polly cried.

"Well, me luvies, that's because she had a most pressing errand to run this morning."

"Then promise us that you will tell her that we will make her proud. Yes, tell her we are going back to school, and we won't ever stop learning until we become winners," a teary-eyed Polly begged.

"You can be sure I will," Aunt Bessie assured the girls.

"Tell her also that one day in the future she will switch on the television and be surprised to see us receiving many awards for all our outstanding achievements."

"Oh, I can tell you now with full authority that she won't be the least surprised if such a thing were to happen, for she firmly believes you girls can achieve anything and everything you put your hearts and minds too. But I promise to pass on your message of great kindness," Aunt Bessie replied as she held both girls to her ample bosom for one long and final bear hug.

"Giles has just informed me that both your suitcases are now safely loaded into the boot, so it's high time you girls let go of me to clamber into the back of this car. I tell you now that Lady B. has many other errands to do before the day draws to a close, and look, Giles is about to start up the engine," she said as she gave both girls one final, tender kiss on the forehead.

"Now take these sweet mince pies to nibble on, on your journey," she insisted as she gave each girl some pies wrapped in a brown paper bag. "And here, take a bottle of our homemade lemonade, and mind you, don't guzzle it down too fast or else you'll have a bad case of the hiccups," she warned. "And girls, please remember, when things seem bad, don't look down; look up."

The girls leaned out of the window as they furiously waved goodbye to Aunt Bessie and all her wonderful staff, who had all come out on the lawn to wave them off.

"Oh, Lucy. I really want to cry and never stop, really I do, for I do so hate good-byes, as they make me truly melancholic," Polly admitted as she sat back in the car and shut her eyes to prevent further unabated tears.

"Me too, Polly. No other holiday could ever begin to match this one," Lucy deeply sighed. "Lady B., please, may I have a tissue? Otherwise you'll be left with one almighty puddle on the floor if you don't pass me one, and quick."

Her ladyship quickly obliged. Both girls then knelt on the backseat and waved out of the back window until the staff on the lawn were nothing more than tiny dots on the horizon. They then turned 'round to blow into large bundles of tissues, as they were both overcome and overwhelmed with strong feelings at leaving the manor house that had been a wonderful refuge to both girls.

Lady B. then broke their mournful silence. "Here, girls, you can look after my little pooch for me," she said as she passed over the pup to Polly in the back of the car. Moments later found Tiddles fast asleep with her paws over her eyes as she lay stretched out on Polly's lap making quiet whimpering noises.

"It's as though Tiddles doesn't want to leave either," Lucy loudly commented.

"Girls, I know you're in no mood to hear it, but all good-byes are to be considered hard. You two must now look forward to your futures. I know for sure that you face extraordinary difficulties, but I also know that both you girls have the strength of character to persevere and come through the other side," she gently counseled.

Both girls independently chose to close their eyes and rest from all ongoing discourse as they tried hard to immediately empty their minds and imaginations of all potentially bad premonitions that had come back to harass and haunt them concerning the future. But it was hard to do, if not downright impossible.

"Girls, it's feeling very much like an abandoned graveyard in here, so tell you what? Let's play I Spy, and I'll start," Lady B. very brightly suggested. "Yes, I spy with my little eye something beginning with L."

Finally, the car pulled up outside Lucy's house.

"Right. Lucinda, sadly this is it. You must quickly say your good-byes to Polly and come with me. I will escort you to the front door, and Giles will follow on behind with your suitcase in hand."

Lucy immediately grabbed hold of Polly's neck and cried, "Good-bye, Polly. I trust I'll see you again."

"Polly I know in your kindness you gave me Langdon for keeps, but that was back then when we all thought I was going to be left alone in the hospital. Now I must give him back, for he truly belongs with you," Lucy very matter-of-factly stated.

"Oh, Lucy, are you really sure?"

"Yes, Polly. I now have my family to cling to; therefore I no longer have any need of him," she whispered as she bravely handed over the elephant. "I now believe that you really need him much more than I do," Lucy gently said as she gave Polly a long, final hug.

Polly thought Lady Butterkist looked quite as wretched as they did watching on as the two friends were forced to part company once more.

"Come on, Lucy, to linger longer will just add to your pain. Polly, please stay in the car. I assure you I won't be too long," Lady Butterkist insisted.

"Can't I also come to the door?" Polly pleaded.

"Sadly, on this occasion I don't think it would be a good idea, so I respectfully request that you do as I ask and stay put while I see Lucinda to the door. I promise I won't be long."

Polly watched like a hawk as Lady Butterkist took Lucy gently by the hand to lead her up the garden path. Giles followed in their footsteps, as he dutifully carried her small suitcase in one hand. The door opened, and Polly got a small glimpse of both parents as they stood at the door, their kind but fragile faces masking great strain. Both parents took it in turn to shake Lady Butterkist's hand, and minutes later their faces lit up as they listened enthusiastically to all her ladyship had to say. Lucinda's father then looked so lovingly at his daughter before taking the suitcase from Giles, and her mother immediately bent down to give Lucy a long and very warm and loving embrace.

Polly watched on as Lucinda's dear mother stooped to give her precious daughter a long and heartfelt hug. Polly, gripped with raw emotion, then picked up Langdon. Clutching him tightly to her chest, she gulped, "I must stay brave. Really I must," as she sat alone feeling very sad and dejected in the back of the large, old car with Tiddles lost to the world as she lay stretched out on Polly's lap.

Chapter Forty-Four
NOW IT'S YOUR TURN TO CRY LIKE A BABY

*M*INUTES LATER, AND THE journey was once again resumed. Polly rather wisely chose to close her eyes as she tried to keep the image of her dear friend Lucy at the forefront of her mind. All too soon it was time for her to alight the car. She felt great waves of apprehension as the large black gates very slowly opened before her.

"Polly, I'm not sure I fully appreciate your loud and disgracefully depressing sighs," Lady Butterkist announced. "So, young lady, before we leave this car, I feel the most urgent need to give you a further little pep talk," she said as she exited the front passenger door to go around and join Polly sitting in the rear of the car.

Five minutes later Polly and Lady Butterkist, holding Tiddles, emerged from out the back of the car and then headed toward the front door, Giles following on behind as he dutifully carried her small, tatty suitcase.

Before they even reached the door, they were enthusiastically greeted by both Mildred and Boritz as they rushed out to greet them.

"Lady Butterkist, how lovely it is to see you again," they both obsequiously fawned.

"Oh, and Polly, this break has obviously done you so much good, for you look visibly happy and relaxed," Boritz superficially cried. "Now come inside, all of you, for we have prepared a light supper for you all, as I am sure it has been quite a while since you've eaten anything decent or of real substance."

"Why, thank you, Boritz, although I must confess that we did stop en route to get ourselves a nice, big bag of fish and chips, and as for the motorway food, I have no choice other than to admit that it was well above average, truly it was."

"Yes, well, I am sure you are in dire need of a decent cup of properly brewed tea, for I feel certain if nothing else that this was not in good supply on the motorway."

"No, you are indeed right about that, for the tea was virtually undrinkable. Yes, put bluntly, pretty ghastly, wouldn't you say, Giles?" she muttered. "So perhaps a teeny cup of Earl Grey would not go amiss," she sweetly stated.

"Well, I am completely at your disposal, so come this way, Lady Butterkist," he beckoned.

After light refreshments of China tea served with finger sandwiches, scones with jam, and finger shortbread, Lady Butterkist announced that it was time to get back on the road.

"Before I leave, Boritz, I wish to know if you have heard anything of dear Dr. Ninkumpoop?" Lady Butterkist fished, all the while trying to keep a straight face.

"Well, madam, as you ask, sadly, the news is not good."

"Not good? How is that?"

"Well, I have to report that the opening ceremony for the new ward did not go as smoothly as planned. Yes, if I'm to be perfectly honest, since that most tiresome event it has been downhill all the way."

"Downhill! What precisely do you mean by that?"

"Well, things went a little haywire that day, and since then I have not been able to speak with him."

"Oh, and why is that?"

"Well, the gossip buzzing around town is that he has been checked into an exclusive rehabilitation clinic somewhere in the Swiss Alps, or so I am led to believe. However, as I had no occasion with which to speak alone with him since the day of the very ghastly and disturbing incident, I can therefore only rely on the small tidbits of gossip that regularly seem to come my way."

"Oh, dear. How very unfortunate."

"Yes, the whole event turned out to be rather disturbing, to say the least, for during the fracas even my darling Mildred sustained a serious bleeding nose. Didn't you, my dear?"

"You mean to say that dear Poopy punched her?"

"Oh no, madam. Please understand it was that mindless, parasitical pop star who goes by the name of Freddie Fruitless. Yes, it's quite amazing what passes for talent these days," he said, giving a deep, all-knowing sigh. "Anyway, with the local and national press covering the event, it was nigh impossible to even begin to attempt to minimize the damage."

"Oh, dear! Well, enough said. Anyway, Boritz, I have one most urgent thing left to settle before I head home, and this is to write a check in show of my support of your orphanage."

"Oh, the check! Well, believe it or not, Lady Butterkist, I must confess to having completely forgotten all about that," Boritz announced.

"Well, Boritz, if you could hold on to Tiddles just for a small moment, then this will not only free up my hands but give me the opportunity to search my purse for my checkbook and pen," she said as she proceeded to unceremoniously dump Tiddles into his empty arms long before she had his verbal agreement.

"Ahh, I seem to have momentarily mislaid my pen," she cried as she continued to rummage through her purse in pursuit of this important item.

"Oh, Lady Butterkist, please feel free to use mine," he quickly said as he whisked a pen out of his top pocket.

"Why, thank you, Boritz, but I would hardly call that a pen, for it neither requires ink nor an ink cartridge," she dismissively snorted. "Forgive me here, but I'm a bit of a puritan when it comes to placing my signature on any document, large or small, so I much prefer to use my own exclusive fountain pen when I write checks, or any written correspondence for that matter," she said, as she finally brought out a very expensive-looking, jewel-encrusted fountain pen.

"Oh, Lady Butterkist, I gave up using fountain pens many moons ago, for I was thoroughly fed up and tired of them leaking and staining the inside pockets of some of my most expensive suits and blazers," he freely admitted.

"Well, that really does come as a surprise, Boritz, for surely you always use a fountain pen when you are required by law to place your signature on the bottom of any legal document?"

"Well, yes, Lady Butterkist. You have indeed caught me out in a little white lie, for as you so rightly state, a proper ink pen is in those cases most advantageous, as the law does, as you so rightly state, suggest that all documents submitted must be signed in ink for the purposes of authenticity. But outside office use I, for one, much prefer to go with the modern invention of a Biro."

"Well, I confess to having a total abhorrence of such things and so am indisposed to use any such vulgar, modern inventions," she insisted, adding a little tut to complete her disapproval.

It took Lady Butterkist just a matter of minutes to write the check, and after popping her special fountain pen back in her purse, she stood up to hand Boritz the long-awaited and much-desired check, as well as retrieve her precious pup, who she could not help but notice looked decidedly uncomfortable in Boritz's outstretched arms.

Boritz eagerly accepted the check, his eyes on stalks as he shuddered at the amount written on the check.

"Boritz, does this check meet with your approval?"

"Lady Butterkist, what more can I say other than 'my cup runneth over,' for this is so terribly kind and generous of you," he stammered.

"Well, Boritz, I hope this money goes some way in alleviating the suffering of these unfortunate young children," Lady Butterkist said as she continued most affectionately to stroke her pup.

"Oh, trust me when I say it most definitely will, your ladyship. It will."

"Well, Giles, please drink up, for we urgently need to be on our way. I plan to visit again sometime in the future, although I have to add that at present I am not the slightest bit optimistic that this promise will be carried out during this next coming year, for out of the blue I have just made plans to do a bit of traveling abroad."

"Oh, really? How wonderful, Lady Butterkist."

"Yes, I'm rather hoping it will turn out to be a most exciting, if not thoroughly exhilarating, adventure," she loudly exclaimed. "Firstly I propose to climb the Himalayan Mountains with a handsome young Ghurka at my side."

"Really?"

"Yes, I was thrilled to bump into the darling little man while purchasing some foreign teas at Harrods, and needless to say, we hit it off instantly. Then my next intended stop is Russia to see my elder sister, who lives somewhere along the Baltic Coast, although I have to confess that at present I'm not entirely sure where on the coast she has parked herself. I then intend to take a long train ride down through Italy and only get off when I reach Tuscany, for can you believe that this is where one of my long-lost cousins has chosen to spend the rest of her days? So, I expect to be eating many olive oil–drenched sardine salads while breathing in the intoxicatingly heady smell of fresh lemons from the nearby groves. I'll not leave Italy until I have paid a much-dreamed-of visit to Florence and Rome. From there I have been invited to stay at a kibbutz in Israel, and then finally when I have tired of everything else, I intend to join a group of hot-blooded, very sweaty Spaniards as we board a tourist bus bound for Puerto Banus in Spain," she announced as she clasped her hands together to control both her delight as well prevent her imagination from running riot.

"Incredible."

"Have you ever been to Puerto Banus, Boritz?"

"No, madam. I don't believe I have."

"Well, it was indeed a wonderful discovery when I first set eyes on the place. It has the most delightful bay filled to overcapacity with the most opulent sailing vessels imaginable. An old school chum of mine named Mrs. Georgia Ganglegoose has invited me to come join her on her extremely palatial craft, and then I believe we will set sail on the high seas in search of some new and exciting adventure. I do believe she has the West Indies in mind, and after that, well, who knows?

"Now, won't that be a lot of fun? So at present I have absolutely no idea as to when I will next visit you good people, for I fully intend to let my wings take me wherever they wish to flutter and with whomever it feels right to be."

"Oh, your ladyship, surely you are not only playing with me but also with fire, for it is most dangerous, if not completely irresponsible, for two perfectly vulnerable creatures to go to sea without a strong, capable man at the helm of their vessel."

"Well, Boritz, I can see that there might be some cause for alarm at two women of a certain age jaunting around the globe on their ownsome lonesome, but as you can see, I am a fairly feisty woman. So if we get boarded by a gang of pirates of—how shall I say?—well, disrepute—"

"Madam, hear me out when I categorically state they are never otherwise," he interjected, "for you will indeed be considered seriously lucky to find even one considerate gentleman amongst them. Oh, no, it is a well-known fact that fiendish pirates have not changed a bit from days gone by. And have you taken into consideration what you will do if you are taken captive on the high seas?"

"Captured? Oh, that does sound so very romantic," she continued to tease.

"Well, there is every possibility that in the event of being captured, you might well be forced to walk the plank!"

"Oh, how exciting!" Lady Butterkist cried.

"I don't understand, for *exciting* was not the first word that sprung to my mind."

"As I was saying, Boritz, I am ready and willing to take on this, as well as any other challenge that is thrown my way, for it most surely is all part and parcel of having this rather late in life lusty penchant for travel," she deliberately teased.

"Well, I can only hope you take my words of caution seriously," he muttered.

"Thank you for your concern, but before I rush to leave, I must request a quiet word in Mildred's ear."

Mildred obliged and calmly walked over to her ladyship. A few words were then exchanged.

"Well, thank you for letting me know, Lady Butterkist. I will do all in my power to ensure such a thing never happens again. You can rest assured on this one," Mildred bristled through tightly pursed lips.

"I would be most grateful if you would see to it that it doesn't," Lady Butterkist retorted. "Now, please show me to the door, for we do need to be on our way."

"I'd be more than glad to," a harassed Mildred meanly muttered.

As they headed toward the door, Polly called out her last good-bye. Lady Butterkist turned around just in time to catch her heading up the oak staircase and called out for Polly to come and see her off.

"Mildred, I do have one final request."

"Yes, Lady B. What might that be?" Mildred attempted most sweetly to ask.

"Well, would you mind very much if I were to have a moment alone with Polly?"

"Oh, absolutely!" Mildred snorted. "I, for one, have need of getting my little ones to bed, and Boritz, well, he has a number of letters that he urgently needs to write. Don't you, dearest?"

"Uh. Oh, yes, if you say so, dearest."

"Well, thank you both once again for your wonderful hospitality, and hopefully I will be in touch sometime in the not-too-distant future," she said, giving a warm, enduring smile.

"Oh, and do please send us a postcard or two," Boritz ever-so-politely pleaded.

"Yes, perhaps I will," Lady Butterkist responded, very tongue in cheek.

She then waited patiently until she was sure that Polly's guardians were well out of earshot. "Giles, be a dear. Hold on to Tiddles for me while you stand on guard," she politely ordered.

"Very well, madam."

"Polly dear, I have something on my person that I believe rightfully belongs to you."

"I'm not too sure what you mean by that, Lady B.," was Polly's initial response.

Her ladyship placed her hand deep into her pocket.

"I am referring to this!"

"Oh goodness. My ring!"

"Yes, my dear, your ring. Now, I would strongly advise that you hide it away in that special place."

"Special place?"

"Yes, dear. Now don't pretend you don't know where I'm suggesting."

"No, Lady B. I have no idea of where you are thinking."

"Why, in young Langdon's belly, of course, yes, for the purpose of safety. And I have every reason to believe that your guardians will never think to look there."

"Thank you Lady B., but as soon as Uncle discovers the ring is missing there will be all hell to pay until it is back in his possession," Polly anxiously cried. "They will strip the place bare and punish us all until someone finally owns up. Yes, our lives would become even more unbearable so you had better take it back."

"Polly, please do not get yourself in a tizzy. I promise you I have taken care of this for I have replaced the ring with something pretty similar, and that, young lady, is all that I'm prepared to say on the matter."

"Oh, Lady B., tell me quickly, how on earth did you come to get it back?"

"Never you mind, dear, for until such a time as I am forced to stand in front of a judge and jury and confess, all I am prepared to say at this moment is 'Finders keepers, losers weepers,'" she said, giving a most wicked smirk.

"Lady B., you are quite something. Truly you are," Polly said as she reached over to give her one final, extremely overzealous Polly hug.

"Keep telling me, my dear. Keep telling me. Now, listen to me, Polly dear. Things will seem much better for a time, but mark my words, it won't be for too long."

"Yes, I realize that, for lepers don't change their spots, do they?" Polly very glumly stated.

"There you again, Miss Malaprop, for it's a *leopard*, not a *leper*, that never changes its spots," she gently corrected. "Anyway, what I was about to say was, if you need to get a message to me, I would suggest you place it for safety in Langdon's belly, and one way or another it will get to me. So promise me, Polly, even if others don't recognize you to be a true princess, you can still act like one. Stay kind and charitable, and trust your conscience to guide you. Until such times as we meet again—and trust me when I say we will meet again—I will have you in my thoughts and prayers," she said, giving Polly one final long hug. "Yes, the real trouble with you, Polly Brown, is that you are truly special."

"And so are you," Polly quipped.

"Oh, Polly, I have no trouble believing it about myself, but you, my dear, well, you still need to work on that one."

"I hear you, Lady B. Giles, may I give you a hug and thank you for everything?"

Giles handed over Tiddles to Lady B. and then gave Polly a long, fatherly hug.

Polly then stood at the front door and waved until the car disappeared from sight.

"Madam, I have to admit to feeling quite teary-eyed and emotional at this moment," Giles confessed.

"Oh, Giles, if that is the case, then I propose we stop on the motorway and have ourselves a nice, strong cup of tea."

"Thank you, madam, that sounds like a very good idea."

———— ❖ ————

Meanwhile, back in his private study Boritz sat in an undeniable stupor with his eyes firmly fixed on the check lying on the desk in front of him.

Then there was a knock on the door, and Mildred quickly entered, holding their youngest child in her arms.

"Dearest, I have just brought Jeremy in for you to give a quick kiss good night."

"Yes, yes, dear."

"Hasn't it been a long and very strange day?" Mildred casually commented.

"Yes, and my, what an eccentric old biddy she is!" he loudly muttered.

"She's no more eccentric than you are, my dear," Mildred quickly retorted.

"Hmm. Mildred, tell me now, precisely what did Lady Butterkist wish to say to you in private?"

"Well, apparently when Gailey returned Polly's dress and shoes, they were virtually ruined."

"What do you mean?"

"Well, the old battle-axe complained that the dress was badly torn, and the shoes were missing some of the sequin studs. As for the tiara, sad to say, she made sure that this too was completely destroyed."

"Oh my goodness. How absolutely embarrassing!" he said, shaking his head in a show of utter disbelief.

"I should say so. We must make sure Gailey never resorts to this sort of ridiculous behavior again, or at least while the old crow is around."

"Tell me, Mildred dearest, were you in any way able to appease her?"

"Well, as I did not wish to exacerbate the situation by defending dear Gailey, I was left with little choice other than to fully humble myself and give the old bat something of a meaningful apology. I also promised it would not happen again."

"Well, for the time being, perhaps it would behoove us all to try and be nicer to Polly, although heaven knows just how difficult a task this might well turn out to be," Boritz helpfully suggested, his eyes remaining firmly glued on the substantial figures written on the check in front of him.

"Yes, Mildred, my sweet pea, if we want to see more money in the coffers, we will have to find other, more preferable ways to discipline her."

"I think you mean 'more subtle' ways. Don't you, Boritz dear?"

"My sentiments exactly."

"Sadly, you could be right on that one, Boritz dearest," she very churlishly admitted, "although the girl is such a problem and headache, it will be difficult to find other, more suitable forms of punishment. Don't you think?"

"Well, Mildred, my sweet pea, let us put all such headaches to one side as we joy and revel in this latest exceedingly charitable donation," he brightly suggested.

"Yes, we'll get Miss Scrimp to organize the foster children and get them to bed early, and I'll get our little brood ready for bed. Then it's high time we celebrated. Here, Jeremy, say good night to daddy," Mildred cooed as she placed their youngest child in front of him for a quick bedtime kiss and cuddle.

"Night night, sleepy byes coochy coo. Daddy loves you. Kissy kissy."

The young toddler began to make pleasurable giggles and gurgles, which encouraged Boritz to continue on with the daft baby talk that, ridiculous as it may seem, all gooey-eyed parents cannot fail but act out.

Suddenly and without warning, tragedy struck. The young infant's foot accidentally hit his father's large glass of water. The glass tumbled over, and the water spilled out all over the desk, drenching everything in its path, the check included.

"Mildred, you stupid woman!" he screeched. "Here, take Jeremy, and then quickly get me a cloth, anything!" he roughly ordered.

A panicked Mildred, with the bouncy toddler in her arms, raced around the room desperately looking for anything that might soak up the water before all documents on his table suffered irretrievably from severe water damage. Sadly, she was not quick enough.

Boritz let out a death-defying scream as he watched the figures on the check disappear one by one, as the ink bled into the rest of the check. He was left feeling wildly impotent, for there was absolutely nothing he could do about it.

"Mildred, how could you possibly let this happen?" he raged.

"Temper, temper!" Mildred angrily retorted.

Boritz ripped off his shirt and vest in his desperate attempt to mop up and thus salvage the check and save it from further water damage. These last-ditch attempts proved just as futile, for the more he attempted to dry the check, the more it smudged, causing the ink to rather sadly stain his expensive shirt as well as his vest. He then resorted to using some old blotting paper, but this too was of no use. This unbelievable and most unfortunate crisis continued on until the check was thoroughly beyond all redemption.

"I, for one, cannot believe this has happened," Boritz woefully wailed as with the tips of his fingers he picked the soggy check up from the desk to wave it in the air. The soaking wet check immediately began to break off into little pieces. "Oh, this is so, so terrible," he wailed and whimpered.

"Well, can't you get her to write another check?" Mildred helpfully muttered.

"Oh, you stupid woman, how do I do that?" he sneered.

"Simple! You put pen to paper and write to her, of course," Mildred quickly retaliated.

"Woman, were you not listening to anything while she was here?"

"What sort of stupid question is that? Of course I was listening."

"Well, it is quite obvious to me that you've failed to clean your ears out; otherwise you would realize that the old boot clearly stated that she was going to be off traveling the globe for many long months," he bawled.

"Well, instead of boohooing like a baby stuck in a soiled nappy, go to your desk and write a letter. Then send it to her estate in Scunthorpe," Mildred snorted.

"Well, if I could do that, then I would, but I don't have her address."

"Why ever not?" a very shocked Mildred dared to ask.

"Because I never thought to ask her for it, you stupid, ridiculous, dumb woman," he indignantly roared. "And before you ask anything else, she never offered to give it to me. I did all my liaisons through Nick Ninkumpoop. I don't even know the name of the place she took Polly to on this so-called eventful holiday." He wept out of pure frustration.

Before too long, the accusations were flying back and forth as the blame game headed into the second round.

"Well, I don't know who you're calling a dumb idiot when it's perfectly clear that you're the one who's been officially dealing with her," a now very irate Mildred cried. "Perhaps you should have shown a little more interest in where she was taking Polly, for not only are you the one with the gift of the gab, but to top it all, you're a jolly lawyer!" she ridiculed. "So perhaps if you'd shown more interest and care, the lady would have happily given an address."

"Oh, like you really cared?"

"Well, no, but all the same, as her official guardians we should have paid a little more attention to all that was going on," she sourly reprimanded.

"Oh, do be quiet, woman, and give me the space to think. No, it's no use," he muttered. "I know she lives somewhere near Scunthorpe, but I would imagine that just like other rich and famous people, her telephone number will not be listed in the book, and her official residence will be just as much a secret."

"Boritz, do yourself a big favor. Pull yourself together and stop moaning and blubbering like a teething baby!" she harshly scolded.

Still, he could not stop bawling as he picked up the soggy shreds of what earlier had been an extremely generous donation.

"Look, at the end of the day there must be a way out. Could we not trace the woman through our dear friend Dr. Ninkumpoop? After all, she gave him considerable financial assistance."

"Woman, I believe you have a brain the size of a mutated door mouse, for where in heaven's name do you get your ideas from? You know full well that Dr. Ninkumpoop has been sent to get help at some very private hospital in a remote part of Switzerland, so I have absolutely no way whatsoever of getting in touch with him," he inconsolably sobbed, tears now streaming down his tersely taut face.

"Oh, what if anything have I ever done to deserve this?" he pathetically cried, as over the next few weeks he found himself sporadically bursting into uncontrollable bouts of deep and powerful anguish, followed by many, many tears.

———◦•◦—◦———

Meanwhile, back in Piadora a tremendously large crowd had quickly gathered to await the arrival of Giles and Ralph, oh, as well as Tiddles the pup.

"Here they come," someone in the crowd shouted as the trumpets sounded to mark this great and splendid occasion. Before too long, great applause broke out.

"Lady Butterkist, can we have your autograph?" many in the large crowd begged as they reached out to shake both his hand as well as Giles's.

"Ralph, you, my dear, are the talk of Piadora, for you gave a truly splendid performance," Mrs. O'Brien cried as she gave him a really big, affectionate embrace. "Yes, we are all so very proud of you. Oh, and Giles, well done for putting up with him. I, for one, would have clubbed him many times over," she freely admitted. "We were all truly amazed, for you really do have the patience of Job."

"Oh, don't worry, for I'm still after some payback," he insisted, giving a gentle smile.

Ralph gave his friend a hug and thanked him. "I couldn't have carried this off without your courteous assistance, Giles," he insisted.

"Well, both you boys were a blast," Mrs. O'Brien happily stated.

"Why thank you, Mrs. O'Brien, and I apologize for giving away Piddles, but I promise, hand on heart, she has gone home with a really kind, loving man who has promised to truly care for her."

"Ralph, I have no objection to you giving her away, for I am well aware that it was for a good cause. But to take Precious and Peaches and rename them Piddles and Tiddles, well, that really takes the biscuit! Yes, it was too much to bear. Really, it was," she gently rebuked.

"Anyway, setting that aside, I freely choose to forgive you, for you have indeed achieved great things. Polly is finally out of that terrible hospital, as is Lucinda. So for today, at least, you are a star."

"Why, thank you, Mrs. O'Brien."

"Now, tomorrow—that's an entirely different matter, for you surely realize that you will be required to return to being a gentleman of the road."

"Yes, but you had better hold on to these clothes for me, for my work as Lady Butterkist is most definitely unfinished. I intend to pay a few more visits to that castle, and just like dear Dr. Ninkumpoop, Mr. and Mrs. Scumberry will eventually either change for the better or otherwise rue the very day they met me."

"Oh, Ralph, I hate to tell you this, but they already do. Yes, they are already in a quandary. At this very moment they are both crying in their soup over the sad and unfortunate loss of your outstandingly generous check. It's all terribly sad, really, for he blames Mildred's negligence for the accident, and Mildred is having none of it, for she most surely blames him. I wonder, is there any hope of a truce?" she asked.

"Not likely. The blame game will surely go on for many weeks more."

"Yes, this loss seems to be affecting them both deeply," she sighed.

"Oh, didums to the both of them!"

"Didums! Oh Ralph, you're sounding so terribly old-fashioned, and—dare I say it?—toffee-nosed English, really you are. So are we to expect you to stay in this modus operandi?" she rather flippantly remarked.

"Dear Mrs. O'Brien, I resent that underhand comment. Really I do," he said, giving an impish smile.

"Anyway, Ralph. Back to my point. I hate to speak ill of anyone, but they are such an unbearably cruel couple. Truly they are," she felt obliged to comment.

"Well perhaps it's because money and power have become their gods."

"Well, they've always loved the finer things of life. Their personal lifestyle indicates that they've been ridiculously lavish, and mainly at the expense of the poor children. So now I suppose they will have to cut their cloth accordingly," Mrs. O'Brien deliberated.

"Oh, more than likely."

"Hmm. And forgive me, Ralph, for sharing this, but Mildred has already called you a number of very impolite and derogatory names that had me as well as many others chuckling."

"Oh, so I expect you will be wanting to share them with me."

"Oh, absolutely! They range from Lady Much to 'the old battle-axe,' and the one I liked the most was when she deigned to call you 'Lady Muck O'Dirt Castle.'" I tell you now, Ralph, that particular insult literally had everybody in stitches for days on end."

"How dare she insult me in such a manner, for there's nothing dirty about me or my castle, for that matter! Oh, no. It's always kept utterly spick and span," he announced, pretending to be more than a trifle miffed.

"Well, she also thinks you're nothing but an eccentric and cantankerous old biddy who needs to be brought down a peg or two."

"You mean cut down to size?" he said, pretending to be hurt.

"Precisely."

"Well, she's got a point, for I really am quite a large lady. I mean, I've got extraordinarily big feet and a large rear end, and—"

"Ralph, dear, trust me when I say that I don't think she is referring to your physique but rather more your attitude and temperament. Yes, she sees you as being, well—how shall I say it?—thoroughly impossible!"

"Well, I never! For it takes one to know one. Anyway, that's pretty rum coming from her," he continued to playfully sulk.

"Yes, well, they both need a mirror to be placed in front of themselves. Don't they?"

"Well then, I will make it my business to make sure they get that opportunity to evaluate themselves, as well as their lifestyle. Those two superior imposters really need a wake-up call, so I fully intend to see they get it. Yes, I will happily set the alarm."

"Hmm, and how do you propose to do that?"

"Oh, Mrs. O'Brien, I'm not at liberty or fully disposed to giving away all my secret plans, at least not yet. Anyway, setting that aside, I have a more impending crisis that needs my immediate attention."

"Oh, and what is that?"

"I am most desperate to get out of these stupid high heels, for they are truly crippling me," he whined, a look of great pain written all over his face.

"Oh, stop being such a moaning Minnie, for you look very becoming in those delicate shoes," she quickly retorted.

"Don't mess with me, Mrs. O' Brien. Tell me now, have you any idea where my hardy old boots might be hiding?"

"Well, I'll only reveal their whereabouts once you've handed me back my pink lipstick," she teased.

"Done! Then I think I could easily murder a nice hot cup of tea. So how about it, Mrs. O'Brien?" he implored, giving her a little wink.

"Well, Mrs. Butterkist, I believe you've really discovered a taste for sumptuous teas, as well as the finer things of life. However, as soon as we've finished our tea, we must find Hodgekiss, as I know he wants to hear everything concerning your latest update. Also, during the time of your absence many delightfully wonderful souls have arrived in Piadora, and they are all dying for the opportunity to meet and speak with you. If you will agree to meet with them later on, then I will agree to make us a pot of tea, garnished with other delectable refreshments. Still, there are still a few small conditions attached to my very generous offer."

"Conditions, Mrs. O'Brien?"

"Yes, Ralph, after all, you've spent the last few months as Lady Butterkist laying down conditions to all and sundry, and I might add, in rather a superior manner. So now it's my turn to be demanding."

"Oh, so what are we hoping for, Mrs. O'Brien?" he playfully moaned.

"Well, firstly I need a proper apology from you for changing my little pups' names to Tiddles and Piddles, for I have to confess I was very shocked by this most mischievous decision of yours."

"Oh, Mrs. O'Brien, I apologize most profusely. I just wanted to have some fun."

"Hmm. All right. Apology accepted, but you still owe me one for that. Next, I'm only prepared to make the tea if you're then willing to play mum by pouring the tea. I would also like to suggest that while we sit back and enjoy the ritual of sipping tea from dainty cups, you use the time wisely by spilling the beans to reveal all your future intentions regarding Polly and her future."

"Everything?"

"Yes, everything! Leave nothing out! I do not wish to be left in the dark a minute longer than I have to," she forcefully declared, "for just like you, I feel very involved in Polly's tough life, so it is only natural that I should want to be in the know long before anything else untoward happens," she adamantly insisted.

"Mrs. O'Brien, you have my word!"

"Oh, good."

"Now, please be a dear and lead the way to the kitchen before I die or faint of thirst," he said as he placed a friendly arm around her shoulder.

Then bearing down heavily, he began to hobble away

"I know I've said it many times before, Mrs. O'Brien, but I really need to take a long break from being a lady, for I can just about cope with the wig, the stockings, and tweed skirts, but these ridiculously high heels really take the biscuit, for they are well and truly killing me."

"There you go again—moan, moan, moan."

"I'm not moaning. I'm just stating fact," he sniffed as he pretended to be most offended.

"Oh, trust me, Ralph, for it's still moaning. So perhaps next time 'round you should consider going back as an entirely different prima donna."

"Oh, and quite who are you thinking of?

"Why, Mona Lisa, of course!"

"Mrs. O'Brien, I can't believe you just said that," he playfully sniffed while giving her a friendly pat on the back.

THE END

CONTACT THE AUTHOR

*I*F ANYTHING IN the book has raised personal issues for you, whatever your age, and you would like to talk to someone, please feel free to contact us. Please also contact us to let us know how you enjoyed the book.

Or should you wish to contribute to our children's work, both here and abroad, please also contact us through our Web site, www.hopeinyourheart.com, or by mail to:

Tricia Bennett
P.O. Box 1167
Wildwood, Florida 34785